Stardust
and
Wolfsbane

M. L. LYONS

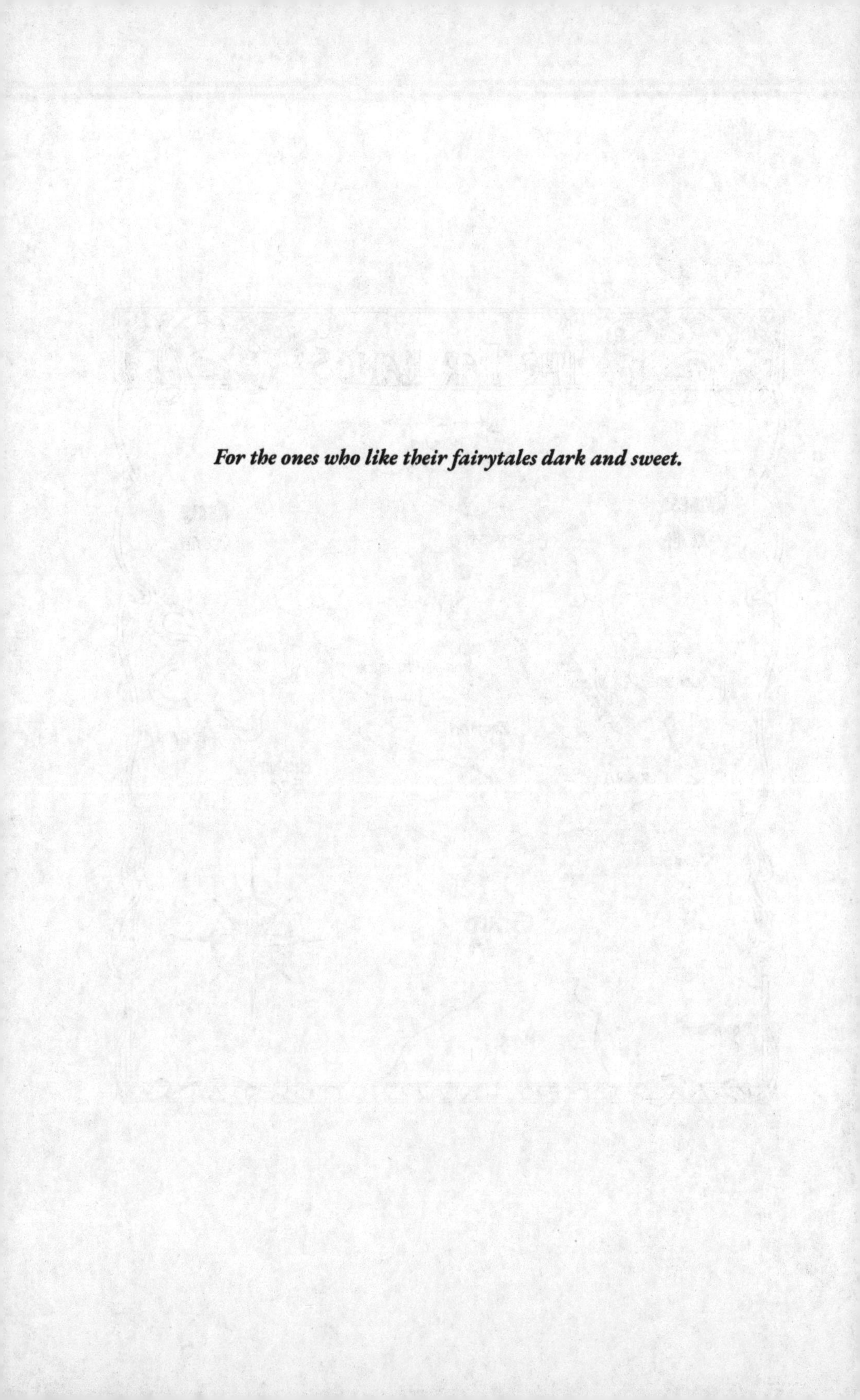

For the ones who like their fairytales dark and sweet.

THE FAR LANDS
NORWIN
ICY PASSAGE
Isle of Fortune
ENDLESS OCEAN
AZURE OCEAN
AUSTVEST
SOLDCROIE
WENDY CHANNEL
BELSTERRE
LOGR
ESTELLEN
ZEEMAA
MOON BAY
SENUAMA
NIGHT SEA
KORALIA
DREAM BAY
CHRYSONERO
GOLD SEA
N
W
E
S
DUHANIBA
EMAIR

A Ravenous Wolf

CHAPTER 1

S pring brings new life and hope but the wolf brings only death.

For three months, the village of Foxglove Grove has lost man and woman alike to the deadly prowler. No hunter in this village, or from the surrounding areas, has defeated this beast. After many losses, the village leaders unanimously voted that none should enter the eastern woods without proper supervision. Upon this decision, signposts leading toward the eastern forest were erected with warnings for both literate and common of the danger that lies there. It was clear to all: no one is to go in the woods alone. Still, Stella does.

The earth squishes beneath Stella's brown leather boots. The ground of the eastern woods is a tad bit sturdier thanks to the cleared path being covered overhead by the ancient trees' extensive branches. Often Stella has walked this path and stared at the branches reaching out toward each other as if they were hands wanting to be held by each other. The desperate reaching has caused a green, leafy ceiling to form from spring to the end of autumn. With spring's recent return, the ceiling has been reformed while the ground has become covered in new colorful blossoms and grass.

An unseasonably cool wind makes Stella pull up the hood of the crimson cape she wears. She had been so upset when she found her violet cape taken by her sister this morning but now with this wind, she is grateful to have the thicker of the two coverings.

Stella's hand tightens around the handle of her wicker basket as she sees the last warning sign in the woods. Neither the cape nor the heat from her basket of freshly baked goods can stop her from shivering. Staring at the crude drawing of a snarling black wolf, her mind races to her friend, Afanen Pugh. Afanen, a maiden with a contagious laugh and rosy cheeks that matched her red hair, was found not far from this path, making her the first victim of the wolf. Afanen had been found by the Bonham brothers who were not shy to share the details of their discovery. Most could not listen as they described how they found her lifeless and pale while her naked body and the snow beneath her were soaked in blood from her ripped-out heart. But Stella listened as her curiosity compelled her.

Soon after Afanen's closed casket funeral, the Bonham brothers' mangled bodies were wheeled to the village by the woodcutter, Mr. Horn, from the woods. Stella had been curious as to why the people were gathering in the center of the village so she joined them. She wishes she had not as her eyes were marred with the image of their bloodstained bodies with open chest cavities and dangling intestines. The thought of them even after three months makes her want to vomit. She never did go out to see the other victims that were found and brought home. She attended every funeral though, all twenty-seven.

About a month ago, as Stella was working at Mrs. Kenwyn's bakery, Stella overheard Dr. Marsh speaking to Father Engel about a very peculiar similarity between all of the victims. Everyone, no matter the level of mutilation, was only missing one thing – the heart. Though things were hanging out, torn, broken, or chipped, nothing was missing.

Why would a wolf only eat a heart? Stella wondered and still does.

Later that same day while the young women of the village worked on the quilt for a newly engaged maiden, Emilia Marsh brought up the information she had learned from her father but added something he left out from his conversation with Father Engel. Afanen and the other four women who had fallen victim at that time had bites on the back of their necks and were found in shreds of their clothes if that. Since then, most of the maidens in the village have worn their hair in fashions that cover the backs of their necks and an extra layer of clothes as if it will keep them safe. Even with their neck covered and extra layers, more women fell to the beast.

Hunters tried their hands at catching the wolf. First came Mr. Beltz, then the Hafners, and then the Pryces. When Mr. Pugh posted a hefty reward for the beast, men from other villages began to come. None succeeded. All claimed the same thing – the beast is as tall as a hawthorn tree and black as night.

Killing it has proved to be as difficult as trying to catch the wind.

Surely, this description is an exaggeration. Stella tells herself though her heart still pounds thinking of the creature.

A rustling to her left causes Stella to freeze. Her hand cautiously slips into her basket. She takes hold of the knife she packed in case of an unfriendly encounter. She pulls it out slowly, ready to take on what is behind the high bushes. The rustling continues. Her throat is filled with a lump she tries to swallow.

Mrs. Kenwyn was right. I should not have gone alone.

Prayers for mercy and protection come from her heart. She closes her eyes and holds it out before her.

"Hello." A low man's voice calls to her.

Stella jumps backward, gasping and clasping her chest where her heart leaps. Her knife thuds on the ground. She tries to catch her breath as her enlarged eyes stare at the man who unexpectedly appeared before her.

The young man is one Stella has seen nearly every morning these past few months. He came to be a woodcutter just a few weeks before the wolf and following hunters appeared. Nearly every young lady in the village had become infatuated with the woodcutter.

*Not just the young ladies…*Stella recalls the numerous glances she has seen the married and widowed women give the young man. There have even been rumors of him having affairs. Of course, Stella knows she should repeat such things given there is no proof. She would hate for someone to make such a malicious lie about her and others believe it.

Stella squats to pick up her knife from the ground. She looks him over as she rises up. He may not be the first man to send the maidens of Foxglove Grove into a frenzy, but despite the influx of new men into the village, it is this woodcutter who remains at the top of the community's eligible bachelor list.

He is also by far the tallest man in the village. It is one of the many differences between him and the other men. His lean physique and smooth fair skin make him look more like a teacher or store clerk than a woodcutter. Over the past three months, his soft hands have not become rough and calloused. She only noticed this from handing him his baked goods last week. He also has not developed a broad chest and muscular arms like Mr. Horn. It is strange but she is not clued into how all men work. The other maidens do not care about any of this. They care about how his dark curls always look freshly tousled, how his nose is straight and unbroken, and how he has all of his milky white teeth. But what has caught her attention are his sparkling hazel eyes with their flecks of gold and silver. She swears she has seen pink in them too.

Though his name is frequently in the mouths of those in Foxglove Grove, his origins are a mystery. When the question arose in the quilting circle after his arrival, many of the women had theories. Perhaps he was a schoolmaster or clerk who had changed occupations. Perhaps he is a bounty hunter seeking a criminal who secretly lurks in Foxglove Grove. The most popular theory came about from her sister Althea.

"Maybe he is the runaway prince. He is only pretending to be a woodcutter to protect his identity. It was said Prince Eirian was pale of skin and dark-haired, like his mother. He could be Prince Eirian." Althea concocted the possibility.

"But why would he come here of all places?" Elspeth Kenwyn, Stella's employer's daughter, asked.

"For us maidens, of course," Afanen joked causing all to laugh.

Despite the theory being outrageous, the rumor spread like fire among the rest of the girls in town. "Prince Eirian'" became his name among the Grove's girls. But at this moment, Stella cannot remember his other name.

"I am so sorry. I didn't mean to frighten you." The apologetic man's voice is low but humored by her reaction. Stella politely smiles as she tucks her knife back into her basket.

"Oh, it is fine." She easily forgives. "I am just glad you are not the wolf."

"Ah, yes, the wolf." His eyes move from Stella to scan the surrounding terrain before returning to her. "A young lady such as you should not be alone walking in these dangerous woods."

"I will be fine. The hunters say the wolf only comes at night." Stella takes a step to move beyond her stopping point only for Prince Eirian to keep at her side.

"Still, wolves can change their habits."

"Perhaps... but I must finish my task." She does not slow her feet.

"Oh? And what task is that?" Prince Eirian purposefully steps into her path making her stop.

"I am delivering some food to Mrs. Beverly. The poor dear has been sick for some time. Since her son is away doing business in another village, I am going to make sure she is well." Stella lifts her basket to show evidence.

"Oh... yes...Mrs. Beverly," He pauses and ponders as if in deep thought. "She is the widow who lives in the cottage between two sycamore trees about a league further in the woods right?"

"Yes."

"That is still a way off then. Please, let me escort you there. I would hate to see you fall victim to the wolf." He offers his assistance with a smile that might have driven her to swoon and blush had she been ten years younger. Instead, she feels as if stones are in her stomach.

I want to get to her and go back as quickly as possible. Having him will slow me down.

"That is kind of you, but I would not want to take you away from your work." Stella gestures to the surrounding trees. Her eyes catch his shiny, sharp ax that is still attached to his back, giving away he has yet to cut anything today.

"The trees can wait. I am sure the wolf has no plan for them. Please, let me walk you to Mrs. Beverly's." He insists and answers the question in her mind.

"Please. I do not want to be a burden to you and keep you from making your wages, Mr..." She pauses, still unable to recall his name.

"Blevins, Lyall Blevins. You may call me Lyall."

"I apologize for forgetting, Lyall. I have many customers at the bakery."

"I understand," then he adds coquettishly, "It is also difficult to remember my name when you refer to me as Prince Eirian with your friends."

Stella's cheeks burn. Lyall chuckles at the reaction. "I am flattered to think you all find me princely." Stella's skin continues to redden. Her tongue sticks to the roof of her mouth, unable to be loose. Not a word can be uttered to save her. "But sadly, I am not Prince Eirian."

"Well, that will disappoint many," Stella mutters with her tongue finally working. Her words are not lost on him.

"Will it disappoint you?" His dark, thin eyebrows raise.

"No. I never really thought of you to be a prince." Stella bites her tongue after hearing how rude her comment may have sounded. "I mean, I did not think you were Prince Eirian, specifically."

"Why?" He continues to question, making her stomach turn.

Why does he care? It's all a joke.

"He is to be older than us and Prince Eirian stutters. You look younger than I and speak clearly."

"How do you know if he stutters?"

"I learned of it when I lived in Rexheart," Stella thinks about one of her previous homes but stops herself from thinking further about it.

"Because of my youthful, handsome looks and lack of stutter, you have deemed me to not be Prince Eirian?" Lyall strokes his shaved chin.

"I did not say you were handsome," She quips, making him blush. "But yes."

"If you have known, then why are all the others calling me so?"

"Well, it is clear you are not a woodcutter. The girls thought it was fun to have the fantasy of a prince being among us in disguise. In a blink of an eye, one lucky girl could be whisked off to her happily ever after."

"Is this your dream too?" He muses.

"I don't know you well enough to say," Stella chuckles before finally realizing how much she has shared with him, "But you have a dream of fooling everyone into believing you are a woodcutter. Why go along with this act?"

Taken aback by the turned question, Lyall grins sheepishly, then chuckles. "It is true. I am no woodcutter. I only recently escaped my father who was forcing me into his trade, a trade I want no part of so I ran away. I have posed as a woodcutter, but I am just a man, a man in search of something extremely rare."

"And what is that?"

His lips curl up and he exposes his teeth pleasantly as he comes closer. His hazel eyes stay on the cloaked woman. A tingling sensation comes from her buttocks and up her spine as her skin is suddenly cold. His hand comes to lightly hold the tip of her chin.

"What every man seeks at least once in his life."

His face draws closer. Her back sweats at the closeness of his lips to her face. She can feel a warmth coming off his body. The hairs on the back of her neck stick up in a mix of disgust and fear.

"Which is?"

"Love. And I have found it."

"With whom?"

"You."

Stella's stomach drops.

"Me?" She barely hears herself.

He shakes his head with a smile still on his face.

"Stella, I..."

Her feet twitch in a need to run, yet they are like stone.

"I have looked everywhere for you." His hazel eyes are soft, as are the corners of his mouth. His smooth hands try to take hold of one of hers.

A confession from the village's heartthrob should delight a maiden. No man has ever searched for her. Her sister Althea, on the other hand, has swells of men lining up for her. Now the young man, desired by so many, claims to love her. Pleasure, giddiness, or even pride should swell in her chest. But her heart sinks.

"We do not even know each other." She pulls her hand from his and moves it behind her back.

"We do not know each other as well as I would wish but we do see each other and speak every day. We are not even remotely strangers."

She indeed sees him every day and they speak. But their words are not of consequence. Every conversation has been something she speaks of with everyone like the weather, the status of the wolf's capture, the goods of the day, and other pleasantries. Only on rare occasions have they held a conversation about something else. None have been of note. She cannot remember a single one now. And every time she feels relieved when he leaves, though she has never been sure why.

"Even so...I have seen how your eyes have turned to my sister when you come into the shop, just like all the other men. I have felt the desire you have had for her."

He blinks several times.

"The desire you felt was not for her but for you."

"Then why did I sense your desirous feelings when you were flirting with other women in the village?"

"I had to test that my feelings for you were genuine by trying other women. I also hoped to create some jealousy in you by flirting with them. I thought then you would want me too."

"So, you do not really love me but simply want me to want you," Stella walks again. Lyall grabs her wrist and pulls her toward him. His eyebrows have come together as his smile has turned into a frown.

"Do you think so lowly of me?"

Stella does not answer making his nostrils flare and his left eye twitches.

"What must I do to change your mind?"

Stella presses her lips together. His eyes convey earnestness.

"You can start by letting go of my wrist."

He does so with a laugh as if he had forgotten his hold on her.

"I am sorry, Stella. I should have been forthright with you. As soon as you drew me in, I should have embraced my feelings rather than testing them with the others in the village. But be rest assured, I will only pursue you now. I cannot resist you. Everything about you draws me in. Your food, your personality, your looks, especially your plump figure, all ensnare me." He turns his focus back on her.

Stella's skin burns at the mention of her figure. His hand comes to her chin and tilts her face upward. Their eyes lock. She can see every colorful sparkle in his eyes.

"And your eyes... I have not seen violet eyes. They are so rare. And this here." He touches the corner of her mouth with his thumb. "I have yet to see a woman with this hidden kiss."

Her body feels fuzzy and pliable the more she stares into his eyes. Still, the sick feeling lingers in her.

"I have grown exceedingly uncomfortable with your presence, Mr. Blevins. Do not escort me anymore." Stella pushes him away.

"I am just trying to be direct with you." He attempts to come to her again. She steps out of his reach and turns with her hand out to stop him. He stops walking. His lips become a line, but his eyes stay on her.

"I am not interested in you at all." She remains resolute.

Lyall's lips scrunch together, then smooth out once more just for the left corner of his mouth to rise. His head is tilted down so his eyes are almost looking through his eyebrows.

"I will have to change that then." He takes one step forward. Stella's hand goes into her basket. She grips the bone hilt of the knife inside her basket, though her body is shaking. Her hold tightens even more as Lyall Blevins takes another step closer.

He is worse than a wolf.

CHAPTER 2

"**S**tella!" A booming voice echoes in the stillness of the woods. Stella looks beyond Lyall, who has also turned his head. Two woodcutters with axes on their shoulders approach the couple. Stella beams seeing they are the jolly, red-faced Mr. Horn and his brawny son, Gus.

"Mr. Horn! Gus!" Stella greets the men. She quickly breaks away from Lyall.

"What are you doing out here, Stella? Shouldn't you be back at the bakery with Mrs. Kenwyn?" Mr. Horn thinks of the widowed baker.

"I am going to visit Mrs. Beverly and bring her some goods," Stella answers.

"Oh, I see. Well, that is very kind of you, Stella, but you need to be careful. I don't want you ending up like all those poor girls," Mr. Horn warns, then looks over to his son, who possesses the same red hair he once had in his youth. "Perhaps I could lend my son Gus to escort you there and protect you from the wolf." Mr. Horn pats Gus's wide back as the young man's freckled cheeks color. Gus breathes out bashfully, "Father..."

"I am already escorting her to Mrs. Beverly's house," Lyall comes behind Stella and places his hand on her shoulder, making her shudder. Mr. Horn frowns seeing her reaction. "She does not need your help."

Stella pushes Lyall's hand off her shoulder. "But you need to get back to work, don't you, Mr. Blevins? I would be happy to have Gus finish your polite mission, should he not mind." Stella steps out of Lyall's reach and toward Gus.

"I do not mind escorting you, Stella," Gus answers. Lyall's lips downturn while Mr. Horn's return upward. Gus doesn't notice how brightly his father smiles at the possibility of setting up his son for success.

"I am not so busy that I cannot keep my word to you, Stella. I like to finish what I start," Lyall insists. His voice is calm but something is radiating from him that makes Stella's muscles tighten.

"Oh, no. You have taken me far enough. Thank you. Gus can finish for you," Stella takes the young, ginger-haired man's arm and quickly pulls him to go with her down the path. "Come with me, Gus."

The two hurry down the path, leaving behind the scowling Lyall and the merry Mr. Horn. Stella's speed and grip are so strong that Gus trips every few steps. Holding on to Gus's large arm makes her feel much safer than the walls of the village.

Eventually, Stella comes to her senses and releases Gus. She sighs relieved and looks up to the man next to her.

"Thank you for agreeing to escort me, Gus."

"It is my pleasure, Stella," he smiles, showing off his overlapping buck teeth.

They continue walking in a relaxed silence. Though she catches Gus's few glances, neither says a word. She is grateful for the lack of conversation or rather the lack of having to explain what just happened with Lyall. Gus is rather the perfect companion for now. He is always rather quiet. He asks nothing too personal of anyone, he hardly asks anyone anything at all. The same cannot be said of his father. Mr. Horn is constantly sticking his cherry red, bulbous nose into everyone's business in town. It has become easier to answer his invasive queries than to not. But Mr. Horn is not a hated or hateful man. He is just... curious.

"I saw there is going to be a village dance on Septday to celebrate spring," Gus breaks the silence first.

"Yes!" Stella brightens up at the mention of the upcoming dance. "Mrs. Kenwyn has been asked to bake several pastries and a ten-layered cake for the event. We have already begun baking some of it so it will not be too overwhelming on Septday."

"Ten layers? Isn't that too extravagant?" Gus questions.

"I think with all the sorrow we had been having, the village heads just want to help us forget it for a night."

Gus smiles softly to himself.

"Maybe so... Will you be able to take part in the dance, or will you only be working?"

"I hope to take part. It will be nice to celebrate the new season in a high-spirited way. Will you be going, Gus?" Stella glances at the tall woodcutter.

"Yes," Gus answers. "Are you going alone?"

"No."

His face falls, though Stella does not catch it as she imagines the event. "I am going with my sister and the Kenwyns."

"I see." Gus's smile returns.

"Oh! And Basil!" Stella remembers the other member who should be in her troop.

"Basil?" Gus has yet to meet anyone named Basil in Foxglove Grove. His face falls, but she catches it this time.

"My brother! He is coming to the village soon. He will want to go dancing," Stella explains. She had forgotten none in her village know of her younger brother or her parents. Of course, that would be the way as she and Althea were not locals but merely traveling workers who had settled in Foxglove Grove.

"I did not know you and Althea had a brother."

"Oh, yes. He left for Belterre before Althea and I settled here in the grove. I have not seen him in the past two years. He is finally coming here, and hopefully, he can help rid us of the wolf."

"Is he a huntsman?"

"No," Stella giggles, "he is a piper."

"A piper?" Gus's brown eyes double.

"Yes, just like my father," Stella warms thinking of her father. She has not seen him or her mother in two years, but at least she knows they are safe and happy in the kingdom of Soldoro.

"I did not know that either," Gus scratches the back of his neck.

"How could you? I think this is the longest conversation we have had," Stella chuckles. His ears turn red.

"Yes, well, um... I... I... It is hard for me sometimes to speak to others." Gus cast his eyes away from her.

"Well, I am glad you have been able to speak with me." Stella smiles at him and stares at her in awe.

"At the party, would you... would you mind sharing a dance with me?"

The question has Stella's skin turning from fair to pink. The corners of her mouth curl up, but she presses her lips together.

"As long as you will not mind my careless feet stepping on yours," she jokes, making him grin.

"I will wear extra thick socks," he chuckles, making Stella laugh lightly.

Stella's eyes leave Gus just as they emerge into an opening where the branches separate enough to allow more light through. In this patch of earth, wildflowers are blooming despite the late frost of a few days ago. Yellow buttercups and trilliums are scattered like drops of sunshine throughout the grass. Bluebells swayed with the tall grass in the breeze. Pink and purple foxgloves also pop up in the patch.

"This view is so pretty," Stella comments aloud.

"Yes. The view is. The flowers, I mean," Gus attempts to compose himself. "Do you think Mrs. Beverly would like some?"

"I think she might. What a wonderful idea, Gus. But I would not want to delay you from joining your father by having you watch me pick flowers." Stella looks back to Gus.

"My father can spare me for a little longer."

Stella steps into the flower patch. She takes out her knife and begins cutting flowers and putting them in her basket so they sit atop the cloth covering her goods for Mrs. Beverly. Gus patiently waits and watches her despite the long time she takes. Having collected enough for a beautiful, full bouquet, Stella finally returns to Gus and the path. They continue toward Mrs. Beverly's.

"Oh, there it is," Stella points to the cottage beyond the little river with a small wooden bridge for crossing. The thatch-roofed home is nestled between two giant sycamore trees. She turns to Gus.

"Thank you for your escort. Come by the shop tomorrow and I will give you anything you want free," Stella smiles.

"You... you do not want me to wait for you?"

"No. I do not know how long I will be with Mrs. Beverly and your father will need your help. "

"Are you sure?"

"Yes. Thank you, Gus." She gently touches his arm.

Stella crosses the creaking wood bridge Mr. Beverly built nearly fifty years ago when the old bridge caved on itself. Stella crosses quickly as if the bridge could collapse. It doesn't. She spins back and waves at Gus who had watched her cross. He waves and begins walking back to find his father.

Stella gathers the collected flowers into her left hand as she approaches the cottage made of hemlock wood. She lifts her right hand and lets her knuckles rap at the door. It becomes ajar at the touch. Stella frowns as the door opens so easily. Mrs. Beverly would never let the door be unlatched, especially with her son away.

"Oma?" She calls out the title Mrs. Beverly has insisted Stella call her since their first meeting.

"Who is it?" She hears a faint, crackly voice from deep in the cottage.

"It's Stella. I have come to see you. May I come inside?" Stella waits for an answer. Sometimes it takes the older woman to reply.

"Come in, dear," Mrs. Beverly gives her permission. Stella opens the door to the dark house. The fire in the fireplace is nearly out, leaving the house dark and cold. Some dried logs sit near the hearth. Stella turns her head to see Mrs. Beverly's bed. The old woman has been using the bed curtains as walls. The one closer to her is open.

"Oma, are you aware your door was ajar?" Stella asks.

"Oh, no. I guess I didn't lock it well enough," Mrs. Beverly guesses.

Stella approaches the mahogany bed where Mrs. Beverly is propped up against two pillows. She is covered in furs and quilts. Stella recognizes the top covering as Mrs. Beverly's wedding quilt. It is much like the one Stella and her friends have been making. This one is yellowing and fraying as it has lost its youth like Mrs. Beverly.

The woman's wrinkled skin is paler than it had been the last time Stella saw the widow. Her thin white hair is barely braided and to the side of the woman. Dark bags have formed beneath her eyes. Her loose lips are chapped. Still, she smiles as her old eyes land on the young woman.

"Come closer, dear," Mrs. Beverly waves her hand to beckon the young woman.

"I brought you these," Stella holds out the flowers to the sick woman. Mrs. Beverly takes the bouquet and inhales.

"They are beautiful and smell so good," she pulls the flowers away, "They are surely a bright presence in this dark hole."

Dark hole? Stella is surprised by the term. Never has Mrs. Beverly referred to home as anything less than charming. Maybe her illness and loneliness have made her depressed.

"I'll put them in a vase with water so you can have them by your side," Stella takes the flowers back as she stands to find a suitable vase, leaving the large basket on the bed. "I also brought you some baked goods."

Stella pumps some water into the found, unused vase then arranges the flowers into a cheery display for the sickly woman's nightstand.

"There." Stella is content with the placement of the floral arrangement at Oma's side.

"What did you bring for me?" Oma points to the basket.

"Well, Oma." Stella unwraps the goods. "I've brought you some scones, banana bread with nuts, raspberry turnovers, brown bread and butter, a cask of mulled wine, a venison pie, and a bottle of fresh milk. I even brought some vegetables and potatoes to put in a stew if you'd like me to make you some." Stella pulls out the many items. She sets the basket which still holds her knife onto the floor beside her.

"Deary me. I cannot possibly eat all of this." Mrs. Beverly shakes her head.

"It is not meant for one sitting of course," Stella chuckles, "I was not sure what you would want most, so I brought enough options for you."

"You are so kind, Stella." Mrs. Beverly puts her hand on Stella's wrist. The icy grip makes Stella jump.

"Oma! You are freezing!" Stella takes the woman's hand and immediately rubs her hands over it.

"It just happens as you get old," Mrs. Beverly sighs.

"No. It's because the fire is almost out. I'll fix it for you." Stella gets up from the bed.

"Oh, no. Sit with me, Stella." Mrs. Beverly grabs Stella's wrist and pulls it rather hard, much harder than this feeble woman ever has. Using her free hand, she pulls a fur over Mrs. Beverly.

"I will. I just need to get the fire going." Stella is let go. She finds her spot at the fireplace and gets to work. Soon the fire has grown, filling the cottage with warmth.

"That should do for a time," Stella pokes some of the wood with the iron stoker.

"Take off your cape and sit with me, Stella." Mrs. Beverly chirps. Stella nods. She removes her sister's cape which she hangs on the hook by the door. She comes back toward the bed but notices the food has remained untouched.

"Let me put this food away unless you would like some now." Stella gestures to the spread of food. The older woman just shakes her head. Stella collects the food and finds the best spots for them to be stored. Finally, she returns to Mrs. Beverly.

"How are you feeling, Oma?" Stella inquires.

"I am much better now with you here, Stella."

"I am sorry I did not come sooner. Mrs. Kenwyn was terrified I might get eaten by the wolf if I came. But I could not sit idly in the village knowing you were ill and all alone out here."

"I hope you were careful on your way here." Mrs. Beverly speaks up.

"I was. Gus Horn escorted me here." Stella refers to the woodcutter fondly.

"Gus Horn? That chatty woodcutter's son?" Mrs. Beverly seeks clarification.

"Yes. You know the redhead with freckles and muscles like mountains," Stella giggles.

"You like him?"

"I mean, I like him as a person. He is kind and earnest. He has also asked me to dance with him at the village dance this Septday."

"He has? You accepted?"

"Yes."

"Do you think you'll marry him, then?"

"Oh, Oma." Stella shakes her head surprised by the question. *Marry Gus? No...I don't want to marry Gus. He's not...**him**.* "Gus Horn is a kind, good man who has flattered me by giving me his attention, but I do not think marriage is in store for us."

"Hmm. Is this because someone else has caught your eye? Perhaps that new woodcutter. What did you say his name was?" Mrs. Beverly tries to recall.

"The fake Prince Eirian." Stella rolls her eyes. "Lyall Blevins."

"Yes...him. I recall seeing him in the village a month ago. He is exceptionally handsome." Mrs. Beverly praises him.

"He is, but I must tell you how he acted. Today he tried to escort me and professed his 'love' for me. He gave me the strangest feelings." Stella's hand goes to her stomach.

"Feelings of love?"

"No. It was a feeling of... I don't know. It was as if every fiber of my body was trying to scream 'run'. Yet I did not and I spoke with an authority and boldness I usually do not have with strangers. Have you ever felt like that around someone?"

"No." Mrs. Beverly stares blankly at the young woman.

"Oh." Stella looks down.

"Besides these strange feelings, was there anything truly objectionable about the man?"

"He's a flirtatious liar, and he frightens me. Right before the Horns arrived and rescued me, I tried to make it clear to Lyall that I was not interested in him. He gave me this look." Stella shudders recalling it. "It was like he wanted to... devour me. He said he would change my mind about being interested in him. I know what he meant to do."

"I'm sure he was harmless, dear. Perhaps he was just being passionate and misspoke." Mrs. Beverly pats Stella's hand again. There is a creeping, slimy feeling coming to the back of Stella's neck. It makes her want to squirm. Her stomach tightens as well.

Is this how Oma's illness is making her feel?

"Perhaps..." Stella still does not smile. "But it frightened me."

"Well, sometimes being afraid of a man makes things more fun," Mrs. Beverly winks.

"That's not what you've told me before, Oma. You said I should avoid men who try to make me fear them." Stella furrows her brows at the change of advice.

"I did?"

"Yes."

"Mmm, I mean, in general, you should. But something is thrilling about being a man's prey. One gets to be the sole object of his attention and lust." Mrs. Beverly's lips spread and curl up. "It is nice to give one's control over completely to another person. You may think you dislike something, but you should still try it. You never know what pleasure you may find."

Mrs. Beverly's wrinkly hands are still icy cold on Stella's hand. Her knuckles and fingers are larger as well. Stella stares at the woman now. The old woman's once brown eyes have gained greenish splotches and speckles of gold, silver, and magenta. Her smile is not one of grandmotherly love. It is...unnatural and otherworldly. Her canines were enlarged and the bottom row of her crooked teeth shifted and straightened into a perfect white row. Her visible ears have a point to them now.

Had they had points before now?

Mrs. Beverly's voice typically crackled like a fire and each word held a similar warmth as well. Now it is cold and croaky, like a bullfrog.

"If I were you, I'd give that Blevins boy another chance," Mrs. Beverly croaks, her large sparkling eyes staring into Stella's.

"Oma…" The slimy feeling oozes down Stella's back. "You're not Oma at all, are you?" Stella's muscles harden like stone. Mrs. Beverly's mouth spreads even wider. Her eyes lock on Stella. Her hands sit on the bed.

"No. I am not." The bullfrog voice is gone and replaced with a youthful, masculine one. Mrs. Beverly's pale wrinkled skin dissolves and the gray hair shrinks until they are replaced with smooth skin and dark curls. Stella trembles.

"I see you have seen through my disguise. You must have known the old hag well," Lyall comments.

"Have known?" Stella feels a lump in her throat.

"Yes. The old crone met the wolf yesterday." Lyall pushes the blankets off of him. Stella clenches her jaw as her ribs ache and her eyes burn to keep back tears. She cannot look at him.

"I see… Where is she?" Her grief keeps her locked in place and her mouth feels as if it is filling with cotton.

"Her remains are out back." He nods toward the back wall of the house. Stella's watering eyes flicker to where he nodded. He picks up the wedding quilt and covers Stella with it. "Don't cry over her, Stella. It was her time. She was a pleasant lady. She seemed ready to go. She didn't fight much." He speaks with a melodic tone which she finds off-putting.

"If the wolf killed her, then…how… do you know all of that?" Stella's voice cracks as she pieces together the information.

He forces her chin up with his finger and thumb. He holds her there and stares at her reddened eyes as he licks his lips.

"Take a wild guess, Stella?" His voice is smooth and dangerous.

Stella wants to speak but nothing escapes her. She cannot move despite her mind screaming for her to do so. She wants to flee but her nerves keep her trapped in her spot. Lyall's hand grabs her wrist. His knuckles grow hair as his nails grow long and sharp. His teeth grow sharper as well. Stella leans away from him but he yanks her back toward him. With her pressed against his chest, he seizes her other wrist. With his firm grip and great force, he pins her beneath him. His knees go to either side of her hips. Her wrists ache and her body squirms. She cringes as he brings his face centimeters from hers. He licks his lips, then grins. Her heart and mind race as he brings his mouth down close to her neck. He drags his sharp canines against her delicate flesh before going up to her ear.

"You should know by now."

CHAPTER 3

Nearly bone-crushing is the hold around Stella's wrists. She knows better than to pull away, as she cannot break the hold with a simple pull. She remains still, not sure what his next move is or hers. Her eyes survey his unkind face as well before briefly glancing down. The nightgown he stole from Mrs. Beverly has opened at his chest. Now she sees what Lyall's always laced up, long-sleeved tunics and black leather jerkin covered. Instead of fair skin to match the rest of his complexion, there are inked symbols. She recognizes none but one at the top of his sternum where it meets his collarbone. It is not a tattoo but a scar. An 'X' with a vertical line going through the crossed line has three lines just above in a vertical style as well. The "Fallen's Star" it is called. Her spine quivers, knowing what it means to wear this symbol. But she cannot show her fear.

Come on, Stella. At least pretend you're not afraid. Don't give him any satisfaction. Be brave. Be brave. Stella tells herself.

"Aren't you going to scream for help?" Lyall chuckles.

"I think you would enjoy that." Stella glares at him.

"A little." He snickers, darkness creeping into his eyes. Bile rises into her throat.

"What are you going to do to me?" Her mind seeks information to be prepared.

"Well... if you were just like the other girls, then I'd ravish you." He brings his lips to her neck and then drags his hot, wet tongue up to her ear. Stella recoils at the touch. Amused, he brings his face to look at her.

"Then, with your heart still racing, I'd take it out to add to my collection." His tongue runs over his teeth. Stella grimaces at the words and actions.

"You're going to force yourself on me, kill and eat me," Stella simplifies the next steps.

"No."

"No?"

"No. Remember, you're special, Stella."

She rolls her eyes.

"These lovely eyes you roll give away what truly makes you special." He brings the attention back to her eyes and her so-called specialness. "Violet eyes are rare as is that hidden kiss in you lip for only those with fairy blood can possess them."

"You are mistaken. None in my family can perform magic." Stella shakes her head.

"Now, who is the liar?"

"We are not fairy folk. We do not practice fairy magic."

"Dear, you're telling lies again. Doesn't your father use a magic pipe?"

Stella silences herself. She thinks of her father. He had just started getting silver in his brown hair and beard when she and her siblings left him and her mother in Soldoro to find their own ways in the world. Even as the three of them sailed away, he held a smile. He always has a smile; it wins over almost anyone he meets.

How is it this... creature knows him? How does he know he is a piper as well?

"How do you know?"

"I know of Lierre Sipos. He is the royal piper of Soldoro, correct?"

Stella's heart grows heavier.

"I am, aren't I? Pipers have to have magic to use their pipes. Unless your father is a wizard, he must have fairy blood in him. If your father has magic blood, then you do. I bet he has this hidden kiss and his eyes are just as purple as yours."

"No, they're blue," Stella blurts out the correction, not intending to do so. But his lack of knowing her father's eye color gives her some relief in that he must not have met her father in person.

"Then your mother must have fairy blood as well. Double lines are better," He mutters the last sentence to himself.

"I-I don't have magic."

"But you do. I can taste it in your food. I can see it in your eyes. I see it in the corner of your mouth. You have fairy blood like me."

"Why do you care so much?" Stella grows frustrated.

"Because I know what you're worth and what you could be capable of," He speaks as if this should flatter her.

"So, what are you going to do with me?" Stella huffs.

"I'm going to make you my wife." His words knock the air from her.

"W-wife?"

"Yes. First, I'll sully you so no one else will want you." He licks his lips as his eyes venture south toward Stella's covered but large chest. "Then I'll take you home with me as my bride."

"I'd rather be slaughtered and left for worm food than marry you," Stella sneers. Lyall only grins more.

"If you don't come with me, then I guess I'll have to go for your sister," He brings up Althea. Stella holds her breath.

Althea... No, he cannot have Althea.

Stella's eyes go in the direction of the door She just needs to escape him. Stella needs to run away. She will get Althea, then head toward Basil if he has not yet arrived. With his pipe, they can protect themselves. She just needs to escape.

"I would rather have you. Your sister... She draws too much attention. My father would become intent on seducing her. But you... you are more my type. But if you will not come, then I have to take Althea. So? Who will it be? You or Althea?" Lyall sets the choice.

"You will not have my sister," Stella answers.

"Good, so I'll have you." He brings his mouth to her neck and attacks her with fervent kisses and bites. Stella steels herself not to react, though she wants to jerk away from his offensive, wet mouth. A reaction would only make him more excited.

She bides her time thinking about what her parents taught her. So often, she and Althea grew bored with the lessons her parents sought to teach them about fighting. Never did she think she would be in a predicament that would call for it. Oh, to return to a time as then... She longs for the days she lived in the care of her parents with her siblings. She could be naïve and innocent then. Alas, this is no time for melancholia.

Lyall's open mouth is brought to her closed, tight lips. His rough tongue demands entry into her mouth while slathering her face with his saliva. His hand moves from her left wrist so it can slip beneath her blue kirtle.

It is time!

Stella bends her knees and slides her left foot to hook over his right ankle. Lyall raises his face, his lips poised for a comment. Stella instantly brings up her palm to strike his cheek. Upon making contact, she claws his face, hoping to gouge his eye. She bucks her hips wildly as she does. Lyall loses his balance as he tries to pull away. Stella turns her body, causing Lyall to fall off her and the bed. She turns back and reaches for her basket on the other side of the bed.

"So that's how you want to play?" Lyall grabs her long braid and yanks her back on the bed. She rolls to come under him. She swings her right hand.

"Ah!" Lyall screams as the knife Stella had grabbed from the basket plunges into his neck. As her attacker is screaming out and holding his injured area, Stella leaps off the bed and runs out of the cottage. She runs without looking back. She runs despite her lungs and legs burning. Her panicked heart cries out, though her mouth cannot. She can hear her name echoing in the forest.

Stella's feet stop dead in their tracks as she finds Mr. Horn, or rather what is left of Mr. Horn. His jaw is ripped off while his chest and abdomen are ripped open. His blue eyes stare out lifeless but terrified. She covers her mouth to keep from vomiting.

"Stella?" A faint, broken sob comes from her left. Stella turns her head to see the wet-eyed Gus sitting on the ground. She grabs one of Mr. Horn's dropped axes from the ground. She holds it toward the standing woodcutter.

Is this the real Gus, or has Lyall disguised himself again?

"Stella, what are you doing?" Gus raises his hands, his eyes giving away his surprise.

"Are you the real Gus Horn?" Her arms shake, holding the weapon.

"Yes!"

"Prove it!" Stella orders.

"What is going on?"

"Prove to me you are not a shifting sorcerer. Prove it!" She barks.

"A shifting sorcerer?" Gus thinks about part of her words. "What are you talking about?"

"A sorcerer is the wolf! He's Lyall Blevins." Stella quickly spits the new facts, making Gus's blood drain from his face at the news. "Now, tell me who you are!"

"Gus! I'm Gus!" He insists. "How can I prove I'm Gus?"

Stella pauses. She does not know him well enough to ask something extremely personal. Today's conversation was the first time they spoke at great length.

"What are you wearing on Septday?" She gives her test. He pauses. A weak smile comes to his face.

"Thick socks."

Stella lowers the ax but does not drop it. She reaches for his hand.

"Gus!" she shrieks. Blood splatters on Stella as a hand emerges from Gus's chest holding his heart. Gus's eyes become as lively as painted glass. His body falls forward. With the redhead fallen away, Stella sees the puffed chest and wicked smirk of Lyall. The stolen nightgown is gone, and he is shirtless. He shows off his Fallen's Star scar and the other unknown tattoo symbols. Great black, leathery wings are out of his back. She trembles at the sight of him and what has been done to Gus. Lyall presses Gus's heart to his skin. He absorbs the stolen organ. He licks his bloody fingers. Stella can only watch, horrified with tears gushing down her red cheeks.

"Now, where were we, Stella?" He takes a step toward her and his wings shrink and disappear into his back. Stella moves her foot to find them being sucked into the ground.

"Get away from me." She swings the ax at him. He catches the ax blade with his hand. She sees blood start down his hand and wrist.

"Stop being so hostile, Stella. It only makes me want you more." He pulls the ax out of her hands, then casts it toward the Horn men. Stella clasps her hands together and closes her eyes.

"Pleading won't work on me, dear," He laughs, stepping forward. Stella does not open her eyes but her lips move without words coming off them. Lyall stops to stare at her. Her face is completely calm despite the blood on it. Her lips tighten to form a tiny 'o'. The wind blows from her emitting a high pitch whistle. Lyall cringes at the sound. He steps back. Stella continues the melodious whistle. The ground retreats from her feet.

Fluttering and creaking wood draws Lyall's attention to the tree branches above him. A murder of crows has darkened the forest's ceiling. They stare down at the couple, unnaturally silent. Stella reaches a high pitch.

Down. Down. Down, the crows dive with their talons out before them. Lyall tries to swat them away, but they still scratch at his lifted limbs and face. They peck viciously when and where they can. Lyall curses and keeps trying to move as the birds do not give up their task.

The crows slash his flesh, causing blood to be drawn. The pecks leave deep holes. His hands do their best to protect his eyes from being plucked out.

Seeing her attacker being stalled, Stella silences herself and makes a run for it again. She will not and cannot stop.

"Stella!" She hears her name shouted again. Looking up, she sees some of her crows have fled in her direction as well. A howl rings throughout the woods.

If only she could sprout wings like the crows, she could reach the safety of her village faster. All she has are short, human legs. A faint growl behind her spurs Stella to push forward.

Catching sight of the east gate of Foxglove Grove, Stella's hope rises. It is not far now. She can see two men standing near the gate.

"The wolf! The wolf!" Stella screams despite her lungs almost bursting. The two men turn to the screamer. She sees them run into the gate only to return with others armed with their bows and arrows. They raise their weapons, ready to shoot.

"Shoot him!" Stella screams, not even turning her head. They still wait. What shame the men would have should they shoot her and not the wolf.

Stella passes the row of men into the gate. Arrows are loosed. Stella collapses to the ground, her legs aching from the unplanned run and fear. She gasps and pants while she tries to push herself up from the ground. Two women come to help the young woman.

"Ahh!" cries of terror arise from the men behind Stella. The women drop Stella as they see the shooters covered in flames. One woman runs to ring the village's emergency bell in the middle of the village while the other only falls to her knees in horror as she watches her husband burn. Stella begins crawling backward from the flames caused by the burning bodies. Lyall emerges scratched and peck marked.

"Look what you have made me do, Stella." He gestures to the running, burning men.

"Get away!" Stella orders.

"Enough of that mouth of yours!" Lyall waves his hand as he speaks in a language unknown to her. Stella's lips burn and melt together before they disappear, leaving only skin. No matter how much her jaw pulls down, her lips cannot reappear or part. Could she scream from the excruciating pain, she would.

Those who were trying to answer the call of the rung bell stop and cower as they see Lyall standing above the mouthless Stella. He moves his hands again. Black smoke wraps around her wrists and ankles, making them bind. He grabs her by her braid and drags her behind him. Stella thrashes about. Only her eyes can speak to her distress. Still, no one dares to come near her.

CHAPTER 4

In the woods west of the village where a group of birch trees is thickest, there sits a hut made of mismatched stone with a crooked chimney. Hip-high stone walls surround the homeowner's vegetable and herb garden which is in front of the home. Rosemary sprouts about the wooden gate door while lavender is against the house. Sage is potent in the old home. Only the truly desperate or curious villagers of Foxglove Grove come here.

Madame Fennella, as she has styled herself, lives in the woodland home away from prying eyes and, more importantly, away from those who oppose the use of magic. On this day, Madame Fennella sits by her fire wrapped in two blankets. Her nose is almost as red as her hair which lies flat about her shoulders. Madame Fenella's puffed brown eyes stare at the flames dancing as they heat a pot of stew. Her sable ferret rests about her neck.

Knock. Knock. Madame Fennella's eyes leave the fire to view the door. The ferret's ears perk at the noise.

"Come in," Madame Fennella croaks. The door scrapes against the floor as it is opened. In the doorway, Althea Sipos stands in the purple cloak she borrowed from her sister without permission. She holds a polite smile on her heart-shaped face. Madame Fennella grins at seeing the young lady.

"Mrs. Kenwyn was worried about you and sent me with some food for you." Althea lifts the basket in her hands.

"That was kind of her. Put it on the table please." Madame Fennella points behind her.

Althea closes the door behind her and slowly walks into the house. Althea is careful not to run into any of the tapestries hanging from the ceiling. She reaches the table close to the slow-rising woman. The table is covered with a purple cloth embroidered with silver and gold thread to make suns, stars, and moons. A brass stand holds a crystal ball and a latched wooden box rests on the far side of the table. Althea places the basket on the table as directed.

Madam Fennella comes forward still wrapped in her blankets and ferret familiar. She opens the cloth covering the food. Her mouth waters. She inhales deeply. Despite the mucous in her nostrils, some of the scent comes through.

"Your sister made these, didn't she?" The redhead guesses before covering her mouth as she coughs. She sees baked pies and loaves of bread.

"How did you know?" Althea looks up, her big blue eyes batting in astonishment.

"My third eye watched her," Madam Fennella taps the center of her forehead where an eye has been tattooed. Althea presses her lips together and stares at the third eye. Madam Fennella cackles.

"I am joking, girl. Your sister always makes her portions larger than either you or Briallen." Madame Fennella covers the food again. "And no slight to you or Briallen, but I am glad your sister was the baker of these. There is just something... special in each bite."

Althea nods in silent agreement, her eyes stay on the basket. It is not the first compliment she has heard about her sister's skill today.

"I see I have hit a nerve," Madame Fennella notes.

"No. Not at all. My sister will be pleased to have the compliment." Althea puts on a smile. Madame Fennella purses her lips, her eyes reading the young lady. She grabs her wooden box.

"You know, Briallen is my sister. She was better at many things than me. But I found my talents as I am sure you will too." Fennella takes some coinage from her box. "How much do I owe Briallen?"

"She said you owe her nothing," Althea repeats the order given to her by her employer.

"How kind." Madame Fennella puts the money back only to pause. "Of course, I should compensate you for your legwork."

Althea eyes the coin held in the other woman's heavily bejeweled fingers. It would be quite nice to have some money. She could add it to her savings for her trip back to Soldoro.

Never take anything from a witch. You can give to them as a kindness, but never take anything in return." Althea's mother once told her and Stella after a witch near Rexheart offered them sweets. She supposes Mrs. Kenwyn has learned this as well and therefore has asked for no payment.

"No, thank you, Madame Fennella." Althea shakes her head in rejection.

"I see you are just as kind." Madame Fennella closes her box. "But I cannot let you leave empty-handed. Please, pick something and take it."

Madame Fennella gestures to a nearby hutch where many filled vials sit. She can see they are labeled for their uses: fertility, virility, sleep, prosperity, small healing, hair growth, strength, and beauty. Many large gemstones sit in baskets as well. She turns her eyes away.

Never take anything from a witch. The words echo in her head.

"That's generous, but no, thank you," Althea rejects the second offer.

"I cannot let you leave without repaying you," the redhead sniffles.

"I need nothing," Althea backs away to return to the door.

"No. No. Come and sit. You may not take anything, but I can at least do a little reading or something." Madame Fennella points to a chair at the table.

"Oh, no, you don't have to…"

"I insist." A pale hand grabs Althea's forearm and pulls her to the table. Althea is pushed into a seat. Madame Fennella steps to her fireplace and grabs a ladle and mug from her mantle. She collects some of her stew from her pot and blows at the steaming cup, then dramatically downs it. She shudders, then places the mug and ladle on the mantle. Madame Fenella sheds her blankets and red nose, leaving her in a simple white nightgown that does not hide much of her womanly figure. She takes her cuddling ferret off her neck. Its ears perk again before it scurries toward the back of the house. Even the woman's hair grows a vibrant vermilion color and gains volume.

The madam takes her seat across the table from Althea. Althea can hardly believe her Mrs. Kenwyn and this woman are sisters given their vocations and difference in age but their red hair, eyes, noses and even build give away their relationship.

Madam Fennella clears her throat, then smiles. She reaches into her sleeve and pulls out a deck of black cards.

"I can read your cards for you." She shuffles them. "Or I can look at your palms."

Althea's hands go to her lap and out of view of the card shuffler. A heavy weight slowly creeps its way onto her neck, shoulders, and chest. The older woman's no longer puffy eyes search Althea's face for some interest.

"Don't you have something you want to know? Maybe about business? Love?" The madam raises an eyebrow.

"No. I'm not exactly interested in knowing about business or love," Althea shakes her head.

"I see. Well, I can do a general reading." Madame Fennella ends her shuffling.

"I don't… I don't know…" Althea bites her lower lip.

"Come on. It's fun. Almost everyone has come to at least have a reading from me," Madame Fennella grins while trying to convince the blonde guest. Althea chews on her lip.

Should I stay or go?

"I… well…"

"It's fun! Trust me! Even that stuffy priest's daughter, Hildegard, has come for a reading."

"Hildegard?" Althea thinks of the local priest's pious daughter. The meek young woman would not venture to a witch's home. Althea does not even think she has seen the girl leave the village walls in the past year.

"Yes. She was pleased. I know you will be. So let me read for you."

"I guess… it would not hurt…" Althea concedes.

"Excellent." Madame Fennella grins and moves her crystal ball. "Think of something you want to know whether it be a specific question or just a general 'what does my life hold' sort of question. Then tap my deck three times."

Althea does not think deeply, then taps. Madam Fennella spreads her cards on the table with a smooth, single motion.

"Pick three cards for your past, your present, and your future."

Althea slides out a card near the left of the deck, the center, then the right. Madame Fennella collects the excess cards and puts them in her box.

"Tap this card three times, then flip it over," the madam points to the card at Althea's right. Althea obeys.

The flipped card is black and blank till it turns white. An image slowly appears. Althea blinks several times as she sees her parents. Her father stands with an arm raised toward ten gold cups resting in the sky while his other rests around her mother's waist and is partially hidden by her golden hair. One of her mother's arms rests at her side while the other is raised. By their sides are Stella and their brother Basil. The brunette children have their arms raised as well. Althea is in between her siblings with arms raised and a smile on her face, like the rest of her family. She does not understand how her family's image has appeared on this card, especially the image of her and her siblings as children.

"Well, this is an excellent card. As the Ten of Cups card has appeared for your past, it means you have grown up in a loving, stable, harmonious family. That must have been nice." Madam Fennella remarks.

"Yes, we were happy even in the rougher times." Althea stares at the card, her heart yearning to be with her parents and brother.

Soon.

"Your mother is quite beautiful, just as you are." Madame Fennella compares Althea to her depicted mother.

Althea has always been told she favors her mother. They share the same peaches and cream skin tone, naturally amaranth pink lips, and a waterfall of goldenrod hair. Their heart-shaped faces, svelte bodies, and even their soft voices are similar. "Fairy-blessed", "peerless flower", "divine beauty", and many more compliments have been bequeathed to Althea and her mother by many, especially by men who have caught sight of them. She did not receive her mother's violet eyes. She gained her father's blue ones. Even without her mother's rare eyes, Althea knew she was just as beautiful if not more than her mother. She supposes this was her gift instead of baking or piping like her siblings.

"Thank you," Althea acknowledges the compliment.

"Your sister is pretty, but not as fair as you. I suppose that is why she *has* to be such an excellent baker." Madame Fennella looks closer at Stella's image.

The words do not exactly sit right in Althea's ears, but she says nothing.

"Does your sister have many suitors?"

"No. I think Gus Horn likes her, though he does not act on it. Otherwise, no one else favors her," Althea answers.

"I see, so there is not much competition for her... Does she favor anyone else in the village?"

"No," Althea shakes her head.

"Not even the new woodcutter?"

"Prin- Lyall Blevins?" Althea corrects herself instead of saying his nickname.

"Yes. I thought every maiden in the village liked him." Madame Fennella scratches behind her ear.

"Not us. I mean, I find him handsome, but as Stella keeps pointing out to me, he is a flirt. That does not interest Stella or me."

"Oh. So, if he were to proposition your sister, would she reject him?" Madame Fennella leans forward and props up her elbow so her chin may rest on her hand.

"I don't know. Why do you ask?" Althea cocks her head to the side.

"No reason. She is staying at the bakery today, correct?" Madame Fennella leans back and begins fingering her green malachite pendant.

"Yes. Oh-wait. No. She is making a delivery to Mrs. Beverly in the eastern woods."

Madame Fennella's face grows contorted in thought while her finger now twists the leather string her malachite hangs on around a few times.

"Is there something wrong?" Althea inquires.

"No. No." A shaken head and smile do not reassure Althea much. "Now, let's move on to the middle card. Tap it three times, then turn it over."

Althea obeys. Like the first, it turns white. Althea appears dressed in a knight's armor while riding a horse. She holds a large coin in her hand. However, it all appears upside down.

"Oh, should I turn it around?" Althea reaches for the card.

"No. It is meant to look this way," Madame Fennella stops Althea's hands.

"What does it mean?"

"In the present, you feel... stuck. You have a routine to which you follow and now you are bored. I am sure working in a bakery every day could become tiresome." Madame Fennella looks up to Althea, who presses her lips together and keeps her eyes on the card.

"You may need to have a minor change in your life. Do something spontaneous. Maybe leave the village for a few days or something." Madam Fennella advises. "Time for the last card."

Althea taps her last card thrice and turns it over. Althea lies on what appears to be the ground with her face turned away to look at the setting sun. Ten swords are in her back. Althea's back shivers at the sight. She looks up at Madame Fennella, who is frowning.

"What does this mean?"

"I am not sure, but... you may suffer a betrayal in the future that will lead to a great deal of pain and loss and an ending. An ending to what I do not know." Madam Fennella keeps staring at the card as if staring harder will help her find an answer. Althea shivers again involuntarily. The weight which was creeping earlier has grown heavier. The card reader easily detects her guest's unease. Madame Fennella attempts to smile.

"Now, this could be a mistake. Let me look at your dominant palm. It might clear up things." The cards are taken away. Madame Fennella reaches for Althea. Althea's hands stay in her lap.

"Come now. Give me your hand." Madame Fennella shakes her outstretched hands in urgency. Althea slowly raises her wrist and then lets them settle in the other woman's hands. Althea nearly pulls her right hand away, feeling the madam's cold, bony hands. Althea's hand is flipped so her hand is upward and able to be viewed.

"Hmm.... hmmm... huh... oh... hmmm," Madame Fennella keeps gazes intently at the hand.

Althea's palm is long while her fingers are short. Her palms have profound extra fleshy sections beneath her thumb, the other bottom half of her hand, beneath her pinky, beneath her middle finger, and her ring finger.

The lines on her hand are even more attention-drawing to the palm reader. Starting at the base of the index finger comes a long, deep line curving upward. However, the line has a large break in the middle and a smaller crossing line on the line. Below the first line is another long, deep line with a curve. The line appears as a chain line but has broken spots and small lines crossing it, just like in the first line. A third line comes around the thumb and ventures toward the wrist in a deep line. A final main line goes vertically through the first two in a light line. It breaks at least once.

"So?" Althea finally speaks.

"You are a passionate, loving person and will live a long life." Madame Fennella pushes the hand away.

"That's it? How does that add or take away from the cards?" Althea leans forward with brows furrowed. Madame Fennella wets her red lips with her tongue. Her ringed fingers go to play with the green malachite dangling from the leather string around her neck.

"Well... do you really want to know?"

"Yes." Althea nods.

"As I said, you are passionate and loving, though a little picky in the love area of your life, at least for now. But I see your emotions rule you, your thoughts often change, and your loving nature will cause you significant loss and pain later. You'll face changes both in your career and personal life. You will live a long life, but soon you will suffer much misery."

Althea breathes heavily.

"I'm cursed to live a long, horrid life?"

"Not necessarily. You will just suffer more often than others, I suppose." Madame Fennella leans back in her chair.

"That's just-just ludicrous!" Althea stands up with her hands balled.

"Now, now, no need to get so upset," Madame Fennella flexes her hands and fingers to indicate for Althea to sit back down.

"But why am I doomed to suffer? What am I to lose?" Althea has not taken a seat.

"Sit, you're making me anxious." The reader's eyes stay on the fists of her new client.

"I'm making *you* anxious? You're the one telling me my life is riddled with loss and pain. You haven't even told me what I'm losing or why I will have so much pain and loss." Althea huffs, her face turning red.

"Sit and I'll consult the ball." Madame Fennella reaches for the once-pushed-aside crystal orb. Althea sits with arms crossed and lips downturn.

"Give me your finger." Madame Fennella holds out her hand again.

"Why?" Althea gives over her hand. Madame Fennella brings it toward a sharp point on the brass holster.

"I just need a drop of your blood." She nearly cuts Althea's hand, but the younger woman pulls away.

"Whoa! No. No. I'm not giving over any blood," Althea holds her hand to her chest. The redhead brings her hand back to the crystal ball.

"Having your blood will help the ball give a more personal and clear vision."

"I am not giving you my blood." Althea shakes her head.

"Fine. Then you will need to hold the ball with me. Get up." Madame Fennella stands up with the ball and comes to the side of the table. Althea stands and joins Madame Fennella.

"Put your hands on the ball with me. Like that. Yes. Now stare deeply into the ball, as will I. Focus all your energy and thoughts on the ball."

The two women stare into the clear crystal. All Althea sees are her and Madame Fennella's hands in it. Smoke fills the sphere, making Althea's eyes widen but lock on the rolling vapor.

Green trees and a dirt path come into view. On the path walks a young man. His brown hair curls are wild, but his light blue attire is kept orderly. His violet eyes are focused on what is ahead. A silver pipe is raised to his lips. His brows are dipped in his concentration.

"Basil," Althea smiles, knowing the man to be her brother. The ball rolls, allowing her to see what is before Basil. Althea gasps as the horrid, giant wolf she has heard of these past three months is snarling there. Next to the wolf is Stella lying on the ground.

"Stella! What is happening?" Althea looks up at Madame Fennella. The pale woman does not answer but keeps her eyes on the ball. She grimaces. Althea returns her eyes to the ball.

"No!" Althea shrieks at what she sees and releases the ball, which falls from Madame Fennella's hands.

Crash! The ball shatters on the floor.

"My ball!"

"What was that? Is that happening now? How can I stop this?" Althea pays no attention to the glass on the floor.

"How am I supposed to know? You broke my ball. Unlike an Ora-Oculist I needed it to see the future. Now, I can't help you anymore," the owner of the broken item scoffs as she bends down to collect the pieces. "All I know is you better not interfere with Bardolph and his plans with your sister."

"Bardolph?" Althea fails to recognize the name.

"Ah!" Madame Fennella drops the glass she is collecting as she cuts her finger. She puts it in her mouth as she stands.

"Who is Bardolph?"

"He's that Blevins boy," Madame Fennella answers, venturing to her hutch. She grabs a small healing vial and pulls the cork out with her teeth before she spits the blockage away. She pours some of the liquid on her injury.

"Lyall Blevins is Bardolph? He wants Stella? I am confused." Althea steps toward the healing woman.

"Yes. Yes. Bardolph is this sorcerer from... I don't know where. He is just having some fun around here playing wolf and woodcutter." Madame Fennella uses her healed fingers to retrieve the cork to put back into the vial.

"How would you know?"

"He came here first. It is only polite to alert other dark magic persons of your presence so you do not have conflicting curses or reveal each other." Madame Fennella turns to go back to her seat.

"You knew he was the wolf and did nothing as he killed all of those people?" Althea is aghast.

"He's a sorcerer. He has fairy blood. I'm just a village witch. He could kill me like that." Madame Fennella snaps her fingers. "Luckily, a couple of nights in my bed keeps him from having my head. Besides, excluding Briallen, no one cares if I live or die. Why should I care if the others die? And he is leaving in the next few days, depending on your sister's answer."

"Her answer to what? Why does he want Stella?"

"You can hide it better than your sister, but your family has fairy blood. He and I could see it in your sister's eyes. So, Bardolph wants your sister for a wife or something. Why he did not choose you is beyond me as you are prettier, but he wants her so he is going to take her. Once he has her, he will leave and everyone can go back to their normal, boring lives here," Madame Fennella explains. Althea gulps at the mention of their blood.

"Even if we have fairy blood does not mean we have great magic. Why would he want her to wife because of our little fairy blood?"

"I do not know or care. It is none of my business. Now, please, leave. I have to clean up this mess." She gestures to the glass on the floor.

"But I have to stop him from taking my sister and from what-what I saw in the ball. How do I do that?" Althea takes hold of the witch's arm.

"There is nothing you can do about it. Even if you have fairy blood, I am sure you have not nurtured it. You will be as powerful as a newborn against Bardolph. The best thing for you to do is just let Bardolph have your sister and let him leave. Find your brother and keep him from trying to confront Bardolph. At least then you will have one sibling left." The advice is given to Althea. The blonde lets go of the redhead.

"You're wrong. I will keep both of my siblings!" Althea declares.

"Good luck then. You'll need it," Madame Fennella crosses her arms. Althea flees the crooked home with the witch inside. She races away. She must stop her brother and guard her sister.

Madame Fennella walks to the doorway of her home to watch the golden girl run off. Her ferret comes to her side. She picks up her familiar. Her hair falls flat again and her chill returns. She sniffles.

"How sad. She truly thinks she will be able to save them."

CHAPTER 5

Althea races through the western woods, not caring to look at where her feet go, causing her to stumble and scrape her recently-read palms on the trees she grabs to regain her balance. Several times, her borrowed cape catches on tree limbs and thorny bushes only to rip by the force of the maiden running.

Reaching the main road leading to the village, Althea can have a clearer path. She wishes she had wings to fly her faster, or at least a horse. Her heavy breathing and wildly beating heart have become so loud in her ears that she does not notice the sound of clopping horseshoes.

"Thea?" The call of her name causes the runner to look backward. Upon a speckled black and white horse with large saddle bags rides Basil, his brown curls bouncing with the rest of his body as he rides. A smile on his face warms Althea's heart as she sees it.

"Baz!" She starts toward him and his horse. Basil stops the horse next to his breathless sister.

"What are you doing out here?" He does not dismount.

"I was delivering food to a witch," Althea answers.

"A witch? Ooh. Mother would not like you associating with witches." He leans back from her as if getting closer would get him in trouble.

"It was a charity delivery." Althea frowns at her younger brother.

"Well..." Basil intends to tease and scold her.

"But forget that! Baz, we have to go to the village now and get Stella. We have to get her and go!" Althea interrupts him.

"Why?"

"There is a sorcerer who wants to take her away and make her his wife. We have to get her first before he can," Althea states. "Now let me up on your horse."

Aghast and confused, Basil gives his sister his hand and helps pull her up onto his horse. He kicks his horse hard so they may be quicker.

"Oh, great El-Yah! What is that?" Althea points to the distance. Black smoke rises high above the trees into the clear blue sky.

"Looks like smoke from a bonfire or something," Basil answers.

"It's coming from the village! We must hurry, Baz!" Althea urges her younger brother.

"Hold on to me." Basil kicks his horse. Althea holds tightly around her brother's waist as the horse takes off at a full gallop.

Growing closer and closer to the village, Althea and Basil hear screaming and shouting. The village's emergency bell rings. The smoke's scent increases in their nostrils. Entering the western gate, Basil pulls his horse to a stop.

The villagers of Foxglove Grove are in a panic. Buildings have caught fire, causing many to form assembly lines from the village's center well to try to put out the fires with passed buckets of water. Some are trying to throw water on men who are aflame. Others tend to the wounds of burnt men. Some cry over charred men who must not have been put out in time.

"Stella! Stella! Stella!" Althea jumps down from the horse. Basil jumps off the horse and ties it to a hitching post.

"Stella! Stella!" He calls.

"Help us, young man," the man Althea knows to be a cobbler calls Basil. Basil moves to help but Althea grabs his arm.

"We have to find Stella and get out."

"I must help these people, Althea. Go get Stella while I help them with these fires." Basil pulls from her and goes to join the assembly line.

"Stella! Stella!" Althea leaves her brother and calls for her sister.

"Althea!" Mrs. Kenwyn runs to the blonde. Althea turns to the graying baker.

"Mrs. Kenwyn! Where is Stella?" Althea thinks only of her sister. Mrs. Kenwyn's brown eyes are wet with tears.

"He took her, Oh, El-Yah... He set the men on fire and then took your sister's mouth. He dragged her away. Oh, it was horrible, Althea. Just horrible," Mrs. Kenwyn weeps. Althea's heart sinks. She does not even have to ask who it had been set aflame.

"Which way did they go?"

Mrs. Kenwyn points toward the eastern gate which is essentially ash now. Althea leaves her employer. She directly goes to Basil. She rips him out of the assembly line, not caring it causes a bucket of water to spill on the ground.

"Thea!" he exclaims, having been splashed with the water meant to extinguish the fire.

"He has her, Baz. He has already taken her. Mrs. Kenwyn said he took her mouth, whatever that means, and dragged her away. We have to go get her!" Althea pulls him. Basil does not argue with his sister. They return to his horse which they quickly ride off out of where the eastern gate was. They must find Stella.

***

The captive of the sorcerer thrashes about despite her back being torn up by the rocky path on which she is being pulled. Breathing is far more difficult as Stella only has her nostrils and the dust of the path keeps rising into them. She is not quite sure what hurts worse, her cut back, inflamed nostrils, or her scalp which is barely held to her head as her captor has yanked her behind him by her braid.

"Stop all this resistance before you make me rip off all your hair!" The sorcerer stops and drops her braid. A muffled response is lost on the sorcerer, as no words can come from the smooth skin which has replaced Stella's mouth. But her purple eyes convey enough contempt now that her voice is taken. He squats down, so he is closer to his face.

"Oh, those eyes... I love the fire in them. It makes me want to take you right here, right now." He takes hold of her by her full cheeks. She tries to jerk her head away, but he squeezes her cheeks tighter. She winces in pain.

"Does that hurt? Good. I can be gentle, Stella. I can be sweet, kind, and loving. But when you act like this, I have to hurt you. I don't want to hurt you but I will make you submit." His hold does not relent. She does not try to move lest she risks more pain. He smirks.

"I will break you and remake you as mine." He drags his tongue over where her mouth should be. He takes hold of her shadow hand bindings and pushes them above her head. She tries to pull her hands down, but she is unable. The shadowy bindings have been attached to the ground. She tries to raise her legs to push against her attacker as he climbs atop her. Like her hands, her bound legs cannot move. She wriggles and writhes beneath him. His hands venture beneath her kirtle and skirt, where no man has dared to venture. She grunts as she tries to turn from his unwanted, wandering hands. Her thighs remain tightly together.

"Stop fighting this!" the sorcerer strikes her face. Tears of pain and frustration spring to her eyes, but she does not stop resisting.

"Get away from her!" Basil jumps from his horse. Lyall turns his head almost to look over his shoulder at who would dare interrupt him. He sees Basil approaching as Althea dismounts the horse as well. Lyall pushes himself off Stella's body and turns around to face the young man and maiden.

"This is the only and last warning you will receive from me. Leave us alone." Lyall is generous.

"Get away from our sister, you monster," Althea barks back.

"Monster? I'll show you a monster," Lyall snickers. Basil steps back with arms spread to block Althea as he watches in horror with her at the man shifting his shape.

Lyall grows taller and taller while his skin sprouts thick, black fur. His nose and mouth stretch out into a snout as his teeth grow into sharp fangs. Lyall gets on all fours since his hands and feet have turned into clawed paws. From his back sprouts large leathery wings. He grows greater than a bear and licks his barred teeth. He charges at the interrupting Sipos siblings.

Althea rummages in the saddlebags in search of anything with which to defend Basil and herself. Basil, on the other hand, reaches for his hip. He pulls from a holster a silver pipe. With a confident smile, he brings it to his full lips.

A low smooth note leaves the instrument only to be followed by a higher long note. Higher and quicker the music grows. The wolf slides to a stop as he whines and lowers his head at the sound. Basil lowers the pitch and slows his playing. The wolf stops his whining but does not move to attack. Stella finds her bindings are loose but her mouth has yet to regain itself. Still, she tries to pass the wolf. She tries to smile seeing the foolish choice to change form has left her captor weak against her brother's playing.

Althea pulls out a knife hidden in a bag. She turns and gasps, seeing her approaching sister is missing her mouth. Just as Stella is about to pass the wolf, he momentarily breaks from his enchantment to block her from joining her siblings. Basil raises the pitch and speed once more to cause Lyall to whimper and lower his head again.

Stella runs. She gets behind her brother to join her knife-wielding sister. Althea takes Stella's face in her hands.

"Oh, Stella, what has he done to you?" Althea's eyes run over her disheveled, blood-splattered sister. Stella would answer if she could. Instead, Stella takes the knife from Althea's hand. She turns around and passes Basil. Althea grabs Stella's arm.

"What are you doing?" Althea asks though she will not get a verbal answer. Stella points to the knife, then to the cowering wolf. Althea lets go of her sister.

Stella passes Basil and confidently comes toward the wolf. Her violet eyes glare at the beast before her that dared to not only hurt her but killed her friends. She raises the knife as she stares into the hazel eyes of the wolf. There is fear there.

"Please," she can hear his fragile voice. His eyes plead for mercy as he whimpers. Stella wants to bring down the knife and end this creature's life. Yet... her hand lowers to her side. She turns away. She returns to her siblings.

"Why don't you kill him? He is evil!" Althea questions her sister, but once more, Stella cannot answer.

Stella takes Althea's hand. Slowly she traces letters in her sister's palm with her finger. Althea nods, receiving the message.

"Baz, lead this *thing* back to the village and let the villagers have their justice."

Basil nods as he continues to play. Stella and Althea climb aboard the horse once Stella picks up Basil's knife. They turn to return to the village. Basil follows behind, playing a peppy melody. He walks backward to keep his eyes on the wolf who is commanded by the music to follow him.

"I still think you should have killed him, Stelly," Althea comments to her sister as they ride.

"Ah!" Basil trips on an unseen root and falls on his backside. As his lips are removed from his instrument. The song has been broken, as has its control.

Before Basil can bring his pipe back to his lips, the beast loses his fur and height and becomes upright as a man. The sisters turn their heads in time to see the sorcerer approaching the fallen Basil.

"You dare to have controlled me!" Lyall waves his hand, causing Basil's pipe to fly out of his hand. Basil looks back to his sisters.

"Ride!" He orders. Stella hops down from the horse then slaps its backside sending it running away with Althea.

"No!" Althea cries out, not wanting to have been sent away.

Stella takes the knife and cuts the flesh formed over her mouth. Despite the pain and gushing blood, her mouth is free to speak.

"Get away from my brother!" Stella orders.

"You do not tell me what to-"

"I spared your life! You are indebted to me! Pay your debt now by sparing our lives in return!" Stella interrupts the sorcerer before he can finish. The sorcerer snorts.

"Fine. I will not kill you or your siblings. You must come with me though and not resist me," he insists.

"No. You are the one who owes *me*. I will not go with you!"

"Then I must make you want to come." His eyes grow dark as his face twists into a cruel grin. Stella keeps her hold on her knife, as she is unsure of what he will try.

The sky grows dark with black clouds as Lyall speaks in his foreign tongue. A boulder of invisible weight keeps Stella and Basil breathless and bound to the earth. The knife is dropped. Their purple eyes are unable to leave Lyall. The sorcerer points his hands toward the siblings. His eyes have gained black veins and his irises start turning red. His exposed fallen star tattoo glows blood red.

"Gahhhh!" Basil screams out in pain. Stella's eyes shift to him. His legs grow beyond normal human length as brown coarse hair pops out. His feet burst through his shoes and become large birdlike talons. His torso stretches and gains fur. From the base of his spine comes a long, scaly tail. His arms spread and grow into fleshy wings.

"Stella! Stella, help me!" Basil cries out, but Stella is paralyzed.

"Baz!" Only her voice can come to him.

Basil's ears grow large and pointed. He gains a long snout as his face is covered in hair. His eyes become so enlarged they are almost on the side of the sides of his head. His violet irises turn blood red. From the top of his head sprouts two large horns like a bull's. His voice turns into a high-pitched screech.

A black smoke chain appears and wraps itself around the monstrous Basil's long neck and connects to Lyall's hand. Basil gnashes his teeth and tries to pull away from the chain to go near Stella. Lyall tugs and Basil's new form is whipped back toward Lyall's feet. Basil rises and proves to be nearly three times larger than Lyall. He attempts to hit Lyall. An invisible force prevents Basil's body from making contact with Lyall. The sorcerer laughs.

"You cannot harm me. I am your master now," Lyall proclaims and flicks the chain, causing Basil to fly above his head.

"Let him go! Change him back!" Stella screams. Lyall walks toward the sister. He reaches her stilled body and wraps his hands around her neck. He speaks again. Stella feels a sharp pain in her throat.

"Listen to me, my dear. I am the one to give commands, not you. Until you come to me on hands and knees begging for me to make you mine, your brother will remain my beastly slave, and you... any who calls you by your name will be as you were when your brother called for your help. Still as stone," Lyall mocks her former stuck self, "It's a shame you cut your mouth free. Your luscious lips are utterly ruined."

"Take me now and let my brother go!" Stella tries to bargain, her eyes watering. "Please, Lyall. I will do whatever you want. Just change him back and let him go!"

"Bardolph. My name is Bardolph," He corrects her.

"Please, Bardolph."

"I like you begging," Bardolph chuckles. "But I want you to suffer."

Stella glares at the curse maker.

"Come to me at my home, east of the sun and west of the moon. Till then, think only of me," He gives her cut mouth a kiss. He pulls away, pleased with himself.

Bardolph lets go of Stella's neck and turns around. He pulls at the chain. Basil's body flies toward Bardolph. Basil lands on his stomach. Bardolph ascends onto Basil's back. He stands on the cursed man's spine and pulls up on Basil's chain, making Basil push himself up.

"Goodbye, my dear," Bardolph waves, then pulls up again. Basil jumps up toward the smoke-filled sky. Stella looks up and watches Basil fly away with Bardolph on his back.

The sky is clear of clouds, and Stella's body regains its ability to move. She falls to her knees and tears overtake her bloody cheeks. Her lungs shudder along with the rest of her body. She hangs her head, ashamed and distraught. Her tears drip from her bloody chin to the dirt below her. She brings her palms to her eyes to wipe away the tears.

You need to find Althea. Find Althea and then Basil. Stella tells herself. She gets off the ground and collects the dropped knife. As she turns to go back toward the village where she had Althea and the horse go, she notices Basil's castaway pipe. She picks it up and holds her to her chest.

I will find and free you, Baz. I swear to El-Yah you will be found and free. Stella vows. She keeps the pipe to her chest and begins walking back to the village.

CHAPTER 6

Althea finally gets the horse to slow down. Althea looks back to where her siblings had been left. There is cackling above her head. Looking up, she can see a dark creature flying through the sky. A person stands on top of the flying beast.

"THEEEAAA!" the creature shrieks making Althea's horse rear, but Althea is not thrown off.

"Baz?" Althea regains control of her horse and makes it run. She must follow her brother.

"Baz!" she calls him. The winged creature begins to descend, allowing Althea to see the rider is Lyall/Bardolph. The sorcerer grins and then jerks on his smoke chain, causing Basil to ascend higher into the sky.

Althea tries to keep her eyes set on the sorcerer and her beastly brother, but they go so high they turn into a speck in the sky and then into nothing. Althea tries to keep on in the direction they had been flying but finds herself at the smoky gate of the village. Her eyes lower. The fires are out. The sooty people are in clusters. Not all buildings have been damaged but there is enough to affect the village. Many of the clusters are with the burn victims as they try to tend to their wounds or weep over their deaths. Her heart keeps sinking.

"Althea!" Mrs. Kenwyn runs to the girl and her horse. Althea gets off the horse in tears.

"Mrs. Kenwyn..." Althea keeps looking around.

"Where are your sister and the young man?" Mrs. Kenwyn looks for a sign of Stella and Basil. Althea shakes her head and hangs her head.

"I have lost them. The sorcerer took them from me. Madame Fennella told me I would suffer a significant loss but..." Althea sniffles and tries to wipe her tears.

"Oh, Althea," Mrs. Kenwyn embraces the young woman. Althea buries her face into the baker's neck and allows herself to cry freely.

"Let's get you inside. I'll put on some tea." Mrs. Kenwyn leads Althea toward the Golden Hearth Bakery, which has remained unharmed.

"No. I need to go get my sister." Althea steps out of Mrs. Kenwyn's hold.

"Let me go with you. If that sorcerer is still there, he-"

"He is not there. I saw him flying away. He has turned my brother into a-I'm not sure but he could fly and had the sorcerer on his back. I did not see my sister with them though," Althea informs her employer.

"Still, I will come with you. You should not have to go alone," Mrs. Kenwyn insists. Althea nods.

"Mother!" Elspeth comes to her Mrs. Kenwyn.

"What is it, Elspeth?"

"Father Engel has called for everyone to head to the church so we may have a head count of who is left and to pray away the sorcerer. Come, Mother and Althea." Elspeth takes her mother's arm and pulls. Althea frowns, having wanted to go immediately to find her sister, but perhaps going to the church would be better so she can gather a search party.

Althea follows the others to the church. Reaching the gate, she ties the horse there. She enters the grounds and building. She takes a seat in a pew with the Kenwyns. Feeling hot from the influx of body heat, Althea removes the purple cape and lets it pool around her on the pew. Some of the gathered villagers weep, others have begun fervent praying, others cling to their loved ones, and a group of men has begun the counting. Father Engel comes to his pulpit.

"We have counted those here, those being treated at Dr. Marsh's, and those who we have lost. We know of those who are ill and homebound as well. There are two missing people, Johannes Horn, and Gus Horn. Does anyone know where they may be?" the priest asks the congregation. No one can answer as none knows of the horrible fate of the father and son.

"I see. Well, as the rest of us are accounted for we should..." Father Engel moves on to another topic.

"My sister is gone." Althea stands and interrupts the priest. The congregation grows quiet.

"Miss Sipos, your sister... She was taken by the sorcerer. She is more than likely dead," Father Engel determines.

"But she may not be. I want to find her," Althea states.

"If she is alive, she will be with that sorcerer. It is too dangerous for our people to battle that sorcerer." Father Engel is unmoved.

"The sorcerer is gone. I saw him fly away over my head. But my sister was not with him. She is still out in the woods."

"Fly?" The word is mumbled among the villagers as they try to grasp the concept.

"I do not know if we should have anyone leave the village as of now. Who knows what the sorcerer has done in the woods. For all we know, he may have cursed it." Father Engel is resistant to giving aid.

"You're just going to leave my sister alone in a possibly cursed wood?"

"Your sister is probably dead. Just let her be until we know it is safe for us to leave the village." Mr. Welch, the village's reeve, stands up from the back of the full church. The bald man receives many agreeing nods as he heads out of his pew and toward Althea's pew.

"Should we leave her to be harmed further by a cursed wood?" Stella's friend, Emilia Marsh, stands to question Mr. Welch.

"I am not going to risk anyone being harmed to look for someone who-"

"Who what? Who goes out of her way to help others like old Mrs. Beverly? Who has never once asked anyone in this village to help? Who is the best baker this village has ever seen? No offense, Mrs. Kenwyn," Emilia praises the absent baker. Mrs. Kenwyn shakes her head to express her lack of offense.

"Who has been consorting with a sorcerer. Why else would he take her away if they were not in some seedy relationship?" Mr. Welch rationalizes as he starts to the front of the church.

"My sister has never consorted with any man in this village, let alone that sorcerer!" Althea defends her sister's honor.

"Maybe not in *this* village. You two have only been here for barely two years. How do we know if either of you has had relations with sorcerers before coming here? How do we know you two did not bring this sorcerer here with you?" Mr. Welch points out the lack of knowledge of the sisters' past. Althea opens her mouth to defend herself and Stella. However, Mr. Welch continues.

"I mean, we have all seen the older one's eyes. They are purple. Only magic persons have purple eyes. I suspect they are witches who have come to our village to scope us out before bringing this sorcerer to wreak havoc on us as that wolf," Mr. Welch theorizes.

"Witches are not born with magic blood. Sorceresses are the ones with magic blood," the comment is made by Father Engel, who only refutes this one fact and brings up another.

"Sorceress then," Mr. Welch corrects himself. "They must be sorceresses. I suppose the sorcerer is still out in those woods with her sister, waiting for us to come so he can curse us all."

"He is not! I saw him..."

"You are the only one to see. We cannot verify this is true," Mr. Welch cuts her off. Utterances of agreement ripple among the congregation.

"We are not witches or sorceresses," Althea refutes.

"Then how is your sister's food by far more delicious than any other? She must have spelled it so no one can have enough of it," the rotund Mr. Garvey adds to the conspiracy.

"And no one is naturally beautiful like you. You must use some spell to look like that," the hook-nosed, sallow Mrs. Welch hisses and points a boney finger at Althea. Many women seem to agree with this.

"And you must do it to try to seduce our men just like the witch Fennella does," Mrs. Engel accuses further. The speaker makes Althea's eyebrows rise.

"We should hold her in custody till we can put her through a trial to see if she is a sorceress." Mr. Welch shocks the accused blonde.

"I am no sorceress or witch," Althea tries to defend herself.

"A trial will determine that. Mr. Roach, take Miss Sipos into custody," Mr. Welch directs. Mr. Roach, the bulky jailer, comes forward to do as told.

"There is no need for this. I can vouch that neither sister has performed any sort of magic or consorted with men." Mrs. Kenwyn stands to block Mr. Roach from Althea as she defends her employees both present and absent.

"Just as you swore your sister Fennella was not a witch?" Mrs. Engel reminds all of the last time there was an accused witch in their midst previously. Mrs. Kenwyn would continue in her defense, but her credibility has been lost since she lied about her sister's dalliance with dark magic. Mr. Roach pushes Mrs. Kenwyn gently out of the way to reach for Althea. Elspeth jumps from her seat and blocks Mr. Roach.

"Has my mother lied since the trial of Madame Fennella? No, and she is not lying now. I have never seen either do magic or consort with men, despite the many who have tried to engage with Althea. There is no need to jail her or put her on trial." Elspeth goes on the defense.

"Let us take a vote, then. Who thinks we should detain Miss Sipos and put her on trial?" Mr. Welch puts the choice on the villagers. Mr. Welch raises his hand along with Mr. Roach, the other Welchs, the Garveys, the Engels, and an uncomfortably large number of others.

"And who thinks we should let Miss Sipos go free and search for her sister?" Mr. Welch gives the other option.

Althea, the Kenwyns, Emilia, and a few others vote this way. This group is far less than the other.

"We have voted. Seize her, Mr. Roach," Mr. Welch orders. Mr. Roach pushes the Kenwyn ladies out of his way and roughly grabs Althea's arm.

"Let me go! Let me go!" Althea resists. Mr. Roach takes Althea's other arm and lifts her. She kicks her feet, but it does not affect the jailer. He carries her out of her pew and into the main aisle. He heads for the door.

"Let me go, please. Please!" Althea pleads. Mr. Roach ignores her as do most.

"Please! I have to find my sister! Please, let me go!"

"Silence." Mr. Roach hits the back of the maiden's head. She goes limp in his hands. Mr. Roach throws the young woman over his shoulder.

Mrs. Kenwyn and Eseld attempt to follow Mr. Roach and Althea out of the church. However, they are blocked by Mr. Welch's large sons, Cordon and Gordon.

"Do stay, ladies. We must figure out a plan on what to do next." Mr. Welch points to the pew where the mother and daughter had been sitting. They stayed behind, hoping for the best for their wrongly accused friend. They wish they could be with Althea.

At the northern edge of town, Mr. Roach had arrived at the iron-covered jail holes dug into the earth. The man drops the unconscious woman on the ground so he can open the iron grates. The grates were large and heavy with an awkward metal pull which requires the use of both hands to open and secure. Once open, Mr. Roach not so gently rolls Althea inside the cavernous space. She lands with a thud on the hay-covered stone slab below. He closes the covering and pulls a lock from his belt to ensure Althea cannot escape.

Mr. Roach starts to the church to rejoin the other villagers. He pulls his snuff-box and takes a pinch. Invigorated, he puts the box back in his pocket.

"Mr. Roach." He stops when he hears his name called. He turns to see the older Sipos sister approaching.

Stella walks slowly toward him as the backs of her legs are exhausted and scraped badly like her back from the dragging. Her dress is torn, loose, and blood-stained. Her hair is greatly disheveled, falling out of her braid and an enormous bruise is forming on her cheek. However, her slit mouth, which has finally begun clotting, draws the most attention.

"Miss Stella?" Mr. Roach recoils at the sight of her.

"Mr. Roach, please…" Stella stops. Her eyes unblinkingly stare as the jailer's once rosy flesh turns to gray stone.

"Mr. Roach!" She speeds up her space and comes to the man. She touches him. Cold, hard, rough. He is stone. She feels no pulse and detects no air from him. Her shaking hand comes to her face to muffle the scream bubbling in her throat. She looks around for someone to help. Alas, there is no one she sees.

"The horse!" Stella catches sight of Basil's horse tied to the church gate. With one hand clutching Basil's pipe and the other picking up her skirt, Stella hastens to the church. She pushes the doors, but they meet resistance.

"Open, please. I need help!" Stella knocks loudly. The doors open. Cordon and Gordon grimace at the sight of Stella as the others gasp and look away.

"My El-Yah!" Father Engel calls out in horror.

"What happened to you, Stella?" Emilia is the first to head toward the returned woman. However, Emilia makes no distance as, like Mr. Roach, she has become stone. Screams emit from the onlookers.

"Emilia!" Elspeth goes to her.

"What have you done, witch?" Mr. Welch booms at Stella as he points at her. Stella steps backward.

"I have done nothing," Stella swears.

"You must have done something, Stella!" Mr. Welch hisses. Instantly, the pointer gains a stone appearance.

"Father! Stella, what did you..." Cordon cannot finish his question as he becomes like his father.

"Cordon! Stop this, Stella!" Gordon moves to grab but his fingers and body are rock before he reaches her.

"Why are you doing this to us, Stella?" Mrs. Engel questions only to become a victim.

"Mother!" Hildegard goes to her maternal statue. She gives Stella a hateful glare. "Why have you cursed my mother, Stella?"

"Hildegard! Sylvia!" Father Engel reaches his wife and daughter.

"Please, stop, Stella!"

"Have mercy on us, Stella!"

"Stella, pl-"

These phrases are uttered throughout the church, but it only becomes quieter as the persons are no longer human.

"I am not doing this!" Stella tries to explain but the panic among the villagers remains at a high.

"Undo this now! Undo this, Stella!" Father Engel demands, stopping his foot. Alas, he is gone now as well.

"Stop saying her name! Stop saying it!" Mrs. Kenwyn climbs onto a pew and screams having put together what is happening. No one listens but Elspeth. Finally, the church grows quiet. How could it not when all but three now are stone?

"I'm cursed. My name is cursed," Stella finally speaks with great pain on her face.

"I know, St-sweetheart," Mrs. Kenwyn approaches Stella. She takes in the injuries of her employee. "What has happened to you? Did he do all of this too?"

"I cut myself but he did everything else that led to this," Stella tearfully gestures to the room of statues.

"I see."

"Where is Althea?" Stella knows Mrs. Kenwyn will not know about Basil.

"They took her to the cells. They thought you two were witches or sorceresses and so they locked her away till they could come up with a trial," Elspeth finally speaks up, having stepped away from Emilia.

"I must get her out of there then." Stella starts for the door.

"Let us come and tell her of your curse first so she does not accidentally say your name," Mrs. Kenwyn suggests, picking up the purple cape Althea discarded earlier. Stella agrees to the idea. The three women leave the church. Dr. Marsh has come onto the street, having left the patients he had been treating in his home.

"Ladies, I heard a commotion. What is going-Whoa! What has happened to Donald?" Dr. Marsh stops as he reaches the stilled Mr. Roach.

"I..." Stella starts.

"My El-Yah! What has happened to you, Stella?" Dr. Marsh gawks at her face. The woman sighs at another loss. A significant loss is this, as he could have treated Stella's wounds.

"We should let no one else see you. Elspeth, go to the Marsh house. Tell the patients to not say her name no matter what. Also, gather some ointment and bandages for her wounds. I will go to Althea. And St-you should go back to our shop and wait," Mrs. Kenwyn devises.

"Yes, Mother," Elspeth goes on her mission.

"Yes, Mrs. Kenwyn," Stella nods. The three split and go their separate ways.

With her head splitting in pain and arm throbbing, Althea wakes grimacing in the dank hole. She looks up to the bright sky tarnished with the iron grate. Althea tries to sit up but finds she cannot put pressure on her sore arm as doing so makes it throb in burning pain. She rolls over and pushes up with her good arm. Upright, she further attempts to get to her feet. Her head is too low to reach the grate, but her arm can go through an opening.

"Hello? Mr. Roach?" She calls for the jailer.

"Althea! Althea!" Althea recognizes her name and the voice calling her.

"Mrs. Kenwyn, over here!" Althea calls, waving her good arm out of the grate.

"Althea." Mrs. Kenwyn gets on her knees at the grate. "Oh my! Your head is bleeding."

Althea reaches up and finds blood coming from her temple.

"My arm is not too well, either," Althea comments.

"I am going to get you out of there."

"No. I do not want you to get in trouble with Mr. Roach or anyone, Mrs. Kenwyn," Althea rejects the baker's statement.

"They will not mind," Mrs. Kenwyn remarks.

"I am sure they will. Please, go. I do not want you to get in trouble." Althea tries to wave Mrs. Kenwyn away.

"I will not. They have been turned to stone."

"What?" Surely, Althea has misheard her employer.

"They have been turned to stone. Nearly everyone in the church has been except Elspeth and me."

"But how? Did the sorcerer come back?" Althea's heart races at the thought.

"No. Your sister came and…"

Althea beams. "Stell-"

"Sh! Do not say her name!" Mrs. Kenwyn cuts Althea off.

"Why?"

"The sorcerer has cursed her name. Anyone who says it turns to stone. Do not say her name."

Althea gulps at the new information.

Just saying Stella's name will turn me to stone?

"I am going to get you out now. I took the key from Mr. Roach's statue. I will take you to your sister then." Mrs. Kenwyn produces a large key ring. She tries three keys before finding the correct one. Opening the grate, she reaches out for Althea's hands.

"Give me your hands."

Althea reaches up. She yowls as her injured arm is yanked, but she does not withdraw until Mrs. Kenwyn has pulled her to the surface.

"What is wrong?" Mrs. Kenwyn puts her hands gently on Althea's arm.

"I think it's broken."

"I will make sure we splint it then," Mrs. Kenwyn plans. She and Althea rise and begin walking back toward the center of the village. They quickly make it to Mrs. Kenwyn's bakery. They venture to the back room where the sisters lived.

Althea's breath catches as she sees her sister's back and legs being wrapped by Elspeth. Althea and Mrs. Kenwyn are quiet until Stella's fresh underdress is over the wrappings.

"Althea!" Stella turns and exclaims excitedly, seeing her sister. Althea jumps at the sight of her sister's bruised, bloodied, cut-up face. She swallows and steps to go on as she cannot let her fear of Stella's new look keep her away.

Stella covers her deformed mouth from her sister's delicate eyes. Stella notices Althea's blood. "What happened to you?"

"Never mind me. What did he do to you?" Althea nods to Stella's face.

"I did this. It was the only way I could speak to protect Basil and me," Stella answers then grabs a clean kirtle to put over her chemise.

"You need to put a splint on Althea's arm. We think it is broken," Mrs. Kenwyn informs her daughter, who nods. It does not take long before Elspeth finishes Althea's arm and dresses Althea's head.

"I need to treat and wrap your face before it gets infected," Elspeth looks at Stella. Stella nods and allows Elspeth near.

"We should write to Mother and Father about all of this," Althea voices her thoughts.

"No."

"No? They need to know what has happened. They can help us."

"No. I am the only one who can break this curse on Baz and me," Stella claims. Elspeth's hands slather ointment on her face.

"Your brother is cursed?" Mrs. Kenwyn raises a red eyebrow.

"Yes. Lyall-Bardolph-whatever his name is- says he will undo it all once I go to him at his home and beg him to make me his. So, I have to be the one, not Father or Mother or you." Stella reaches and touches Althea's good arm, but lets Elspeth keep working. "You should go to Soldoro and stay safe with Mother and Father until I can break this curse."

"Absolutely not! Where you go, I go," Althea refuses.

"I cannot let you get hurt like Baz because of me," Stella gently pushes down Elspeth's hand.

"Well, too bad. I'm going with you. You're not Mother, so you can't tell me if I can or can't go." Althea puts her hand on her hip and sticks her tongue out childishly. Stella rolls her eyes. She pulls up her covering again and mutters a 'fine'.

"You two will not do well to travel in your condition, but I fear for you two. Stay here to recover. When word gets out about people turning to stone because of you, they might try a witch hunt and lynching," Mrs. Kenwyn points out some of her developing fears.

"We will just leave. Althea and I need to find Baz quickly anyway."

"But your injuries are terrible, St-," Elspeth bites her tongue as she does not want to turn to stone.

"They will heal."

"You need a different name so no one slips up and calls you the cursed one," Mrs. Kenwyn recommends.

"Just go by one of your middle names. They are nothing like your first," Althea chimes in a solution.

"What name is it then?" Mrs. Kenwyn asks.

"Gloria," Stella gives the first of her two middle names.

"I will only think of Grandmother if you go by that. Go by the other name," Althea gives her opinion.

"What is your second middle name?" Mrs. Kenwyn inquires.

"Hajnal."

Elspeth chuckles at the name.

"Go with Hajnal. It's not close to your first name at all," Althea gives her opinion. Stella nods her head to agree to the choice.

"Well, Hajnal and Althea, I think you will need a proper doctor or a healer to treat you two before you go off too far on this journey. Your wounds can get infected, Hajnal, and your arm can heal incorrectly as well, Althea," Elspeth comments.

"We will keep that in mind." Althea smiles at Elspeth.

"But we must go as soon as possible. I do not want to let Baz suffer too long." Hajnal looks at the door.

"But you're not going to give yourself to Bardolph, are you?" Althea grabs Hajnal's arm.

"I don't know how else to break these curses," Hajnal admits.

"I might know someone who could help," Mrs. Kenwyn interjects.

"I don't think a dark magic person is a good way to go for them, Mother," Elspeth steps close to her mother.

"I know that, dear. I know of a fairy. She is old and lives in the Violetwood. But she knows much about curses and healing. Maybe she could help you find an alternative as well as heal you. She may even tell you which way to go," Mrs. Kenwyn steps closer to the sisters.

"A fairy?" The sisters lean in with wide eyes.

"Yes. You will have to find the Moon River in the Moonwood and follow it down to the Violetwood. She lives in a cottage with a yellow door. Tell her Briallen sent you," Mrs. Kenwyn instructs. The sisters nod soaking in the directions.

With the help of Elspeth, the sisters pack up their few belongings. Elspeth wraps the lower half of Hajnal's face. The Kenwyn women escort the sisters to Basil's horse. They add their small bundles to the beast and then make their way to the ashy gate for a farewell to their dearest friends.

"Thank you both so much," Hajnal speaks, though muffled. She embraces Mrs. Kenwyn, then Elspeth.

"Yes, thank you," Althea copies her sister's actions.

"Be careful and be treated as quickly as possible," Elspeth gives her last words.

"May El-Yah protect you both," Mrs. Kenwyn blesses them as she puts the once discarded purple cape around Hajnal as it is she to whom the cape truly belongs. The rips in it have been quickly stitched up by Mrs. Kenwyn while the sisters were packing.

Out of Foxglove Grove and into the Moonwood, the Sipos Sisters go, neither knowing what lies ahead for each of them.

CHAPTER 7

"There it is!" Althea points ahead with her good arm to the flowing water in the distance. Hajnal would smile if her cheeks were not partially split. They quicken their pace to the river they have easily found.

Reaching the river's edge, they stop and allow the horse to drink. Althea looks into the water and sees white stones sitting at the bottom. She reaches into the river to pluck a stone. As she pulls it out, the white stone immediately darkens till it is pitch black. Althea returns it to the water, where it regains its white appearance. Hajnal looks up and down the river for signs of anyone. Finding themselves alone, Hajnal is surprisingly pleased.

"Mrs. Kenwyn said to head toward the Violetwood so we will have to go south." Althea points to her right. Hajnal nods in agreement to save herself from pain.

Traveling along the river's side proves easier than the woodland trail they took. The ground may be softer but there are no roots to hurdle or fallen trees to go over or around.

As the sun begins to set, causing the once blue sky to turn a romantic shade of pink, the sisters find the green grass has become splattered with purple flowers. The trees which once had brown or whitish bark have gained a purple hue to them as well.

"I think we are in the Violetwood," Althea comments, taking in the change of nature. "We should make camp for the night, then. Who knows how far the fairy's house is."

The sisters decide to make their camp in a pleasantly situated piece of land amid the grove. Hajnal ties their new horse to a surrounding tree before she begins to unload the bag so the horse may not have to be burdened through the night.

"Can you start making a fire?" Hajnal asks her younger sister.

"I thought you would want to do that," Althea sheepishly grins.

Hajnal looks down at the ground. "I don't know how..."

"But you always make the fires at the bakery," Althea points out.

"Matches."

Hajnal thinks back to the many nights their family had to camp outdoors during their travels. The sisters and Basil would always be sent off to find kindling while their father and mother made preparations for the rest of the fire. Then, when it had been just the siblings, Basil always jumped to make their campfire.

"Well... I don't know how to make a fire, either," Althea admits. They stand awkwardly silent together.

"We can wear more clothes," Hajnal figures.

"Yeah. Of course, I don't have a cloak now since you lost mine," Althea huffs as she recalls not being able to find her scarlet cloak when they were preparing to leave.

"You stole mine," Hajnal points out Althea's fault.

"I borrowed it by accident. I wasn't paying attention to what cloak I was grabbing when I left to go see that witch," Althea claims. Hajnal sniffs.

"Looks like we won't need to make a fire, since your dress will catch fire with your lies soon," Hajnal snaps though it hurts.

"Alright. Alright. I took your cloak because I think it looks better on me. The red makes me look too pale," Althea confesses. Hajnal would smile in satisfaction, but it would only cause her pain. "You didn't have to lose mine though. It is the last thing Grandmother made for me."

"I didn't mean to leave it behind at Oma's but if I had hesitated..." Hajnal's mind refills with the memories of the day. Her hand begins to shake while tears fill her eyes. Althea notices the tremor. She tries to reach for Hajnal but Hajnal looks away from her. "You...you should just see if Baz has a cloak."

Althea turns her attention to their brother's set-down and rapidly packed bags.

"His bags were surprisingly heavy. He must have a lot of dirty laundry in them," Althea comments, having set down the last of Basil's bags.

As Althea starts to go through the bags, Hajnal removes the saddle from the horse. Hajnal stops as she looks at the leather item. She rubs it, feeling its softness. On the back edge of the seat is engraved in silver lettering 'Meteora'.

"Baz named the horse, Meteora." Hajnal continues to remove the saddle. She turns around with it in her arms. "Althea, look at this saddle. It must have cost a lot of-" Stella stops, seeing her sister on her knees with one of Basil's bags open. "Is that..." Hajnal's eyes stare at the pack's contents.

"It's gold!" Althea runs her hands through the large gold coins filling the bag. She bites a piece and finds the metal soft. "It's actual gold!"

Hajnal drops to her knees to touch the coinage herself. She hops up and begins grabbing the other bags to open them.

Gold. Gold. Gold.

"It's all gold in these bags!" Hajnal exclaims, astonished.

"How in the world did Baz get all this gold?" Althea questions, moving to the last of Basil's bags. *I guess he was an exceedingly successful piper.* Hajnal has to assume. Althea opens the last bag.

"I found his greatest treasure," Althea announces in a sing-song voice.

"Really?" Hajnal comes to Althea's side excitedly. She looks in the bag. Hajnal rolls her eyes and laughs. She holds her face with her hands to calm it.

"I can't believe all the gold is his. I didn't think he was as good a piper as Father or you," Althea comments, rummaging in the laundry bag. She pulls out a clay bird. She smiles, looking at it.

"Better than the average piper," Hajnal praises the brother. "Must have been a big job."

"He did have Phila tell us he was hired by a duke in Belterre. I guess he was rewarded handsomely," Althea holds up the named clay bird.

Hajnal takes the bird from Althea's hand. "She's in good shape."

"We should send her or Galatea to tell Mother and Father what has happened," Althea suggests. Hajnal moves to her bag. She opens it and finds her clay bird inside. She has Basil's Phila set next to her Galatea.

"No." Hajnal covers up the clay birds.

"But they may be able to help." Althea brings up the possibility of coming to her sister's side.

"No. They will want to intervene and they may get hurt or killed. I think it will just be better to leave them out of this. Besides, if we can't figure out a way to get Basil freed and back to normal, I will give myself to Bardolph. Mother and Father would not silently allow that to happen."

"I will not either. You will not enslave yourself to that monster." Althea's hand goes to Hajnal's shoulder.

"I will do what I must, Thea." Hajnal stands.

"But Basil wouldn't ask you to do that for him."

"But it's my fault we've all ended up like this. If I had gone with Bardolph when he first proposed, then Baz would be fine. No one would be stone, burnt, or dead, and we wouldn't be all battered, broken, and bloody."

"Do not blame yourself for his actions. You did what was right and we are going to make this all right. And that sorcerer is going to get what he is owed." Althea squeezes Hajnal's shoulder in reassurance. Hajnal just nods.

"We should rest," Althea directs seeing blood coming into her sister's bandages.

The sisters close Basil's bags and put them in a pile. Hajnal allows Althea to take the saddle for her makeshift pillow. Althea rummages through Basil's laundry bag once more and pulls out his blue cloak to use for her blanket. Hajnal spreads the blanket from under the saddle to cover Meteora better and returns to lie down next to the pile of bags, using her own for her pillow and her purple cloak as a blanket. Both she and Althea stare at the sky which has turned a navy blue with the faintest speckling of stars. They barely see them through the thick branches of the surrounding trees.

Althea is quick to find her sleep but Hajnal lays awake with her eyes lifted to the heavens. She tries to close her eyes only for flashes of Gus's heart bursting from his chest to appear. She feels Bardolph's hands and tongue on her. The scent of burning flesh lingers in her nose. Since Althea is asleep, Hajnal can finally cry. She cries for her brother, Gus, and his father, for Mrs. Beverly, and for those hurt and killed trying to help her. She weeps till her body gives up.

Just like every night, Hajnal stands before the protruding stone gatehouse with a lowered iron gate. Ivy creeps up the gatehouse walls and the towers on either end of it. Hajnal merely has to step forward for the gate to rise creakingly. With the round-top entry open, Hajnal ventures inside the grounds. Hajnal gazes at the white stone castle which seems to glow in the moon's light and millions of stars not obscured by the forest outside the border walls. The rectangle pool with scalloped corners before the main entrance of the castle shines as if the waters were made from celestial bodies. In the center of the pool are two marble unicorns rearing up and facing each other.

Hajnal's feet have somehow become covered in pointed, white leather shoes with a bar strap to keep them secured to her. Her blue kirtle has been upgraded to a white gown with silver and gold embroidery. Her hair has been braided, pinned up into a coif, and covered by a rounded, white velvet hood with an intertwined silver and gold trim and a white veil coming off the back. Another veil has been pinned into the side of the hood to cover the lower half of her face. Only the upper portion is free from cover. Over the years, she has tried to remove the veil and different clothing items. She fails each time and so she has accepted her attire. No longer does she feel any pain in her face.

Drops of blue flames flicker and jump toward the castle's main entrance. Hajnal follows them. The purple wood doors are closed, allowing the iron inlay in them to create an eight-point star. She does not have to touch the doors for them to open. Hajnal enters the dark hall with the jumping flames to lead her. She heads toward a back spiral staircase. Up four floors she goes with an ease not known to most who walk four flights of steep stairs without stopping.

Exiting the stairwell, she comes into a dark hallway with a few candles lit. The dancing guides continue this way. Following the trail of lights, she comes to a pair of open doors. The walls are white with golden pillars between each of the floor-to-ceiling windows. Hanging from the ceiling are several golden chandeliers lit to illuminate the entire room. Many times she has come to this ballroom. The blue lights disappear.

"Stella!" She hears her name. Hajnal excitedly spins around to look at the room's opening.

Tall is the man who enters. He has not turned to stone, giving her some relief. Everything about his clothing is white like hers, from his boots to his hose to his long tunic embroidered with a large, silver eight-point star trimmed with gold. His belt is silver and the buckle is gold. Unlike her hair, his thick but wispy curls freely bounce with each step. In some lighting, his hair is blond, while in others it appears to be a shade lighter to match the stars. A golden circlet with silver stars sits upon his head. Coming down from the crown are two golden chains attached to a white veil covering the lower half of his face, just as it does Stella's. Still, she can look into his large cornflower blue eyes. His long dark lashes around the eyes make it appear as if his eyes were painted on his face.

"Astro!" She smiles at him, though he cannot see it. They quickly step up to each other. He holds out his large pale hands to her but she passes the option of taking them. Instead, she embraces him and buries her face into his shoulder.

His oddly natural musk resembles the semi-sweet aroma of applewood and has a warm, resinous odor similar to heated amber. It fills her nose and causes her body to become lax in his hold. The comfort of his hold is the perfect amount of whelming. Her eyes release her tears.

"Stella, tell me what is the matter?" He tightens his hold on her instead of pushing her away. Her tears darken the white linen he wears. He strokes her back. She leans more against him.

"Pray, tell me what upsets thee so. Thou have not come to me in such distraught spirits since the passing of thy grandparents. Has another tragedy struck thee?" He inquires. Stella finally moves backward. Astro's arms allow her to come away from him.

"Oh, Astro, I have caused something horrid to befall my brother and my village," Hajnal sniffles, wiping her tears. Astro produces a handkerchief for her use. She accepts the cloth. She quickly wipes her face.

"I am sure thou are not at fault for whatever has happened," he speaks without knowing.

"It is my fault, though. I am the one who brought the sorcerer's wrath on us," Hajnal's glistening eyes go to her hands holding the soiled handkerchief. Astro's hands cover the outside of her thick ones. Her hands are warm like her kitchen's oven while his are soothingly cool like a northern mountain stream.

"Please, elaborate, Stella, so I may perceive who is truly at fault."

Sighing, Hajnal looks up toward the ceiling to one of the hanging chandeliers. Her gaze finally lowers to meet Astro's.

Hajnal proceeds to tell him everything. She does not hold back even though she knows it may upset Astro. When she does cry while reliving the trauma, Astro brings her close to his chest. He understands her words despite the sobs.

"I do not want to be with him at all, but unless I can break this curse, it is what I will have to do," Hajnal finishes defeated, and pulls back from his chest.

"No!" He speaks suddenly, almost making Hajnal jump. Her cheeks redden at his dislike of her marrying someone else. He clears his throat.

"Thou should not be forced into such a dreadful union. There are always ways to reverse curses. Some can be broken just by saying the sorcerer's true name. Some just require an elixir or a rare magical fruit. Some just require an act of true love, like kissing someone." Astro presents many options.

"You sure seem to know a bit about breaking curses," the maiden notes.

"I have a few books about them. But I think thou should seek the counsel of a fairy." He suggests.

"Althea and I are going to find the one who lives in Violetwood."

"Althea...it is good she is with thee."

"Yes and no. I'm glad to not be alone but I'd rather her be somewhere safe like with our parents back in Soldoro."

"Will thou send word to thy parents?"

"No. I am twenty and five. I need to be able to settle my problems without having to run to my parents for help. I also do not want to cause any stress to them. I'd rather find Basil and tell them afterward."

"There is no shame in asking the ones thou love for help, especially thy parents."

"I know they will try but it will only hurt them. I do not want to be responsible for more harm to my family. If I break the curse, I will tell them."

"Thou will break it." He put his hand on her shoulder.

"Thank you for your confidence in me. I hope you are right."

"I am as I often am," His hand slides down her arm from her shoulder to her hand. The motion makes her skin raise and warm further.

"Perhaps you could show me your books on curses in case I cannot find the fairy," Stella suggests.

"Of course," Astro offers his arm to her. She takes hold of it ever so lightly.

Astro leads her out of the room and takes her to a higher level of the castle. He takes her into a room almost as big as the ballroom had been. The walls are made of bookcases towering so high rolling ladders are needed to reach the higher shelves.

Hajnal has been here many times. She watches as Astro climbs and slides around on the ladders. He tosses the book down to her when he finds the ones he desires. With arms full, she ventures to a velvet couch near the fireplace burning on its own. Astro slides down the ladder and comes to join her. He takes most of the books from her so she is not burdened by them.

"I also selected geography books so we may find this place the sorcerer mentioned," Astro points to one of the larger books. Hajnal looks up from the book and stares at the young man with all the books.

"Astro...you are simply wonderful," Hajnal smiles at him though he cannot see it.

"I do not deny that," he laughs confidently. Hajnal smiles and tries to pick up a book. Her hand passes through it. Astro's light eyes give away his displeasure.

"I suppose my time is up for the night," Hajnal watches her hand fade.

"I will read while thou art gone and share what I learn with thee when thou return," Astro promises.

"Thank you." And with that, Hajnal disappears from the other world.

CHAPTER 8

"Is that it?" Althea catches sight of a cottage by the river. The structure is made of stacked stone with a thatched roof. a spinning water wheel attached the cottage to the river and a small barn stood a few meters away. But as they grew closer to the home, they could see the entrance is closed, allowing the sisters to see the color. Though chipping away, a dark mustard shade of yellow was there giving way to the dark wood beneath it.

"Mrs. Kenwyn said the door would be yellow, right?" Althea looks back to Hajnal and seeks confirmation. Hajnal nods. Althea smiles.

"Then this must be the place!" Althea faces toward the cottage again and ventures forth confidently with Hajnal leading Meteora close behind.

Coming to the door, Althea knocks on the door cheerfully as Hajnal ties Meteora's reins to a hitching post. Hajnal comes to Althea's side as they wait for a response from the home. There is only silence. Althea knocks again, a tad harder in case the first one was not heard. Several moments pass without an answer.

"Maybe the fairy is not home..." Althea frowns.

"Then we will just have to wait," Hajnal states their only option.

"But what if she does not live here anymore? What if she moved away or died?" Althea voices the possibilities.

"We will just wait and if someone comes, we can ask them," Hajnal gives the simple solution.

"I guess...but what if no one comes? We did not see anyone today as we were traveling and we have been traveling since sunrise and it is nearly sunset. What if-" Althea rambles her concerns.

"Thea, please. My mouth hurts. I can't answer your questions to calm you down," Stella's hands are holding the sides of her face.

"I'm sorry, St-Hajnal," Althea notices her sister's discomfort, "I'm just so... anxious."

Hajnal nods to show her understanding then reaches over to her sister to touch the unharmed arm. Althea sighs, an unexplained relief coming over her. With her sister more at ease, Hajnal can be eased as well.

A dark spot comes into the corner of Hajnal's eye. She turns her head to make sure it is not a beast or man who intends them harm. She pats Althea's arm so she will turn and see what she sees.

Coming from the trees saunters a voluptuous woman in a gray and black striped skirt and a simple black bodice piece to go over her cream chemise. On her left arm rests a basket full of apples while her right hand brings a long, thin smoking pipe to her full lips. She sucks in, then exhales a puff of gray smoke matching the natural streaks of gray in her long black curls. A gold ring dangles from the approaching woman's septum.

"That can't be her. Fairies don't look like that," Althea whispers.

"How many fairies have you seen, Thea?" Hajnal quips, making Althea press her lips together momentarily.

"Well, hello, young maidens." The questionable fairy waves her pipe-holding hand at them. Her voice is loud and shrill. She smiles at the sisters.

"Hello," Althea returns the greeting to the stranger with a civil but uncomfortable smile.

"I see you two are all bound up. Are you here to see if the old crone will help?"

"Um, we are seeking help." Althea does not want to insult their possible helper by calling her an 'old crone'.

"Well, you might want to seek a physician in town, or maybe the witch further down the river. I hear they ask for far less from you," this woman advises as she takes another drag on her pipe. The sisters exchange a side glance before looking ahead again.

"Thank you for your suggestion, but we will seek the woman here," Althea states. The woman begins nodding, then her eyes shift to Stella. She lowers her smoking pipe.

"Your eyes." She leans close to Hajnal's bound face. Her voice has grown soft and almost soothing, "You're a fairy."

"Do you know if the woman who lives here is at home, or is she in town?" Althea tries to take the attention off Hajnal and get some information. The stranger does not seem to hear Althea's words as she is too busy staring into Hajnal's eyes.

"You're the one Zarin has been waiting for," the stranger starts smiling.

"Zarin? Is that the old fairy who lives here?" Althea questions. Finally, the woman leans back and registers Althea.

"Oh, no. I'm the old bat who nests here," the woman laughs and passes the sisters, "Come with me."

Althea and Hajnal look at each other before following the older woman. Stepping into the house, the sisters find themselves in a large living area with walls covered in books. Plants hang from the ceiling and a stone fireplace lights the room with its burning fire. A pot hangs above the flames. Hajnal's stomach growls as the scent of beef, garlic, cabbage, potatoes, tomatoes, and other vegetables comes through her bandages. Four large wooden chairs with hand-stitched pillows rest near the fireplace. Small tables sit at the sides of the chairs. A floral tapestry with many creatures like unicorns, deer, and phoenixes woven among the flowers hangs in the house to separate this area from the rest of the home.

"Zarin!" the homeowner calls loudly as she walks. There is no response.

"Please, take a seat," the woman gestures to the chairs. Hajnal and Althea take the chairs sitting closest together. The curly-haired stranger puts her basket of apples and pipe on a table next to a chair.

"Zarin!" The name is called again but there is no response. The pipe smoker huffs and takes a seat next to the table covered in her previously carried items. She mutters under her breath of her curiosity about where this Zarin is.

"You're a fairy?" Althea asks.

"Yes. I'm Huldah Holle," she introduces herself properly.

"Then why did you make it seem you were not? Why suggest we go elsewhere?" Althea questions instead of introducing herself.

"People often scurry when they think they have to give up something," she answers.

"So, do you want payment or not?" Althea seeks a straightforward answer.

"You two should know I do not," Huldah laughs, as if Althea and Hajnal are joking. "Now let me look at you."

Huldah moves from her seat so she may grow closer to Hajnal. Hajnal does not move from Huldah's reach.

"I've introduced myself. Now you may do the honors," Huldah glances at Althea before returning her focus to Hajnal. Her fingers delicately loosen the bandages.

"I am Althea Sipos, and this is my sister Hajnal." Althea is sure not to mess up the name.

Huldah gasps covering her mouth as she sees the inflamed gash making the opening for Hajnal's mouth. "What happened to you?"

"She cut her mouth open," Althea answers for her sister.

"Cut her mouth open!" Huldah's brown eyes grow as did the volume of her voice. "Why? Why did you do this?"

"A sorcerer cursed her mouth to be sealed and she cut it open," Althea gives the short answer.

"A sorcerer?" Her head whips to look at Althea.

"Yes, he came to our village. He has been killing many of our villagers. He cursed our brother and took him away. He sealed my sister's mouth. Our employer, Mrs. Kenwyn, sent us here to you for help," Althea shares their purpose here with great exactness.

"Kenwyn, Briallen Kenwyn?"

"Yes."

"Hm... well," Huldah turns to face Hajnal "Let me heal this so you can tell me what is going on as well."

Huldah raises her hand, allowing Hajnal to see a thin light line making a circle on the palm of her hand. She places it over Hajnal's mouth. Huldah closes her eyes and mumbles words neither sister knows. She inhales, then exhales deeply. A cool rush comes over Hajnal's mouth, then a tightness. There is no pain anymore. Huldah removes her hand, pleased is she as she looks upon Hajnal's face. Hajnal raises her hands to touch her once-marred face. She grins, feeling the smoothness of her rosy cheeks, the proper spacing of the corners of her mouth, and her soft lips.

"Thank you!"

"You are most welcome. This is how she looked before, correct?" Huldah looks to Althea for confirmation who nods.

"Oh, and I see you're a feeler and an Air Elemental. What a fun combination," Huldah points to the right corner of Hajnal's mouth.

"A what?" Hajnal brings her fingers to the spot.

"I can see you're a Feeler by your eyes and try as you might to hide it, I can see your Elemental mark there," Huldah points once more to the corner of Hajnal's mouth. "There is no need to act surprised or try to hide it. I'm of mixed fairy blood, too. I'm Healer and Earth-Elemental."

Huldah shows off the faded, circular line in her palm, then pushes back her curly hair to show off the pointed tip of her ear. The sisters gawk at the unnaturally sharp ear.

"Why do you two look at me as if I have sprouted horns?" Huldah snickers, not ashamed of her ear.

"We've never had much experience with fairies, so we have not seen these marks or know really what you are talking about," Althea gives their explanation. Huldah blinks her dark eyes several times as she attempts to process this statement.

"But aren't you fairies yourselves?" Huldah raises one of her thick eyebrows.

"We just have the blood," Hajnal answers.

"Oh, were you two born void?" Huldah describes what they must be.

"Void?" Althea questions the word.

"Without magic. Oh, I should not have embarrassed you two this way. I am sorry. If I knew you two were void, I would not have gone about what gifts you should have and acted as if we were the same. Let me heal your arm and I'll get you some tea to make up for my lack of grace," Huldah moves to do as she said to Althea.

"Well, I am not without magic," Hajnal corrects Huldah before the older woman can put a hand on Althea's injury.

"Oh?" Huldah's attention leaves her task.

"Yes. If I use a special pipe, I can manipulate animals like our father can. Sometimes I can do it by just whistling," Hajnal shares this with the fairy.

"And sometimes she can make my feelings change," Althea adds.

"A Feeler and Air-Elemental fairy-like I thought!" Huldah grins, satisfied with knowing she had not been wrong.

"But I am no fairy. Neither of us are. We know nothing of your ancient words, spells, or ways." Hajnal wants her identity to not be confused.

"I don't do spells, but that's a different discussion," Huldah waves off the topic before continuing, "Being a fairy does not mean you must know the Starrling language or our ways. You must simply have the blood in your veins and faith in El-Yah to do what you need to be done. Do you have these things?"

"Yes," Hajnal nods.

"Then you are a fairy. You are the same as well?" Huldah looks to Althea.

"Yes, but I've never been able to perform magic, ever." Althea shares the difference between her and her sister.

"Let me have a closer look at you," Huldah reaches out for Althea's face then stops, "I should probably heal your arm first, shouldn't I?"

Huldah puts her hand on Althea's arm again. She closes her eyes and speaks what the sisters must assume is the "Starrling" language. Her weak, sore arm regains strength, and the pain is gone almost instantaneously. Huldah removes her hand, allowing Althea to twist, straighten, and shake her arm at her pleasure. She removes her sling easily.

"Thank you," Althea smiles in her gratitude.

"You are welcome, dear. Now let me look at you." Huldah takes Althea's face in her hands. Huldah takes her time scanning the heart-shaped face of the beautiful young woman. She can easily note despite Althea having large, sparkling eyes, they are simply blue instead of violet, magenta, silver, or gold. She is not a feeler, discerner, scouter, or ora-oculist. Her full, pink lips lack the dimple in the mouth's corner which Air-Elementals possess. Although she quickly sees the lack of gift marks on the maiden, Huldah continues to stare, almost entranced by Althea's beauty.

"See anything?" Althea asks, snapping Huldah from the trance.

"No. Let me see your ears," Huldah moves to push back some of Althea's golden hair covering the tops of her ears. Unlike Huldah, there are no points. Instead, the ears are perfectly rounded.

"Open your mouth and stick out your tongue," Huldah orders in a tone not giving off an arrogant air of authority. Althea complies. Huldah stares at the pink tongue. It lacks the circle and semicircle indicating she can speak all human languages or animal languages. She looks to the roof of Althea's mouth in search of the Water-Elemental's double horizontal lines but finds nothing.

"You may close your mouth. Let me see your hands." Huldah moves her hand to take hold of Althea's. She examines the palms of Althea. An uneasiness comes to Althea as the last one to look at her palms gave her disheartening news. But this must be different. Huldah is not reading her palms, but merely observing them.

Huldah detects no unnatural lines. Her inner fingers do not possess the extra vertical, light lines of a Fire-Elemental. Her palms lack the circles Huldah has which allow her to have some control of the earth.

"Do you have any discoloration on your back?" Huldah inquires not wanting to make the young woman strip to see if she has one of the rarest of abilities.

"No."

"Stand for a moment," Huldah stands up herself. Althea follows Huldah's example. Though she is not extraordinarily tall herself, Huldah looks down ever so slightly to look upon Althea.

"You are not an Endurant," Huldah lightly remarks, taking her seat once more. Althea sits not knowing what an Endurant is.

"What is an Endurant?"

"Fairies with great strength and endurance. They are always tall if not gigantic unless they are a product of mixed blood and loss some stature."

"Oh..."

"Have you ever changed forms?" Huldah continues the questions.

"Never," Althea shakes her head.

"I see. Then I suppose you are void then, my dear," Huldah pats Althea's legs kindly, "There is nothing wrong with this, though. Many of fairy descent have no gift."

Althea just nods. It has been several years since Althea felt lesser for not being able to use magic like her sister and brother. Even though this Huldah woman is attempting to make her feel as if it is not an issue, Althea finds no comfort.

"Let me go make some tea," Huldah rises and heads towards the animal tapestry. The sisters must assume her kitchen is behind the cloth.

"Zarin!" Huldah's call can be heard by the sisters.

"When she returns, we need to ask her about what to do about Baz," Hajnal keeps her voice low.

"Zarin!" Huldah's voice rings again as she comes through the tapestry with a tray of cups of a steaming beverage. Huldah puts the tray on a table and begins handing out the cups.

"I am so sorry Zarin is being unresponsive. But please enjoy the tea." Huldah takes a seat and blows on her drink to cool it. She brings it to her lips and takes a sip before either sister does.

"Who is Zarin?" Hajnal inquires about the absent person.

"My apprentice."

"Oh."

"What has brought you sisters here besides needing healing?" Huldah takes another sip.

"As we mentioned earlier, a sorcerer cursed and took our brother away. We were hoping a fairy such as you might have some knowledge as to what we could do," Hajnal gives their purpose.

"Interesting... What sort of curse did he place on your brother?"

"He turned him into a horrid creature unlike any I've seen before in my life. It was like a horned bat with a lizard tail," Hajnal describes.

"I see... Did the sorcerer give any sign as to undo this?"

"Yes... he said he would change Basil back if I found him and submitted myself to him," Hajnal answers, looking down at the light green liquid in her cup. Huldah's large lips purse displeased.

"I see. And where did he say you could find him?"

"East of the Sun and West of the Moon."

Crash! Huldah's cup shatters upon the floor, causing hot tea to spill freely on the wood there.

"East of the Sun and West of the Moon..." Huldah's lips tremble as they speak the words. Althea presses her lips together as Hajnal swallows the lump rapidly forming in her throat. Neither expected that reaction.

"Who... did... the sorcerer... was his name... did you learn his name?" Huldah finally forms a question.

"Yes. He was called Bardolph," Hajnal gives away the sorcerer's identity.

"Bardolph? Was he a tall man with a light tan, black hair, and black eyes?"

"No. He was pale and he had brown curls and hazel eyes."

"Oh... I see..." Huldah brings her bent index finger to her chin as she thinks about this information.

"So, will you be able to help us break these curses and find that place?" Althea speaks, wanting to come to a solution.

"I-I need to consult my books," Huldah stands, her shoes crushing her broken cup further but she moves away from the circle not fazed. She moves to one of the walls of books. Her finger drags across a few as she searches for the one she believes will help her.

"Mother Huldah, whose horse is out-" A maiden comes into the house with a question coming from her lips but she stops upon seeing the guests. The Sipos sisters gaze at the newest addition to the cottage. Her beige apron is covered in stains but has saved her mustard-colored kirtle. Her linen chemise hangs off her arms in large puffs as her kirtle tries to give the illusion of a bell shape. Her figure resembles Althea's, except it lacks curves despite the woman being beyond puberty.

The newcomer's long, slender neck is exposed as her hair is hidden beneath a white coif. There were bits of smeared product on her left cheek and forehead. The maiden's plump lips spread, giving a view of her teeth. The front upper two are more sizable in comparison to the rest, but charmingly. Above her smile, her nose stayed straight but short and wide. It also remained a perfectly equal distance between her eyes. Though large, her eyes have sharp corners and long, black eyelashes. But her irises draw the most attention. One would think the woman's copper skin, which is not common in Austvest, would be what captures onlookers. Alas, it is not. Hajnal had been told before how her own uniquely colored eyes drew the eye most. Unlike Hajnal's violet eyes, this young lady's eyes were the most dazzling gold. It was almost as if the rings around her pupils were meant to be around a king's fingers. Hajnal and Althea, like most, had heard of those with golden eyes, Ora-Oculists, or more commonly called 'seers'.

"It's you," Zarin's focus is on Hajnal.

"Zarin," Huldah addresses gold eyes.

"Yes, Mother Huldah?" Zarin answers but does not look away from Hajnal. The staring makes Hajnal's stomach gurgle uncomfortably.

"Where have you been? I've been calling you," Huldah comes toward her apprentice. Zarin pulls her gold eyes from Hajnal so she may look at her mistress.

"I was painting in the barn. I'm sorry I did not hear you," Zarin offers her apologies, then turns her eyes back to Hajnal, "But you're finally here."

"Do I know you?" Hajnal feels she should ask.

"Not yet, but we are going to be the truest friends," Zarin keeps up her smile. Hajnal politely smiles back but turns to Althea, whose eyes are lowered to the right, and lips are pressed but curled up in humor.

"I did not know you would come so soon. I had hoped it would be after I finished my training, but I am happy to know our friendship can begin sooner in life rather than later. I will go pack my belongings," Zarin begins to walk but Huldah grabs her arm.

"What are you talking about, Zarin?"

"My friend-what is your name?" Zarin looks back to Hajnal.

"Call me Hajnal."

"My friend Hajnal and I will have to leave to begin our journey," Zarin answers her mistress.

"Your journey?"

"Yes, I've seen it. She and I will travel far and wide. Why and for what, I do not know. But we should get started as soon as possible."

"Am I not there?" Althea leans and whispers to Hajnal who only shrugs as she had no idea who this girl even is.

"Wait, Zarin. These sisters are here for help," Huldah attempts to slow down her apprentice. "Fix them some stew and some for us as well."

Zarin nods and starts for the tapestry. Huldah grabs a large book from a top shelf, then a small one from the lower one. She comes back to her seat just as Zarin returns with bowls, spoons, and a ladle. She hands out the spoons before taking the bowls and ladle with her to the pots over the stove. She carefully scoops out enough to fill each bowl. Zarin gives out the bowls to the sisters and then to her mistress who sets it aside before taking her seat near her mistress.

"Oh, no," Zarin notices the broken cup. She holds out her hand and rotates her hand in a circular motion. Hajnal and Althea watch in amazement as the pieces of the cup seal themselves back together in the air, then land on Huldah's side table. Zarin then waves her hand over the spilled tea, sending it into the fire. The fire hisses at the moisture but does not go out. The sisters clap at the display. Huldah pays it no mind as she is scanning through her books.

"Oh, thank you," Zarin giggles.

"That was amazing. How did you do that?" Althea asks.

"It's a simple sealing blessing for the cup and since I am a Water-Elemental, I know how to get the tea moving," Zarin shares another of her gifts, "Oh, what is your name? I forgot to ask."

"Althea Sipos," the blonde sister answers.

"Althea. That's a lovely name."

"Thank you."

"Ah ha!" Huldah exclaims.

"Did you find the cure for my brother?" Hajnal lowers the spoon of stew she was about to put in her mouth.

"Yes. From your description, it sounds like your brother was turned into a Flottdyr." Huldah turns the large book around which shows a beast nearly identical to the one Hajnal had seen. Althea is cringing at the sight.

"They can be hurt like most beasts but killed only by piercing the heart. Of course, you don't care about how to defeat one since you want to change him back from it. True Love's kiss, like almost any curse, is a cure. Do you know if he has a lover you could bring to him?" Huldah wonders.

"As far as we know, he has none," Althea answers.

"The other option is to have the sorcerer change him back, which I know you would not want to do given the conditions your sorcerer gave you, Hajnal. So, the only other option is to make the All-Cure elixir. This potion could also undo your name's curse."

"If we make this All-Cure, we would still need to find Basil, correct?"

"Yes, he would need to ingest, as you would need to do."

"We would still have to go to that place East of the Sun and West of the Moon," Althea brings up the location of their brother. Zarin gasps and nearly drops her bowl, but Huldah catches it and then passes it back to the younger woman.

"Yes. Sadly, I do not know how to reach that place. But I may know someone who does." Huldah closes the large book holding the illustration of the Flottdyr.

"And who would that be, Mother Huldah?" Zarin looks to her mistress. Huldah stands and walks away to put up the book.

"Her name is Tzafrira. She knows how to get there. But she lives in the capital in Koralia. That is far from here," Huldah points out the distance between them.

"If she is the only way for us to find Basil, I'd travel across the Endless Ocean to find her," Hajnal states. Althea nods in agreement.

"Your devotion to your brother is touching. But I cannot promise she will help you."

"We will still try," Althea puts her hand on her sister's arm. Huldah comes back to her seat and picks up the smaller book she left there.

"As you are traveling, you should look for the ingredients of the All-Cure elixir," Huldah flips through the book then stops, "Zarin, get some parchment, ink, and a quill."

Zarin moves to fulfill Huldah's order. She returns quickly with the items.

"Write this down, Zarin. The All-Cure elixir requires a cup of water from a blessed spring, powdered blue pearls, a single mustard seed, the root of aconite, and a dash of stardust. These ingredients must be mixed by a virgin with a love spoon. After mixing, the elixir must be blessed by a fairy before being ingested by those afflicted. The blessing must be the one written here," Huldah continues to read the Starrling language from the book. Zarin diligently takes down the information given. Once finished, she hands the parchment to Huldah, who compares it to the book.

"What is aconite?" Zarin asks her mistress.

"Wolfsbane," Althea answers.

"Here is the list, my dears. Be sure to get everything correct on your journey," Huldah hands the list to Hajnal before closing her book, tucking it at her side, and picking up her bowl of stew for her first taste.

"The items on this list are not easy to come by except for the mustard seed and maybe the wolfs-bane. Blue pearls are expensive and blessed springs are rare," Hajnal sets out listing the challenges of making this cure. "Where are we to get a love spoon or stardust? And who will bless our elixir once we've made it? Would you come, Huldah?"

"Oh no. I cannot leave my village here. They need me," Huldah rejects the quest.

"I'll go with you as your fairy as I know how to speak like the Starrlings," Zarin volunteers.

"Wonderful," Hajnal smiles, pleased with the volunteer.

"Zarin, no," Huldah shakes her head.

"Why not?"

"You are not finished training. Your training is of the utmost importance."

"Helping those in need is what I have been training to do. This is a perfect opportunity to show not only you but myself, my capability. I will come right back home to you after we make this elixir." Zarin takes hold of Huldah's hand.

"It is dangerous, especially for one like you," Huldah's voice is hushed as she focuses her attention on the younger fairy.

"I know. But it will be even more dangerous for them not to have me. Besides, Hajnal is the one who keeps appearing in my visions. They must have been signs for me to go with her and Althea." Zarin does not forget Hajnal's sister. Huldah bites her lower lip. Her dark eyes search Zarin's gold ones for some sort of faltering. The golden rings remain strong, determined, and fearless.

"Fine. But you must come back after the elixir is finished to complete your training with me," Huldah sets her terms.

"I will! Oh, thank you, Mother Huldah!" Zarin embraces her mistress. Huldah pats Zarin's back, then breaks the embrace.

"Once we finish eating, I will prepare a map and items for your journey. You may house your horse in the barn. Zarin will stay in my room with me tonight and you two may stay in Zarin's. You all will need much rest before you begin your journey tomorrow," Huldah gives the night's impromptu itinerary.

"Thank you so much, Huldah," Hajnal thanks their hostess. Huldah nods with a sigh. She brings another spoonful of stew to her mouth. As she swallows it down as looks at her grinning, eating pupil. She hopes she will not live to regret this allowance.

CHAPTER 9

Sharing a bed with each other is not unusual for the Sipos sisters. Zarin's humble bed is intended for one person but the sisters squeeze together on the mattress.

"Do I really have that dimple in the corner?" Hajnal asks as she and Althea lie face to face. With the candle on the table at their heads, the sisters can see each other.

"Yes. Now as I think about it, Father and Baz have the same dimple." Althea considers her father and brother. Hajnal smiles to herself at the similarity between her and her family.

"Another fairy thing to pass me," Althea mumbles. Stella loses her smile. She takes hold of Althea's hand.

"Thea, there is nothing wrong with missing these things. You know the risks for people with fairy blood, especially those with obvious signs. You have so many wonderful things about you. Being 'void'-Huldah's word not mine-does not make you lesser than anyone else."

A warmness comes upon Althea as her insecurity starts to slip from her body. Although comforted by the words and feelings, Althea grabs hold of Hajnal's wrist.

"Stop. Don't... don't make me feel different," Althea knows of her sister's influence.

"Sorry," Hajnal apologizes.

"We need to sleep. We've got a lot to do tomorrow." Althea turns away from Hajnal. Hajnal blows out the candle and turns so her back meets Althea's. In the still darkness, the sisters seek sleep. As Althea finds herself lost to dreamless sleep, Hajnal finds herself once more in white and outside the opening gates of the fortress.

Blue flames lead Hajnal into the castle and up the tower's stairs. This time she is not led to a ballroom. Instead, she is led level after level till she is allowed to walk on the floor higher than the ballroom. The flames cease, but she is not left in the dark.

From the doorway, light leaks in the hallway. Hajnal walks comfortably to the room. It is right where she disappeared last night. Candles burn all around the library, though the wax does not melt.

Books have now covered most of the floor in piles towering almost as high as the ladders leading to the higher shelves.

"Ugh." Stella hears a groan deeper in the mountains of books.

"Astro?" she calls out.

"Stella?" a voice calls for her. Hajnal carefully continues on the thin trail between the piles and even steps over a few fallen books. Sitting on a sliver of a covered settee, Astro holds a book in his hands. His blue eyes shine as they meet hers. She can sense his smile beneath his facial covering. She hopes it truly is a smile, for she smiles beneath hers. He sets down the book and comes to her. He takes her hand.

"I am overjoyed with thy return," He cautiously leads her to the larger open space around his former seat.

"I am too."

"I have been reading since thou departed. Pray, tell me, did thou find the fairy?" He has her sit in his former spot. He sits on the floor before her.

"Yes. We have."

"Excellent! Did she have a solution to these curses?"

"Yes."

"Wonderful! And what was her solution? I have struggled in vain to find a cure excluding True Love's kiss," Astro brings up the option Huldah had mentioned to Hajnal.

"Well, she mentioned True Love's kiss as a cure. But as far as I know, my brother has yet to even meet his true love. And my true love is-" Hajnal stops herself. Astro's eyes do not deter from her eyes. Astro's dark eyelashes, the only dark hair on him, provide the perfect frame for the blue eyes glistening in the candlelight. They wait for her to finish the sentence. She cannot bring herself to finish it. She does not even know the ending of the sentence.

"True Love's kiss is just not an option. But she told us we could make the All-Cure Elixir," Hajnal quickly gives the second solution.

"The All-Cure Elixir? I read about it in the past few hours. It can cure nearly all ailments and curses. But the name is not fully true. Some curses are simply too strong." His eyes look toward what Hajnal assumes is the book with this information, then come back to her, "But it may solve these curses."

"I hope so. Huldah was most confident in it."

"If I recall correctly, it is mostly a mixture of rare items," Astro rises. He ventures into a pile and pulls a book from the middle. Amazingly, the stack does not topple. He brings the green book with him as he returns to sit on the floor. He quickly searches the book and finds the instructions.

"The All-Cure Elixir..." He mumbles the title.

"You have a fairy book?" Hajnal questions the possession.

"Yes, of course. This castle used to house many fairies, so their books were stored here."

"Oh." Hajnal had not known this. Astro's eyes quickly scan over the words before he looks up at his guest.

"The ingredients are important, but the ones to mix and bless the elixir are equally as important. Do thou have persons in thy party to match these descriptions?" He lifts his eyes to look at her.

"A fairy has volunteered to come with us to bless the elixir. Althea and I are both qualified to mix the elixir," Hajnal remembers the details of the stirrer. As far as she knows neither she nor her sister have been with a man.

"Excellent. Then thou should not have much to worry about then." He smiles.

"My greatest concern, though, is finding stardust for the elixir. I know of nowhere that has it," Hajnal brings up the one elusive ingredient.

"Stardust? My country has an abundance of stardust!" Astro exclaims.

"Your country?"

"Yes. Estellen. Many stars fell in our kingdom. The fairies found the stardust helped enhance their magic. Stardust was collected and kept in safe crypts made so no single fairy could not hoard the stardust for himself or herself. They are practically impervious to magic. This is a secret, of course. No one would want the crypts to be raided by our enemies," Astro enlightens her. "I do believe one of these books has a map marking the locations."

Astro gets to his feet. He ventures toward the entrance of the library. Hajnal stays seated waiting for his return.

Estellen... why does it sound familiar yet foreign? Is it a country from the Old Lands?

"Ah ha!" Hajnal hears his excited voice. Astro returns with a tiny opened book.

"Here! These are the locations. The closest one to me is the one near the border between Estellen and Aust." Astro pushes one of the piles of books off the settee so he may sit next to Stella and show her the book. There is a small map of Estellen on the pages with dark markings on certain spots. He points to a blot she sees is in a county labeled 'Vespera'. There is a thicker black line separating 'Vespera' from the land simply labeled 'Aust'. Right at the border is a small black blot that indicates the location of the stardust crypt. A circle is around the blot at the border. It is labeled 'Violet Star Gate'. The crypt and 'Violet Star Gate' are near a triangle with the words 'Castle Evensong' beneath it. It is strange 'Aust' is simply labeled 'Aust' instead of 'Austvest'. Of course, this must have been made before the unification of Aust and Vest.

"As thou can see, this crypt is at the borderline. It is immune to magic, so there should be no difficulty reaching it," Astro continues. Hajnal smiles, though he cannot see it beneath her veil. But Estellen still bothers her.

He must not know…

"What is wrong?" Astro's attention leaves the book to focus on Hajnal who stars hard at the book but says nothing.

"Nothing," She shakes her head and puts on a cheery voice.

"Thou can tell me if there is." He places his hand atop hers so he may pat it gently. "Oh, no," He remarks as his hand passes through her hand.

"Already? I have not been here long, though," Hajnal comments.

"Do not fret. I shall see thee tomorrow night," He reassures her. Hajnal sighs and evaporates.

Hajnal opens her eyes to find Althea already awake in the room and putting on her clothes. Hajnal yawns, drawing her sister's attention.

"Oh, good. You're awake," Althea comments.

"What time is it?" Hajnal looks for a window to show the hour.

"I am not sure, but the sun is not up yet. I hear Huldah and Zarin, so we should get up and ready," Althea refers to the other occupants of the house. Hajnal nods in agreement and joins her sister.

By the time the sun rises, all in Huldah's cottage and even Meteora have been prepared to leave the homestead. The women gather in the cottage before the fireplace. The sisters have their hair braided in single braids to make sure their manes would not become a burden in their travels while Zarin keeps her hair hidden beneath her coif, but somehow Huldah's hair has grown curlier in the night.

"Here is a map with the three fastest paths to Tzafrira's location," Huldah presents the map. There are three lines of different colors that lead to Koralia.

"This red line is the fastest. It would require you to go through Logre after going through Zeemaa. This would put you three at risk of capture by Ogres. The green line is the second fastest. It takes you through Zeemaa again, but you would need to take a ship through Mermaid's Lair instead of Logre. You would have to risk those vicious sirens and pirates. So, your third option is this blue line, which is the longest. You will have to travel through Belterre, then Koralia. This would be the safest route," Huldah explains as she shows each line on the map.

"Which path would allow us to gather more of the items we need for the elixir?" Althea poses the important question.

"I suppose the Belterre path would allow for the collection of most items," Huldah figures.

"But Belterre does not have stardust. No country in the Far Lands do except Estellen," Hajnal brings up the fact she now knows.

"Yes, that is a problem since Estellen is cursed and impenetrable," Zarin looks down at this defeat.

"For most, but I know there is one spot not affected by magic. We could enter there," Hajnal shares.

"You know a spot to get in Estellen?" Althea guffaws.

"Yes, I do. It is here at the border between Austvest and Estellen," Hajnal points at the spot on the map she remembers seeing in her sleep.

"The Violet Star Gate?" Huldah gives the title of the border opening.

"Yes. There is a crypt holding stardust around there which is unable to be affected by magic. We could try to cross there. We could get the stardust we need and then choose our path from there," Hajnal explains.

"How do you know this? No one of the last century has found a spot to enter Estellen," Huldah questions the violet-eyed woman. Zarin and Althea look just as curiously at Hajnal. Hajnal clears her throat and lowers her eyes demurely.

"From... my dream friend," Hajnal answers, mostly in a mumble.

"Dream friend?" Zarin's head cocks to the side.

"I have a friend who I see in my dreams who tells me things." Hajnal is embarrassed at how it all sounds.

"It's true. She's been talking to him since we were children," Althea backs her sister.

"And what is this dream friend's name?" Huldah does not hold any judgment in her voice, merely a tone of interest.

"It's-" Hajnal stops.

What is his name?

"I honestly cannot remember. Althea, have I told you his name before?" Hajnal turns to the blonde.

"Um..." Althea pauses as she tries to recall if her sister did share a name for the friend. "No. Not that I can recall."

"Interesting..." Huldah takes hold of her own chin lightly, "I have heard of persons having their mind bound to another but I have never met someone who has had it. Is it the same person every night?"

"Yes. Every night for as long as I can remember, he has been in my dreams," Hajnal answers.

"And you trust him and this information he has given you?"

"Yes. I would trust him with my life," Hajnal answers.

"I think you three should try to enter by the Violet Star gate then. It would be easier to find stardust there than by any other way," Huldah gives her thoughts on the detour.

"If you think so, then we should," Zarin nods in agreement.

"You can see on the map how to get there. I suggest going to the village and buying a horse or two, Zarin, to help hurry things along and not burden yourself," Huldah continues with her advice.

"How will I pay for these horses?" Zarin inquires.

"We have money," Hajnal gives away the little secret. Mother Huldah smiles.

"I also have something else for you three," Huldah walks to the mantle above the fireplace where a small box sits. She opens it, having come back to the group. Inside are four rings. Huldah pulls out three. The rings are all gold and large enough to be a child's bracelet. She puts one on Zarin's right middle finger. Huldah begins to sing in the Starrling language. As she does, the gold ring shines and shrinks to fit Zarin's finger. With the ring fitted, Huldah ends her song. The shining stops as well.

Huldah brings a ring to Althea's hand. Althea bends her fingers instead of allowing the ring to be put on her.

"What is it?" Althea questions.

"These are protection rings. As long as you wear them, you will be protected from great harm and unable to have any additional curses harm you. But as Hajnal is already cursed, that will still be in effect," Huldah explains.

"Oh," Althea extends her fingers. Huldah places it upon her middle finger and does as she had for Zarin. Hajnal willingly allows Huldah to give her the ring as well.

"These rings are unmovable, but they are only temporary. Once at least one of you reaches..." Huldah pauses and whispers, "Your brother on East of the Sun and West of the Moon, it will break."

The three maidens nod understanding the limit of their rings. Huldah rolls up the map.

"Now, go. You have a long journey," Huldah hands the map to Zarin who puts it inside her large pack. The women venture out of the cottage to where Meteora waits at the hitching post. The Sipos sisters thank their hostess before going to their mare.

"Goodbye, Mother Huldah," Zarin smiles at her mentor. Huldah pulls her pupil into her arms.

"Be careful, Zarin. Do not take any unnecessary risks." Huldah charges her golden eye protege.

"Do not be afraid for El-Yah watches over me," Zarin kisses her mentor's cheek then leaves her at the door to join the sisters. Huldah watches with arms crossed and heart heavy till the young walking women and horse have disappeared beyond the trees in the direction of the village. Huldah returns inside and refills her pipe.

On the little foot trail toward the village closest to Huldah's cottage, the three women walk at a decent pace that will not cause them to grow weary quickly. Zarin leads the way as she is the one who has been on this path more times than she would care to count.

"How far is the village?" Althea is the one to ask.

"Not far. Mother Huldah wanted to be closer to the village than the witch, so they would come to her first. Sadly, many still go to Brunhilda before Mother Huldah," Zarin shakes her head in disappointment over the villagers' past choices.

"You know of someone who sells horses in the village, then?" Hajnal wants to make sure this detour is not fruitless.

"There is always someone trying to sell all kinds of beasts in the village. For the past week, the circus has been in town, so even more people will be around trying to sell their wares," Zarin brings up the festivities.

"The circus? How exciting," Hajnal smiles.

"When was the last time we went to a circus?" Althea looks back to Hajnal, who brings up the rear of their group with Meteora. Hajnal does not speak as she ponders the question.

"Yes. That was about ten years ago. We had to sneak away to see it," Hajnal recalls.

"I know. We got in so much trouble when Mother found our bed empty," Althea giggles now though when it happened, she was terrified.

"I would love to go to the circus again. It is a shame we will not have time."

"After we get Basil back, we can find a circus and go all together this time," Althea proposes.

"Yes. He would like that. He was so upset that did not take him with us."

The sisters smile, amused with the memory of the pouting ten-year-old. The feelings of nostalgia turn to feelings of melancholia. Hajnal shakes her head as if this will shake off her feelings.

"Zarin, did you get to go to the circus?" Hajnal tries to turn the focus away from Basil.

"Oh, no. Mother Huldah thought it might be too dangerous for me," Zarin replies.

"Too dangerous?" Althea does not understand why.

"Yes. I am sure you both know how rare Ora-Oculists are in these parts. Many greedy people would love to take in an Ora-Oculist to tell people's fortunes for a price. Mother Huldah did not want me napped by these performing nomads and forced to waste my gift," Zarin explains Huldah's reasoning.

"Do people still nap fairies to exploit their gifts?" Hajnal has not heard of the frightening tales of fairy napping since she was a child.

"Oh, yes. I have had four attempts made on me since I arrived here in the Far Lands."

"Four times!" Althea exclaims.

"But I always got away, by one way or another. Oh! Here it is," Zarin points ahead cheerfully. Where the trees part, the group can see the single-level, stacked-stone buildings making up the village. The closer they come, the more the colorful tent on the other side of the village becomes visible. Zarin leads them into the empty streets. The baker's light is dim in the window, but they do not head to the shop.

"There is a stable on the other side of the village that typically has horses for sale. We will start there," Zarin keeps heading straight forward.

Coming toward the far edge of the village, the tent of the circus begins to fall. Coming to the stable, the three can see the carnies packing up the circus into mule-pulled carts.

"Mr. Lovasz. Mr. Lovasz," Zarin knocks on a side door of the stable. She continues to knock till finally the door is opened by a tall, lanky man with a thick brown mustache in a beige nightdress. One eye seems stuck to be closed, and the other is half open.

"Where is the fire?" The man huffs.

"No fire. I need to buy two horses," Zarin answers.

"Come back later." He closes the door. Zarin stops it with her hand.

"We cannot wait. We need them now."

"You can wait," He tries to push it again.

"Will this change your mind?" Althea pulls a piece of gold from Basil's bag. The precious metal causes both eyes to open wide as well as the door.

"Yes. Follow me," Mr. Lovasz puts on a smile.

"I'll stay out here with Meteora. You go on with Zarin," Hajnal directs her younger sister. Althea follows the other two into the stable.

Hajnal stands with Meteora and calmly strokes the beast's nose. She patiently waits for the return of her sister and new travel companion.

"Excuse me, Miss."

Hajnal jumps startled at the sudden voice behind her. She turns around and finds a short but burly man standing behind her with a yellow rope in his hand which is tied around the neck of a bridled black stallion.

"I'm sorry. I did not mean to scare you, little lady," He apologizes in a laugh at her reaction.

"It is alright. How may I help you, sir?" She asks as he approaches her.

"I was hoping to help you, Miss. I see your horse is heavily loaded down. I thought you would like to lighten your beast's load and dispersed it on the back of another fine animal such as this horse I have here." The man gives a little tug on the yellow rope to indicate the horse.

Hajnal's eyes run over the tall stallion. His dark eyes are clear and open. He does not favor a specific leg or hold one up to relieve it of pressure. He appears to be of a healthy weight.

"May I look in his mouth?" Hajnal asks.

"Open up," the man tells the horse who complies. Then the man comments. "As you can see, he is an extraordinarily obedient horse."

Hajnal looks in the mouth. The gums are a perfect pink, and the teeth are solid and a surprising shade of white.

"Why are you selling this horse?" Hajnal inquires, unsure why this man wants to be rid of a healthy horse.

"Oh, I need the money. The circus did not do as well as expected, so we are selling some of the excess animals and materials," the man explains. Desperation is not the feeling she is getting from this man. She cannot quite put her finger on it.

"I see...'" Hajnal looks the horse up and down again. His eyes glisten as if sad. She feels unease coming from him. It is strange. She has never felt an animal's feelings.

"How much is the horse?"

"Well... he is a strong, obedient horse and does well for riding. Such a horse is worth about... two hundred shillings." He smiles again.

"Two hundred shillings?" Hajnal balks at the price.

"He is an excellent horse, and if you do not take him, I will have to sell him to the local butcher."

"Why not sell him to Mr. Lovasc?" Hajnal brings up a different solution and the name of the stable's owner she has just learned.

"He refused to take my poor horse as he says his stable is full. I've tried to sell him to anyone who passed in this village yesterday but no one would buy him," the man sighs, defeated. Hajnal frowns. She is no discerner, but she is also no fool.

"Why are you trying to get rid of this horse?"

The man loses his smile. He looks over his shoulder, then back to Hajnal.

"I owe many men in this village many debts, including Mr. Lovasc. I am trying to make money honestly by selling this horse. So, will you buy him or not?" The short man loses any sense of politeness in his voice. Hajnal purses her lips.

"I'll buy him for a hundred shillings," Hajnal barters.

"Fine. Just get me the money quickly," the man agrees. Hajnal steps to one of the bags. She looks in a pouch and only finds gold coins. She grabs two of the gold coins. This would be equal to one hundred shillings.

"This will do?" She holds up the two coins, having come back to the man and horse. His eyes light up greedily.

"Yes. Yes. Here," He hands over the yellow rope while keeping his hand out. She takes the rope as she hands over the coins. He closes his hands around the gold.

"Nice doing business with you and whatever you do, don't take the rope off," He smiles then runs off.

"That's not suspicious at all," Hajnal comments to herself sarcastically. She looks at her purchase. "I hope there is not anything wrong with you."

Hajnal looks beyond the horse to the stable where one door opens, allowing Althea, Zarin, and one chestnut-colored horse to exit. Each of the exiting women carries a saddle. Hajnal can see how Althea's face goes from curious to shock as she looks from Hajnal to Zarin. The women come close quickly.

"Hajnal, this is unbelievable! Zarin said for us only to buy one horse but two saddles because you would have a horse when we came outside. Then we came outside, and you had a horse!" Althea gushes over her amazement at Zarin's prediction. Hajnal laughs as Zarin snickers to herself.

"She is an Ora-Oculist, Thea," Hajnal reminds her sister.

"Yes, but, still, it was something to experience," Althea brushes a stray hair from her forehead.

"We should distribute the bags on the three horses and get moving," Hajnal pulls her black horse to follow her to Meteora's side.

"Where did you get this horse?" Zarin asks.

"Some man from the circus," Hajnal answers. Zarin "hmms" to herself. The women saddle and spread the bags out. With each horse situated, the women select a horse to mount. Althea takes Meteora, Zarin her brown purchase, and Hajnal the former circus horse. Zarin takes the lead. And so, mounted and ready, they begin their journey for the Violet Star Gate.

CHAPTER 10

Zarin leads her troupe of three southeast alongside the Moon River as dictated by the map. Her recently purchased mare moves beneath her with ease as if they had always been together.

Meteora submits to Althea's lead as well. Only Hajnal finds resistance. Instead of following the mares, the stallion keeps trying to turn away. Hajnal must work the reins and her heels to keep him in line.

"Obedient horse my foot," Hajnal mumbles under her breath, having to pull the stallion toward her sister again.

"So, tell me, my friends, from where do you come?" Zarin asks, wanting to learn more about her traveling companions.

"Most recently, Foxglove Grove. It's a small village where Stagpool, Doesvale, Moonwood, and Violetwood counties meet," Althea answers for the two sisters.

"Most recently?" Zarin questions the phrase.

"We have traveled a lot since we were born so we do not have a true home although I would say Austvest is our home as we have spent most of our lives here but our parents now live in Soldoro," Hajnal shared once more, making her horse turn forward and not off the path, "What about you, Zarin?"

"Yes. Are you originally from this village?" Althea gives her version of her sister's question.

"Oh no. I was born and spent most of my formative years in Gold Haven."

"Gold Haven? Isn't that the city-state with the thirteen marble temples?" Althea's eyes light interested in the far off place.

"Yes. Have you been there?"

"No." Hajnal shakes her head.

"We've never been south of Belterre," Althea adds, "But how did you end up here?"

"Well, after my failure with Hadiakbar, my mother thought it would be best to smuggle me out of Gold Haven so I would not be executed. So, she-"

"Wait a moment! You were going to be executed?" Hajnal interrupts though her steed as she turns in a circle both trying for control.

"And who is Hadiakbar?" Althea interrupts as well.

"I should have known my friends would want more details," Zarin chuckles to herself.

"Well, Hadiakbar is a sorcerer in Gold Haven. He is one of the most powerful men in all of the Southern Continent because of his magical skill, fortune, and place in the Gold Haven council. He personally sees to it those in service to the temples are truly dedicated to following the practices of the Thirteen."

"You are a follower of the Thirteen?" Althea arches her eyebrow.

"At the time I was supposed to be, but my mother had taught me the truth so my faith is in El-Yah. We had to hide our faith to survive."

"I thought Gold Haven was supposed to be open to all religions," Althea brings up what she had heard over the years.

"Not for those in the temples. We are only allowed to worship the Thirteen."

"Oh..."

"I was born with many gifts. The priests and priestesses took notice and spoke with Hadiakbar. He sought me out and desired for me to train under him as an apprentice. When I came of age in the temple, he wanted me to make my blood pact with the gods. As sorcerers and sorceresses do, but- oh! We are nearing the bridge," Zarin stops herself and points ahead. Althea looks forward as Hajnal does another full turn with her horse. At the river's edge begins a slope of stones creating a high and rounded bridge over the rushing water.

The bridge is not flat, the group learns. Instead, it makes a high arch. The higher it goes, the thinner it becomes. No longer can two horses fit side by side. They must go one by one. With no railings on the side, the horses must be sure-footed to avoid losing themselves and riders off the sides.

Zarin keeps her eyes on the bridge before her. Althea looks to the sky so as not to look down and become afraid of falling. Hajnal closes her eyes, fully trusting in the beast to step where he should. A loose pebble causes Hajnal's horse to begin to lose its balance.

"No, do not fall," Hajnal braces herself. The horse regains his footing. Hajnal holds her breath, unsure if they will make it to the other side.

"We are almost there. Just hold on a little longer." Zarin can see the other side of the river. The sisters hold tight. By the time Hajnal needs to take a breath, her horse steps onto the solid ground on the other side of the bridge. Hajnal finally inhales only to sigh, relieved.

"We made it," Zarin smiles back to the group.

They continue to the other half of the Violetwood. Just as before, Hajnal begins losing control of her horse. Each turn she makes is turned into a full circle or a sharp turn in the opposite direction. She huffs in aggravation.

"Why don't you pull out the pipe and make him submit?" Althea looks back at Hajnal and offers the option.

"I want him to submit of his own free will," Hajnal feels him turning beneath her again. She pulls again. He resists.

"Just follow Zarin and Althea," Hajnal huffs. The horse shudders, then turns. He follows the other two horses. Hajnal grins.

Did he just obey me?

"Thank you," she pats his neck. As she brings back her hand, she scrapes it against the yellow rope she did not remove. Her hand is unharmed but her eyes go back to the neck where the rope is. She carefully pulls the rope to look at the flesh underneath. She frowns, her eyes landing on the hairless, tender red skin beneath it.

"Oh, you poor creature," Hajnal pulls on the reins, making him stop. She dismounts.

"What are you doing?" Althea pulls at her horse to stop. Zarin stops as well.

"This rope is hurting him," Hajnal grabs the rope where it is knotted. The rope sticks her as she tries to loosen the knot, she does not give up. The horse remains exceptionally still as she works the rope. Hajnal pulls out the knife she got from Basil. She brings the blade between the rope and neck. She clenches her teeth and as she saws at the thick, tight rope.

Slowly, the fibers break. One by one they sever, bringing the horse one more step to freedom from the scarring rope.

"Ah ha!" Hajnal brings the knife and rope away from the horse. Hajnal smiles only to lose it as the horse immediately rears up. Zarin grabs Hajnal by the arm and pulls her back and out of the way in case the horse would come crashing down on her.

The horse does not come down, though. No, he stays on his hind legs, front legs reaching up toward the air. The beast seems to be screaming.

Meteora backs away as Zarin's horse tries as well. The women can only gawk at the horse. A bright light finally causes the women to look away to avoid being blinded.

"Neeeiiiiigghhhhhaaaaahhhhh!" The horse's scream turns into a human one. With the light's disappearance, the women uncover their eyes. Hajnal's bags and saddle lie on the ground. Amid the fallen items stands a youthful man.

His hair is black as the horse had been. The lengthy mane falls flat on his back, shoulder, and chest. His skin is rather fair with golden undertones. Unlike his large round horse eyes, his eyes are small, sharp, and rather pointed at the corners. He pulls the bit from his mouth and removes the bridle. Upon realizing the man has no clothing, the three maidens look away.

The nude young man exclaims joyfully in words not from the Common Tongue. He laughs in his jubilation. He runs his hands over his face, shoulders, arms, and chest. He grazes the horrid wound around his neck, but he does not let it steal his joy. His hands stop moving as he sees the women. He looks down and realizes his lack of clothing. He picks up the saddle to cover himself. His eyes shift to and from each blushing woman.

"Pardon my undress, ladies. I-uh-I can explain," He speaks in a language they understand.

"There is no need. I know exactly what you are," Zarin speaks, her head still turned.

"You do?"

"You are a shifter, yes?"

"Yes, but I mean none of you harm, so please do not harm me." His eyes go to the dagger in Hajnal's hand.

"We will not harm you," Hajnal drops the dagger.

"Great. So, I will just go my way and you all can go yours," He decides.

"You cannot just go away like that. You need to at least be clothed," Zarin brings up his lack of clothing.

"As handsome as I'd look in a kirtle, I'd rather not wear it," He remarks.

"We have our brother's clothes. Let us get them for you," Hajnal offers, still not looking at him. The changed man considers the offer.

"I guess that wouldn't be a terrible idea," He decides.

"Just keep yourself covered and I will get them," Hajnal says. She walks toward this man since one bag on the ground holds Basil's clothes.

Hajnal keeps her eyes focused solely on the bag. She pulls out enough items to properly cover the saddle holder. Hajnal tosses the items in the male's direction before standing up. She turns her back on the man, as do Althea and Zarin.

"When was the last time these were washed?" The comment comes at the man sniffing the clothes he puts on himself.

"Who knows? Our brother is not exactly the cleanliest person," Althea answers. Even with this information, the man keeps dressing.

"Well, beggars can't be choosers," He mumbles to himself. The man exhales having finished dressing.

"Thank you for the clothes. I'll be on my way now," He nods to the women. They finally look at him.

"Wait! Where are you going?" Zarin shouts and holds out her hand. He stops.

"Away."

"Away?"

"I'm free, so I'm going to leave."

"And go where?"

"I do not see how that is any of your concern."

"Well, you are a penniless shifter in borrowed clothes who until now was under a form of binding and obedience curse. Right?"

"Yes. So?"

"So, I assume those carnival people were the ones to do that to you"

"Yeah. For the past six months, I've been cursed to be silent and to remain in my horse form. Thanks for cutting it off." He looks at Stella.

"If you go back their way, they will just recapture you and force you back into that life." Zarin brings up the likely possibility.

"I do not plan to go back toward them."

"Then where are you planning to go?"

"I do not know, but why do you care so much?"

"Look at my eyes and hers," she points to her golden orbs and then to Hajnal's eyes. His dark ones go between the two sets.

"You're a seer and she's a feeler. What does that have to do with me?"

"I know what it is to be on your own and be taken advantage of repeatedly because of your gift. If you go off on your own, you'll be used again. Maybe not by the carnival people, but by someone else."

"And?"

"And I think you should stay with us. We fairies should stick together. We are much stronger in larger numbers," Zarin proposes. The man crosses his arms and stares down the women.

"I'm not a practicing fairy. And you want me to turn back into a horse so you can keep traveling, don't you?" He guesses.

"That would be helpful, but you do not have to do so if you choose to stay with us," Zarin clarifies. He grabs his lower lip and twists it as he intently stares at Zarin.

"Where are you headed?" He needs to add this to his consideration.

"Our final destination is Koralia, but right now we are headed east toward Estellen," Zarin informs him.

"Estellen? But that place is cursed!"

"Yes, but we must go there if we want to save our brother," Althea explains, partially drawing the man's eyes to her. He stares at her. He finally registers what she looks like. His muscles relax and he releases his lip.

"You're trying to save your brother?" He speaks directly to Althea in a soft, caring tone.

"Yes. He's been cursed and we have to find him and treat him with the All-Cure Elixir. But we have to get the ingredients first, and one is in Estellen."

"That is terrible. But you are such a wonderful sister to be trying to save your brother," he walks to Althea as he speaks as if entranced.

"I try to be. But now we are down one horse, it will take us longer and make it hard to save him," Althea lets her eyes grow wet.

"What's your name?" he asks, now face to face with Althea.

"Althea," she answers.

"Althea," He whispers the name as if saying it louder would break it. He gazes at her, still amazed by her beauty. His warm amber eyes glaze over. "I would hate to make things harder for you, Althea. If you need me, say so." He offers himself. Althea glances over to her sister and Zarin. Hajnal rolls her eyes, then nods.

"You would be a great help to me and my family," Althea bats her eyes.

"Then I will help you. If you need me to be your horse, I'll gladly shift my form again," He pulls at his shirt.

"I have a horse, but if you will be sister's horse, I would be exceedingly grateful." Althea gestures to Hajnal, but he does not even look in the sister's direction.

"I can do that," he nods.

"Splendid!" Althea smiles. He smiles as well. Althea turns her head to grin at the other women. The man blinks and shakes his head. He blinks a few more times and looks down at his body.

"Why did I just agree to this?" He mumbles under his breath then looks up to Althea again. "Are you a witch? Have you bewitched me?"

"No, not at all. I'm void of magic," Althea shakes her head, appalled at the suggestion.

"Oh... I'm sorry. It's just one moment I was ready to leave, then I looked at you. Then I was..." He pauses, trying to find the words to explain the phenomenon.

"It happens a lot to many people," Hajnal states, allowing the shifter to know he is not alone in his experience.

"I see... Well, I offered my help, and you accepted, so I should be a man of my word."

"Thank you. We do appreciate it."

"Yes. But if anything goes wrong in Estellen, I will take my leave." He sets his limitations.

"We will not hold it against you should that time come," Zarin agrees to the limit.

"Alright. And who am I carrying?" He asks, waving a pointed finger toward the ladies. Hajnal raises her hand. He runs his eyes over the full-figured woman. She will not be as light a load as the other two women would have been.

"We will not look if you want to change back into your form," Althea breaks the temporary silence.

"Shouldn't we see if we have anything to help treat his neck?" Hajnal points at the blistered circle around his neck.

"I'll take care of that," Zarin crosses over to the shifter. She comes between him and Althea. Zarin stares at his neck before putting her hands on him. She closes her eyes and begins her blessing. The skin regrows.

"There you go," Zarin smiles, removing her hands. He rubs his hand over his neck and smiles at the lack of pain and ridge.

"Thank you..." he pauses and waits for her to fill in her name.

"Zarin."

"Zarin. And you are Althea," He points to Althea.

"Yes. Althea Sipos."

"And you are?" He points to his future and past rider.

"Hajnal Sipos," Hajnal gives her alias.

"Hajnal," He almost cringes at the name.

"And your name is?" Hajnal returns the question.

"Tyr. Tyr Dahl," He makes his introduction. The women repeat his name to themselves.

"Welp. I better get back into horse form if we want to get moving," he pulls off the borrowed shirt. The women turn their heads sharply.

"I'm ready to be saddled," they hear Tyr's voice. Zarin looks first and finds the black stallion ready.

"Excellent."

Hajnal saddles and ties her belongings to Tyr as Althea collects and puts away Basil's clothes and knife. She and Althea regain their positions atop their horses. Hajnal mounts a tad more gracefully than she had earlier. She cannot help being more self-aware. Now she knows she does not have just any ordinary horse beneath her. She has a man.

When the traveling group makes their camp for the night, Zarin makes a fire with a wiggle of her fingers. The lines on her fingers emit a light amber glow from them as the flames come forth. Stella and Althea smile at each other knowing they will not be freezing this night of camping. Tyr has to hide away to change back into his human form. They all come together to share some of the provisions packed by the Sipos sisters before they left.

"Zarin, you never did finish telling us what happened when it came time for your blood pact?" Althea's mind has not forgotten the story Zarin had previously begun.

"Blood pact?" Tyr lowers the food he was bringing to his mouth. "I thought you said you were fairies, not witches. I'm traveling with witches."

"We are not witches. We are fairies. I was given the opportunity to become a sorceress, but I did not," Zarin looks back to the sole man.

"And how am I to believe that?"

Zarin comes and sits next to Tyr and unlaces the front of her kirtle. The young man blushes at her sudden action.

"Zarin, what are you doing?" Hajnal gasps as the woman pulls down on her chemise.

"I have my proof here. You all can see I am telling the truth." Zarin moves her chemise enough to show the flesh above her left breast but below her shoulder. There remains a wound made from a blade. It looks to be a simple 'X' with another line starting at the top in the area between the upper portion of the 'X'. It comes down to divide the 'X' vertically. However, it stops when it reaches the intersection of the other lines. Hajnal recognizes the mark as almost the same as the mark on Bardolph's chest. However, his vertical line went all the way through the horizontal line so it divided the 'X' again. Bardolph's mark had been the mark of the Fallen. Zarin's is just short of being the mark.

"Had my mark been finished, I would have made my pact with the Fallen One and I would have gone on to be a sorceress. I stopped them as I knew I did not believe as they believed," Zarin states, and Tyr stares at the unfinished mark. Zarin also turns so Althea may see.

"I thought you were being forced to follow the Thirteen, not the Fallen," Althea brings up the information given earlier. Zarin fixes her clothes.

"Gold Haven's temples are supposed to follow the Thirteen, but in truth, the higher ranked follow the Fallen. They cover it up with the worship of the Thirteen. As Hadiakbar wanted me to be his apprentice, he was having me join the Fallen," Zarin answers. "So, there is a fun secret fact of the Gold Haven elite for you."

"They cut you to make that mark?" Althea asks.

"Yes. Blood is needed for a blood pact after all." Zarin returns to her original seat and the food she left there.

"If you are uncomfortable, you do not have to tell us more," Hajnal offers Zarin a way out of continuing.

"Oh, no, I'm not uncomfortable at all. This is a sign I did not give in to Hadiakbar. I am proud of it. It is just rather indecent to show it off all the time and at a glance, it looks like a sign of loyalty to the Fallen. Anyway, I was cutting myself as required. But I knew I could not go through with it. I had to decide then and there what was more important: to be true to myself and die in mere minutes or live a lie for decades to come. It is better to live briefly in truth than to live for centuries in a lie."

"True," Hajnal agrees.

"Hadiakbar and the other temple leaders were enraged. They demanded that I finish. Some even came to lay their hands on me to force me to continue."

"How did you escape then?" Tyr is the one to question now.

"I could manipulate the blood I had spilled to rise and blind some leaders. I also caused the ground to break and begin swallowing them. Hadiakbar could lasso me with the ridiculously long golden chain he always wore about him. He was going to kill me right there on the cold, broken marble floor. He had the dagger I had used earlier in his fat hand. By the grace of El-Yah, one of the other leaders intervened. She... she said they should execute me publicly. They could claim I was trying to follow the Fallen and, as that goes against the law of Gold Haven and the temples. This would also get those who were questioning them about being a part of the Fallen to stop."

"How devious!" Althea gasps.

"Yes. I was imprisoned and was to be executed in the morning. As dawn was coming, there was a commotion outside my cell. I had been bound, gagged, and blindfolded in my cell therefore I could not tell what was going on outside. Then I felt myself being grabbed and thrown into a hard wooden box. I could barely breathe in it. I was tossed about in it like common cargo. When the box finally opened and my blindfold was removed, I found myself on a ship. My mother was there! I was so relieved. She had left the temple. I expected an embrace and freedom from my restraints. Instead, my mother grabbed my bound hands and put them in the hands of the ship's captain. In exchange, he gave her a bag of silver. I would have cried out to my mother, but I was still gagged. She left the ship and me. I have not seen her since... After two years as Captain Kolar's personal slave, I escaped him and arrived at Austvest. I was found by Mother Huldah and she made me her apprentice. And that is how I got to Austvest," Zarin ends her story with a cheery tone and a small smile.

Hajnal and Althea stalled internally at the lightheartedness of how Zarin ended her story. Tyr puts his food down having lost his appetite. A horrible thing had been done and Zarin acts happy.

"I'm so sorry you had to go through that." Hajnal offers her sympathy.

"Oh, it is all well. It helped form who I am now and who I will be." Zarin brushes off the pity then addresses the horse-boy. "But what about you, Tyr? When did you leave Senyama for Austvest?"

"I'm from Norwin, not Senyama."

"Norwin? You exclaimed in Senyamese how happy you were when you transformed the first time," Zarin gives her observation. Tyr snorts.

"It was my mother's tongue but I am of Norwin, not Senyama," He disregards the other island nation.

"I see. I did not mean to offend you," Zarin apologizes.

"You did not offend me. It is a common mistake. I am surprised you would know Senyamese," He expresses.

"I have the gift of all-speak, so I understand all human languages, including Senyamese."

"How many gifts do you have, Zarin?" Hajnal asks as Althea tries to calculate the number of gifts Zarin has shown or listed previously.

"Only six. I have the gifts of prophecy, all-speak, control of fire, earth and water elements, and healing."

"You act as if that is not much," Tyr scoffs.

"It is not compared to some. I am sure you all know of Rastaban Rumplegeist. He had eleven of the fairy gifts." Zarin brings up the person. The other members of the group have indoctrinated disgust come over them at the mention of Rastaban's name.

"And it has been prophesied there will be one who will have all of the gifts," Zarin continues.

"The New Starrling," Hajnal recalls the word. It had been many dreams since her nighttime friend had told her of the prophecy. It was one of the many ones he spoke of during their time together over the years.

"Exactly," Zarin nods.

"The what?" Althea is unfamiliar with the term as is the silent Tyr.

"The New Starrling. It was prophesied a fairy will be born with all the fairy gifts making him or her equal to a Starrling. The New Starrling will be the most powerful person in the world. The New Starrling will either bring peace and unity or will bring death and destruction. As it is uncertain what will be brought, fairies have been striving to avoid intermarrying with fairies of differing gifts thus postponing the prophecy. As far as I know, Rastaban is the last known fairy to have nearly all of the fairy gifts," Zarin explains further.

"How do you know what a New Starrling is?" Althea looks at her older sister curiously.

"*He* told me of it," Hajnal refers to her dream companion. Althea presses her lips together and nods.

"'He' being the one to whom your mind is bound?" Zarin grows excited to bring up the rare bond.

"Yes. He has an extensive library and tells me stories, histories, and prophecies," Hajnal divulges.

"Interesting..." Zarin's voice trails off.

"Wait. You have your mind bound to someone?" Tyr raises his eyebrows. "How is that possible?"

"I don't know. I was just born bound to have my mind linked to another's." Hajnal shrugs.

"Your mother must have been cursed when she was with child." Tyr assumes.

"Having one's mind bound to another is not exactly a curse. Some fairies bless others with that ability for a time. This is done to help connect persons who must be separated for a long time or are prophesied to meet," Zarin gives a different explanation.

"I suppose we are destined to meet then..." Hajnal whispers to herself, her heart skipping and cheeks flushing at the idea she could meet her longest friend in real life one day. She loses her excitement as she thinks of their last talk. He had spoken of his homeland. It would be impossible for him to be in his homeland and for her to meet him. It is impossible.

"Do you also have your mind bound, Althea?" Tyr speaks to the other sister.

"Oh no. I have no special gifts or mental bindings like my sister. I'm void, void, void," Althea speaks passively and gives a smile as if she were fine with this.

"Well, you are not void of beauty," Tyr gives his opinion. Althea laughs.

"How sweet you are. How old are you?"

"A man's age," He answers with a wink. All three women guffaw at his answer. He turns pink.

"We should probably take shifts keeping watch at night. Of course, whoever is awake needs to have a weapon." Hajnal considers. "I have my pipe to help protect us and a knife."

"I can shift into a great beast, if need be," Tyr offers his talent.

"I do not think we need to do this. We are protected, remember," Zarin raises her hand and points to the ring matching Althea and Hajnal's.

"From what kind of physical harm do those rings actually protect us?" Althea questions.

"From any harm, physical harm. Did you suffer a wound when you touched that rope around Tyr?" Zarin looks at Hajnal who shakes her head.

"I felt a mere prickle for an instant then nothing and I had no mark."

"Right. Now watch this," Zarin pulls out a knife from her bag. She raises the knife and angles it toward her chest.

"No!" the sisters shriek as Zarin plunges the knife down toward her chest. With heavy panting, the group gawks at the knife meeting the chest.

"See? I press and press, but I cannot penetrate anything. Slaps and kicks are mere taps. And if a man of any age tries to do what he should not..." Zarin glances at Tyr. "He will be kept at bay."

"I would not do such a thing," Tyr states.

"Good to know." Zarin smiles.

"So where can I get one of these protection rings?" Tyr gazes at the magical marvel.

"My mistress gave them to us, so I do not know where you can get one," Zarin explains.

"Could you not make me one? Are you not a fairy as well?" He asks, leaning toward the golden-eyed maiden.

"I am not there yet in my training," she looks away from him. He sighs and distances himself again. He mutters to himself in his mother's tongue. Althea yawns, signaling her need for rest. Hajnal catches the yawn only for Zarin to catch it as well.

"We should sleep now. The sun will be back before we know it," Zarin urges. No one protests. Instead, they lie down and cover themselves. The fire's warmth almost makes their bodies forget they lie on the cold ground.

CHAPTER II

Blue flames bounce at Hajnal's feet. They pass through the open gate to lead her to the small castle. They do not go into the castle this time. Instead, they lead her around, allowing her to take in the dark and still grounds. She sees where the flames lead.

A glass, rounded building with iron trim, is the only thing lit out in the yard. The doors open on their own, allowing the heat from the house to waft over Hajnal. As none of the flowers are in bloom, there are no floral aromas to greet her. Lanterns hang from the ceiling. The blue flames disappear from her view, only to reappear in one of the unlit lanterns. They change from blue to white.

"Stella," Astro stands amid the sleeping plants. Hajnal steps swiftly to meet him. She feels his smile, though she cannot see it.

"Astro, I am sorry I left before we could do more research."

"It is not thy fault. Besides, I hath done much research while I waited for thee."

"Why are we here and not in the library?" She questions, though they both know their control of their placement is limited.

"I have something to show thee." He takes her hand gently. His touch is gentle but leading. Keeping in step with him, Hajnal makes her way to the back of the greenhouse. Astro stops them at the sight of a vegetable bed. She recognizes them as the tops of carrots.

"Carrots?"

"They may look like carrots but-" Astro reaches to take hold of two of the carrot tops. He pulls, lifting the dirt, which proves to be a facade. With the fake dirt up, Astro releases a carrot top to pull down the wooden box, revealing a stairway heading downward.

"It is a secret passage," Astro finishes. The warmth of the grin hidden beneath his facial covering reaches her, making her smile as well.

"Where does it go?"

"While I was doing research, I learned this is a passage to the stardust keep," He answers.

"Interesting."

"Will thou join me to see it still is joined to the keep?"

Hajnal nods and takes Astro's empty hand. He holds it as she takes a few steps down. He steps down as he lowers the fake dirt panel. Once his head is cleared, he keeps to Hajnal's side. He does not release her hand until they reach the stone ground. They find themselves in a black corridor. The faint blue light from the upper level gives the faintest light below. Astro notices a torch on the wall as well as striking stones. Astro takes the stones and hits them till their sparks ignite the torch in his hand.

"Oh, my." Hajnal's eyes move from wall to ceiling to the other wall. They sparkle and shine from the torch's flame. The walls and flat ceiling sport iridescent tile which have been creatively pieced together. Gardens of floral mosaics are upon the walls while the ceiling has numerous eight-point stars to reflect the nation of Estellen's sigil.

"This is so beautiful." Hajnal cannot tear her eyes away.

"It is. Shall we venture forth?" Astro seeks her decision. She nods and the two step forward together. Though the hall is beautiful, it is narrow. The two stay with nearly no space between their arms.

"Why would there be a secret passage from here to the stardust keep?" Hajnal's hand cannot stop grazing Astro's as they walk in the narrow hallway.

"The tunnel was built by Prince Caradoc so he could meet with his love, Lady Blodeuwedd. She had been selected as the keeper of the stardust vault."

"Why did they have to meet through a tunnel?"

"It was unlawful for fairies and royals to marry at the time. To keep their meetings a secret, Prince Caradoc built the tunnel. He made these mosaics as his lady should not have to live like a mole to be with him," Astro explains further.

"I see. And what happened to Prince Caradoc and Lady Blodeuwedd?"

"He abdicated the throne. He took residence in Castle Evensong, taking the role of protector of Vespera, and married Lady Blodeuwedd. Lady Blodeuwedd removed herself from being the keeper so she could teach her children and other fairies magic."

"So, they lived happily ever after?" Hajnal summarizes the end.

"No."

"No?"

"They lived happily for many years, but a careless servant accidentally set fire to the castle. Prince Caradoc died when he became trapped in a tower while trying to save his youngest daughter, Blodwen. Lady Blodeuwedd died of a broken heart seven days after the funeral," Astro shares the fate. Hajnal's heart sinks at the end.

"How tragic."

"I thought so as well when I read it earlier." He agrees. "I pray we meet no such end as theirs."

We. The word sticks out to Hajnal. *Does he pray for us as a couple not to meet such an end or just for us in a general sense? In a general, completely platonic sense?*

"Astro, do you mean-" Hajnal asks, only to stop when her body walks into a clear, texture-less blob. This blob prevents her from any further steps, yet also forms to her body. As if to let her sink into it before repelling her.

"I see the barrier reaches us even under here," Astro sighs. It is not the first time the two have run into this clear force. This surrounds the outskirts of the castle's grounds.

"I guess we have to turn back then," Hajnal tries not to let on too much about her disappointment.

They both turn but as they do their bodies collide. The bumping causes Hajnal to stumble backward. Astro reaches out and catches the small of her back before she can hit the wall. Instinctively, he pulls her against him.

The flames of the torch cause a gorgeous gleam to come into Astro's light eyes. She is unsure if the warmth kissing her skin is from the torch or Astro. Her heart races.

Astro releases her now as she has sure footing. She smooths out her dress before they continue walking back toward their entrance.

"Do you know where the tunnel comes out on the other side?" Hajnal brings the attention back to the hallway.

"I read it comes out in the vault behind a crest of Estellen."

"Hmm...Did I tell you my group is coming to the stardust keep?"

"Thou art?" His voice jumps an octave positively.

"Yes. We intend to arrive tomorrow."

"Then thou could see me." Gleeful tingling comes over Hajnal's skin from Astro.

"I would like that... I would like to meet you in true flesh and not just in this dream world."

"As would I."

Hajnal smiles to herself but loses it when she thinks of the probability of not being able to come to him or the stardust vault. Astro hangs the torch into its holster as there seems to be nothing to end the flame. He takes Hajnal's hand as he escorts her up the stairs. Once back in the greenhouse, Astro resets the carrot container to cover the secret entrance.

"I see our little leaders are leaving," Hajnal points at the blue flames hopping down from the lanterns and to the floor. They head for the main entrance.

"We must follow then," Astro offers his arm for her to take so they may walk on together. Hajnal takes his arm.

As they promenade, the will-o'-the-wisps hop like rabbits around the grounds. They do not head inside the castle. Instead, they keep jumping around the estate. It has not been the first time Hajnal has been led to walk the grounds. It can be refreshing being in the clean, night air with the dazzling stars and brilliant moon lighting up the land.

It is quiet. Nothing but their steps and breathing can be heard. No owl hoots. No crickets play. Not even the wind whistles.

"Stella."

"Yes?"

"When thou arrive tomorrow at the vault, will thou promise to come to me?"

"I do. It will be by force of others to prevent me," she promises. He pats the hand on his arm.

"I do hope thou could overpower thine own sister," he chuckles.

"I would have two others to contend with though."

"Two? I thought thou only attained one more companion."

"We have accidentally attained a shifter," Hajnal updates her walking partner.

"How does one accidentally attain a shifter?"

"I thought he was a horse. I purchased him but he transformed back into his human state later," Hajnal explains away the situation.

"Hm..." his pale eyebrows dip.

"Does something trouble you, Astro?"

"No. No. I...uh..." He clears his throat, "I hope this new man's presence is not upsetting to thee given thy last experience with a shifter."

"You are so sweet, but I have no issue with him. He only has an interest in my sister and I...I don't get the feelings I did when I was around Bardolph from him."

"Good. I would hate for thee to be forced into the company of an unsavory sort."

"Yet I'm forced to be in yours every night," Hajnal jokes.

"As am I," He teases back. She laughs lightly. She leans her head fondly on his shoulder as she did often. He does not stiffen, shudder or pull away. Why would he?

Hajnal's heart is warm and at ease as it always seems to be with him. There is such peace being with Astro in this place. What a refuge this world and he is to her. How fortunate she has been to get to spend every night in this place with him since infancy.

Will I truly be able to find him tomorrow? Is all of this truly real or a sickeningly realistic figment of my imagination? Huldah stated our minds are bonded but how could this be? It is said there is no one in Estellen. Has everyone been wrong? Do the people of Estellen still live? Will I be able to find Astro? If I do, will he know me? How will he feel about me when he is awake? What does he feel now?

Hajnal slows her pace, which causes Astro to do the same, and lifts her head from him. She speaks his name, gaining his attention.

"Do you... are you... how do you..." she struggles. His eyebrows bend and dip curiously. Hajnal pauses, pressing her lips together. She stares into his clear blue eyes.

"I'm sorry. My question just fell out of my head." Hajnal shakes her head.

"Do not apologize. Oh! Look! The will-o'-the-wisps are heading inside," Astro points to the blue lights. The couple follows them inside. Up they go. They ascend higher than she has gone before in years past. As they near the top of the tower they have been climbing, Astro stops.

"Is something wrong, Astro?" Hajnal turns to her partner.

"I think we should turn around," He turns.

"But the lights are going up," she points ahead. Sure enough, the lights remain still at the top of the stairs at a closed door with a rounded top.

"I think we should turn back."

"Why?"

"It would be inappropriate for us to go there together," he claims.

"Why is that? We have gone up there before when I was younger."

"Thou were a child then, not a woman. And this is... a bedchamber," he answers shyly. Hajnal immediately releases Astro's arm and puts her hands behind her back.

"Oh..." She blushes, though Astro cannot see. In truth, this would not be the first time she would have been alone in a bedroom with a member of the opposite sex who was not from her family. The only other time had been when that dastardly Bardolph had tried to assault her in Mrs. Beverly's home. Every good, chaste girl in Austvest knows being alone with a man in a bedroom could ruin more than just her reputation.

"Seeing as thou art now a young woman and I am a man, we should not venture further. I would not want to dishonor thee," Astro explains.

"I doubt you would ever hurt or dishonor me, Astro. I trust you."

"Still, let us turn away and go elsewhere," Astro urges. He takes a step down and holds his hand out to Hajnal. She takes his hand and his offer. She smiles to herself. Even though they are in a world separate from all others, he intends to not "dishonor" her. No one would know if he did. Would it even matter, as this is all a dream world? Still, he sees her as a young woman now. That must count for something.

The further down they walk, the less she can see. She holds onto him tightly, afraid of falling.

"Can you see anything, Astro?" Hajnal whispers.

"No," He admits.

"Could we stop then? I do not wish for either of us to fall."

"I suppose we could sit here and wait for the lights to return this way," Astro proposes. The two sit down on the stone stairs. Hajnal removes herself from him.

"Why hast thou let go? Have thou disappeared?" He reaches out for her in the dark.

"I am still here. Given the reason we have turned around, I thought you may not want to touch," Hajnal answers.

"No. This is fine. We are merely keeping close so as not to fall after all," he finds her hand. She lets him take it. She grins to herself.

"Oh, if you say so," she feigns some naivety.

They sit in silence.

"Stella," Astro breaks.

"Yes?"

"Does thou think when we meet in the other world, we will-thou will-" It is Astro now who struggles to vocalize.

"Will what?" She means to encourage him to finish his questioning.

"Thou will think of me as more than thy brother?" Astro's low-tone words make her heart jump.

"I think not of you as a brother now, Astro," Hajnal answers truthfully.

"Thou do not?" His voice grows light and high.

"No."

"I do not think of thee as a sister, Stella." His hands find her upper arms.

"Is that so?"

"Yes. Thou art closer to my heart than that."

"Am I?"

"Yes. Do I have the hope that I am closer than a brother to thine?"

"Yes."

Astro releases a quick but joyful breath. He brings her closer and holds her against him in an embrace. She sinks into his hold.

"My heart is filled with jubilation, my dearest Stella. This means when thou come for me, thou could-" He stops and sighs happily again.

"I could?" Hajnal does not know what.

"Thou could...Stella? Stella, thou art...so soon?" He feels her body losing form. Hajnal frowns. Sure enough, she evaporates.

Hajnal inhales deeply before opening her eyes. She finds herself back on the ground next to her sister. The grass beside her is covered in dew. The fire has turned to smoke and ashes. Tyr and Zarin lie still on the ground nearby. Hajnal looks up at the high trees above her. The sky is still dark but has turned bluer as the sun intends to rise soon. She exhales. Her heart is racing. He held her in his heart, closer than a sister. That must mean the man in her dream loves her.

What did he think I could do? And what was his name?

The others wake up and share some of the packed food before setting off again. Hajnal rides quietly on Tyr's back, thinking only of her veiled night companion, as Zarin and Althea sing songs to entertain themselves. When the women's voices grow tired, Hajnal plays her pipe, rejoining her daytime companions.

The ground grows steeper as it turns more mountainous. Still, they follow the road even as it becomes overgrown with grass, vines, and tree roots as the sun is in the west but ready to set.

"We should be reaching the border any moment now," Zarin looks down at the open book in her hand where a map is drawn. The air grows chilly and the surrounding trees become dark and dead. The light from the still-shining sun has become obscured by dark lowering itself enough to create a dense fog at the tree line. If one were to look back, they would see a bright blue sky but looking ahead it is not so.

Dread creeps upon the group as a spider climbs up from one's foot to one's neck, only to turn into a snake wanting to squeeze the life from its prey. The sisters grip their reins tighter. The horses press on, though Meteora shudders beneath Althea.

Coming around the bend of the road, a gasp comes from the group. The horses stop as their riders become motionless.

From the earth has emerged and stands, giant thorns from a thicket not even a giant could surpass. Like steel spikes, these thorns stick out daring a brave person to touch them. Up toward the dark sky they extend as if trying to poke a hole in the clouds. This dense briar patch is higher and thicker than any wall any of the group has ever seen.

"What is this?" Tyr backs away, taking Hajnal with him.

"This is the border of Estellen," Zarin proclaims, then looks into her book at her map. She points to the left. "The gate you mentioned, Hajnal, should be that way."

Following Zarin's lead, the group turns left. They do their best to steer clear of the dangerous thorns. Hajnal and Althea cannot look away.

"What happened here?" Tyr is left out of the loop.

"The curse," Althea answers.

"What curse?"

"The curse of Estellen," Althea speaks slightly slower in hopes it would register in Tyr's head.

"The curse of Estellen? I've never heard of it."

"You haven't heard? Everyone in the Far Lands knows about the curse of Estellen!" Althea is aghast at Tyr's lack of knowledge.

"I must have slept through that lesson," he remarks with his excuse. "What happened?"

"You tell it, Hajnal. You know it better."

"Well... a century or so ago, Estellen was this glorious kingdom known to have the most beautiful royals. The Queen of Estellen gave birth to a daughter who was hailed as the most beautiful woman in all of the Far Lands. No one could deny it. All in the land were invited to celebrate the baby's christening. A vain fairy who had secretly become a sorceress came to the christening to see the child. While the fairies were giving their gifts, the vain sorceress came to gaze upon the child. Seeing the princess was even more beautiful than described, the fairy cursed the princess so when she turned sixteen, she would prick her finger on the spindle of a spinning wheel and die," Hajnal begins the story.

"What does that have to do with the thorn wall?" Tyr brings up the barrier.

"After the sorceress gave her curse, another fairy used all the magic she could to reverse the curse. She stated the princess would not die but instead would fall into an ageless sleep. She would one day be awakened by true love's kiss. So, when the princess turned sixteen and fell into her sleep, she was put in a resting place. The king and queen were eager for someone to break the spell but the sorceress was not. To keep the princess's true love from coming, the sorceress cursed the land to grow these horrible thorny thickets to surround the barrier of Estellen to block any entry from anyone from other lands. No matter what magic or force people tried, no one could break the barrier. Without access to other lands, their resources diminished. One brave fairy rode a Pegasus up into the sky to take a look at the land. He saw people lying on the ground, dead. He was then blown away out of the land. All knew then the people of Estellen must have died. So now the princess must sleep for eternity, never to wake as no one can ever come and break her curse," Hajnal ends the sad tale. Her heart weighs like a stone in her chest as her thoughts go to the Estellen man who persists in her dreams. He surely is a victim as well.

"Wait. I have heard something similar to this. But the kingdom was Starland, and it was a princess who was guarded by a forest filled with evil creatures," Tyr gives the version he remembers.

"Starland is another name for Estellen," Althea remembers a fact she was once taught.

"I had heard the princess was kept in a tower with a dragon guarding her. But the barrier of thorns was also in the version I was told," Zarin gives another adaptation.

"It is sad. A whole kingdom lost because of vanity." Hajnal shakes her head.

"Pride can be so destructive," Zarin murmurs.

"Do you think there is an opening?" Tyr's eyes keep looking around for such.

"I can only hope," Zarin replies.

The three make it a little over a league when Zarin stops. The sisters follow seeing Zarin doing so. Zarin dismounts gracefully and approaches the thorny wall. Hajnal jumps down, trusting Tyr not to run off, and comes to Zarin's side to look at the wall. There is a patch of grass with no growth sprouting from it, but just above it, the briars have grown together from the sides to hide it.

Hajnal reaches out and takes hold of one branch. She feels the pressures of the thorns in her hand but no pain. She pulls it from another. Zarin joins her and pulls apart the branches. Althea leaves her horse to join her sister and Zarin. Slowly, they pick apart the thicket. A path begins to show.

"Oh, my." Zarin gazes upon the rounded stone arch they uncover. In the middle of the archway is the eight-point star of Estellen painted a violet color.

"This is the Violet Star gate then," Althea deduces.

"Yes," Zarin nods.

"We need to keep clearing," Hajnal pulls more diligently. She has to see if they can get to the other side. The other women keep up with Hajnal.

Hajnal beams as they push through the last poking hazard to the dense forest of oak trees with soft, lush grass serving as the floor of the woods. She barely can register she is the first to step into the cursed land in a hundred years for her eyes are searching for any sign of the place her dream friend spoke of previously. In the not-too-far distance, under a giant oak, is nestled a stone building resembling a mausoleum.

"There!" Hajnal steps forward excitedly, only to be grabbed by Althea.

"What?" Hajnal looks back at the blonde.

"We should get Tyr and the horses to come with us," Althea points back at the opening. Hajnal tries not to frown. She looks forward again.

"Let me see if that is the vault while you two get Tyr and the horses," Hajnal suggests. Althea purses her lips and lowers one eyebrow.

"It will take just a moment," Althea pulls on her sister. Hajnal exhales heavily. She returns through the opening to fetch what was left behind them. They find the horses with a humanized Tyr loading them down with the bags he formerly carried.

"I got tired of being a horse," He quickly explains his change of appearance. Luckily, he did dress after shifting.

"We have made a path into Estellen. You should come in with us." Zarin grabs her horse's reins. Althea takes Meteora. Tyr walks behind the horses and women through the passage to the other side. Coming out, Tyr looks around at the serene woods.

"That's odd," Tyr mumbles.

"What?" Althea looks at the shifter.

"Do you hear that?"

All go silent.

"I hear nothing," Zarin comments.

"Me too," the sisters speak in unplanned unison.

"Exactly. There is no sound. I do not hear birds, squirrels, or even a fly," Tyr points out. A chill runs down Althea's spine.

"Did all the creatures die as well in the curse?" Althea looks at Hajnal as if she is the expert. Hajnal shrugs.

"Do you think the air is cursed as well? Shall we die if we stay in here?" Tyr voices his fears.

"Wouldn't the trees and grass be dead, then?" Zarin tries to remain logical. Tyr does not relax.

"Let's get the stardust and go," Althea urges. Hajnal says nothing but walks to the stone structure. The others remove the bits and reins from the horses, then tie them with ropes to a tree, thus allowing the horses to rest and feed, while they search.

Coming closer, Hajnal finds the small, rounded mausoleum covered in patches of moss. Spiderwebs are in between the columns. The spiders sit in their webs but do not move, even as the intruders come near them. A rectangular cut-out holds a copper door that has turned into a green patina. There is no handle on the door.

"There's not a doorknob," Hajnal feels her veins tightening like her stomach.

"Let me try to open it," Tyr volunteers. Hajnal steps out of his way. He backs up before running at the door angling his shoulder to take the brunt of the door. He groans, holding his shoulder. The door remains unmoved.

"Maybe if we all push," Althea suggests. Hajnal, Althea, and Tyr all begin pushing. Grunting and huffing, the three put all their effort into pushing it. It has to open. It does not.

"Help us, Zarin," Althea calls to the one human not participating.

"Step aside and I will," Zarin answers. The three steps aside, breathing heavily.

"If we three couldn't open it together, I doubt you can open it on your own," Tyr comments as Zarin walks to the door. Zarin ignores him. She lays her hand gently on the door before closing her eyes. She opens her eyes, makes a fist, and knocks.

Creaking, the door swings open. Zarin looks at Tyr and smirks. He rolls his eyes.

"Let's go inside," Hajnal steps eagerly to the open door. Going inside, there is only darkness. The little light coming from the opened door only allows them to see there are stone floors and walls.

"I can't see anything," Althea states, the thought Hajnal has as well.

"I think I see... yes. I'm right," Zarin smiles, looking upward. She thrusts her hand out. From her palm comes sparks. The sparks fly into lanterns hanging above their heads. The sparks hop from lantern to lantern in the hallway, creating a lit path.

How like the will-o-the-wisps. Hajnal thinks.

Once Tyr enters, the door closes. The hanging lanterns allow them to see the four of them are in a narrow marble hallway. They walk until they reach the end where a wooden door awaits. This door has a handle. Opening the door, the group can step into a round room. The walls have many shelves covered with books, bottles, and small lamps. A few empty beds are against different parts of the wall. In the center of the floor sits a circular altar made of stone with the top of the altar dipping down into a bowl. Coming around the altar, the group sees a pile of silver and gold sparkles. They shine dimly in the room.

"Is this the stardust?" Althea looks down at the bright powder.

"Yes. We just need a pinch," Zarin recalls the ingredients of the elixir. She reaches into her satchel to pull out a vial. She uncorks it before stretching out her forefinger and thumb to get a pinch of the glittery residue.

"Maybe you should take a little more. We may need it for something else," Althea suggests.

"I'm sure it could fetch a decent amount of gold." Tyr's eyes stay on the dust.

"We should only take what we need," Zarin sprinkles the dust into the vial.

"But-" Althea begins to protest.

"We should listen to Zarin. She knows more about these things," Hajnal puts her hand on her sister's shoulder. Althea sighs. Tyr groans.

"We should go now," Zarin seals and puts away the vial.

"Yeah. Who knows how long we will survive in the dead land," Tyr starts for the door. Althea follows, as does Zarin. Hajnal lingers behind. Her eyes search the walls. The walls are not bare.

Besides the shelving, tapestries are hanging. The art on them is mostly of nature. There is one hanging lower than the others. The threading is dark except for the silver thread making an eight-point star and the gold thread making rays behind the star. Below the star, more gold thread was used to stitch the words "Faith Fidelity Fortitude". Hajnal walks to the sigil. She pushes it aside and finds the wall here is discolored in comparison to the rest of the wall. She pushes it. The stone quietly slides out of her way. A set of stairs is behind it.

"What are you doing?" Zarin's appearance makes Hajnal jump.

"I found this secret passage," Hajnal answers truthfully.

"Oh!" Zarin bends down like Hajnal excitedly. "Where do you think it goes?"

"What are you two doing?" Althea and Tyr have turned back for the others.

"Hajnal has found this passageway," Zarin answers.

"Where do you think it goes?" Althea asks what Zarin did.

"Maybe to treasure," Tyr suggests.

"No," Hajnal shakes her head.

"Then to what?" Tyr asks. Hajnal presses her lips together. To the dream world is what she wants to say, but knows she will sound silly.

"Let's find out," Hajnal lets herself start down the stairs.

"I don't know…" Althea is hesitant.

"Stay here if you want but I'm going," Hajnal does not stop for her sister. Zarin shrugs and follows Hajnal without a second thought. Not to be shown up by her sister, Althea starts down.

"Wait for me," Tyr cannot let the beautiful Althea be unprotected.

Reaching the bottom of the stairs, Hajnal finds a torch on the wall. She turns to present it to Zarin. The golden-eyed maiden needs not be asked before she sets the torch aflame. The light causes the floor, walls, and ceiling to shine against the beautiful tiles around them.

"How beautiful," Zarin looks around, as do the others. Every nerve in Hajnal buzzes.

I know this place. I was just here. Well, not here, but like here. Her feet yearn to run but she knows she cannot run off and leave the others. This does not mean she cannot step quickly.

"This is amazing. How did they do all of this underground?" Althea wonders.

"I wonder who made all of this," Zarin comments. Hajnal knows the answer but does not share. She wants only to get to the other side. Her heartbeat increases with each step.

"Is that a light?" Tyr points to a distant brightness in the distance. Hajnal carelessly hands the torch to Zarin, then runs. She cannot stop her mouth from smiling as she comes closer to the light.

Sure enough, on the wall is a torch burning. It is near the end of its burn but it still burns. Hajnal looks at the staircase by it. She starts up despite hearing her sister calling for her to slow down.

"How is this lit? Is there someone else here?" Tyr looks around the narrow hall.

"But no one is alive in Estellen," Althea claims.

At the top of the stairs, Hajnal pushes up on the wooden, slanted roof. It lifts and so she pushes the wall in front of her. It moves. She steps up and out. She stands still in awe.

"Hajnal, why did you-oh my," Althea comes up and stops her questioning as she sees where they are.

Hajnal steps out into the glass greenhouse. Althea joins her only for Zarin and Tyr to come up as well. They all look around the plant nursery.

"I've been here before, Thea," Hajnal speaks to her sister, though she does not look at her.

"How?" Tyr is skeptical.

"In my dreams, I've been here in my dreams."

CHAPTER 12

*O*ne. *Two. Three. Four. Five. Six. Seven. Eight. Turn.*

One. Two. Three. Four. Five. Six. Seven. Eight. Turn.

One. Two. Three. Four. Five. Six. Seven. Eight. Turn.

Sir Artegal Belamour no longer has to count the paces he takes but does as to keep his mind wandering from the darkness there. Outside the castle he guards, his feet have made a worn path, but they have never grown tired. His dragon skin boots have not worn away either. His gloved hand rests on the pommel of his sheathed sword while his eyes survey the perimeter for any disturbance in the castle's grounds. Just like every day, there is nothing. There is no sound but his breathing, the rustle of the grass beneath his feet, the patting of his sword against his body, and the voices from his memories. There is no sound of a whistling wind, a babbling brook, a bird's song, a cricket's chirp, or anything else that might cause him to hope for a return to normalcy.

One. Two. Three. Four. Five. Six. Seven. Eight. Turn.

One. Two. Three. Four. Five. Six. Seven. Eight. Turn.

One. Two. Three, Four. Five. Six. Seven. Eight. Turn.

The sky above him grows darker, showing it will soon be night. He knows there will be no moon or stars visible to him. There has not been a sun, a moon, or the stars for him all these years. There are only clouds occasionally releasing rain and lightning bolts. As he inhales the air, his nose tingles at the scent of rain. His lip twitches at the simple pleasure of tonight being different. There will be noise - glorious, thunderous noise. He will feel the refreshing droplets on his face. How long has it been since he has been touched by something other than himself?

One. Two. Three. Four. Five. Six. Seven. Eight. Turn.

One. Two. Three. Four. Five. Six. Seven. Eight. Turn.

One. Two. Three, Four. Five. Six. Seven.

"What is this place?"

Sir Artegal turns early at the sound of the voice.

Is it a true voice or my imagination again? He shakes his head, ready to regain his routine.

"Do you think...." The words become muddled. Sir Artegal stops again. He knows this is a true voice.

Unsheathing his sword, he bolts. His feet fly toward the glass greenhouse around the corner from him. Coming around the wall, he does not stop. How can he? Coming from the unused greenhouse are four strangers.

A plump woman with her brown hair tied into a single braid falls down her back, contrasting against the blue dress she wears. Beside her, a blonde woman sports a simple outfit but her figure is far slighter. She is fair of face; he admits to himself. He is not blind after all. In a yellow kirtle is a third woman with skin like copper and a coif covering her hair. The lone man in the group is tall, but not as tall as Sir Artegal. His clothes do not fit well. His lengthy inky hair flows freely down his back.

"Halt!" Sir Artegal yells with his sword ready to swing. The four turn to look at him but freeze like deer who catch sight of a hunter. The wide eyes catch Sir Artegal's attention. The brunette has purple eyes while the covered maiden has gold ones. The small man moves. Like lightning, Sir Artegal is before this intruder with his blade at the man's neck.

"I said halt," Sir Artegal does not express any kindness in his voice. No one dares to move, especially the young man who could be decapitated easily. Sir Artegal's eyes run over the young man. He notes how his monolid eyes are sharp but nervous.

"Who art thou?" Sir Artegal speaks, giving the one he questions permission to speak.

"I am Tyr Dahl," Tyr answers.

"That is no name from Senyama," Sir Artegal comments, thinking of the names he recalls from the island nation in the Azure Ocean.

"I am from Norwin," Tyr insists. Artegal presses the sword into the skin but still does not draw blood.

"I know thou art lying," Sir Artegal is unconvinced. His blade draws a drop of blood. Tyr grows white.

"I am from Senyama. But I swear I am called Tyr Dahl," Tyr insists. Sir Artegal's blade moves once more, but only to lessen the trauma it inflicts.

"Who art these maidens?" He keeps his eyes on Tyr still.

"My traveling companions," Tyr tells truthfully.

"I am Zarin Almanzar of Gold Haven," The one with the covered head and brilliant gold eyes introduces herself to the sword wielder. He notices how her golden eyes shine like sunlight. How long has he seen such a warm shine? "These are the Sipos sisters, Hajnal and Althea, from Austvest."

Sir Artegal glances at the women now.

"Why is it thou hast come here?"

"We have come for stardust. We require it for a All-Cure elixir," Zarin answers.

"But how hast thou come here?" Sir Artegal insists on knowing.

"I learned of the Violet Star Gate. It is close enough to the stardust keep that it was not allowed to be affected by the magic cursing this land. We had to merely find the gate's position in this thicket to enter." The one with purple eyes, called Hajnal, speaks now.

"How then did thou come into these grounds without using the front gate?"

"The tunnel from the vault to the greenhouse," Hajnal answers.

"Tunnel?" Sir Artegal's eyes slip from the group to the greenhouse.

"Prince Caradoc and his lady Blodeuwedd's secret tunnel," Hajnal clarifies. Sir Artegal's eyes snap back to Hajnal.

How could I forget about the tunnel? How does this outsider know of the lovers?

Sir Artegal looks into her violet eyes. They sparkle like starlight used to in the Estellen night sky. Her honesty and calmness are evident in the steadiness of her heartbeat. He feels it in his chest. Zarin has the same peace. The blonde one has a racing heart like Tyr. But only Tyr has a sickening fear aching in his kidneys and stomach. Sir Artegal lowers his sword from Tyr's neck. He sheaths his sword.

"Have thou found thy stardust?" the swordsman checks.

"Yes, we have. We will go. We will go the way we came." Zarin takes the lead on answering for the group.

"Wait," Hajnal speaks up, gaining the eyes of the others.

"What is it, Hajnal?"

Hajnal looks to Sir Artegal not Zarin.

"May we stay here? It looks as if it will rain. I can smell it in the air. Could we stay until the storm is over?"

Sir Artegal stands still like the stone walls around the grounds. He considers her request. The clouds release their excess fluid. One by one, the raindrops come down. They are spaced in their timing.

"I will let thee into the castle till the storm passes," he decides. He turns around. He walks toward the castle's entrance. The foursome follows. Hajnal walks the quickest to keep up with their guide.

Coming around to the front, Sir Artegal bypasses the scalloped, cornered, rectangle pool where marble unicorn statues stand facing one another. The rain splashes into the pool's water, causing ripples. Sir Artegal approaches the large purple wood doors. The new group admires the eight-point star made from an iron inlay in the door. Sir Artegal uses both of his hands to push open the doors. The hinges screech and creak as they allow the doors to create a path inside the castle. A dark hall greets those who seek shelter. Sir Artegal lights no candle or lantern. Still, he walks further into the castle without faltering or stumbling.

As they walk through the dim rooms, they can barely see the furniture or tapestries of the walls. Artegal finally stops at a table where a lantern sits. Fire appears inside, giving light to the room.

Finally, the group can see they are inside the great hall. There are long tables, including the table where the lantern sits. Many chairs are set along the tables as if they expect to be sat in by numerous guests.

"Make thyselves comfortable here till the storm ends," Sir Artegal gestures to the chairs. The women and Tyr take seats. "I do not suggest wandering around this castle. It is ancient and may require repair. If thou seek to leave this place as thou came, thou will heed my words. Stay and rest here," Sir Artegal advises. He turns around to walk away.

"Wait," Hajnal jumps up from her chosen seat. He looks over his shoulder at her. The walls of her heart tighten in concern. "Where are you going?"

"Outside. I must protect the castle," He answers. Her eyebrows furrow, unsure of what he must protect the castle from now.

"But it is raining. Would you not rather stay inside with us?" Hajnal suggests. Her concern has not left her chest.

How strange.

"Rain does not harm me," he takes another step.

"Sir!" Zarin stands up to speak now, causing him to stop once more. He looks at the golden-eyed woman. Her chest is also tight like Hajnal's.

"What is your name, sir?"

Sir Artegal pauses. How strange! He did not even think to give his name.

"Sir Artegal Belamour," He answers.

"Well, Sir Artegal, it is still not good for your health to trudge around in the rain," Zarin takes note of his health.

"I will be well," He replies, nodding his head. He takes his leave. Sir Artegal returns to his position outside. He begins to walk as he had before but now in the falling rain. He savors the wetness on his skin.

One. Two. Three. Four. Five. Six. Seven. Eight. Turn.

One. Two. Three. Four. Five. Six. Seven. Eight. Turn.

One. Two. Three. Four. Five. Six. Seven. Eight. Turn.

For hours, Sir Artegal keeps at his post. The rain does not relent. Lightning flashes giving him some light on this night. He is not afraid. He must do his duty.

One. Two. Three. Four. Five. Six. Seven. Eight. Turn.

One. Two. Three. Four. Five. Six. Seven. Eight. Turn.

One. Two. Three. Four. Five. Six. Seven. Eight. Turn.

Sir Artegal should try to be vigilant on this stormy night. His mind should focus on protecting the castle. But he has let these travelers inside the castle. No one has been inside this castle since the curse. No one has even given signs of existence in this land since the curse. Now four people have discovered him and the castle via the lover's secret tunnel.

How could an outsider know of the lover's tunnel? Only the residents of Castle Evensong know of it. Hajnal is no resident of Evensong let alone Estellen. How could she know? How could she know of an entrance into Estellen at all? No one is to know how to come into the land.

One. Two. Three. Four. Five. Six. Seven. Eight. Turn.

One. Two. Three. Four. Five. Six. Seven. Eight. Turn.

One. Two. Three. Four. Five. Six. Seven. Eight. Turn.

These people... two are clearly of fairy descent. I know by their eyes. I see the dimple in the corner of Hajnal's mouth and the marks on Zarin's hands. They could be descended from the fairies of Estellen who dispersed before the curse came. That could explain how Hajnal knows of the entry point and the tunnel. That must be it. No other explanation makes sense.

One. Two. Three. Four. Five. Six. Seven. Eight. Turn.

One. Two. Three. Four. Five. Six. Seven. Eight. Turn.

One. Two. Three. Four. Five. Six. Seven. Eight. Turn.

"But why now?" He stops suddenly and speaks aloud to himself. "Why would the fairies come back now? Why would they come for stardust for their elixir instead of coming to break the curse? Have they been coming all these years for lousy stardust instead of trying to break the curse?"

Sir Artegal's cheeks grow red as his heart pumps his anger and confusion through his veins. He inhales sharply through his nose. Sir Artegal palms his pommel more though not sure if he should draw it. He shakes his head and moves his hand away.

One. Two. Three. Four. Five. Six. Seven. Eight. Turn.

One. Two. Three. Four. Five. Six. Seven. Eight. Turn.

One. Two. Three. Four. Five. Six. Seven. Eight. Turn.

Sir Artegal runs a gloved hand through his drenched hair. He looks at the closed castle doors and frowns.

Sir Artegal passes through the doors he opens. He travels straight for the great hall. The lantern still burns, giving some light to the room. Tyr's head lies on the table as he has fallen asleep there. Althea's face is hidden in her folded arms resting on the table. Zarin leans back in her seat with her head thrown back in her sleep. Sleep is only natural, especially as the night has come and the rain has not ceased. He begins to turn, then stops. His eyes run over the group.

One. Two. Three. Where is the fourth? Where is Hajnal?

CHAPTER 13

The low light of the lantern in the dark hall and the beating of the rain create an atmosphere that could lull many to sleep. Though her companions succumb to slumber, Hajnal does not. There is no rest for her mind or her heart. How can there be?

Seeing Zarin, the last of three, has given in to sleep, Hajnal rises from the seat she previously claimed. She is careful of her steps to not knock into any furniture, thus causing a ruckus to wake the others. She does not take the lantern with her. Had she, traveling in the unlit rooms of the castle would be easier. Her hands and memories serve as her guides. She needs to exit the Great Hall by going the way she had been led in by Sir Artegal. With the faint light from the lantern behind her, she finds the doors and slips out quietly. In the hallway, Hajnal feels about the wall. She moves alongside it. Her hands stroke some tapestries. Her hips bump into a few pieces of furniture. It goes unheard.

"Oof," Hajnal falls forward onto a set of stairs. Fortunately, the stairs are headed upward, therefore she does not fall further. She regains her footing and climbs. Up. Up. Up, she goes. The stone beneath her feet is as familiar as the flooring in Mrs. Kenwyn's shop. She does not even have to touch the walls now to know how they turn.

Coming to a landing on the stairs, she leaves the stairwell. She walks in the hall till her hand extends to grasp a handle. She pushes the door open.

Floor-to-ceiling windows give some natural lighting to the room when the lightning flashes. With the bright bolt giving a moment of light, Hajnal finds herself in the ballroom she knows she had been in recently.

Coming into the center of the room, Hajnal inhales deeply. Her eyes close. So often she and the man in her dreams would come here to dance to the music of unseen instruments. The last time she had been here, he had comforted her after all that Bardolph had done.

Her eyes open.

"Is he here?" She asks herself. Is her lifelong friend here in this castle?

Lightning flashes only to be followed by an immediate boom. She blinks her eyes only to find a small blue flame on the floor in front of her. She gasps.

"Am I dreaming?" She asks at the sight of the will-o-the-wisp she has only seen when asleep. Hajnal looks at herself as there is more light from the flame. She is not dressed in white and she has an uncovered face and hair. She smiles.

"Where do I go?" She asks.

Hopping, the wisp passes Hajnal. She turns around more than ready to follow its lead. Out the doors, down the hall, and to the stairwell it goes. Up again Hajnal steps. Her heartbeat rises as she does. Her lips spread into a smile.

Breathing heavily, Hajnal begins to slow her steps. Perhaps it is the speed she has gone, maybe it is the sudden altitude change, or it could be the excitement making her lungs unable to control the receiving and giving of air. The little guide does not slow or stop. It continues without her. Hajnal pauses to gain some control over her breathing. Once more a master of herself, Hajnal climbs.

"There?" Hajnal reaches the top of the stairs where the blue fire waits. Her cheeks color.

This is where it took me last time. I can't go inside. He thought it would not be proper. Oh, what is his name?

The will-o'-the-wisp disappears leaving Hajnal alone at the door. She reaches out for the door. She draws her hand back and brings it to her chest.

"What if he is not in there?"

Her light spirit falls. She could open this room and find nothing but an empty room. No other room has been filled. And Sir Artegal made no mention of there being anyone else around the castle. Her friend could be like her only showing up here only when he is asleep. But he knew the place more than she did and claimed this door to be to his bedroom. That must mean he lives here. Or he lived here.

What if he is in there? What will he say? What will he do? Will he know me? Will I be a stranger? Does he know my name? Has he forgotten it just as I have forgotten his?

"Please, remember," she whispers, then shakes her head remembering her curse, "No, don't."

If he does not remember my name, then he will be safe. If he does not remember me at all, then… then he cannot be disappointed to see it is me and not someone else. Would he be disappointed to see his dream friend look like me? Would he prefer I look like someone who resembles Althea?

Hajnal turns away from the door with her hands clasped together at her chance. Perhaps it would be better for her not to even see if he is there. This will spare her feelings and will keep him from disappointment.

This will also protect him. For him to turn to stone would be…

Hajnal's eyes water, recalling seeing the painful stone faces of the Foxglove Grove. She could not let that happen to him as well. She may not know what his face looks like but she is sure it would devastate her to see it distorted in fear and pain only for it to be kept eternally in stone.

No, I should go. I should go right back down to the group in the Great Hall. I should get some sleep and leave in the morning

Hajnal takes a step down but stops.

How could I explain this to him once I fall asleep? He would be so upset to have missed this opportunity.

Standing still on the steps as if her shoes were in pitch, she considers her options. She makes her choice.

Slowly, with breath held, Hajnal opens the door. She steps inside with eyes wide, having found candles all around lit with blue flames which quickly turn white. The illuminated room is circular in construction. The walls are white with four high arch windows. There are marble columns placed evenly but sparingly about the room. A wardrobe, a few tables, and chairs are also dispersed about the room. The floors are made of dark mahogany. Between two of the columns on the eastern side of the room is an open fireplace, the mantle is made of marble, like the columns. However, the mantle has been cut and carved to depict an eight-point star in the middle. Above the mantle is a sword. The blade points downward toward the fireplace. The ceiling reaches far up to make a point. But it is painted blue with silver and gold stars as if to cause the heavens to be visible indoors.

Hajnal faintly recalls entering this room in her past as a child, but despite years being from it, she does not pay attention to the details. Her eyes go to her left where a four-post bed sits with sheer linens, making a canopy over it. The candle on the nightstand next to the bed is still blue. She knows this must be where she is meant to go.

Coming closer to the bed, she sees the bedding is white with silver and gold embroidery which creates a pattern of braided stars. More importantly, she sees the figure of a body behind the canopy. Having reached the bed, the candle turns white. Hajnal looks at the figure, but the person is still obscured a bit. Cautiously, she draws back the curtain.

Gasping, she covers her mouth as she catches sight of the body there. Beneath the blanket is a man. He has been tucked into the bed with his arms atop. His hands have long fingers but little color. Despite being in bed, he has on a sapphire tunic with a gold braided pattern going about the neck. His clothes are not what is important to Hajnal. No, it is his head which is most important to her.

Upon a silk pillow, his head lies. Pale gold is his thick but somehow wispy hair. His curls have grown from his head toward the base of his neck. Some of his hair has expanded out to make a small pattern on the pillowcase while some hang down to obscure his forehead from her eyes. His skin is pale as porcelain. There is no color on his cheek. His blond eyebrows are relaxed, as are his closed eyes. Dark eyelashes are a welcome contrast to this polished ivory skin. His nose is straight, unbroken, and proportional to his face. His eyes are evenly distributed as well. His jaw is sharp enough to be defined but soft enough to touch it seems to be welcomed not prohibited. His lips are plump but not so large they overpower the lower half of his face. The upper lip is a perfect hunter's bow, while his lower lip is a symmetrical half circle. The color of his lips reminds her of the pink insides of a summer watermelon. They even look as if they were made freshly wet by his tongue. But there is no movement from him. Is this the beautiful face hidden from her for so long?

Hajnal wishes to wake him. She has found her friend after all. But is she to call him? His name still escapes her.

With what does it even start? It is a vowel I know for sure. E? I? O? U? No. A. It is definitely A. It sounded simple but not common in Austvest... Oh, what is it? A-A-As-Ast-Asterion! That has to be it! She clears her throat, then looks down at the sleeping man.

"Asterion," she calls him.

He lies still.

"Asterion, it's me, your dream... friend," she repeats.

No answer. Hajnal purses her lips. *How odd.*

"He must be a deep sleeper," she mumbles. She pokes his chest.

"Asterion," she speaks louder.

Nothing.

"Wake up. Wake up!" She pokes his chest harder, then his cheek. He does not stir, moan or react at all.

The longer she stares, the longer she finds he is not breathing. His chest does not rise or fall. His lips are closed and his nostrils do not fold and expand with the passing of air. Her heart stops.

Is he dead?

Hajnal kneels and presses her ear against his chest. A sigh of relief comes when she hears a heartbeat. It is slow but there. She inhales and is pleasantly surprised to find he smells of apple wood and amber.

"What is that?" She notices something beneath the hair on his forehead. She lifts his hair a little and sees what she assumes is a birthmark. It is a pale pink mark in the shape of an eight-point star. As she shuffles on her knees to get closer to his forehead, her back knee slips followed by her legs. Her upper body falls forward. Her hands catch hold of the bed and his chest. Her face, however, is caught by his.

Hajnal is frozen with her lips pressed against his. His and hers pulse as if filled with an electric current. Yet his lips are soft and wet enough to please. Hajnal pushes herself up and away as she comes to her senses. She scoots back from the bed, red-faced from the accidental action. She raises her fingers to her still-tingling lips.

"I must go." She gets to her feet. Goosebumps appear all over her body, and her heart cannot be slowed. She searches for the door.

"It is broken," a voice most familiar to Hajnal comes from the bed. Her eyes stop their search for the door to return to the bed.

Sitting up with a cheerful grin is the blond man. He looks at his hands before he feels his face, body, hair, and bedding. His smile grows wider and wider with the more he touches. His open eyes are the cornflower blue Hajnal has always known. They look at her. His joyful face turns quizzical.

"Who art thou?"

The three words have Hajnal's heart drop to her feet. He does not know her or remember her. It is understandable, she supposes. He never saw her complete face.

How could he know me?

"Pray, forgive me, fair maiden. I should not have greeted thee with such a sudden question. I assume based on the lack of anyone else's presence thou art my savior. I should greet thee with the deepest bow and express my eternal gratitude." The man leaves his bed and gets on the floor before her. He bows fully to her.

"Please don't do that," Hajnal waves her hands.

"Thy wish is my command," He raises himself from the ground. His skin has gained a healthy, albeit still fair, shade of skin. He comes toward her with a soft smile and focused eyes. He steps right before her, leaving little space between them. She does not have to look up much to keep looking into his bright eyes. His aroma fills her nose. Hajnal swallows, not aware her mouth was filling with saliva.

"Pray, tell me thy name so I may know what to call my heroine?" he asks. Hajnal yearns to speak her name, but to turn to stone now would be most unfortunate.

"Hajnal," she answers. His smile twitches.

"Highball?" He bats his eyes.

"No. Hajnal."

"High knoll?"

"No. Hi-Nawl."

"Hajnal? Hajnal? Hajnal. Hajnal. Hajnal!" He tries out the name as if it were a new word. He takes Hajnal's hands into his own. Hajnal can feel his chest filling with a light but powerful heat. "It is the sweetest name to have ever passed these lips."

"Well, that is kind of you to say," she pulls her hand from his. They are growing hot along with the rest of her body.

"I am sorry. Did I offend thee by touching thee?" He comments on the withdrawal. Hajnal shakes her head.

"Good. I found it strange thou would kiss me yet be opposed to holding my hand," he laughs lightly. If her skin was not red before, it is now.

"It was an accident, I swear!" Her hands try to cover her cheeks. His eyebrow raises.

"An accident?"

"Yes."

He smirks.

"Thou must jest. Kisses are not accidental."

"This one was. I slipped and when I fell, my lips hit yours," Hajnal tries to explain. He loses his smirk but none of the warmth from his chest.

"Thou did not intend to kiss me?"

"No."

"Oh." His hair somehow wilts while his cheeks grow pink. He swallows, then regains a smile and the curl in his hair. "Of course, thou would not intend to kiss me. That would not be improper. But I am glad thou did."

Hajnal merely nods, unsure of what to say or do now.

"We will need to leave for Starsfall, immediately. My parents must be worried sick about me. And they must meet thee. I must meet thy parents as well. Are they nearby? If not, we will fetch our fastest coach or ship to retrieve them," He rambles.

"Why would I go with you to Starsfall? Why would you send for my parents?"

"We must be married then we will go to Starsfall to spend the rest of our lives together," He answers simply.

"I-I-" Hajnal cannot make a sentence, let alone a full thought.

The door to the bedroom slams open. Hajnal turns her head as the blond looks past her. In the doorway stands Sir Artegal. His eyes are enlarged and teary. The corners of his mouth twitch between a smile and stoicism.

"Thou art here as well, Artegal? How full is my heart now!" The former sleeper beams. His heart, though described full, is lighter now. Sir Artegal's heart weighs like stone and therefore Hajnal feels the weight. Sir Artegal strides to the blond and kneels before him with his head bowed low.

"Thy Highness, I swore to never leave thee unprotected. I broke my vow. Please, forgive me." Sir Artegal keeps his head lowered. The man bends, grabbing the knight by his shoulders.

"Rise, my friend. Thou know I shall never deny thee forgiveness." The trespassed man smiles. Sir Artegal stands with the other. The weight is gone. The heart is air. Hajnal notices how much taller Sir Artegal is.

"If it were not for my failure, thou would not have been cursed," Sir Artegal insists.

"It was inevitable. It is all well. I am free from it and now I have been found by my true love: Hajnal." The curse-free man looks at Hajnal. Sir Artegal faces Hajnal. He bows to her.

"Thank thee for freeing my prince."

"You're a prince!' Hajnal gasps before covering her mouth.

"Yes." The prince nods. Hajnal sucks her lips into her mouth now, knowing she has kissed a prince.

"Artegal, I need thee to perform the rites of marriage now so I may bring home Hajnal as my wife," the prince speaks to the knight, his body tingling.

"Yes, thy Highness," Sir Artegal clears his throat. "We are gathered here in the sight of El-Yah to join together this man and this woman in the sacred union of marriage. Marriage is-"

"Whoa. Whoa. Whoa. I am not marrying you!" Hajnal steps back from the two men.

"What?" the prince's jaw drops as do his curls.

"I have just woken you. You just learned my name. I don't even know yours. We cannot get married right now. Why would you think we would?"

"Because thou art my true love. We should be married as soon as possible," the prince answers in a matter-of-fact tone.

"True love? Why do you think I'm your true love?"

"Only my true love's kiss could break my curse. Thou kissed me and I awoke. Ergo, thou art my true love." The explanation is quite clear.

"How could I be your true love? We are strangers," she speaks, though it hurts her heart to say so. In the real world, they are. He has forgotten her, and she is unsure of his true name.

"Everyone is a stranger till thou come to know them," Sir Artegal comments.

"Exactly," the prince nods, agreeing with the knight's words. Hajnal exhales exasperatedly.

"We have just met. We cannot be married this instant," Hajnal argues.

"Many couples do not meet till their wedding day," Sir Artegal makes another observation. The prince nods in agreement with the argument made by his friend.

"I will not marry you on this day. Do you understand?" Hajnal snaps. The prince steps toward Hajnal and takes her hands in his again.

"I know this is a shock to thee. I do not intend to frighten or force thee. I was merely excited. I have waited my whole life to meet my true love. I wanted to be joined to thee forever as quickly as possible. I should not have rushed thee. I am sorry," he apologizes.

"It is well. I understand waiting to be with someone your whole life...but I am not ready for marriage now," Hajnal explains with a calm, still voice.

"We can wait. We can go to Starsfall. We may get to know each other better there and then wed," he plans.

"I cannot go to Starsfall. I do not have time to settle there and get to know you." Hajnal shakes her head pulling her hands from the prince again.

"Why not?" His warmth turns cold in disappointment.

"I have to save my brother. I cannot veer from my mission till my brother is found and freed from his own curse."

Warmth returns.

"Thou art an honorable woman. I shall not deter thee from this."

"Thank you."

"Artegal, we shall go with my Hajnal to save her brother," the prince looks to the much taller man.

"But, thy highness, thy parents will expect our return, the entire country will." Sir Artegal has not forgotten the rulers and people of Estellen.

"I will not return to Starsfall until Hajnal comes with me," the prince states.

"But thy mother–"

"Will understand. I will send a bird with a letter to her to explain everything."

Sir Artegal nods, though he does not agree.

"Yes, thy Highness."

"Enough with the 'thy highness', Artegal. Thou art as my brother. Call me by name." the prince grows tired of the title.

"What is your name?" Hajnal finally asks.

"Oh! I have not told thee?"

"No."

"I am Astrophel Leander Vercingetorix Wencelaus Amvrosiy Caradoc, son of Queen Aurore and King Philip, prince of Estellen." The prince bows.

Astro... My Astro. She remembers. *Perhaps if I say my true name, he will remember me? No! No. That is too risky...*

"Thou may call me whatever thou desire," Astrophel informs her of the allowance.

"Astrophel. Look!" Sir Artegal points toward the windows. It is now Hajnal realizes the tower looks over the treetops. She walks with them toward the windows.

The sky has been cleared of the storm's clouds. The edges of the sky are navy mixed with dark purple. The purple fades into mauve and magenta only to be met with bursts of tangerine and lemon. The sun's head is mostly hidden by the treetops. The trees, once dead or dull, are now vibrantly green and lush. Blossoms pop from the branches. In the silence, they can hear the song of the thrush which soon flies past the window with its mate. Sir Artegal's breath is shaky. Hajnal's eyes look at him. Once more his eyes have watered. The eyes she thought recently turned silver show touches of magenta and purple in them. They are not reflected from the sunrise.

"How beautiful," Prince Astrophel comments.

"Thank El-Yah. I have not seen a sunrise since... What year is it?" Artegal tears his eyes from the window to look at Hajnal. The prince joins his knight in looking at Hajnal.

"The year is 2320," Hajnal answers. The prince and knight gaze at each other with necks and chest swelling in what Hajnal feels to be shock.

"Thou are sure?" The fair-haired prince's eyes return to Hajnal.

"Yes. Is there something wrong with the year being 2320?"

"No. However, this means I have been asleep for a hundred years." He grows pale but not as pale as when Hajnal first saw him in the bed.

"That's impossible."

"I have been keeping watch. I must have miscounted the years. I thought it had been ninety years." Sir Artegal admits.

"How could you be alive for a hundred years?" Hajnal runs her eyes over the knight. He cannot be over thirty. He is a handsome man with a firm jaw covered in black stubble. His lips are rather thin but still pink and chapped. His nose is straight and ends in a little bulb at the end. His eyebrows are thick and dark but not overgrown. His skin is tan letting you know he must often go into the sun. His hair is black and reaches for his shoulder. What she does not see are wrinkles, gray or white hair, or age spots. He looks as young and healthy as any man around thirty. There is no way he is over a hundred. The same goes for the prince, though the prince looks much younger.

"A spell was placed on me to prevent me from aging, growing weary, or dying so I may protect my prince," Sir Artegal answers.

"Thou did what?" The woken prince puts his hand on the bearded man.

"I could not leave thee unprotected. I had to guard thee. If a dark sorcerer or sorceress had found a way in, they would surely kill thee. I could not let that happen."

Prince Astrophel smiles.

"Since thou have awakened the rest of the land will as well. The fairy council placed a spell on everyone else in Estellen to sleep agelessly as long as thou did. The walls of protective thorns will fall away soon." Sir Artegal brings up the barrier separating the nation from the others for the past century.

"Then we will travel faster to Koralia," Hajnal deduces, growing cheery at the thought of getting closer to Basil faster.

"Koralia?" Sir Artegal repeats the name.

"We are to find a woman there who will tell us where the place east of the sun and west of the moon is. We will be able to find my brother then," Hajnal clarifies.

"Is the All-Cure elixir thou are making for him?" Sir Artegal recalls the purpose of the travelers to Estellen.

"Yes. He has been cursed and taken away by a sorcerer. I must make the elixir and find my brother to save him." Hajnal's heart turns cold having to speak of it. Her body can still feel Bardolph's hands molesting her, the warmth of his breath as he gave her orders and his foul lips. Basil's desperate pleas for help ring in her ears. Her chest recalls the panicked racing heart of her brother when he was being transformed into that monster.

Warmth spreads from her shoulder to the rest of her body when the prince puts his hand on her shoulder. Looking into the blue eyes of her dreams, her heart slows.

"We will go with thee and protect thee. None shall harm thee." He looks deeply into her eyes before turning back to the knight. "We must go immediately. Artegal, help me pack!"

The prince starts to the wardrobe in his room. The dedicated guard goes right with him.

"I will wake my group then," Hajnal excuses herself.

"Group?" Prince Astrophel spins around.

"My sister and two others are on this journey with me," Hajnal answers.

"Thy sister and two others?" He repeats her words.

"Yes," she nods.

"Hmm…" Prince Astrophel looks down; his tongue goes into his cheek. His eyes lift to look at the woman. "We will be with thee and thy group soon, my love."

Hajnal's heart jumps at the term of endearment. Flushed, she escapes the room. She races down the steps. Althea will not believe this.

CHAPTER 14

"**W**here were you? I was beginning to get worried," Althea huffs when her sister comes into the great hall. The younger sister speedily walks to the older one. Hajnal takes her sister by the wrist and pulls her outside of the Great Hall.

"Althea, I met him."

"Him? Who?"

"Astro, the man from my dreams," Hajnal answers in a hushed tone to not be overheard by the others.

"What?" Althea raises an eyebrow and scrunches up her nose.

"When all fell asleep, I went up a tower here in the castle..."

"Sir Artegal said not to!" Althea interrupts.

"I know, but, Thea, this place is the place I've been in every night in my dreams. I had to search for Astro. And I found him. He was asleep in the tower."

"He was asleep here?"

"Yes. I accidentally woke him."

"Accidentally?"

"Yes..." Hajnal's cheeks turn pink. "I fell on him."

"Oh."

"But he woke up and informed me he was cursed to sleep. He was asleep for a hundred years."

"That's impossible."

"That's what I thought, but you know magic has weird abilities which could include preserving someone in sleep for a century. Sir Artegal also said he had magic put on him to preserve him for the past century as well."

"You fell on this man and it broke the curse?"

"Yes."

"I feel like you're not being totally honest." Althea crosses her arms.

"Well, I fell on him and my lips happened to hit him and woke him up." Hajnal looks down rather than at her sister. Althea grabs her sister and grins cheekily.

"You kissed him awake!" Althea squeals.

"Shhh! It was an accident!" Hajnal whispers.

"Accident-smaccident. You kissed him awake. And if your kiss broke his spell, then this means you're his true love!" Althea pieces the situation together further. Hajnal's burning ears match her face.

"He certainly thinks so, but I don't know..." Hajnal shakes her head.

"You don't know? What more proof do you need? Your kiss broke his spell and you two have been mentally bound forever," Althea scoffs.

"Well, I know, but he... he doesn't remember me."

"What?"

"He doesn't remember me from the dream world. He seems to not know me at all." Hajnal loses her coloring.

"Then tell him. Tell him you are St-"

Hajnal covers Althea's mouth.

"Don't say my name."

Althea nods, which lets Hajnal know she can uncover Althea's mouth.

"I would tell him my name, but he probably will not remember it, anyway. And I do not want to risk turning him to stone. We must keep it all a secret-my name, the dreamworld, everything," Hajnal decides.

"But maybe he just needs a little nudge to help him remember," Althea suggests.

"No. I don't want to risk it." Hajnal shakes her head. Althea sighs.

"Fine. I won't tell."

"Thank you."

"But where is your dream guy? Why isn't he with you?"

"He and Sir Artegal are packing. They want to go with us to find Baz. Well, I should say the prince wants to go and Sir Artegal is just following," Hajnal corrects herself.

"Prince?" Althea straightens up at the word.

"Astro is a prince, Prince Astrophel," Hajnal gives the longer yet still condensed version of the royals' name.

"Astrophel? That's pretty," Althea thinks aloud.

"Isn't it?" Hajnal smiles to herself.

"There you two are." Zarin exits the great hall with a smile. Tyr follows. "I was thinking you two took off without us."

"Oh, no. We couldn't leave you two behind."

"We should probably get back to the horses and out of the knight's way." Tyr's feet itch to go.

"Well, actually-" Hajnal starts.

The footsteps from the nearby stairs draw all eyes. Sure enough, down comes Sir Artegal with large packs in his arms. Behind him is the dazzling prince. He has changed from the blue tunic he wore when he slept. Prince Astrophel sports a silver-trimmed lapis doublet with a white chemise beneath. His doublet reaches his knees which are covered, like the rest of his legs, with white breeches and navy hosiery. His dragon-skin boots are black and cover up his calves. About his waist is a black belt holding a sword. His clothing almost makes Hajnal chuckle. Though richly made, the style of the prince's clothes is something they have not seen since her grandfather.

Still, Prince Astrophel's curls are bouncing with life and excitement. His eyes find Hajnal immediately. He beams. His eyes leave her to look at the others.

"Good morning," He greets them. The three who have yet to meet the prince gaze upon him. Zarin smiles at the new man while Tyr stares him down as if it will let him know who he is without asking. Althea cannot take her eyes off him. She has a pink tint to her cheeks. Her full lips part in want to say something, but nothing except air comes from them. Her skin tingles.

Hajnal glances at her sister, having felt the tingling. Hajnal's stomach begins to squeeze and her heart quivers. Her eyes dart to the prince, who now looks directly at Althea.

Does he see he has been kissed by the wrong sister?

"Who are you?" Tyr crosses his arms. Hajnal makes the introduction of the prince to her companions. Both Althea and Zarin bow before the prince while Tyr remains upright.

"Gentlewomen, please arise. There is no need to bow before me." Prince Astrophel waves them up. Zarin and Althea straighten. "Please, call me Astrophel, Zarin and Tyr."

"If you wish," Zarin nods. Tyr simply shrugs still unimpressed with the royal.

"And as sister to my sweet, Hajnal, I ask thee to call me brother," Prince Astrophel practically sparkles as he speaks to Althea.

"Brother?" Althea repeats the word.

"Yes. Soon we shall be family," the prince informs the sister.

"What?" Althea blushes.

"After we find thy brother, Hajnal and I shall be wed," He proclaims the plans. Hajnal could burst into flame from the heat rising in her face. All eyes go to Hajnal.

"Um, I-I-I-I did not agree to marry you." Hajnal holds up her hands. The statement makes the prince lose his smile for an instant only for it to return.

"Thou did not disagree either. Thou said thou could not marry me *this* day. That does not mean thou will not marry me *another* day." the eager young man points out.

"Well, um-uh-um…" Hajnal is unsure of what else to say. His logic is sound. Althea does her best to cover her mouth to keep in her desire to laugh.

"Wait. You want to marry Hajnal?" Tyr wants it to be clear.

"Yes."

"Oh." Tyr smiles, well pleased the prince's object of desire is not the same as his own.

"We should be going. Koralia is still far from here," Zarin speaks, noticing Hajnal's state.

"Yes! We need to get our horses and go." Hajnal steps toward Zarin.

Hajnal takes Zarin's arm to wrap hers around as they briskly make their way toward the entrance serving as their exit.

"Thank you," Hajnal whispers to the Ora-Oculist. Zarin nods.

Out of the castle, Hajnal and Zarin pause. The world is green and vibrant. The air is light but filled with the scent of blossoms and the sound of rejoicing songbirds. Althea, Tyr, and the prince come out into the yard with them.

"Which way will take us to the stardust vault?" Zarin asks Prince Astrophel, realizing she does not know the way.

"It will be west of here. But, please, wait for Artegal and me to get our transportation and for me to send a letter to my mother. It will take only a few minutes," Prince Astrophel requests, then walks away. Hajnal knows he is going to the stables she has visited before in her dreams.

"You didn't tell me he was gorgeous and wanted to marry you!" Althea swats Hajnal's arm once the marriage-minded man is out of sight.

"I was going to tell you, but I did not get the chance," Hajnal explains. "But I told him I would not go off and marry him when we are still searching for Basil. So now he is coming with us."

"That is fine with me. Who knows what skills they may have to benefit us," Zarin comments.

"True. Sir Artegal seems to be an excessively dedicated knight, so he should have combat experience. And the prince…he is…well, he is easy on the eyes." Althea thinks fondly of the other blond and giggles. Hajnal feels her stomach squeezing again.

Has Althea begun falling for the prince?

"Of course, his fine eyes are solely on you, Hajnal." Althea wiggles her eyebrows suggestively to her older sister.

"As they should be," Tyr mutters. Althea rolls her eyes.

"How odd is it that Sir Artegal did not tell us of the prince earlier. And why is it this prince is so invested in you, Hajnal?" Zarin thinks aloud. Hajnal swallows before sharing a summary of the events from the night and morning.

"He thinks I am his true love and we should be wed," Hajnal finishes.

"Do you think he is the one to whom your dreams are connected?" Zarin asks what Althea and Hajnal know.

"Yes. Though I believe he has forgotten his dreams," Hajnal tries not to give away her disappointment.

"I never remember my dreams," Tyr interjects.

"Perhaps that is a part of the curse breaking. As he was under a curse when your minds were connected then he lost all his dream memory when his curse was lifted," Zarin rationalizes.

"That makes sense. I would appreciate none of you mentioning it to him. It is not important after all," Hajnal makes her request. The group nods their heads.

Hearing approaching feet as well as hooves, the attention of the troupe is given to the direction of where Prince Astrophel had gone.

Prince Astrophel may be handsome and Sir Artegal may be a tower of a man but neither can attract more attention than the beasts they have walking beside them. With manes and bodies white like untouched, freshly fallen snow, eyes like indigo blossoms, and ivory horns protruding from their foreheads, the unicorns are on what they focus. Though saddled, neither is bridled. None have ever seen equines this large except for draft horses.

"Unicorns," Zarin whispers, her gold eyes gleaming with delight and wonder, just like the others. Of all things to see, two unicorns, let alone one, are not what Zarin had expected to see.

"You ride unicorns?" Hajnal asks in complete awe.

"Yes. This is Cornelius." Prince Astrophel strokes the nose of the magical creature next to him and then points to the one nearest to Sir Artegal. "And that is Isra."

"They are so beautiful." Althea cannot take her eyes off them.

"I have never seen a unicorn in real life," Hajnal admits.

"Neither have I," Zarin and Tyr speak simultaneously.

"Then come. They are friendly." Prince Astrophel motions for the others to come forward. Hajnal steps forward toward Cornelius. She hesitantly extends her hand toward the nose. The unicorn stands still questioning the hand held out toward him. Finally, he steps forward to let the hand, which he has decided is good, touch him. Hajnal glows excitedly.

"I'm touching a unicorn," she nearly squeals. Cornelius's human delights in Hajnal's reaction. Isra nudges her nose against Hajnal, who presents her hand to the beast only for it to accept her as well. With both hands on the two unicorns, butterflies flutter in her stomach and chest.

"May I try?" Althea steps forward. She steps forward and copies her sister. Once accepted, she reacts similarly to her sister. Zarin takes a step then stops.

"Come, Zarin," Hajnal waves her hand to the other woman. Zarin comes closer to the unicorn who without any prompting comes to her. Zarin pets Cornelius tenderly.

Tyr comes forward as the others had. Cornelius and Isra bray and step backward from him. He frowns.

"What is wrong?" Althea questions the reactions of the unicorn.

"Usually, unicorns are wary of men," Sir Artegal answers.

"They prefer children and women," Prince Astrophel adds.

"But they are fine with you two," Tyr crosses his arms.

"Well, they have known us since we were children so they know they can trust us."

"Ah," Tyr accepts.

"Won't they bring much attention?" Althea thinks about the rarity of these beasts.

"I can mask their horn when needed or shrink them to hide them," Sir Artegal replies.

"You can shrink things?" The question comes from all but the prince and Zarin. Sir Artegal nods.

"Wow. You were born with that gift?" Althea is the one to ask.

"No. It is teachable. But let's make haste. I would like to return home sooner rather than later," Sir Artegal replies.

"I agree. We should be on our way. Our horses are waiting for us." Zarin steps back from the white rides.

"Yes, they've been alone all night," Althea remembers Meteora and Zarin's horse.

"Sir Artegal, please, lead the way back to the Stardust Vault," Zarin requests of the knight. He accepts the charge.

Instead of riding the unicorns, the prince and knight walk alongside the beasts. It would be shameful for the men to ride while the women walk.

"What led thee all to Castle Evensong from the stardust vault?" Prince Astrophel inquires as they walk.

"Hajnal found an entrance to a secret tunnel," Zarin nods to Hajnal.

"Oh? How did thou find it?" He gives his attention to the woman he made sure to stand close to during the small journey.

"Luck, I suppose," she remains vague.

"It was more than that. You were feeling the walls, remember?" Althea does not allow her sister to be aloof.

"Why would thou do that?" The prince is intrigued.

"I don't know..." Hajnal faces away from him. She does not want to tell him she was looking for a way to get him.

"Hm, I suppose El-Yah was leading thee to me," the prince remarks. Hajnal's face remained turned from him now as to find her bashfulness.

"There it is," Sir Artegal points forward to the building the foursome had entered previously.

"There are the horses!" Althea points to the grazing steeds still tied to the trees.

"It looks like thou hast lost a couple," Prince Astrophel notes the amount.

"No. We have not," Hajnal shakes her head.

"But there are only two horses," he counts again.

"Yes, there is Meteora, which Althea rides. There is Zarin's horse. What have you decided to call the horse, Zarin?" Hajnal takes her attention away from the prince to look at the woman with the covered head.

"I think I like Safa," Zarin keeps walking to her brown mare.

"So Zarin has Safa and I have Tyr," Hajnal gets back to speaking to Prince Astrophel.

"What do thou mean, thou have Tyr?"

"I ride Tyr," Hajnal answers. The prince's jaw tenses.

"What?" The prince turns his eyes on her.

"Oh, I forgot to say Tyr is a shifter. He's been shifting into a horse for me to ride," Hajnal expounds. Relief should have come over the prince, but Hajnal does not detect this.

"I'll start shifting, so look away, ladies," Tyr announces. The women do just so, giving him privacy to undress and shift. Once in his horse form, Tyr allows the women to look again. He trots up to Hajnal to be saddled and loaded. She begins her work quickly and easily.

"My darling, please, allow me to ride Tyr. Thou may have Cornelius to ride." Prince Astrophel approaches Hajnal with his unicorn and a smile.

"Really?" Hajnal grins.

"Yes."

"Well, if you don't mind, Tyr," Hajnal looks to her former horse.

"Not at all. My back could use a lighter load," He mutters the last part so Hajnal does not hear. Astrophel is quick to help Hajnal onto the unicorn before getting on Tyr.

"Onto Koralia then," Zarin smiles, seeing all settled.

"Yes," Sir Artegal agrees, and the party turns south toward the country where the desire to go.

***

For hours the group has ridden. They have passed a few newly woken farmers who bow before the prince as he passes. Astrophel is gracious to smile, wave and wish them well as he passes. Hajnal smiles to herself as she sees how loved he is by the people.

"It is so lovely here," Hajnal comments, looking around the land.

"There is no better land." Prince Astrophel takes pride in his country.

"It is a shame we must leave it for Koralia," Sir Artegal mutters.

"Koralia is lovely this time of year, Artegal," the prince tries to lighten the negative attitude.

"But we could go to Starsfall and ask if the location is known there," Sir Artegal suggests.

"We know someone in Koralia definitely knows where to go. We do not have time to waste," Althea interjects before the idea can be discussed further.

"And Mother Huldah is sure this woman will help us," Zarin adds.

"Who is this Mother Huldah and how can thou be sure to trust her?" Sir Artegal look to Zarin.

"My mistress."

"Thy mistress just happens to know someone who knows where the place east of the sun and west of the moon is?"

"My mistress has come to know many people throughout her life. This person is just one of them.

"If your mistress's friend is so knowledgeable about how to find this legendary place, why has she not made her fortune by revealing it to all?" Sir Artegal keeps up his questioning.

"Not everyone seeks wealth."

"How sure are thee she will even tell thee of the location, then?"

Zarin pauses. Sir Artegal has brought up a potential issue. Hajnal and Althea both catch their breath, realizing the woman they seek may not share the coordinates with them.

"We will trust in El-Yah to show us favor just as he has in allowing us to find Tyr and you two," Zarin's response causes Sir Artegal to grow a slight smile.

"I shall pray El-Yah continues to grant thee favor." Sir Artegal nods.

"I shall pray the same for you." Zarin nods to the knight. Hajnal yawns.

"I am sorry. I did not sleep last night. I think my fatigue has caught up with me." She apologizes.

"Little lambkin, do not apologize. Thou need rest. I know thou do not want to stop, but perhaps we should have a midday meal. Thou could rest for a short while." the prince suggests. Hajnal turns red at the suggestion. She opens her mouth to reject the offer.

"That sounds like a wonderful idea, Astrophel," Althea turns her head to the prince and her sister with a big smile.

As Prince Astrophel has Tyr stop, Hajnal looks to Althea with wide eyes darting between the prince and her sister. Althea mouths 'Do it' to her older sister.

"Please, Sister, call me 'brother'," the prince speaks kindly to Althea.

"Oh, right. I will, Brother."

All stop and dismount. Tyr runs off to change back into his human form. They sit on the soft grass and begin to pass out the rolls Hajnal packed. They unload the horses to give them some reprieve.

"Mmm! This is divine!" Prince Astrophel exclaims.

"It is delicious. Art thou sure this is days old?" Sir Artegal questions Zarin after taking a bite.

"I can taste hints of... lemon in it. I can feel my body tingling with... excitement." Prince Astrophel touches his chest.

"I do as well... I have not eaten in so long... this is a welcome introduction back to food. Who made these?" Sir Artegal stares at the roll he eats.

"I made them," Hajnal answers.

"Thou did?" Prince Astrophel beams.

"Yes, I am a baker. I made those the day before we had to leave. I am glad they are to your liking." Hajnal comments.

"I need to taste these rolls," Tyr takes one and bites into it. His lips uncontrollably curl upward. The hair on his arms raises. "They're right."

"Wasn't that the day we learned Basil was coming to us?" Althea recalls.

"I believe it was. I was so...excited," Hajnal remembers. Sir Artegal stares at Hajnal. His eyes look her up and down several times before he nods. He leans over and whispers in his liege's ear. The prince nods. The sisters take some bread to eat. Hajnal takes a bite but unlike her sister does not gain the tingles of excitement. She yawns again.

"Lie down and rest," Althea pats the soft grass.

"Do not let me sleep long. We must keep going."

Hajnal closes her eyes. When she opens them she finds all, including the unicorns and horses, are gone except for Astrophel. With eyes wide she looks around confused and honestly, startled.

Why is everyone gone? How long was i asleep? I did not dream. Do i no longer get to the castle now that Astro is awake?

"Thou have awaken, little sunspot," Astrophel smiles and comes to sit by her. "The horses told Artegal they needed water, so the others have gone to fetch water. I stayed behind to defend thee should a beast approach."

"Sir Artegal can speak to horses?"

"He can speak to all animals. Animal speak is one of his many gifts."

"We should go and join the others," Hajnal begins to rise but he grabs her wrist.

"They will be back soon. We can just enjoy sometime alone together."

"The last man who wanted to be alone wanted to attack me. I have been tentative to be alone with a man since then," Hajnal recalls her encounter with Bardolph again, summoning some anxiety. Hajnal senses rage simmering in Astrophel's chest.

"Thy sister informed us of what happened with that Bardolph. I assure thee. I will protect thee from such a man and do not have any intention to harm thee, in any way."

Hajnal smiles at his earnest words. "I know you will not hurt me. I doubt you have ever even had a mean thought in your head." The prince laughs and shakes his head.

"Thou think too highly of me, my unblemished blossom."

"And you of me. I am no unblemished blossom, Astro." Hajnal bites her tongue, having called him by the name she uses in her dreams.

Have I given myself away?

Astrophel's lips spread into a wide smile, showing off his pearly teeth.

"Astro? I have not been called that in quite some time," He remarks.

"Oh?"

"Yes. Only my parents have called me Astro." His eyes grow distant as he thinks of the king and queen of his country.

"I am sorry. I should not have called you that," Hajnal quickly apologizes.

"No. No. I prefer it," He insists, putting his hands on her shoulders. "Thou may call me anything thou wish."

"I suppose it is fair given you call me many names," Hajnal chuckles.

"If it displeases thee then I shall stop," He grows panicked.

"Oh, no. I find it sweet. Do not feel the need to stop." She turns her red face slightly. Thought the names are slightly odd sometimes, she enjoys the affection though she may not admit to it.

"If thou should dislike them, tell me at once and I shall cease. A man should not displease his wife," He states. Hajnal burns. The prince notices the flushed maiden.

"We are not married," Hajnal reminds him quietly.

"Not yet. But soon, my dainty duck," he speaks so assuredly.

"You are decidedly sure of that."

"I am, though since our meeting thou art doubtful," He comments, his smile fading.

"I just think the more you see of the world and get to know me, you will change your mind." Hajnal is more honest. Astrophel pauses and stares at the woman he intends to wed.

"I see. Thou art insecure," He states bluntly. Hajnal's mouth drops open at the statement. Though she knows it is true, she cannot believe her over-complimentary beau is saying this to her.

"I-I-" Hajnal stammers.

"Do not be. I have waited my whole life for thee. We may find qualities in each other that are not ideal but they will not make us unworthy or unable to love and be loved. Nothing and no one in this world will change my mind or my heart."

Hajnal soaks in his words like a sponge. He always did seem to know what to say. Even now when he does not remember her, he is sure of what to say to her.

"You think there will be things about me that will not be ideal?" Hajnal teases.

"About thee? No. No. I misspoke. I am the only flawed one," He is quick to jest. She giggles.

"Thy sister has mentioned the rings of protection given to she, thee, and Zarin, but-" Astrophel pulls a sheathed knife from inside his doublet. "Thou need a defense."

The ivory handle is simple in design, while the ivory sheath is covered in etched filigree. He presents it to Hajnal.

"Use this to protect to thyself. And should some licentious curse befall me and I should I try to harm thee, plunge this into my heart. I should never be able to recover with the knowledge I harmed even a single hair on thy head," He claims.

"That is sweet of you, Astro, but this ring will protect me from all harm." Hajnal holds up her hand.

"Still, take it. Rings of protection do not last forever." He takes her hand and puts the weapon in it. Hajnal accepts the gift.

"Hajnal! Prince Astrophel! Are you two still out there?" Zarin's voice can be heard calling. Hajnal leans back from Prince Astrophel. He stands.

"We are here," Prince Astrophel calls back to reassure the approaching members. All but Tyr, who has changed himself into a horse again, are atop their rides.

"Were you successful in finding water?" Hajnal asks the group walking toward her sister and Zarin. Prince Astrophel helps Hajnal to mount Cornelius. He then climbs atop Tyr. Prince Astrophel goes closer to Sir Artegal, who has already started leading again.

"Yes. Zarin found the water with such ease! It was truly a sight to see. But I'm sure you two were content here." Althea raises her eyebrows a few times while smirking. Hajnal glares at her sister who giggles. "What did you two do?"

"We just talked," Hajnal remains vague.

"About?" Althea is not wanting to drop the issue.

"About how large your mouth is compared to your ears," Hajnal claims.

"My mouth is larger than-hey! That's not funny." Althea understands her sister's jab. Hajnal smirks.

"It is none of your business what he and I speak about, Althea."

The younger sister scoffs, "Well then."

Althea has Meteora take her away from her sister. Hajnal chuckles to herself at the sister's reaction. She will tell her sister about these things later. Now is not the time or place.

"You will not tell me either then," Zarin comes beside Hajnal, "But I can guess what it was about."

"Oh? And what do you guess, Zarin?"

"Love," Zarin answers.

"How-how did you know?" Hajnal's hands go to her cheeks. Zarin laughs.

"Anyone could have guessed," Zarin giggles.

"I thought you had a vision or something."

"Well, I have but not about this."

"Have you foreseen anything else with the prince and me?" Hajnal whispers her query.

"I have."

"And?" Hajnal eagerly leans toward Zarin.

"I cannot tell you. It will ruin the surprise of life," Zarin refuses to answer with a cheery smile. Hajnal sighs but knows Zarin is right.

"How often do you get visions, Zarin?" Hajnal becomes curious.

"Oh... well, it depends if I'm trying to see a vision or if I am letting it happen naturally to me," Zarin responds.

"You can make yourself have visions?"

"Yes. I was trained in the temple of Ender to do so."

"Can you make yourself specific people's futures, or are they random even when forced?"

"I was trained to do so, but I do not let myself do it anymore."

"Why?"

"I'd prefer to let El-Yah determine when and what I see. It makes me feel more connected to him rather than to my own power." Zarin looks up to the sky peaking between the leafy branches overhead.

"Do you recommend training with your gift or just letting them be?"

"I think training would be wise. We are given these talents by El-Yah so we should learn to use them properly. That is why I am training under Mother Huldah so I can master not only my gifts but other uses of magic so I may help others. You have fairy blood. You should try training with me so you can learn to master your abilities!" Zarin comes up with the idea.

"Do you think you could train me?"

"Sure. I can show you some basic lessons and let you read my books. I did not get the gift of air or feeling but I am sure the books will have information," Zarin pats one of her bags which Hajnal assumes holds her books.

"That would be... amazing. I would like to know how to control my gifts more," Hajnal smiles.

"Then we should begin tonight when we rest!" Zarin squeals.

"Sure!" Hajnal tingles with her and Zarin's excitement.

"Oh my-look!" Althea gasps, looking ahead. The group looks forward. Not too far in the distance, beyond the trees, a wall of thorns can be seen. Or rather, a wall of fallen thorns is beyond the trees.

"That must be the border between Estellen and Zeemaa," Prince Astrophel deduces.

"Then that is the way we must go," Zarin has ridden up next to the front group.

CHAPTER 15

Elecampane is heavy in the air. As it is inhaled, it clears the mind but fills the lungs of Bardolph. He stands before the crystal bowl of water sitting on the table. His eyes are closed while his arms remain at his sides. His lips move with faint dark words leaving them. Opening his eyes, he takes hold of the knife resting on the table next to the bowl. He holds his empty hand above the bowl and brings the blade to it. He slices his hand with the wavy blade of the dagger and does not grimace at the cut. Bardolph sets the dagger back down on the table. He clenches his cut hand causing the blood to build and drip into the water. Six drops are given to the water before he pulls his hand away. The wound heals. His eyes stay on the water. The blood begins to swirl on its own in the water.

"Show me. Show me the one I desire. Show me where she is," he orders the water in a hushed voice. The water turns crimson before turning black. The dark water separates. He gazes intently into the space. He dips his face into the clear water.

The forest is lush and green. Birds sing from the branches while rabbits race from bush to bush out of sight from the main path. On the formed nature road is a group. Bardolph nearly steps back, seeing the large unicorn being ridden by a knight.

Where could he have gotten this unicorn?

Behind the rare beast and rider comes the fair Althea on a common horse while another woman rides next to her. In the back of the group, Bardolph sees who he desires. Again, he questions how Stella came to ride a unicorn. Stella glows with her cheery smile. Bardolph frowns at her happiness.

She should be miserable. She should be desperate and on the verge of collapse, searching for her brother. How could she be happy?

"Oh, really Astro?" Stella laughs. Bardolph finally notices the blond man on the black horse. The blond man in old fashion clothing seems to have a light shining from him. His looks are dazzling and Stella does not take her eyes off him. Bardolph grits his teeth.

Who is this 'Astro' person?

"I swear it. I can ride a horse backward. Shall I show thee?" Astro turns in his saddle.

"No. I don't want you to get hurt," Stella reaches over to touch his arm.

"I shall not be harmed. Watch," Astro does not even stop his horse as he turns around in the saddle. He faces behind him but turns his face to look at Stella. He smiles at proving his claim. Stella laughs at the sight.

Bang. Bang. Bardolph hears the noise but knows it is not from where Stella is.

"Show me where she is," Bardolph grumbles. The woodland scene disappears and becomes a map of Zeemaa. A little red light moves in the northwestern portion of the map close to where Estellen, Zeemaa, and Logre meet. Ink appears on the map with the word "Sterhout".

Bang. Bang. Bardolph pulls his head from the bowl. He whips his wet hair back, splattering water all around him. The water becomes murky and brown like rust. Bardolph runs his hand over his tense face to collect the water there, then throws it off to the side. He stomps to the door of the room just as the banging comes again.

"What?" He roars at the knocker, making his canines significantly large to appear more frightening.

A squat man with a wide face and eyes so far apart they look to almost be on the sides stands with a raised hand. Bardolph looks down at the person with skin tinted green with brown spots. He wears simple brown trousers and a brown vest over his dirty white linen shirt. His feet have no covering.

"Y-Young M-master, I-I-I-" He stammers with a low croaky voice.

"I-I-I- what? What is it?" Bardolph mocks then snaps at the cowering servant.

"We have received word that Countess Yelena has given birth," the servant answers clearly.

"Is it a boy or girl?"

"I-I-I am not sure," the servant braces for impact. It does not come.

Bardolph loses his sour expression. He grins to himself with his dark eyes twinkling with evil intent.

"Then I will go find out, Natterjack." Bardolph exits the room. Natterjack half hops, half walks behind Bardolph. Bardolph runs his hands through his dark curls to style it as he makes his way down the stone steps. Reaching the bottom, he finds a large mirror there. He checks himself in the mirror. He wipes off the little bits of water on his white and red kosovorotka. Bardolph licks his thumb before running it over his eyebrows. He keeps smirking at his reflection.

"Prepare the east tower. I will not be gone long." Bardolph walks away from the mirror. He walks down the hall to a door. It opens to a balcony. Once out, he shifts into a falcon, clothes and all. Bardolph's wings flap and take him into the air.

***

His Serenity Count Terenti has another bottle of wine opened for him and his friends as they continue to celebrate this joyous occasion. The balding count's exposed scalp and the rest of his face are red like wine.

"A son! A son! I have a son!" His Serenity sings the chant.

"A son! A son! He has a son!" his comrades sing along with him repeatedly as they guzzle down more wine. The servants happily work around the drunken men, as they know they will surely receive gifts during this joyous time.

In the countess's room, Her Serenity, Countess Yelena, sits up in her bed cuddling her newborn boy. He stares up at her sleepily as he has had such a stressful day, being born and all.

"He is beautiful, Your Serenity," the attending midwife comments, looking at the tiny pink boy.

"Where did he get such lovely eyes?"

Her Serenity looks into the eyes of the boy. They are large with gold, silver, and magenta speckled throughout his brown and green irises. They are stunning. Her Serenity knows she never had such speckles in her brown eyes and her husband's eyes are the plainest of blues.

"I think from my mother," the new mother lies.

"What name shall be given to him?" the midwife inquires.

"My husband wants to call him 'Varfolomey' after his father. But I do not think it fits," the countess replies.

"Oh? And what do you think does?"

Tap. Tap. A falcon sits at the window as if waiting for entry. The midwife stares at the window bewildered by the sudden appearance of the bird. The countess smiles and sits herself up straighter despite the pain it causes her lower half.

"Tuula, could you open the window and then leave me?" Her Serenity asks.

"But the falcon could get inside, Your Serenity." Tuula shakes her head.

"I will be fine, Tuula. Please do as I ask," the countess urges gently. The midwife shakes her head but obeys. As Tuula approaches the door of the bedroom to leave, the falcon flies and lands on the bed next to the mother and child. The bird shakes, grows, and finally morphs into the fully dressed Bardolph.

"Hello, Rurik," She greets warmly.

"Yelena." He greets her with a kiss.

"Careful. Do not crush the baby." Yelena pushes him back gently.

"Oh, yes, the baby. You sent word so I came." Bardolph looks at the infant. Yelena adjusts the infant so the guest can see him clearly. Bardolph looks over at the babe and pauses looking into the eyes of the child.

"He has your eyes. See?" Yelena points out the similarity between the man and the child.

"He? The baby is a boy?"

"Yes. He is a fine and healthy boy. I want to name him Rurik after you, seeing as you are his father," Yelena gives away the relation.

"Will you let me have him?" Bardolph holds out his hands.

"Of course." Yelena hands over her son. Bardolph takes the boy into his arms. As Bardolph cradles the child, he strokes the boy's soft head.

"You are sure he is mine?"

"Yes. Remember, I traded you my virginity for the spell to turn pebbles into jewels. I did not sleep with anyone else until I married Terenti. I was already pregnant by you on that day, so you see, he can only be yours," Yelena explains. Bardolph licks his bottom lip.

"I do remember," his voice is deep and husky.

"But we can never tell the truth about his paternity. Terenti would be merciless," Yelena brings up her husband again.

"Terenti is as vicious as a butterfly," Bardolph snorts.

"You do not know him as I do." Yelena looks away from Bardolph.

"Then I should not give him the satisfaction of having my son as his heir," Bardolph acknowledges his paternity.

"What will you do then? Take us away?" Yelena's eyes light up hopefully. Would the magic man her heart longs for finally whisk her away to a life even grander than the one she acquired by the gift given to her by her Rurik?

"I will take my son," Bardolph stands up.

"What?"

"I will not let that fool have my child. I will take Rurik with me now," Bardolph informs the mother of his child.

"But what about me?"

"You will stay here. You can give that oaf a child of his own to raise," Bardolph replies.

"But..." Yelena grabs Bardolph's pants. "You cannot take away my child."

"My dear, you have already given him to me, remember? He is all mine now."

"What? No. Give me back my son. You will not take him from me. I am his mother. He needs me." Yelena keeps her hold on Bardolph's pants but uses her other hand to reach for her son.

Bardolph backhands her, causing her upper body to fall back onto her set-up pillows. She holds her cheek, tears already bursting from her eyes. Yelena sobs.

"Don't start, Yelena. I have no time for your tears. I thank you for the child and that is why I am not wiping your mind of the spell."

"I don't care about the spell. I only want my son," Yelena answers.

"No. I will not leave him here."

"Then take me with you. You loved me once. Once I am healed, I can show you all I have learned. I can bear you more children as well. Let me come with you, Rurik, and our son."

"Take you? Nothing you have learned will ever impress me. And I want no more children from such a pathetic and unremarkable slut like you." His words are venom in her soul.

"I thought you loved me," Yelena weeps. Bardolph laughs.

"You're a fool then. Men like me don't love girls like you," He hisses. He walks toward the window.

"Stop there!" Tuula enters the room with a yell. Bardolph looks over his shoulder at the large woman.

"Tend to your mistress." He steps forward. The woman stomps her foot. The floor shakes and rumbles as it splits. The sorcerer turns, having avoided falling through the split floor. His eyes sparkle with piqued interest.

"Witch or Sorceress?" He asks the midwife. She tucks some of her hair behind her right ear showing off the point there.

"Fairy. Now give back the child," Tuula demands. He scoffs.

"He is my son. I will do with him what I wish," Bardolph declares.

"Raise him to be another dirty sorcerer who steals, rapes, and kills?"

"No," Bardolph shakes his head.

"No?"

"I swear I will not." He lifts a hand to make his oath.

"I do not trust sorcerers. Give me the child now!" Tuula orders.

"You'll have to come and take him," Bardolph sets the challenge. Tuula runs toward him with hand raises. Pieces of the floor rise with her. She throws her arms, causing the flying flooring to head straight for the man. Bardolph waves his hand, causing the wood to fall onto Yelena. Tuula comes just after the last piece with a fist aimed at Bardolph's face. He catches her fist with his hand. From his finger sprout talons that dig into the flesh of her hand. She raises her other hand to land a blow. He surely cannot block it as he is holding the sleeping babe.

Tuula's fist meets Bardolph's face like a glass vase meeting a wall. As she grimaces at the shattering of her bones. He releases her bloodied hand, only to immediately grab her throat. His talons dig in there as well. Despite his grip and her pain, Tuula spits at Bardolph's face. He catches the spit and swallows it. He grins. A forked tongue like a snake shoots out of Bardolph's mouth. He uses it to lick her lips.

"How many gifts did your fairy blood give you?" He asks.

"Why do you care?" Tuula does not understand his questioning.

"You're a healer and earth elemental, aren't you? It is a pity I have those gifts already."

"Gifts can't be transferred. Why does it matter?" Tuula has to ask as she claws at the hand around her throat. Her eyes go to the boy. "You cannot take whatever gifts the boy has or mine."

"I know. I don't want your powers or his."

"Then why are you taking him?" Tuula chokes out.

"So, I can find the one who will give me the New Starrling," Bardolph answers. Tuula's bloodshot eyes widen more though they already almost pop.

"How many gifts do you have?"

"Almost all. I am only short two and I have found a maiden who has the two I need to make the child. I just need this little one to help me," Bardolph nods to the babe.

"No. I won't let you use him to..." Tuula's sentence is cut off by the cracking of her neck.

Bardolph throws Tuula's body to the side. He hears the servants, the guests, and the count making a commotion as they are on their way to the room. Bardolph goes to the open window. He sprouts wings out of his shoulder blades, causing his shirt to rip. He jumps out and takes flight.

At no time in the flight did the baby awaken. He stayed comfortably in the arms of his father. Reaching the balcony from where Bardolph had taken off earlier, the wings return inside Bardolph's body.

"You have returned, Young Master," Natterjack bows to the returned sorcerer.

"Yes."

"What did that Countess have?" Natterjack inquires.

"A healthy baby boy," Bardolph passes his servant and continues down the hall to the stairs he had come down earlier.

"Congratulations, Young Master," Natterjack hops up the stairs behind the young master.

"Thank you."

"Do you want me to inform the Great Master about the child?" Natterjack checks. Bardolph stops causing Natterjack to run into the back of his legs. Natterjack jumps back.

"Do you want me to split your head in half?"

The servant covers his head and squeaks out, "No, Young Master."

"Then keep it to yourself. My father does not need to know of this. Go and fetch me the magic thread. Bring it to me in Amraphel's tower," Bardolph turns back around to keep up the stairs.

Natterjack turns greener but nods. He hops down the stairs to obey the young master. Bardolph keeps ascending till the steps stop. He turns into the hall there. Through his home, he ventures not paying any care to the servants of various sizes and likenesses to other creatures, until he reaches the eastern part of his home. Up he goes to the tower. The stairs made of white marble slowly gray the further up he goes until they turn black. At the top, Bardolph sees the red door with the star of the fallen burned into it.

Bardolph opens it without knocking. The air is icy. Bardolph can see his breath though the windowless room is dark. Bardolph does not shudder in the temperature change though he feels his small son do so. With a flick of his wrist, Bardolph sends a fireball into the fireplace in the room. With the fire, the room lights up. Bardolph lights the six unlit candles in the room by touching the wicks. He walks to the stone table in the room where he lays down his son. The babe begins to fuss as he finds himself cold and discomforted. He moves to the iron candle stands to place them at the six points of the drawn star on the floor.

"Y-Y-Young M-Master," Natterjack cracks open the door.

"Did you bring the thread?" Bardolph holds out his hand.

"Yes, Sir," Natterjack shakes from the top of his head to the tip of his toes as he creeps forward into the room. He holds out a needle and spool of iridescent thread.

"You can get out," Bardolph snatches it from the servant, who immediately flees the room. The door slams behind him, but it does not bother Bardolph. He takes the threaded needle. He begins to needle the air. As he does. He creates an outfit similar to the one he saw Stella's Astro wearing. Once it is finished, he puts on the clothes.

Bardolph looks back at the fireplace. The fire burns brightly inside the opening that by design is the opened mouth of a skull with sharp-pointed, stone teeth. Bardolph bites his thumb, drawing blood. He sucks some of the blood out then spits it into the fire. He breathes out a quiet incantation. A cloud of black smoke bounces and creeps out of the fireplace and into the shadow of a corner.

"Bardolph," The shadow calls from the corner. The brunet smiles.

"I have brought my new son, Great Amraphel." Bardolph gestures to the table where his son has started whimpering.

"I see. Born just this day, isn't he?" the shadow notes.

"Yes," Bardolph nods.

"You surprise me with a liveborn child. This will be the first one you've let be born of your ten offspring," the unshaped Amraphel comments.

"Yes. I learned, despite your neglecting to tell me, the children outside of the womb give more power than the ones I take from within," Bardolph remarks.

"The more powerful the child, the more powerful you can become. What is it you are seeking, then, Bardolph?"

"I want passage to and from Sterhout in Zeemaa through the portal, as well as more strength in my shifting skills," Bardolph answers.

"Hmmm. Is this to seek the Sipos girl?"

"Yes."

"Good. Good. Now, give me my share and I will give you passage and strength," Amraphel states.

The smoke leaves the corner to return to the fireplace. Bardolph walks back to the stone table where the baby now cries loudly. Bardolph is unconcerned with the crying. He unwraps the baby, exposing him to the now-hot air. Yelena's child flails his arms and legs as he does not know what else to do.

Bardolph walks to the closed door. On it is hung a blood-stained sword made from bone. He brings it to the now screaming newborn. Bardolph holds up the weapon and looks down at his son. The wet eyes look up at the man. The babe stops crying for a moment. He reaches out toward his father.

With a swift motion, the child can no longer cry. Bardolph dips his finger into the fresh, innocent blood and rubs it on his tongue before he grabs the separate remains and tosses them into the roaring fire. The evidence of his relationship with Yelena is gone. His eyes glow red as smoke leaves the fire and fills the room. Bardolph breathes easily. He feels his nerves, muscles, and bones strengthen. He stares at the red flames. They turn white and then form an oval. Bardolph steps forward. As he does, his hair grows light and curls more. His skin becomes paler, and his face shifts from his handsome one to the more dazzling one of the man he has seen only once on this day. His eyes fade from red to blue. He steps through the oval smiling.

CHAPTER 16

The festival of the goddess Zola's Return is not forgotten by the members of Sterhout. Most of the population there are followers of the Thirteen, after all. As such, they should celebrate their goddess coming back from hibernation and giving them spring once more. Nearly every house and storefront have large, brightly colored floral wreaths on their doors. The streets are lined with pots of differing sizes holding differing flowers. The boxes of the windows are filled as well with floral arrangements. As it is the second day of the festival, the townsfolk are gathered in the middle of the town's square.

The women wear petticoats of red, yellow, orange, pink, or light purple with silk jackets with florals embroidered there to match their skirts. The older women wear scarves around their necks to cover their bosoms while the younger women are not as modest. They show off their clavicles and the tops of their breasts. The older women have their hair up in linen caps or straw hats. The younger women let their hair be in braids with flowers or scarves entwined there.

The men have brown or tan breeches, white linen shirts, and jerkins with floral embroidery. Their stockings come in the same colors as the women's petticoats. The older men cover their heads with short-brim hats with colorful hat bands. If the man has a beard, there can be flowers found there. The young leave their heads uncovered.

In the center of the square is a large stage decorated with flowers. On the stage are two thrones. Both are decorated with flowers. There sits a young woman all in white with her hair loose about her and horns like a cow's on her head. They are not natural horns as they are made of bronze. A crown of flowers also sits on her head. She laughs as she watches the young children and adults dancing around the stature of the horned goddess Zola made of flowers as well. The band plays lively music making it easy for all the dancers to move.

Interwoven with the floral perfume in the air are the aromas of spiced brandied raisins, apple pie, ham glazed with honey, trout, and cooked greens. Many sit at the tables set in a circle around the stage and statue. Beer and wine fill the glasses of the adults while the children drink the mixed juices from oranges, lemons, and grapefruits.

"I see the spring festival has begun," Sir Artegal comments, despite still being outside of the town.

"I am surprised to know Sterhout celebrates. I thought this was a prominent home for fairies." Prince Astrophel gets off Tyr's back.

"Many of the fairies from Sterhout came back to Starsfall to try to find thy cure as well as protect Estellen. I suppose without them there, the people turned from El-Yah and followed the Thirteen," Sir Artegal figures.

"I wish they would have stayed then," Prince Astrophel mutters. Tyr walks away to hide himself in the trees so he may change his form.

"If they are having the spring festival for Zola in there, I do not wish to enter the town." Zarin brings her horse next to the knights.

"Why? If you do not believe in Zola, then it is nothing more than a flower festival for us to enjoy." Althea does not understand Zarin's lack of desire.

"I want nothing to do with that festival. I can stay here and watch our beasts if you want to go into the town for supplies." Zarin dismounts Safa.

"But it's not a big deal to..."

"Althea, Zarin has made it clear she is uncomfortable with this sort of thing. Let her be." Hajnal shakes her head disapprovingly at Althea's insistence.

"Whatever." Althea rolls her eyes. "I, for one, want to go into the town and see the festival."

"I will go with you!" Tyr volunteers from a distance.

"I'm fine to go alone, Tyr. Thank you," Althea yells back to him.

"No, we will go as well. Artegal and I do not participate, but we need to get supplies. Morning Glory, will thou come?" the prince looks to Hajnal. She smiles at the pet name as morning glories are her favorite flowers.

"Yes. If that is fine with you, Zarin. I do not want to leave you all on your own." Hajnal looks at the gold-eyed maiden.

"I will be fine. Leave all the beasts with me. Be quick," Zarin urges the others. Free of their riders, the horses and unicorns gather about Zarin just as Tyr comes out of his hiding spot to be with the travelers who intend to go into the town. Since the troupe had discussed their needs when they woke in the morning, they take the appropriate amount of funds with them. They do not want to be empty-handed.

As they walk toward the town's wide-opened gate, Althea has locked her arm to her sister, who walks close to the prince though she touches him not. Tyr stays as close as Althea will let him, as

Sir Artegal stays at the prince's side dutifully. Althea gapes and gasps at the many beautiful flowers around them when they enter. Hajnal too takes in the beauty with awe.

"For you." Tyr picks a blossom from a pot holding the last of the town's cyclamens. The purple blossom is lovely, but Althea smirks.

"That is sweet, Tyr, but you are aware to give me this is to tell me 'Goodbye'." Althea gives him the meaning of the flower. He turns red.

"What? I do not want that!" Tyr throws down the blossom.

"Do not waste the blossom. It is not its fault to have such a meaning." Althea unhooks herself from her sister to pick up the blossom. She puts it in her hair.

As the group enters the main center where the celebration is, they watch the merry folk. Tyr taps his foot to the beat of the song playing. He turns to Althea with an outstretched hand.

"I know this dance. Dance with me."

"I-I don't know…" Althea starts to reject.

"Come, just one dance." He grabs her hand and pulls her toward the other dancer.

"Well, only because I haven't danced in so long." Althea gives in to Tyr's request. Prince Astrophel looks at the smiling Althea, who dances, then looks to Hajnal, who watches her sister and others.

"Hajnal, I would ask thee to dance, but I do not want to honor Zola." Prince Astrophel turns to Hajnal.

"Oh, that is fine, Astro. I try to never take part in the festivals of the Thirteen." Hajnal has not been offended. The prince smiles. Hajnal looks at the dancers to watch her sister.

"Thy sister does, though. Does she follow the Thirteen?"

"No. She just thinks as long as she does not believe that it means nothing." Hajnal explains, her eyes not leaving the blonde dancer.

"Wow. Tyr, you are good on your feet," Althea compliments her dance partner.

"I better be. I did not suffer dance lessons for nothing," He laughs then spins Althea out only to spin her back into him. He dips her. As he does, he stares deeply into her eyes. They shimmer.

"You took dance lessons?" Althea asks once upright again.

"Mother insisted. What about you? You are light on your feet."

"We did not have professional lessons, but my mother taught my sister and me."

"Your mother did well. You are an excellent dancer," Tyr praises her.

"Thank you, Tyr." Althea accepts the compliment.

"If you let me, I can show dances your mother may not have even known," Tyr offers, bringing his mouth close to her ear. The heat of his breath and the lowness of his voice make Althea blush.

"Do you mean the dances of Norwin, or the dances meant for the dark?" Althea keeps her cheek to his cheek as is required for this part of the dance. His cheeks redden.

"I-I-uh..." He fumbles over his words as well as his feet. Althea laughs lightly and Tyr spins her out again. She comes back to him smiling.

"You're secretly a pure boy, aren't you?" She teases. He looks away bashfully.

The dance concludes, causing the participants to stop and clap. A man with buttercups in his white beard steps on stage. Tyr and Althea return to their group.

"Good people of Sterhout, I have the most joyous news. The thorn wall separating us from Estellen has fallen!" He announces. Gasps arise from the crowd.

"This must be the work of our great goddess Zola. Let us praise her!" He calls the people. They all cheer, then face the flower statue. Those who were sitting stand. The horned maiden on the stage stands as well. They all bow down to the flower statue. Prince Astrophel, Sir Artegal, Hajnal, Althea, and Tyr do not.

"Praise Zola! Praise Zola!" they chant.

"They praise flowers when in fact the wall fell because of thee," Prince Astrophel shakes his head.

"They do not know that," Hajnal points out their ignorance.

"I should enlighten them." Prince Astrophel takes a step. Hajnal grabs his arm.

"They will say Zola sent me to you."

"I will tell them it was El-Yah," the prince decides.

"Do you think they will believe you?" Hajnal raises an eyebrow. "Just as you believe it is El-Yah and they mistake it for Zola, they will believe the opposite."

"It may be best for us to not address it at all, Astrophel. We need to get our supplies and leave. Bringing it up may cause a riot, as it is a Zola festival," Sir Artegal advises. The blond frowns. He would prefer to tell the people of the events and El-Yah but Hajnal and Sir Artegal make good points.

"Very well then. But if anyone ever asks me how the wall fell, I will not hesitate to tell the truth," the prince determines.

The Zola worshipers arise and look at the stage again. Buttercup Beard speaks again.

"Let us continue with our festivities. As we do, our Zolan Maid will be seeking her Himmelite Lord."

Many of the young men grin at each other and begin preening. The Zolan Maid comes off her stage and starts to walk about the area.

"We may need to split to find our supplies." Sir Artegal begins talking to his fellow travelers.

"I can go get the extra clothing," Althea volunteers.

"I will go with you," Tyr raises his hands.

"I'm sure I will be fine to-"

"You do not know my measurements, so I must come," Tyr interrupts with reason.

"I will get the water." Sir Artegal picks his job.

"Hajnal and I can get the food." Prince Astrophel picks his job as well as Hajnal's.

"I need to see an apothecary." Hajnal changes her job.

"Art thou injured? Artegal heal her!" Prince Astrophel looks to his knight concerned.

"It is not an injury Sir Artegal can fix." Hajnal turns red.

"What injury cannot be healed with magic?" Prince Astrophel dares to ask. Hajnal wants to crawl out of her skin and away from the answer. Sir Artegal leans down to whisper into his liege's ear. The prince turns redder than his love.

"I am so sorry. Please, do what thou must!" Prince Astrophel apologizes. Hajnal nods.

The quintet search for their desired stores. Most are closed with signs showing the owners are celebrating. Those whose suppliers are in the festival head back toward the town square. Hajnal continues walking as she sees the apothecary's sign at the far end of the street.

Hajnal finds the door with a lavender wreath to be unlocked and so she enters the shop. From the ceiling hangs many drying plants. There is a large counter made of dark wood. Behind it is a wall of shelves filled with jars and containers of items unknown to Hajnal.

"Hello?" Hajnal calls out, hoping the Apothecary is in the shop. A thud from beneath the counter lets Hajnal know someone is home. Some frustrated murmurings follow the thud. Up from beneath the counter emerges a tall, lanky, pale man with long gray hair and large spectacles sitting on his hooked nose. Unlike the other men of the town, he is dressed in all black.

"Can I help you?" he looks down at Hajnal.

"Yes. I need a special tea," Hajnal answers.

"A special tea for what?" He gains a look as if he has smelled something foul.

"A tea to help with...My courses are upon me," Hajnal gives her reason.

"Oh. I'll get you some peppermint tea then." He turns from her. He grabs a jar of green leaves from a shelf. He begins his work as Hajnal waits. When the apothecary finishes, he gives Hajnal a bag with the tea.

"I was also wondering if you have any mustard seeds or wolfsbane root?" Hajnal thinks of some items from the list of the needed ingredients for the elixir.

"I only have the mustard seeds. How much do you need?" He turns around.

"Just a handful," She answers. He grabs the desired amount and puts it into a small pouch for her. Before the man can give her the cost, she lays a gold coin on the counter. His eyes light up at the sight.

"Thank you. You are most generous." He quickly slips it into his pocket. She nods to him.

"Enjoy the festivities," he conjures a smile. Hajnal nods once more to him, then leaves. She tucks the bag into a pocket of her dress. She looks up and sees Astrophel leaning against the door of a closed shop across the street.

"Astrophel!" She smiles at him, "I thought you would still be looking for the baker."

"I found what I needed, my dear. I came here to help," he comes to her.

"That's sweet of you, but I have what I need," she answers.

"Good. Then there are no more errands."

"Not unless the others are not finished with theirs."

"They are," He informs her.

"That was fast." She considers the time it might take to find the shopkeepers, get them to sell their goods, and regather.

"Gold is a great influencer," Astrophel remarks.

"True."

"I found something special. Do we have time to see it?" the prince asks.

"I suppose so."

"Come with me," He offers his arm to her. Hajnal takes it. She allows him to lead her from the apothecary shop and further from the town square.

Hajnal turns her head hearing the cheering in the town of which she is just a little out of bounds. She looks back to her escort.

"They must be having fun back there," Hajnal comments.

"If I am correct, the time has come for the Himmelite Lord to be chosen," Astrophel exclaims the reason for cheering.

"Oh, right. I had forgotten about *that* part of the festival. We should probably go back before the Zolan Maid and Himmelite Lord are to publicly consummate their union. Neither my sister nor I need to witness such an act."

"Why? It is only natural," the prince comments, making Hajnal stop.

"Astro, where are you taking me?" Hajnal finally asks.

"To a tulip field, I saw. It is close." He points ahead.

"I care little for tulips. Let's go back," Hajnal lies and begins to turn. She feels a creeping, slimy feeling coming up the back of her neck.

"Come now, my dear. These tulips are extraordinary."

"How did you come by these extraordinary tulips? I doubt you had time to go through town and find a tulip field in the time it took me to get my tea from the apothecary."

"I found time. Come." He pulls on her.

"Astro," She does not move.

"What, my dear?" His aggravation is not missing from his voice. The term of endearment he uses does not ease her nerves.

"Do you think we will live happily ever after like Caradoc and Blodeuwedd?" She asks innocently.

"What?"

"When we wed, will we have a long, happy life like Caradoc and Blodeuwedd?" She repeats.

"Yes, of course," He answers smiling. Hajnal grabs Astro by the face. He is surprised by this and smiles.

"What are you doing, my dear?" He asks. She stares at his eyes. They are blue but something else is in them. Something is behind the blue.

"Kiss me," She orders.

"Very well," He grins. His lips start soft then turns forceful, his tongue plunders her mouth. Hajnal pushes him off and wipes her mouth.

"What? You said to kiss you," he is confused.

"You are not Prince Astrophel," She backs up from him.

"What? Of course. I am," He steps toward her.

"No. I know Astro and you are not even an ounce like him," Hajnal states.

"I guess you've caught me." He turns his hand's palm up and shrugs. As he does, he fades from Astrophel to Bardolph. Every muscle in Hajnal's body tenses.

"Miss me?" he asks mostly jokingly.

"Why are you here, Bardolph?" She keeps stepping backward. She slips her hand into her pocket.

"I am so glad you got someone to fix your lips. I was worried you'd remain disfigured." He keeps walking toward her. Every step back is matched with a step forward.

"Why are you here?" She asks again.

"You don't know?" He cocks his head to the side. Hajnal shakes her head. He snorts. "Well, dear, I've come to make a deal."

"A deal? I want no deal with you, Bardolph," She states.

"Really? Even though it would let your brother be free?" He brings up Basil. Hajnal stops. Bardolph does not. As he comes closer, Hajnal pulls out the knife given to her by Astrophel. The sorcerer stops.

"What a beautiful weapon." He points to it.

"Isn't it? I'd hate to have to dirty it with your blood," Hajnal says. Bardolph laughs.

"I am loving this fire in you. It's getting me... excited," He shows his teeth as he grins.

"What is the deal you wish to discuss, Bardolph?" Hajnal wants him to get to his point.

"I'd feel more comfortable if you would put the knife down, my dear," he points to the weapon.

"I feel more comfortable with it up."

Bardolph purses his lips then snaps his fingers. From the ground come roots. They wrap over Hajnal's feet and then grab her wrists. They make the weapon fall to the ground. Hajnal feels no pain but feels the pressure and her lack of ability to move.

"This is better," Bardolph comes up to Hajnal.

"Let me go," Hajnal demands.

"Not if you're going to be hostile. Now, shut up and listen to my offer."

Hajnal keeps her mouth closed but glares at him.

"Good girl. I have come here today to help you and your brother. I know I said I would not free him until you came to my home and begged me to take you, but I have cooled off a bit since then. I know it will be nearly impossible for you to find my home so I have come to you with a revised offer. You can come with me now to my home, be my wife, have my children, and I will let your brother go," He ends his proposal with a smile.

Is it my life or Baz's? I cannot believe I would have to do those things with someone other than Astro...But how can I delay his freedom for my own selfish sake?

"Have you made your decision? Will you come with me now or let your brother suffer more?"

Hajnal breathes in deeply before answering.

"I'll come with you but I want to say goodbye to my sister first."

"I guess I can allow that," Bardolph smiles and with a snap of his fingers the roots fall from Hajnal. He takes her by the arm. "But we will go together so you won't be tempted to run off."

"Of course." Hajnal nods.

With his arm tight on hers, Hajnal turns to her walking partner.

"Bardolph," she says his name softly.

"What?"

"Why do you want *me*? I do not understand it."

"You have what I need."

"Which is?"

"The last two gifts. You and I will combine our gifted bloodlines and bring forth the all-gifted child, the New Starrling."

Hajnal tenses at the mention of this plan.

"Why would you want to make that?"

"The New Starrling will be the most powerful being in the world and as his father, I will control him and his power." His eyes are light with his thoughts of having power over something even greater than himself.

"What would you do once you had control of the child? What would you use the child for?"

"To take over the Far Lands then the rest. I will achieve what my ancestors could not," he laughs pleased with his plans.

"What a foolish idea," Hajnal murmurs.

"Foolish?"

"If the child is anything like you, then the child would usurp you and make himself or herself the ruler of all instead of you. Your plan leaves you dead and useless," Hajnal points out the flaw.

"Ah, but this is where your gifts help me out more. You will make the child feel devoted to me. And if you cannot, I'll kill our child before he can kill me then make another one," He gives away his backup plan.

"You would kill your own child?" Hajnal is aghast.

"I've already killed ten of my children both in and out of the womb. I will soon have another one from another woman. I will not hesitate to kill it either," He brags. Hajnal feels tears in her eyes. Though none of the children were hers and he only speaks of a pretend child with her, her heart breaks over their deaths.

"You're horrid."

He shrugs.

"You'll come to accept it."

Hajnal looks down to the ground beneath her.

How can I agree to take part in this terrible plot? If what he says is true, everyone will suffer, not just me and Baz. I cannot let this come to be. I have to do something...

Hajnal wets her lips with her tongue before pursing her lips. A little noise escapes only for it to be silenced with a slap from Bardolph.

"Do not try any of your piper or whistling tricks on me." He grabs her face and makes her look at him. Neither the blow nor the grabbing of her face hurts. She looks back at him with no tears or signs of pain. Bardolph stares at her confused.

"I have a ring of protection. You cannot do anything to me." It is Hajnal's turn to laugh. Bardolph snarls. He strikes her again, but she does not indicate she is harmed. He opens his mouth before her eyes. She can see a light in the back of his throat. Soon comes the fire. It is but warm air against her.

"I guess you are protected from physical harm." He steps back from her. Hajnal remains smug, but Bardolph smiles thus making her lose hers.

"What about your sister?"

"You cannot hurt her. She also has a ring of protection!" Hajnal informs him quickly so he knows he cannot harm her.

"But does your little Astro?" he asks. Hajnal pales then opens her mouth to lie to protect the prince but Bardolph knows the truth before she can speak.

"Maybe if I remove my rival for your affections, you will be more pliable," He steps back from Hajnal. From the back of Bardolph's clothing come his large black, scaly wings. He jumps to start flying into the sky.

"No!" Hajnal screams. Bardolph ignores her as his body shifts into a great and terrible flying wolf. She runs toward the town.

***

In the town square, the selected Zolan Maid walks about the people earning many eager smiles and hopeful looks. She is fully aware of why so many of the townsmen are excited. She smirks proudly at the power she has. As the Zolan Maid, she must simply choose a mate, conceive and give birth to a healthy baby as a sign for a future healthy harvest. Not only does she get to avoid working for the rest of the year, but she also has her choice of any unmarried man in town. She prays to Zola and the childbirth goddess Sormus for the healthy birth of twins.

"Who is she? She is so beautiful," the Zolan maid hears the comment from some men to her left who do not look at her.

"Exceedingly. I'd say even more so than Klazina," another says referring to the Zolan Maid's true name.

"She must not be from here," Another speaks. The Zolan Maid maneuvers her way through the crowd to see who dares to steal her spotlight and title as the most beautiful in the town.

"I must say she is not. I have never seen her before now." Another man claims.

"And she has come into town with the Senyamese fellow and knight," one points. Klazina finally comes close enough to see of whom the men speak. Klazina scowls, seeing the blonde maiden walking through the other women. Klazina has never seen this woman but can tell by her clothes she is not from Zeemaa, at least this part of Zeemaa. Klazina does not fail to see the attention the blonde walker has received. Klazina looks to the maiden's companions.

There is the obvious Senyamese man who holds packages as well as the colossal knight, who is busy speaking with the grocer. The knight is handsome she notes but her eye is quickly turned from him to the hoard of women near him. Some look at the knight, but the rest are near another man who stands in the midst as if trying to appease them. Klazina's mouth waters as she gazes at the man. Although he wears old clothing from a time most definitely gone by, he is by far the most handsome man she has seen in her life. His starlight hair, gods-molded face, and enchanting smile draw her across the way to him without her noticing. Realizing she is near the holder of the finest blue eyes in Sterhout, Klazina clears her throat. All grow silent except the knight still trying to speak with the grocer. However, the grocer goes quiet and looks at the Zolan Maid. The knight becomes quiet.

"I have chosen the Himmelite Lord. I choose this man," the Zolan Maid announces loudly. Loud cheers emerge along with many disappointed groans.

"What?" the chosen man is confused. The women around him lay hands and lift him.

"Astrophel!" the knight calls to the uplifted man. He cannot get to him though as the many women now joined by men create a sea sweeping Astrophel toward the stage.

"And we have our new Himmelite Lord," the woman with yellow roses announces, bringing a crown of flowers with copper lightning bolts on them as Prince Astrophel is set on the stage.

"You're not of Sterhout," The older woman comments not recognizing the chosen man but crowning him. Sir Artegal finally makes it to the stage and walks up behind the prince.

"No. I am not. I should go," Astrophel tries to walk away as he takes off the crown.

"Wait. You must stay. You are the Himmelite Lord. You must do your duty as such," the Zolan Maid grabs the prince's sleeve. He pulls away from her.

"Touch me not, woman."

"But you have been chosen. We must continue the ritual or we will be cursed." Klazina stomps her foot.

"She is right." The woman tries to make Astrophel put the crown back on his head. Astrophel throws down his hand and drops the crown. The woman easily catches the crown.

"You must wear the ceremonial crown and carry on with the ritual." Yellow Roses tries to force the crown back onto Astrophel's golden head.

"I am not taking part and I will not wear this crown." Astrophel catches her wrists.

"You must!" The woman tries to force her hands down once more. Astrophel lets go of her and grasps the flower crown again. He pulls on it making it break. He throws the bit he got to the ground. As his parts and more of the broken flowers fall everyone becomes silent.

"What have you done!" The old woman cries out in horror.

"Now we are cursed." The Zolan maid falls to her knees. The people of Sterhout wail in despair.

"You did this! You will pay!" The older woman raises her hands, conjuring fire in her palm.

"Do not threaten my prince." Sir Artegal steps in front of Astrophel with his hand on his sword. The woman's eyes leave Sir Artegal as she sees something else in the sky.

"What is that?" A boy in the crowd points up to the sky. All look up. Screams of terror fill the people as a black wolf with great wings dives toward them. Many duck while others run. Loud howls boom from the beast that lands on the stage. The force of its landing makes the stage shake off the two women while Astrophel and Sir Artegal fall on the stage.

"There you are," the creature speaks and grabs Astrophel in his claws.

"Unhand me!" Prince Astrophel orders.

"Shut up," Bardolph replies and jumps up to take to the air again. The wolf does not get far as Sir Artegal takes hold of the animal's tail. The beast kicks at the knight with his back legs. The knight suffers the blows.

"We need to get out of here," Tyr tries to pull Althea so they can be safe.

"We have to help Astrophel and Sir Artegal." Althea pulls away from Tyr. The young man groans but follows the blonde against the scattering crowd. He shifts allowing his clothes to tear away. Althea's mouth drops as a black panther passes her and leaps up. Tyr jumps up onto the wolf and bites its leg. The beast cries out in pain before kicking the panther off. Tyr hits a wall rendering him unconscious.

"Astro!" Hajnal calls out seeing her prince in the clutches of her enemy. Both Astro and the transformed Bardolph look at the running Hajnal. Though growing breathless from the running, Hajnal purses her lips and blows. A few birds come and start pecking at the creature. As Bardolph goes to block his eyes, he drops the prince who is caught by Sir Artegal. The knight puts down the prince. They both draw their swords. The swords burn with flames.

Hajnal trips over a dropped plate. Having heard her sister, Althea changes course to head to her sister. Since Hajnal's whistling stops, the birds fly away. Bardolph stays in the air and looks down at the armed men. Seeing how their blades burn, Bardolph is hesitant to attack them. He sees Hajnal on the ground with her sister heading toward her. Althea reaches Hajnal and helps her up.

Bardolph dives down, not toward the men of Estellen but toward Hajnal. With claws spread and paws open, he dives. Althea pushes Hajnal to the ground and is captured by Bardolph. He takes off.

"Althea!" Hajnal screams rising up. She runs after Bardolph who flies above her and toward the outskirts of the town where he had tried to take Hajnal. Althea cries out for help and reaches back for Hajnal. Hajnal falls behind as the beast is just too fast.

Althea cries out as Bardolph takes her into the woods. A bright light there claims them. Hajnal eventually makes it into the woods but there is no trace of her sister or the sorcerer.

"Althea! Althea!" Hajnal keeps calling while walking in the woods.

"Hajnal." Astrophel finds Hajnal having caught up to her.

"She's gone, Astro. My sister is gone. Bardolph has taken her." Hajnal falls to her knees helpless. Astro takes to his knees and wraps his arms around his lady. Hajnal sobs into his chest. Now she has lost both of her siblings to Bardolph.

HEARTS ALIKE

CHAPTER 17

ALTHEA

With a thunderous thud, the great creature falls out of the light portal, with Althea still in his clutches. Lying on the floor, Bardolph shifts from his winged wolf form back into his human one. He releases Althea who lies on the floor breathless despite attaining no injury thanks to her ring of protection. Althea looks over to Bardolph who groans and puts his hand on his leg. She sees the large portion of his leg missing due to Tyr's bite. She smiles at knowing Tyr injured the sorcerer.

Althea's eyes wander around the dark room she is inside now. The floors and windowless walls are stone. Just behind her head is a stone table. Before her is a fearsome fireplace appearing to be an open-mouthed skull breathing fire. There are candles around, but placed in specific spots. Looking down at the floor she is on, she sees the drawing of the Fallen's Star.

What is this place?

Bardolph speaks to himself and his leg heals. Althea frowns. He looks over to Althea once his leg is healed. She draws back as if to brace herself for an attack.

"Get up," He orders, getting to his feet. Althea pushes herself up from the floor and grabs onto the stone table for support. Feeling a wetness on her hand, she looks down at it. She gasps, seeing the blood there.

How is there blood? I have a ring of protection.

Her eyes look beyond her hand to the table. There she sees blood. She must have stuck her hand in the already present blood.

"Whose blood is this?"

"No one of importance to you," Bardolph answers, walking to the closed door. Althea looks at the table again and sees a dagger. She grabs it.

"Where are we?" Althea questions, holding the dagger behind her.

"My home. Come with me." He opens the door. She slips the weapon into a pocket of her dress.

"Where are we?" she asks again.

"My home."

"Which is where? Near Sterhout?"

Bardolph rolls his eyes, then puts on a false smile. Althea feels sick to her stomach.

"Congratulations, you have made it to the place East of the Sun and West of the Moon." He gives her mocking applause.

"Basil is here?" She gains some hope.

"Yes, not that you'll find him," Bardolph smirks arrogantly. "Now, move."

Althea obeys. Though she knows he cannot harm her, she knows if she stays here, she cannot find Basil. She leaves the tower room and finds she must immediately go downstairs. She puts her hand against the stone wall to keep her steady.

"Wow. You think you're sneaky, don't you?" Bardolph reaches into her pocket. Althea inhales sharply as her weapon has been discovered. She turns around to look at him.

"You cannot blame me for trying," she responds. He throws his knife back into the room.

"Try all you want. You'll never be able to fool me," he claims.

"Well, I think-" Althea disagrees.

"I don't care about what you think."

With great force, Bardolph pushes Althea down the stairs. Down she tumbles. When she can grip some stairs to stop falling. Bardolph comes over and with his foot kicks her down. This repeats over and over till finally, she falls flat on a polished floor. She looks at her ring of protection. She will never not be thankful for it. Althea gets up and smiles proudly at the man who abuses her. She shows off her ring.

"You cannot hurt me. No matter if you strike, push, or kick me, I cannot be hurt," she snorts.

"Those rings have limitations, Althea. It won't last forever and when it is done protecting you, I assure you, I will do as I please with your body," Bardolph remarks.

"You are mistaken. You can never harm me. This ring will last longer than my captivity here."

"You are so confident like your sister and just as stupid," Bardolph compares the sisters.

"Insult me if you wish, but your words cannot harm me either," Althea laughs.

"I may not be able to hurt you, but I can most assuredly harm your foolish brother. He has no protection from my hands or curses," Bardolph brings up the lost brother. Althea loses her confidence and smile. Bardolph takes it.

"If you don't want him harmed, then you will do everything I say. Understood?" He grabs her roughly by the chin. Though it does not hurt and she pulls away.

"Yes."

"You will refer to me as 'Young Master' as all the other servants do. Understood?"

She looks at him, unimpressed with the title.

"Understood?" He repeats sternly.

"Yes, Young Master." She rolls her eyes at him. He grabs her by the throat. He lifts her off the ground so their eyes meet.

"Don't disrespect me, Althea. Every eye roll, annoyed sigh, and snide comment will earn a lash to your brother. You are to be as submissive as a well-trained bitch. Do you understand?"

"Yes, Young Master," she answers without the eye roll. He drops her, so she lands on her feet.

"Good. I will take you lower in the castle, then have a servant come and take you to get proper clothing and show you what pigsty will be yours. Then they will put you to work," Bardolph informs her of his intentions. She nods, as she does not know what else to do or say. Bardolph comes before her to lead the way.

The hallway where they walk has rounded ceilings with wooden beams cut and styled to make large, layered flowers. Large windows made of glass with wooden panes let Althea see the lit sky outside. She cannot see if there is any ground.

The squat servant Natterjack walks with a lowered head toward his young master and the young lady. His round fingertips fiddle with his vest. His wide-set eyes keep looking to the ground, then briefly upward.

"Natterjack! Just who I wanted to see," Bardolph greets the warty underling.

"Young Master," He bows.

"This is a new addition to the household. Have her changed, show her a place to sleep, then put her to work. Do not be afraid to give her to do what the others will not," Bardolph pushes Althea toward the short man.

"Yes, Young Master," Natterjack nods obediently. He grabs Althea by the forearm. His hands are moist and sticky like mucus. He pulls her to go with him. She tries to pull her arm away as she dislikes his touch, but as she does, she notices his fingers do not come unstuck from her skin. Althea looks back to Bardolph, who watches her smugly.

"Come on," Natterjack pulls her toward another flight of stairs.

"Where are you going to take me?" Althea asks.

"Below as Young Master ordered," the servant answers. Natterjack takes Althea through many hallways and stairways. She tries to take in the beauty around her, but Natterjack pulls her so quickly she cannot enjoy the details. She can peek out some windows. On one side she could see rolling hills, manicured lawns, and trees. On the other side, she can see they are on a cliff overlooking a beach with black sand.

Throughout the trip from the tower to below, Althea catches sight of many different servants. The women wear brown cotton dresses with little aprons but no shoes. They keep their hair tied up. The men dress as Natterjack does in brown trousers, a white shirt, and a brown vest with no shoes.

Even in passing, Althea can tell there is something different about these servants. Just as she easily noticed with the near-green, toad-ish Natterjack. There is something just off about their physicality. One maid she passed was about the same height as she with a large, rounded white face. But on her face were black lines hooked coming from the outer corners of her eyes, a yellow line going around the structure of her nose and mouth as if to outline it, orange dots in the corners of her mouth, and her mouth and nose were red. Never has Althea seen someone look like that. Many others had strange markings on their faces or oddities about their bodies.

"Here is where the females sleep," Natterjack brings Althea into a room with rows of beds stacked on top of each other. Some of the wooden frames have pillows; others have hay, leaves, and even twigs. One or two have mattresses. There are blankets randomly out there as well.

A rotund woman with no hair but white skin with dark gray and black freckles and large brown eyes walks into the room. She almost steps back out seeing Natterjack and Althea.

"Pinni, have this one changed, then set her to work." Natterjack releases Althea's arm. This Pinni woman nods. She steps to Althea and gently places her hand on Althea's back to guide her further into the female quarters. Natterjack leaves the women.

"Our uniforms are back here," Pinni points toward a back wall where a hutch is. Pinni takes her hand off Althea as they reach the uniform holder. Pinni gives her the clothes.

"So, what are you at night?" Pinni asks.

"What?" Althea does not understand the question.

"At night, when you are in your true form, what are you?" Pinni asks again.

"I am just myself." Althea stares at Pinni, utterly confused.

"Which is a-?" Pinni pauses and waits for an answer.

"I'm sorry, but I don't understand what you're asking," Althea confesses.

"I need you to tell me what you are so I can find the right habitat for you. Like if you are a bird, you will want a nest and not a mattress. So what animal are you?" Pinni is clearer.

"Animal!" Althea steps back.

"Yes. Are you not aware you are not in your animal form?" Pinni stares at Althea who must be soft in the head if she does not realize she is not in her true animal form.

"I am no animal. I am human," Althea responds. Pinni's already large black eyes grow larger.

"Human?"

"Yes. You are not?"

"No. I am a seal. All of us are animals the Master and Young Master have changed in the day to be human-like servants," Pinni explains. Althea blinks several times, trying to process this information.

"I guess you will want the mattress," Pinni walks to a nearby bunk with an unused mattress.

"Thank you." Althea walks over with Pinni.

"You will need to hurry and change. We have much work to do." Pinni steps back from Althea. Althea nods and changes her clothing. Despite changing, she keeps on her shoes.

Pinni goes to a closet in the hallway, and Althea follows.

"There are buckets, rags, scrub brush, and soap in here. There is a water pump down this hall. You will need these to clean the floors."

"Which floors?"

"All of the floors," Pinni answers, "But I will show you where to start."

Althea grabs the supplies and fills the water at the pump. She follows Pinni to a stairwell.

"Start here."

Althea nods and gets on her knees.

Though Althea's ring has protected Althea's hands from blistering and her knees from going numb with her hours of scrubbing, it does not protect her from growing tired and frustrated with the work. With the sun gone, the lights in the stairwell are replaced with lanterns lighting themselves.

Scrub. Scrub. Scrub. Scrub. Scrub. Scrub. Scrub...Scrub... Scrub...

Althea opens her eyes to find her face resting against her hand which still clutches her scrubbing brush. She pushes herself up and tries to look around, though her eyelids want to stick together. She gazes at the floor. White marble stairs, unmarked by shoes or food, are below her. Althea stands up and sees her hours of work finished. She smiles. She must have fallen asleep as she finished.

She drops her brush in the bucket before picking up the pail and putting it back where she had found it originally. She walks toward the doorway. Her stomach growls. She touches it.

Should I find some food or find a bed?

She ventures to the doorway. Hopefully, she can sleep away the hunger. Reaching the opening. Althea puts her hand forward. A smile graces her face once more, seeing she can now leave the kitchen. Of course, now she must try to find the dormitory she was shown earlier.

Was it to the left or the right?

Althea takes a turn and starts walking. She lets her hand run across the cool stone of the wall to help her keep her balance as she walks. Soon she finds a door. She blinks several times before realizing this it is the dormitory. Althea passes many animals tucked away in their beds and nests. She makes her way to the bunk intended for her. Her stomach roars in hunger while her limbs ache. She sits down when she sees half a loaf of bread on her bed. She picks it up and looks around. Someone, or rather some animal, brought her food. The animals are asleep, so she does not know who. Althea does not care much and eats the stale bread. She wishes it were her sister's warm, cloud-like bread. Still, she is glad to have something in her body. She does not finish the food for fear she will not get any more, then lies down to sleep.

Every morning, Althea wakes before being forced to clean. After a week, Althea finds she has cleaned the kitchen floors, pots, pans, dishes, laundry, hallway floors, a few stairwells, and the lavatory she and the animals use when in human. Every night she returns to her hard bed to find small morsels of food from her mysterious benefactor.

After cleaning, scrubbing, polishing, and waxing the floor in a corridor, Althea sees some animals scurrying in the distance, allowing her to know it is now night. She stands up, bone tired from another day of slaving away. She inhales deeply, only to catch a savory scent. Her mouth salivates. She dreads having to go back to the dormitory and eating the piddly food she will find on her bed. Her stomach growls at the food she smells. Maybe just finding the source will give her some comfort.

Following her nose, Althea leaves the cleaned corridor. Finding a flight of stairs, she climbs them. Another hall she walks until she sees an open door. She walks through and stops as her feet squeak on the polished wooden floor.

"Oh, wow," Althea takes in the room. The ceiling is high with a rounded arch. From it hangs two circular chandeliers with lit candles. The walls are made of limestone. One wall has tall windows with rounded arches and stone lattices over them. The wall across from it has grand openings meant to lead to other parts of the castle. The wall across from where she entered is built-in wooden shelves covered in precious crystals of various sizes. Above the shelves is a balcony. The base of the balcony is wooden with a golden inlay with wooden figures styled on top of the gold. On the balcony is a giant organ. The pipes seem infused with the wall. On either side of the organ in the limestone are some carvings, but she cannot tell what it is as she is too far from it. She steps forward and finds next to her a three-opening fireplace. The limestone mantle has many figures carved into it. A fire rages in each of the three spots. Armor with swords hangs on either side of the fireplace. Hanging from the walls are many tapestries depicting nature scenes while the stuffed heads of killed animals line the walls as well.

In the middle of the room is a banquet so large it could fit thirty-two people. Large cushioned seats surround the table. Many more seats are placed along with walls. Against the wall are two benches with large wooden backing with awnings. Gold is laid in the awning. There are many rugs laid on the floor including two bearskin ones.

Althea walks to the table. She salivates, finding the table still has the food prepared from earlier. There is a plate with scraps and a glass half full of wine. Another plate is still full of food. A glass is with it full of wine.

Does Bardolph have a guest? Who cares! There is food!

Althea darts for the food. She stuffs the untouched fowl, sugared almonds, and potatoes in her mouth. Althea chokes on the meat. She grabs the glass of wine and tries to take a swig to remove the blockage. Though the liquid has some heat, she ignores it as it allows her to breathe again. She takes care not to eat too quickly to prevent any more mishaps.

"What are you doing here?" A voice makes Althea stop and drop the almonds in her hand. She swallows what is in her mouth and turns around slowly. Althea presses her lips together as her eyes run over the other person in the banquet hall. The young woman who looks to be about her age, if not younger, stands with her hand on her hip. Her wide, navy sarafan is fastened just below her bust with a gold belt matching the trim and the pattern of flowers on the dress. Large, white puffed sleeves are a vast contrast to her small hands, long slender neck, and thin face. Her black hair falls loose around her fair face which is angular but no less beautiful. Her lips are full and pink and her eyes rest beneath a set of thick, dark eyebrows. She is much taller than Althea.

"I-uh," Althea is unsure of what she can say.

"Why aren't you back into your beastly form?" the young woman comes closer.

"I am not a beast. I am human," Althea states her manner of being.

"Human?" The dark-haired beauty comes closer. "Did my brother bring you here?"

"Who is your brother?" Althea has to be sure with whom this woman is connected.

"Tell me the name of the man who brought you and I will confirm or deny if it is he," the woman remains rather formal and cryptic.

"Bardolph," Althea gives away the name.

"You know his true name?" the woman's eyebrows raise as does her voice.

"Yes. So, is he your brother?"

"Yes. I assume you are one of his new lovers," the dark-haired woman picks up an almond and pops it into her mouth.

"Ugh," Althea is not shy about gagging. The woman laughs at the reaction.

"No?"

"Absolutely not." Althea shakes her head. Bardolph's sister kindly offers Althea an almond. She takes and eats it.

"Then why has he brought you here? We do not need more servants," Bardolph's sister claims.

"He is using me as leverage to lure my sister here." Althea has no problem sharing the reason for her presence.

"Why does he want your sister?"

"I'm not sure. She's a splendid cook and all, but I am far prettier. Oh, I should not say that. It is not kind. My sister is beautiful, just not as beautiful as I am. That still sounds so vain." Althea does not know why she cannot stop speaking her thoughts. The woman snickers.

"But I know my sister has magic, so he may want her for that," Althea continues to think.

"You have magic too?"

"No. I am void," Althea shakes her head.

"Oh... well, that is fine. But if you are void and my brother's captive, why aren't you tied up in his chamber? Why are you dressed as a servant and stealing from the meal prepared for me?"

"I did not mean to steal your food. I am just hungry."

"It's fine. I'm not very hungry, anyway. Sit and eat more." The food and seat are offered. Althea sits and eats some more. The woman sits as well next to Althea.

"But answer my other questions, please. This is confusing for me."

"Well, Bardolph cannot hurt me or have his way with me so he's put me to work." Althea tucks a loose hair behind her ear, causally showing off her ring of protection as she continues to tell the truth to this stranger.

"I see. How fortunate for you. But I do not see why you would allow yourself to be his servant if he cannot hurt you. I would do whatever I wished as he could do nothing to hurt me," the woman snacks on almonds.

"Well, he has my brother imprisoned here as well. I know he can hurt him so I am forced to comply to spare my brother." Althea looks down sadly, thinking of Basil.

"Ah." The woman puts the rest of her almonds down. "My brother is a prick."

Althea sort of smiles at the remark. *This woman is rather likable.*

"I wish I did not have to live with him let alone deal with him, but we are blood."

Althea stops eating.

"Wait... so does this mean you are a witch?"

"I'm a sorceress in training," the magically inclined maiden corrects. Althea stares at the woman's eyes. The outer rim of the iris is silver and fades into a beautiful light blue color. Around the pupil is a starburst of gold with tiny magenta stripes in the burst. Althea leans back.

"You're afraid. Do not be. I have no intention to harm you," The well-dressed female tries to squelch Althea's apparent unease.

"I cannot trust that," Althea shakes her head, blurting out her thoughts again as she stands.

"Because I am training to be a sorceress? I suppose it makes sense. You've probably only been taught about how evil we are. But that is a stereotype. Besides, why would I want to harm you? I just met you."

Althea stays still and quiet.

"You don't believe me, do you?"

Althea remains silent.

"That's fine. I know it takes time to build trust. And we will probably have time to build it as you may be here for the rest of your life." The wannabe sorceress flips some of her hair.

"The rest of my life? No. No. I will leave once my sister gets here," Althea rejects the timeline.

"Listen, this place is enchanted to only be found by my bloodline and a select few of my father's associates. Unless we are actually related, or you are on good terms with my father, your sister is not coming here," the woman states. Althea feels nauseated. The black-haired one stands.

"It will be alright. I'll be your new sister," the young woman smiles.

"I need no other sister."

"Then let us just be friends. You won't be betraying your sisterly bond with us being friends." The woman offers her hand to Althea. Althea does not take it.

"Come now. It is better to be friends than enemies. We can despise Bardolph together." The hand stays outstretched. The friendly smile on the sorceress's face weakens.

"You are keen for someone who does not even know me. Which only makes me only more suspicious of your motives," Althea keeps her hand to herself.

"I have lived here my whole life. The only non-animal people who come here who are not kin to me are my father's unsettling friends and my brother's conquests, who are cast away as soon as he is finished with them. I do not have friends. I never have. You probably cannot relate to this given you are beautiful and have a sister to help you socialize. Seeing as you are stuck here as I am, we can make the best of your time here and become friends. So, please be my friend," the girl explains, ending with a sigh. The honesty is rather refreshing for the speaker. Althea stays unmoved. She glances between the hand and the pretty young woman.

"Will you help me find my brother?" Althea brings up a condition.

"I do not see why not. If it ruins whatever my brother is cooking up, I'm all in," the magical girl smirks.

"Truly?"

"Must I make a blood pact to prove my honesty?"

"No…" Althea says though one would prove the severity of her word.

"I swear I will help you as long as you are my friend," the woman swears.

"Fine. Let's be friends," Althea takes the hand. The young woman smiles brightly.

"Excellent. Now, let me get you a place to stay. I will not let my brother make my friend a servant," The dark-haired woman takes Althea by the shoulders and leads her away.

"What is your name, by the way?" the question comes.

"Althea. Althea Sipos," Althea answers.

"Pretty."

"And what is yours?"

"Odile."

Having been led up many flights of stairs, through a hallway, and across a glass walkway, Althea hopes the next door this Odile girl takes her through is to a bed where she can rest.

Odile pushes open the door before taking Althea inside the room. Althea's body automatically relaxes at the sight of the bed in the room. If it were day and she was alert, she may have tried to take in the details of the room, but all she wants is the bed hanging from the ceiling by ropes with ivy wrapped around them. Althea's feet move themselves toward the bed.

"I take this room is acceptable?" Odile assumes.

"Yes. Yes. Thank you," Althea touches the bed. Her fingers are met with a plush, downy blanket. She wants to crawl in and rest. Althea stops herself. She looks back at Odile, who holds a kind smile.

"Your brother... will he come to seek me?" Althea thinks of the sorcerer.

"He will, but he can't hurt you and he cannot even enter this part of the castle."

"Really?"

"Yes. My father made it so. No man may enter here unless I permit him, except for my father," Odile states.

"Where is your father?" Althea wonders where the third family member is this evening.

"I don't know. But do not fret. He will not come here. He is off and away. Sleep well." Odile leaves the room. Althea shrugs, having to accept this. She kicks off her shoes and sheds her clothes except for her chemise. Althea crawls into the bed. It sways gently with her entry. She finds the bed to be overall warm, soft, and welcoming as if she crawled into a freshly baked yeast roll. Her eyes flutter. She looks for a candle to blow out to darken the room. But she finds none. She does not know where her light source comes from now. However, she blinks and the room darkens. She may not know what turned out the lights, but she accepts it. She lets herself rest.

CHAPTER 18

HAJNAL

S terhout is silent except for the sound of crying coming from Hajnal. The villagers are in shock at what has happened. The selected Himmelite lord rejected his duties and a flying wolf appeared, taking away a young woman. If this is not a sign that gods are displeased with them, then what is?

The priestess, Jetta, comes to the stilled center of the village and with a great cry she rips open her dress. The villagers begin to copy the woman. Sir Artegal ignores them as he goes to check on the unconscious Tyr who has changed out of his panther form. The knight takes Tyr into his arms.

From Sir Artegal's back sprout a set of large white wings. Hajnal and the other onlookers are astounded by the wings but it does not stop the crying. Sir Artegal takes to the sky with Tyr in his arms.

Hajnal hears the others weeping. She knows their cries are not for the same reason as hers.

"You! You have cursed us. You have cursed us!" Jetta points to Astrophel who holds Hajnal close to his chest to keep her protected as they both come to their feet.

"I have done nothing of the sort," Astrophel refuses to take the blame.

"You refused and now we are cursed. Flying wolves are coming for women. It can only mean the gods will rip away our land's fertility, which will leave our lands barren! We will all starve because of you!" Jetta contrives. The people of Sterhout wail and lament their future loss.

"Thou art all cursed because thou hath strayed from El-Yah and cling to false gods," Astrophel states as their true curse.

"How dare you!"

Hajnal senses a burning, boiling sensation growing in Jetta's body, but there is a dark coldness in her as well. It is strange how polar feelings are combined in one person.

"We should leave," Hajnal puts her hand on Astrophel's chest. Agreeing, Astrophel turns his back on Jetta and the others with his arms still around Hajnal.

"Seize them!" Jetta orders. Many of the men start toward Astrophel and Hajnal. Astrophel moves Hajnal behind him before gripping the handle of his sheathed sword.

"Stay back!" Astrophel gives the counter order. The men do not listen to the prince. Prince Astrophel pulls out his weapon. Hajnal gasps as do the other men as they all see the blade looks to be made of pure, burning light. The men who had come with ready hands step back, fearful of the unusual weapon just as Bardolph did during his attack.

"Thou shall not harm us or I shall send thee all to pits of eternal torture!" Astrophel bellows in a low voice Hajnal has never heard before, even in their world. Like fearful rats, the men scurry away.

"We are leaving and none shall follow lest he desires death," Prince Astrophel keeps up his violent threats. No one moves. Jetta glares at the group. Her hate and anger sicken Hajnal's stomach.

"We need to go," Hajnal touches Astrophel's shoulder. Astrophel looks back to the teary-eyed maiden.

"You may leave but you will leave cursed as us!" Jetta screams, then shouts out the dark words of the Fallen. The villagers back away to not get in the line of fire as the woman points her finger toward the prince. A black bolt of lightning flies from her finger and toward the prince.

Hajnal pushes down Astrophel, who falls to the ground with the sword still in hand. With horror, he finds Hajnal being struck by the bolt. He cries out but stops. The bolt bounces off the woman and, in a flash, disappears. Hajnal stands unaffected and with curled fists. The wind suddenly begins to blow. Hajnal breathes heavily and shakily. With each breath, the wind grows stronger and wilder.

"HOW DARE YOU!" Hajnal shrieks. The shrill noise causes all to try to cover their ears, but doing so leaves them unable to grip onto something, thus causing them to fall over in the high-speed wind. Jetta flies back, flipping thrice until she slams into a building. Only Astrophel, who is behind her, is unaffected but awestruck.

Hajnal inhales sharply. Her eyes go over the villagers. The fear fills them and reaches her. Catching glimpses of children clinging to their mothers and many cowering in fear, Hajnal grows sick to her stomach. The gentle hands of the risen Astrophel on her shoulders cause her tears of frustration, anger, and slight regret to come out. She turns and lets him hold her. As his sword has been sheathed, he can have her in both arms. Once more, he begins to take her away. This time, none dare to try to stop them.

Astrophel speaks not as he guides her back toward where Zarin said she would be waiting and where they hoped Sir Artegal and Tyr would be. Halfway there, Hajnal stops.

"What is wrong?" Astrophel gives her some space from his chest but keeps his hands on her shoulders.

"I'm sorry," Hajnal apologizes softly.

"Why? Thou hast saved me once more." Astrophel did not fail to notice.

"I let my hate and anger overtake me and I hurt those people. I hurt people who did not know better and I could have hurt you. I am sorry."

"I am well. Do not apologize."

"But I... I acted so horribly in my anger."

"As did I. I am sorry thou had to see me in my anger as well," Astrophel recalls his threats to the others.

"I am not upset with your actions. You were protecting us."

"As were thee."

Hajnal becomes quiet again and looks to the ground instead of Astrophel. She takes a breath.

"Astro, I saw and felt the fear in those people. It is like what Bardolph put in me and the people of my village. I know some were intent to harm us but not all of them were. I hate I could leave someone as scared as Bardolph has left me. I don't want to be like Bardolph," Hajnal confides her fears and feelings to the young man. His hands slide down her arms and take her hands.

"Thou could never be like Bardolph. I may not have met him as himself, but in our brief interaction and from what I know of his deeds, he is cruel, wicked, and hateful. But thou... thou art kind, compassionate, warm, and loving. Thee and he are completely different entities. Thou shall never be as he," Astrophel renounces the idea. Hajnal leans her head against his shoulder.

"Astro... I pray you are right." Hajnal stays settled in her spot with Astrophel.

"We must go. We should see our friends are well," Astrophel reminds her of the others. Hajnal removes her head but keeps a hand in his. They return to the spot where they left Zarin. Sir Artegal and Tyr are there with her. Tyr appears conscious and unharmed but dressed in different clothes which is reasonable as his clothes were lost in the village when he shifted.

"Oh, Hajnal!" Zarin rushes to embrace the other woman when she comes near. "They told me what happened. I'm so sorry."

Hajnal holds onto Zarin and only lets go when her eyes go to Tyr. Hajnal goes to the shifter.

"Are you well, Tyr?"

"Yes. Artie and Zarin fixed me up. Is it true, it took Althea?" His eyes are quite concerned. Hajnal nods solemnly, pain entering her heart again. Tyr frowns with the confirmation.

"It's a shame." He shakes his head. It is Hajnal's turn to frown. She senses his dismay as well as his hopelessness of finding her.

"Do not give up hope so quickly." Zarin puts her hands on both Hajnal and Tyr's arms.

"She is gone, and we have no way to find her. This whole mission is..." Tyr begins.

"Stop. Do not lose hope. We will find Althea and Basil." Zarin refuses to listen to Tyr's negative talk.

"Only you seem confident in this," Tyr remarks.

"I too have faith the Sipos family will be reunited," Astrophel takes Zarin's side.

"As am I." Hajnal has to be. Tyr looks to Sir Artegal who remains quiet, but all know he will take to Astrophel's side.

"If you do not believe in this quest, then feel free to part from it, Tyr. I thank you for your aid up to now and I will wish you well on whatever journey you undertake. But I do hope you will continue with us," Hajnal speaks peaceably to the youngest of the men. Tyr closes his mouth as he considers his options.

He could search for the beautiful maiden who had an unexplainable hold on him, though he doubts he will ever find her or the mysterious place east of the sun and west of the moon. Or he could go off and be free. He is no longer cursed by that infernal rope or with that traveling show. He is his own person...with no real place to go or real purpose other than surviving...

"I will stay with you and search for Althea," Tyr decides. Hajnal and Zarin both smile at the decision.

"Let us away from this place and put distance between us and Sterhout before nightfall." Prince Astrophel looks back toward the village.

"Yes, we should depart," Sir Artegal agrees.

The group gathers together and takes to the horses. With Althea gone, Hajnal takes Meteora to ride. Tyr allows himself to transform into a nightingale so he may fly.

***

Hajnal rises before dawn ready to continue her search for her stolen siblings. It does not take long for all to be up and traveling again.

With Tyr flying ahead in the form of a nightingale, the others ride their horses and unicorns on the bright and sunny day. Sir Artegal leads the group with Astrophel close to his side. Hajnal, who has requested lessons in magic from Zarin, rides behind the men alongside her new teacher.

"Am I saying it correctly?" Hajnal asks her teacher as she repeats the incantation just taught to her.

"Yes, Hajnal, you are saying it correctly, but remember, these are merely words in the mouth of one who does not have faith in them," Zarin adds.

"I must believe I can do it?"

"Yes, and no. You should be confident in yourself and your ability, but the power does not come from you. We may have been born with some natural gifts which allow us to have more ease with certain things, but these words we say are prayers to El-Yah to allow us to do what we otherwise are not capable of doing."

"But I asked nothing of El-Yah when I did my magic?"

"You have never prayed while using her magic?"

"Well… yes, I have, but not every time and I did not say these sorts of words."

"One does not always have to pray to use magic. The gifts our blood predisposes us to often allow us to use the bare minimum of our gifts. If one practices without seeking El-Yah or another higher power, their talent might grow, but not to the point it could. It is like when a piper learns to play the pipe. At first, the piper can blow and play with the instrument. The piper may be able to make a pleasant noise with some practice and then even be able to make up original songs. However, it is when he learns to read and play notes the piper may learn songs even better and prettier than the ones he made at first. Soon the piper has learned more songs than he could have come up with on his own and over time he does not even need to read the notes to remember them and play them. Did you not find this to be the case when you started piping?"

Hajnal smiles. To recall back to the days of her childhood when her father taught her to play a pipe. She remembers the cool silver pipe in her warm hands. The grooves made from the holes in the pipe sucked in her fingertips. Her playing was pitchy, breathy, and in every way flawed. Her father would smile and encourage her to try again despite the way the sounds made any passing dog yowl and birds fly away. She cannot believe how patient he was with her. For so long, he taught and practiced with her. Such moments were not fruitless. She learned the piper's songs and even the ones her father created. It took many years for her to reach the point where she knows all the songs he could teach her without having to look at the music sheets or even think much about the notes. The songs come as easily to her as breathing sometimes.

Will this magic be the same?

"I did," Hajnal finally answers.

"It will take time but if you practice and keep your heart sincerely focused on and open to El-Yah, you will find it will take no time at all to learn these simple blessings," Zarin speaks with great lightness in her voice.

"Only simple blessings? Will you not teach me greater magic? Like the sort to fight Bardolph?"

Zarin pauses.

"Fairies are not supposed to use their magic to harm others. We are to use it to help others. We should use it as a defense not to take offense," Zarin clarifies. "Did you not recall this from the beginning of the book?"

"I do, but I also recall fairies fought in the Great Fairy War and used their magic for other purposes other than defense," Hajnal points out the known history.

"Fairies can learn offensive magic, but again, this is for when one has been attacked first. A fairy should not strike first," Zarin claims, earning a soft "humph" from Sir Artegal in front of them.

"Do you disagree, Sir Artegal?" Zarin asks the knight. The knight looks back.

"I do not fully disagree with thee, but I have found in times of war, fairies may and sometimes should take offense in battle."

"But we are to be peace-keepers," Zarin speaks to the principles she has been taught.

"How can one keep peace when there is no peace?" Sir Artegal returns with his query. Zarin keeps her mouth shut as she considers the best answer she can muster.

"Thou speak as if we were at war before my sleep. I do not believe we had a war in Estellen since before either of us was born," Astrophel tries to laugh off the tension growing between the knight and young maiden.

"Do not forget, we have had to battle sorcerers for the sake of helping our neighbors. Also Estellen has had wars before and I do not doubt the resurface of a lost nation will stir up some trouble around the surrounding countries," Sir Artegal does not talk lightly.

"You think there will be war?" Hajnal asks now.

"I know the hearts of men are full of greed. The surrounding lands may think our country will be behind in the advances of weaponry by a hundred years and, therefore, an easy target. I should not be surprised if there are invaders who come to strip our land of their riches and claim the land as an extension of their own countries' boundaries. I doubt any will recall all the aid we once gave," Sir Artegal shares his thoughts on his nation's doom.

"That is a bleak view, Artegal," Astrophel frowns.

"But I fear it will be our fate."

"But the closest countries to Estellen are Austvest, Zeemaa, and Logre. King Eric is known for his desire to keep peace and Zeemaa's new queen-well, I know little of her, but if she follows the footsteps of the previous queen, then she will be of the mindset to keep peace as well. And we all know the Ogres of Logre never leave the mountains. If anything, I think Estellen will be greeted with astonishment and ambassadors seeking to curry favor with the returned monarchs," Hajnal gives a far more positive outlook on the future.

"I think I prefer thy prediction, my sunbeam," Astrophel smiles at Hajnal.

"Thou know as well as I, peace is not permanent," Sir Artegal is set on the darker outcome. "And one day the Ogres will leave the mountains."

"What make you say that, Sir Artegal?" Hajnal questions the action.

"Ogres leaving the mountains for the sea is one of the signs of the coming New Starrling," Sir Artegal gives more.

"Right. But there have been no signs of this particular prophecy coming true any time soon," Zarin finds ease in this.

New Starrling... The word stands out in Hajnal's mind. *That is what Bardolph said we would have should we conceive. It is for this New-Starrling that my life has been shaken. Now I know a sign of this prophesied person, will the Ogres go to the sea and war start in Estellen? What other horrible things must come?*

"Do any of you remember what the prophecy said about the New Starrling?" Hajnal tries to speak without giving away her concern.

"Um... when the ogres leave the mountains for the sea, the Great Water Dragon kills his bride..." Sir Artegal begins.

"No. No. That is not how it goes," Zarin cuts off the knight.

"I have been alive for 130 years. I am sure I know that prophecy," Sir Artegal asserts his age, therefore his knowledge.

"It must be your age affecting your memory then because that is not how the prophecy goes."

"And how would thou know?" Sir Artegal is annoyed with Zarin's disagreement.

"Because it is written here in this book of prophecies," Zarin digs into her bag and pulls out a book.

"Why in the world does thou have that?" Sir Artegal gaffes at the bringing of the book.

"It is important to know what to expect. And it is convenient for times such as this when one may misquote an important prophecy," Zarin flips to a page and reads.

"The New Starrling Prophecy as given by the prophetess Lady Evangeline in the year 2014, at the betrothal of Lady Estelle and Sir Rastaban Rumplegeist.

'From the seed of Rastaban will come a trueborn heir who will have all the gifts of a Starrling. The all-gifted will be born after the Great Water Dragon takes the final bride, the Ogres march to the sea, and a lost star is made one with a lion's heart. The Far Lands' calamity or continuation will be by the hands of the New Starrling.'

That is what the prophecy said." Zarin closes the book before she begins to put it back in her bag. "Lady Evangeline's prophecy has been expected for centuries. The likelihood of this prophecy coming to fruition in our lifetime is unlikely."

"But not impossible," Sir Artegal adds.

"Must you seek to disagree with me, Sir?" Hajnal feels Zarin's frustration tightening in her forehead and her heart in her chest.

"'Twas thee who sought my opinion first," He points out to their earlier conversations.

"Let us have peace among ourselves, Artegal. We have no enemies here," Prince Astrophel intervenes, wanting no more animosity to grow. Sir Artegal nods in respect for the request of his prince. Zarin keeps her lips closed.

"Zarin, let us return to our lesson," Hajnal tries to get back on her track.

"Yes, Hajnal. Now, repeat after me," Zarin begins to speak. Hajnal does as bid, keeping in mind what Zarin had said earlier.

At first, the words come out simply as words, but then there is a change. She can hear the music in the phrases she speaks. She can feel a tingle of a power not her own, warming her chest and then flowing over her body. It is almost as if it has replaced her blood.

Astrophel watches the maiden and finds she radiates a lightness. Hajnal stops and looks behind her just as Zarin does. Hajnal beams. Behind her and Meteora is a new trail of yellow and purple flowers.

"Teach me another one!" Hajnal turns her eyes to her teacher, thrilled with the positive outcome. Zarin happily complies.

Some blessings are easier to perform than others, but Hajnal does not let a little failure stop her from trying. It is when the sun begins to set and camp is being made Hajnal and Zarin break from their learning so they might eat and rest. As they bed down in the forest, Astrophel stays close to where Hajnal should sleep. Tyr, then Zarin, and finally Sir Artegal fall asleep to the crackling fire, leaving only Hajnal and Astrophel awake. Hajnal lies on her side and looks at the upright Astrophel near her.

"Are you not going to sleep?" She whispers.

"I do not believe I shall."

"Oh? Are you not tired?"

"Having slept for a century, I find I do not need sleep now."

"Ah," she nods. It is no wonder to her now she does not have any dreams then.

"Do you think you will ever go back to sleep?"

"I do not know. Perhaps when I am more at peace, I will be," he replies.

"You are not at peace?" She sits up.

"Art thou at peace?"

"Well...not exactly. I am rather distressed over the events of the past few days."

"Then how could I be at peace when I know thou art distressed?"

Hajnal bites her lower lip softly at his response. *My distress disturbs him?*

"That is not to say I blame thee for my unease, for I understand why thou art troubled. I also know until I am reunited with my loved ones in my own home with thou as my wife, I will not be at great enough ease to even try to sleep." He is very open about his thoughts and plans. Hajnal looks away from Astrophel. She is sure of the sincerity of his feelings and his desire for their marriage. She is not opposed to this but thinking of the details of the prophecies Zarin read presses on her mind again. Zarin had read this child would be from the seed of Rastaban. Bardolph was so certain the two of them would bring forth this child.

Is Bardolph a descendant of Rastaban? If he is, then are we destined to have this child? Am I destined to be part of Bardolph's plot and not be free to be with Astrophel? Is it because I will need to give in to Bardolph to save Thea and Baz?

"Thou art troubled again. Pray, tell me what is on thy mind?" Astrophel softly puts his hand on hers.

"I worry about the future."

"Did Artegal's talk of doom and gloom harm thy mind, Hajnal? He has a penchant for that sort of thing. He does not intend to depress others. I believe he merely wants us to be on guard for what could happen," Astrophel tries to give a defense for his knight.

"It was not Sir Artegal. It was more about that prophecy Zarin read."

"Ah. But I agree with what Zarin said. We have expected it for centuries and none of the signs have come."

"But...they could and soon. I am no Ora-Oculist but I do know there is someone who has begun their plot to bring about this child."

"Who?"

"Bardolph," Hajnal answers. Astrophel's ivory brow wrinkles.

"How does thou know?"

"He told me that is why he chose me. He has all but the two gifts I have. If we were to have a child from our mixed bloodlines then the child could be born with all the gifts."

"But thou shall not have his child."

"I do not know of this. I fear that because he will harm my siblings, I may have to concede to his desires. I do not want to but I cannot bear the knowledge they could be tortured the rest of their lives when I can prevent it," Hajnal confesses. Astrophel goes quite surprising Hajnal slightly. She would have thought he would pronounce loudly and with many flowery words his disagreement with this possibility.

Tenderly, Astrophel reaches and takes Hajnal's hands. His cool hands soothe her warm ones. His true-blue eyes stay focused on hers. The firelight makes his eyes sparkle.

"May I pray with thee, my love?" His request is simple. Hajnal is taken aback.

Of all the things he wants to do, he wants to pray. It is not that she finds this off-putting but rather more endearing.

"Yes."

He closes his eyes and so does Hajnal. He inhales before reaching out to his voice and spirit.

"Magnificent Creator, we come before thee as thy humble creation to seek guidance, grace, and fortitude. We know not what the future holds for either of us but thou do as thou art the great author of our lives. Let it be thy will to be done to us whether it be to remain together for the duration of our lives or for us to be parted. Let our hearts be not easily swayed from thee in fear but strengthened in the knowledge we are under thy protection no matter the roughness of our paths. We ask for thou to keep thy hedge of protection over both of our families in these uncertain times and over our friends both old and new. Please, lead us safely where we are meant to go and find those we are meant to find. Let us grow in our love for thee and grow in the power and grace thou continuously bestow on us. Give us patience and self-control in place of our anger. We give thee our cares as thou dost care for us. We ask this all in thy name," Astrophel prays with such conviction and earnestness that Hajnal feels tears in her eyes, calmness in her spirit, and great affection in her heart.

"Try to sleep, sweet Hajnal, and put away these thoughts for the night," Astrophel encourages. Hajnal nods and releases the prince. She lies down and then puts out her hand.

"Will you hold my hand until I fall asleep?" She gives the request.

"Of course!" He excitedly changes his position to sit closer to her. He takes her hand. Hajnal relaxes with his touch. She easily goes to sleep under the watchful eyes of her prince.

CHAPTER 19

ALTHEA

A ceiling of ivy intermixed with blooming morning glories greets Althea's opening eyes. The ceiling she sees more clearly now is made of glass and iron. She blinks when an uncontrollable yawn jumps out of her. The hanging bed in which she lays sways as she sits up. She looks around her. The walls she had thought to be painted dark are also made of glass with plants both potted and creeping there. Natural light shines in from the window, illuminating the room further. Althea slips out of bed and finds the floor beneath her feet not cold.

Is this a greenhouse?

Bending down to pick up her clothes and shoes, she finds them gone. She looks under the bed and around the floor, but there is nothing.

Has someone been in here?

"Good, you're awake." Odile comes through the door in a green linen dress with flowers embroidered there in yellow, orange, and red. Her black hair is braided to form a crown around the back of her head.

"Where are my shoes and clothes?" Althea's searching eyes still do not find them.

"I had them removed. I have brought something more suitable." Odile snaps her fingers. A servant with red hair, yellow eyes, and a pointed nose comes with a dress in her arms and a pair of black slippers hanging off two of her fingers. The servant lays the items on the bed, then walks out of the room.

Althea looks at the dress intended for her. It is like the one Odile wears except hers is white with red embroidery. She puts it over her chemise before slipping on the shoes.

"Let me fix your hair" Odile comes behind Althea. She skillfully undoes the braid Althea made last night. Odile's fingers rake through the golden waves before her hands begin their work.

"I can do my hair," Althea makes a single attempt to pull away only for Odile to tug her back.

"Not as well as I can do it." Odile does not release the hair. "I have a real talent for hair." Althea stays still and lets her eyes go around the room again.

"So, is this a greenhouse?"

"It's my conservatory. Do you like it?"

"It's very pretty. But I am curious how there was a light in here last night. I saw no candles and the know the strong light did not come from the stars or moon."

"Oh, that is because the plants are enchanted to give light when it senses it is dark and there is a movement in the room," the explanation comes.

"You enchanted them to give light? That is... amazing." Althea can hardly fathom this ability in the plants.

"I think so." Odile smiles. "I am all finished with your hair now."

Althea reaches back to touch her hair. Odile snaps her fingers and from the walls comes a set of mirrors. Odile hands one to Althea while she holds the other. Getting the right angle, Althea can see the back of her head. Her hair is plaited as if it were meant to resemble billowing waves, while two braids come together and ripple through the center of it like a chain.

"Oh, that is... that is nice," Althea runs her hand over her hair, pleased with the looks.

"You're welcome," Odile tosses her mirror on the bed. Althea puts her mirror on the bed gently. "Come." Odile starts for the door.

"Come where?"

"To eat.

"I'd rather go straight to my brother."

"We must eat first," Odile insists. Althea's stomach gives a perfectly timed growl, urging her to follow Odile. She walks down the hall instead of going in the direction where the dining area would be. Odile opens a large door made of purple wood.

Althea walks inside with Odile. The circular room has windows with pointed arches going around the room. So much natural light comes from the windows, causing there to be no need for artificial light. In between the windows are mirrors in ornate gold frames. There are chaises and chairs in the room. A few tables are spread out, with stacks of books and parchment on them. In the middle of the room is a table with two chairs at it. On the table are two plates, a tower of pastries, a variety of preserves, a platter of meats and eggs, a teapot, and teacups.

Odile claims the chair to the left, leaving Althea to take the chair to the right. Althea looks over the baked goods. She and Stella have made so many of these over the past couple of years. Thinking of her sister and baking makes her homesick. Her appetite leaves her.

Odile grabs a hot cross bun, a few slices of crisp bacon, a blood sausage, and a boiled quail egg. She pours herself some tea before pouring some for Althea.

"Eat." Odile smears some raspberry preserves on her hot cross bun. Althea reaches out and grabs a cinnamon roll. She picks at it.

"Is something wrong with the food?" Odile takes a bite of her own.

"No. I just... I'm not hungry now," Althea answers.

"Come on. I heard your stomach earlier. Eat," Odile points to the plate. Althea brings a piece to her lips and takes a bite. The sweet, warm treat is welcomed by her tongue.

It is well made but... it lacks... the special quality in Stella's cinnamon rolls. There is no extra burst of happiness. Stella's always had extra happiness in it since she wakes happy almost every day from her nights with Astrophel. I hope they are well and safe.

"When can we go to my brother?" Althea asks.

"Not now. We are eating."

"Once we are finished eating, when can we go to him?"

Odile brings her teacup to her lips. "I don't know."

"What?"

Odile swallows her tea and calmly lowers it to the table.

"I don't know when we will be able to go."

"Why?"

"Because I don't know where he is." Odile looks away from Althea.

"You don't?" Althea's disappointment and anger make her voice raise. "You said you would help me find him."

"Yes, and I will. I will just have to find him with you," Odile clarifies. Althea frowns at this news. "Do not be so upset."

"How can I not be? I thought I would find him quickly now as I am here and with you but now, I am delayed again."

"You are on a faster track than if you were not here, though. And I am extremely good at finding things." Odile tries to point out the positive.

"Is that so?" Althea is not impressed.

"Yes. I bet I can find him today," Odile brags. This makes Althea's eyes flicker back to the other woman.

"Truly? How?"

"I'll show you. But we must get our strength up. Eat," Odile points to Althea's plate. With the possibility she and Basil can be reunited today, Althea eats vigorously. Once finished, Odile stands up from the table and saunters toward one of her mirrors. She waves for Althea to come with her. Althea comes to her side.

"Since you share blood with your brother, I can use it to find him." Odile pulls a knife out from the side of the mirror. Althea instinctively puts her hands behind her back.

"Come on, give some blood and I'll find him." Odile holds out her hand.

"I will not take part in blood magic. Even if I wanted to, you cannot harm me, remember?" Althea brings up the ring.

"Right... well," Odile pauses to think and flips the knife several times in her hand. A faint buzzing catches Althea's ear. She stops and throws the knife across the room. The buzzing stops.

"Give me some spit. It could be a viable substitute for blood," Odile holds out her hand.

"You want me to spit in your hand?"

"Yes. Do a big one." Odile keeps her empty hand out. Althea cringes. She purposefully moves her cheeks to build up the bodily fluid.

Feeling a large production of saliva in her mouth, Althea leans over Odile's hand and spits. Odile does not flinch at the sudden wetness on her hand. She walks to the mirror and wipes it on the glass. As she does, she speaks in dark words unknown to Althea. The glass turns black except for the spit being slowly sucked into it. The black glass begins to warp and ripple. Odile's strong, confident words suddenly become hesitant. She stumbles over her words as if she is struggling to remember them. The glass resembles a dark sea's stormy waves. It rises and crashes within the ornate trim around the mirror. Odile tries to recover words.

The waves calm and return to their original still and reflective state. Odile sighs, staring at her reflection in the clean mirror. Althea sees Odile's growing frown.

"You couldn't do it, could you?" Althea calls out the troubles of Odile. Odile flips her frown so she holds a smile.

"Oh, no, no, no. I was doing everything right," Odile denies her struggles. Althea crosses her arms and raises an eyebrow in disbelief at Odile's statement.

"I believe my brother has hidden yours somewhere not be easily detected with simple scrying. We will just have to figure out a different way to find him," Odile puts her hands together. Althea remains unmoved by this information.

"I am sure he is somewhere on this island. We will just have to go looking, the old fashion way," Odile tries to keep up a smile and positive attitude.

"He could be here in the castle." Althea lowers her arms.

"No. I would have heard about it from one of the servants by now," Odile rejects the suggestion, giving Althea less hope.

"We will just go adventuring." Odile grins as if they were going to go look for wildflowers or a waterfall, instead of Althea's cursed brother.

"Let's go!" Odile takes Althea by the hand as a friend might to lead her out of the room. Again, instead of going toward the way they came from the previous night, Odile takes her to a different door. A spiraling staircase waits there.

Down they go, flight after flight. Althea cannot believe how quickly and far they go until they reach the bottom. Odile has let go of her by now and opens the door. A fresh breeze welcomes the women. Althea can hear ocean waves but cannot see them. Althea steps out onto crushed stone. There are lawns of green grass with pools placed in the centers to connect the lawns. Hedges surround this courtyard. Marble statues are spaced out to decorate the area. Althea recognizes them from her schooling.

On each side are six statues. To the right are females. They are the goddesses of the Thirteen.

First, there is the goddess of marriage, childbirth, family, and love: Sormus. The favored goddess has a bee resting on a raised finger. She looks as if she is about to speak to it. Her other hand rests atop the head of a tall stork. A crown of peonies rests atop her head.

A few paces down is Zola with horns growing out of her head, a third eye in the middle of her forehead, a stalk of grain resting in her arm, and a female goat with large teats standing at her side.

Beyond Zola comes Uk, Zola's daughter, who rules the daytime and sun. From her head comes the sun's rays making her halo. Her arms are stretched up as to be reaching for the sun. Her face also is tilted upward. Soon after Uk is her twin Kuu, the goddess of the night, stars, and moon. Her arms are holding a mirror. She has a full moon with stars on either side to make her a diadem. Her eyes look straightforward.

After the twin sisters are their individual daughters. Uk's daughter Taide is first. She stands with a lute in her hands, as to be expected by the goddess of the arts and languages. Her mouth is slightly open. Her hair has a trail of cosmos in it. One of her shoulders holds a nightingale while the other has a mockingbird. Her cousin, Belast, who is the last in the lineup is the only one who sits. She sits on a bench. Olive branches have been woven to make her crown. Her ears are depicted as pointed at the top. In her lap lays the head of a stag. One of her hands rests on his neck which connects him to the rest of the body that lays at her feet. Her other hand holds an arrow that she may have pulled from the beast.

On the left side of the courtyard are the male gods of the Thirteen. Mirroring Sormus is her husband, Vitor, the god of wisdom, education, and justice. He holds scales in one hand while the other tries to hold the multitude of scrolls beneath his arm. A laurel crown rests atop his head.

Next to the wise god is the statue of Zola's husband, Himmel. The god of the sky, wind, weather, and lightning has a pair of large wings protruding from his back. Lightning bolts emerging from clouds around his head give him a kingly look. He holds lightning in his hand while the other faces out as if he is pushing toward something.

Himmel's son, Vindur comes next. The boy god of travel, change, and youth has large wings liken to his father. His hands rest on his hips confidently. Feathers give him a circlet.

Vindur's neighbor is the water god, Meer. Seaweed and a few starfish cover him instead of clothes. An eel hangs around his neck while ocean waves rise at his feet, obscuring them and his legs.

Naked Blig wears only a crown of grape leaves and grapes in his hair. One hand holds a goblet raised toward his wife, Taide. The other holds a jug about to spill its contents. A chameleon clings to his leg.

Though placed beside Blig, his brother Vig is covered almost entirely in armor. Only his face is uncovered so his eyes may look across the way to his own wife, Belast. He is much larger than the rest of the statues. He has a quiver of arrows on his back, a sword on his hip, and a bow in his hand. He wears a stony expression as expected of the god of war as well as a statue.

Odile walks casually between the deity statues while Althea looks at them, amazed at the craftsmanship. She counts them as she passes them. She begins walking backward when she reaches the mirrored Vig and Belast.

"Twelve," Althea mumbles as she reaches the other side of the courtyard where Odile has stopped to wait for her. One is missing she mentally notes.

"You're probably thinking about how one is missing," Odile seemingly reads her mind.

"Yes."

"Ender waits at the gate," Odile points ahead to the hedge. Althea turns around to see a wrought-iron gate is there. A statue is next to it. There is the god of death, time, and wealth. Ender, as he is called, has a hand open and gesturing to the gate. He holds a giant scythe in the other hand. He wears many necklaces, rings, and bracelets as well as a crown like a king. At his feet is an hourglass. Althea involuntarily shivers at the sight of the death god.

"Come, let us go through Ender's gate," Odile opens it. The two pass through; Althea is the one to do so the quickest.

Beyond the gate, the ground is flat, then shoots up into mountains. The trees covering them are not all green. Some have a purple, blue, or even pink coloring to them.

"Don't like Ender?" Odile snickers, staring to walk toward the mountains.

"He is the god of death," Althea replies.

"And fortune," Odile reminds her.

"Yes.... well, I don't believe in the Thirteen."

"Hmmm. Well, I find them fascinating."

"Do you follow the Thirteen?"

"No. I just enjoy their stories and the festivities with their holidays. The Zola festivals should be going on now. I wish I could go to one, but I never leave the island," Odile sighs longingly.

We are on an island. Althea retells her information to herself and then speaks to Odile, "You never leave here?"

"No. I'm not allowed to yet," Odile shakes her head.

"You're not allowed? You look to be of age. Shouldn't you be able to decide whether you can leave or not?"

"An apprentice cannot leave their place of training without permission from his or her master or else he or she can be cut off from further training," Odile explains.

"Ah, I see," Althea nods understandingly. "How long have you been training?"

"All of my life."

"How long is that?"

"I am sixteen," Odile smiles brightly.

"You are so young."

"How old are you? You don't look much older than me."

"I'm twenty and three. I suppose I'm not much older than you..." Althea does the math between them.

"Since you are of age and not bound to an apprenticeship, you must be free to do as you please and go where you want," Odile is inclined to suppose.

"Not really."

"Oh, are your parents overbearing?"

"No. No. Once we came of age, my parents strongly encouraged us to find our ways in the world. Of course, my siblings had my father's talents with a pipe, so it was easier for them to make plans for their future. They planned to go to Belterre together to become pipers."

"They did not want to stay with your parents?"

"No. My father has been made one of the royal pipers there and my siblings wanted to earn a spot on their merit somewhere else."

"I see. What were you going to do?"

"Well, I... I am not talented like my siblings. I cannot play the pipe and I am merely decent at baking. I have no other true skill except being beautiful which has only lead to marriage proposals by men I do not care about. I had to choose: stay in a life of monotony or go off on an adventure into the unknown. I chose the latter."

"And you three have just been wandering around piping for money since then?"

"No. My little brother's pipe was lost in a storm when we were crossing the Windy Channel. But my sister gave her pipe to Basil so he could continue to be piper. I think she is a better piper but it was his dream to be a piper."

"What was hers then?"

"To...you know what. I'm not sure. I mean she talked about the literal dreams she would have at night but I don't know what her dream for life is. I thought it might be to be a baker like our grandmother since she started working as one when we went to different villages. I always felt so bad when we'd have to leave because I kept rejecting the proposals of overzealous men. That's how we ended up splitting. Basil wanted to stay in Belterre and my sister thought we would do better in Austvest. I apologized to her about how I kept ruining her dreams of having a bakery but she assured me that wasn't her dream. She didn't tell me what it was though... Maybe it was for all three of us to be together again. Basil was on his way to visit us when... when your brother came and ruined it all," Althea stops walking as she recalls who she is sharing all this information with and her relation to the Sipos family's oppressor.

"He tends to do that." Odile stops, so she does not go ahead of her walking partner. Althea keeps her mouth closed, not sure of what to say or do next. "I sense you're uneasy with me again. It's because Bardolph is my brother, isn't it? Would it make you feel better if you knew he is only my half-brother? We did not even share the same womb."

Althea does not respond. She is unsure if it is comforting or not. Althea exhales and begins to walk again.

"Do you know of any places nearby where my brother can be hidden?"

"We must just keep looking," Odile keeps at Althea's pace.

The two women continue walking up a hill rather quietly. Althea takes in the surrounding land. She hears rustling and leaves moving in the distance, but has yet to see any animals. She does not see birds in the sky or insects in the grass. It reminds her of walking in Estellen before Prince Astrophel woke. Of course, there wasn't rustling or proof of life in Estellen.

Coming to the top of the hill, Althea sees there are three directions they can go. They can go to the left or the right. Either way will take them toward opposite-facing hills. To go straight will take them down into a valley where Althea sees a lake of shining waters with a small white castle on its edge. On the water are several swans swimming.

"We should go look down there," Althea points toward the lake.

"No. He will not be there," Odile shakes her head.

"Why?"

"No men go there, especially Bardolph. He will not be there."

"Then which way should we go?"

"Let me see..." Odile reaches into a pocket of her dress. She pulls some small bones of different sizes and cuts. She shakes them in her hands, then throws them up into the air. Althea watches them fall to the ground. Odile squats down to look at them. She suddenly points to the right.

"We should go that way." Odile picks up the bones and puts them back in her pocket when she stands back up. Althea nods to agree. They go to the right.

Walking through the pastel-colored trees covering the hill they have chosen is rather peaceful and pretty. Of course, Althea cannot enjoy the walk entirely, as she is looking for any signs there could be a place to hide her brother.

The once clear sky grows dark with gray clouds. They roll in unannounced and unwanted. Odile looks up through the branches to the darkness taking over midday.

"We should start back to my place," Odile turns around to face the direction from where they started.

"What? Why?"

"It's going to storm soon."

"Storm?" Althea looks up and finally notices the dark clouds. "When did this happen? It was so clear."

"Storms are always coming suddenly. It means someone is near the island but is not supposed to be. We are in the Icy Passage so Norwin and Austvest trade ships are always coming nearby." Odile does not wait for Althea to stop looking upward. Finally looking down, Althea follows her guide.

By the time they reach the divided path, raindrops begin to spray them. They start to run to avoid being wet. However, before they can reach Ender's gate to let them back into the courtyard, the clouds dump buckets on them and the earth. Pink and yellow lightning light the sky. Althea can barely hear anything over the rain and howling wind.

Once in the door leading to Odile's stairwell, the drenched women take deep breaths. Water pools at their feet as it drips from their dresses and hair. Odile and Althea look at each other. Both snicker, then laugh as they find the other looks to resemble a drowned rat.

"Let us get upstairs. We need to get out of these wet clothes," Odile grabs hold of the railing on the wall. Althea agrees.

As they ascend, the wet shoes slip on the smooth stone floor. They giggle when either one slides but neither lets the other fall. Reaching the top, they come back to the hall leading to Althea's room, as well as the one with the mirrors. Odile does not lead Althea to either room. Instead, she takes her into yet another room.

Althea almost mistakes the room for another hallway but quickly realizes it is a room. The walls are covered in mosaics made from polished citrines, amethysts, and rose quartz. On the wall next to the entrance are shelves with towels, vials, and small baskets. The left wall looks to be brass doors. To what Althea does not know.

Pinkish marble pillars appear like torch stands with the light pink ceiling billowing from it instead of flames. Ornate brass lamps hang from the ceiling. They are lit and from the cutout are made beautiful geometric patterns of light on the walls and floors.

The floors are made of red travertine tiles placed precisely to make a herringbone pattern. From the wall, the floors stay as they are for three feet before dropping into what looks to be an empty pool. Steps lead down from the entrance into the dropped floor.

At the far end of the room, there are stairs again. They lead to a landing where some chairs sit with a small table. A circular window of stained glass is on the wall there. Althea cannot tell the design from her position.

"Get undressed, I'll start the bath." Odile points to cut out as she walks toward the wall with the handle.

"This is the bath? This is far too big to be a bath." Althea does not believe the size.

"Really? I think it is rather small myself," Odile comments.

"In what world is this small?" Althea asks herself under her breath. Odile twists the handle.

Althea's eyes bulge as she sees water leaking onto the floor in the empty pool. Her mouth drops open. Never has she seen such a sight. Water is just coming into the bath without anyone fetching buckets.

"Go on, now. Get undressed and get in." Odile comes back to Althea's side. The blonde undresses. Odile takes the wet clothes and tosses them to the side. Althea puts begins down the steps. As her toes dip into the water, she gasps.

"What?" Odile seems concerned.

"The water is warm!" Althea remarks.

"Of course," Odile replies flippantly. Althea blinks, then continues into the water.

How amazing is this!

Odile walks to a shelf. She takes hold of a vial.

"I think we will have a little bit of verbena oil," Odile comments, then opens the vial. She pours it into the water. The water bubbles and releases a flowery scent. Odile seals the vial before putting it away.

"And some rose petals." Odile reaches into a small basket and brings forth a handful of rose petals. She scatters into the water. Odile waves her hand to waft the aroma into her nostrils. She smiles as she inhales.

"Wonderful. Now you stay here and enjoy while I go send for some tea and food." The still-dressed Odile leaves.

The water continues to rise, with more and more foamy white bubbles being made. She finds herself delighted with the new experience. The warm water relaxes her muscles. The sweet perfume of it is soothing as well. She feels her body start to float some. It has been so long since she was able to bathe. When she last bathed, it was quick with cold water and plain soap. She could not enjoy it much. She could enjoy this.

She releases her hair so it may freely spread into the water. With the water rising to her ribs, she feels like she is in a swimming hole. She lies on her back and starts to float. She looks at the light shapes on the ceiling and the hanging lamps.

The creak of the door makes Althea sink. She turns to look for Odile.

"Odile, is it true that-" a voice speaks but is not Odile. Althea covers herself and crouches down beneath the bubbles to hide from the intruder. If it were a woman, Althea would not be the color of a carnelian stone and wishing to be invisible. At the door stands a man. She is unsure if it was because she is lower in the floor than him or if it is because he is in fact of great stature he seems to be a tower of a man.

Black boots go up to his knees. He wears maroon velvet breeches and a long maroon coat with golden filigree with a matching waistcoat. From the sleeves of his red coat come the frilly cuffs of a shirt. About his neck is a neckcloth as frilled as his sleeves.

His hair, black and curled, is cut so it barely passes the line of his collar. His jaw is sharp and triangular. His nose is long, pointed, with evenly shaped nostrils. On either side are hooded, almond-shaped eyes with eyelashes so dark she sees their dramatic outline despite Althea being so far away that she cannot see the color of his eyes. Above his eyes are thick, black brows raised in surprise. His proportional brow has a few wisps of rebellious dark curls coming across it.

It is not just her nakedness making Althea blush, but the way the man looks at her and the man looking at her is handsome. An all-too-pleased grin comes to his face.

"You are not Odile."

CHAPTER 20

ALTHEA

Althea sinks so far into the bath that the bubbles around her are now over her up to her chin. She watches the man's movements. The man removes his coat.

"What are you doing, sir?" She watches the removal of his coat. He tosses it onto the floor.

"She speaks... and so politely. I am glad you are not mute." He takes off his waistcoat.

"Why are you taking off your clothes, Sir?" she asks more clearly.

"It is hot in here," He answers, tossing the waistcoat to the side with his coat.

"Step out of the room then, sir." Althea gives him a solution to his problem.

"I do not know if I should. I am rarely in such a situation as this." He returns, his boots coming off as well as his white stockings leaving him only in his pants and shirt. "It has been a long time since I came home and found a beautiful maiden alone, armed only with her... manners."

His husky voice combined with his sharp, watching eyes and smoldering smile make her spine tingle. She gains an ache in her lower belly. These feelings are irksome. Never has looking upon a man given her such physical feelings. Not even Prince Astrophel inspired these sorts of reactions. Of course, Prince Astrophel gives her no fear either.

"I am armed with more than that, so you may want to leave," Althea speaks hoping to pose a threat. The young man pauses, then snickers.

"I can tell you are lying and not just because of my gifts." He sits and puts a foot in the bath. He keeps one on the floor with his knee bent. He rests one arm on the knee while his other hand supports him. He pulls at his neckcloth. She takes a step back. If he joins her, she must be able to get away.

"But do not fear, little lotus, I have no intention of harming you." His words ring sincerely and stop Althea's feet from moving.

"What is your intention, then?"

"I just want to chat."

"Can we not chat when I am dressed and decent?"

"Hmmm, we could, but I find when put in a compromising or desperate position, people are freer with the truth." He nods toward her and then winks. She sinks deeper, so the water covers her mouth. The bubbles pop and tickle her nose.

"Now, give me your name." He does not ask.

"I can tell you it, but not give you it," Althea replies.

"Ah, I see you know of the old ways... good. Tell me your name then," He repositions the phrase.

"Tell me yours," Althea responds without answering.

"I am not the intruder here."

"I would beg to differ," Althea quips. He smirks.

"I may have intruded on your bath, but you have intruded into my home. I am being polite by merely asking about you instead of dragging you by your pretty gold hair and casting you out of my home in nothing but your skin." He points out his rights. Althea deters her eyes from him.

"Tell me your name."

"Althea," she murmurs.

"Althea," he repeats it, having heard it despite her lack of effort to project. "From where have you come, Althea?"

"The Far Lands." She remains vague.

"Well, Althea of the Far Lands, how is it you have come into my home? I know I did not bring you. If Bardolph had, I doubt he would let you stray from his bed. Do you have the blood of Rastaban in your veins?"

"Rastaban? As in Rastaban who started the Great Fairy War?" Althea can only think of one person named Rastaban.

"Yes, Rastaban the Conqueror," He nods.

"Of what I know, I am no relation to him," Althea denies any familial link.

"I did not think so. If you are not of his blood, not brought by me, and not one of Bardolph's acquisitions, that only leaves that Odile brought you here," He deduces. "Of course, this means she broke the terms of her apprenticeship and will be cut off by her master."

"She did not bring me. She did not break any terms." Althea is quick to defend the other young woman.

"Then how are you here?"

"I am not one of Bardolph's women. But he brought me here. Odile took me into her care, though. I am to be safe here, as no men can come. I guess she lied since you are here." Althea has to assume Odile misspoke.

"No man may come unless he has permission or is her-"

"I have returned!" The door opens, revealing Odile with a tray of food, a teapot, and teacups. When she sees the man, she drops the tray.

"Oh, Odile, don't make such a mess." The man waves a finger and causes the falling items to float and land in order back on the tray that he then has sit on the ground.

"I did not know you were here," Odile states. He gets to his feet and waves his hand. The tray comes up to land on his fingertips, which he holds out to Odile.

"I am early, but I see you were not lonely," the man looks back to Althea. Having taken the tray, Odile begins to walk along the side of the water as she heads to the table on the other side of the room.

"Why have you come back early?" Odile inquires.

"Must I have a reason? And must you ask so harshly? You wound me." He touches his chest. Odile rolls her eyes with a little smile. She puts the tray on the table, then begins walking back to the man. Althea stays concealed in the bubbly water.

"I just was not expecting you, and I doubt Bardolph is, either."

The man rolls his eyes at the mention of the sorcerer.

"I did not think he would be back early. And I suppose he did not expect you to take away his new plaything either," he references Althea.

"I did not take her away. I found her and she willingly came with me," Odile states, coming back to the front of the room.

"I am not Bardolph's plaything."

"Pardon me, his lover," the man gives a mocking correction.

"I am NOT his lover or anything that would want to have anything to do with him," Althea rebukes him. The man is puzzled.

"Why would he bring her here, then?"

"You should ask Bardolph," Odile suggests.

"Oh, I will, but I would like her side of the story."

"Can it wait till we are finished bathing?" Odile speaks softer.

"I suppose it can. Have her dressed and sent to me in my study," He orders.

"I will," Odile agrees.

The man collects the items he shed earlier, then leaves the room.

"He speaks to you with such authority as if he were master of this place. Why did you allow him here?" Althea questions.

"He is the master here, and I am unable to keep him away from here. I am sorry for his intrusion, though. I did not know he was coming so soon and he'd come here," Odile apologizes as she removes her clothes. Odile joins Althea in the bath.

"I thought your father was the master here and the only one not affected by male blockage around your quarters?" Althea recalls.

"I know. He is my father."

"Your father!" Althea gasps.

"Yes."

"But he-he-he looks so young!"

"It's the fairy blood. It does wonders for our appearances."

"It has done a great wonder," Althea mutters. Odile shrugs.

"Now, once we finish bathing, I have some yarrow tea and a fruit tray. Given we had such a large breakfast, I thought we could use a light lunch."

Althea wraps herself up in one of the available towels before walking to the table where the food is set. The tea steams while the fruit tray lays with a little moisture. Althea stares at the fruit. Some are white with black speckles. Some are green with a dotted black circle in the middle. She recognizes the yellow fruit belonging to pineapples, and the red ones are clearly strawberries and raspberries. She picks up one of the green ones. Her tongue is met with a burst of sweet citrus. She smiles at the taste. She picks one of the speckled white ones. The flavor is a bit more complex. It reminds her of the fruit she had just eaten, but also a pear or a watermelon. It is strange but it delights her.

"Do you like it?" Odile joins her at the table.

"Very much so." Althea puts more in her mouth.

"Good." Odile picks up the yarrow tea. She takes a sip without even blowing it.

"Once we are dressed, we can go back out to look for my brother, correct?"

Odile swallows her tea.

"No. It is storming. We cannot go back out into it." Odile shakes her head. Althea frowns.

"We will go out again tomorrow when the storm is over." Odile gives her a date. The blonde just nods, accepting what she must.

"Do not stress," Odile puts her hand on Althea's. Althea does not ease but continues to eat.

"If you want, I can read your palms. That could be fun." Odile tries to offer some form of entertainment to distract her guest.

"The last time they were read, things went awry." Althea pulls her hand away from Odile.

"Oh? Did you get some bad news?"

"Yes. And then bad things happened."

"Perhaps I'll see something your last reader missed. I am a sorceress, after all. I bet you got read by some backwater witch who will say anything for money," Odile refers negatively to this supposed person. Althea's hand goes up. It is true Odile is a sorceress, while Madame Fennella was just a witch.

Could Odile find something else?

Do not do it. Althea hears Stella in her head. Althea stops her hand.

"No, thank you," Althea rejects the offer.

"If you change your mind, I'd be happy to do a reading." Odile keeps the offer out. Althea responds by eating more fruit.

Fed, the women leave the bathing room. Althea watches in great astonishment when the water sinks back onto the floor before they leave. Wrapped in their towels, Odile has Althea follow her to another room.

The walls are dusty blue with some white moldings. The white crown moldings are trimmed with gold. The ceiling is a blush pink with dusty blue panels lined with white pieces. Swans are painted on the panels. In the center of the room is a crystal chandelier hanging from a giant, oval ceiling medallion.

There is a glass door Althea can see leads to a balcony. Althea notices the storm continuing outside. Near it is a marble fireplace. On the mantle is a large, floral bouquet complementing the room's colors. Althea sees a large standing mirror in the room as well as a desk with an accompanying chair, a chest of drawers, and a bed. The bed with his heavily framed headboard, beaded and carved motifs, and champagne finish is covered in dusty blue and pink blankets and pillows. Above the headboard is a large canopy of silk curtains with the ability to be pulled around to surround the bed at night.

Odile comes to the chest of drawers and pulls out two chemises. She hands one to Althea. They both slip on the undergarments. Odile picks up the soiled towels and steps to a small hatch on the wall and throws them inside it before closing the hatch back.

"Over there is my closet." Odile walks to the door in the room. She opens it and steps inside. Althea is taken aback once more at the large room filled with faceless statues wearing what seem to be hundreds of different gowns and accessories. Though the bedroom had a definite Belterre feeling, no gown is stuck to a singular, cultural fashion. On a wall are rows of shelves covered in shoes.

"You have so many lovely things."

"I know. Go ahead and pick a dress and some shoes," Odile encourages. Althea begins to walk among the dressed statues. Althea soaks in the myriad of fine dresses. She sees some are silk, satin, and even velvet.

What fine materials.

"I do not mean to offend, but why do you have so many dresses when you do not leave this island?" Althea inquires.

"Just because no one sees me does not mean I cannot dress well. And sometimes we have parties here." Odile gives her reasons.

Althea's eyes catch sight of something pink. Althea walks slowly, pretending to observe other clothes until she reaches the dress she desires. The kirtle is light pink with a pattern of shimmering silver flowers. The gown on top has an opening to show off the kirtle is magenta. It is trimmed with white rabbit fur. She reaches to touch, then pulls her hand away.

This will not be practical for going out to find Baz. Althea can hear Stella in her head.

"Find something you like?" Odile comes behind Althea.

"It is not practical. I need something practical," Althea states. Odile scoffs.

"Why?"

"So, I can wear it to find my brother," Althea answers. Odile rolls her eyes and sighs.

"You can still pick other dresses just for wearing around here."

"I do not plan on being around here long, so I think it will be best to only pick practical clothing." Althea stays focused.

"Then you will want to look over there." Odile points to a back corner. Althea leaves the pink dress to go to the section pointed out by Odile. Odile settles on a gray wool apron dress with large brass buttons carved to have the images of unending knots. From the buttons hang a chain with brass triangles hanging from it. Around her waist, she ties a navy belt with a brass color thread making a knot pattern around the belt.

Althea walks to the wall of shoes. She finds a pair of ankle boots she believes will be durable for walking. She puts them on and ties them. Althea is glad they fit.

"It is fortunate you have a beautiful face, for those clothes make the rest of you so plain," the magical maiden comments, coming toward Althea. Her choice of dress is far finer than Althea's.

Odile wears an emerald green skirt with a matching long-sleeved top. The two pieces do not meet, however, allowing Althea to see the fair flesh of her stomach. Draped from one shoulder across her body to the opposite hip is a sheer scarf with a gold patterned trim. She has gold bangles around her wrists. A gold necklace hangs from her neck with gold leaves coming from it. She has large golden-leaf earrings. With a flick of her hand, her hair is dried and braided. A golden headpiece comes to lie in the part of her hair and allows an emerald to hang about her forehead. Althea has only ever seen women wear such clothes in drawings.

"Let me fix your hair." Odile comes behind Althea. She uses her hand to touch instead of waving. Odile repeats the braid she did earlier for Althea.

"That's better." Odile smiles, proud of her handiwork.

"Thank you." Althea touches the braid.

"We should go to my father now," Odile reminds Althea of the man's order. Althea clenches her jaw. She knows she cannot refuse. There is nowhere for her to hide or go.

"Come, his study is not far." Odile takes hold of Althea's arm kindly. Together, they leave the closet and bedroom. A series of halls, walkways, and stairs take the women away from Odile's tower and to the door for the master's study.

Odile knocks. The door opens on its own. The man in the study sits on a large desk with a book in his hands. He no longer wears the red velvet attire he had worn earlier. Instead, he wears a loose white shirt beneath a half-unbuttoned black jerkin embroidered green filigree. He wears black breeches and black boots to his knees.

"Come in." He waves, not looking up from his book. Althea and Odile begin to cross over.

"Not you, Odile."

Odile lets go of Althea, but the blonde grabs onto Odile.

"I do not want her to leave," Althea states.

"I will not harm you. I cannot." The man snaps his books shut, then points to Althea's hand holding Odile. "I see your ring."

"It is well. I will wait out of here." Odile pats Althea's hand, then steps back out of the room. The door shuts without any hands laid on it.

Althea stands quiet and motionless. Her eyes stay focused on the floor and not on the man. He sets the book in his hand on the desk. He stares at the young woman in the room.

"I see Odile was not generous with her clothes," he observes Althea's dress.

"She was. I chose this, however." Althea feels a need to defend her choice and Odile's generosity.

"You chose this?" he snorts, amused.

"Yes. Is it humorous?" Althea stretches out her skirt.

"To me it is. Of all the fine dresses to choose from, you pick the one I gave Odile when she idealized the peasants in her storybooks and wanted to dress like them," He states.

"Well, it was the only dress I found to be the most practical."

"I suppose you are correct. Now, come and sit." He gestures to a large chair in front of his desk. Althea obeys. She comes to the chair and sits. She folds her hands on her lap. The hand with the ring lies on top.

"That is a fine piece of magic there. May I look at it closer?" He holds his hand out to Althea.

"It will not come off if that is what you want to do to it." She does not move her hand.

"I am aware of how rings of protection work, little flower." He snickers but keeps his hand out. Althea lifts her hand. As the man takes it, he kneels. His hands are warm and soft. Althea pinkens at his position. As he stares at her ring, Althea finally looks at his face and inhales his scent. It reminds her of orange, cedar, and jasmine. But there is amber and sandalwood as well as something else she cannot describe.

His face is so handsome and young. There are no lines about his eyes that come from decades of laughter. There are no lines on his forehead from decades of worrisome thoughts. He looks a little older than Stella, but not by much. His fairy blood must do wonders to keep him this way.

How old is he?

"This ring is excellent work. What sorcerer formed it?"

"It was not a sorcerer." Althea shakes her head.

"Sorceress then?"

"It was not a sorceress, either."

"I know of no witch or wizard who could do as good of a work."

"It was a fairy."

"A fairy... I should have known. They are lovers of giving protection." He seems a bit disgusted but does stop his looking. "How long is this supposed to last?"

"She said it would last until-" Althea stops herself remembering to whom she is speaking, "I do not think I am supposed to share that information with you."

The man knows he has been caught but is not upset. He looks up with a smirk. Their eyes truly meet for the first time. His eyes, defined by the dark lashes around them, baffle Althea. Never has she seen such a pair. A set of warm brown irises plays a simple background to a kaleidoscope of intertwining silver, gold, and magenta. They shine like precious metals in sunlight. Just as the pattern in his eyes is established in her mind, they begin to shift into another. They sparkle.

His hands lose their stiffness, allowing her limp hand to fall back onto her lap. With her lips parted, her breaths are heavy. From her neck down, her skin prickles like it would when the first breeze of fall comes early in the last days of summer.

It is when he blinks and looks away Althea comes to her senses once more. He stands while clearing his throat. He walks around to the other side of his desk to the large black chair there.

"We are not here to talk of your ring," he says as if reminding her. "We are here, so you may tell me how you came to be here."

He takes his seat. Althea straightens up in the chair and swallows the knot formed in her throat.

"Bardolph proposed to my sister. When she rejected him, he burnt my village, cursed my sister, transformed my brother, and stole him away. As my sister and I were traveling to find my brother, Bardolph came and took me away. He brought me here. When he realized I could not be hurt, he sent me to be a servant in the kitchen with the threat of death to my brother. Odile found me and took me. And that is how I came to be here." Althea keeps the story short. The man sits staring and listening.

"How beautiful is your sister?" his question is not one she expects.

"Why does that matter?"

"It matters a great deal," He answers.

"She is beautiful in a way different from me," Althea replies.

"She is ugly," He deduces.

"She is not! She is lovely in looks, but I know when we are compared, I am the victor," Althea spits out, then bites her tongue. Guilt comes over her for comparing her looks to her sister again.

"What is it about your supposedly attractive sister that has drawn Bardolph to her instead of you?"

What if this man has the same thoughts as Bardolph? What if he will seek out Stella for nefarious purposes because of her gifts?

"What insight do I have into the mind of a murderous villain?" She huffs instead, though she knows this is not the same response she gave Odile last night.

"I shall have to ask him then," He replies.

The door swings open. Bardolph enters. Ironic is what Althea thinks when she sees the black-hearted terror walk into the room dressed all in white. His eyes immediately go to Althea, but he walks to the other chair that is open next to her in front of the desk. The door closes again blocking out Odile.

"Bardolph," the master of the room addresses the newcomer.

"Hadion," Bardolph finally looks at the other man and calls him by name rather than his parental title.

"I have heard you have been busy of late," Hadion begins.

"Yes. What of it?" Bardolph crosses one of his legs over the other to grow comfortable.

"I think it is rather clear what has come from it." Hadion nods toward Althea.

"I brought home another servant." Bardolph remains collected and cool.

"Oh, because we are running short on our animal staff." The stoic Hadion keeps his eyes locked on his son. Bardolph shrugs.

"I have been told this is all just part of a bad reaction to being rejected by a semi-attractive woman. Is that why you've brought this woman here?" Hadion gestures to Althea. Bardolph's jaw tightens. His eyes dart over to Althea, then back to his father.

"This is all a part of a strategy," Bardolph calmly replies.

"A strategy for what?"

"To make you a grandfather."

"A grandfather?" Hadion raises an eyebrow.

"Yes. I think it is time for me to put down some roots. I have found a suitable woman to give me what I want. She is just a bit resistant to it all at the moment. I am merely trying to encourage her to change her mind," Bardolph explains.

"By cursing her and my brother? And kidnapping us?" Althea interjects.

Hadion looks to Bardolph for a response to these questions.

"Why is she here? She should be in the kitchens or something," Bardolph sneers.

"She has become your sister's new pet and my eyes enjoy the sight of her," Hadion gives his reasons. Bardolph rolls his eyes while Althea's grow.

"Next, you will tell me to take her back to her sister and abandon my pursuit of her," Bardolph scoffs. Althea's heart leaps at the possibility.

"No. I will not have Odile sulking over losing her new companion. And this courtship-I use the term loosely- is up to you to end. If you truly want this girl, do what you must." Hadion dashes Althea's hopes to the ground while giving Bardolph a reason to smile. His smile makes Althea's blood boil.

"You will fail," Althea snaps, standing. "My sister would never stoop to marry the likes of you."

"I have you and your brother. Unlike you, your sister is not selfish. She will do anything to save you two." Bardolph remains seated and smug.

"Do not speak of my sister as if you know her."

"I know what I need to about her. I am doing something right if she is trying to find me.'"

"She is trying to find Basil, not you."

"Either way, she is trying to come here, and the only way she can save your stupid brother and you is to give in to me."

"Then I will pray that El-Yah wipes us from her memory so she will not come for us and you will never be satisfied."

Bardolph laughs.

"They will be wasted prayers. But should your useless El-Yah or some other deity take heed of your prayers, then I shall pick another to steal away to draw her to me. Perhaps her little prince or your parents. They are in Soldoro, correct?"

Before Althea can comprehend her actions, she snatches a sharp letter opener off Hadion's desk and raises it to bring down on Bardolph. A hand grabs her wrist, preventing her from plunging the office supply into the sorcerer. She looks back to see Hadion. How he got to her so quickly is baffling.

"Now, let's not have any bloodshed in my study. I would hate to have to get the stains out of the carpet." Hadion takes the letter opener from her hand. Althea looks down. Though she loathes this man and is itching to kill him, she knows now is not the time.

"I think it might be best if you rest now. I'll have Odile take you to whatever room she has for you." Hadion puts his arm around Althea and begins to lead her to the door. Bardolph stays seated. As Hadion opens the door to show the waiting Odile, Althea looks back at Bardolph. He gives her a rude gesture with his fingers. Althea glowers at him. She faces forward again.

"Take her to rest. I will speak with you later." Hadion lets go of Althea. Odile nods and takes Althea's arm. Althea looks back again as she is being led away. Hadion closes the door, separating her from him and Bardolph.

Odile speaks to Althea, but her anger and embarrassment block out the words until they reach Odile's former greenhouse room. Althea sits on the bed as Odile uses waving hands to make the plants grow to block out the light in the room.

"I will come back later. You rest," Odile smiles and leaves. Althea kicks off the boots and lies on her bed. She closes her eyes, but not so she can sleep. In the quiet, she hears it. There is no more rain.

Althea puts her borrowed boots back on her feet. She comes to the door of her room. Slowly, she opens it just enough for her head to poke out. She looks left to right to see if anyone is nearby. With no soul in sight, Althea slips out of the door, which she closes behind her. Remembering how Odile led her earlier, Althea finds the stairwell. She quickly descends.

Stepping out into the courtyard, her feet sink slightly into the soft earth. But she does not tarry. Speedily she makes it through Ender's gate and out toward the path leading to the mountains. She must continue her search.

When the road divides, she goes the opposite way than what Odile had chosen. Up she begins to go. She looks for any sign of someone or something has been in these woods. Such a great creature as Basil had been transformed into, he would not make small effects. There would have to be large signs. He could not just hide in a tree, either. He would have to be hidden somewhere large, like a cave. Up she continues with careful eyes, going side to side for a sign. Althea turns off the path. Carefully she steps over risen roots and large, random stones on the ground.

Coming beyond the last trees, Althea gasps as she nearly walks off a cliff. She backs up and clings to the nearest tree. She leans enough to look over the edge of the cliff. Dark waves of the sea beat against a rocky show. Her pounding heart almost drowns out the sounds of the ocean.

"SQUAWK!" A bird suddenly flies down at Althea with its talons out. Althea yelps and steps back from the bird. As she does, she loses her ground. Down she goes.

CHAPTER 21

Hajnal

In the many days following their departure from Sterhout, Hajnal has realized three things.

First, if she falls asleep with her hand in Astrophel's hand when she wakes from her dreamless sleep, her hand will still be in his possession. Such a gesture guarantees her prince will be the last face she sees at night and the first she sees wakes. She is not opposed to this arrangement. It is rather comforting to be able to see him in the real world, as she can no longer see him or anything in her dream world. Though her sleeping arrangements are not ideal as sleeping on the floor of the forest is not as comfortable as the bed she used to share with Althea back in Foxglove Grove, his face is a far more pleasant sight to see when she opens her eyes instead of Althea's drooling one. Of course, she would give just about anything to see that drooling, mouth breather next to her as well as the little brother who used to kick her in their sleep when they were little. As she has yet to find her siblings, Hajnal is more than content to have Astrophel be her bedside companion.

Second, Hajnal enjoys magic. There is a joyful surge going through her each time she can perform a spell. Though her lessons are on simple tasks, she is happy to do them. She cannot believe she did not learn more in her youth. Well, she did learn some magic, but not all Zarin has taught and will teach her. Of course, Hajnal looks forward to learning more about harnessing her natural gifts.

Third, Sir Artegal and Zarin do not mind exchanging passive-aggressive comments about how Hajnal is being taught magic. It is not that Sir Artegal is against Hajnal learning magic or that she is being taught to gain it through faith. Rather, Sir Artegal thinks there are areas of magic more beneficial for Hajnal to learn than what Zarin teaches. Today is no different.

"Excellent, Hajnal. This is a perfect morning glory. Now try some other flowers," Zarin encourages Hajnal.

"Why should she learn to grow flowers when learning to call down hail is far more helpful to protect her?" the question is brought up by the knight.

"Everyone should master the simple blessings before trying to do more grandiose ones, or did your master not give you a strong foundation, Sir Artegal?" Zarin answers coolly with her own question though Hajnal feels the heat of frustration and pride swelling in Zarin's chest.

"Have no concerns about my foundations, Zarin. I was brought up and taught by members of the Estellen Fairy Council. I finished my apprenticeship long ago," Sir Artegal defends himself.

"Perhaps it is because it has been so long since you were trained, you have forgotten the order in which a student should be trained?"

"Correct me if I am wrong, but art thou still an apprentice and not yet a master of magic like myself?"

"I am still in my apprenticeship but should not that make me even more aware of what should and should not be taught to one new to magic?"

"Perhaps, but given thy age, I would think thou would be already finished with thy apprenticeship. It concerns me to think one struggling with magic is even training another," Sir Artegal dares to question Zarin's abilities. Hajnal feels no true concern in Sir Artegal's being. There is not a quivering in his kidneys or the turning of his stomach. Instead, she can feel or believes she feels the swelling of his head.

"Artegal." Prince Astrophel gives his friend a disapproving look. The knight does not hear or selects not to hear the prince.

"Fear not, Sir Artegal. I understand under normal circumstances a fairy is trained and finished with his or her apprenticeship in his or her teen years. Unlike you, who was born in a manner to be trained up by highly esteemed fairies, I was born and trained to be a sorceress in temples of Gold Haven. It was only after escaping there, as well as slavers, I found a fairy who took me to train. So, I would hope knowing now what my background is, you will be kind enough to understand why I am more advanced in my years instead of my fairy training," Zarin leaves Sir Artegal silent. Hajnal feels shame burn in his cheeks and regret pinching his stomach. How could he have known Zarin's background?

"I was unaware of thy origins, Zarin. I am saddened by the thoughts of what atrocities thou may have experienced in those years, but I am in awe of thy evident victory over such circumstances. I also think even if thou art a mere apprentice, thou art still an excellent teacher. I see how well Hajnal responds to thy lessons. I am sure thou art the right teacher for her and are teaching her exactly the way she should learn," Astrophel speaks instead of the knight and takes the side of the young apprentice. Sir Artegal keeps his eyes lowered and away from Zarin.

"You are kind to say so," Zarin smiles at the golden prince, her body coming to more ease.

"Please, continue with the lesson." Hajnal encourages the other woman.

"Yes. So not only can you grow flowers, you can start to grow other plants. You can grow herbs, fruits, and vegetation. This will be helpful if you are put into a situation where you need a medicinal herb or food," Zarin smiles, thinking of the possibilities.

"Wow. That would be convenient when I am cooking," Hajnal thinks of the many times she was missing a specific ingredient in a recipe and had to substitute. Then her mind goes beyond her own cooking.

"Could we then grow the wolfsbane root we need for the All-Cure Elixir?" Hajnal lights up with the possibility.

"I did not even think of that! Perhaps we could try. Let me bring out my book to look at the recipe!" Zarin begins to rifle through her belongings in search of the book. After a little search.

Zarin finds the right book. She flips the pages until she finds the correct one. She smiles as she looks it over.

"I have heard that before somewhere," Astrophel mutters.

"Despite its name, it does not truly cure all curses," Sir Artegal claims.

"Oh? How do you know that?" Hajnal's stomach drops.

"When a curse is said by one with enough power and with a specific set of rules, this elixir will not be enough. The cure allowed by the cursing one is the only way to get rid of it. For instance, Astrophel was cursed by a sorcerer so powerful, and with such specifications when we attempted to give him the All-Cure elixir, it failed. That is why thou had to kiss him. Only true love's kiss was allowed to save him," Sir Artegal gives more insight into the abilities of the potion or rather the lack thereof.

"Was Bardolph specific with his instructions about your brother?" Zarin looks to Hajnal as she was the only one present at the cursing.

"I do not know. When he was cursed, Bardolph spoke in a language I did not understand. Bardolph also said he would be the one to return Basil to his human form, but only when I did as Bardolph asked," Hajnal thinks back somberly.

"Then he might have set a curse on thy brother unfixable with this elixir," Sir Artegal brings the negative news.

Hajnal's heart sinks to join her already fallen stomach. Sir Artegal swallows and licks his lips before speaking again.

"But he may not have. And if that sorcerer is still young, his power may not be strong enough to put a strong hold on thy brother to prevent this elixir from working. I think we should still try to make it." Sir Artegal tries to uplift the crestfallen maiden.

"Do you think so?" Zarin does not ask to provoke the knight but rather as an apprentice asking one who has already become a master.

"I do." He answers softly and not with arrogant authority. "What were the ingredients again?" Zarin is happy to read the list to him.

"We have the stardust already and the mustard seed," Hajnal accounts for the two ingredients.

"We cannot make the blue pearls and we must find a blessed spring. We also lack a lovespoon," Zarin thinks about the other ingredients.

"There is at least one blessed spring in Koralia. It is halfway between the northeast coast and the capital, I believe," Sir Artegal recalls the legendary location.

"And I will make the lovespoon," Astrophel volunteers.

"You will?" The women ask simultaneously.

"Yes. I need to make one for my intended after all. I am surprised I forgot about it till now." Astrophel looks at Hajnal. She smiles mostly to herself about his thoughts and the future gift from him.

"When is thy birthday, Hajnal?"

"The first of Bodza," Hajnal answers.

"I see. Then the first elder tree I see, I will use to make thy spoon," the prince decides.

"When is yours, Astro?" Hajnal asks, realizing she does not know his.

"Ah, it was the seventh of Celyn," He answers. Hajnal's mouth falls open.

"That was merely days ago. In fact, I believe it was the day on which I found you!" Hajnal creates the timeline.

"Was it?" He is just as surprised.

"Yes. You should have told me. We could have celebrated." Hajnal's shame comes over her.

"I think being free from my curse and meeting thee was enough of a celebration," he decides. Hajnal cannot argue.

"Next year we will celebrate properly then," Hajnal states pleasing Astrophel's ears and heart.

"When we make camp, we can try to grow the wolfsbane," Zarin gets back to discussing their important task.

"Yes. What art thou capable of growing, Zarin?" Sir Artegal inquires.

"I can grow nearly anything. I was born with the earth elemental gift. What about you, Sir Artegal?"

"Look! An Elder tree!" Astrophel points ahead. He rides to the large tree though it causes him to leave the others behind. Hajnal blushes, knowing it is for her he rides off excitedly. Astrophel unsheathes his sword. Hajnal is shocked to see it no longer lights up. Instead, it is steel. He cuts at the branch.

"Sir Artegal," Hajnal comes to the knight's side as they draw closer to the tree.

"Yes?"

"When we were in Sterhout, the prince's sword was lit yet now it is metal. How can this be?"

"His sword is blessed, as is mine. It will change depending on the level of danger. If there is no danger like now, the sword will stay steel and be of use. But as the danger increases, the sword will begin to heat, and eventually, if the danger is terrible, it will turn into flames which will render most weapons useless against it," Sir Artegal explains.

"How amazing," Hajnal looks in awe at the sword still in Astrophel's hand.

"Thank you," Sir Artegal gains a proud smirk.

"Did you bless the swords?"

"I did," He nods.

"I am truly in awe. Is that something that can be taught?"

"Yes. But it will be long before Zarin will teach thee such things and that is, of course, if she has learned them herself," Sir Artegal thinks of the possibility that Zarin is untaught.

"I see."

Having removed a decent-sized branch from the elder tree, Astrophel returns to the other three with his sword put away. He is utterly pleased with his acquisition. He slows again so he may be near Hajnal.

Hajnal feels warmth throughout her body as well as from Astrophel's, despite the distance between them. A part of her knows that she should be sad and downtrodden over the taking of her siblings. Another part is ravenous for more knowledge of magic and to find what she can accomplish. However, the biggest part of her that is relishing the joy-inducing, romantic connection with Astrophel is taking over her at present. Even with the stress and sadness that is dominant in her life at this time, the prince makes her feel...differently. It is most welcome.

"How old are you, Astro?" Hajnal asks having stared at him for a solid minute without speaking.

"Oh... um, what year is it again?"

"It has been 2320 years in the time of magic," she gives him the proper answer.

"Well... then I am... a hundred and twenty-one years of age," He calculates and smiles at his answer. Hearing the exact number aloud makes Hajnal's eyes bulge for a brief second. She had forgotten he was cursed for a century but did not know he was only twenty-one when he was cursed. She blushes.

"Am I too old for thee now?" Astrophel looks to his heart's desire.

"No. No. I am just surprised that despite being alive for a hundred and twenty-one years, you are really just twenty-one."

"I suppose thou art correct. Does this bother thee?"

"No. It is just surprising that you are younger than me," Hajnal blurts out her thought.

"Am I? How old art thou? I-I mean, I apologize, I should not have asked about thy-"

"It is quite alright. I am twenty and five years of age," Hajnal shares her age. Astrophel's eyes widen for a moment, then he smiles widely.

"I suppose it is better to say that we are merely four years apart instead of ninety and six."

"I agree," Hajnal nods.

"Shall I call thee 'madam' then, as thou art my elder?" He poses the question with a playfully raised eyebrow.

"I suppose so, but only if you want me to refer to you as a 'boy'?"

"I assure thee I am all man," his voice suddenly deepens and he winks causing a tingle to come over Hajnal.

"Yes... yes, you are," Hajnal turns away for a moment in hopes of hiding her colorful skin.

Before anything else can be said, Tyr flies down from the sky. In his nightingale form, he lands on the hand that Hajnal raises for his perch.

"What is it, Tyr?" Sir Artegal is surprised at the bird's sudden return.

"We are nearing the coast," he chirps.

"Excellent." Astrophel smiles.

"It is not too far, so I think I will change back into my old self," Tyr states then flutters away toward some trees. Sir Artegal dismounts and takes clothes from a bag before taking them to where Tyr hides. Sir Artegal quickly returns to his unicorn before Tyr finishes dressing and comes out of the woods.

"Artegal, dost thou think we should have the unicorn's appearances change to not draw unwanted attention?" Astrophel looks at his friend after looking at his beast.

"I think it might be wiser and more cost-effective if I shrink all the beasts before we get to the port. Then we will not have to pay to ship them," Sir Artegal gives an alternative.

"I must see this," Zarin comments excitedly.

Before the group comes to the town, they all dismount and step away from their equines with their bags in their arms. Sir Artegal speaks clearly as he holds his hands out to the beasts. Quickly they shrink to the size of nuts. Sir Artegal waves his hands over the small horses and unicorns causing them to fall asleep. In their unconscious state, he puts them into a jar he had taken out from his bag earlier and put the animals inside it.

"Amazing," Hajnal, Zarin, and Tyr all comment in awe. The corner of Sir Artegal's mouth twitches with some pride.

"Can you shrink most of our bags too?" Hajnal holds up the objects in her arms.

"I suppose so." They place most of their belongings on the ground and with a few words, the items shrink so they are easily stuffed into the pockets of the owners.

"You should have done this the whole time, Artie. It would have saved our backs." Tyr touches his back.

"It is only temporary for a few days, horse boy," Sir Artegal explains the time limit. Tyr rolls his eyes at the nickname the knight has given him during their journey

"And you said this can be learned," Zarin asks earning a nod from the knight.

"Even by someone like me who is just a shifter?" Tyr touches his chest.

"Yes. As long as thou have fairy blood, thou can learn it. But it comes easier to those with more gifts, like me."

"What gifts do you have?" Tyr asks what Hajnal has been wondering.

"Well, I have the gifts of flight, healing, discernment, pathokinesis or 'feeling', visual scouting, control of water and air, speaking all languages including animal, shifting, and compulsion," He lists.

"So many," Hajnal murmurs.

"You've been able to shift this whole time! You could have been flying around as a bird this whole time instead of me!" Tyr complains. Sir Artegal snorts.

"You say, compulsion, but I have never heard of that gift," Zarin admits.

"I suppose because it is so common on fairies that it is forgotten."

"But what is this gift?" Tyr remains curious.

"It is the gift to use thy physical looks to compel others to do as thou wish. It is not a gift that lasts long, especially on those of strong minds," Sir Artegal gives his explanation.

"I might have that gift," Tyr grins.

"Thou do not," Sir Artegal answers dryly. Zarin and Hajnal cover their mouths to keep back their laughs while Tyr scowls at the knight.

"Come now, we should get in before it gets too dark. We still need to find a ship," Astrophel has not lost track of their purpose despite the astonishing display of magic. With everything collected, the group ventures forth to the port town.

CHAPTER 22

ALTHEA

The sea's cold-water splashes over the rocks and Althea's body. Sitting up and gasping, Althea looks at her hands. She feels her body and finds no injury. She feels the pressure of the stones under her as well as a dull pain on the backside of her body, but nothing so terrible it would imply she just fell off a cliff. She looks at her ring and kisses it. Another wave hits her. She stands up in her soaked dress and looks around at her new surroundings. The cliff's face is jagged but smooth at the bottom so she will not be able to climb it. Behind her is the sea. Though her ring may protect her from drowning, swimming away will not lead her to Basil. The little bit of beach she sees is rocky, with no inclination of growing to a larger dry portion.

Althea comes as close as she can to the wall of stone. She keeps her hand on the wet stone as she carefully walks on the land. Seafoam tries to stick to her dress, but the lapping water washes it off. She looks at the water often. The choppy waves are rather dark, as is the sky. There are large stones in the water. It is almost as if they are teeth meant to bite anyone who comes near the island. But she can see the fins of sharks, which lets her know even if the stones do not bite, the sea creatures will.

The icy wind sends a chill into her. She shivers but does not stop walking even when her feet sink into the moving sand in the water.

"Ah!" Althea yelps as her foot plummets into a hole hidden by the water and sand. She falls as the hole swallows up her leg to her upper thigh. She receives a face full of water as she tries to push herself out of the hole. Each time she pushes up, her leg gets sucked back down and receives watery smacks to the face. With great force, she finally frees herself from the sinkhole. She takes several breaths; she looks at the salty water. A piece of wood floats nearby. It is not some branch or shred of bark. It's the stem post of a ship. Its dragon figurehead is still intact. Its lack of wear gives Althea reason to think the ship to which this piece belongs wrecked recently. Sure enough, Althea notices more pieces floating in the water. She finds the one smooth wall now has large rocks in front of it. Althea climbs up to have sturdier ground.

Climbing from boulder to boulder, she begins to come around a corner. She is astonished when her eyes lie upon a beach with black sand. Close enough, she jumps from a rock into the drier sand. She sees how it goes further up into the island, leading to green grass. Though she is unsure of where she is, surely getting to the grass will lead her back to the castle.

Should I go back or keep on this beach to look for Baz?

As Althea stands trying to decide, a hand grabs her ankle.

"Eek!" She shrieks and looks down.

A man in a white tunic and black breeches lies face down in the sand. His boots are gone, revealing his bare legs and feet. Like the rest of him, his short hair is wet. He lifts his sand-covered face. His brilliant blue eyes are a contrast to his darker skin.

"Help" is the only word to leave the mouth of the ankle grabber. He releases her as his face falls into the sand again. Althea kneels and turns the man over so he is on his back. She sees the front of his shirt is turning red with his blood. She rips his shirt where it is torn about his injury. She sees a cut. How he attained it is a mystery to her.

If only I had magic, I could heal this man. I guess I can just do what Mother taught me instead.

Althea removes the overlayer of her dress, leaving her solely in her chemise. She ties her borrowed apron dress around his waist. She ties it tightly to apply pressure to his wound. She grabs him from underneath his armpit and begins to drag him further away from the water. It is a challenge given he is larger than her and the sand is not sturdy ground. With much effort, she reaches where the sand meets the grass. With a great huff, she lets go of the stranger so she can take deep breaths and try to slow her pounding heart.

The man moans but does not speak or open his eyes. She bends down to clean his face of the sand. As she does, she finds herself not displeased with his looks. She looks away from him so she can fix her eyes on the grassy land near her. She frowns, seeing it is all uphill to get away from the beach.

Can I drag him all the way up? Will I even be near anything once I do so? Will anyone even help me? Maybe I should just leave him be and let nature take its course.

'I must help these people, Althea.' She remembers Basil's words when he stopped to help the people of Foxglove Grove after Bardolph set it on fire. She did not think about the villagers, as she was only focused on Stella.

Am I being... selfish? Is Bardolph right?

"I will come back for you with help," Althea pats his chest lightly. He groans in response. Althea rises and begins her journey uphill. She looks back often at the young man until she gets so far up she can no longer see him. Reaching the top of the hill, she finds no sign of the castle or any built structure. She sees only fields and mountains. She sighs at her predicament.

"I think the castle is on the eastern side of the island and I came west, so let me see where the sun is." Althea looks to the sky. Sure enough, the little bit of sun not hidden by the dark clouds is westward and ready to hide in the horizon.

"Oh no," she mutters, knowing night is soon to be had.

Has Odile noticed my absence? How will I see in the night? Will the tide come too high and sweep away the injured man? Althea's mind is plagued with questions and worry. She shakes her head.

"Shut up, brain," she tells herself and begins heading east.

The sun quickly disappears, taking the clouds with it. Althea is surprised at how clear the night sky becomes. It is so clear she can see many stars and the rising moon. The light from the heavenly bodies gives her surprisingly enough light to find her way.

Unlike her earlier walk with Odile, Althea hears crickets in the grass, owls hooting in their trees, and notices some furry, tailed creatures running around in the distance. It is almost like traveling at night back home. Then Althea hears it. It is no animal noise but rather stringed instruments and woodwinds. It comes beyond the crest of her next hill. Althea reaches the top and finds herself looking down upon the valley with the lake and a small white castle. There are no swans now. Instead, there are young women in white. Some sit playing music while others dance. Althea quickly but quietly begins her way down the hill toward the gathered women.

The closer Althea comes, the more she sees how their dresses shine as if reflecting the moon and stars. Even the women playing instruments seem to sparkle. The ones who dance do so in such graceful, elongated moves astonishing Althea. They stay in sync despite twirling and leaping. By the time Althea comes close enough to the group, she stops by some bushes to watch them longer.

Althea had seen this sort of dancing before at the royal court in Soldoro. She remembers her excitement to be attending the royal birthday party for Princess Julissa after her father became a royal piper for the king. The dancers came from Belterre to perform their elegant dances for the princess's delight. She remembers the comment of an attending countess that the dancers from Norwin were much better, but Althea could not be sure as she was only able to see the ones from Belterre. But as Althea looks at these dancers, she may think they can rival the ones she saw.

The dancers stop with their bodies bent downward but mirrored in a manner as to make a path. Coming practically out of nowhere comes a maiden in a gown dazzling the eyes. But not only does her dress draw attention but her flowing, golden hair. Unlike the others who keep their hair up, she is allowed to flow freely. Atop her head is a diadem. Before Althea can notice more of this woman, she begins to dance. The woman's moves are far finer and more purposeful. Every stretch of her arm, bend of her back and tiptoe step are so precise, it is almost as if this is the only way one should move. The other women join the star among them. They dance nicely, but none are as divine as the perfect one.

But all too soon, they all stop their dancing as the musicians end their music. Though saddened by the loss of beauty, Althea's hands give a signal of her praise with a clap. With a single clap, the eyes of the women turn on her.

Some cling to each other while others stand in front of the frightened ones. Others look ready to approach but hold back. Althea steps out. She comes toward the women.

"I am sorry to disturb you all." Althea apologizes.

The crowned one comes close to Althea to stop her a few feet away from the others.

"Who are you?" She asks, not afraid to get into Althea's space.

Althea finds herself struggling to say her name as sees the woman more clearly. Though her face is thin and angular, it is angled and cut in a manner most pleasing to the eye. Her lips are thick and pink. Her skin is fair with golden-pink undertones, like a peach. Her eyebrows are thick, but their pale color makes them not look so. Her nose is short and upturned at the end. Her eyes are a shade of blue Althea would compare with the sky on a clear spring day. There is something familiar about her face. On her head rests a tiara. The bottom band has tiny diamonds bordering larger diamonds cut to look like leaves leading to perfectly spaced and placed pearls. Atop this first band is a much larger one with small pearls making the border around the leaf-cut diamonds surrounding large pearls surrounded by tiny diamonds. In her most secret vanity, Althea would consider this woman her equal in beauty, which has never happened.

"I am Althea." Althea finally gets her name out.

"Althea? What has brought you here?" The beautiful woman questions.

"I need help," Althea remembers the man she found as well as her own origins on being on the island.

"Are you also seeking shelter from Bardolph?" A woman holding a piccolo asks. The other women seem to lean toward Althea curiously.

"I am seeking help to treat an injured man who I fear will die if I do not help. I cannot carry or tend to him on my own. If any of you can help, please come with me," Althea requests. The women look at each other exchanging quiet looks.

"Who is this man?" The leader asks.

"I do not know. I found him on a beach."

"If this is a ploy set by Bardolph then say so now," A taller dancer crosses her arms in the background.

"No. I want nothing to do with Bardolph, especially helping him lure women." Althea shakes her head.

"How do we know she speaks the truth? She could be another enchanted animal or desperate lover." One holding a violin brings up the possibilities.

"The moon is out. The animals have returned to their true form," the harpist of the group points to the bright moon.

"That does not mean she is not a lover of Bardolph," The tall dancer brings up the other possibility again.

"True. How is it that she is out wandering and not with Bardolph? This has to be a trap," the violinist insists.

"I escaped the castle and ended up on a beach. You do not have to believe me. But there is a man who needs help. He is a shipwreck survivor who will bleed out if he is not tended to soon. You do not have to come with me, but I would appreciate it," Althea points her finger back to where she came from earlier. The women stand silent.

"I will go back myself and pray El-Yah heals this poor man since I cannot," Althea turns to walk away.

"Swear to El-Yah you are not lying about this man and are not a lover of Bardolph," the tall woman hisses. Althea raises both hands.

"I swear to El-Yah I am not lying about this man, and I am not a lover of Bardolph."

The women are quiet.

"I will come," the leader of the group speaks up again. There are looks of surprise among many of the women.

"Then I will come with you in case this is a trick," the tall dancer volunteers.

"So will I." The harpist stands.

"And I," Three other dancers pipe up simultaneously.

"Someone fetch my healing bag," the leader orders. A young, petite dancer runs toward the small castle.

"Someone gets us lanterns. The rest of you, make ready some food and a place for our future guest as well as for Althea," the leader gives more jobs. The women scatter to do as their leader bids.

"Will this man even be able to come to our place?" The tall dancer asks her leader.

"If I welcome him, then he will be, Darya," the golden-haired woman answers. The petite dancer runs up swiftly with a leather satchel in her hands.

"Thank you, Yaffa."

More women come with lanterns. They hand them off to four of the seven travelers. With some extra light, it seems the group is set to depart.

"Lead the way, Althea." the direction is given. Althea does her best to recall the way she has come. She does not speak much to the other women except to give directions. She prays she has not lost her way back to the man.

Hearing the crashing waves of the sea, Althea picks up speed knowing she is close. Almost excitedly she maneuvers down the hill leading to the black sands beach. She holds the lantern out in hopes the light will shed on the body she left behind.

"Over here!" Althea calls to the others, trailing behind her when she notices the body of the man. She kneels beside him to make sure he still breathes.

"He is breathing."

The others come. The most beautiful of them comes to kneel. She opens her bag.

"Unwrap him carefully, ladies."

Darya, Althea, and the others do so. His moan is weak. The crowned woman lifts his shirt, showing a deep gash in his side. She pours a liquid over her hands, then on his wound. He cries out, though he does not open his eyes or register that others are there. She pulls out a dry cloth and proceeds to dry the area. Once satisfied, she pulls out a needle and thread. She begins to sew. Althea wants to look away but figures it will be better for her to learn. Some sort of ointment is applied before orders are given for him to be lifted gently so bandages can be wrapped around his torso.

"He does not seem to be waking, so we will have to carry him. We will need to work as a team. Katia, Nadia, take his legs. Darya, take him by his shoulders and support his head. I will support his side and back. Althea, take the other side. Rufina, take some lanterns and lead the way. Susanna, keep some lanterns and stay at the rear so it does not get too dark." Each woman accepts the assignment.

With great effort, the women lift the man. Having five to one helps the carrying of the load. Rufina, the harpist, eagerly leads the group toward their abode despite the terrain and distance they must face.

With arms and legs burning from the continuous weight lifting and walking up hills, Althea is ready to drop this man and collapse herself by the time they reach the little white castle. Fortunately, some of the young women come to meet them with a stretcher. Althea happily gives him over to it. They take the man away to the building. Althea sits down having given him up, but most of the other carriers go on with him. Althea waits by the water, unsure of what to do now except rest. Soon, she is approached by Darya. The woman of great stature looks down at the sitting Althea.

"Come. Her Highness wants you to come and eat," Darya invites Althea inside unenthusiastically.

"Her Highness? I did not know there was royalty here."

"Only she is royal here," Darya answers. "Now, get up and come inside."

Althea stands up sore. She begins to follow Darya.

Althea is greeted by a polished floor made of black-and-white marble squares. A grand staircase of stone grows, then curls along the wall to a second floor. Its railings are made of wrought iron and gold. The marble walls have been sculpted to make borders and pillars. From the ceiling hangs a long chain interwoven with golden vines. The chain holds a cage with large candles inside giving brilliant light. However, the chandelier is aided in giving light by tall candlesticks around the entry hall.

"This way." Darya walks on through a door under a higher part of the staircase. There an arch hallway waits only to lead them to a long rectangular room.

The white walls are decorated with golden accents to create rounded arches. There are many glass windows with doors. The white ceiling allows for two giant crystal chandeliers to hang from it. Below the light givers is a long dining table. It is almost as long as the one Althea saw in Odile's home. There are chairs upholstered with gold or white fabric. Many are filled with the women Althea saw before interrupting their gathering. Each has a gold bowl before them but none touch their food.

"Come this way." Darya does not stop in awe like Althea has. Althea quickly moves to follow Darya to an empty seat to the left of the empty head of the table.

"Here." Darya points to the chair. Althea sits. Darya takes a seat across from her. Althea looks down at the table. The women speak quietly among themselves but none touch their food. Feeling a rumbling in her stomach, Althea looks at the steaming soup before her. She grabs her spoon, only to receive a kick under the table.

"No one eats till the princess says so," Darya snaps. Althea releases her spoon.

"You could have just said that instead of kicking me," Althea comments, though the kick did not hurt.

The group becomes quiet suddenly and all stand. Althea follows suit, confused, until she sees the beautiful woman coming.

She is a princess...It makes sense as she is wearing a crown and all seem to obey her.

"Thank you all for your patience. Our new patient is resting well now." The princess comes to the head of the table. "Say your blessings and then begin."

The princess sits down. Many mutter prayers aloud, while others keep their lips closed. But the hushed words are soon replaced with conversations among the women who talk as they eat. Althea picks up her spoon and takes part of her soup. Warm tomato and basil soup soothes her chilly body.

"Althea," the princess addresses her.

"Yes, your highness."

"I suppose Darya has told you to call me this." The princess glances at her right-hand woman.

"Not in so many words."

"I see. Well, I wanted to speak with you. First, I commend you on helping that poor man. He surely would have died had you not tended to him before getting help. It was kind and brave." The princess praises the blonde who blushes at the compliments.

"I was just trying to help."

"Yes, even when faced with resistance and disbelief. I am sorry my ladies were hostile. We must be here on this island."

"I suppose you must be, considering who lives here." Althea thinks of a particular sorcerer.

"Yes. Every woman here has been in a position similar to you. We have all been captives only to seize an opportunity to flee the big castle. We have banded together here in this place of safety and sisterhood." The princess eyes the many women. Althea looks and counts them quickly in her mind. She is appalled at the number of women in the room.

All of them were victims of Bardolph's abuse?

"You are more than welcome to join us here. We will get you some proper clothing, food, a bed, and a strong sisterhood."

"Thank you, your highness, but I do not plan on staying on this island for long," Althea states. This makes the table go quiet.

"Excuse me?" the princess asks.

"I am not going to stay here long. I will get off soon."

Darya snorts, then begins to laugh.

"You think you will get off this island? You are a fool!" Darya belittles Althea as some laugh along with Darya.

"I am not! I am going to find my brother and leave this place."

"Brother?" The princess is confused.

"Yes, my brother was brought here by Bardolph and hidden away. Once I find him, we will leave this place."

The princess puts her hand on Althea's wrist.

"Althea, no one except the sorcerers can leave this island. I have tried for many years as have the others. The only way one of us can escape this place is death," The princess claims. The room is quiet with heavy and dark truth.

"I can't believe that," Althea shakes her head.

"Some truths are harder to swallow than others. But you must accept this or you will waste so much time and energy," the princess claims. Althea furrows her brow, confused at how they can accept just a dreary outlook on the rest of their lives.

"I know this is heavy talk, but I do hope you will join us here. As you can see, we live well here and we are protected from men. Only those given permission may come here," the princess continues.

"If I stay here, then will I be allowed to look for my brother?"

"I do not see why not. But you should know to join us you will have to undergo a change to protect yourself," the princess states.

"A change?"

"Yes. Those who stay here are given a special gift," the princess chooses her words carefully.

"What sort of gift?"

"Well, it is a gift to protect us. It makes us unattractive to men who would wish to take advantage of us."

"I do not understand."

"We turn into swans," Darya blurts out.

"Swans?" Althea repeats.

"Yes. When we are touched by sunlight, we turn into swans, which keeps us safe. Then in the moonlight, we return to our human form."

"That sounds like a curse." Althea is blunt.

"It is just a blessing in disguise. If any of us stray from the grounds here, we are still safe from the men," the princess tries to make the situation better.

"But how do you change?"

"There is a curse on this place for women who live here. Spend one night and-poof!- you're a partial swan forever," Darya shares. Althea gulps at the situation.

"It is not a curse. You all know because of this none of us have been hurt again," the princess addresses the other women, rather frustrated with having to be defensive. They all nod in agreement. The princess is not wrong. The princess takes a breath, then looks at Althea again.

"So, you see, you can stay here at Sommerstern Castle and be as we are or you can try to survive on this island alone and more than likely be a victim of Bardolph again. I recommend you stay. But it is up to you."

Althea sits, considering the invitation. She is aware her ring should protect her from this swan curse, but she cannot be so sure.

Did Mother Huldah say curses were covered too, or am I mistaken? What if I stay and do not change? Will they think I'm a sorceress or spy? But it would be nice to not be forced to be near Bardolph. And if I'm here I probably won't get in trouble for running away. But there is a chance I could turn into a swan... What should I do?

Althea looks at the women at the table who eye her as they wait for her choice to be made. Excluding herself and the princess, there are twenty women. Twenty women have been brought to this island to be abused, then discarded by Bardolph. Althea knows there have been more women hurt by Bardolph.

How many girls died in Foxglove Grove village at the hands of Bardolph? I cannot even imagine the number of women he may have hurt around the rest of the Far Lands.

Looking at the women, she can see they are from different countries. Some even look to be from the Southern Continent and the Senyama islands.

Does his wickedness know no boundaries?

"Your Highness, is there any way to break the swan curse?" Althea inquires since if she must meet that fate, she will want a way to be rid of it.

"There is one way, but it is not one that can be done in a place like this," the princess answers.

"Still, what is it?" Althea questions.

The princess opens her mouth to answer, but the table begins to shake as the windows rattle and the chandeliers jingle. Althea grasps the table, unsure of why the room shakes. Many of the women hide beneath the table. The shaking stops just as suddenly as it had begun.

The glass doors in the room fly open, letting in a chilly breeze. Althea's head turns to look at the doorway.

Hadion stands at the doorway. His eyes go to Althea. He smirks, then runs a hand through his black hair as he walks close to the table. The princess stands up and faces the sorcerer. She comes between him and the table of mostly fearful women. His eyes slowly move from Althea to the princess.

CHAPTER 23

ALTHEA

"What are you doing here?" The princess demands to know glaring at the intrusive Hadion.

"It seems my guest has gotten lost and ended up here. I am here to collect her and return home with her," Hadion explains, holding his hand toward Althea. Darya looks at Althea appalled.

"This place is a sanctuary for women. You cannot take her back to that place to be abused." The princess steps in front of Althea.

"She is far from being abused," Hadion contradicts.

"If she goes back to Bardolph-"

"She is not for his entertainment," Hadion cuts off the royal. The princess raises a golden eyebrow.

"No?"

"No. Come, Althea." Hadion walks around the princess with his hand still out toward the maiden. Althea flushes. She does not take his hand.

"She is staying here. She will join our sisterhood," the princess interjects, despite Althea making no such claim.

"Is that so?" He lowers his hand.

"Yes." The princess nods. Hadion stares at Althea, who turns her eyes, finding his eyes to be too piercing. Hadion turns his attention to the princess.

"Your Highness." His words are formal but his tone is not. "I think we need to speak privately."

The seemingly fearless woman swallows, then nods in agreement. The princess follows Hadion to the opened doors. Once outside, they shut keeping the women separate from the couple.

"You are that man's lover!" Darya accuses Althea.

"No. No. Not at all!" Althea denies.

"Then why would von Rothbart want you?" the red-haired Rufina snaps.

"I-I-I don't know."

"He said you were not here for Bardolph, then you must be here for him. Why did you lie about being with Bardolph?" Darya looks ready to gouge out Althea's eyes with her soup spoon.

"Bardolph did bring me here but he never-we never- he couldn't…" Frazzled, Althea struggles to clear things up. "But I swear I am no one's lover."

A few roll their eyes or frown in disbelief just before the doors open again. All eyes are drawn to the entering princess. Her eyes are on the ground while her downturn lips give away her displeasure. Hadion on the other hand maintains an expression border-lining between arrogance and delight.

"Come, Althea," Hadion beckons her with an outstretched hand.

"But-" Althea starts.

"Go, Althea. You are not welcome here," the princess speaks up retracting her earlier statements.

"What?" Althea is baffled.

"You heard her. Now come." Hadion bends his fingers in toward his palm to wave her to him.

"But, your highness," Althea starts again.

"Go," the royal one orders, looking up with sad eyes. Althea swallows her disappointment and walks to Hadion. She slowly takes his hand. He begins to lead the young woman out of the room. She looks back at the women who gawk at them, excluding the princess, who does not look at the excited people at all.

Hadion shakes, and from his back slips out two large wings. Althea jumps at the unexpected sight of the pair of large, black feathered wings. Without warning, Hadion lifts Althea into his arms as if to cradle her.

"Hold on to me," he tells her. She does not obey until his jump and the flapping of wings takes him high into the air. She grasps his clothes and closes her eyes tightly. Her heart beats like a festival drum. She holds her breath as she feels them moving faster than a galloping horse. She can only liken the speed to when Bardolph whisked her off in his flying wolf form.

Hadion stops abruptly, but Althea is not jerked about in his arms. Then, as gently as a feather floating, the two reach the ground. Althea does not even feel when Hadion's feet settle on the green grass of Odile's courtyard.

"Must you also be carried inside?" Hadion's words make Althea open her eyes. Realizing they are no longer flying; Althea turns red at her clinging to this man.

"Let me go!" Althea demands, pushing away from him. He shrugs and drops his arms, causing Althea to fall to the ground. Althea glares up at Hadion who is not bothered by her foul look. He is rather amused.

"Come, come." He holds his hand out to her. Althea ignores his hand and comes to her feet on her own. She brushes off her chemise. Upon realizing she is only wearing a chemise; she covers herself with her arms. Hadion laughs.

"Do not fear, little flower. The shadow of your figure beneath that sheet will not drive me to ravish you," He snorts.

"I should hope not. I would think a man of your age would have self-control." Althea lowers her arms.

"My age?" He is confused.

"It does not matter. What lie did you say to the princess to cause her to cast me out?" Althea changes the subject.

"I only told her the truth. I am not fond of lying," he claims. 'Dubious' is the word Hadion would give Althea's expression.

"I know you must think a sorcerer such as myself would have no morals, unlike you followers of El-Yah. But I know the price paid for lies and I would rather not pay," he states firmly but sincerely. His sincerity is not lost on Althea.

"What truth did you tell her?" Althea still desires to know.

"That is private," he declines to answer. Althea purses her lips, displeased.

"What am I to do now that you have taken me from the others?"

"You will return to being Odile's companion." He walks toward the castle. Althea steps quickly to keep up with his long strides. "She has been worried about you since you disappeared. Do not do that again," he orders. Althea thinks of the maiden, who was far more welcoming to her than any of the other women.

"I did not mean to make her worry. I just wanted to look for my brother," Althea tries to explain her disappearance.

"You will not need to do that anymore."

"You have found him?" Her eyes light up in hope.

"No. But it is too dangerous to go around this island looking for him."

"I cannot be harmed." Althea stops when they reach the door to the stairwell.

"Odile can." Hadion reminds her of her voluntary seeker.

"I do not want Odile to be hurt or anything, but I must find my brother. I will do whatever it takes to find and save him."

"Is that so?" Hadion rolls his eyes and begins to open the door.

"Yes. I'll do anything to save him," Althea proclaims.

Hadion pauses the turns so he may make eye contact with the younger, smaller woman. His eyes shimmer for a moment, causing the hair on the back of Althea's neck to rise.

"Anything?" His voice is soft and husky. Her body seems to numb hearing his voice.

"Yes," she merely breathes the word.

"Even sell your soul?" He poses the question, his voice barely above a whisper. Althea stands silent, her brain slowly comprehends his query. Once it does, her lips open, though no answer is formed on them.

Would I sell my soul for Baz? She shivers.

"It will not come to that," Althea finally speaks

"And if it does?"

Althea lowers her eyes.

"Then I suppose your definition of 'anything' is different from mine," Hadion returns to opening the door. He leads the way up the stairs, with Althea following.

Is there a limit to what I will do for Baz? Is it wrong to value my own soul over his? Am I selfish? Would Stella give up her soul for Baz?

Having lost her mind to these thoughts, Althea does not notice she has reached Odile's bedroom door, or Hadion has stopped. Althea bumps into his back. She jumps back from him, coming back to her senses.

Hadion knocks on the door. It opens without anyone there. Hadion steps inside, with Althea following. The air is thick with the smell of elecampane. Odile is bent over a table with her face in a glass bowl full of water. She pulls her face out.

"I cannot find her even using this thing!" Odile whines, knocking the bowl off the table. Water and glass spread over the floor. Odile turns around, pouting. When her eyes move from her father to the woman with him, Odile loses her pout.

"You're back!" Odile glows. Althea cannot believe she had forgotten, even in this short time, how beautiful a girl Odile is.

"Yes." Althea nods.

"I knew you'd come back!" Odile rushes to Althea and embraces her.

"I'm sorry if I worried you. I was just out looking for my brother." Althea pats Odile's back awkwardly.

"You should have come to get me. I would have gone with you!" Odile pulls back from Althea but keeps her hands on Althea's arms. Her eyes look over Althea's body. "Good grief! Look at you. What happened to your clothes?"

"I..." Althea is unsure how to answer without speaking of the shipwrecked man. She does not believe Hadion knows of the man yet.

"This wasn't your handiwork, was it?" Odile questions Hadion.

"No." Hadion is not bothered with the accusation and leaves.

"Come, let us get you some night clothes," Odile starts to lead Althea to her closet. Odile waves her finger. The water and glass on the floor fix themselves and return to the table. Odile quickly changes Althea into a clean chemise, then wraps her in a silk robe lined with rabbit fur. The wet, sandy boots are removed and replaced with fur slippers.

"Were you able to find your brother?" Odile asks as she dresses Althea.

"No."

"We can try another time."

"Yes... your father does not want us to go look." Althea shares Hadion's opinion.

"Well, he often has work to attend to elsewhere. And when the hawk's away, we doves can play." Odile grins, mischief coming into her eyes.

"When will he leave again?"

"I do not know, but he is never here for too long. Bardolph will have to leave first. He does not like to leave when Bardolph is still here." Odile thinks about the man's scheduling.

"You're often here by yourself?"

"I have the servants and now I will have you." Odile smiles. Althea is not sure if she should be happy for Odile to have a companion or uncomfortable she is somewhat of a pet.

"You must be tired. I am as well. We should go to bed." Odile takes Althea's arm to escort her from the room. Althea does not resist the suggestion. Fatigue is upon her. Odile takes Althea into the greenhouse room. The plants give light to the entering women.

"Sleep well, Althea." Odile steps out of the room. Althea walks to the bed. She removes her robe and lies it on a chair in the room. She removes the slippers before getting into the swaying bed. Althea begins to relax in the cloud of a bed and rests her eyes when she hears a 'click'.

Althea sits up at the little noise. She flies out of the bed and to the door. However, when she reaches it, she taps the door's handle. She tries to open the door, but it does not move. She gives her hands more strength to try again. Alas, it is still secured.

"She locked me in?" Althea lets go of the handle.

I can't be so surprised. I did run away earlier, but still... Althea sighs and returns to bed as she must resign from this predicament.

***

The warmth of the risen sun streaming into the windows of her room and the faint clicking of the door again awakens Althea almost better than a crowing rooster. She shoots up in her bed but tries not to look as if she were bothered at all by her internment.

The door creaks open only for Odile to enter the room. She is already dressed in a pearl gray taffeta gown possessing two skirts styled to create a layered look and add a train. Her corset has a broad trim with gold, crimson, and mauve thread to create an intricate design going even into the front of the skirts. The gown and corset are richly decorated in pearls and precious stones. She wears no chemise, but from her golden shoulder straps come sleeves so long their hem nearly reaches her ankles. Odile's black hair is tied up into a high large bun with two large braids coming down to make intertwining circles at the base of her neck, while two smaller braids wrap around her bun. Two even smaller braid loops over the bun. In the middle is pinned a floral comb made of pearls and precious stones. Two sections of her hair are curled and let loose to frame her face. Her pierced ears hold large pearl earrings. On her feet are pearl gray slippers to match her dress.

Odile comes carrying clothing and shoes in her arms and hands. They are obviously not meant for herself.

"Good morning," Odile greets Althea, who returns the greeting. She lays the clothing on the bed. Althea climbs out.

"I have brought some proper clothes for you this morning." Odile pats the gown she has brought. Althea stares at the dress. A giddiness grows in her to see the dress is the pink one she desired the previous day. She reaches for it and then pauses. *Is it a treat in hopes of keeping me happy to stay Odile's pet?* Althea looks to Odile who seems happy and guileless. *It is probably just generosity.*

"Thank you," Althea finally touches the dress.

"I will help you dress after you take care of your morning needs," Odile offers. Relieved of her morning needs, Althea is ready. Working together, Althea is quickly dressed. Odile happily plays with Althea's hair. The result is a long bubble braid down her back while a small braid goes around her head like a circlet.

"Perfect. Now, we should go eat." Odile takes Althea by the hand to pull her from the room.

"Are we not going into the room?" Althea asks, pointing to the far room in the hall once she finds Odile is leading her in the opposite direction toward the stairs connecting to the main part of the castle.

"No. We are expected in the dining room," Odile shakes her head.

"And who is expecting us?" Althea dreads the answer she knows is coming.

"Just my father," Odile answers. Althea's stomach twists. She has not forgotten his question from last night.

"Can we not eat alone together?" Althea stops.

"No. My father is waiting and has made plans for us." Odile shakes her head again.

"What sort of plans?" Althea does not move.

"Lessons. Now come, I am famished," Odile pulls on Althea. The maidens make their way down. Before they enter the dining room, Althea can smell a medley of pork and tea. Coming into the room, Althea sees the table set with three place settings. One is at the head of the table and the other is on the left and right hands of the seat. Sitting already in his place at the head is Hadion. He rises at the sight of the ladies.

His sky-blue doublet with gold trim and embroidered gold mandalas is more fashionable than his simple knee-length blue trousers. His high black boots are well polished so they shine similarly to the gold garter chain and aquamarine jewels about his neck. His black curls are mostly pushed back but one stubborn curl comes down at the corner of his forehead. Some of his hair is tucked behind an ear allowing her to see he has small points at the top of his ears.

"Good morning," He welcomes them.

"Good morning, Father." Odile comes close enough to her father for him to kiss her cheek before she takes a seat at his left hand, her chair moving on its own for her to be seated in it.

Althea stands away from the table, unsure of her move.

"I see Odile has been more generous with her closet. You are a vision this morning, Althea." The compliment is not lost on Althea, who turns pink as her dress despite not wanting to show she was affected in any manner by his words. But of course, her body betrays her.

"Come, sit," Hadion offers the seat in his right hand. Althea comes to the available seat. When she sits, it moves on its own so she is closer to the table. She looks down to see a plate with two large sausage links, two pieces of bacon, three poached eggs, grilled tomatoes, fried mushrooms, buttered toast, black pudding, and beans. Three cups are set before her. One is a goblet of water, one is a cup of steaming tea, and the other is a glass of milk. There are jars of preserves on the table to be used as well. In addition to it all are a bowl of bright green apples.

Given what Odile had them eat for breakfast the day before, Althea thinks she should not be surprised by the spread, but she is. She is not sure if she will be able to eat it all. She looks to the other members of the table who eat without hesitation. Although they have started to eat, they do not eat like animals, but in a refined manner. There is no smacking, slurping, or burping. Althea watches for a few moments. How dazzling they both are. She wonders if she looks pleasant when she eats.

"Is something wrong with the food?" Hadion interrupts her observing.

"No. No." She quickly picks up a fork so she can start her meal.

"So, father, how long will I get to have you?" Odile looks over to her father.

"Well, seeing as I have ordered Bardolph to stay put for three months, I will be here for at least that long," He answers. Althea chokes on her poached egg when she hears the time limit. She coughs it up and embarrassedly covers her mouth with a napkin.

I have to postpone my search for three months!

"Are you well?" Hadion looks at the coughing Althea. She nods before taking a large gulp of her water.

"Three months is a long while," Odile comments to bring her father's eyes back to her.

"Do you not want me around that long?" Hadion raises an eyebrow.

"That is not it at all! I just don't want Bardolph around that long." Odile waves her hand to dismiss her father's thought.

"Well, we must give the rest of the world some respite." Hadion brings his tea to his lips. Odile smirks as she drinks some tea as well.

"You know your son wreaks havoc yet you do nothing more than make him sit around and wait, thus giving him more time to plot? Are you sure this is the proper way to deal with him?" The questions fly out of her mouth before she can bite her tongue. Odile bites her lip as Hadion turns his eyes to the one dressed in pink. He does not glare at her but maintains a civil expression.

"How many children do you have, Althea?"

"I do not have any."

"Have you ever taken care of children as a sort of governess, schoolmarm, or caregiver?"

"No."

"Then why do you speak about my parenting with such authority?" He poses the question.

"One does not need to be a parent or highly experienced with children to see the issue with the discipline of your son," Althea does not hold her tongue.

"How would you suggest I discipline my son, then?" Hadion leans on his fist and waits for her answer.

Althea opens her mouth but stops, as she cannot find a suitable answer. Bardolph is of age, he is powerful, and she knows not of the relationship between the father and son. It is surely not a great one, as Bardolph refers to his father by his name and not his paternal title. Yet she does know Hadion does have some authority in that he can confine Bardolph to this island for a time.

What could I recommend? Althea closes her mouth.

"Have you no advice for me?" Hadion's lips start to curl in the corners, pleased at her lack of an answer. Althea's tongue stays hidden in its fortress of protection. She lowers her eyes then raises them.

"I suppose I do not, for it should have been in your son's boyhood that you should have sought advice on discipline. It is clear by his actions now you did not." Althea's words jab at her host. He sticks his tongue into his cheek but keeps his eyes on the young miss. He inhales before speaking.

"I should have," He admits, then brings his tea to his lips.

"I think you have done a splendid job in raising me, father. I am not even a tad as horrid as Bardolph," Odile pipes up. Althea bites her tongue this time at the childishly vain claim. Hadion holds back a laugh with pressed lips as he lowers his tea cup.

"It amazes me at how self-aware you are, Dilly," Hadion pats his daughter's hand. Odile smiles proudly as if her father has confirmed her statement.

"Master," a brown-haired man-creature, comes to the table. His eyes are large as saucers and orange. His nose is hooked and starts to cover his thin lips. His brown skin is speckled with white spots.

"What is it, Tellu?" Hadion turns his attention to the other male. Tellu leans down and whispers into the ear of his master. Hadion sighs before Tellu pulls away.

"Excuse me, ladies. Do finish your breakfasts, then wait for me in your parlor, Odile," Hadion gives direction then leaves the table. Althea waits till Hadion leaves the table before speaking.

"What is he off to do?" Althea asks.

"I don't know. It could be an issue with one of the servants transforming or something." Odile takes a bite of one of her sausages.

"Hm..., I suppose you will do your lessons in your room this morning?"

"We will do them in my parlor."

"I see. And what will I do then? Stay in my room?"

"Oh, no. You will come with us," Odile smiles. Althea nods, though she is not sure she would like to see them do their dark lessons. Still, Althea eats her breakfast until she cannot squeeze another morsel into her mouth lest she burst.

Finished, the young ladies venture back to Odile's quarters and into her parlor. Althea takes a seat in a chair, as does Odile. Althea looks at the numerous books in the mirror room again.

"What sort of books do you have here?"

"Well, most are books for me to study, like herbology, herpetology, zoology, astrology, spells, etc., etc. I have some books of poetry I like but none interest me as much as my volumes of the histories of the world. I love reading about the places I have yet to go to as well as the fascinating events that took place. I especially like the tales of adventures." Odile fondly looks at the books on the shelves.

The door opens and Hadion walks into the room with a large book that looks to be bound by patches of different leathers. He lays it on the table. Odile stands to come to the table.

"What will you teach me today, Master?" Odile asks giving him the title an apprentice should.

"We shall be working on your levitating spells," Hadion decides.

"Levitating myself or objects?" Odile sets the options.

"Other people," Hadion gives the unknown third option. Odile immediately looks to Althea who in turn leans back.

"You do not mean me, do you?" Althea speaks up for herself.

"Not yet. Odile will begin with trying to levitate me." Hadion does not totally squelch the fact. Odile will try to levitate Althea.

"Is it the same incantation as before?" Odile looks at the book.

"Yes. See here. You must focus only on me to begin to raise me." Hadion points out the words on the page. Odile nods, then steps away from the table. Hadion walks away from the table and comes across from Odile. Althea watches, curious as to if Odile will succeed. Odile inhales and exhales deeply many times with her eyes closed, but she opens them and sets them on her father. She holds out her hand toward him before she begins to speak words unknown to Althea's ears.

Althea holds her breath in anticipation of the man in the room being lifted upward. The speaking goes on for five minutes and the man does not rise. Not even a hair on his head moves. Twenty more minutes pass and still there is no change. Althea wonders if magic always takes this long to work.

"Am I saying it wrong?" Odile asks her teacher once when she lowers her arms, dissatisfied with her work.

"No. You speak clearly and with great diction. Just keep trying," Hadion offers an encouraging smile to his pupil.

"Perhaps if I gave some blood-"

"There is no need for that. You need to learn to do this without extra help. Now, start again."

Odile raises her arms again and her voice.

Hours upon hours pass with the members of the room still waiting for Odile to change any part of Hadion's firm state. Althea has many times changed her position in her, watching as Odile has many times sought for some sort of correction. Each time, Althea notices Hadion, not to be bothered by the failure. Instead, he continues to be encouraging with his words and reassuring touches.

Surely it should not take hours of raising arms and speaking the same words repeatedly to get the spell cast? How is this difficult for someone who is not void like me?

There comes a question to Althea's mind.

The words Odile says, are they useless when said by someone like me?

Althea's hands are kept in her lap, but she secretly points a finger at Hadion. As Odile's now raspy voice stays loud and proud, Althea whispers the words.

"I-I-I did it!" Odile exclaims in glee as Hadion floats an inch off the ground. Althea stares, curling her pointed finger back into her palm. Hadion comes back to the ground.

"I did it. I did it!" Odile squeals in delight. Hadion smiles and pats her on the head.

"Go and fetch us some water now, Dilly," Hadion bids his daughter. She nods. Odile is so enthralled by her success she does not care if she is sent on an errand. She leaves the room.

Hadion walks to the chair across from Althea and sits. Althea keeps her hands folded neatly in her hands.

"I know what you did," He states.

"Hm?" Althea hopes he means something else.

"I heard you say the spell. I have excellent hearing. You did not tell me you could use magic," he focuses on Althea's eyes. She tries not to match his.

"I cannot use magic. I am void."

"Yet when you spoke, magic left you and lifted me," Hadion claims.

"It was Odile."

"I know what Odile's magic feels like. Your magic feels different. It was your magic that lifted me."

Althea finally meets his eyes. They hold no guile in them.

"That is impossible," Althea insists.

"It is not. You have fairy blood in you, don't you?"

"Yes, but it is not active in me. I cannot do the magic my sister does." Althea thinks about her lack of talent with feelings for others, and playing the pipe.

"So? Sometimes siblings do not share the same gifts. I see you have the gift of a compeller."

"What?"

"You have been gifted with an incredible beauty that makes people feel compelled by you. It is a gift often overlooked, as it is common among fairies. Have you not always been surrounded by those who favor you, especially once you look them in the eyes?" Hadion elucidates.

"Um... I suppose so, yes."

"Then you are not void. You have magic in you and magic you can use." Hadion is certain. Althea is at a loss for words.

"Odile will be back soon. I do not want to take away her little victory of the day, so I will not tell her it was you who levitated me. But should you want to learn to use magic, ask, and I will teach you," He offers. Althea keeps her mouth closed. Odile enters with water for the three of them. She happily passes them out before Hadion tells her to do it again.

As Odile tries again and again to lift her master, Althea looks down at her hands and wrists. She looks at the veins there. In them are the fairy blood. It is not as inactive as she thought.

So, I'm not void. But does this mean I should take on Hadion's offer to learn magic from him?

CHAPTER 24

The morning sunlight streams through the windows of Althea's temporary room onto the beautiful florals as well as the equally beautiful maiden. She has already dressed in the borrowed pink dress from the day before as she has no other dresses and does not seek to get another as this is lavish enough. She combs her hair with her fingers. The golden hair almost shines in the light. She thinks about what Hadion suggested the previous day. It plagued her all night. Should she allow him to teach her magic or should she resist?

Althea could imagine her parents standing right before her. Her mother would have her hands on her small waist and an angered expression on her otherwise beautiful face. Her father would have his arms crossed before his chest and a stony expression.

"No. No. No. Do not even think about it! This is all a ploy for-for something else. You can never trust a sorcerer! He will only lead you to destruction." Her mother would say. Her father would nod his head in agreement. They always seemed to agree on such matters. Of course, they would disapprove. They have never been supportive of anything to do with those who do not follow the way of El-Yah.

Althea could also see Stella there. She would probably hold a stance just like her mother but with a face more flabbergasted than angered. She would probably say, "How could you even consider this? His son is the reason our family suffers! He probably taught Bardolph all of this so isn't he also to blame?"

Basil would probably sigh and say one word. "Seriously?"

"I should not do it," Althea tells herself, having thought of her family. "If he asks me again, I will tell him 'No'."

Feeling resolute in her decision, Althea finishes her hair. A knock and click at the door alerts Althea to the arrival of Odile to the room. Althea beckons her to enter which Odile does instantly. The young sorceress in training glides inside in a white organza gown. The sleeves are large, puffed, and sheer. They have ruffles at their edge. The bodice is cut in a manner exposing much of Odile's collarbone and upper chest but the fabric covers that which would make her indecent. The bodice fits tightly around her chest almost to suppress the growths there. Just after her bust, the dress decides to puff out into a full skirt. It is surprisingly lovely on Odile despite the dress making Althea think of spun sugar. Her black hair is left down in loose curls as a contrast to the lighter colored dress.

"If you want another dress do not hesitate to go into my closet, Althea." Odile takes notice of the repeated outfit.

"Thank you, Odile, but I am completely fine in this dress."

"Suit yourself then." Odile shrugs.

"Since food was brought this morning, I assume we will not be meeting your father for breakfast." Althea looks at her empty plate once covered in fruits and pastries.

"Correct. Father wants us to meet him on the beach." Odile shares the new location.

"The beach?" Althea thinks of the beach she had been on to her day when she found the wounded man.

Would it be the same beach? Is that man well? Is he still with the swan women? Did he get kicked out? Did Hadion learn of him?

"Yes, we will go to the beach. Come." Odile walks out of the door with Althea right behind her. They go down to the garden of the Thirteen. Instead of going through Ender's gate, they stay close to the castle and go through another iron gate leading to more grounds. They walk far through these grounds till they reach an exterior stone stairway. It zigs and zags down a hill. As they go down, the sounds of the sea grow stronger in Althea's ears. Finally, they reach the beach. Althea finds the sand to be white instead of black. The sand sinks slightly with each step but Althea does not lose her balance as they walk closer to the blue water with small rolling waves. She looks back and sees the castle foundation is made atop a hard, rocky cliff.

At the water's edge stands Hadion. He wears his knee-high boots, a pair of black knee pants, and a white blouse with billowing sleeves fluttering in the sea's breeze. The red waistcoat he wears is buttoned up properly. He smiles as the women approach him.

"You look fetching in that new frock, Dilly." Hadion comments looking at his daughter.

"Thank you." She does a little twirl for him.

"You...you did not change, Althea," Hadion notes. Althea's cheeks burn as his piercing eyes run over her before returning to her eyes.

"I did not soil it so..." Althea is not as confident in choosing to repeat her outfit now.

"Sensible." He keeps a smile that gives Althea some ease.

"What are we to do today, Father?" Odile brings his attention back to her.

"You are going to practice your shapeshifting," He answers.

"Well, that won't be too hard." Odile smiles more excited about this task than the one from the previous day. "What will I be shifting into? A bird? A mouse? A cat?"

"A seal," He chooses.

"A seal?" Odile raises an eyebrow.

"Yes. You need to turn into a seal and swim about the sea without getting eaten or harmed by a predator," Hadion instructs.

"You want me to swim in the sea?" Odile looks at the water with widened eyes.

"You know how to swim," Hadion reminds her.

"Yes...but you don't usually let me swim in the ocean." Odile does not look away from the water.

"Today is a special exception as I want to make sure you can master this shift." Hadion pats her on the shoulder.

Odile swallows her words and looks back to her father.

"You can do this." He is positive. She nods and takes a deep breath. She takes a step back from him and Althea. She takes a few more deep breaths. Althea watches intently as Odile's black hair shrinks back into her head as her skin darkens and becomes spotted. Whiskers begin to sprout from her face. Her nose shrinks back till they are just two slits on her face. Her pink lips are replaced with thin black ones lining the large lumps on her face. Her eyes grow larger but do not lose their color. Her fit body grows larger and smooth. Fins replace her arms. The dress however does not rip. Instead, the dress changes to make her new body. It is as if it melds to her. Her legs come together and finish making the portly body. Laying on the beach, Odile is almost indistinguishable from any common seal except for her light eyes.

"Good. Now get in the water." Hadion points to the water. Odile turns her new body toward the waves. She somewhat bounces her way into the water. Both Althea and Hadion watch as Odile goes further into the sea.

"That was amazing. I did not know one could shapeshift with their clothes as well." Althea keeps looking at the swimming seal.

"Only untrained shifters cannot shift their clothes," Hadion comments.

"I guess Tyr is not trained," Althea tells herself.

"Tyr?" Hadion catches the name. "Who is that? Your lover?"

Althea laughs. "No. No."

"Then who is he?"

"He is a shifter traveling with my sister and me." Althea thinks of the once cursed horse man.

"You fancy this shifter?"

"No," Althea answers lightly. She does not feel inclined romantically toward Tyr though she supposes she is fond enough of him to be his friend.

"Why not? Do you have a lover somewhere else?"

Althea looks from the sea to Hadion whose eyes are still on his shifted daughter.

"Why do you care?"

"Who says I do?" He turns to meet her eyes and smirk.

"You ask many questions like a man who cares."

"Can a man not just be curious?" he responds.

"I have no lover." Althea looks back to the sea though she cannot see Odile now.

"I know you are not lying but I admit I am surprised."

"Why is that?" Althea turns her eyes to him but not her face.

"Look at you."

Althea rolls her eyes. If she has heard a compliment about her looks once she has heard it a thousand times.

"You are beautiful, but even in this short time of knowing you, I have found you are rather resilient, brave, and kind, well, kind to Odile," He lists her virtues causing her to turn her whole face so she can look better at him. She stares into his eyes. She inhales deeply but quietly.

"Such traits in a woman are desirable. When these are put into such a body as divine as yours, it is a wonder you and your heart have not been claimed." His fingers push back some of her hair the wind has blown out of place. They rest on her cheek. The colorful spots in his eyes twinkle as if they were gems being shined with light.

"Is it because you know no common man is worthy of you?"

"Yes," the words slip out though she does not know why she speaks to agree with him.

"That is a bit vain, isn't it?" He snickers. The change in tone causes Althea to blink and end her eyes' fixation on his. She pushes his hand away.

"I am not vain. I just have high self-esteem. I will not allow myself or my heart to be claimed by any common man who may want me. I know my worth and I will wait to meet someone who not only sees my worth but proves his own to me," Althea claims, earning silence from Hadion. His judgmental smirk shifts into a smile.

"I see. I was wrong." He swipes back some of the curls bouncing against his forehead in the wind. "It is good you know your mind."

"Yes."

"Then you should know if you want to learn magic from me," He brings up the topic she dreads.

"I do."

"So? When do you want to start?"

"Oh, I do not want to start."

"What?" His face falls.

"I do not want to learn magic from you?"

"Why not?"

"Because...my family would be displeased."

"Are they here?" He looks around as if they should be anywhere close but clearly, they are not.

"No."

"Then how could they know?"

"I am pretty sure when I am reunited with them, they will want to know where I learned magic."

"They would be happy to know you are not void," he counters.

"No. Not if it is magic taught by-" Althea stops herself.

"By what? A handsome man?" he finishes for her with a rather vain smile.

"By a sorcerer," Althea corrects. Hadion pauses.

"I see...Your family...are they religious?"

"Yes. We all follow El-Yah."

"Yes. I should have remembered since you mentioned praying to El-Yah when we met with Bardolph," he recalls.

"Yes..." Althea also remembers the meeting.

"So do you follow El-Yah because of your family?"

"What?" Althea is rather shocked by the question.

"I know many people follow the way of their parents as they are either not taught any other way or find it easier than finding their own way."

"I-I do not follow El-Yah just because my family does," Althea is not sure if she should be insulted by his questioning of her faith.

"Did you live your life and one day heard of El-Yah and changed? Or did you research all the different faiths and pick that one as it lined most well with what you wanted to believe? Or did you have an encounter with him?"

"I-um...I..." Althea stops as she tries to find an answer.

Why do I follow El-Yah? I have only ever been taught to follow El-yah but it's not like I only believe what Mother and Father said to believe. When I studied other faiths, I did not care for them. I have had no encounter with El-Yah either. So...why do I believe in El-Yah?

"I have not gone through any of that so I cannot explain why," Althea admits, her eyes lowering as if ashamed.

"Then maybe you should try to learn more so you can make a more informed decision," Hadion suggests, causing Althea to raise her eyes.

"Who do you follow then? Or do you not believe in gods?"

"I am not foolish enough not to believe there isn't something out there," He scoffs.

"So, who do you follow?" Althea seeks an answer.

"You call him the Fallen One. I call him Eous," Hadion answers. Althea's body tenses at the name.

"I know you must have been raised hearing the story of Eous's fall and how he only wreaks evil since," Hadion assumes.

"Yes, of course," Althea's mind goes to the many times she was told by her mother and father of the Fallen One.

"But that is merely based on the perspective of followers of El-Yah."

"Oh? And what is your perspective on the one who calls for blood and death?" Althea does not know why she spits out the facts she has been told about the followers of the Fallen One.

"My dear delicate flower, don't you know everything comes with a price?"

Althea frowns at the phrasing of the question and his continuation with the pet name.

"Nothing is free, especially power and magic. That is why I am willing to shed a little blood here and there to strengthen myself."

"Well, fairies don't have to do that and I didn't shed any blood to perform that little magic before," Althea points out to him.

"Their magic is inherited in their blood. They and you can do a little magic due to your naturally born abilities but you will find unless they sacrifice their time and free will they do not gain more."

"Their free will?" Althea raises an eyebrow.

"Fairies are required to follow a strict code of conduct. They are not free to make their own choices. They make themselves slaves to an oppressive dogma and a deity who does not care about them."

"You think El-Yah does not care about us?"

"Correct."

"Then do you believe the Fallen One cares about you?"

"No. I don't," He shakes his head. Althea stands still so confused.

"Then why follow him?"

"Following him has led to my enlightenment, power, and freedom."

"And you could not have that by following El-Yah?" Althea crosses her arms.

"No. Haven't you noticed those who follow El-Yah forgo their wants and desires to follow oppressive rules?"

"I don't know if they are oppressive..." Althea disagrees.

"Come on, how many times have you or those you know who follow El-Yah restrain from doing something because of fear of displeasing El-Yah?"

Althea's cheeks color as she can think of many times she or her family prevented her from doing many things for the sake of not breaking one of El-Yah's laws. Even her dancing in the Zola Festival with Tyr was something most followers of El-Yah would disapprove of despite her having no faith in the Thirteen.

"I can tell it has been many times," Hadion comments. Althea nods affirming this.

"With Eous it does not matter what I do. I do not have to seek any forgiveness or permission. I do what I want when I want and do not have to fear anything. I give a little blood here and there but I am always making more blood," Hadion chuckles with his last statement. Althea absorbs his words with a closed mouth and eyes settled more on the sand beyond Hadion's body than on Hadion.

Is the way of El-Yah truly repressive? Is it better to follow the other as there is more freedom? But with the Fallen One, the price is paid in blood...

Much splashing makes the duo on the beach look to the sea. Odile has swum back to the shore still in her seal form. She looks to Hadion for instructions.

"Now, turn into a bird and fly to the far side of the island then back here," Hadion gives the orders.

"But I just did so much swimming," the seal pants.

"You must build endurance, Odile," Hadion pushes. The seal nods. With a deep breath the silky, spotted seal begins to shrink and sprout black wings. The rounded head and face become oblong with a long beak. Her neck stretches. Althea admires the beauty of the now black-feathered swan.

Odile quickly takes to the sky. Althea watches as the swan flies away. Hadion watches as well. Once Odile is out of sight Althea looks back to the sorcerer.

"Why is it you have to use blood?" Althea's question makes Hadion blink and turn his attention to her.

"It is just payment."

"But why do you have to make a payment?"

"Because our natural power is limited. We need power from a superior being. We shed some blood, say some words, and we have it," Hadion simplifies the process.

"I did not see Odile shed blood to shift or yesterday when she was trying to levitate you."

"Odile is squeamish when it comes to blood, well, her blood," Hadion laughs.

"Then how can she do beyond her natural abilities?"

"She practices diligently. That is how fairies get their magic. They practice their spells over and over. But that is why Odile and fairies do not surpass sorcerers and sorceresses who do blood magic," Hadion explains the difference.

"If I wanted to learn magic but not give blood, would I be able to do it?"

"Yes, and even though I think you would excel in blood magic, I am willing to teach you as I teach Odile without it. Besides, with your ring of protection, you could not give blood," Hadion offers and reminds.

"Will I have to convert to the Fallen?" Althea voices her other concern. Hadion pauses for a beat.

"No."

Althea presses her lips together as she considers this information. She is not exactly sold on the Fallen ways but would it hurt to learn magic if she does not have to stop following El-Yah, does not have to give blood, and can help save her brother?

"Althea," Hadion calls her name drawing her eyes to his face. Her lips relax only for her teeth to lightly bite her lower lip. Everything from the the curve of his lips to the softness in his eyes to the dark curls framing his face just makes her want to keep staring at him. He is entirely too handsome but she would not necessarily say that is a bad thing.

"Althea," he says her name again and takes her hand in his large one. His skin is warm despite being in the wind for so long as her cold hands. The hairs on the back of her neck stand before a rush of heat goes down her spine.

His dark eyes suck hers in again. They sparkle and shine. The colors in his iris almost dance. Her body grows slacker.

"Let me be your master and I will show you the wonders you are capable of," His voice is soft but rich.

No voice but his is in her head when speaks. Nothing in her says to decline.

"Will you say 'yes', Althea?" he poses the question, his face coming closer to hers as his free hand comes to hold her cheek.

"Yes," She does not hesitate. His lips curl up pleased with the answer.

"Excellent," He murmurs. He slides his hand down from her cheek to her shoulder. Once Hadion blinks his eyes, Althea blinks her eyes several times. She steps back, moving her hand from his and her body from his other hand.

"W-when do we start?" Althea tucks her hands behind her back.

"Now, if you like. Odile will be taking some time," Hadion brings up the absent girl.

"I-I guess we could start now."

"Grand. Let's begin," he smiles.

Hadion takes large steps as he turns and backs up to be at her side. He begins to put his arms around Althea. She stiffens as he does as she does not understand why he is starting to touch her.

"Does learning magic require you to hold me?" Althea questions his method.

"I am merely trying to support you," He speaks tenderly. Althea does not relax unlike before when he held her hands.

"Support me in what?"

"Support you as we begin. It can be physically taxing sometimes," Hadion gives more reason for his touch.

"Oh..." Althea accepts his reasoning.

"Now, when you are going to use magic, you need to follow four steps," Hadion begins. Althea takes a step forward and counts it.

"What are you doing?" Hadion steps up with her.

"You said to take four steps," Althea answers earnestly, earning a laugh.

"Not physical steps."

"Oh," Althea blushes. Hadion's laugh dies down.

"I will try to be clearer with my teaching," he gently pats her upper arms.

Althea nods.

"When you start using magic you need to follow four steps, not literal ones. The first is focusing. You must be able to focus. You need to cut out all distractions from your mind. Most find closing their eyes helpful to this when beginning," Hadion offers a tip. Althea closes her eyes as suggested.

"Now, I want you to tune out everything and focus on your breathing. Do not listen to the waves crashing, the seagulls flying near, or any other sound. Ignore the feeling of the wind and my hands on you. Ignore the smell of the sea air. Focus only on your breathing. Breathe deep. Breathe clear. Once it is all you know, speak," Hadion instructs.

Althea keeps her eyes closed. She purposefully inhales and exhales deeply. However, doing as Hadion says is harder than it seems. Each crash of the waves seems to roar louder than the last in her ear. The passing seagulls practically scream to each other now that her eyes are closed. The wind has sure picked up as well bringing with it a salty and almost fishy scent. However, another scent overpowers the sea. It is the smell of citrus, cedar, jasmine, sandalwood, and amber. It lightly exudes from Hadion as if he were a flower near her nose. It is far more inviting than the sea. It grows stronger as she feels his chest against her back and his arms over hers. But she is to ignore it, ignore it all. She must only focus on her breathing.

In....out...in...out...in...out...in...out...in...out...

The seagulls' song begins to fade as does the sound of the waves.

In....out...in...out...in...out...in...out...in...out...

Her body grows numb to the wind and to Hadion's touch.

In....out...in...out...in...out...in...out...in...out...

The wind's salty smell leaves her nose but Hadion's scent still lingers. It is sweet but bitter and masculine. It is entirely too enticing. But she must ignore it.

In....out...in...out...in...out...in...out...in...out...

He is almost gone.

In....out...in...out...in...out...in...out...in...out...

"In...Out..." She speaks aloud now all is gone except her breathing.

"Now, visualize what you want to do," Hadion says, making his voice the only thing she hears beside her breathing.

"Like what?"

"Like drawing the water to us," Hadion speaks when the water is rather far from where they stand. "See it in your mind. Visualize the water coming to our feet at your command."

"And then?" She asks her eyes still closed.

"Then believe you can do it. Believe you can control the waves. Believe then command it."

"How?" Althea seeks what will make it possible. Hadion whispers a phrase into her ear. It is the language she has heard him and Odile use when they have performed magic. Althea nods and begins to envision the beach in her mind. She pictures the water rushing to her feet. She keeps on with her deep breathing. She lifts her hands so they are stretched out toward the water.

I can do it. She begins to whisper the spell. The water does not come.

"Louder," Hadion advises. She does so but the water does not come to her feet.

"Speak clearly and confidently," Hadion further instructs. With head high and back straight, Althea loudly speaks the spell.

"Ah!" She squeals, feeling a wave crash into the hem of her dress. She opens her eyes delighted to see despite being so far from the water, she made it come to her.

"I did it! I did it!" Althea turns around to look at Hadion. Her eyes are lit in her amazement and glee. Hadion smiles pleased as well.

"Splendid, Althea. Now do it again," He turns her around by her shoulders. Althea closes her eyes and begins breathing again.

In....out...in...out...in...out...in...out...in...out...

She tunes out everything and then pictures the water in her mind. She visualizes waves coming to her feet again. She holds her hands out. She repeats the words Hadion told her the first time. She speaks with a great commanding tone. Feeling the cold water splash her, she smiles delighted with her success again.

"Again," Hadion whispers in her ear. Althea sets to it again. Over and over, she finds she is successful in bringing the water to her now-soaked feet. It is no bother though. How can it be when it is proof, she can now do magic?

"Here comes Odile," Hadion touches Althea's arms so she will lower them. Althea opens her eyes and turns her head so she can look at the sky. Hadion removes his hands from her arms and steps back to give some space between himself and his new student.

The black wings shine in the sunlight hitting the swan flying toward them. As Odile begins her descent, she stretches out her wings as a sort of parachute to help her slowly and gracefully fall to the sand. As her webbed feet reach the sand, she takes a few steps and flaps her wings before finally stopping. Now stopped, she lifts her wings and slowly shifts back into her naturally beautiful human self.

"I have done as you asked," Odile looks at her teacher almost out of breath. He pats her on the shoulder.

"Very good."

"Odile, look what I can do!" Althea excitedly speaks up drawing Odile's attention from her master to the blonde. Althea closes her eyes and repeats the lesson she learned. When the water hits her feet, Althea opens her eyes with a wide smile to look at Odile.

"I thought you were void." Odile's forehead wrinkles.

"I have just recently found I am not." Althea keeps a smile.

Odile's eyes go from the blonde maiden to the man. She does not smile like Althea. Instead, she has a rather stony expression.

"You are teaching her magic?"

"Yes."

The familial duo keeps their eyes on each other but remains silent. Neither one breaks eye contact. Althea watches the staring contest not sure why it is even happening.

"I think you should go to your rooms and study up on some spells." Hadion breaks the awkward silence. Odile sneers in displeasure but starts to walk away.

"Use your wings," Hadion gives the little order. Bursting out of her back comes a set of beautiful, large black feathered wings. Odile takes off flying toward the castle.

"Is Odile upset?" Althea immediately asks while Odile is away.

"Yes. She is jealous she will not have my undivided attention now that I have a new student," Hadion answers. Althea frowns.

"I don't want to do this if it is going to cause issues between you and Odile." Althea puts her hands behind her back.

"Do not worry. Odile never stays upset with me for long. She is not one for grudges," Hadion praises the other girl.

"That is good to know."

"You should get back to practicing." Hadion gestures to the water. Althea agrees and starts breathing with closed eyes. Time flies but Althea hardly notices. She only knows she finds her control over the water to be easier and the small portion of water she could draw toward her has grown. By the time Hadion puts his hand on her shoulder to tell her it is time for them to go back to the castle, she can raise, curl, and crash large portions of water onto the beach.

"Well done," Hadion praises.

"What will you teach me next?" Althea turns to him eagerly.

"We are going to focus on the elements for now, specifically water and earth."

"Then fire and air?"

"Yes. But they are a bit more difficult so it may take a week before we get to that," He answers.

"I see. So, after this week, I should be a master of water and earth control?"

Hadion snorts but tries to cover his mouth with the back of his hand.

"What? Why is that funny?"

"It takes years to master an element, especially when it is not your natural gift."

"Years?"

"Yes. That is why those with fairy blood should begin training as children so by the time they are in their teenage years they will be masters of basic magic and get to turn their studies to specific areas of magic that interest them," Hadion explains.

"Is there not an accelerated way to study and master magic for late starters like myself?" Althea inquires.

"There are some avenues but I doubt you would like them," he replies.

"What are they?"

"Well, you can make a blood pact but we both know you are unwilling and physically incapable of doing that. You can begin an intensive course of training but that will be physically and mentally draining. Of course, the more natural talents you have the easier magic comes to you. However, as you only have the natural gift of compelling, it probably will not be as easy as it would be for one such as me who has all but two gifts," He brings up the options.

"What two do you lack??"

"Feeling and air just as Bardolph said he was missing."

"You two have the same amount?"

"Yes, as does Odile."

"But she struggles even with the many gifts. But you said it would be easier with more gifts." She brings up his words.

"Yes...well, when it comes to her natural gifts, she does well enough to get by but she struggles to be the master of them. My father said it was because Odile's mother lacked fairy blood," Hadion mutters the last sentence. Althea is surprised at Hadion bringing up the person she has yet to see on this island.

"So...she was human?"

"Yes. But Odile has my blood and gifts. She can do more."

"Did Odile spend her childhood learning magic or did she wait?"

"She started in childhood but even then, she struggled. Like I said before she is squeamish about blood so I cannot help her accelerate that way."

"Why not do the intensive one then?"

"I...I cannot do that with her," He shakes his head.

"Why not?"

"I am her father."

"Is it so intense you fear hurting your child by it?" Althea is rather touched he cares so much for his child to not put her through such a mental and physical challenge.

"I suppose so...There are many lessons in it that I do not think are right for a father to teach his daughter," Hadion adds more to his reasoning.

"But if I asked for the intensive course, would you teach me?"

"I doubt you could handle it," He snorts. The suggestion of her lack of ability to handle some mere magic lessons stirs something in her. Her eyebrows sink as her lips purse in a sour expression.

"You think I can't handle it? Why? Because I am too new to magic? You said yourself I have great promise!" Althea starts to bring up his words.

"It's not that." Hadion turns his eyes from her but keeps an arrogant look.

"What then? Because I have too few gifts? Because I am young? Because I am not a part of the Fallen? What is it?" Althea lists a few other options standing up frustrated.

"It's none of that either."

"Then what? What is it about me that makes you think I could not handle it?" Althea steps up to him with her fists on her hips. She is not quite sure why she is angered by his lack of faith in her but it is too late for her to change her feelings.

He tenderly grasps her jaw. He has her look up at him. He leans over bringing his face so close that with a single purse of a lip, their lips would touch. Althea freezes in his hold to not accidentally kiss him. Her breath becomes ragged in anticipation. Her racing heart bumps so much blood it becomes evident underneath her skin. Althea closes her eyes to prepare for contact. Althea feels the rough friction of his face against her cheek as his lips move to her ear.

"You are too innocent, little flower," He whispers. Althea pushes him back from her with skin still pink as the inside of a grapefruit.

"I am mature and I am capable of this accelerated course of training." Althea is determined to prove this man wrong. He grins wickedly.

"Then I will let you try to prove me wrong."

"Good!" She crosses her arms over her chest.

"Good."

"When will we start?"

"We will begin now. Go to Odile's room and memorize every spell in her spell book."

"What?" Althea raises an eyebrow unimpressed with the challenge.

"Memorize every spell," He repeats.

"Okay...and then what?"

"Then we will start to use them," He answers in a matter-of-fact tone.

"So, I memorize spells over the next weeks then we will do them? That does seem too h-"

"No. You will memorize them in the next three days."

"What? Three days!" Althea balks at the time constraint.

"Yes. If you do not want to go slowly then we cannot spend weeks learning phrases."

Althea frowns at the challenge but does not want to back down from it either.

"Fine," Althea sighs, her arms going down to her sides.

"Excellent. Now, if you fail on your first task then I will stop teaching you magic altogether and have you go back to being a scullery maid," Hadion adds.

"What!" Althea balls her hands into fists.

"Do not be so upset. You can do it..." He pats her shoulder as he begins to pass her then looks back at her over her shoulder. "Maybe."

Hadion keeps walking away.

"I can and will do it! You'll see, Hadion. I will memorize every spell in that book!" Althea proclaims.

"We will see..." He shrugs.

"I will, Hadion!" She yells after him. He stops and looks over her shoulder.

"Oh, one more thing, Althea."

"What?" She puts her fists back on her hips.

"It's 'Master' to you," He winks then walks on his way. Althea scowls at his back.

Althea stomps up to Odile's tower and finds the young woman at a desk reading from a large brown book. Althea walks directly to Odile.

"Althea, what is wrong?" Odile sees her displeasure.

"Where is your spell book?" Althea asks.

"Right here. Why?" Odile pats the massive book she has on her table. Althea gulps and the incredibly thick book.

"I made a deal with your father and I must learn every spell in that book in the next three days," Althea informs the young sorceress in training.

"Oh, Althea. What have you done?"

CHAPTER 25

Of the forty sea ports in Zeemaa, the grandest is at Queen's Harbor. It is no surprise this coastal city is the capital of the country with its caverns of black pearl-producing clams, easy-to-maneuver canals, and vibrant art scene. But it is not Queen's Harbor where Hajnal and her friends arrive. They come to southern border of Zeemaa at Port Whitrock.

Finding shelter at an inn, Hajnal and Zarin take a rest along with Tyr while Sir Artegal and Prince Astrophel volunteer to find a ship to charter.

"Thou should not use thy true name when we speak with the captains. We do not know if we can trust them," Sir Artegal watches every man they pass on the way to the docks.

"I agree. I shall be Mr. Sidney like my father before me," Astrophel decides on his alias.

"There is the dock master. He should be able to help us." Sir Artegal points to a little box not far from them where a man sits with a little lantern hanging high and a smoking pipe in his mouth.

"Excuse us, sir, where might we find a captain to take us to Koralia?" Sir Artegal speaks first.

"Depends, are ya lookin' for a leisure or somethin' quick?" The dock master lays out the option.

"Quick," Prince Astrophel answers.

"Well, the *Aldegonda* leaves to sail across Dream Bay in four days. She's pretty quick. Captain Klerken can get ya there in a week."

"Is there anything that will leave sooner and will take less than a week?" Prince Astrophel presses.

"No." The man shakes his head and takes a puff of his pipe.

"Not even for a generous benefactor?" Sir Artegal asks.

"The safest route takes a week or more."

"But the map shows Port Ondabianca should be reached in a day from here," Sir Artegal points to the map of ports hanging in the little box.

"Ya have to go through the Mermaid's Lair to do that. No man in his right mind would that. Especially in mermaid mating season," the man shakes his head the stops, "Well...actually, I think I might know someone."

Sir Artegal and Prince Astrophel leaned in interested.

"His name is Captain Kolar. He'll be down at Moll Doll with what's left of his crew. If you've got the money, he's got the ship and the balls to do what you want," The man crudely remarks.

"Thank you, sir. Where is the Moll Doll?" Sir Artegal asks. The man points out the direction. The young men thank the older one and depart.

"I do not know if we should go to such a place, Astrophel," Sir Artegal doubts as they reach the large wooden building. The sounds of singing and congress can be heard from outside.

"I know it is a den of iniquity but...if this will help Hajnal, I must do it." Astrophel takes a big step forward then looks back at Sir Artegal with a sheepish grin. "But we do not have to tell her we came here."

Sir Artegal smirks. "No, we do not."

The men enter and greeted with a waft of tobacco, beer, and cheap perfume. Some women dance and sing in nothing but their undergarments while men laugh and watch. Astrophel keeps his eyes on the floor.

"We should speak to the barkeep," Sir Artegal looks across the room to the bar. Astrophel nods but keeps his face lowered. They reach the bar.

"What can I get ya?"

"Do thou know of a Captain Kolar?" Sir Artegal asks.

"Over there," the barkeep points to a dark-haired man with bright blue eyes drinking a pint of ale.

"Stay here and I will negotiate."

Astrophel agrees not wanting to see more than the wood of the bar. Many women approach and try to coax a conversation from the man who is by far the most handsome in the room if not the whole town. However, when he would speak with them with his eyes closed they parted from the bizarre man.

"Mr. Sidney," Sir Artegal returns to Astrophel's side. Astrophel turns to the voice and opens his eyes. "Mr. Sidney, this is Captain Kolar," Sir Artegal introduces Astrophel to the other man.

"Hello," Captain Kolar salutes Astrophel with two fingers. Astrophel nods to him.

"I'll show you my ship," Captain Kolar waves and slightly stumbles away.

The men walk together until they reach the end of a pier where a ship is anchored and waiting to be boarded. The large boat is not especially new as can be seen by its chipped and faded paint. The sails look to have been patched. The topless woman at the front has a face showing the carpenter who made her was not exactly trying to go for beauty. There is an odor that wafts from the ship as the wind blows. The smell is like a mixture of manure and oakum, salt, and tobacco.

"This is my new ship the *Marisa*. Will she do for you?" Captain Kolar is more than proud of the vessel. Sir Artegal and Astrophel look before nodding in agreement.

"Good. It will take me the night to get the crew together. We will sail by the afternoon's high tide so be here by noon," Captain Kolar states.

"We will."

"How many will be in your party?" the captain questions.

"Three men and two women," the dark-haired one answers.

"Women?" The captain raises his eyebrows.

"Is there a problem?" the blond inquires.

"No. I guess not. We've had women on board before, it's just the women...are they beautiful?" the captain checks. Astrophel begins to gain a displeased look.

"They are. What of it?"

"I just want to make sure they are worth risking bad luck is all," the captain laughs. The other men do not.

"We will see thee at noon," Sir Artegal gives a bag of money to the captain. He peaks and finds gold. He grins.

"Oh, wait. I need your names for my log," the captain remembers.

"I am Artegal Belamour," Sir Artegal one gives his identity.

"And you?" the captain keeps his eyes on the blond.

"Leander Sidney," he answers.

"I look forward to our adventure, Sirs."

Sir Artegal and Astrophel nod and go on their way. Captain Kolar grins devilishly having secured such a lucrative contract. He pulls a piece of gold from the sack and takes a bite. Feeling it bend in his teeth he knows the gold is good. He puts it back in the bag and ties it to his waist.

"I better get them lazy maggots working," Captain Kolar mutters to himself as he boards the ship. He is quick to rouse the men sleeping below deck. He set them to work despite their moaning and complaints.

"You lot," he addresses four of his crewmen, "Go into the taverns and find drunk able-bodied men. Bring them back here."

"Yes, Captain," They nod. Captain Kolar returns to his quarters.

Sitting on the bed with her hands in her lap is a young woman with long black her. Her skin is tan with golden undertones. Her eyes are large and light brown. She wears a simple dress but a golden bracelet on her wrist. Everything about her is so close to what he wants but she is still not the one he desires most.

"Welcome home." She forces a smile.

"Take off my boots, Nafisa." He sits on the bed. She quickly slips off it and begins removing his shoes. "We got a contract. We'll be sailing off tomorrow."

"Will we be going back to Gold Haven?" She looks up hopefully. He grabs her face roughly, bringing tears to her eyes.

"You would like that, wouldn't you? I bet you'd try to run off back to your family. As if they'd take back an ungrateful, sullied cow like you." He lets go of her face. She looks away from him.

"We are not going to Gold Haven then."

"Correct. We are going to Koralia. The men who hired me have promised a great sum of money. I will be able to buy a new ship in Koralia and if you're a good girl, I might even buy you something nice."

"Another cursed obedience bracelet?" She mutters and earns a slap across the face. He grabs her by the wrist where the bracelet is.

"Do not forget I saved you, Nafisa. You owe me more than just your obedience." He bares his teeth at the cowering woman.

"Captain," His first mate, enters the room and draws all attention to himself.

"Can't you see I'm in the middle of something here, Phan!' Captain Kolar looks over his shoulder to the quartermaster.

"I see, but there are more important things you need to do right now."

"Like what?"

"Like help us fix the leak in the bottom of the boat," Phan answers.

"There's a leak! Why did no one say anything sooner!" Captain Kolar releases Nafisa and quickly puts his boots back on his feet. Nafisa rises to her feet and steps away from the captain.

"Go sit in the desk chair and don't move until I return," He orders.

Nafisa's body begins to move on its own. She takes her spot in the chair. She sits still and unmoving. She wants to speak up and move out of it but no matter how much she mentally tries, she cannot. She is stuck as if she were encased in amber.

"Much better," Captain Kolar smirks then leaves the room. He does not return anytime soon. After fixing the leak there was the matter of putting golden bracelets on the unconscious crewmen who are brought aboard.

By noon, the *Marisa* is set to leave with the nearing high tide. The captain stands proudly on the main deck. He watches the large man he recognizes as Mr. Belamour come aboard with the other man he remembers as Mr. Sidney. Another man of clear Senyama descent stands near two women who have their backs to the captain. He sees the curviest maiden to have a long braid down her back while the other, small woman hides her hair in a cap.

"Mr. Sidney, Mr. Belamour, welcome aboard!" Captain Kolar approaches the beautiful, men with a wide smile.

"Thank thee, Captain," Astrophel offers a small smile.

"Who have you brought aboard with us today?" He looks at the other members.

"This is Tyr Dahl," Astrophel gestures to the man at his side. He then turns to introduce the women but only the woman with the uncovered head has turned around. The captain is surprised to see the violet eyes she possesses. "This is my betrothed, Hajnal."

Captain Kolar gives her a gentlemanly bow which she accepts with a nod of her head.

"And this is-" Mr. Sidney looks to the other maiden who has yet to turn around. Hajnal puts her hand on the other woman's shoulder. She slowly turns around with her head high.

Captain Kolar loses his breath as his eyes recognize the golden eyes, plump lips, and pleasant face. Oh yes, he knows this face. It has plagued his mind for years. It is the face that has overtaken all of his fantasies. It is the face that caused him to be drawn to taking Nafisa. He knows this woman.

"Zarin," He addresses her before her introduction can be finished. The woman looks at him coldly.

"Captain Kolar."

CHAPTER 26

Hajnal

Great unease comes upon Zarin as she boards the ship called *Marisa*. Though she has never been on this ship before, the smell and movement beneath her feet as she came aboard reminds her all too well of the ship she had once lived on years ago. Even thinking of it makes her want to vomit.

"Is something wrong?" Hajnal asks, putting her arm around Zarin.

"It has been a long time since I've been on a ship." Zarin touches her unsettled stomach.

"I understand. It has been a few years for me too. This smell does not help," Stella addresses the odor.

"Perhaps looking at the solid land will help," Hajnal suggests and turns with Zarin to look over the side of the boat toward the solid land.

"Who are you?" Ludo, one of the sailors, walks up to the newest people to board the ship in a puffed-up manner as if to try and intimidate these people.

"We are the ones who booked passage on this ship to Koralia" Sir Artegal answers, slightly offended by the attitude.

"You lot?" Ludo looks them over then turns around. He walks to a tall but rather rotund man with thick, white mutton chops, and skin damaged from years of exposure to the sun. The man walks away.

"I see the captain coming," Astrophel informs the little group. Zarin and Hajnal are prepared to turn around with this new information then the captain speaks.

"Mr. Sidney, Mr. Belamour, welcome aboard." The tone is friendly as he addresses Astrophel.

Zarin grips the boat's edge as every fiber of her being stiffens. A cold sweat comes over her. Her chest races as it is prepared to help her body flee.

"Are you alright, Zarin?" Hajnal once again puts her hand on Zarin as she feels the mix of terror and disgust come over the younger maiden. Zarin nods just in time for Hajnal to turn around and be introduced to the captain.

Zarin hears the prince begin to introduce her. She feels Hajnal's hand on her shoulder. Zarin knows she has two options. Jump off the boat and escape or face the captain. She chooses the latter. She straightens herself as if she had an iron rod in her back. She keeps her head high as if she were aristocratic. She turns and looks at the captain.

He is a man of medium stature but confidence radiates from him. Dark boots, pants, and jacket are contrasted by his white shirt and his blue vest. It all fits in a way to flatter his built figure. His curly brown hair reaches his shoulders. His face has a five o'clock shadow. His eyes are blue, bluer than sapphires, bluer than the sky. They are the eyes haunting her nightmares. His face, his voice, everything about him is what makes her wake in the night full of fear and terror.

"Zarin." His call of her name sends ice through her.

"Captain Kolar," She addresses him in return. Seeing him grin as she speaks makes her skin crawl. She thought she was over this. She thought she could push him aside. She thought she could keep the memory of him suppressed enough he was nothing more than a vague memory. Alas, seeing him face to face floods her mind with the past she shared with him.

"Do you know each other?" Tyr asks the question in the minds of the others. Hajnal has a sense she has heard this name before now.

"Yes, but that was many years ago." Captain Kolar keeps a wide grin. Zarin does not give the same expression.

"I thought your ship was the *Acrasia*," Zarin brings up the ship she recalls.

"Sadly, she sank a few years ago but she and the memories made with her are still present in my mind." He does not turn his eyes from the maiden. Zarin tries to ignore the ice in her veins so she will not shiver in front of him.

However, Hajnal does shiver. She feels as if she were seasick but knows it is not the sea making her sick but rather it is Zarin's emotions. Hajnal also feels an overwhelming burning coming from Captain Kolar. It is not the burning one feels in anger. They are more like the burning coming from one's desire for another. Hajnal wonders what happened between them. Sir Artegal steps in front of Zarin and Hajnal.

"Eziz!" Captain Kolar suddenly yells. The young cabin boy appears at his captain's side. "Take our guests to their rooms then give them a tour of the ship."

"Yes, sir!" Eziz smiles at the ship's new guests and waves for them to follow him. They begin to follow but Hajnal purposefully intertwines her arm with Zarin's. Sir Artegal steps behind the women. Captain Kolar watches the party though his focus is on the back of Zarin.

Eziz shows the fivesome to two cabin rooms. The one designated for the women has three small beds in it and not much walking room. The men's room is the same. The group regathers in the hall to be met by young Eziz. He happily shows the people the different parts of the ship. Even when the boat begins to set sail, Eziz continues the tour.

Astrophel proves to be the most attentive tourist. The others, however, only listen to the placement and not much of the extra details Eziz shares. Eziz returns the new guests to the deck so they may watch as they sail.

As they stay on deck, Zarin feels eyes on her. She looks around as carefully as she can and notices many sets of eyes she has known from long ago. But none are so dreaded as the captain who steers the ship but watches her. Her skin feels clammy and her seasick-like illness is still upon her.

"Zarin," Sir Artegal draws her attention.

"Yes, Sir Artegal?" She looks up at him.

"Thou seem to be ill. Do thou need to lie down and rest?"

"I-I suppose I may need to do that." She nods.

"Let me escort you." He holds out his arm. She takes his forearm. As they begin to walk, she looks up and sees the captain scowl. She knows why he does. Her scalp instantly hurts.

"Thank you, Sir Artegal." Zarin goes to open the door to her cabin.

"I can sense something is distressing you, Zarin. What is it?" He asks directly.

"I am just seasick," She lies.

"I am a discerner, Zarin, and a feeler. I felt thy distress. What is wrong?" He remains unmoved.

"I do not want to talk about it now," Zarin answers. The knight inhales sharply but when he exhales, he nods accepting this answer. Zarin steps into her room and lies down on a bed. The blanket is scratchy, the mattress hard, and the pillow is so flat it is as if it is almost not there. Still, it is more comfortable on this bed than on the deck in the eyesight of Captain Kolar.

Zarin tries to get some rest but it is pointless. No matter how long she lies on the bed with her eyes closed she cannot seem to find peace from the fear trying to choke her. She remembers how she used to gain some temporary relief from such feelings. But she has sworn to give up poppy tears and strong liquor. She gets off the bed and onto the floor. She settles on her knees and then bows so far that her forehead rests on the ground.

A knock at the door immediately makes Zarin jump. She rises from the floor. She wipes her wet cheeks.

"Who is it?" Zarin asks.

"Artegal," answers the knight. She cracks open the door. The tall knight stands at the door calmly.

"Have you been out there this entire time?"

"Yes."

"Why?"

"I can feel thy distress," He answers.

"Oh...well, I'm sure if you return to the main deck, you will not feel it anymore."

"Unfortunately, that is not true." He shakes his head.

"Ah...I'm sorry. I have tried to soothe myself but I fear I cannot," Zarin admits. Sir Artegal opens his mouth then shuts it only to open it again.

"I can help thee," He claims quietly.

"How so?"

"I can help thee feel differently," He merely says instead of going into detail.

"Alright...what do you need to do?"

"I need to come inside," he points to the room. Zarin steps back and allows him.

"I will keep the door open so none may claim us wrong." He leaves the door open. Zarin takes a seat on her bed. The knight comes and sits next to her but leaves some space between them. They sit in silence for a moment before Artegal begins to remove his gloves. He puts them together and then lays them across the knee furthest from Zarin. He then holds out one of his hands to her. Zarin stares at his large hand. She had never seen his bare hand up close before as he has them covered nearly all of the time. She then looks up to his face which is turned from her.

"What am I to do?" She asks.

"Take my hand," he answers, still not looking directly at her. She puts her hand in his. His hand is almost comically bigger than hers.

"Take deep breaths," He instructs. Zarin does. Sir Artegal closes his eyes.

A prayer in the words only fairies and Starrlings know is whispered by the knight. Usually, when Zarin hears the knight speak, he speaks with great authority and confidence. He does not speak often but when he does, he is also sure to give his opinion which often is counter to hers yet in the end she supposes they agree. Even so, his voice is different now. It is low and soft as if he might break his words should he say them any louder.

Zarin feels a tingle in her hand. Her cramping, burning, twisting, painful body begins to feel something like a cool, calming stream come over it. The cramp ease, the twisting undoes itself, and the burning is squelched. The thoughts about Captain Kolar begin to drift away. Thoughts do not come to her at all. It is like her mind has gone to sleep. She breathes easily and her body begins to go slack. Her body leans and lands on Sir Artegal who does not move as he does not wish to interrupt her relaxation. He too eases and finds some rest.

"Zarin? Sir Artegal?" the questioning voice of Hajnal startles the knight whose eyes open wide and go to the doorway. He removes his hand from Zarin who wakes up from the rest she had. Realizing she is on the knight she removes herself completely by standing up. The knight stands up as well. He quickly puts on his gloves.

"Hajnal." Zarin stares at the brunette at the door rather flustered. "We were just..."

"I was easing her anxiety. I am sure thou has done so before given thy natural gift," Sir Artegal is forthright and brings up the gift with which Hajnal was born.

"Ah, yes." Hajnal nods in understanding. The three stand in an awkward silence before Hajnal speaks again. "We have been invited to dine with the captain."

"Oh..." Zarin looks down. Her stomach does grumble. She did not realize how much time has passed.

"If you do not want to go, that is fine. I can stay here with you if you wish instead," Hajnal offers. Zarin takes a minute to consider the options.

"I would hate for you to miss out on dinner to sit here bored with me," Zarin says.

"If I am with you, I will not be bored," Hajnal replies with a gentle smile.

"Would you stay with me then?"

"Of course."

"I will send thy regrets," Sir Artegal states then walks away. Hajnal goes into the room and closes the door behind her. She takes a seat on a bed as Zarin takes the other one. Hajnal looks at the quiet Zarin.

"Zarin, what is wrong?" Hajnal asks directly.

The golden-eyed woman inhales deeply before exhaling with tears growing in her eyes. She does not look at Hajnal.

"You could feel it, couldn't you?"

"Yes." Hajnal nods.

"I...I told you I was a slave on a ship after I ran away from Gold Haven, correct?"

"Yes, and I do believe you said it was on a ship with Captain Kolar."

"Yes."

"And this is *that* Captain Kolar."

"Yes."

"Do you want to tell me what happened?"

Zarin pauses and remains silent though she does not indicate whether or not she does. Hajnal says nothing but just waits as she does not want to rush her friend.

"I know every experience we have is for a reason though it might not be for a reason we may ever know. My years with Captain Kolar are ones I try to forget and often wish never occurred. I...I struggle to even say what happened though my mind is quick to remember every detail." Zarin clutches the scratchy blanket beneath her.

"If it is too painful, you do not need to say anything more." Hajnal leans across and touches her friend's knee.

"Mother Huldah says it is good to share both good and bad stories with friends, true friends. We are true friends, right?"

"Yes, of course." Hajnal grips Zarin's hand. Zarin smiles at the affirmation but it begins to fade as her eyes turn to remember the woeful experience.

"I think I told you how my mother smuggled me away from the temple in Gold Haven. She brought me to the *Acrasia* which was captained by Captain Kolar. He had just replaced the old captain who died from falling off the boat mysteriously. But their ship was paid to procure young maidens from the Southern Continent with magical abilities to take them back to a wealthy benefactor in the Old Lands. Money was supposed to be given to the families of the girls as compensation. We girls were told we would be entertainers for this man. Being the only ora-oculist, my mother knew I would be desired to be taken. I truly do believe my mother thought it better to sell me to be an entertainer than to be a sorceress," Zarin thinks of her mother. She need only look in a mirror to see her mother's eyes but her face is growing more and more unclear as the years pass.

"To prevent us girls from using magic on the sailors or using it to escape, they had these cursed bracelets we all wore that made us entirely obedient to Captain Kolar." Zarin's hands grab her naked wrists.

"Like the rope Tyr wore as a horse?" Hajnal brings up the item that harmed Tyr.

"Yes! Of course, Tyr's rope was a bit more of a crude spell as anyone who held the rope could be his master while these bracelets were more refined. We only obeyed Captain Kolar," Zarin explains the difference.

"I see."

"So, from the first night on the boat, it was clear Captain Kolar abused his position and his power over us girls. He... would pick a different girl or set of girls to join him in his cabin. Many were of age like me but some were...younger. I had been spared the first part of the journey across the Azure Ocean and heard of the many things he did to the others. I prayed I would not be subjected to those horrors. But I had a vision of what was to come for me and that same night, I was chosen." Zarin's tears run though her voice remains slow. She stops closing her eyes and lips. She exhales a shuddering breath. Hajnal's heart aches and not just in mimicry of Zarin's.

"I pleased him greatly. I pleased him so well that he decided to only call me after the first night together. I hated it but I thought about all the girls I was sparing. It gave me a small comfort. But many of the other girls came to begrudge me. I understand why. I was sleeping in a bed and not on the floor. I was being fed the captain's food instead of scraps. I was dressed up in Senyamese silks instead of the rags I arrived in. I had no friends in those days as we sailed to the Old Lands.

When we arrived, I was excited. I was excited that I would finally be free of Captain Kolar. Even though I was being forced to entertain someone with my gift, it was better than entertaining Captain Kolar with my body.

It was in the middle of the night when the girls were unloaded. I had no idea as I was asleep. I awoke and found I was sailing back across the Azure Ocean. Captain Kolar decided to keep me as his private slave. I was trapped on the *Acrasia* for two years. For two years I did everything and anything he asked in and out of his bed. I told fortunes for those he brought to the ship. I cleaned for him. I fed him. I waited on every need he had. When he was cross, he would abuse me or humiliate me in front of his crew. He would grab me by my hair when he would do this. He already had control over me by the power of the bracelets but taking hold of my hair was just...I don't know...another way to take control of me." Zarin reaches up and touches the coif on her head.

"I prayed so much to El-Yah. I prayed for my suffering to end, to be rescued. I prayed for harm against Captain Kolar. I prayed for death...my death. I prayed so hard but...it felt like El-Yah did not hear me. He was not going to help me. I wondered if he was having me suffer because I started the pact with the Fallen One or because I had not been faithful enough to him since I lived in the temples or because I just did wrongs," Zarin confides further with Hajnal. She does not say it but Hajnal understands a fraction of what Zarin describes.

"But El-Yah was listening to me. He... gave me a friend, Mr. Phan. He was the quartermaster on the *Acrasia*. He was the only one of the crew who pitied me. He did his best to try to squelch Captain Kolar's anger towards me and to give me privacy from the other crew members. He did not treat me as lowly as the others. He treated me like a real human being. He...he was the one to help me escape."

"How?"

"The only way to remove those bracelets is for the owner to remove them. Mr. Phan told me to convince Captain Kolar that I loved him and perhaps then the captain would remove the bracelets as he no longer needed them to control me. The two months I spent playing the adoring lover were sickening to my core. But it did cause him to trust me to remove them. I stayed on and did as he said for another month to prove I was not lying. But when we ported in Soldoro, Mr. Phan gave me a strong wine to give the captain. He drank and when he slept, Mr. Phan helped me escape. He paid for me to take a ship to Austvest. I have never forgotten Mr. Phan's kindness and help. I would be...I don't even know what I'd be if he had not helped me," She thinks fondly of the man.

"So that is the history between the captain and me. Being back here on this ship with the man who hurt me, and broke me is...almost unbearable. That is why I do not want to be even in his eyesight. But because I know our trip is short, our cause is great and I am protected, I can make this trip," Zarin proclaims.

"Yes. But I am sorry for what happened to you and that of all the ships for the men to get us on it is the one under his control."

"It is not their fault. You know no one else would even try to cross the Mermaid's Lair at this time of year."

"Why is it so dangerous at this time of year?"

"I am not sure but the weather is rougher this time of year in that area and mermaids lurk in the waters. A storm may rock your boat and cause you to fall over but the mermaids will make you jump off, or so Mr. Brames would say. I think he is being dramatic," Zarin thinks of the older man who used to be on the *Acrasia*.

"Hmm...Well, we will be protected," Hajnal lifts the hand with a ring on it.

"Yes," Zarin agrees with a smile.

***

Up in the captain's quarters, Captain Kolar sits at the head of a table with a glass of wine in his hand. He looks at the feast he had the cook prepare for him and his guests. He had given the cook some gold to get such good food for the trip as Captain Kolar and his men were sick of eating stale bread and something resembling porridge. His eyes go off the meal to look at the guests at his table. He has his usual companions of Mr. Brames and Mr. Phan to his right while Mr. Belamour, Mr. Sidney, and Mr. Dahl have taken to his left. Two spots have been left empty due to the missing Hajnal and Zarin. Having learned of the ladies' rejection of his invitation has assuredly soured Captain Kolar's mood. A young woman walks around serving the guests. It does not go unnoticed by the three guests the woman holds a resemblance though faint to Zarin.

"Tell me, gentlemen, what is it in Koralia that makes us take such a dangerous journey this day?" Mr. Brames asks the three young men in front of him.

"My betrothed is trying to reach her family. We cannot be wed until we are reunited with them," Astrophel answers.

"Ah. Marriage. That's a rough path to take. Believe you me," Mr. Brames snorts.

"I doubt he will be marrying three different women at the same time, Mr. Brames. I am sure his path will be far smoother," Mr. Phan brings up his shipmate's polygamy earning a laugh from Mr. Brames.

"Is your betrothed the woman with the long brown hair?" Mr. Phan inquires.

"Yes."

"I heard there were two women with your group but I only saw one," Mr. Brames brings up the other woman.

"Our companion felt ill so she went to her room," Sir Artegal answers.

"It may be better for her to get fresh air than to stay cooped up in her room," Mr. Phan suggests.

"Yes, then we'll be able to meet her." Mr. Brames licks his lips as his eyes go to Nafisa who silently pours more wine for him.

"Well, you've already met her," Captain Kolar finally speaks after learning of the women's refusal for dinner.

"I have?" Mr. Brames raises an eyebrow.

"All three of us have," Captain Kolar picks at his plate.

"Who is she?" Mr. Phan asks.

"Why, it is our dear, sweet Zarin," Captain Kolar reveals.

"Zarin!" Mr. Brames chokes on his wine but quickly regains his airflow. Mr. Phan's jaw clenches.

"Yes, Zarin." Captain Kolar smiles.

"How is it you know Zarin?" Tyr asks.

"She used to sail with us," Captain Kolar answers.

Mr. Brames smirks at the response but takes in more wine. Mr. Phan keeps a stony expression.

"Surely not as a member of thy crew. Thou seemed rather unenthusiastic to have ladies aboard thy ship when we were making arrangements last night," Astrophel reminds the captain.

"I do prefer to keep ladies off ships as they are bad luck. But sometimes journeys are long and it does no harm to have a little female companionship. That is why I have Nafisa here." He wraps his arm around the passing girl who almost drops the bottle of wine from her hands. She smiles but it does not reach her sorrowful eyes. Captain Kolar gives the girl a pat on her backside then releases her. She takes a step and trips. When she does, the bottle falls and breaks. The wine spills all over the floor.

"Clean it up quickly!" Captain Kolar barks at the girl. She drops to her knees and begins to clean up the pieces of glass.

"Let me help," Both Astrophel and Sir Artegal stand up.

"Sit. She is fine to clean it on her own," Captain Kolar waves his hand at the men.

"I will help," Sir Artegal puts his hand on Astrophel's shoulder. The prince takes a seat and the knight goes to help the silent Nafisa.

"I say she can do it alone, Mr. Belamour." Captain frowns at the large man. Sir Artegal ignores the captain. Nafisa gasps as she cuts her hand on a shard.

"Allow me," Sir Artegal takes her hand. He pulls the glass from her finger then with a simple touch he heals the wound. She looks at the healed digit and then smiles at him truly grateful. Sir

Artegal waves his hand and bottle pieces come together and reform the bottle. It flies through the air to a rubbish bin. He then waves his other hand causing the wine to come from the grown. He sends it flying out of the window and into the sea. He helps Nafisa back to her feet.

"I haven't seen someone do that since Zarin was with us," Mr. Brames comments.

"Yes. She was extremely talented," Mr. Phan comments.

"You have fairy blood like her?" Captain Kolar asks the tallest man in the room.

"Yes, though we do not have all of the same talents," Sir Artegal takes his seat.

"I am sure you do not," Mr. Brames chuckles.

"What does thou mean?" Astrophel looks at the oldest man.

"There are certain talents only a woman can do, if you catch my meaning," Mr. Brames winks. Tyr drinks quickly while Mr. Brames earns a rather disgusted expression from Astrophel. Sir Artegal's face appears as unmoved as a cut stone.

"Mr. Brames, how crassly you speak," Captain Kolar admonishes the older man despite having spanked a woman before the men just minutes ago.

"Apologies," The man huffs.

"It is true Zarin did have many talents both in and out of the bedroom. Which is why I have a proposition for you gentlemen. I will trade you Nafisa and the rest of the fee you owe us for Zarin." Captain Kolar smiles, setting out his deal.

Tyr freezes in shock at the audacity of the proposal. Astrophel stands up infuriated while Sir Artegal remains calm in his seat.

"How dare thee! How dare thee ask us to trade her and to trade Nafisa as well as if they were animals or-or property and we are their owners! Zarin is her own person and our friend. I am absolutely disgusted at this utterly indecent proposal!"

"Surely this outburst of horror is a farce. You must have bedded her and that is why you want to keep her. She is much prettier than your fiancée and she is a bit of a wanton minx. Zarin has always been eager to please whether she is on her back or her knees," He remarks.

"That is enough!" Tyr slams his cup and fist on the table.

"I see. You have bedded her as well. That little whore," the captain mumbles the last phrase.

Wham!

All are silent as the captain spits out the blood. He rubs his almost dislocated jaw. He looks back at the one who dared to assault him. Sir Artegal stands with his hand still fisted as if ready to strike again. The captain glares at the secret knight.

"How dare you! I am the captain of this ship!" Captain Kolar rises to his feet.

"If thou speak of Zarin in such a manner again, I shall not be held responsible for my actions," Sir Artegal speaks coolly though his eyes are full of fire.

"It is a good thing I planned for such a possibility," the captain speaks calmly.

"What do you mean?" Tyr questions.

"I was prepared for a refusal or some sort of outburst so I added a little potion for tonight's meal. In a matter of moments, all of you will find your body unresponsive and will become completely paralyzed," Captain Kolar claims.

"What!" Mr. Brames shoots up out of his seat. His legs lock causing him to fall. As he lies on the floor, he contracts his upper muscles leaving him with bent hands and fingers. Mr. Phan falls victim next as he simply falls face-first into his dinner. Tyr stands up and tries to flee the table but falls to the floor. Astrophel begins to feel his legs locking. As he falls, Sir Artegal catches him. He gently lays the prince on the ground before taking out his knife. He charges for Captain Kolar who remains calm in the face of danger. Sir Artegal grips the captain by the neck and throws him to the ground where he pins him. He replaces his hand with the knife.

"Give me the antidote!" Sir Artegal demands.

"I am surprised at your strength and how long it is taking for the potion to work," Captain Kolar remarks.

"Give me the antidote now!" Sir Artegal orders, his toes stiffening.

"Why?"

"I will kill thee if thou do not." His legs are gone.

"Then how will you get the antidote? Illogical," Captain Kolar mocks the knight. Sir Artegal draws blood with his blade but the captain is not moved.

"Three. Two. One," the captain counts down and just as he counts, the larger man's body flops down. The captain pushes the knight off him while keeping the knife away from his throat. He kicks Sir Artegal in the ribs. He dusts himself off and grabs a clean cravat from the small wardrobe in the room. He wraps it around his neck to keep it from bleeding more. Nafisa watches horrified at the display of men lying about with eyes wide open but bodies unmoving.

"You have killed them," Nafisa feels tears in her eyes.

"They aren't dead, just temporarily paralyzed. They'll regain some function by the time we are crossing the mermaid's lair. Then they will be at their mercy," Captain Kolar explains.

"Why have you drugged your own men?" Nafisa keeps questioning. Captain Kolar walks over to Mr. Brames and Mr. Phan. He kicks the floor-bound Mr. Brames in the crotch a few times.

"This old fool knew his brat of a boy had contracted the purple fever and brought him aboard anyway. Because of him, we lost our income and many men,'" Captain Kolar explains then walks to Mr. Phan. He grabs Mr. Phan by his hair, lifting his face out of the food.

"But this son of a whore did an even worse transgression," Captain Kolar keeps his eyes locked on Mr. Phan's eyes that are still able to move enough to look at the captain.

"What did he do?" Nafisa is almost scared to know. Captain Kolar grips the hair tightly and then slams Mr. Phan's face into the table only to lift it again.

"He."

Slam!

"Stole."

Slam!

"My."

Slam!

"Property."

Slam!

Mr. Phan is slammed a few more times into the table before Captain Kolar lets him go. Nafisa looks away as she cannot bear the sight. She covers her ears to block out Mr. Phan's choking on his blood. Captain Kolar breathes heavily and then composes himself.

"I do not tolerate betrayal," He runs a hand through his hair. Nafisa stays still and quiet.

"Now, I am going to reclaim what is mine. You will stay here." The captain points to the woman. She cannot help but obey. He straightens his clothes and then walks out of the room.

CHAPTER 27

ALTHEA

"I am merely making a point with your father. Now, please let me look at the book," Althea answers Odile's question. Odile moves aside so the determined Althea could look into the spell book. Althea takes Odile's seat and stares down at the words written on the page.

"What sort of point are you trying to make with my father?" Odile questions.

"I am a capable person that can do what he thinks I cannot," Althea flips a page to look at the words on the next. She clenches her jaw as she looks at the words.

"Ah...I see. Well, I think it would be better if you just give up now," Odile comments. Althea looks up from the book to the other woman.

"What? Why? Is it because you are jealous of him teaching me magic as well?" Althea brings up the reason Hadion gave earlier.

"No. I just..." Odile trails off.

"You just what?"

"I just...know sorcerers sometimes can use...interesting means to get the results they want to see."

"Like what?"

"Well...my grandfather, Kazimeer, would make Bardolph stand in a pot of boiling oil and make him learn to levitate himself out of it. The longer it took for Bardolph to levitate the more oil he would add to the pot. Bardolph learned to levitate quickly that way. My father did too."

Althea grimaces at the training method. *How could a man boil his son and grandson?*

"Well, I have my ring of protection so any sort of physical harm he might do will not affect me," Althea tries to comfort not only Odile but also herself.

"It is not just physical incentives that can be used against you. Grandfather Kazimeer drowned my pet cat when I failed to perform a spell correctly just as he had done with my father's pets. Though I was not harmed physically...." Odile divulges more but trails off as she thinks of atrocity. Althea continues to be appalled.

"Well...I hope your father does not resort to such tactics," Althea fears he will though.

"I say it is better to give up. Just take the slow path with me."

"If I fail this challenge then I will not be taught magic anymore," Althea gives the condition.

"Well, that's not so bad. You've gone your whole life without doing it. It shouldn't be too bad to return to that lifestyle. And you'll just be my companion." Odile flips some hair from her shoulder.

"No. If I fail, I will be made a scullery maid again," Althea corrects the job placement. Odile's mouth drops open at the change.

"That's not fair!"

"Not much about this is," Althea mutters.

"Well, I can't have you back in the scullery. I will help you the best I can," Odile pledges.

"Thank you." Althea smiles then looks back to the spell book.

"This isn't written in the common tongue." Althea frowns, finding the words to be written in a language entirely different from hers. Even the letters look different.

"That is because it is written in the language of the Starrlings," Odile states what she thinks is rather obvious.

"Oh..." Althea's face falls. She knows nothing about the language of the Starrlings. She only ever learned to read and speak the Common Tongue.

"It is not so hard. I have a cheat sheet with a phonetic way to pronounce these phrases since a single mispronunciation gives things a different meaning. And each spell just starts the same but has a different ending. Let me find my sheet," Odile starts looking through different drawers in the room in different furniture. It takes some time but Odile finds what she desires with a cheerful shout of 'Here!'.

Odile brings the paper to Althea. Althea finds the handwriting tiny but with great focus, she can read it. Odile begins her lesson on what the different symbols sound like. Odile is surprised by the many "sh", "zsa", "ah", and "el" sounds she repeats as well as the many times she must make a sort of hacking noise in the back of her throat.

Hours they spend just matching sounds to letters. Althea kins the process to when she was a child and had to learn the letters and sounds of her own language. Althea is happy to see however in the spell book, there is a label for each spell written in the common tongue. She does note, however, the spell labels are written in a different ink than the phrases. They are a bit sloppier as well. It is as if a child came through the book and labeled the spells. Child or not, Althea is grateful to whomever wrote these notes.

Feeling more confident, Althea digs into her work more. Odile, having grown tired, leaves to fetch herself something to eat as she did not stop for a midday meal. She ventures to the dining room far lower than her protective tower. She finds four plates out and platters of food waiting to be eaten.

Odile sits in her usual spot and serves herself a small roasted hen with a spicy apricot glaze, mushroom rice, scalloped potatoes, sugared almonds, boiled greens, and a roll. She pours herself some plum wine to drink with her meal. She begins to eat when she feels another presence in the room.

Odile stiffens when she sees Bardolph enter the room. He dons a loose white tunic with gold embroidering around his neck and wrists and matching pants. He walks barefoot, however. He enters the room and scowls when he sees Odile.

"There she is...Daddy's little princess," Bardolph pulls out his chair and sits. Odile rolls her eyes.

"How are you getting along with your new little pet?" Bardolph stabs his hen to bring it to his plate.

"She's not my pet, she's my companion." Odile corrects him. "And we are getting along well."

"Oh? You don't find her utterly boring?" Bardolph pours him a glass of plum wine. He breaks off a leg from the hen and puts it in his mouth. He removes the bone which is now clean.

"No, not at all. We have fun together," Odile sips her drink, "In fact, she's starting to learn magic."

"Magic? A void can't teach a void, Odile," Bardolph brings his glass to his smirking lips.

"I'm not void, Bardolph!" Odile slams her fist onto the table making Bardolph snicker.

"Could have fooled me," He murmurs, earning a hateful glare from his sister. "Besides, I know for sure that Sipos girl has no power."

"But she does."

Bardolph puts down his glass.

"I spent three months in that village with her. Except for her pretty face, there is nothing special about her."

"Well, you're wrong."

"What kind of magic can she do then?"

"She is a compeller like you and me."

"A compeller? That is the least of all the gifts." Bardolph rolls his eyes.

"Well, she still has it so that means she has fairy blood and she can learn to do magic." Odile gains a smug look on her face.

"You're teaching her?" Bardolph scoffs. "You're not even close to finishing your sorceress training."

"I'm working on my training." Odile crosses her arms and looks away from her brother, frustrated and insulted. Delighting in her anger he breaks off the hen's other leg to eat.

"And I'm not training her. Father is," Odile informs him more. Bardolph chokes on the meat. After much coughing, he spits up the bone and meat.

"He is what?"

"Father is teaching Althea magic. He thinks he sees great potential in her," Odile smiles at Bardolph's reaction or rather at his choking. Bardolph remains quiet for a moment as she thinks about this news. Slowly a grin comes to his face.

"What are you grinning about?" Odile loses her happy expression as she sees his. Bardolph begins to chuckle.

"You know sometimes I wonder about Hadion. But then he goes and does something like this...Kazimeer would be pleased," Bardolph remarks. Odile stares not sure of what Bardolph means.

"What? Why would he be pleased? What is Father doing?"

Bardolph snickers.

"I guess you're still too naive to know about these things," Bardolph remains vague.

"About what things?"

"If I told you, Hadion would be livid. I guess you will just have to wait and see." Bardolph finishes his glass of wine. Odile grinds her teeth at being left out of this joke Bardolph is suggesting is between him, their father, and anyone else who is not "naive".

"I don't know what you're talking about but I am sure whatever you think it is, is not right and you will feel stupid when you're wrong." Odile stands up.

"I doubt I'll be wrong." Bardolph starts to pour more wine into his cup.

"But you have been. Like about Althea's power and her sister's willingness to be yours," Odile brings up the Sipos sisters including the one she has never met. Bardolph loses any mirth on his face and looks coldly at Odile. He squeezes his bottle of wine and his glass so tightly that both shatter in his hands. Odile leans back only to have the chair press into the back of her knees. She falls back into her seat as Bardolph stands up. He keeps balling his hands ignoring how the glass presses and cuts his hands deeper. Odile sees his eyes darkening. She has seen this side of him many times and reaches subtly for the knife on the table by her plate.

"What is going on in here?" Hadion enters the room drawing attention to him. Bardolph loosens his hands as Odile moves her hand away from the knife.

"Bardolph, your hands." Hadion walks directly to the bleeding, wine-splattered man. He gently takes hold of his son's wrists.

"I can heal myself." Bardolph pulls out of Hadion's hold and storms away from the dining room.

"He has not cursed you again, has he? I will get the All-Cure elixir if he has," Hadion steps closer to his daughter.

"No. I'm fine. We were eating and I mentioned he isn't always right like how he was wrong about Althea having magic and how her sister is not interested in him," Odile rambles off the events he missed. Hadion sighs and rolls his eyes as he goes to take his seat at the head of the table. He begins to take food for his plate. He is sure not to get glass in his food.

"So, Father, is it true you're going to make Althea a scullery maid if she fails this test with you?" Althea seeks confirmation.

"Yes." He brings some of the mushroom rice to his mouth.

"But she's supposed to be my companion! You can't make her a scullery maid!"

"I can do whatever I please, Odile. I am the master of this island," Hadion states almost casually as he brings more food to his mouth.

"But she's the first real friend I've had. You can't take her from me and put her to slave away in the kitchen when she fails," Odile whines.

"When she fails? Do you think she will fail?" Hadion lowers his fork but raises his eyebrow.

"How can she memorize every spell in that book in three days? I have not even done that and I've been reading it for years," Odile compares.

"But she has pressure. Pressure is what makes diamonds," Hadion states.

"Or breaks ice," Odile brings up the alternative.

"Do you think she will fail, Odile?" Hadion asks again.

"I...I hope she does not but realistically, I think she will." Odile looks down at her food, her appetite leaving her. "And I do not want to lose her to the scullery."

"Well, if you do not want her to fail and go back to the scullery, then I suggest you do everything in your power to help her pass this," Hadion recommends.

"How?" Odile looks up to her teacher.

"I'm not going to tell you how, Odile. You are both big girls. You two can figure it out." Hadion shakes his roll at her.

"Fine. I will try to help her as best I can." Odile stands up. She leaves the room to return to her tower and her friend.

Despite being a student for over a decade, Odile never studied as intently as Althea does now before her. For the past thirty-six hours, Althea has not slept or eaten. Instead, she has had her eyes glued to the pages of the spell book. Her lips move as she repeats the words in the book in hopes speaking it aloud fourteen times will lock it in her mind.

"You need a break." Odile sits across the table from Althea who is only a quarter of the way through the large book. Althea ignores her as she repeats the latest spell she has read.

Odile takes the book and slams it shut earning a gasp and an angered look from Althea.

"What are you doing?"

"I'm serious, Althea. You need a break. You need to sleep and eat. If you overdo it, you'll pass out and then not remember anything. Go to sleep for at least an hour," Odile urges Althea.

"I have to learn-"

"You will but take a break," Odile refuses to move her hand from the now-closed book. Althea groans but does feel the wear in her body. She looks over to the futon in the room.

"I will lay here but you must wake me in an hour." Althea starts toward the futon.

"I will," Odile agrees. Althea yawns as she begins to lie down. Odile grabs a blanket and covers up the eager student. Althea slowly bats her eyes as Odile goes to the door. She waves her hand extinguishing the candles in the room to create a dark room for Althea to sleep inside. Althea inhales deeply once and is quick to fall asleep.

When Althea wakes, she finds the room as empty as when she closed her eyes. She looks at her lap and finds a piece of paper there. She picks it up to read.

Althea,

I tried to wake you but you would not. I am going to bed. I am sure you will wake up soon.

-Odile

"Oh, no. How long have I been asleep then?" Althea frowns but finds no clock in the room. She inhales deeply and accepts the fact she lost some time studying as there is nothing else she can do.

Slowly, Althea gets up from the futon and returns to the table to the closed book. She opens the cover to return to the first page so she might see if there is an index and therefore a shortcut to the passage, she was last at before Odile made her sleep. She finds the first page is no index but an introduction page. Althea exhales not caring to read anything unnecessary. She goes to finger the top corner of the page when she notices small handwriting there. She looks closely at the tiny words there. She stares until she realizes it is a page number and not the one indicating what page she is currently on now.

Althea begins flipping the pages in search of the page number written in the corner. She turns and turns till finally, she finds it near the back of the book. She covers her mouth in surprise as she reads the translated words written beneath it. She starts to giggle giddily

Is this my solution?

She reads over the spell in the Starrling language. She slowly says the spell out loud fourteen times. Having felt she knows the words now; she knows she must do as Hadion taught her on the beach. She needs to focus, visualize, believe, and act.

Althea closes her eyes and finds it easy to shut out the rest of the world as there is no one else in the room. She begins to visualize what it is she desires. She smiles as she begins to put her faith in it. She speaks the spell out loudly and confidently.

A tingling sensation comes over her body. From the tip of her toes to the hairs atop her head, she feels a buzzing sensation. The buzz of her body begins to travel and stick to her head. It is not painful but unusual. She opens her eyes and turns the book's pages back to the first one to have a spell. She reads it once and then goes to the next. She flips through the book, her eyes scanning the spells. Her brain begins to gain a feeling of swelling but it does not stop her from reading.

It takes many hours but Althea reaches the end of the book. Althea closes it. She takes several deep breaths as she stares at the back cover of the book.

"I know it. I know it all." She brings her hands to her cheeks and smiles giddily. Her happiness is interrupted when she yawns again. Her head rather hurts and her limbs are weak from hunger and incomplete sleep long for some rest. Her eyes go to the futon.

"I can lay down for a little bit." Althea looks at the futon. She comes back to her temporary sleeping place and covers herself up with the blanket. She happily returns to her sleep.

"Althea! Althea! Wake up!" Althea hears Odile yell as her body is shaken. Althea opens her eyes to see the young maiden standing over her. To keep solidarity with Althea, Odile has not changed her clothes.

"Odile, what's wrong?"

"You do not have much time left! You have slept too long just as I have. You have to get up and study!" Odile grabs Althea's hands to pull her upright. Althea yawns but is yanked out of the resting place.

"Come on, Althea." Odile leads Althea to the table and chair. Althea pauses, having taken a seat. She blinks several times and then lays her hands on the table. She closes her eyes.

"What are you doing? Open the book! You need to learn the spells!" Odile cannot understand Althea's current ease.

Althea just smiles.

"Odile, can I have something to eat and drink? I think it might help me." Althea puts in her request.

"Um...Yes? Just get back to studying and I'll get you some food." Odile is lost on Althea's willingness to eat when before the girl refused everything. Odile leaves to send for nourishment.

Althea stretches a bit and yawns more. She takes a walk about the room and even opens the curtains. She enjoys the sunshine she sees outside. She takes a deep breath before going back to her seat.

When Odile returns to the room, she has her foxlike servant enter with steaming tea and a platter of meats, cheeses, and bread. Althea happily eats the items on the board as well as drinks the minty tea.

"You need to be reading." Odile cannot understand Althea's calm.

"Do not worry, Odile. Everything will be well," Althea speaks though her mouth is rather full.

"My father could be here at any moment and you are eating as if you have all the time in the world. What happened to your determination? Do you want to be a servant?" Odile's hands find her hips.

"No, but-" Althea starts.

"Good day, ladies." Hadion enters the room. His lilac linen shirt is only loose about his arms. Silver designs are on his high collar and his bishop sleeves. There is a Silver and white belt around his waist and dark pants underneath. His gray boots look to be made of elephant leather.

"Good day," The women greet him. Odile's heart races in her anxiety as Althea sits calm and relaxed.

"Are you ready for your tests, Althea?" Hadion asks the student directly.

"Yes," She stands up. Odile eyes her and begins grinding her teeth.

"Yes, what?" He tilts his head in anticipation. She sighs.

"Yes, Master," She adds the title.

"Good. We will start with something easy from the start of the book." Hadion grabs the book and flips to one of the first pages. Althea waits with hands folded together before her.

"What is the spell for the growth of flowers?" He asks.

Althea does not even blink an eye and the words for the spell come out of her mouth.

"Good." Hadion flips further into the book. "What is the spell for multiplication of gold?"

Althea does not hesitate in answering. Odile's eyes widen at the quick response.

"Very good." Hadion keeps flipping. Several more questions are asked. Althea answers without flubbing any words. Odile is rather amazed at Althea's memorization. She knows she cannot even give half of the spells in the book.

"One more." Hadion closes the book and puts it behind his back.

"Yes?"

"What spell is for rapid memory absorption?"

Althea smiles to herself thinking of the little note she found. How lucky she was someone who left such tiny notes that have gone undetected by Hadion? Althea easily gives away the answer.

"Excellent," Hadion remarks and puts the book on the table.

"She has passed?" Odile asks for Althea.

"Yes." Hadion nods. A squeal comes from Odile who embraces the smiling Althea.

"I knew you could do it!" Odile claims. Hadion restrains from exposing Odile's former doubt.

"Now, I think you two need to bathe," Hadion comments, making Althea blush.

Do I smell?

"Once you are dressed, Althea, you will meet me in the courtyard. You, Odile, will get back to studying these spells," Hadion gives directions to the two women and then leaves just as quickly as he came.

"Let's get going. I reek!" Odile takes Althea's hand. Althea does sniff at Odile as they walk but finds no ill smell about Odile. But she is forced to wonder, if Odile thinks she smells, what does she think of Althea's odor?

One perfumed bath later, the robed maidens walk to Odile's room. Before they can reach the closet, Odile quickly notices two boxes on her bed. The women go to inspect. Each box has a piece of paper. One reads "Odile" as the other reads "Althea".

"I wonder what this is?" Odile squeaks happily as if she already knows what is inside the box.

Odile opens her box and gushes as she pulls out a new, shimmering green dress. Althea opens hers and finds a purple dress.

"I guess Father kept himself busy these past few days," Odile comments.

"What do you mean?"

"Father made these dresses," Odile smiles and changes into a new dress. Althea touches the purple dress and finds the fabric to be made of satin.

"Try it on, Althea," Odile urges the other girl. Althea nods and begins.

In the end, Althea is pleased with her dress, or rather that it is not the same as Odile's. It is not because Odile's dress is ugly but rather more immodest than what Althea wants. The emerald dress, though flowing, has no sleeves leaving her white arms bare. The front also has a deep 'v' cut that would expose her breasts if it were not for a large shining silver band that covers them.

Althea's dress, though fitting to her torso, also begins to flow at her hips. A dark purple fabric makes the tops of her off-the-shoulder sleeves. She feels rather lovely in it despite her exposed shoulders.

"Aren't these just lovely?" Odile plays with the skirt of her dress.

"Yes," Althea nods in agreement.

"Well, we better hop to doing what Father says." Odile starts for her bedroom door. Althea agrees and goes. She knows where she must meet Hadion.

Arriving in the courtyard, Althea quickly sees Hadion leaning against the goddess Sormus's pedestal. She notices he is eating something. She quietly approaches him.

"There you are, Althea," he takes notice of her. She simply nods in acknowledgment. Having come closer, she sees a half-eaten fig in his hand.

"So? Do you like it?" He asks.

"Like what?"

"Your dress."

"Oh!" Althea looks down at her new dress again. "Yes. It is beautiful."

Hadion nods content with the comment and takes the last bite of the fig before throwing away the stem.

"What are we going to do now?" Althea questions.

"You keep forgetting to speak properly, little lotus. Do you think because you happened to find my note and memorized those spells you are too superior to call me 'master'?"

"Your note?"

"Yes. It is clear you read my note in the corner and found the memory spell," he brings up her success-leading tip.

"You wrote me that note?"

"No, I wrote it for Bardolph when he was learning magic with my father," Hadion denies purposefully helping her.

"Oh. I see. You did not teach your son magic?"

"No. And again you forget to speak properly to me. I think I may have to send you to the scullery to teach you your place," he brings up the dreaded place.

"No. I am sorry, Master," Althea makes herself apologize for the sake of saving herself.

"That is better."

"What are we going to do now, Master?" Althea asks again.

"We are going to start putting those spells in your head to use. You may know them now in words but you need to be able to execute them."

"Sounds good to me, Master."

"Now, since you were able to perform the memory spell, I know you are capable of performing spells of a more complicated nature. Therefore, you should be able to cast simple spells easily."

"That sounds logical."

"Then you feel ready?"

"I suppose so."

"Excellent. As I know you are new to spell casting, I will give you three tries on each spell to get it right. For each spell you correctly perform, I will reward you." He smiles rather nicely, Althea mentally notes. Althea nods agreeing with these terms rather surprised at his positive reinforcement.

"Of course, if you fail to perform the spell after three tries, you will be punished," he keeps his smile.

"Punished?"

"Yes. I will punish you."

Althea snorts and chuckles.

"How would you punish me, Master? You cannot hurt me?" Althea is rather amused and pleased she has her ring of protection which makes physical punishment impossible.

"I have ways not involving harming a single hair on your head." He reaches out and softly strokes her hair then her face. The skin tingles where he has touched.

"Well, I doubt I will see these ways as I intend to get each spell right." Althea takes a step away from him.

"Then let's begin," Hadion grins.

CHAPTER 28

ALTHEA

Althea readies herself for the supposed challenges Hadion may throw her way. She stares at him as he keeps grinning.

"Make flowers grow," Hadion gives the challenge.

"Okay," Althea accepts. She closes her eyes. Holds out her hand and breathes deeply before speaking the words that come easily from her memory. When she opens her eyes, she smiles seeing roses springing up near Hadion's feet.

"Very good."

"I know. So where is my reward?" She reminds him of his word. Hadion reaches into his pocket and pulls out a diamond shining in the light of the sun. He tosses it to her. She catches and stares in awe at the precious jewel. The size alone amazes her as it is at least five carats. The clarity is nearly perfect as well. Never has she had such a fine gem.

"Put that away so we can continue," Hadion brings her attention back to him. She nods and puts it in her pocket. She smiles excited for what other rewards she might attain.

"Will I always get diamonds?"

"No."

"No?" Her disappointment is not lost on him.

"You get diamonds if you succeed on the first try. Sapphires are for the second try and emeralds for the third try," He informs her of the other rewards. She regains her glee. Sapphires and emeralds are just as good to her.

"Now, make the roses grow ten hands high," Hadion gives her next challenge. Althea nods determined to succeed on the first try again. Closed eyes, deep breaths, outstretched hands, and confident words are followed by the sudden and impressive growth of roses. She stares proudly at them then looks to Hadion with an outstretched hand. He reaches into his pocket again and places the diamond in her palm. She tucks it away.

"Now shrink them back to their original size," Hadion points downward.

"Will do." Althea is more than ready. She begins her routine. The words leave her mouth and she opens her eyes excitedly to see the small flowers. She frowns when she sees the flowers have not shrunk. She closes her eyes and tries again. When she opens her eyes, she is pleased they did as she bid. A sapphire is given.

Four diamonds, three sapphires, and two emeralds later, Althea begins to feel the drain on herself from using magic. Her breath becomes more labored and her limbs heavy.

"Are we wilting, little flower?" Hadion observes her slouched stance.

"No," She denies and rolls her eyes at the nickname.

"I can see you wilting, Althea. Do you want to stop?"

"No. I'm fine," Althea insists.

"Then turn yourself into an animal."

"What animal?"

"What animal do you want to turn into?"

"I don't know..."

"Well, what is your favorite animal?"

"Um...well..." Althea looks to the ground as she thinks of the beast she most likes.

"What is it?"

"Well, my favorite animal, though I have not seen it in person, is a phoenix," She answers.

"A phoenix?" Hadion is rather surprised by the answer.

"Yes. They are so beautiful in paintings. They are powerful and able to be reborn from their ashes. I saw one in a traveling show once. They are simply incredible!" Althea gushes.

"They are. There are some here on the island," Hadion states.

"Really?" Althea's eyes light up.

"Yes. But they do not come too close to the castle."

"They probably don't want to be turned into servants," Althea speaks before she can hold her tongue.

"Yes."

"I suppose I will not see them since they are so far," Althea sighs disappointedly.

"You never know. Sometimes they come toward the gardens." Hadion gives her a little hope. "Now you should try to turn into one."

"Oh, I could not do that. They are far too complex." Althea shakes her head.

"Then turn into my favorite." He suggests an alternative.

"Which is?"

"A lamb," He answers. A laugh jumps out of her mouth but she puts her hand over her mouth to stop herself.

"Is there something funny about me liking sheep?"

"No. No. It is just...I would think you would say something like a dragon or griffin or wolf or lion or something fearsome, not something...simple, docile and sweet," Althea explains her thoughts.

"I like what I like. Now such a creature should not be hard for you to shift into with your magic spell." Hadion gets back to the task at hand. Althea nods and begins her process.

A sheep. A sheep. I am a sheep. She tries to visualize. The spell leaves her mouth. She feels her skin thickening and her hair curling. Her body begins to bend but the force she feels in her body weakens. Her skin returns to normal. Her hair does as well. She straightens and she opens her eyes. She takes several deep breaths.

"Try again," Hadion orders, seeing she has failed to change herself.

A sheep. A sheep. I am a sheep. Althea tells herself again and tries again. She feels her face begin to elongate. The sensation frightens her, making Althea stop. Her face reverts to its original state. She touches her face.

"That's two tries, Althea." He holds up two fingers. Althea frowns. She knows she must get over the strange sensation.

A sheep. A sheep. I am a sheep.

Althea puts all her focus on shifting herself into a sheep. She will not the strange sensation of her face growing or any parts keep her from failing her third try.

Her face elongates, her skin thickens with wool, and a growth comes at her backside. She feels her ears holding and drooping while her waist starts to widen.

"Squaaaaaaaaaaaaaaaak! Squaaaaaaaaaaaaaaaaaaaaaak!"

The sound rings in Althea's ears. She shakes her head to ignore the passing bird.

"Squaaaaaaaaaaaaaaaak! Squaaaaaaaaaaaaaaaaaaaaaak!"

The bird continues over and over taking Althea's mind away from her task and onto the irritating noise. Her body, already weak, begins to lose the sheep form it was attaining. Finally, Althea opens her eyes and loses the animal form she wanted. She looks at the sky and sees a greenish bird flying around in the sky. It reminds her of the one she saw before she fell off the cliff the other day. She glares at the creature who soon flies away.

"Well, well, well, looks like you failed your task." Hadion points out the third failure.

"I only did because that bird was distracting me," Althea blames the avian creature.

"It should not matter if a bird is singing in the sky or a dragon breathing fire in your face, you should never let anything break your focus and execution of a spell."

"But-"

"No. You must also take responsibility for your mistakes."

Althea pouts.

"You failed, and now you will be punished." The corners of his lips start to twitch with anticipation.

"What are you going to do?" Althea asks rather smugly as they both know there can be no physical punishment.

"I will just take back what is mine," He answers.

"The jewels?" Althea loses her smugness. Her hand goes into the pocket weighed down with the precious stones.

"No. No." He relieves her of the concern. He walks up to Althea and takes hold of her sleeve.

Rip!

Her right sleeve comes clean off with the yank of the teacher. Althea grabs at her now naked arm. She gapes at him.

"What did you do that for?"

"I just took back some of what is mine,"

"You took the sleeve?" She does not understand.

"Yes. For every spell you fail, I will take a piece of the dress I made," He states. Althea hides the lower half of her face.

"But-but I could end up..." She cannot even say what could be her final state should you have many more failures. Hadion twists the fabric in his hands.

"I guess you need to not fail anymore," he teases. Althea grimaces.

"Now try again to turn into a sheep."

Althea tries to do as bid but she is distracted again, not by a bird but by fear. *What if I get all the tests wrong and he takes all of the pieces? How will that leave me?*

Fear and fatigue make for a lack of results again. Althea breathes heavily and looks at the unemotional Hadion. He approaches her and grips her other sleeve.

"What are you doing? I only failed once."

"No. No. You have failed five times now. You do not get to restart your count of misses on the same spell," Hadion states then rips off the other sleeve. Her hand goes to touch her newly bare arm.

"Try again." Hadion backs away from her. Althea takes a few deep breaths and then closes her eyes. She tries to clear her mind of anything except her goal to turn into a sheep. She ignores her weakening muscles, the breeze blowing against her, and the thoughts of what Hadion might tear off next if she fails. To be a sheep is the only important thing now.

Althea's body begins to stretch and grow. She repeats the spell a few times and finds her voice is starting to change as well as she speaks. She feels some relief as this must mean it is working.

Hadion loudly yawns. The unexpected sound breaks her focus and makes her jump. As she does, she remains human.

"What was that? You scared me!" Althea glares at Hadion whose hand is over his open mouth.

"I had to yawn. I did say you have to be able to focus no matter what is going on around you. That includes me yawning," Hadion grows rather cross in his tone. Althea scowls as she is further exasperated by this.

"Do not look at me like that. I am trying to teach you." He comes to her again. His hand goes to her chest as he wraps an arm around her.

"I do not like this way of teaching." She brings up her hands to grip his hand on the collar of her dress.

"Trust me, this is better than what I could do if you weren't protected."

"What would you do then?" She tries not to get distracted by his scent.

"I would take you across my knee and make sure your rear would bear the mark of my handprint. Of course, if you continued to fail and your backside was completely overtaken with proof of me, I would..." He stops himself and smirks, then raises the hand that had once been at her chest to her ear and softly rubs the earlobe between his finger and thumb. "I should not say what else I would do with you possessing such innocent ears."

Althea burns with mixed feelings. She is close to humiliation while full of frustration and anger as well as a desire to prove this man wrong. However, there is something else in her that makes her heart race, the hair on her tingling skin raises, and her lips want to close the vast space between them.

"Try again and if you fail, you know what will happen." Hadion releases her earlobe and steps back.

"Alright."

"Alright, what?"

"Alright, Master," she adds the title she keeps forgetting. She keeps what is left of her dress against her and brings her cycle. She shakes away the strange effects Hadion had on her body as she quiets her mind. She hears Hadion yawn again but ignores it this time.

A sheep. I am a sheep. I am a sheep!

Althea opens her eyes. Her vision is quite different than it had been before she closed her eyes as is her view. Her body feels heavy. The dress she had held is on the ground close to her. She tries to look down at her hand but is met with a face full of wool. Althea bleats and jumps about as she rejoices in her success. She is a sheep.

"I did it!" She baas and wags her little tail.

Hadion smiles.

"Excellent," he comes to her, kneels, and pats her wooly head. She finds she enjoys this touch.

"Now turn back."

"Yes, Maaaaa-ster."

She closes her eyes and thinks of her true form and the words she needs to say to return to it. Hooves turn into hands and feet. Her body sheds weight and wool as it stretches back to her proper size. Her face regains its perfect shape. She opens her eyes and finds she is still on the ground with Hadion kneeling next to her. He smiles as does her.

"I did it," She giggles ever so pleased with herself.

"Yes." He takes her hand and helps her come back to her feet. His hand is so much larger than hers but it does not crush hers. Instead, it supports hers.

"Where is my reward?" She asks, having yet to move her hand from his warm one. He does not answer. She notices how his eyes are not on hers. They are lower. She looks down. Her hand flies away from his to cover herself which she finds completely uncovered now due to the dropped dress. Hadion covers his mouth as he chuckles watching her try to cover up with her hands and then the fallen dress.

"You are vile!" She screeches but he keeps laughing. She wraps the fabric as she would a towel so she can cover her front and back. She turns to leave him. He grabs her wrist.

"Come now, Althea. You are the one who dropped the dress," he reminds her to put some blame on her.

"I was a sheep! How can a sheep hold that?" She barks and tries to pull away from him. "Now, let me go, you lecher!"

He does not release her.

"I have done nothing to warrant this fleeing," He defends himself.

"I am naked. Let me go!" She yanks but his hold is too strong though not painful. He rolls his eyes.

"It's time for a new lesson, Althea." He keeps his hold but loses the merriment he had.

"I doubt it is one I want to learn." She does not pull away but keeps her hand fisted.

"Still, you need to learn it. Modesty is a hindrance."

"What?" Althea is unimpressed with the statement.

"If you are concerned with making sure you are never exposed or indecent in appearance, you will severely limit yourself in your magical abilities. You were afraid of being naked when you were turning into a sheep, weren't you? Wasn't that why you were struggling?"

Althea looks away. *How did he know that?*

"See? If you had just focused on completing the spell instead of whether or not I might see you naked, you would have succeeded faster," He points out the reason for her shortcomings.

"So, you think I should just be fine with anyone and everyone seeing me naked so I can do magic?" She questions.

"Yes."

Althea is stunned by the blunt answer.

"Then why teach Odile to shift with her clothes?" She points out the hypocrisy she sees.

"That is a lesson I will teach you as well. But until you can master shifting itself, I cannot teach you to shift without losing your clothes. When you worked in your bakery and made bread you had to mix the ingredients, knead, let it rise, then knead it again before you baked it or it would be ruined, correct?" Hadion brings up her old occupation.

"Yes..."

"You are still being kneaded and once you have risen to know how to shift without fault, then I will knead the lessons with keeping your clothes so you will be a full master of shifting. Understand?" Hadion sets out his process.

"I do...but I still do not like the idea of being naked."

"You don't have to like it; you just have to accept it. To make you learn to adjust to it, I am now making it a rule you must be naked when we train."

"What? No!" Althea steps back.

"Yes."

"At least let me wear my chemise." Althea tries to find a compromise. Hadion pauses to consider the option.

"You may start in a chemise but once you falter on a spell, it will be removed," he decides.

"But-"

"Or you can just be naked," He brings back his original choice.

"Fine. Only if I falter on a spell three times," Althea sets more to the conditions. Hadion nods in agreement to the deal. He offers his hand to shake on the deal. She shakes it.

"Now, I think you should get dressed and rest." He lets go of her hand.

"I agree."

"I will see you later." He sprouts his large wings and then jumps into the air where his wings carry him off.

"Too much of me..." Althea sighs and then begins her long walk back to the castle.

Althea received many side glances from the servants she passed on her way back to Odile's tower but none spoke to her. She hates the looks she receives.

"Will I have to end up like this every day? Will they look at me like this every day?" Althea walks in Odile's hall. She raises her hand to knock on Odile's door but stops. She looks down at herself embarrassed by her appearance.

"Is it really worth it to learn magic just to end up like this?" Althea asks herself. However, she knocks on the door.

"Althea, what happened?" Odile opens the door with wide eyes.

"Modesty is a hindrance," Althea repeats Hadion's words while she enters the room.

"Oh...I see. You've reached that part in your lessons." Odile heads towards her closet with Althea.

"Your father had you train naked too?" Althea asks seeking some solace this is not uncommon. Odile stops.

"He is having you train naked?" Odile is rather surprised.

"Yes. Is that not normal?"

"Well, I have never trained with him naked," Odile's statement makes Althea's anger rise as well as her blood pressure.

He tricked me!

"But that is only because I did my naked training as a child. All sorcerers and sorceresses do as children. It's to teach us to be confident and not to worry about unimportant things like accidentally ending up naked. I guess I was just surprised since that type of training is for children but then again you were not trained as a child and so you need to go through it. I guess I was also surprised my father was doing that with you since I did not do that with him. When I was at that stage, I was being trained by my Aunt Odessa then Bardolph's mother." Odile thinks back to her younger days. Althea's tensed muscles start to release as she is glad to know naked training is not a lie. However, her curiosity rises.

"Bardolph's mother?"

"Yes. Livia started training me young and so I was naked when I trained. She believed modesty to be a hindrance. I did not train with her long," Odile continues into the closet.

"Why is that?" Althea accepts a chemise Odile hands her. She drops the remains of the purple dress to put on the chemise.

"I don't know. I think Livia just liked being naked and having everyone naked as well," Odile answers.

"Not that. I mean why did you not train with her long?"

"Oh! Well, my mother wasn't very happy for me to be under Livia's wing so Father became my master instead." Odile holds up two dresses for Althea to choose one of them. Althea points to a blue dress. She is handed the dress.

"Your mother and Bardolph's were around here at the same time?" Althea throws the dress over her head.

"Yes." Odile helps to pull it down so Althea's head can be exposed again.

"Are they still around?" Althea pulls her hair out of the dress.

"What do you mean by around?" Odile makes sure the skirt of the dress did not get tucked up under as it was being put on by Althea.

"Are they alive?" Althea rephrases the question.

"Yes. As far as I know." Odile walks away from Althea towards the shoes.

"I assume your mothers do not live in the castle. I have yet to see any women besides us in the castle here. But to be fair I have yet to see the rest of the castle."

"You are correct. They do not live here anymore." Odile brings Althea a pair of slippers. Althea takes them to wear.

"Oh, you look splendid." Odile admires her friend.

Odile smiles looking at the dressed Althea who thanks her. The blonde finds a mirror to look at herself. The silk dress is a pale blue with double-layered chiffon sleeves nearly touching the floor. Silver filigree decorates the collar of the modest gown. It is far more comfortable than being naked. Althea touches her long yellow hair. It makes her think of her mother who also shares her hair.

"Do you miss your mother?" Althea's question surprises the young maiden.

"Not really. I see her sometimes," Odile runs her fingers through her hair as she looks at herself in the mirror.

"You do?"

"Yes."

"Does Bardolph see his mother at all?" Althea asks mostly due to the thought he must not with how he acts.

"On occasion. Bardolph is free to see her when he leaves the island but she has to have permission from Father to come back to the island." Odile fixes her dress.

"Did your Father and his mother have a bad falling out?" Althea is not sure why she is curious about Hadion's past with this woman but as long as Odile will answer her questions, she will feed her curiosity.

"I don't know exactly what happened. One day she was here and the next she was kicked out. I don't think Bardolph has forgiven Father for that," Odile recalls.

"Did your mother get kicked out as well?" Althea tries again to get more information on Odile's mother.

"She left of her own accord."

"I heard your mother is not of fairy blood. How did she leave?" Althea is shocked a human could just leave the island.

"Father let her."

"Ah...Did your father love her immensely?" Althea's question pops out of her mouth before she even realizes she formed the question.

"Uh..." Odile pauses to think. "I don't know if they were in love but I suppose they had to like each other long enough at some point to make me."

"I'm sorry if I'm making you uncomfortable with my questions. I am just so curious about your family." Althea notices Odile's shoulders tensing and puts her hand on Odile's arm.

"It is fine. My family is rather complicated which can make one more curious about it. But I would rather speak of yours. It would be nice to speak of a family not all twisted and divided," Odile admits.

"I do not mind speaking of mine though there are some mysteries in mine as well," Althea smiles.

"Such as?" Odile takes a seat on the bed. Althea joins her

"I have no idea who my mother's family is."

"You don't?"

"No. I know some things about them like they lived in Chrysonero, my mother has a twin sister with whom she did not get along, and her father disapproved of my father so when my parents eloped, all contact was cut off. I suppose they were a bit wealthy as my mother is well-educated. Other than that, I know nothing of them," Althea shares.

"Hmmmm. I suppose we are alike in this," Odile comments.

"How so?'

"I barely know anything about my mother's family. I know where they are from, their names and positions, and what part my mother was in the family, but other than I know nothing. I never met them and my mother rarely speaks of them."

"Did they disapprove of your mother's relationship with your father as well?"

"They never knew of it."

"Oh? How could they not?"

"My mother was kidnapped and has not had contact with her family since then."

"Kidnapped! Did your father kidnap your mother?" Athea's mind is immediately appalled Hadion would do such a thing.

"No. No. They met later." Odile shakes her head.

"Has your mother been able to return to them now that her relationship with your father has ended?"

"No. But I do not think it would be wise for her to go home to her family either. Her parents are dead now and her brother is in bad health and may die soon."

"How do you know that?"

"My father did some scrying and learned of this," Odile explains though Althea is not sure what scrying is.

"But your mother may want to go home to her brother if he is so unwell. I know if my brother or sister were on their deathbeds, I would want to be with them at least one last time before they died."

Althea feels tears in her eyes thinking of her own siblings she has not seen in so long.

"You must love your siblings," Odile pivots the conversation away from her mother.

"I do. That is why I am here. Well, that and being taken off by Bardolph."

"I know you want to find your brother. And I think...I might know of a spot he could be," Odile's words make Althea's heart jump and eyes light up.

"Really? Where?" Althea grasps Odile's hands.

"It would be on the other side of the island. I saw a suspicious spot while I was flying the other day. He could be there..." Odile tries to not get Althea's hopes up too high.

"Could you find out if he is?"

"I cannot go to that specific place alone. You would have to come with me," Odile claims.

"Absolutely! Let's go!" Althea stands ready to find her brother.

"It is not that simple, Althea," Odile remains seated.

"What do you mean?"

"Where he is will require you to cross much terrain and to be able to do much magic. You are not trained enough to do the magic needed and frankly, I am not skilled enough to do what I will need to do alone. Also, without you being able to fly, we will have to cross the island on foot."

"Where is he?" Althea cannot understand what would cause all these hoops to jump through.

"Again, I am not certain if this is it, but he might be in what I call the cave of...terror," Odile grows pale, saying the name.

"Cave of terror? What is that?"

"It's a cave on the far side of the island. The only opening is on the side of a cliff. I never go in there because...it is cursed. But knowing Bardolph, he may have stored your brother there because only my father and Bardolph have strong enough magic to counter the curses in there."

"I see..." Althea sits next to Odile once more.

"But if you keep training and do well then maybe together, we can face it and see if your brother is in there." Odile takes Althea's hands this time.

"Alright. Then I will do all I can to learn as fast as I can. But you must also keep up your studies and training so we will be strong enough to do this together," Althea charges Odile. She nods in agreement.

CHAPTER 29

ALTHEA

Althea was up and dressed when she received a knock on her door the morning after she and Odile agreed to give their all to training. She gave word for the knocker to enter as she does not have the key to the locked room. The opening of the door allowed Hadion to enter. He is dressed all in black from his knee-high boots to his bottoms to his tunic. Only the braided embroidery at the hem of his shirt and the belt around his weight are not black as they are gold.

"Good morning," he greets. She returns the greeting.

"Are you ready for training?"

"I suppose so."

Hadion takes Althea back to the courtyard where he had trained her the previous day. He has her perform many spells, most of which she did the previous day but with some new additional spells including making their meal by growing fruit. When it came time for her shift, she was feeling weak and failed thrice to shift. This resulted in the loss of her chemise.

"Do not try to cover up, Althea." Hadion crosses to her and pushes away the arms trying to cover her. Her flesh burns with humiliation.

Bear it. Bear it for Baz. She told herself as she tried to ignore Hadion's attentive eyes.

"You do not need to be ashamed of your body. It is perfectly natural to be nude. You were born naked, correct? What is wrong with being in the state in which you were born?" He brings up the universal fact for all births.

Althea looks away uncomfortably.

"Would it make you more comfortable if I were naked as well?" He moves his hand to grab the hem of his shirt.

"No!" She grabs his wrists to stop him. He laughs.

"I suppose that would be wise. I would not want *you* to get too aroused."

"As if anything you could do would arouse me," Althea snorts, crossing her arms.

"Don't tempt me to prove you wrong, Althea. We might enjoy it too much." He winks.

"I think not. I have no interest in a man like you."

"What? Handsome, powerful, generous," he lists some qualities he believes to possess.

"Arrogant, controlling, lecherous," Althea lists her own. He laughs at her barbs.

"I promise having you practice naked is not for my satisfaction even if I do enjoy seeing such a beautiful sight."

His last comment does not fall on deaf ears but she chooses to ignore it. It is surely a ploy to flatter and make her think kinder of him.

"Odile told me it is to help build my confidence as well, so I guess I will endure it."

"It does. Of course, now I have to think of true punishment if you fail," He thinks of his new challenge.

"I suppose it will be hard given you can't hurt me." Althea smiles smugly.

"I may be a physical man, but I am creative enough to find ways to reach you without touching."

Althea's smile drops. She steels herself in the idea she will not fail anymore.

"Try again now to turn into a sheep," He instructs. Althea sets her focus. Sure enough, she succeeds this time. When told, she changes back into her human form.

"Good, Althea. Now shift into a horse," he challenges.

"A horse?"

"Yes."

"Alright. I will become a horse."

I am a horse. I am a horse. I am a horse.

Althea is indeed not a horse. Even after six attempts she fails to shift into the majestic sort of beast.

How did Tyr do this?

Unfortunately, she is spent before she can attempt another time. She pants and sweats as she grips the pedestal of the nearest statue.

"I think you may have overexerted yourself," Hadion comments.

"I'm fine." Althea pushes herself off the statue to give the appearance of fortitude. Of course, the moment she stands up for herself, her legs cramp and cause her to start to fall. Swift as the wind, Hadion catches Althea before she can hit the ground. His arms wrap around her sturdily while his hands are gentle but firm on her bare skin. The warmth of his clothed body is welcomed against her cool skin.

"I see I was right again." He has her stand upright. She keeps her hands on his forearms to keep her balance as she feels her legs weak again.

"Hold onto this." He puts her hands on the pedestal. He grabs the discarded chemise and puts it over her. She is surprised at his dressing her but does not dare to question it. Then without so much as another word, Hadion swoops Althea up into his arms. Her arms instinctively go around his neck to keep her from falling from his arms.

"I'm not going to drop you." He feels the tight squeeze of her arms. She loosens them, allowing herself to trust his hold.

"Why are you picking me up?"

"You need to rest. I will take you back to your room." He starts to walk.

"I can walk by myself." Althea starts to turn as if to step out of his arms. He does a controlled toss to keep her in his hold.

"No. I will take you up. You'll need to save up your energy."

"You're not going to fly me up there, are you?" Althea checks quickly looking up at the great height, her buttocks tingling in fear of the height they would have to go.

"No. I'll just carry you."

She does not want to admit it but she is rather comfortable in his arms. She also finds this training, though not terribly physical, has left her body weak in feeling. It is nice to not have to climb up the several steps to get back to her room. She supposes she can allow him to carry her. He is supposed to be her master after all and does not a master take care of his students?

Leaning her head against his chest, Althea inhales his smell and listens to his heartbeat. It thumps at a regulated speed. It is consistent and soothing.

"If I get too heavy, you can put me down," Althea informs him of the option.

"Do you not think I'm strong enough to carry you?"

"No. I just...don't want to be too taxing on you." She shakes her head.

"If you are fishing for a compliment on how light you are, then please, be direct with what you desire me to say to flatter you."

"I am not fishing for a compliment."

"No? Well, I would have gladly supplied you with an earful had you wanted them."

"Oh, please, I do not want any of your false compliments. I despise insincerity in a man."

"Who is to say they would be false? I am not known to be insincere."

"I doubt you have many compliments for me given my rather hostile attitude toward you and my lack of compliance to your rules as your student."

"It is true I dislike hostility and disobedience. Anyone in my place would. Most would have ended their tutelage of you, but I enjoy a challenge. And I admit I like watching you grow and learn."

"Really?"

"Yes. I especially enjoy the way you squeal in delight and smile when you get a spell correct. And I do not mind your anger much as you are lovely in any temperament." His words make her skin flush.

"You're just flattering me in hopes of making me more compliant, aren't you?"

"No. You're too smart to fall for that."

"You think I am smart?"

"Why would I waste my time teaching you if I did not think so?"

Althea presses her lips together and stays silent.

"Are you not used to people confirming your intellect?" His question makes her stomach tighten. Her mind goes back to the scores of men and boys she has known growing up who have paid hundreds upon hundreds of compliments to her.

"When one is a great beauty, other characteristics are not so important." Althea holds up her head high.

"You do not believe this, do you?" He raises an eyebrow.

"No, but every man I've met who has sought my affection, if not just my attention, has made it clear my beauty is my greatest accomplishment. It is...concerning to know one's worth is based on something that will not last." Althea gives voice to her thoughts then stops and looks down as she realizes to whom she speaks. "I do not mean to be oversharing like this. I'm sure none of this is of interest to you."

"Of course, it is of interest to me." His reply makes her eyes go back to his face.

"It is?" Her stomach has something fluttering in it.

"I am your master. I need to know of your feelings and thoughts so I can find the best way to guide you," He answers, looking down at her.

"I suppose that makes sense." Her eyes do not meet his.

"Do feel free to confide in me, Althea. I only want to help," he insists.

I wish that could be true. Can I really trust this man?

Before Althea can realize it, she has been set down at the door of her room. Her legs have regained their strength.

"Go and rest. I will come for you at supper time tonight." He opens the door. She enters the room then turns back. He has forgotten to punish her. She opens her mouth to remind him then closes it.

Why would I want him to do that?

"I did not forget about your punishment. It will be later tonight." Hadion leaves.

Althea does not remember falling asleep but sharp poking in her cheek wakes her.

She sleepily opens one eye to see Hadion sitting on her bed and poking her with his long index finger. She gasps and jumps in the bed resulting in her falling from the bed. Hadion laughs then lays across it to look at her on the floor. She clutches her racing heart.

"What are you doing in here?" She is scandalized.

"I told you I was coming for you. Come," He gets off the bed. She gets off the ground and straightens out her chemise. He starts for the door. Althea puts on some slippers but does not put anything over her chemise nor does she remove it.

Althea stays on her master's tail as they venture down. She finds the halls to be lit with lanterns since the sky outside of the windows is getting darker. She yawns several times as they go down to the dining room. Once there, Hadion takes his seat at the head of the table. He has a plate covered in rocks, nails, and maggots. She cringes at the sight.

"Turn it into supper," Hadion points to the plate.

"You want me to turn all of that into food?" She brings her hand to her chest. He looks at her with a raised eyebrow. She knows she has forgotten the key word so she adds it. "Master?"

"I do."

Althea sighs and mumbles an 'okay' before setting her mind fully on the task at hand. She stares at the items and closes her eyes. She breathes deeply and speaks clearly as Hadion taught her.

It would be good to have hot, soft rolls. Just like the ones Stella makes with melted honeyed butter on top. She thinks and makes her stomach growl.

She peeks out of one eye after casting the spell. She beams seeing the steaming, glossy rolls on his plate.

"Now the rest." Hadion gestures to the leaves and maggots. Her eyes go to the chubby, squirming maggots making her gag. She searches her mind for something for it to turn into as well as a spell to do it. She snaps when she comes up with the solution. It takes two attempts before the maggots are changed into large, brown sausages. When she sees the nails, she does not feel so disgusted, and with great ease, she changes them into asparagus.

"Excellent job, Althea." Hadion looks up from his plate. She smiles accepting the praise.

"Now come and taste it." He waves her over. She comes to his side only for him to pull her into his lap. She nervously grabs one of the rolls. The smell entices her enough to take a bite. She is pleased to find it soft, warm, and delicious. She next goes for the asparagus. They are rather raw but not unbearable. She picks up a sausage. She prays it will not turn back into a maggot. She takes a bite and finds her prayer answered.

"It is good," She declares. With his arms on either side of her, he gathers some of the food to taste.

"It is," he agrees. Althea smiles pleased she succeeded. They eat their fill.

Once finished, he orders her to follow him. He leads her from the dining room and takes her toward the inner parts of the castle.

Althea looks around as she follows him. She is amazed at the rooms she passes and crosses through. Each room is different but all are ornate in their furnishings, art, and style. She supposes she may have been this way before when she was taken to Hadion's study that other time but the doors were closed then. She notices now how the ceilings are unique as well. Some have painted murals on them depicting different scenes she knows she has read about in old tales and myths as well as intricate moldings and carvings.

Hadion enters his study. Althea looks around more carefully this time. Last time she noticed hardly anything except Hadion for he had entranced her. She remembers the large desk with large chairs as well. Hadion's chair is made of brown leather while the ones where she and Bardolph sat were a plush green velvet. She catches sight of the letter opener she attempted to stab Bardolph with on the large desk with many papers, an ink well, feathers, and books. Everything else she sees as if for the first time.

The wood in the room making up the vast bookshelves with their accompanying ladders, the moldings, the desk, the legs of the chairs and couches in the large room, the small tables placed about the room, and the door are made of walnut. The walls not covered by bookshelves have been painted hunter green. There are plants placed about the room but known are set in a manner indicating they are meant to be a centerpiece. On the marble floor are a few rugs including one made from the body of a bear. Lanterns appearing to be held by brass hands are placed about the room so the room is well-lit. Althea is not sure how necessary they are since behind Hadion's desk is a large fireplace so high it is halfway up the wall. Like the marble floors, the mantle is made of marble. The top is flat but the corbels on the side have carved dragons facing each other from opposite sides. Their mouths are open giving the appearance they are the ones breathing fire into the hearth. The dragons' bodies go up and intertwine in the center of the mantle. Just above the mantle is a large painting in a brass frame with two large circular windows on either side of the picture. Further up, is a simple cream ceiling.

Althea's eyes go back to the large picture in the room. She is surprised to see it is not a singular portrait but of a family. Just as she starts to focus on it, Hadion steps in front of her blocking her view.

"As punishment for your earlier failure, I want you to dust this entire room then sweep it, mop it and wash the windows."

"And with what tools will I clean, Master?" She questions.

"Over there," he points to a corner she did not notice.

"Then I will get to work, Master." She nods but sighs thinking about the amount of work she will have to accomplish. With the size of the room, it could take hours.

"Good. I will leave you to it." He walks back to the door only to stop. "Oh, Althea."

"Hm?"

"I need this all cleaned by sunset," he states.

"Sunset?"

"Yes. That's about a half hour from now. You can do all of this by then, right?"

Althea's mouth falls open at the ask.

"I will be back soon." He does not continue to wait for an answer. Instead, he leaves the room, closing the door behind him and locking it.

"Uhhhhhgggggggggg!" Althea groans loudly in her frustration. "How am I supposed to clean everything so quickly? He is crazy!"

Althea huffs as she stomps over to the corner where the supplies are. She looks at the feather duster and then turns to look at the rest of the room.

"Did it just double in size?" She asks aloud though the room had not grown at all since her taking the duster.

She starts at the furniture next to her. She sneezes a few times as the dust is removed.

"This is going to take forever... I wish I could just snap my fingers and have it down for me," She whines to herself. She stops. She smiles. She looks at the duster and points her finger at it. She speaks what her brain recalls.

The duster jumps out of her hand and begins to dust without any help from Althea. She smiles pleased. The duster finishes the room quickly and with much more ease than if Althea had done it herself. The duster returns to her hand once finished.

"Now you, broom." She points to the inanimate object and spells it. It hops off to work. Althea spells the dustpan as well to accompany the broom and mop with the pail of water to follow behind the broom and dustpan. Spelling rags to go wash windows was not hard either. Althea walks to Hadion's chair and sits in it with a smirk. She had bested her master after all.

Althea turns the chair so she may face the fire warming her rather chilly body. As she enjoys the heat she stares up at the picture in the room.

At the center of the picture and standing tallest is a tan man dressed all in black. He has a black cape covering most of what he wears. Golden thread makes a stunning filigree on the cape. The gold matches the belt around his obscured waist and the three large, thick neck rings covering his neck. He has a pin on his lapel of an iron wolf's head with wings coming out of it. He bears a similar resemblance to Hadion but he is not him. His eyes are dark and sharp in shape like Hadion's. He is clean-shaven but his curly brown hair is short and rather pushed back around his forehead hosting a golden circlet with a large red ruby in the center. His nose is a tad wider than Hadion's and his face seems fuller. He holds an all too pleased smile much like the one Hadion gives when her clothes come off.

To the left of the man Althea assumes is a relation to Hadion, who is a young woman. She looks about Althea's age. Her loose hair is long, brown, and curly. She has the same sharp eyes as Hadion as well as the other man. The color is not the same though. They lack some of the colors Hadion has. Her nose is small and thin like her body. Her high-collared dress is black and tight with a copper and golden twisted belt at her waist. The billowing sleeves of her dress are white. On her head is a golden and copper woven circlet like the other man's but she lacks a central ruby. Instead, Althea finds the ruby in a pendant attached to a long lariat necklace. The young woman gives a soft smile.

Seated before the man and just off-center is another beautiful woman about Stella's age. Althea is stunned at how even in the painting the woman's skin looks luminous and golden. Her white-gold hair is loose and cascades in waves about her body. Her small eyes with long black lashes are mostly green with touches of other dots of color giving away what gifts she may have. Her snub nose is a little wide but fits perfectly on her wide face. Her lips are full, even spread into the smile she wears. Her scarlet dress covers her neck but not much else. Her skin is covered with red tulle. From the waist to the floor, the dress is full and dark. But her torso is easily seen through the sheer tulle. Only red lace going down vertically from her shoulder to the waist covers her breasts. Her sheer bishop sleeves have a few horizontal stripes of lace. She too has a circle but with no ruby. Instead, Althea finds her ring finger is the keeper of a large ruby ring.

With the blonde woman stands a young boy around five years old. Her hand rests on his shoulder showing her attachment to him. Simple black attire is suitable for him. His skin is pale except for his rosy cheeks. His dark hair is curly and his eyes sparkle with many colors though form a distance they look simply hazel. Althea knows these eyes.

To the right of the centered people is a male teenager. He is tall and dressed in an outfit identical to the other. He shares the headpiece the women did. Althea cannot find the ruby on him. Looking at his face, Althea knows right away this teenager is Hadion. She is surprised to see him looking this way. He is handsome, of course, but different from his current self. His current self is young looking already but not this young. Now, he has the mature look of a young adult while this painted Hadion is practically a child. However, in his arms is a baby wrapped in a red blanket. The baby has some black hair and large blue eyes with hints of other colors Althea has come to know as well.

Althea is rather confused. Hadion is a teenager, Odile is the baby and Bardolph is the child.

Who are these other people?

"What is this?" A voice booms making Althea jump up from the chair. She turns around to see Hadion in the doorway and a chaotic scene before him. The broom has begun sweeping dirt into the water bucket. While the mop uses the dirt dust pan to help "clean". The wet rags have left the windows to "dust" the books.

"I thought I would use magic to clean up faster. I didn't know they started doing this!" Althea gasps.

"Well, stop them. They are going to ruin this room!" Hadion makes her take responsibility. Althea nods but winces thinking she might make things even worse by trying to stop it. She holds out her hands and closes her eyes as she tries to remember the spell to stop these things.

With a shout and the right word, the objects stop and drop. Althea opens her eyes and looks at Hadion. She cowers and blushes embarrassed by her failure. Surely, he will be furious and punish her.

Hadion just exhales.

"Althea, your mind was in the right place to use magic to clean but when you are using such a spell on multiple items for the first time, you must pay attention to them as you may have made a mistake." He picks up the broom.

"I-I'm sorry. You're right. I should have been paying attention," Althea apologizes.

Hadion comes and puts his hand on her shoulder. She looks up at him. He offers a smile.

"It is fine. I'm impressed you were able to have so many moving pieces on your first try," He gives her a little positivity. She starts to smile. He snaps his fingers and the tools begin their work again but properly this time. Althea watches, rather impressed he did not even need to speak to get the items to work.

"How can you use spells without even speaking, Master?" Althea sincerely wonders.

"You will get to a point where you know the spells so well and can execute them so well you do not need to even speak the words to cast the spell. It takes years to reach that though," he informs her.

"I see," She nods. She watches the cleaning intently curious if it will go wrong like hers. It does not.

"So why weren't you watching when you cast the spell for the cleaning?" He inquires breaking Althea's concentration on the tools.

"I-uh-was distracted." She will not meet his eye.

"By?"

"The portrait," She mumbles.

"The portrait?" He repeats then looks up from her. His eyes go to the picture above the mantle.

"I see." He walks toward it. Althea walks with him.

"I was surprised to see Odile as a baby and Bardolph as a child," Althea comments. Hadion keeps staring at the portrait.

"I suppose it is strange for you as you have only known us a short while."

"Yes, and because I have no idea who these other people are," Althea adds.

"Well, she is Livia." Hadion points to the blonde woman in the rede dress.

"Livia," Althea repeats. "She is Bardolph's mother, correct?"

"Yes." Hadion nods, not even questioning how Althea knows other than the juxtaposition of the mother and child's seating.

"She is beautiful," Althea comments.

"Yes."

"Odile says she does not live here anymore."

"No, she does not and that is best." Hadion keeps his eyes on her still.

"Who is that woman? Is she Odile's mother?" Althea points to the brunette.

"No. No. She's my half-sister, Odessa." He smiles looking at the other woman.

"Odessa..." Althea whispers the name.

Odile did say she had an aunt with that name. But it still sounds familiar...

"Does she live here?" Althea questions.

"No. She lives with her husband now," Hadion states.

"Hm. So Odile's mother is not in the portrait," Althea states rather than asks.

"Correct. She is not gifted," Hadion states.

"Hm...And who is that man?"

"My father, Kazimeer," Hadion answers.

"He is very handsome," Althea observes, "You look like him."

"I suppose he was and I do."

Althea turns her eyes to Hadion. Now as she thinks about it, Odile had mentioned how Hadion's father would boil Bardolph in oil to get him to levitate. She implied he did the same to Hadion.

What other horrible things did this man do to his own son and grandson? And he says 'was', I guess he is dead now.

"Odile is adorable there. And you...you look so...young, not quite a man yet," Althea decides to take the attention off Kazimeer.

"Well, I was only eighteen in the portrait," He gives the excuse for his youthfulness.

"Eighteen? But Bardolph is about five or six years old in the portrait," Althea guesses.

"Yes, he was five years old then and Odile was just a few months old," Hadion sheds more light on the ages.

"But if you were eighteen and Bardolph was five then you became a father at-"

"Thirteen," Hadion answers, so she does not have to do any more calculations.

"You were practically a child. Is it common for sorcerers to begin fathering children at that age?" Althea attempts not to show her concerns and shock.

"Not necessarily. It is the age we begin to learn more about sex magic and sometimes children can result from that but typically precautions are taken to prevent progeny," Hadion tries to explain.

"But you...and Livia loved each other so you decided to have a child young together?" Althea asks.

"More like I was just lonely and horny and she was just bored." His response strikes a nerve in Althea, not the usual one of anger. Hadion continues still staring at Livia. "Her pregnancy was a total accident and for a long time I was not sure if the child was even mine."

"What? How could you not be sure?" Althea cannot hide her surprise anymore. Hadion is taken aback then answers.

"She was my father's wife. It is understandable for there to be a question of paternity given the situation."

"Your father's wife! Your stepmother?" Althea gapes not sure how to process the information she is receiving.

"Yes," he shrugs.

Althea's lips twitch, not sure of what to say or do. She has a hundred more questions in her mind and on her tongue. She cannot get them out.

"This must all be shocking for someone like you. I doubt you've ever even heard of such a thing." Hadion's tone is meant to convey a humorous approach to this topic. He even smiles but Althea sees his eyes.

"You are right. I have not. I am sorry your stepmother took advantage of you."

Hadion is quiet, his smile twitching. He opens his mouth then closes it. He pauses before speaking again in a jovial tone.

"I am grateful to her. She taught me many things both in and out of the bedroom." He purposefully brings up a topic to make Althea blush and look away.

"I need some tea. You must too," Hadion changes the subject. Althea nods.

"Take a seat and I will return," He points to a chair. She takes a seat but stares back at the portrait. She looks at young Hadion then this Livia woman. She is beautiful but it is clear she is older than Hadion. How much older, Althea is not sure but more than likely older enough to know having an affair with one's husband's thirteen-year-old son is clearly not right. It makes Althea's stomach sink.

Althea then looks to Bardolph. The little child looks like both Hadion and Livia as well as Hadion's father. It makes sense there could be confusion about the father, especially given Bardolph's way. Her eyes go to Livia again.

"I suppose he really favors his mother," Althea mumbles to herself.

CHAPTER 30

ALTHEA

Hadion returns with tea which Althea drinks slowly to keep other comments and questions from coming out of her mouth. She does not think it wise for her to speak anymore on it.

"Now that you're finished, let's get on with our evening." He takes the tea cup and saucer from her to put on the desk. Althea dutifully rises from her seat. Hadion leads her out the door. She is not quite sure where he intends to go but follows. Back into the hallways, they go. She peeks at the different open rooms. They reach a stairwell and climb it until they reach the top which Althea knows must be several floors given how tired she is afterward. Hadion opens the door and steps out onto a flat area. Althea walks out and immediately clings to Hadion's arm as he finds she is only on a small platform that can only seem to hold only herself and Hadion. Looking down she can see the top of the castle. She feels much higher up than she has before including when she fell from the cliff.

"Do not be afraid." He softly pats the hand grasping his arm. "You can't get hurt."

"W-what are we doing up here?" Althea asks, closing her eyes still not feeling safe. "I do not like heights."

"We need to go look over the island to make sure nothing is out of sorts," He claims.

"And I must go?"

"Yes."

"But it is dark out."

"The moon will light the island and I have scout eyes. I will be able to see."

"Why don't we get down and walk it?" Althea tries to step back inside. Hadion grabs her and keeps her out with him.

"Because it is quicker and easier to fly and observe than to walk." Hadion gives his sensible reasoning.

"Well, I can't fly…"

"You're going to figure it out," he states then having let go of Althea who does not hold onto him either, he steps off the platform. Althea screams as he falls. He rises back up with his large black wings. She clutches her chest.

"Had you forgotten my wings?" He laughs.

Althea frowns unamused.

"Now, come." He holds out his hand toward her.

"Are you going to carry me?" She asks.

"No. You're going to fly."

"But I do not have natural wings and I doubt I can turn into a bird since I can barely turn into a sheep." Althea holds her arms instead of reaching out to Hadion.

"You can do this," Hadion insists.

"I cannot." Althea shakes her head. "I will fall!"

"Then you will have to get back up and try again."

"No. No. I'm too afraid. I do not want to fall," She admits with tears coming into her eyes.

What if the ring does not work this time? What if I am too high up? I hate falling. The cliff fall was awful. I do not want to fall again! No! No!

Hadion comes and stands on the edge of the podium.

"Althea," His voice is calm. She looks at him. He holds out his hand to her.

"I will not let you fall," He promises. "Take my hand and I will be your wings."

Hesitantly, Althea obeys. Having taken his hand, she is drawn close to him. He wraps his arms around her securely. His wings flap taking them higher and higher into the sky. She keeps her eyes shut tight.

"Open your eyes, Althea. You need to look out with me." Hadion's finger taps her to get her attention. She opens one eye and looks over his shoulder. She sees now the sky has turned to navy and small stars try to come out to shine. A brilliant moon is already out and shedding light everywhere. She opens her second eye and slowly turns her head to look at the ground.

Althea finds them soaring over the lush, green island illuminated under the moon. The are many hills with cliff drop-offs, random gardens of beautiful flowers, fields, lakes, waterfalls, forests, and black sand beaches as well as white sand ones. Basil is somewhere out there. She does not fail to see the castle for the swan women. She notices the many women in white around the lake. There are few animals Althea sees given the height and the coverage by the leafy branches of the trees. Althea begins to enjoy the flight but does not release her hold on Hadion. He does not release his hold on her either.

"Oh, no," Hadion mutters.

"What is wrong?" Althea asks not seeing anything amiss.

"Hold on," he says in response, and with a greater flap of his wings they speed across the sky. They begin to descend. Althea sees now a white stag limping.

Hadion's landing is smooth and effortless. He releases Althea to the ground safely before he retracts his wings inside of his shoulder blades. He walks toward the large stag that does not run at the sight of the island's master. Hadion begins to speak but the noise coming from his mouth is anything but human. Althea almost laughs at the strange sounds leaving his mouth when the stag begins to make a similar noise. Hadion kneels and looks at the affected leg of the stag.

"What is wrong with him?" Althea inquires.

"He says the pain is in his joint here." Hadion touches where the joint is. The deer stays calm even with Hadion touching his injured leg.

"Can you help him?" Althea asks.

"Yes." Hadion nods. His hand stays on the affected area. He closes his eyes and makes no sound. When Hadion opens his eyes and stands, he makes the deer's noise and the stag begins to walk. The stag jumps and prances a little before coming back to Hadion who rubs his head. The stag then walks off pleased.

"Did you just heal him?" Althea's heart flutters happily at the sight.

"Yes."

"How? I saw no spells in the book about healing," Althea recalls from her absorption of the book of spells. It only surprises her now there are no healing spells in the book.

"Well, first of all, I have the natural gift to heal so when it comes to minor animal issues and small injuries like cuts, I need no spells. Second, the spell book you have learned is magic you can do without using blood. In our magic, there must be a blood price paid to heal something. If not your own blood, then the blood of another or an animal," Hadion explains.

"Oh..." Althea supposes she is glad to not know these healing spells then.

"Of course, there are other methods to help heal such as making potions, elixirs, and the like. However, they take longer and sometimes fail to work due to the wrong amount of ingredients," Hadion gives an alternative.

"Will you teach me how to make such potions, Master?" Althea asks.

"Yes. I will teach you anything you wish to learn." He smiles. Althea returns the smile with her own.

"Come, let us see if there is anything else needing attention." He holds out his hand to her as his wings come out. Althea goes to him and enjoys his embrace as they fly up again though she would not say such a thing.

Soaring through the sky, Althea begins to like this way to observe. But the flight is soon ended when Hadion lands on a black sand beach at the farthest part of the island. Having let go of Althea, he pulls in his wings.

"We've reached the furthest point on the island from the castle," Hadion states.

"Then I suppose we will be turning around?"

"Not quite yet," he says and begins to lay on the sand.

"What are you doing?" She stares at him.

"Come and lie down." He pats the sand next to him. Althea comes but sits instead of lying down.

"I said to lie down," he repeats. Althea moves to fulfill his demand.

She looks up to the sky and finds the stars to be bright and prominent in the sky. With the shining stars above, soft sand below, and the crashing of the nearby waves, Althea finds herself comfortable.

"What are we doing?" Althea feels compelled to ask after lying on the ground for a few minutes.

"We are observing the stars."

"Why?"

"You need to learn to use them."

"For?"

"Navigating."

"Are we going to travel?"

"Not that sort of navigation though that can be helpful," Hadion keeps his eyes on the sky.

"What sort then?"

"To navigate the courses of our lives and others so we know how best exploit our potentials to the fullest."

"Like prophesying?"

"Not exactly. It is to help predict or indicate when it is the right time to do something. Planets are always moving and as they move different people act on different things. We must study the stars and the planets to know when something may come," He explains.

"Would not prophesying be clearer on such things?"

"No. I have the gift of prophecy so I may be able to see something that may happen but I do not know when it will happen. So, I look to the stars and planets." His claim of the gifts reminds Althea of the gold in his eyes like Zarin.

"Is seeing the future so unclear?"

"What do you mean?"

"Do you not see clearly who and what is involved in the future as if you are watching it play before you?"

"It depends. Some visions are so clear I can identify who and where things are taking place while other times it is flashes and symbols are rather vague. I study them to understand them. Of course, sometimes I'm wrong on their meaning until it has come to pass and I gain clarity."

"You can be wrong?" Althea teases looking over at him. He looks over at her for a brief moment.

"On rare occasions," he concedes, then returns his eyes to the sky. Althea giggles.

"What would you say was the vision you saw the most...unclearly?" Althea seeks to know of one of the few times he will admit to being wrong.

"Sometimes I get visions of golden hair and wolfsbane," He answers, making Althea laugh which in turn makes him as well.

"Why those two things?"

"I have not the slightest clue. It is odd, but visions can be like that," he shrugs.

"Hm....so would you say relying on cards or palm reading to be better to tell the future?"

"No. They are vaguer. Besides, I rarely use cards or palm reading to tell the future since those are more for those who do not have the gift of prophecy."

"Ah...so are they all a farce?"

"No. You can learn from them but it will not be as clear as a vision."

"What do you think is the clearest vision you have ever had?" Althea stares at Hadion curious. He keeps his eyes on the stars. He is quiet for a minute as he thinks.

"When I was a child, I foresaw my mother's death. I saw her using what magic she could to fight but ultimately, she was pinned down and beheaded. Three days after the vision I saw it come to pass," He recounts.

"Oh, Hadion, I'm sorry," She reaches over and touches his arm. He looks at her hand then over to her.

"You sure do apologize a lot for things that are not your fault," he replies.

"I know I am not at fault but it does make me sorrowful to know you have experienced this. I have not lost a parent but I have lost ones I have loved before and it is not something to wish for others to experience," She explains her words.

"Who have you lost that you loved? A former lover?"

"No. No. I lost my grandparents. My grandmother caught a lung fever and died. My grandfather's heart broke so he died just after she was declared dead," Althea shares.

"Your grandfather died of a broken heart?" Hadion raises an eyebrow skeptical.

"Yes. He loved her most ardently. I do not think I have ever seen two people more in love with each other than them. He would always say he could not live without her. And when she died, his words proved true." Althea thinks of the couple.

"Hm..."

"Was your father upset when your mother died?"

"No. He was the one who killed her."

"What?" Althea's eyes bulge not believing what she is hearing.

"My parents were not in love. My mother hated my father with every fiber of her being and I do not blame her. He kidnapped her, forced himself on her, impregnated her, and kept hunting her from the moment she escaped him." He dives into his family history. Althea listens rather horrified.

"That is...horrible," Althea gives her comment on the matter.

"That was my father," Hadion scoffs.

"What happened to him?" Althea hopes justice was somehow served.

"I killed him," Hadion replies without hesitation. Althea sucks her lips into her mouth then releases them to speak.

"To avenge your mother?"

"No."

"Oh..." Althea is not sure why but she is not necessarily upset over Hadion killing his father given what she has come to learn about the man. But murder is still murder.

"Why then?" She feels she should still ask.

"He tried to kill Bardolph and me when he learned the truth. It was either him or my son and me," he answers.

"Oh. Then it was self-defense."

"Yes. You seem pleased," Hadion notes.

"I am not pleased but it is better to know it was to protect yourself rather than because you're a heartless murderer or something," Althea clarifies.

"I assumed you've never killed anyone before then."

"No...but you have seen I have been tempted." Althea thinks of her encounter with Bardolph in the study.

"Bardolph is great at pulling out that desire."

"You...You feel like killing him sometimes?"

Hadion is quiet.

"I get angry with him and know he needs to be punished but I...I could not kill my own child. I am not my father," Hadion speaks slowly.

Althea smiles at the response. She has no care for Bardolph but even so, he is a person.

"There you are, pleased again," Hadion points out the smile.

"It is sweet to see you love your children even with one who is not so easy to love," Althea replies.

"It's easy to fall in love but hard to come out of it. I fell in love with him the moment I held him. And though I despise what he does and is trying to become, I have not completely lost that love for him."

Althea keeps her eyes on the face of this man. There is no arrogance in his face or voice as she shares these things with her. There is softness in his colorful eyes. He is different than usual yet not at all. She cannot explain it but she has more ease with him now especially knowing more about his past.

"Why do you stare?" He calls attention to her actions. She blinks several times and looks away at the stars.

"I-I was just waiting to see if there was anything else you were going to say."

"You're lying," He half grins.

"What? No."

"I am a discerner. I know you're lying," he pokes her cheeks.

"Ow," she groans though it does not actually hurt.

"Lying again," he teases.

"Weren't you going to teach me something about the stars and planets or something?" Althea points to the sky.

"Yes. I almost forgot. I am going to teach you about astrology." He looks back to the sky and moves his finger from her face so he can point it into the air. "You see that planet right there between those stars?"

Althea tries her best to see this planet but her eyes only see small dots and says so.

"Oh, right. You do not have the scouting gift either," He remarks then starts to dig around in his pockets, "It is a good thing I brought this."

"Brought what?"

Hadion pulls out a gold telescope. He hands it over to Althea. She brings the tube to her eye with Hadion's hand helping to guide her. With the device, she sees the stars a bit more clearly.

"Do you see the red dot now?" Hadion asks moving the tube more in his direction.

"Yes!" She beams.

"Good. That is the planet, Vig," He informs her.

"Wow. I have never seen a planet. I would have thought it to be another star." Althea admires the red dot. Hadion smiles watching her enjoyment.

"What are you going to tell me about this?" Althea brings back the attention to the lesson.

"Ah, yes." Hadion turns his eyes back to the sky.

Althea is not sure if it is minutes or hours that pass as Hadion tells her of the stars, planets, their placements, and what they mean. Of course, he cannot share centuries of knowledge in one night.

He comes to his feet and holds his hand out to Althea who takes it to make her rising easier. He tucks away the telescope.

"We must be getting back," Hadion states. Althea begins to nod in agreement but is interrupted by a yawn. She covers her mouth embarrassed.

"Now. Now. Do not fall asleep on me yet. There are still things to do."

"There are?" Althea cannot believe what he says.

"Yes. We have to fly back and I don't want to have to carry dead weight across the island," he claims.

"I am not dead weight. I-"

"You are going to fly." Hadion cuts her off and gives her the task.

"No. No. No. No. I cannot." Althea waves her hands at him.

"Yes, you can and you will. We do not have to fly too high but you will fly."

"How? I have no wings." She reminds him of one of the many differences between them.

"You can shift into a bird or merely change your arms into wings." He pats her arms.

"I cannot. I have already told you this," Althea shakes her head set on her lack of ability.

"Listen." He holds her shoulders in his hands and brings his face close to hers. "You are capable of more than you think. You can do this. It will be hard but you will succeed. Do not let fear take away your power."

Althea swallows the lump in her throat but nods. She knows he is right.

"Try." He releases her and steps away.

Althea takes several breaths.

I will try. I will try. She focuses on what it is she desires to become.

A bird. A bird. I must be a bird. Oh, but what bird should I be? A raven? A crow? A robin? A swan? Althea tries to think of the different birds. But she knows in her heart what bird she would prefer to be. She sets her mind to the task at hand with her choice in mind.

Once. Twice. Thrice. Six times she tries and fails. But Hadion does not grow impatient or cross. Instead, he waits and encourages her to try at least once more.

"Ender's Gate! Look at you, Althea!" Hadion's eyes light up as he sees the changed girl before him. Althea twists her head and squawks pleased. She was successful!

Hadion picks up her far too big chemise and wraps it around his arm before putting his arm to the bird's chest. She instinctively climbs onto his wrapped arm. Hadion raises her and admires her. She is a rare sight. Though there are phoenixes on the island, none are white and gold like her.

"Truly splendid work, Althea," He praises her. She enjoys the praise.

"Now we must fly." His wings come out.

"How?" She asks.

"Just flap. If you start to fall, struggle, or change back, I will catch you," he says. Althea takes him at his word.

Althea begins to flap her wings. Unaccustomed to being in such a state, she struggles to remain level and not sink. Hadion flies near her and is sure to catch her when she coasts too long and starts to fall. But sure enough, flying becomes a bit easier.

The night air moving through her feathers and on her face is sweet. Her eye turns up toward the starry sky. She cannot explain it but she has the sudden urge to fly as high as she can. Her wings do their best to comply with her sudden wish. Hadion follows.

Althea spins in the air as she finds herself no longer afraid of falling. She cannot fall. Her wings, her beautiful, magnificent wings will not fail her. She can fly as high and as far as she wants. She will fly to the cave where Basil is held and save him. Then maybe she will fly away back to the Far Lands with her brother in her large talons.

Just as Althea thinks she can touch the moon, she feels a cramp in her leg. She feels aches in her back. Wings grow heavy. It has become hard to flap them. Her breathing is labored and fatigue hits like a slap to the face. In an instant, her feathery body is gone and her human one is back. Like an acorn in autumn, Althea falls.

"Hadion!" She tearfully screams his name as she drops.

Swooping in like a hawk, he catches her in his arms. He holds her close to his chest.

"I told you I wouldn't let you fall."

She exhales relieved.

Hadion flies her the rest of the way back to the castle. Once in the tall tower, Althea puts her chemise back on herself with Hadion's aid as all of her limbs are sore and weak.

"I'll carry you to your room." He picks her up to cradle her again.

"No, I-"

"What? Crawl? It is too far. I will carry you." He does not let her go. Althea does not protest any longer. He is right. She does not have much strength.

"I am sorry I failed to fly back," Althea apologizes.

"Do not be. I did not expect you to be able to fly the entire island. You have to build up endurance."

"Right..."

"You did a fantastic job though. I was impressed with the phoenix form you chose."

"Well, it is my favorite animal." Althea smiles.

"You did it justice. We will practice again when we go back tomorrow night."

"We are going back again?" Althea is not upset but rather excited at the prospect. She did enjoy herself this evening.

"Yes. You need to learn astrology and astronomy as well as shift and fly. We will also continue our daytime lessons." He gives the schedule.

"That is a lot of time for us to be...working."

"Yes. You'll have to get used to it," he states.

"Yes, Master," She sarcastically refers to his title.

When reaching her room, Hadion lets her down and trusts her to get to her bed which she does. Althea lay in her bed long after he had gone to think about the night she has had.

Althea learned so much about her teacher, both good and bad. She did pity him but he was not pathetic. She is not sure what he is or why she cannot get the smell of him or the look in his eyes out of her head. She tries to shake it out as she tosses herself on the bed. She turns to the side and with great determination blocks him from her head so she may sleep. Of course, in dreams, she is not as in control because it seems her mind would like to relive the night.

As Hadion makes his way back to his private chambers, he is sure to stop and check on Odile who sleeps soundly on her bed. She sleeps atop her blankets with the giant spell books open next to her and candles still burning about the room to help her sleep. Hadion picks up the book and sees she still has not reached the spell for mental absorption. He closes the book and puts it on a table. He comes back to remove her shoes and jewelry before moving her to put her under her sheets. With a wave, he extinguishes all of the candles. He kisses her temple lightly then leaves.

Having spoken of his son with Althea, Hadion makes a detour on his way to his chambers. He climbs up the tower he designated for Bardolph. He finds the door of his son's bedroom to be ajar. He peeks around the door to find candles lit as well. He wonders if his son has also fallen asleep with the candles lit.

"Bardolph?" Hadion calls softly stepping into the room. Bardolph is not asleep but sitting in a Savonarola chair in front of a large mirror with an ornate gold frame. He has a small table next to him with a bottle of wine on it. He holds a glass of red wine and brings it to his lips.

"Shouldn't you be asleep?" Hadion speaks up.

"Shouldn't you be knocking?" Bardolph asks the entering Hadion as he catches sight of him in the mirror. Hadion gives the door a knock with an annoyed expression.

"What are you still doing up?" Hadion rephrases his earlier question.

"Minding my business. What are you doing up, old man?" Bardolph talks to the reflection.

"I was out with Althea," Hadion answers as he walks to the mirror and blocks it with his body. Bardolph smirks.

"Is she finally starting to like you?" Bardolph sniggers.

"I am likable, boy. No woman has rejected me twice," Hadion jabs.

"A woman's 'no' is just an issue of a challenge and we know I don't back down from a challenge." Bardolph puts his glass of wine on the table. Hadion frowns at the words leaving his son's mouth. Hadion notices a fresh scar on Bardolph's palm.

"What is that from?" Hadion points to the hand. Bardolph looks at his hand and shrugs.

"Who knows?"

"You know." Hadion does not put up with his son's vagueness and grabs Bardolph's hand.

"I am a sorcerer, not an apprentice anymore. I can do whatever magic I want," Bardolph states, pulling away. Hadion grabs it again.

"Yes, you are but sometimes you are sloppy." Hadion puts his hand on top of the palm. The scar begins to fade. Bardolph looks up to the other sorcerer who finally lets go of his hand.

"Not that you care, but I am being extra careful with this new spell," Bardolph claims.

"And what spell is that?"

"I am doing what Kazimeer did with Odessa's mother."

"Lucrece?" Hadion remembers the name then turns to look at the large mirror. "Who are you trying to contact?"

"Who do you think?"

"Your mother?" Hadion is at a loss.

Bardolph rolls his eyes and scoffs. "I have other means to reach her. I am going to speak with my bride."

"Your bride?" Hadion crosses his arms.

"Yes. Althea's sister. She is going to be mine. I am going to be in every mirror she passes and sees so she cannot forget about me and or ignore me," Bardolph smiles proudly at his plot.

"That is a stupid plan."

Bardolph stands up furious.

"She will only come to despise you more if you are haunting her in mirrors," Hadion expands on why he is against the plan.

"I don't care if she despises me. She will never be able to forget me or ignore me. I will consume her."

"Why do you want this woman so much?" Hadion cannot fathom this reason for obsession, especially given the description of this woman being lesser in beauty than Althea.

Bardolph retakes his seat and takes another sip of his wine. He gains a small but twisted smile.

"Because...I love her."

CHAPTER 31

Hajnal

The calming camaraderie formed between Hajnal and Zarin in their shared cabin is ripped away from Hajnal. Hajnal suddenly stands up clutching her chest with one hand and her stomach with another. Zarin stands up and puts her hands on Hajnal's shoulders.

"What is wrong, Hajnal?"

"People...people are in great distress near us. I think-I think they are in danger." Hajnal looks at the closed door.

"Who is in danger?"

"I think Astrophel and the others." Hajnal's horrible feelings do not leave her.

"It must be Captain Kolar." Zarin's stomach twists.

"We must go help them." Hajnal finds her bag and pulls out her pipe and a knife. Zarin's limbs are stiff in her distress. She is not sure what the captain has done but she is not surprised he would. Hajnal puts her pipe into the deep pocket of her dress. She holds her knife in her hand but turns it so that when she holds the weapon, the blade is hidden by her wrist and arm. They hastily leave their room. Hajnal is determined to find the others by sensing the strengthening of these horrid feelings.

Coming to the deck, they find it rather dark. The moon is bright in the sky just as the stars are. However, dark clouds are creeping up. There are some lanterns lit around the ship allowing them to have some vision. Some sailors are standing atop some doors leading to the lower floors of the ship. They put a chain between the handles and lock it.

"Eziz, go on to the big room. We'll be there soon." One of the sailors sends off the cabin boy. He runs. He narrowly misses the women. Hajnal hides her knife behind her back.

"Excuse me, ladies," he nods respectively while he keeps running.

"What are they doing over there?" Hajnal looks toward the sailors.

"I don't know. Is the distress coming from over there?"

"No. It's that way." Hajnal points in the opposite direction. As they both turn their heads to see where Hajnal points, they are greeted by the smiling, approaching Captain Kolar. Zarin steps back as Hajnal's stomach tightens.

"Good evening, ladies. I missed you two at supper," he claims. Both notice his split lip and his swelling cheek.

"Zarin was feeling so unwell so we did not come to eat," Hajnal informs him.

"You are unwell, Zarin? You never had seasickness before." He looks around Hajnal to the woman he is addressing.

"It has been many years since I have been on a ship. I am well now," Zarin speaks softly.

"I am glad to hear it," He claims.

"What happened to you?" Zarin inquires and nods to his face.

"Oh, Mr. Brames had a few too many drinks and started reenacting his days in the royal navy. I was standing too close with the lout hit me." He touches his injury.

"Where are our companions?" Hajnal brings the attention back to their current purpose.

"In my cabin," he answers.

"Then please, take us to them. We need to see them."

"I will be happy to take you. Come." The captain holds out his arms for the ladies to take. Hajnal is sure to take the arm allowing her to keep her knife hidden. Zarin's hand trembles before taking his arm. She does not allow it to shake while gripping him.

"Zarin, you must have noticed that this ship is bigger than the *Acrasia*. You've noticed, haven't you? I bought her after the *Acrasia* sank. It is a grand ship, obviously," the captain brags then grows a bit more sincere in his talk. Zarin stays quiet. Hajnal feels the pain increasing. She knows this must mean the men are in the cabin harmed. The overwhelming pain blocks all other feelings around her.

"But I must admit I do miss the paintings you would make on the boards of the ship. It made it all feel much more...homey." The captain slows his walk. Zarin turns her eyes.

"Surely someone on your crew could paint pictures around the ship for you," Zarin mumbles earning a laugh from the captain.

"They can barely mop let alone paint and should any of them want to paint a picture it wouldn't be of the beautiful landscapes or portraits you painted. It'd be of bawdy women and beasts," the captain stops. Zarin removes her hand from his arm.

"Here is my cabin." He turns his focus to the door in front of them. He opens it. Hajnal and Zarin step inside. He closes the door behind him after stepping inside.

"Dear El-Yah!" Hajnal gasps seeing the men lying on the floor and Mr. Phan's caved-in face. Nafisa kneels next to Sir Artegal who she shakes gently but stops when she sees the captain and the women. Zarin stands in shock and horror at the sight of the dead Mr. Phan.

"What have you done?" Captain Kolar roars, stepping between Hajnal and Zarin as if to accuse Nafisa of wrongdoing.

"I didn't do anything, sir," She gets to her feet.

"What did you do to our guests?" He grabs her by her arms.

"I didn't do anything!" She shakes her head.

Hajnal immediately goes to Astrophel's body. Tearfully, she takes him into her lap after setting down her knife.

"Astrophel, speak to me," She urges him.

"Did you poison my guests? Tell me if you did!" Captain Kolar continues to berate the young woman.

"I did not!" She shakes her head.

"Tell me you did!" He orders.

"I did," She falsely confesses.

"Why? After all I have done to help you? You would kill our esteemed guests and my crewmates?"

"I-I-I-" Nafisa struggles to speak.

"Astrophel?" Hajnal puts her head on his chest. His heart is beating rapidly.

"And what did you do to Mr. Phan? What has possessed you?" Captain Kolar gestures to Mr. Phan's corpse. Zarin cannot take her eyes off him.

"I-I-I-"

Captain Kolar slaps Nafisa across the face then gripping her by her long hair drags her to the door. He yells out for Ludo and Loke. The men come running.

"Take this wench and tie her to the main mast," Captain Kolar hands over the young stuttering woman to the sailors.

"I'm so sorry. I had no clue she would do such a thing. I hired her to cook but I never thought...I'm so sorry." Captain Kolar comes behind Zarin and puts his hands on either side of her shoulders. What he intends to be comforting is painful.

"They aren't dead. I hear his heartbeat," Hajnal announces, then looks to Zarin. "Come and heal them!"

Zarin blinks and finally hears Hajnal's words. She moves to take a step forward but Captain Kolar already has his grip on her.

"Are you sure you are not mistaken? You are practically hysterical. You may be conjuring heartbeats in your head as a part of your denial of his death."

"I am not hysterical and I am not making this up. He is not dead. Zarin, please come help him. I do not know the spells to heal yet." Hajnal holds out her hand toward Zarin. She remains in Captain Kolar's hold. His hand has come to hold the back of her bare neck. Zarin is frozen in his hold.

Shivers run up and down Zarin's spine. Her buttocks tingle with the adrenaline running through her. She wants to run. She wants to fight. She wants to be out of his hold and presence.

But...my friends...they are hurt. Mr. Phan is...he is dead. Mr. Phan...the friend El-Yah gave me. Zarin cannot even recognize his mutilated face now. She knows it is not that young girl's fault. *It has to be Captain Kolar's. He did this before when I admired that sailor Yared. This is the same way he killed Yared.*

Zarin returns to that state of hopelessness and helplessness. She is once again shackled in golden bracelets and at the mercy of the captain as are her friends. She looks as if they lie still on the ground. *They're not moving. They must be dead. He has taken away my friends. I'm alone, alone, alone.*

"There is no point. They are dead," Captain Kolar insists. Hajnal picks up her knife and stands.

"They are not! Now let Zarin go so she can save them before they are!" Hajnal holds out the weapon toward the captain. His eyebrows raise in surprise. Then he laughs.

"You think you could even get close to harming me?" he lets go of Zarin and steps forward.

Zarin stays still, her eyes remain closed. She cannot bear to look at her dead friends.

How could I have let them come to this ship? I should have made them leave as soon as I realized the captain was Captain Kolar. Now they are all dead because of me. How will Hajnal ever forgive me? How will we ever leave this ship? Captain Kolar will keep us imprisoned here. He will keep us slaves. He will break and humiliate me again.

"Stay back," Hajnal orders.

"I am the captain of this ship." He does not stop. Hajnal moves to strike him as he is near and senses such wrath from him.

Captain Kolar hits the back of her hand and the front of her wrist, and sends the weapon to fly out of her hand. It lands on the floor. Captain Kolar's hand crosses his body and takes hold of Hajnal's wrist. She puts her free hand atop his grabbing one then swings her grasped arm so she can move this hand to grab his wrist. The swift and forceful movement causes the captain's arm to twist and lock with his head lowered. Feeling confident in her move, her hold relaxes. Captain Kolar escapes the hold and turns around again to face the young woman. His face is red in his rage.

He charges her and punches her in the face. Her head moves but she feels nothing. He punches her in the gut but again she feels nothing much. She swings up her arm and lands a hit on the captain. As his head lowers and turns from the hit, Hajnal puts her hands on his shoulders and raises her knee to knee him in the chest. However, he picks her up from under her legs and throws her down to the floor. The force of it makes Hajnal's back tingle but nothing hurts. The captain puts his hand around Hajnal's throat as he straddles her. He punches her as she claws at his arms.

Zarin cries dreading her fate as the captain's slave again. Of course, now Hajnal will be forced into it too.

Poor Hajnal...She just wants to find her family. Now she is going to be a slave...No. No, Hajnal isn't meant to be a slave. I have already seen that. She has seen a great future that does not involve being a slave to this man. I have seen what is to come for me too. El-Yah has given me the visions before and therefore the promises of the great things to come. I must not fold now. I must not break.

Zarin finally opens her eyes and sees the captain trying to beat Hajnal. Of course, it is all futile as she is protected by the ring. Still, Zarin grabs Captain Kolar by his shoulder and throws him off Hajnal. Zarin holds her hand out to Hajnal to help her up from the ground.

The surprised and tossed-aside captain scowls.

"How are you not hurt?" he demands to know.

"I have a ring of protection." Hajnal shows her ring. He glares at the ring before looking over. He smirks.

"But he doesn't," He states.

"Don't you dare-" Hajnal starts to threaten.

"Oh, but I do dare." He quickly rolls, grabs the fallen knife from the floor, and grabs Sir Artegal's body. He holds the knife to the motionless man's neck.

"No! No! Please! Please, do not kill him." Hajnal pleads.

"Captain, please, let him go," Zarin steps forward.

"Why? Because he is your lover?" The captain glares but keeps his voice calm.

"No. He is not."

"Then which of the other men were?" he refers to Tyr and Astrophel. Hajnal steps in front of Tyr and Astrophel's bodies which are close to her as if this will protect him from the semi-distant, knife-wielding captain.

"None. I have been with no man since you. These men are my friends. Please, do not harm him further." Zarin shakes her head. He cracks a smile.

"Am I still your only, Zarin?" He grins. Zarin does not express any happiness on her face as she nods.

"Please, let him go. He is nothing to you," Zarin tries to turn the focus back onto the hostage.

"But he is. He is my way of reclaiming what is mine."

"What do you want?" Zarin's hands ball up into fists.

"You," he chuckles as if it is the most obvious answer there could be.

"We are in free lands...," Zarin mutters.

"The seas don't count. If you agree then I will spare this man's life. Refuse, and I will kill him." He presses the knife just enough to draw blood. Hajnal and Zarin shout at the sight of blood.

Hajnal grows pale. Sir Artegal's lifespan will be determined by Zarin's acceptance or refusal of a miserable life with this man. Hajnal knows to accept will cause Zarin to be tossed right back into the abuse she had escaped from years prior. But to refuse will mean Sir Artegal's death.

"I can't wait much longer for an answer, Zarin," the captain presses her.

"If I accept, you have to not harm any of my friends and safely deliver them to Koralia as promised. And that girl you had in here before who you blamed for this, she must be unharmed and allowed to leave with my friends as well. And you can never bring another woman on this ship to use for your carnal desires or the carnal desires of your crew members," Zarin lays out her terms.

"Zarin, would you go back with him?" Hajnal grabs her friend's arm.

"I can handle him," Zarin pats Hajnal's hand then turns back to the captain. "So do we have a deal?"

"Hm... I don't know. You are asking me to give up a lot of things," he considers.

"I would be giving up my life to be with you," Zarin points out.

"I can refrain from bringing lovers on the boat for me or the crew as you asked. I can also free Nafisa as long as you service me daily. But as for the safe delivery of your friends...that is something I can no longer control."

"What do you mean?"

"Soon we will be reaching the Mermaid's Lair. It will be every man for himself then. I cannot guarantee the survival of your friends. I cannot even guarantee it for my own men. But I can say if they survive tonight after the paralytic potion wears off and we pass the lair, then I will deliver them safely to Koralia," He counters.

"So as long as they survive the night you will fulfill my terms?" Zarin seeks clarification.

"Yes," Captain Kolar nods.

Zarin holds out her hand to the man to seal the deal.

"Now swear to your god you will not go back on this promise." He brings her faith into this. Zarin frowns.

"I swear to El-Yah, I will not break this promise."

The captain puts away the knife and drops Artegal with a thud to the ground. He takes Zarin's hand to shake then pulls her close to him. He grabs her by the back of the neck and forces a kiss on her lips. Zarin pushes Captain Kolar off and wipes her mouth with the back of her hand.

"Go tell your men to free that poor girl." Zarin gives him a job.

"Now, now, I am the one who gives orders, remember?" He points out her place. She closes her mouth and struggles not to let her anger make her use magic to strangle him.

"But I will let Nafisa go. I have no use for her now, of course, since you're back." He smirks. He walks out of the room leaving the women alone with the still bodies. Zarin rushes to Sir Artegal and heals the cut on his neck.

"Can you heal them?" Hajnal asks.

"I can. Now listen to the words with me so you can help the others," Zarin instructs. Hajnal nods and listens carefully. Zarin puts her hand on Sir Artegal's chest as she speaks. As she repeats the phrases Sir Artegal's feet begin to move then his legs till finally all of him shakes. He is still again but able to turn his head.

"Zarin," He addresses her and begins to sit up.

"We must help the others," Zarin turns from Artegal before he can say anything else. The knight moves swiftly to his prince as Zarin goes to Tyr. When Astrophel rises, he quickly embraces Hajnal who holds him tightly.

Sir Artegal rises from the ground and sees Mr. Phan's body. He moves the man so he lies on his back He then takes a clean napkin from the table to cover the bloody face as none should see such a sight.

Tyr sits and holds his aching head in his hands. He looks at Zarin and thanks her. Hajnal and Astrophel help him up to his feet. Zarin moves on to Mr. Brames.

Sputtering, Mr. Brames comes back to his senses. He stares at Zarin who looks upon him rather emotionless.

"Zarin," he says her name with the start of a smile then stops and looks downward. He remembers what he had done to her when she used to be on the ship. Though he never helped the poor girl, she is here now healing him.

"Thank you," he says. She nods and stands up to get away from him.

Sir Artegal takes hold of Zarin's arm with much concern in his eyes.

"Thou surely are not going to keep that promise to him." Sir Artegal reveals he heard everything.

"I must."

"They were made under duress," He points out.

"I know but I must keep my word this time. I don't know what he'll do to all of you if I do not."

"We can protect each other," Sir Artegal states.

"I swore to El-Yah. You know I cannot break an oath made to El-Yah." Zarin feels tears coming back into her eyes. Sir Artegal turns his eyes from Zarin.

"I suppose thou cannot then."

"But I will be safe. I have my ring of protection," She points out the silver lining.

"I think we should kill the captain when he comes back," Tyr suggests.

"While I am not entirely opposed to this plan, killing him could cause the crew to rise against us," Prince Astrophel points out the possibility.

"But we cannot just let him get away with trying to kill us and for forcing Zarin to stay with him," Tyr glances over to Zarin.

"She has made an oath to El-Yah. She cannot break it," Sir Artegal repeats what Zarin told him. Tyr scoffs and rolls his eyes.

"People break oaths to gods all of the time. She'd be fine to break this one," Tyr argues.

"Do thou think Zarin is the sort of believer to break oaths to her god?" Astrophel questions the youngest man. Tyr exhales and looks away.

"No."

"Woah!" Many exclaim as the ship seems to hit a large bump which shakes it.

"What was that?" Hajnal asks no one in particular.

"Maybe we bumped a whale," Tyr answers.

"No. That wasn't a whale," Mr. Brames shakes his head, growing paler than he was before when he was first drugged.

"No?" All eyes turn to the older man.

"We need to lock ourselves in here," Mr. Brames heads to the door.

"Why?" Tyr questions. The ship bumps again causing them to jolt with it.

"Don't you know where we are? We're getting to the Mermaid's Lair! We need to lock ourselves in!" He reaches the door but finds the key is missing.

"Where is it? Have any of you seen the key for the door?" He looks around the floor.

"No." Is the resounding reply. Mr. Brames curses then gets on the ground.

"Don't just stand there! Help me find the key!" He yells.

"Why do we need to lock ourselves in here? Mermaids cannot reach us if we are in such a large ship." Tyr does not aid the man. Mr. Brames gets up and grabs Tyr by his collar.

"These aren't normal mermaids, boy. They do not even need to get on the ship to have you drown." He grows red in the face.

"And how could they do that?" Tyr pushes the man off him.

"I don't know but I've lost many good friends through here. We need to lock ourselves up!" Mr. Brames gets back on the floor. "Help me!"

The others get on the floor and begin looking for the key but they cannot find it. The bumping of the ship also becomes more frequent. With each bump, more profanities fly from Mr. Brames's mouth.

"Kolar must have taken it! We won't be able to find it! Just find something to plug your ears with!" Mr. Brames jumps up and goes to the tables as the ship begins to rock back and forth unnaturally. The others get up but find themselves struggling to walk with the ship's rocking. Mr. Brames grabs a napkin and tries to stuff it in his ears but the linen keeps falling out.

"Close and latch those windows!" Mr. Brames points to the windows against the wall.

Hajnal goes to the windows and begins to latch them. She looks out one of the windows. She notices the ship has sailed into an area with giant sharp rocks. The ship is avoiding them which raises the question as to who is driving the ship.

The boat's rocking stops suddenly. Everything becomes still and quiet. Mr. Brames only becomes more panicked. He falls to his knees with napkins in his ears.

"Meer, great god of the sea, protect this poor sailor. Call away your daughters from me. Spare me. I will give you half my portion of gold when I reach one of your temples. Protect me, Meer," He prays and bargains.

It is like a whisper, a melodic whisper catching the ears of those who have not plugged their ears. The whisper is more of a low-sung song. It is not unpleasant by any means. It is both soothing and moving. The words being sung do not exactly make sense to Hajnal as she cannot understand the language. She keeps looking out of the window and sees something swimming in the water. It has a large tail which is all she can tell given it is night and this creature is in the water.

Suddenly, the stones around that have algae begun to glow. Bright blue goes up the rocks and even below the surface into the water giving some illumination too deep. Hajnal can finally see the creature. She gasps at the sight.

Beautiful is the woman swimming in the water. Her hair is long and black. Her skin is paler than the moon. Nothing but water covers her toned torso. But at her rounded hips begins a long silvery tail. Though most of the woman's detailed features are unclear to Hajnal she can see the woman has large, luminous purple eyes. This mermaid sings behind the boat. She looks up at Hajnal and winks.

Stepping back, Hajnal finally closes the window and latches it. It does not completely shut out the singing though. She turns around and sees Mr. Brames on the floor covering his ears while the door to the room is open. All of the other men have walked out. Zarin is also out of sight.

Where have they gone?

CHAPTER 32

Hajnal

Sweet, soft, and soothing is the melody that has come into the captain's quarters. The harmony is ever so pleasing as well. The music is enchanting but as Zarin hears the words of the bodiless song creeping into the room, her skin turns cold as ice.

"Oh, no," Zarin mumbles.

Eyes glazing over and ears full, Prince Astrophel, Sir Artegal, and Tyr no longer know anything except the song filling their ears, calling them to find that which men desire. A word does not even leave their mouths when they three just up and walk out of the captain's quarters. Zarin notices the sudden departure and follows after them.

"Stop." She tries to pull on them but she is not strong enough to pull any of them back. She runs before them and tries to block them. She sees then how their eyes are not focused and are somewhat misted. She calls their names but none respond to her. They just keep walking and run through her. Zarin falls into the wall as the men pass on to follow the song.

Coming onto the deck, Zarin sees the ship has entered a cavern of sorts. The rocks and cave surrounding them are covered in glowing blue algae. Mist and fog have come over the deck. The lanterns' lights grow in the vapor. Sitting around on some of the rocks are creatures, half-human, half-fish. She can see rather clearly these women-animal hybrids.

From their hips up, these beings have the appearance of naked women. They all have long hair of varying colors. They are all fair of face and possess giant purple eyes. It is almost unnatural how large their eyes are. Zarin notices on one of them who has her hair pushed back there are gills on her neck. Starting at their hips, however, are long tails like a fish.

Many of the mermaids sing their beautiful song full of words Zarin dreads. She knows what the words mean and what it can mean for her friends. The men split and head for different sides of the ship. If she stops Prince Astrophel then she cannot stop Sir Artegal and Tyr and vice versa. She must find a way to keep them still despite their separation.

Zarin's eye catches on the abundance of seaweed attached to these mermaids' hair and tails. With a few words and a waving of her hands, seaweed flies in the air and takes the three men down by going around their ankles, wrists, and necks and sticking to the floor of the ship. Zarin can heal their headaches later. She looks around for proof of life anywhere else on the ship. She sees the chained doors to the lower decks. It clinks as it is pushed up over and over by a multitude of hands. The chains keep these men trapped below deck. Zarin looks to the helm as she wonders who could be steering the ship if all the other men are locked up. At the wheel stands a terrified and tearful Nafisa. Zarin runs up hoping the seaweed will be strong enough to hold the men down.

Seeing the three men bound to the ground, the mermaids increase the sound of their voices. Some descend from their rocks into the water. They swim up to the boat.

"Who are you?" Zarin asks Nafisa. The younger woman sobs out her name.

"I'm Zarin. Who tied you here?"

"The captain. He said that since I'm a woman I'll be immune and it is my job to steer us out of here safely or we all die." Nafisa keeps sobbing, "I'm so afraid. I don't know how to get us out of here safely. I've never steered a ship before in my life! I don't want to die here."

Zarin tries to pull on Nafisa's arm but her hands refuse to move from the wheel. Zarin notices the golden bracelets around Nafisa's wrists. Zarin knows Nafisa will not be able to break Captain Kolar's order.

Hajnal comes on deck and sees the astonishing sight of the singing mermaids atop the glowing rocks in this cavern. She also sees her friends struggling against the seaweed keeping them down. She rushes to help Tyr, who is closest to her. Surely these mermaids have caused the men to be pinned down with the seaweed. She tries to pull on it but it will not break. Hajnal keeps pulling till finally the piece breaks.

"Tyr, what is going on?" Hajnal asks him but he looks away from her toward one of the mermaids who is now holding onto the side of the ship. She sings and holds her hand out toward Tyr. She curls her fingers slowly to summon him. She flips back some of her hair to show off her long neck. Hajnal notices the gills there. Tyr bucks wildly against the seaweed trying to free himself while not breaking his eye contact with the mermaid. Hajnal looks over to where Sir Artegal is then Astrophel. They are all writhing beneath the seaweed while staring at the singing mermaids.

"Don't move the seaweed!" Zarin runs down to where Hajnal is.

"They're cursing them, aren't they?" Hajnal puts the pieces together.

"Yes. We have to keep them restrained. Nafisa is steering the ship until we can make it out of this cavern. We need to go faster. I'm going to manipulate the water to increase the current and get us moving faster," Zarin shares her plan.

"What can I do?"

"I don't..." Zarin begins but a thud on the ship draws their attention. Another mermaid has climbed over the railing. She sits there and calls Prince Astrophel. He breaks through the seaweed.

"Oh no!" Zarin and Hajnal exclaim.

"Get the water moving! I'll take care of Astrophel," Hajnal directs. Zarin nods and runs to the side closest to her. She comes to the mermaid trying to lure Tyr. Zarin pushes the woman off the side of the boat and into the water. When she leans over the side, she sees the mermaid glaring at her and baring fangs. Zarin ignores her and holds her hands out toward the water.

Astrophel walks slowly and is dazed by the songstress. Coming into the mermaid's reach, she puts her hands on either side of his face. The touch of her cold, wet hands does not concern the entranced prince. She smiles seeing this man is far more attractive than any man she has come through here previously. She pulls him close ready to lock lips and pull him overboard with her.

"Let him go." Hajnal appears behind Astrophel, glaring at the mermaid. The mermaid looks beyond the prince to the rosy-faced maiden. She is taken aback at the sight of the purple eyes but remembers her purpose. She returns to trying to claim Astrophel's lips.

"I said Let. Him. Go." Hajnal pulls Astrophel back by his collar then punches the mermaid directly in the face causing her to fall off the boat. Hajnal faces the prince, grabs hold of Astrophel's shoulder, and tries to shake him to his senses. He tries to move Hajnal aside. She looks at Astrophel's eyes are misted and unfocused. He keeps walking and starts pushing Hajnal with him. He traps her between himself and the side of the ship.

Hajnal sees Sir Artegal breaking out of his seaweed now. She knows he will seek another singing mermaid. She cannot control both men. She either needs to break the curse or duplicate herself. Hajnal wraps her arms around Astrophel's neck and pulls him down into a kiss.

Astrophel's eyes clear and he blinks several times. Once he realizes where his mouth is, he does not move. Instead, he savors the kiss. Hajnal pulls back and looks into his face. Their lips tingle. She sees the blushing prince looking directly at her.

"Um...uh...Hajnal...I...What...uh-" The prince tries to speak but is flustered.

"The mermaids are cursing the men on this ship. I need you to subdue, Sir Artegal." Hajnal points behind to the knight. Astrophel looks around and is surprised by his surroundings then lands on Sir Artegal who is not in control of himself. Astrophel does not hesitate to run and tackle his lifelong friend.

Hajnal notices the ship moving a bit faster which must mean Zarin can manipulate the water. She looks over to Zarin. The woman is hunched over on the side of the ship but appears to be struggling to not fall over. Hajnal realizes hands are trying to pull Zarin down. Hearing some thuds, Hajnal sees some of the mermaids have climbed aboard the ship. They crawl past her and toward the men at a surprisingly fast pace.

Hajnal screams at the larger hoard approaching her as she had in Sterhout. This sends many flying off the ship. The screaming hurts Hajnal's throat causing her to stop. As she rubs her throat, a set of wet, cold hands grab Hajnal's arm and yanks her.

"Astro!" Hajnal shrieks as she feels herself falling overboard.

Hajnal crashes into the water and immediately sinks. The water is well lit from the algae allowing her to see the numerous mermaids heading toward the ship speeding away. Two mermaids grab her by her ankles and pull her downward.

Being brought down into the wreckage of ships, Hajnal sees skeletons upon skeletons of unlucky sailors. Hajnal tries to pull away from the mermaids but another comes. This one takes Hajnal's braid and begins to wrap it around Hajnal's neck.

Hajnal should be strangled by the braid and suffocating from the water. Her neck does not concave and her lungs do not fill with water. She feels no need for air but she still feels the need for freedom.

Swinging her arms, Hajnal strikes the one attempting to strangle her. The hit makes the mermaid let go of Hajnal's braid only for it to be grabbed by one of the mermaids holding her feet. Hajnal is dragged inside one of the wrecked ships. There her hair is tied to a post inside. They use some seaweed to tie her hands in front of her. Laughing, they leave Hajnal behind.

Hajnal struggles in vain to free herself. She tries to use her teeth to chew through the seaweed but fails. She looks for anything sharp. Her eyes search the submerged room. There are some tables and chairs but none that look sharp.

There! Hajnal sees a mirror close to her on the wall. *I can break it and use the shards.*

She begins to swim as best she can toward the mirror. As she comes closer, the reflection is not of herself or the ship. She freezes seeing the one she dreads most.

"My dear, what has happened to you?" Bardolph asks, half amused and half bemused.

Hajnal does not understand how this man is in the mirror and talking to her.

Am I hallucinating?

"Don't worry, you have not lost your mind. I am here, my dear. I'm just on the other side of this mirror."

This brings no comfort to Hajnal who has no time to understand the mirror man. She begins to look for something else to help free her.

"Are you in trouble? Do you need my help?" He continues with his questions and a smirk. Hajnal notices a nail. She begins to swim toward it but her hair is only so long. She pulls and pulls but her hair remains tied.

"I guess you do need my help," Bardolph remarks. "Come close to me again, my dear."

Hajnal shakes her head and continues to try to pull away. How could he help her?

"Come here," he calls. His hands begin to emerge from the mirror. Hajnal stares in shock at the action.

"You're going to be stuck if you don't come to me," Bardolph points out.

I guess he's right. Hajnal swims toward the hand. His hands take hold of the seaweed and rip it apart. She smiles rather surprised and grateful for his action. As she moves to go, he grabs her hand. She tries to pull away. He holds her hand tighter.

"Don't forget my kindness, my dear. I'll see you soon," He lets her go. She swims back and unties her braid from the post.

Hajnal swims out of the ship and up toward the surface. As she swims, she sees on a skeleton she passes, a string of blue pearls. She takes it from the skeleton who no longer needs it.

Breaking through to the surface, Hajnal takes a deep breath. She looks eagerly from side to side for signs of the ship. It is no longer speeding away as it has hit a wall. Hajnal frantically swims toward the stalled vessel.

Coming closer, Hajnal knows she cannot just jump aboard the ship given its height. Her eyes search for another way aboard.

"The rocks," She breathes. Toward the sharp stones she goes. Reaching them, she puts the pearls around her neck. She begins to climb the rocks. The water and algae make it difficult. Slipping and falling thrice does not deter her from trying again. Up she goes still she sees the deck.

Several mermaids are on the deck. Many are trying to unlock the door going to the lower deck where the men have been locked. Zarin is using water and parts of the ship in hopes of fending the mermaids away from Tyr. Some Mermaids have taken hold of the willing Sir Artegal and unwilling Astrophel. Hajnal knows there is not much they can do to fight off these half-fish creatures.

Wait.

Hajnal searches her wet clothes and pulls out her pipe. She empties of water and wets her lips before bringing the instrument to them. She inhales deeply and calmly. As she blows into the instrument, her notes are quick and have a bounce to them. She plays as loudly as she can. She taps her foot as she plays them and keeps her eyes closed as she tries to recall the beat and rhythm once taught to her by her grandfather.

Astrophel feels the hands of the half-women leaving him. Many of the mermaids stop singing and have started to try to cover their ears but their tails twitch then tap along with the pipe's music.

The lovely song of the mermaids begins to turn sharp and out of tune the more Hajnal plays. The tails of the mermaids bounce and move with Hajnal's beat. Though the mermaids try covering their ears or try to lock their nails into the ship or the rocks where they sat, their tails keep moving and dragging them toward the water as if they are all being pulled by an invisible rope. Soon the mermaids are removed from the ship. Hajnal opens an eye as she hears splashes. She looks over the edge as she places. The mermaids, led by their tails, swim in the water away from the ship.

Having been released from the mermaids' song, Sir Artegal is quick to realize what has happened and is happening. Astrophel sees Hajnal and grabs a rope on the deck. Making a loop, he throws it toward her. She puts it around her waist. With help from Sir Artegal, they can pull Hajnal back onto the ship.

"We need to get off the rocks," Sir Artegal states the obvious. Zarin faces the rocks and stretches out her hands. The rocks shake then crumble freeing the ship. Zarin turns her attention to the waters. She commands the waters to rush.

Sir Artegal in turn stands up and moves so he is behind the mainsail. He takes a deep breath and then begins to blow. The air leaves his lips and creates a strong wind. The wind in the sails propels the ship forward even more.

Approaching the exit of the cavern, Zarin and Sir Artegal do not ease up on their work nor does Hajnal with her pipe. They cannot risk slipping in their duty and becoming victims to the mermaids. Though Nafisa's driving skills lead to a few bumps she cannot let go of the wheel.

Out under the starry sky and away from the lair of the singing mermaids, Hajnal, Zarin and Sir Artegal finally stop. Hajnal lowers the pipe and takes several breaths as she tries to regain her regular breathing. Astrophel is quick to come to her side and give her physical support after such an effort. Sir Artegal and Zarin look at each other briefly.

"What in the world happened?" Tyr regains his senses. Sir Artegal can update Tyr on the situation as he rips away the seaweed keeping Tyr down.

Zarin runs to the helm to find Nafisa. Cutting her free, Nafisa falls to her knees, exhausted from the experience.

"You did well." Zarin pats the young woman on the back as she kneels beside her. Nafisa looks at her own hands. They are bleeding and splintered from her tight grip. She cries at the sight of them.

"Let me see." Zarin takes them in hers. She closes her eyes and quickly the palms are healed. Nafisa's eyes light up.

"Thank you." She smiles. Zarin helps Nafisa to her feet. The others on deck go to join the two women at the helm as it should not be left unattended.

"What finally got rid of those mermaids?" Tyr asks Sir Artegal.

"I...I do not know," Sir Artegal furrows his brows.

"Hajnal got rid of them. She played her pipe and got rid of them," Astrophel turns to the soaked Hajnal. All eyes go to Hajnal.

"Thou play the pipe so well like a master," Sir Artegal comments.

"Thank you."

"I saw thou are marked for the gift of air but I did not know thou were this skilled in it," Sir Artegal admits. "Thank you for saving our lives"

"Of course."

"Since we are in the clear, we need to find Captain Kolar," Zarin brings up the missing person.

"Why?" Tyr starts to scowl at the name.

"He needs to get a helmsman and free Nafisa," Zarin shows the bracelets to the others.

"I'll stay here and steer," Tyr volunteers.

"We will go with thee to find the captain," Sir Artegal decides for the rest of them.

The group leaves Tyr to steer while they begin looking for the captain.

"Hajnal, where did you get these pearls?" Zarin notices the jewelry.

"From a skeleton under the water."

"We will need to crush them for the elixir," Zarin notes as they head toward the captain's private quarters. Hajnal nods knowing it is true.

In the captain's private quarters but they only find Mr. Brames on the floor still covering his ears. Zarin goes to him with a gentle touch and informs him they are in the clear.

"Thank you, Meer!" Mr. Brames exclaims praising his god who must have listened and answered his prayer.

"Has Captain Kolar returned here?" Zarin asks.

"Not that I have seen," Mr. Brames shakes his head.

"Then we must keep looking." Zarin turns from Mr. Brames. Captain Kolar enters the room while pulling cotton from his ears. His eyes run over the group.

"Did your other friend not survive?" the captain notes the missing Tyr.

"He is steering the ship. You need to get someone who knows what he's doing to steer."

"Brames, go and do it," the captain orders.

"You think I'm going to listen to you after you tried to kill me?" Mr. Brames snarls.

"You caused me to lose a fortune. I drugged you temporarily. I think we are even. Now do as I say or I'll cast you into the sea."

Mr. Brames grumbles but leaves to do as Captain Kolar orders. He supposes they are even now.

"Since you lot survived, I will make sure to get you to Koralia as I promised." The captain walks over to his desk.

"You need to free Nafisa." Zarin gestures to the young woman next to her.

"I will not free her till we arrive at Koralia." The captain crosses his arms.

"Why? We have no way to escape before reaching Koralia. Just let her go," Zarin questions him.

"I know you and your fairy friends could find a way to sneak off. I'm holding onto her for leverage. Of course, if you were to take on the bracelets and stay here tonight in her place, then I'll let her go now."

"No," Hajnal objects.

"You have no say in this matter." The captain does not take his eyes off Zarin.

"It's fine, Hajnal. Take Nafisa and go to rest in our cabin," Zarin gives instructions.

"No. You-"

"I am fine. Please, go. All of you, please just go," Zarin bids them all to leave.

"Zarin," Hajnal calls her friend's name once more.

"I am fine. Go."

The captain pulls the bracelets off Nafisa who sighs relieved of the burden of obedience. Hajnal frowns but leaves with Nafisa. She knows Zarin is protected by her ring but that is only physical harm. The captain follows behind and shuts the door and locks it once all are out. Sir Artegal stays put outside of the door.

"What are you doing?" Hajnal asks.

"I am staying here and will listen if she needs help," the knight answers.

"I will stay as well," Astrophel volunteers. Hajnal smiles at their attempt to help Zarin then leaves with Nafisa to get to their cabin.

The captain walks toward Zarin with them. He holds the bracelets out to her. She stares at them. They appear as adornments but in truth they are shackles. Zarin knows putting these on means putting her old self back on as well.

Can a snake put on its shed skin?

Zarin slips on the bracelets. They hang loosely from her. The captain's brows furrow seeing they have not conformed to her wrists as they should.

"I am tired and I am sure you are as well from all your scheming." Zarin tries to take his focus off the bracelets.

"Yes, though I could muster some energy to reclaim what is mine." He licks his lips looking her over.

"Why not wait till tomorrow when I am more awake?" She tries to push back any attempts against her.

"I suppose I can wait one more night. Then I'll have enough energy for tomorrow to properly reacquaint ourselves." He grins. Zarin does not give any pleasant expression.

"Now, get in the bed." He points to the bed. Zarin goes and removes her shoes before getting in bed. She turns on her side so she will not have to look at the man. He comes into the bed after blowing out the candles in the room. He is quick to wrap his arms around her to spoon her though his hands go to grope her. She closes her eyes and puts her hands on his. A little prayer leaves her lips and the captain stops moving. His breath becomes deep and ripples with some snoring. She removes his hands from her. She sits up in bed. She feels her tears returning to her eyes. She closes her eyes again and brings her hands together. Her lips move though no words come out. Still, her words are heard by the one to whom she speaks. Zarin lies back down and pushes the captain over more. She then does her best to rest. But how much sleep can a doe get when bedding down next to a wolf?

CHAPTER 33

Hajnal

When Captain Kolar wakes, he finds himself alone in his bed. He does not remember falling asleep but does remember who was supposed to be with him when he did. He sits up with a start and begins looking around for Zarin. His anger rises as he begins to assume she had fled and thus broken her vow to him. He catches sight of the back of a woman. Her head is covered with a coif but her exposed neck is enough for him to identify her. He smiles. Of course, his Zarin is still with him. She was never the type to break her promises. He has long wondered what these past years would have been like had Mr. Phan not tricked her and forced her away from him.

"Zarin," he calls her name. She turns around with an expressionless face. "Good morning."

"You should get dressed and get back on deck. It is already late," She responds. Not caring to exchange pleasantries.

"Such a cold greeting. I expect far sweeter greetings from now on." He gets out of bed, "And I will want you to stop covering your head. Your hair is one of your best features."

"We will arrive in Koralia today then?" She focuses on their destination.

"If we have been kept on course, we should arrive by noon," He puts on his boots.

"I need to prepare my things before we dock in Koralia. Please, unlock the door." Zarin gestures to the door.

"You will need nothing but what I provide and after the rest of this payment from your friends, I will buy you anything you want," He promises.

"I just want what is in my cabin. I also would like some time to bid farewell to my friends," Zarin claims. Captain Kolar pauses then sighs.

"I suppose I can indulge you." He unlocks the door

The captain opens the door. He scowls as he sees Sir Artegal and Astrophel standing at the door.

"What do you two want?" the captain crosses his arms.

"To escort Zarin back to her cabin," Sir Artegal answers.

"Thank you." Zarin steps out before the captain can say anything. Zarin hurries in her step and so the patient men do as well.

"How fare thee, Zarin?" Astrophel comes to her side as they walk.

"I am well enough. I hope you two were able to get some rest last night," Zarin says though she herself was more than restless.

"We stayed at the door all night," Astrophel informs her.

"Oh, I am sorry you did. You both should have rested especially after the whole mermaid ordeal," Zarin apologizes.

"Do not apologize. We wanted to make sure if thou needed us, we would be there in an instant." Astrophel does want her to take on the blame.

They reach her shared cabin where Tyr stands outside of the door. When they knock, Nafisa and Hajnal come out.

"Oh, Zarin!" Hajnal hugs the other woman and then pulls back but keeps her arms around Zarin. "Are you well?"

"I am. He did nothing to me and even if he tried, he would not have been successful." Zarin tries to push away her friend's worry.

"Still, having to be with him must be…" Hajnal is not sure of what words to say.

"It was fine. Do not fret. I am fine and I will endure what it is to come without fear."

"No. You will not." Tyr speaks up. "We aren't going to let you do this."

"What?"

Hajnal lets go of Zarin.

"I have a plan. When we dock, I will shift to look like you and…" Tyr begins.

"You can shift to look like people?" Hajnal asks, shocked.

"I used to shift to look like my sister all of the time. I'm sure if I focus hard enough, I can shift to look like Zarin. Anyway, I'll shift to look like you. So, while I go off with the captain, you can escape with the others off the ship. Then I will shift into a panther and kill the captain then shift into a bird and fly away to meet you." Tyr smiles, finishing revealing his plan.

"We cannot do that." Zarin shakes her head.

"Why not?" Tyr frowns.

"First, you are not sure if you can fully shift into me. Second, you cannot kill him. It is wrong. Third, I made an oath and I cannot break it."

"You could. I am sure your god would understand and forgive you," Tyr huffs.

"I know El-Yah is a forgiving god but breaking an oath made in his name will only show I do not keep my promises and I do not give true reverence and power to my god. I have to keep my oath no matter how much I do not want to do so," Zarin explains to the disappointed shifter. "Also, if I do not keep it, how many more girls are going to be taken to be used and abused by him like Nafisa and me?"

"That's why we kill him," Tyr brings up the previous point from his plan.

"No. Tyr, I cannot let you murder him. I will not let you have his blood on your hands." Zarin shakes her head.

"I am happy to have it. He deserves to die." Tyr crosses his arms.

"Vengeance is not ours to take." Zarin reaches out and touches Tyr's arm.

"Still, there must be a way to get out of this situation without you breaking your promise," Hajnal insists.

"He has upheld his part. He spared Prince Astrophel, he freed Nafisa, and once we dock in Koralia unharmed, he will have held his part of the promise. Unless he takes another woman aboard to abuse, harm befalls one of us or he changes his mind, I am obligated to go through with this. And I would feel guilty should he break his side by hurting one of you or another woman."

"Prince?" Nafisa picks up on the word and whispers it to herself then looks at Prince Astrophel. She had not known he was using an alias. She wonders who these people really are. Nafisa then looks to Sir Artegal. She sees the knight walk out of the small room. Astrophel notices as well and goes after the knight.

"But what about your promises to others? You promised Mother Huldah you would return to her. You promised to help me," Hajnal brings up the other promises.

"I know Captain Kolar ports in Austvest. I can send word to Mother Huldah and therefore see her again. And I have helped you and I will give you my books and map so you can continue to learn without me. I am sure Sir Artegal can continue to teach you the ways of magic," Zarin comes up with solutions to these problems. She looks for Sir Artegal to get confirmation he would teach Hajnal. It is easy to notice he and Astrophel have left.

"Where did they go?" Tyr looks behind him.

"I just saw them walk out," Nafisa speaks up.

"I guess they are preparing to leave." Zarin looks away from the door.

"I will go and look for them," Tyr volunteers. He leaves the cabin. Zarin walks to her bed where her belongings are stowed below. She pulls them out from under the bed.

"You must take care of these books and return them to Mother Huldah for me." Zarin pats the bag.

"You should keep them. You should keep practicing magic even if you are trapped here on this boat," Hajnal urges.

"No. I don't want to learn anything that will empower Captain Kolar to do worse things," Zarin admits.

"He can't make you do anything. These bracelets will not work with your ring still on." Hajnal grabs Zarin's adorned hand.

"I know but there will come a time when you find your brother and this ring will stop working. Then I will be up to his mercy." Zarin looks at the bracelets then back to Hajnal. "But do not let this stop you from finding your brother."

"Zarin, I don't-I don't understand you. I have faced this dilemma and you encouraged me to not give in to Bardolph. But now you are not letting me encourage you to refuse the captain. Why do you encourage me to not sacrifice myself yet you are in a similar situation and are sacrificing yourself?" Hajnal seeks to understand her friend.

"Would you have rather I let Prince Astrophel die?" Zarin questions.

"Of course not! But you did not have to agree to the captain's terms. You could have also sworn to a different god so you could have broken your oath," Hajnal provides alternatives to the past.

"He knows what god I believe in and if I had not agreed to his terms and set my own, our friends would be dead and Nafisa would still be imprisoned by him." Zarin glances at the quiet Nafisa.

"I know. I know, but..." Hajnal feels herself losing the argument and her ability to hold back her tears. "Zarin, you don't deserve any of this. You deserve to be happy and free. You should be training under Mother Huldah back in Austvest and becoming a full-fledged Fairy. You should be safe. You should not be here facing the one who hurt you most and having to submit to him. But you are because of me. Because I chose myself, you cannot. Zarin, I'm sorry. I'm so sorry."

"Shhhh. Stop. Stop." Zarin takes the crying Hajnal in her arms though she is tearful as well. They sit on the bed together. Nafisa excuses herself feeling out of place watching them.

"Hajnal." Zarin leans back and wipes at her eyes. Hajnal tries to wipe her face but more tears keep coming.

"Hajnal, this is not your fault. I wanted to come with you. I wanted this adventure. I chose to follow you and do what I can to help you and our dear ones. It is not for us to say where we should and should not be. My footsteps are guided to where I should be. Yours are as well. So, I...I will have courage as I find out why I should be here and have the faith we will meet again." Zarin takes Hajnal's hands again. Hajnal tries to regain her composure.

"Where are the men? They have been gone for a bit too long," Zarin looks around.

"I thought they were just in the other room," Hajnal looks toward the door.

"Let's go look," Zarin suggests. Hajnal nods. They get off the bed and Hajnal wipes her face not wanting to look like a watery mess.

They go to the men's cabin and are rejoined by Nafisa. They knock at the door but there is no answer. They open the door and find Astrophel and Tyr inside.

"Where is Sir Artegal?" Zarin asks. The prince sighs.

"He has gone to the captain." The prince answers.

"Why?"

"For you," Tyr answers.

Captain Kolar trims his facial hair when he hears a knock at his door. He smiles at his reflection before lowering his compact mirror and walking toward the door of his cabin. He opens the door and loses his smile.

"What do you want?" Captain Kolar sees the large Mr. Belamour before him.

"I have come to bargain for Zarin," Sir Artegal states his purpose. The captain smirks.

"There is nothing you could have that I would want in replacement for my Zarin." The captain begins to shut the door. Sir Artegal puts his hand out to stop the door.

"Do not try to intimidate me, Mr. Belamour. I have handled men far bigger than you," the captain asserts.

"Thou art lying but I am not here to intimidate thee," Sir Artegal is quick to call the captain's bluff who narrows his eyes at the taller man.

"As I have said, I am here to make a bargain for the breaking of thy deal with Zarin," Sir Artegal continues.

"As I have said, you have nothing I want."

"Not even the ownership of a profitable ruby mine?" Sir Artegal poses the question making the captain raise an eyebrow.

"I am intrigued."

"I have the right to one of the most lucrative ruby mines in all of Estellen," Sir Artegal claims.

"Estellen? That place has been shut off for over a century," the captain scoffs.

"Hath the news not reached thine ears that the borders have reopened?" Sir Artegal brings the news. The captain pauses to think. Now as he does think about it, he does recall the gossip going around the taverns in Zeemaa.

"I see."

"With this mine, thou will no longer need to struggle for thy income or sail about for the needs of other men. Thou will live as rich as any aristocrat and do whatever thou please," Sir Artegal sets the stage.

"That is tempting," the captain admits. He can see his life in a castle with walls and floors encrusted with rubies, tables full of the finest foods, bottles of his favorite wines, and closets of fine clothes. He licks his lips. Then he thinks of his large and grand bed made of marble with ruby-red silk sheets. On his bed, he sees his demure and obedient Zarin waiting.

"That is a pretty picture you paint me, Mr. Belamour, but in truth, if I do not have Zarin with me as mine, I am not sure I want it," Captain Kolar begins to reject the idea. Sir Artegal's jaw clenches.

"Dost thou love her?" Sir Artegal asks the captain.

"Aye," the captain nods. The knight pauses. He does not detect insincerity in this statement. He knows a man in love is harder to break than one who is simply greedy.

"Even though she does not love thee in return?"

"She will come to love me again. She did before Mr. Phan stole her from me and had her brainwashed." The captain is sure of this. Sir Artegal notices now Mr. Phan's corpse is missing. He assumes the captain tossed the body out one of his open windows.

"Why do you care so much about keeping Zarin when you claim she has not been your bed-mate?" the captain points the question to the knight.

"She is my friend," the knight answers.

"I have many friends but I'd never give away such a great fortune to keep them near me. It must be more than that. Are you in love with her?"

"No," Sir Artegal answers without missing a beat. The captain stares down at the knight.

"I don't believe that in the slightest." The captain crosses his arms.

"I do not care if thou believe me. I do care that we seal this deal so thou can release Zarin of her oath and allow her to continue with myself and my companions," Sir Artegal returns to his purpose of this meeting.

Captain Kolar puckers his lips then sucks on his teeth as he continues to stare at the man before him. He grins as he finishes thinking.

"I have an idea myself."

"And what is that?"

"As much as I like the life of luxury you spoke of, it would not be right without my dear Zarin. I want both but I know you will not give the mine for nothing. So...I think it is only fair for us to try to have both."

"What dost thou mean?"

"I'm saying that let us have a little gamble. Winner takes the mine and the maiden," Captain Kolar proposes.

"What shall the game be then?" Sir Artegal inquires.

"Do you know the game, The World's Master?" Captain Kolar inquires. It has been over a century since Sir Artegal last played any sort of card game but he has not forgotten this one. His fingers tingle thinking of it.

"Yes."

"Let's play that." The captain smiles but the knight does not. Sir Artegal still nods to agree.

The captain steps aside and allows Sir Artegal to enter. The captain tells Sir Artegal to sit at the table where he was drugged the previous night. It is clean now since the cabin boy Eziz came in to work shortly before Sir Artegal came. Sir Artegal takes a seat on the side of the table. He waits for the captain to sit across from him.

Captain Kolar comes to the table with a stack of cards as well as a piece of paper and a quill in its inkwell. He sets them all down on the table.

"I am writing on the paper so you cannot back out when you lose," Captain Kolar begins to write on the paper.

"Then let us set the terms clearly," Sir Artegal wants no tricks.

"Should I, Captain Valter Kolar, win this game of World's Master then I will receive the rights to the ruby mine in Estellen belonging to Mr. Belamour and I will hold Zarin accountable to her oath," Captain Kolar speaks as he writes. He slides the paper over to Sir Artegal as well as the quill and inkwell.

"Should I, Sir Artegal Belamour, win this game of World's Master then I will keep my rights to my family's ruby mine, and Captain Kolar will release Zarin of her oath and allow her to freely continue with my traveling party who he must continue not to harm including the freed Nafisa." Sir Artegal is specific. He signs the paper then gives it all back to the captain. He signs it as well and shows the knight.

"Now that this is settled, shall we begin?" Captain Kolar puts the contract to the side.

"Yes."

The captain picks up his stack of cards and begins to shuffle them. When the captain slides them across the table, he is quick to count there are seventy-eight cards before him. He is rather pleased the captain had not already begun cheating. He still watches the captain's hands closely so there is no trickery.

Captain Kolar gives Sir Artegal six cards then takes six for himself. He sets the cards to the side and turns over the top card. He reveals the five of wands.

"Wands will be the trump suit for the minor arcana," He states and puts the card underneath the stack of extra cards. Sir Artegal nods in understanding. He glances at his hand before returning his eyes to Captain's Kolar's card-holding hands. He must make sure there will be no cheating.

Captain puts out his first card the two of swords. Sir Artegal puts down the six of swords thus winning the first play. He sets the cards aside for his victory pile. He then lays down the five of coins. Captain Kolar takes his prize. The men replenish their set as they do after each play.

Knocking is at the door. The captain bids the knocker to enter. Zarin enters the room with Astrophel, Tyr, Nafisa, and Hajnal behind her. Captain Kolar smiles looking at the entering woman. Sir Artegal keeps his eyes only on Captain Kolar's hands.

"Ah, if it isn't my Zarin!" He greets Zarin.

"What are you two doing?" Zarin walks to the table.

"Playing a little, friendly game of World's Master," Captain Kolar answers, laying down the three of wands.

"World's Master?" Hajnal finds herself unfamiliar with the game.

"Sir Artegal, that game..." Zarin begins as Sir Artegal lays down the two of wands.

"Is fun?" Captain Kolar interrupts.

"Involves cards of which fairies should not associate," Zarin finishes.

"I am aware, Zarin. That is why I keep my mind focused on what is true." Sir Artegal still does not look at the woman. Captain Kolar takes the cards.

"Why are you playing this?" Tyr comes closer to the table.

"Have a look and see." Captain Kolar points to the contract then lays down the seven of cups. Sir Artegal responds with the ace of wands thus giving him the win.

Tyr picks up the contract and reads it aloud for the others to hear. Astrophel frowns.

"A ruby mine? You have a ruby mine?" Tyr is most surprised by this.

"Yes, it has been in my family since the founding of Estellen," Sir Artegal gives the tidbit as he lays down the two of wands. Captain Kolar wins with the page of wands.

"You two need to stop this. You cannot risk even more in such a card game," Zarin's hands go to her hips as she is mostly scolding Sir Artegal.

"I will do as I please," Sir Artegal answers, still not looking away from his opponent.

"Well said," Captain Kolar laughs and puts down the magician. Sir Artegal simply responds with the two of swords. Captain Kolar takes a look in the deck to see what is the next card. After he and Sir Artegal claim their replenishing cards. Sir Artegal senses a jolt of excitement in Captain Kolar as he looks at the card. But the captain does not expose it in his face.

"I am not a prize so do not continue with this game," Zarin hisses.

"I know what thou art not, Zarin, but as thy senior in age and rank I am to do what I must to protect thee when it is in my ability." Sir Artegal watches Captain Kolar put down the ace of swords. Sir Artegal matches it with the ace of coins. Captain Kolar's mood sours as he and Sir Artegal are now in a duel and the card he had been hoping to take next will now be among the unturned three he has to put down. Both men line up their three cards before taking a fourth to lie down.

Captain Kolar's secret happiness returns as he reveals his card is the priestess while Sir Artegal only has the six of swords. Captain Kolar takes all of the cards to his victory pile. The hands are replenished before Captain Kolar takes a peek and the next two cards in the deck.

"Just sit and watch, Zarin. I will soon be winning us a ruby mine and the luxurious life I deserve," the captain brags. Zarin's frown deepens. She sits at the head of the table and watches the men. Tyr takes a seat to watch as well, thoroughly curious of the outcome of this game. Nafisa stands behind Zarin's chair.

Hajnal senses tension beside her. She looks to Astrophel who has a less than pleased expression.

"What is wrong?" Hajnal whispers. Astrophel makes eyes to the door. Hajnal understands their meeting and the two leave the room. They walk to the deck.

The deck is busy with the sailors going about their duties as well as some new faces being trained on the ship. Hajnal notices the newer faces have gold bracelets on them. But she gives her attention to the prince who stops by the railing of the ship.

"What is wrong, Astro?" Hajnal asks, putting her hand on his arm.

"It is not that anything is wrong yet, but I am...displeased with this gamble."

"You are afraid of him losing the mine and Zarin?"

"Yes, but it is more than that. He is right that he has a duty to protect Zarin. He is ranked as a master among the fairies while she is an apprentice so it is his duty to try to protect her. He mentioned he would try to bribe the captain to break the oath which I was not against but I had no idea he would try to bribe him with the ruby mine."

"What about the ruby mine distresses you so much?"

"The ruby mine has been in our family since the founding of Estellen. It is the royal ruby mine. To have it owned by someone who cares not for the people of Estellen and could decide to sell the rubies to other nations or overcharge Estellen could be dangerous to the Estellen economy. And having a sea captain with no experience in the management of mines could be dangerous to not only the business but the miners who do the work. As the heir of Estellen, I must make sure I do not let harm come to my nation whether that be in protecting the people, protecting the land, or protecting the economy," Astrophel begins voicing his concerns. Hajnal is surprised to hear Astrophel refer to the mines as belonging to 'our' family.

Are Astro and Sir Artegal related?

"These are understandable concerns. It must not be easy to have to worry about such things," Hajnal validates his fears.

"The crown is such a heavy burden. I know I have been raised to carry it but I have always had Artegal by my side to help me. I rely on him as if he were my own right hand. I thought he too was of the mindset I am when it comes to Estellen's protection. This reckless gamble has me questioning if this is so. Perhaps in the hundred years, he has been waiting, he has changed. Maybe living dully this past century has led him to want a taste for excitement, to live on the edge without having to concern himself about the state of the kingdom." Astrophel lets his thoughts pour out of his mouth. Hajnal takes in Astrophel's words of his suspicions. She has not known Sir Artegal long but she has not seen him as someone who is reckless or thrill-seeking. In fact, to her, this is the only time he has done something that has greatly displeased Astrophel.

"I do not think Sir Artegal is the sort of man who would risk what he knows will harm others for his own pleasure or pride. I do not think Sir Artegal would do anything he knew would harm you or Estellen. He was the one who was most upset you did not return home when you woke. He wanted you to reclaim your position and carry on with your role in Estellen. You chose to follow me instead. If anyone has acted recklessly and against the best interest of Estellen, isn't it you?" Hajnal poses the question. Astrophel's cheeks redden.

"I had to come with thee. Thou art my love and I must do what I must to keep thee safe and protected even if it means..." Astrophel stops and more thoughts come into his mind. A look of understanding comes but then more confusion.

"I understand what thou say but it is different. I love thee," Astrophel confesses, making Hajnal's heart flutter, "but Artegal does not love Zarin in the same manner."

"Even if his affection for her is not the same that you hold for me, it does not mean the affection he has for her is less important or less worthy of taking action. I love my siblings differently than I love you. But I have chosen to go after them instead of easily going away with you because they need me to do this to save them." Hajnal's words are absorbed by the prince. His heart races and his smile spreads in delight.

"Thou love me?" He asks making Hajnal blush.

"Is-is that all you have taken from what I have said?" Hajnal wants the attention off her slip of a confession.

"I have and I find thou art wise and more understanding than I. I shall attempt to relinquish my frustrations toward Artegal. However, the most important words to me are of thy feelings. Tell me, thou art earnest in thy words. Do thou love me?" He takes her hands in his gentle ones.

"Yes," Hajnal admits softly.

"I would kiss thee now and crow to the world of how my heart is filled with rapturous joy if I knew thou would not be embarrassed by the display," he states. He squeezes her hands tightly. She feels a surge going through him and how he almost glows. Her heart is more inclined toward his respect for her reservations.

"Perhaps one day thou will let me?" He poses the future possibility. Hajnal nods to confirm.

"We should get back to the others." Hajnal thinks about their friends.

"Yes. Yes," He agrees. As they walk, the prince does not let go of one of Hajnal's hands. How can he be upset with his friend when he is filled with so much joy? He does hope, however, his joy can be increased with Artegal being the victor of this game.

Sir Artegal has not let his eyes leave the table or his opponent for a moment, not even when Tyr sneezed so loudly it made everyone else turn to look at him after jumping at the sudden sound. He knows Astrophel and Hajnal have returned and felt the positive difference after their brief absence.

But he cannot focus on their current feelings of love and happiness or Tyr's nervous excitement or Nafisa's stress or Zarin's concern. He needs to focus on feeling Captain Kolar's. The happier the stone-faced captain is, the more likely Sir Artegal is to lose. Sir Artegal must also be careful to allow his feelings to spread out and affect others.

Though the game has been going on for an hour and Eziz, the cabin boy, has come to alert the captain the ship is about to dock, a victor has not been named. Sir Artegal knows this means the captain has not yet found the world card for surely the captain would have already played it to claim his prizes and move on to docking.

Captain Kolar puts down the queen of swords. Sir Artegal matches him with the queen of cups. This means another duel must be played. Each man reaches for three cards from the deck to lie face down. Captain Kolar goes back for his fourth card before Sir Artegal.

The players meet eyes. It is Captain Kolar's turn to reveal his fourth card. Slowly, he overturns it and lays it flat for all to see. The onlookers lean to see clearly.

In an instant, the despair, fear, and grief fall onto the sojourners and nearly knock them off their feet as if elephants had been dropped upon them. Zarin clutches her chest and loses all of her breath at the sight of the card. Captain Kolar is lighter than air and smiles so widely that almost all of his teeth are visible.

"I am the world's master!" He announces giddily then turns to Zarin. "Now that we are docking, we're heading straight for Estellen, Zarin!"

The slave-to-be becomes paler by the moment. In truth, she had gained some hope in the game that Sir Artegal might be able to save her. But this gamble was just that, a gamble.

"Thanks for the game and mine," Captain Kolar chuckles.

Astrophel steps up to Sir Artegal and puts his hand on Sir Artegal's shoulder in reassurance and support despite the loss. Hajnal looks to the downcast Zarin while Tyr stares at the cards as if staring at them will change it.

"I suppose I should start cleaning up these cards," Captain Kolar starts to gather the cards from his victory pile. He looks at the unmoved knight.

"Let me see what your card was," The captain asks.

"What is the point?" Tyr snaps.

"I want to see if he was even close," The captain snaps back then reaches across to grab the card. He and Sir Artegal turn the card over at the same moment. Their eyes widen at the sight.

Between Sir Artegal's fingers is a card with a naked woman in the sky with a staff in each hand, a green wreath around her, and is being watched by four different creatures. It is the world card.

"How is this possible?" Tyr is the first to speak.

"You must have cheated!" Captain Kolar exclaims trying to rip the card from the knight's hand but Sir Artegal holds it still.

"I have done no such thing. Thou must have. Thou were the one to bring out the cards and to deal them. Thou must have replaced the card with an extra world card to increase thy chances of victory or somehow slipped it in just now," Sir Artegal deduces.

"You're calling me a cheater?" The captain turns red in his face.

"Yes." The knight stands to his feet.

"How dare you! If anyone here is a cheat it's you!" The captain points his finger up into Sir Artegal's face.

"Really? Thou would proclaim I am less trustworthy than thou when thou hast poisoned not only thy own men but thy guests?" Sir Artegal brings up the previous night's events. "I shall be taking Zarin back into my care since thou cheated."

"You will do no such thing!" Captain Kolar grabs Zarin by her wrist. He yanks her, causing her to fall toward him. "I won and I will have my prizes!"

"No. Thou shall not," Sir Artegal bellows. The captain pulls the sword from behind his side.

"I will kill you before I let you have her."

Sir Artegal draws his sword and holds it out to meet the captain's. It burns brightly. The burning blade though shocking to the captain does not stop him from lunging at the knight.

"Stop!" Zarin cries out. The men do not listen and swing their blades. As Captain Kolar comes near Zarin, Hajnal and Nafisa pull her back. Astrophel comes to be a barrier between the women and the men.

"Go from here," Astrophel pushes them out of the door then closes it keeping the fighters and women apart.

"Let me in! Stop fighting! Please!" Zarin bangs on the door tearfully.

"Sir Artegal will win, Zarin. Do not fear," Hajnal tries to encourage her and move her from the door.

"I don't know, Hajnal. Captain Kolar is a skilled swordsman. And either way, a life will be lost on my account and no matter who it is I am grieved." Zarin leans her head against the door.

"But surely, a man like Captain Kolar should die given he hurts so many," Nafisa tries to rationalize this man's possible death. Zarin draws back from the door to look at Hajnal and Nafisa.

"I know what kind of man he is and I have no special love for him. But he is my fellow man. I know him inside and out. I know his soul is not right and if this is his final fight, he will never be able to change that. I have prayed he would but I fear this will prevent him," Zarin shares the thoughts of her mind.

"You pray for him?" Hajnal is baffled at the concept as is Nafisa.

"Who needs our prayer more than our enemies?" Zarin replies.

Hajnal looks down from Zarin while Nafisa looks away.

She is far more merciful and caring than I am. She prays for this man who has wronged her far more than Bardolph has me.

In the room, furniture is sliced and burned. Tyr and Astrophel do their best to avoid being victims of chance. Their swords meet again with both pressing forcibly. Back and forth goes the power of who keeps their sword out from them. Sir Artegal finally pushes, causing Captain Kolar to move backward.

They lunge at each other. When their swords meet, Captain Kolar brings up his leg and kicks Sir Artegal in the stomach. With a groan, he stumbles back. Captain Kolar rushes forward. Sir Artegal meets him. Their blades clash several times in quick succession. Sir Artegal uses his shoulder to shove the captain away briefly. They only draw back together like moths to a flame. Whilst their swords are stuck, Captain Kolar feels the heat of the flames he careful not to be burnt. Feeling his sword bending, the captain headbutts the knight. As Captain Kolar is short, he breaks the knight's nose who stumbles away. He brings his hand to his nose gushing blood. The captain goes forward seeing the knight distracted by his own pain.

Captain Kolar raises his sword to strike the knight but Sir Artegal's blade catches the other just in time. Their faces meet again.

"Not so pretty now, are ya?" Captain Kolar remarks with a smirk but Sir Artegal smiles then laughs.

"Why are you laughing?" the captain does not understand.

"Because thou hast given Zarin her freedom," Sir Artegal answers.

"How so?"

"Do thou truly think Zarin will stay with thee should thou win? Thou hast harmed me already, therefore, breaking thy oath. Zarin is no longer bound to the oath she gave. Even if thou kill me, she will not be thine," Sir Artegal grins. The captain does not share the knight's merriment. He scowls fiercely. He begins to put the pieces together.

"You planned this all along, didn't you?"

"Aye. I changed the card with magic to provoke thee to harm me. Now, no matter the outcome, Zarin is free of thee."

Captain Kolar gives a shove to break their lock. His sword's blade is now melted on the side from the flaming sword. Sir Artegal still comes back to the captain and swirls his sword around till his blade cuts through the captain's. He goes to swing at the captain's head but the man squats down. Captain Kolar jumps up with a start and a knife from his boot. He thrusts it up into Sir Artegal's ribs.

"Artegal!" Astrophel screams and tries to run toward the knight but Tyr holds him back in fear of what may happen to the prince.

"I guess neither of us will have Zarin then," Captain Kolar turns the knife. Sir Artegal grimaces in pain. He drops his sword. Captain Kolar is more than pleased with his obvious victory. He pulls out the knife causing a spurt of blood to come out with it. Sir Artegal grabs the wrist of the hand holding the bloody knife. The captain looks into the eyes of the knight.

"As long as she is free, let us both die," Sir Artegal heaves. His other hand goes to the captain's throat. His hand is tight and unyielding. The captain tries to pull the hand away with his free one but cannot. Sir Artegal's fingers squeeze and squeeze. Captain chokes as he claws the hand.

Crack.

Captain Kolar's body goes limp. Sir Artegal lets him go. The body falls to the floor. All look at the now-dead captain. Sir Artegal breathes heavily as he falls to his knees then his side. Astrophel and Tyr finally go to the knight. Astrophel wraps his arms around his loyal friend and the knight proceeds to collapse in the prince's arms. Tyr rips his sleeve off and tries to apply pressure to the wound. Astrophel cradles the knight.

"What can I do? What can I do for thee?" Prince Astrophel is desperate to know as he holds the increasingly paling Sir Artegal.

"Zarin..." Sir Artegal mumbles the name.

"Tyr, get her!" Astrophel order. Tyr jumps up leaving Astrophel to press on the wound.

"Send...send my heart home. I want it to be buried with my m-mother and father."

"Do not die on me, Artegal. I forbid it!" Prince Astrophel gains tears in his eyes. Sir Artegal gives a weak smile and touches the prince's cheek tenderly to move a tear from it then lowers his hand.

"Thou cannot stop El-Yah's will."

"Who is to say this is his will? Not I. Thou will stay with me. Thou must."

"Astrophel, I..." Sir Artegal begins but his eyes flutter and his breathing struggles.

"Great Creator of the world and giver of life, I beg thee to spare this man. If it is thy will heal him of his wounds, strengthen his body and restore him. Save him. Show grace and healing to him," Astrophel prays fervently.

Tyr opens the door to find the woman standing by Nafisa who gawks at the bracelets falling from her wrists. None understand how the enchanted jewelry fell off. Tyr urges them to come into the room. When they do Zarin, Nafisa, and Hajnal see Astrophel holding the fallen knight. They race to him. Nafisa takes charge of pressing the fabric into the wound instead of Astrophel.

"He has bled through. Let me help." Nafisa has come by the prince. She removes the blood-soaked cloth and replaces it with a bit of her torn dress. She presses down on the wound of the knight as Astrophel continues to pray.

Zarin has stopped her approaching as she catches sight of the dead one being the captain. She sees the bruising on his broken neck and the bloody knife in his hand. She should feel relief and in truth, she feels some but there is sorrow in her for him. Still, she must turn her attention to her friend whose life is fleeting. She and Hajnal take to their knees by the knight.

"Sir Artegal? Sir Artegal, can you hear me?" Zarin speaks loudly. The knight gives faint moans. Zarin grabs Nafisa's hands to move them and the soaked cloth. Nafisa starts to protest but sees Zarin put her hands directly on the wound.

"Hajnal, place your hands on him. Repeat every word I say and put all of your heart and faith into them," Zarin directs, closing her eyes not caring about the warm blood pooling about her hands. She places her hands on Sir Artegal's chest. She feels it is not rising with a breath.

Has he already passed?

Words flow from Zarin's lips. She speaks loudly and clearly. Hajnal repeats the words just as Zarin does. Hajnal does not know the words she says but given what little blessings she has learned from Zarin she knows some of the words already. She puts in her all as Zarin does.

The words become louder and follow a rhythm. Hajnal does not intend it but her chant turns into a song. Zarin begins to sing the words as well. Nafisa sits, watches, and listens. She sees the blood continue to pour out of the wound. She fears their attempt at healing is all in vain. She thinks a witch or some sort of sorcerer would cast a better spell.

Prince Astrophel, on the other hand, grips his knight tightly and continues to pray his prayer. He has faith in his deity and his friends.

Tyr listens to the song but knows not what he can do. He was not born with the gift of healing. But he has seen how Hajnal's ears are not pointed yet she tries to heal Sir Artegal. Tyr reaches out and touches the head of the fallen knight. He closes his eyes and begins to mumble the words of the women's song.

Nafisa watches with a gaping mouth and enlarged eyes as the knight's nose resets itself to its former glory and the fountain of blood beneath Zarin's hands begins to stop. With a gasp, Sir Artegal opens his eyes and mouth. He looks around and then grabs Zarin's hands. Only then does she stop praying. The maiden with wet, golden eyes looks at the knight.

"Artegal!" Astrophel turns his cradle into a hug. Hajnal smiles, wiping away a tear breaking from her eyes.

"I thought thee dead," Astrophel confesses.

"Thou forbade it," Sir Artegal snorts. He looks back to the women who prayed over him.

"Thank thee." He looks up to Tyr though Tyr just nods not sure how in the world he was able to help.

"And thee two as well. I know thou must have been the key to this success," he looks to Hajnal and Zarin. Hajnal nods with a smile in acceptance of his gratitude. Sir Artegal keeps his eyes on Zarin.

Slap!

All are shocked by Zarin's actions. She stands up still wiping tears from her eyes. Sir Artegal gawks at her as she stands over him.

"Do not ever do something like that ever again!" Zarin points her finger at him then storms away. Hajnal rises before going to follow her friend. Sir Artegal touches his cheek. Though the broken nose and stabbing were painful, it is the slap and words that stick with him.

Prince Astrophel and Tyr help raise Sir Artegal back to his feet. It is then he recognizes Nafisa and sees her bloody hands.

"Thank thee for thy help as well," He acknowledges her.

"I did nothing in comparison," She remains timid.

"Still, thou helped when thou could." He bows his head to her. She smiles softly and accepts it.

"Let us leave this place, Artegal," Prince Astrophel pats the knight's back. The knight nods in agreement. The two Estellenians start back for their room. They need to be properly attired as they enter Koralia.

"What are we to do about his body? And his crew?" Tyr asks the women who are left in the room with him.

"Dump it out of the window?" Nafisa suggests.

"No. We must tell the crew the truth," Zarin decides.

"I will find Mr. Brames to tell him to come and see," Tyr leaves the room.

Zarin stands over the dead captain. Her eyes are closed but her hands are together. Zarin separates her hands then allows the tips of her three tall fingers to touch her forehead then go to her chest. She opens her eyes and begins to remove her hair covering. Hajnal stares as she has never seen Zarin without the coif.

There is hardly any hair there. It only looks to be a few weeks' worth of dark hair sprouting on her head. Hajnal covers her mouth, understanding why the hair is so short. The points on the stops of Zarin's ears are now visible too. Zarin covers the captain's face with her coif and drops the gold bracelets onto him.

Tyr returns to the women without Mr. Brames.

"Where is Mr. Brames?" Hajnal asks.

"He is gone. The crew is too. All I could see up on deck were gold bracelets." Tyr shares his findings.

"Those cursed bracelets must have been undone by the death of Captain Kolar," Nafisa looks at her wrists with a smile.

"We are all free now then." Zarin smiles.

Tyr and the woman go back to their cabins to get the belongings they had left behind. Those who had blood on them from Sir Artegal clean themselves before all rejoin on the deck.

They all leave the ship and find the escaped sailors either celebrating or going to the port master to seek help to go home. Looking at her map, Zarin knows the way they must go from this port, Ondabianca, to reach the capital. Sir Artegal unshrinks their animals and travel bags. The troupe prepares to leave.

"Sir Artegal," Nafisa comes to Sir Artegal before he joins the others who have begun to walk. "Thank you for helping me."

The knight just nods to the young woman.

"You must let me repay you." She touches his arm.

"What have I done to deserve payment?"

"You helped me with the broken glass and killed Captain Kolar," She sets out his two actions.

"Thou helped me when I was wounded. I need no more than that."

"But I feel I have not done enough for you." She tightens her hold. He feels the stirring emotions in her. He has no time for such things.

"I know what thou can do for me," he claims.

"What is that?" She lights up.

"Go home and live wisely," he answers. Her spirit falls.

"I...I have no money for traveling back to Gold Haven. But I can travel with you instead and take care of you," She offers.

"That is kind of thee, but..." Sir Artegal looks over to his group. "I have enough people to care for me."

Nafisa frowns disheartened. Sir Artegal notices and reaches into a saddle bag. He pulls out a bag of coins. He puts them in her hand. She is surprised by the weight.

"Take this and buy thy way home," he instructs. Nafisa opens her mouth to protest but Prince Astrophel speaks.

"We should go now, Artegal." The prince who is already mounted on his beast speaks to the knight. Sir Artegal climbs upon his unicorn. Tyr comes and climbs on behind the knight having already helped the women onto their horses.

"Farewell, Nafisa." Sir Artegal bows his head to her before taking off after Prince Astrophel. Nafisa watches as the strangers ride through the docks and toward the center of the Koralian town.

She sighs then looks down to her new small fortune. She supposes she will do what Sir Artegal said after all.

CHAPTER 34

Hajnal

Ever since joining in on the healing of Sir Artegal, Tyr has felt weak. He has felt like this before when he attempted to shift into something far different than his regular animals. Having been poisoned, nearly killed by a mermaid, having no sleep, and performing magic he has never done has proved almost too much for Tyr. He has nearly fallen off the back of Sir Artegal's unicorn in the last five hours. Seeing the village ahead gives some hope for rest.

Tyr is not alone in his exhaustion. Both Zarin and Hajnal have reached their limits. There is some reprieve in the fact they can ride instead of walk the seven leagues but there is still much effort in the riding. They had passed through other villages and towns but Sir Artegal insisted they push further. It is unclear whether his desire to put such great distance between himself and Port Ondabianca is because he desires to get to Liboria quickly or because he does not want to be questioned about a dead captain. Either way, the group can understand.

"We will rest there, yes?" Tyr points to the village they are near.

"Yes," Prince Astrophel answers instead of the knight. Long has the prince noticed his lady love's weariness while also understanding his friend's need to be far from the dead captain and questions.

They keep to the road taking them up to the village with a sign reading "Aura". Instead of going straight through, they turn in search of an inn. It is easy for them to locate such an establishment when a large building near the bottom has a large sign indicating it is an inn. Prince Astrophel had barely asked for two rooms when the owner's wife darted off to the kitchen to start cooking for the travelers and the owner's young sons were out the door to take the horses to their stables. Prince Astrophel went out to fetch his bags and companions after securing the rooms.

Prince Astrophel was quick to help Hajnal down from her horse and with her bags. Tyr slipped off the disguised unicorn and grabbed the bags from it. Sir Artegal dismounted and went to Zarin who looks most haggard of all. She had already started by the time he reached her. His hands carefully went to her waist. The sudden touch surprised her, making her jump and fall back into the knight.

"Fair thee well?" Sir Artegal asks.

"You scared me." She moves his hands from her waist. She goes to reach for her bags but Sir Artegal reaches them first.

"I do not need your help, Sir Artegal," She snaps at him.

"Thou hast been through much today. I can carry thy bags." He ignores her words.

"I think you have helped me enough today." She takes the bags from him and walks to the Inn's entrance. The knight goes to get more of their belongings before following inside.

Mr. Zini, the owner, shows his new customers to their rooms. Tyr enters and finds the two queen beds waiting for someone to flop upon them. Tyr goes to the left one.

"Finally," He exhales, laying across it. The straw mattress is soft as a cloud to the weary man. Sir Artegal puts his belongings on the other. Prince Astrophel sees a suitable chair available for him given he needs no sleep and therefore no bed.

Hajnal and Zarin find their room to have simply one large bed, a chair, a dresser with a pitcher and bowl for water, a lit lantern, and a mirror. They put down their bags and eye the bed. Both want to lie down and sleep. But as they were walking up the stairs to their room, they learned Mrs. Zini will soon have a hot meal ready for them downstairs. Hajnal can smell the herbs and spices sneaking up through the floorboards and into their room. Her stomach grumbles. As they have not eaten much in the last few days, such a meal is appetizing. They return downstairs and are shown to a room with a few tables. Hajnal and Zarin take a seat only to be joined by Prince Astrophel and Sir Artegal.

"Where is Tyr?" Hajnal asks after the shifter.

"He has fallen asleep," Prince Astrophel answers.

"I will soon enough as well after we eat." Hajnal feels a yawn coming upon her A bowl of hot soup warms and relaxes the travelers. Zarin quickly finishes her bowl before letting out a yawn. Hajnal puts her hand on Zarin's shoulder.

"You should go to sleep. You look exhausted."

"I will." Zarin nods and stands.

"I will escort thee." Sir Artegal stands as well.

"I think I can manage on my own," Zarin rejects him but trips as she tries to leave. Sir Artegal catches her.

"You're so tired you can barely walk. Please, let him take you." Hajnal pleads. The short-haired woman nods and sighs. Sir Artegal walks alongside Zarin who has no trouble walking now.

Neither one speaks or even looks at the other as they go up the stairs. Reaching her and Hajnal's room, Zarin opens the door and wishes him 'goodnight'.

"Zarin." He puts his hand on the door before she can close it.

"What?"

"I need to speak with thee," He states.

"About?"

"This morning,"

Zarin frowns.

"Please, let me speak with thee," he requests. Zarin opens the door and allows him to enter. He leaves the door half open for privacy but also transparency of their actions. Neither sit but stand a few feet apart.

"What is it you want to say?" She asks, arms already crossed.

"Shall thou be sore at me forever?" he asks.

"You speak as if what happened was a faux pas like spilling wine on my dress when what you did end a man's life."

"It was not my intention to kill him. I merely wanted him to injure me so thou were no longer bound to your promise to him. He was the one who stabbed me."

Zarin had not known of his plan and pauses for a moment.

"Still, you put yourself in that situation against my wishes." Zarin crosses her arms.

"If I had done as thou asked, thou would be on that ship with who knows how many enslaved men at the mercy of that sick man. I could not abide knowing thy life would be in his hands."

"I have my ring of protection."

"They are not eternal. When it finally broke, thou would have no protection against him."

"Hopefully by that point, I would have been able to sway his heart toward El-Yah."

"And what if his heart remained to be a stone? What if thou only caused him to harden it more?"

"We shall never know now because your pride led you to plot this fight."

"Pride? Pride! Thou think I did this all for pride? I assure thee, it is not out of pride or vanity I did this."

"Then why?"

"It is my duty."

"How so?"

"I am a fairy knight. It is my duty to protect those to whom I am sworn."

"You have made no vows to me."

"I have. Indirectly, I have."

"How so?"

"When thou end thy apprenticeship and are made a master, thou will make vows before El-Yah. Thou shall make vows to protect other fairies who are in training and to those in true need who ask for aid."

"I see. That is why you threw your rank in my face on the boat?"

"Yes. Thou put thyself in an inescapable situation that I had to intervene."

"He was going to slit your throat while the prince and Tyr were no better than two sacks of potatoes lying on the floor. I had to step in or you would be dead."

"I do not regret trying to protect thee. Though I suppose partly of why I did it was to help make up for my earlier deficiency. And because I was fearful of losing thee."

Zarin's lips pressed together and she inhales softly.

"I think partly of why I am so upset, besides the death, is that you put your faith in yourself and not in El-Yah. I know you are a master fairy and therefore I thought you should be so close to El-Yah that you would never fall to such things as fear or anger. I forgot that even master fairies are not...perfect." Zarin speaks further of her deeper thoughts.

"I am far from perfection and I did put my faith in myself over El-Yah. But does thou not think that perhaps El-Yah used my lack of faith as his way to deliver thee?" Sir Artegal suggests the possibility.

"It would not be beyond his ability to use something bad for something good. But I still hold to my wish that you never do such a thing again for my sake."

"I cannot make any such promise, but I can promise that I will think twice before acting in such a manner again."

"I guess I can accept that."

"Can we be reconciled then? I should not like for us to be in this...uncomfortable, angry place."

"Yes. I should like to be beyond this as well."

Sir Artegal takes her hands in his gloved ones. They are so large in comparison to hers. But everything about him is larger than her.

"Oh, excuse us," Hajnal speaks making the knight and maiden see Hajnal and Astrophel have come to the door. They lower their hands but do not indicate embarrassment.

"Good night, Zarin, Hajnal." Sir Artegal nods to each woman who nods back to him. They close the door. Hajnal, though tired, finds a new energy having caught the two. Zarin yawns and begins to undress for bed. Hajnal grins at Zarin.

"What were you and Sir Artegal speaking about?" Hajnal inquires.

"We were merely discussing the events of earlier," Zarin answers and sits on the bed as she takes off her shoes.

"I see. And that called for hand-holding?" Hajnal raises an eyebrow.

"It was just a friendly gesture. Do not read more into it, Hajnal," Zarin stretches her legs then yawns again.

"If you say not to." Hajnal takes off her shoes.

"I am so exhausted. I do not know if I will wake by dawn tomorrow," Zarin slips under the blanket on the bed.

"I do not know if I will either. We need our rest. Last night was...awful. Tonight, will be much different," Hajnal assures her friend.

"It better be."

"Oh, I should have told you but if you want to have a hot bath, Mrs. Zini has a bathroom for women that we can use. She mentioned it to me when I finished my food."

"Perhaps in the morning. I am too tired tonight."

"I understand. But I think I will go tonight. I stink of fish and sweat," Hajnal remarks.

"Be careful," Zarin yawns.

"I will. Good night."

"Good night." Zarin has to merely close her eyes and put her head on the pillow for her to fall asleep.

Hajnal grabs her relatively clean spare clothes to take with her to the bathing room downstairs. She is quiet as she walks down the stairs. Mrs. Zini meets her at the bottom and escorts her to the private room. She brags about how she had a fairy customer once who liked her so much, they blessed their bathing room water pump to always have warm water. Hajnal is glad for such a blessing. She cannot remember the last time she bathed in warm water. Mrs. Zini gives Hajnal a bar of soap, towels, a robe, and a nightgown of her own with the guarantee Mrs. Zini will wash and return the clothes to Hajnal in the morning. Hajnal is almost overwhelmed by Mrs. Zini's hospitality and generosity but is happy to have it. Once she is alone and the tub is full of steaming water, Hajnal slips inside. She scrubs away the stink of the past few weeks. She washes her hair and combs through her curls with her fingers. Having dried off, dressed in the borrowed nightgown, and covered up with a robe, Hajnal goes back up to her room.

Hajnal finds Zarin fast asleep. A little snore comes from the unconscious woman. The lantern is still lit allowing Hajnal to see where she goes. She removes the robe to hang on the back of the chair. She takes off her shoes and then sits in the chair. She looks in the mirror and begins to braid her moist hair. She hums and bats her sleepy eyes. She looks at her face having finished her hair. A pair of eyes that are not hers flicker in her reflection. She shakes her head and looks again. The eyes reappear. Hajnal's reflection disappears.

"Good evening, my dear," Bardolph speaks to her.

"H-how are you in there again?" Hajnal questions rather terrified and tries to cover herself with her nearby cloak.

"Magic," he replies with a chuckle. Hajnal rolls her eyes.

"Go away." Hajnal is not amused.

"Is that any way to speak to the one who saved you from a life under the sea?"

Hajnal presses her lips together. *It is true he helped me.*

"Thank you for your help. But I do not understand how *this* is happening," Hajnal gestures to the mirror.

"I want to talk to you so I have spelled mirrors to let me see and speak to you."

"I don't understand why you would want to do that."

"Why would I not?"

"Because I despise you."

"Something I hope to change."

"Unless you are going to give me back my siblings now and ask sincerely for my forgiveness, I will not stop despising you."

"I can do that but of course, I need something in return."

"And that is?"

"You."

"I do not understand your obsession. Find another with my gifts if you so desperately want to create the New Starrling. You're handsome and obviously powerful. You can find a woman easily to do this for you so stop tormenting me."

Bardolph holds a soft smile.

"I don't want anybody else." His voice is soft and tender. It is different than any voice he has used before with her.

"Because I rejected you? Is this a pride issue?"

"No...well, maybe a little bit."

"Then what is it?"

"It is love."

"Love?" Hajnal laughs. Bardolph shows no signs of humor. "What do you know of love?"

"I know that is something I never felt before until you."

"You're lying."

"I am not," He firmly denies.

Hajnal shakes her head in disbelief.

"It is true. When I came to your village, I saw you and wanted you as I wanted every maiden there. But then I tasted your first-morning batch of bread. And with that first bite, I tasted it."

"Tasted what?"

"What it is like to be loved by you."

Hajnal sits still trying to understand what he means.

"You must know how your emotions affected your food. That's why I came every morning. It felt so good like...I don't know...Not even the thrill of killing or bedding maidens compared to it. No one has ever made me feel like that and no one else but you can."

Hajnal retains a stony expression during the confession.

"It is funny, I liken myself to a moth. They are these intelligent creatures of darkness and magic but fire, a simple element full of both light and warmth, draws moths to them. Neither have anything in common and fire can destroy a moth. Still, the moth cannot help fluttering to the flame. There is no reason to explain it. I feel I am a moth and you are a flame. I will forever be drawn to you, but you have no care for me," Bardolph compares them.

"You say I am fire as if I am the one who hurts you but you are the one who has set out to destroy my life and the lives around me."

"*You* wound *me*. I keep offering my love to you but you reject me."

"Can you blame me?"

"I am capable of change. I just need you to teach me how. Come to me. Teach me the way into your heart," He pleads with his eyes large and wet.

"Return my siblings to me and I will consider forgiving you."

"Will you not love me if I give them back?"

"Maybe as my fellow man." Hajnal thinks of what Zarin referred to Captain Kolar as.

"Fellow man?" Bardolph snickers. "I think we can do better than that."

"Bardolph, I-"

"Stop. Stop before you wound me again. I want to make you another offer."

"You and your offers," She groans.

"You'll like this one." He claims.

Hajnal sits and listens for what he will say.

"In exchange for marrying me, I will break the curses and free your siblings as already promised. I will also guarantee no harm comes to your traveling friends including your little prince. I will rebuild Foxglove Grove so it is even better than it was. *And* I will compensate each family I have hurt there as well as my atonement." He puts out the offer.

Hajnal remains quiet as she is stunned by the additions made.

"Of course, if you reject me, I may act out in my heartbroken state. I think you would hate to see what could befall your friends and family when I'm like that."

Dread fills Hajnal.

"I'll give you some time to think about my offer before I contact you again." He winks before disappearing from the mirror leaving Hajnal looking at her reflection. She wraps her arms around herself and finds herself chilled. Grabs the mirror and turns it around so if he decides to look again, he will see only the wall. Hajnal goes to bed where Zarin has stayed asleep. She turns off the lamp and crawls beneath the blanket with her heart troubled.

CHAPTER 35

Hajnal

For hours, Hajnal lies next to Zarin thinking of her conversation with Bardolph. With each thought the bed feels hotter and harder. She cannot stand it. She gets up and walks around the room. She finds the room cold but she does not want to be in the stifling room. She puts on some shoes and her purple cloak. Perhaps some fresh air will do her good.

As soon as Hajnal steps out of her room, the door to the men's room opens. Astrophel walks out with a knife and a piece of wood in his hands. He tosses them back into his room upon seeing Hajnal.

"Hajnal," he calls to her in a whisper.

"Astro," She addresses him feeling some relief upon seeing him. He closes his door and comes to her.

"Is something wrong?" He whispers.

"I am having trouble sleeping. I thought a stroll in the night air would help," she answers.

"Let me walk with thee then," He offers.

"Are you not tired?"

"I do not sleep, remember."

"Yes. Yes." She does remember. He offers his arm to her and she takes it. They leave the inn and step out into the quiet town. There are no lights except the stars and moon.

"Stay close to me, it is dark," He puts his hand atop the one holding his arm. She nods.

"Where should we walk?" She realizes their lack of destination.

"Mr. Zini told me there is a legendary, blessed spring here. Do we not need water from such a spring for thy elixir?"

"We do! We should go there," Hajnal smiles.

"Then let us go." He smiles.

"Can you tell me what they told you about this spring?"

As they Astrophel recounts the tale of Aura's spring, the fairy who blessed and how it saved the life of the infant princess Aura of Koralia decades ago, the couple walks up the vast stone stairways leading up to the top of the hill. Reaching the top, they find a sizable red stone building with a circular dome atop it. They come to large wooden doors with brass handles.

"It is said new mothers still come here to drink of the water so they may nurse their children," Astrophel finishes the story.

"I see. Do you think it is open now?" Hajnal looks to the prince.

"We shall find out," he pushes on the door. He smiles at his partner as the door opens. Hajnal and Astrophel go inside. Unlike the village, the church has lights. There are lamp stands against the stone walls. The entryway is rather large and leads to another set of doors. Going beyond this they enter a room with a high dome ceiling. The floors are made of dark and light wood styled to go in a herringbone pattern. The otherwise white walls have long oval windows going around. Hanging lanterns hang around from the domed ceiling meets the walls. The ceiling has a stained-glass window in its center. In the middle of the church is a circular stone with a little spring of water bubbling up. Hajnal and Astrophel go forward to the center of the church together and stop at the spring. Hajnal stares at the water. She wonders if it truly is blessed.

They take a seat together in a front pew. They stare at the water with arms still linked. Hajnal leans her head against Astrophel's shoulder. Sleep tries to creep onto her but just as she closes her eyes, she sees Bardolph. She lifts her head abruptly.

"What is wrong?" Astro asks.

"Nothing," She shakes her head while not making eye contact.

"Do not lie, Hajnal. We are in a holy place, after all," he brings up their location. Hajnal does not want to tell him of her mirror conversation with Bardolph but she also does not want to lie.

"I...if um...I..." Hajnal exhales as she tries to formulate her question. Astrophel is patient. "If it were guaranteed your family, your friends, your country, and even me were to be kept safe and well, would you marry someone else?"

Astrophel clenches his jaw and looks away from Hajnal.

"I want to say I would not, for I love thee as thou know but...I must do what is best for thee, my family, and my country. If to marry another meant protecting thee all I...I do not know. I would have to consider many things and seek much counsel. Why art thou asking such a query?" His eyes go back to her.

"Because I am seeking counsel on what I should do," Hajnal admits.

"This is about Bardolph then."

"Yes. I have told no one yet because...well, we've been through so much in the last day I have not had time, but Bardolph has contacted me."

"He has?"

"Yes. He first found me when I fell into the water at the mermaid's lair. He helped actually. I was stuck but that doesn't matter. What matters is he has just reached out to me again tonight in the inn. He-"

"He did? How?" Astrophel interrupts.

"He is using mirrors. He has spelled them."

"Then we must be rid of all mirrors and-" Astrophel stands but Hajnal grabs his arm.

"Stop. I need you to listen, not act, at least not now," Hajnal states. Astrophel sits back down and apologizes for his zeal.

"When he spoke to me tonight, he made an interesting offer, one affecting more than just me or my siblings."

"What was the offer?"

"He would not only free my siblings and cure the curses, but he also would not harm you, Zarin, Sir Artegal, or Tyr. He would also help rebuild my village and try to make atonements to the families of his victims," Hajnal voices the pros of the offer.

"Thou would trust in the promises of a liar?"

"Zarin accepted a similar offer from a man we could hardly trust and-"

"Thou art not Zarin! And her choice was made because there was no other way. Thou hast other options," Astrophel snaps. Hajnal is taken aback by his reaction. She has not seen this anger since they were in Sterhout.

"But what if I don't? What if my rejection of this offer causes everyone to die? I cannot do that to the people I love. I cannot do that to you," Hajnal grabs Astrophel's hands.

"Thou art speaking as if thou know it is marriage or death. The whole purpose of our quest is based on the belief thou will be able to save thy family without having to give in to Bardolph. So far, we have faced adversity but have overcome it. El-Yah has granted us victory after victory. Why art thou so full of doubt now?" Astrophel questions her.

"Because what if El-Yah is only allowing us to go closer to Bardolph so that I will marry him? What if all the horrible things that have happened were a punishment for trying to thwart my destiny?"

"Thy destiny?"

"Yes. What if I am destined to be with Bardolph? What if that is the only way El-Yah will have me save my family and friends? What if I am meant to have the New Starrling who will destroy the lands?" Hajnal's fears run out of her mouth as tears run from her eyes.

"Stop. Stop," Astrophel takes hold of her shoulders. She brings her hands to cover her face.

"Astro, I-I-I" She blubbers. He pulls her into his chest. His arms are tight around her. She sobs into him.

"The plans I have for thee are of hope, not of evil. I will protect thee and uphold thee even in the face of thine enemies. Call upon me and I will hear thee. I will save thee. Do not fear for I am with thee all the days of thy life. What man may intend for evil I shall turn it to good. Thou art my beloved," Astrophel speaks of the recorded promises of El-Yah. Hajnal has heard and read these promises before but it has been a long time since then. Hajnal's breath remains shaky but her sobbing ceases. He has not held her like this since they were in their dream realm.

"Do not forget these promises, my darling beloved. Though I do not know all that is in store for us, I know even if thou art taken into the wolf's den, El-Yah will not abandon thee. Please, have courage, beloved. Remember all El-Yah has done. Do not give into fear." Astrophel's soft words are like a balm. Hajnal takes deep breaths and relaxes in his hold. She finally leans back from him so she can look at his face.

"And if it truly is thy destiny to be with Bardolph-which I pray it is not so and thou shall never be forced to be his- I will still love thee all the days of my life."

Hajnal embraces him again. She can feel his warming love.

"My beloved," She calls him. Astrophel kisses her shoulder. His lips begin moving up slowly. On her neck and jaw, he plants soft kisses. He kisses her cheek once before she turns so he may kiss her lips. Hajnal touches his cheek then pulls back. She admires his lips. How stranger that there was a time she could not see or feel them.

"I am glad the veil is gone," Hajnal mutters to herself. Astrophel leans back with his eyes wide.

"What did thou say?"

Hajnal blushes and looks away. "Nothing."

"No, thou were glad the veil is gone. Why did you say that?" He will not let her avoid it.

"You may not believe me but ever since I was a child, all of my dreams have happened in the same place. All have been in a castle in the woods. And there every night was a man in a veil who was my friend and confidant. And it may sound like wishful thinking but I believe the veiled man is you," Hajnal admits.

"I have waited so long for thou to remember," Astrophel smiles brightly.

"What?"

"I thought thou forgot me and that is why thou were reserved with me."

"I thought you forgot me. When you woke, you did not know me but I knew you. I was afraid you would be disappointed to see it was me and not someone else," She confesses.

"I admit I did not know thee when I saw thee but the more I looked at thine eyes and heard thy voice, I knew thee. And I was not disappointed. How could I ever be disappointed with thee St-" The prince is glowing but Hajnal covers his mouth.

"You cannot say that name. You can never say that name. That is my curse. My name is cursed, Astro. Don't you remember?"

He nods. She lowers her hand.

"But that curse should be broken. We have kissed, more than once now, and as it is true love, thy curse should be broken as well," Prince Astrophel rationalizes.

"It broke your curse. But I do not know if it has broken mine," Hajnal disagrees.

"Why would it not break thine? I am thy True Love," Prince Astrophel claims the title.

"You have said yourself different curses have different ways to be broken. My curse may be one not fixed with True Love's kiss. It may only be cured with the All-Cure elixir like my brother," Hajnal argues.

"I am not afraid to try. No one should be deprived of being called by her own name," the prince makes his case.

"Even so, I will not risk you turning to stone. Please, do not say my name."

"If I do become cursed to be stone then would not a kiss from thee free me?" He logically deduces.

"Well...perhaps..."

"Let me say it. Let me call thee by the name, beloved." He squeezes her hands.

"Why not stick with 'beloved'? I do love it."

"I still want to say thy name."

Hajnal sighs then nods to bless his request.

"Stella," he calls her and every fiber in her body vibrates with delight and joy. Tears spring to her eyes and a smile spreads widely across her face as does one on Astrophel's.

"Am I stone?"

"No. No! You're just your wonderful self!" Stella cries and embraces him. He wraps his arms around her tightly.

"Oh, Stella. Stella. Stella," he repeats her name over and over into her hair as he kisses the top of her head. When she pulls back, he holds her face in his hands. She smiles then yawns unexpectedly. She covers her mouth and apologizes for the action.

"No apologies are needed. We should get thee to bed."

Stella pulls and nods in agreement.

"Wait!"

"What is it?"

"I just remembered! We need water from a blessed spring for the elixir!" Stella points to the water. Astrophel searches himself and finds his canteen still tied to his side. He quickly drinks the water in it and then fills it with the water of the spring.

"Now, we are set. Thou need to rest now." Astrophel takes the maiden by the hand and escorts her from the church, down the stairs of Aura, and to the inn. He bids her good night and returns to his room while Stella gets back in bed with Zarin.

Astrophel picks up his wood and knife and gets back to carving. His elation with the truth is darkened by the problem his dear one shared. He hopes neither of them ever has to truly face that sort of choice.

CHAPTER 36

ALTHEA

In the weeks following her first lessons in flying and astrology, Althea has seen little of anyone except Hadion. A routine has been established. In the morning, Hadion comes to her room to fetch her, then she is to make food from random objects. Post breakfast, they train outside for hours only to come back inside to study astral charts, spells, and other ways to conduct magic. In the evening, they take to the sky before lying on the beach to look at the stars and planets. Each night, she transforms into a phoenix and attempts to fly back to the castle. Each night she lasts a little longer but has yet to make it on her own. She is not too disappointed. She does not mind the way Hadion safely secures her in his arms.

Althea has found each morning she is excited for Hadion's knock at her door. She looks forward to strengthening her magic under Hadion's patient tutelage. As she is getting better, she is having to strip less. Though she finds herself not as embarrassed as she had first been. Why should she be? She has a beautiful body. She has always thought so and Hadion has reaffirmed this many times. However, it is his compliments of her skill and intellect she prefers.

Her preferred time of the day in her opinion is when they fly. She knows she does not have to be afraid to fall as Hadion is always there to catch her. His large, strong hands grip her tightly but tenderly. His arms secure her to his chest when she gets to inhale his sweet scent over and over. No matter how long she is against him, she does not get used to the smell and does not want to either. Her eyes too have grown accustomed to lingering on him. He is not an eyesore, after all. Despite his looks and smell drawing her in, she has found her feelings growing to be more...fond of him.

They lie together now on the beach so they may look up at the speckled sky. They should be talking about what the current star and planet placement means but instead, they look to one another.

"Althea," he addresses her softly.

"Yes, Master?"

"Can you swim?"

"...Yes...why?"

"We are going for a swim," Hadion stands up and begins to remove his shirt. Althea stares at him startled but curious. In the light of the half-moon, Althea can see upon his muscular torso, numerous black lines upon his otherwise pale skin. She is surprised not just by the dark marks but by the lack of hair on his torso. They are all symmetrical in design but different and connected by their centerlines coming to a line from the six-point falling star in the center of his chest. Unlike the tattoos, she can see the falling star is a scar.

"Like what you see?" Hadion catches her staring.

"Oh, please!" Althea looks away with cheeks aflame.

"I saw you staring," He continues to tease.

"Of course, I stared. I have never seen so many tattoos before in my life," Althea defends her action. Hadion looks down at his torso.

"Ah, yes."

"Why do you have so many?" Althea dares to question.

"They help to maintain certain spells on my body," He answers honestly.

"So, your looks are spelled," She is quick to assume. He laughs.

"No, my looks are all mine."

"Oh...so what sort of spells have you put on yourself?"

He comes by her and gets on his knees. He takes her hand and puts it on his right arm.

"This one is for endurance and strength."

He moves her hand to his other arm.

"This is for prolonged memory."

Her hand moves to the right shoulder.

"This is for cloaking my whereabouts from the prying eyes of other sorcerers."

To the left shoulder, her hand goes.

"This is for protecting me from minor curses."

He places her hand on the right side of his chest.

"This is for rapid healing."

She feels his steady heartbeat when he moves her hand to the left side of his chest.

"This is to maintain good health and protect from diseases."

When he brings her hand to his abdomen, she feels the hardness of his muscles beneath his smooth skin.

"This is for balance and this one is for restful sleep."

He lets go of her hand but she sees her has another mark on his pelvis with part of his hidden by his pants. She points to it shyly.

"And that one?" Her curiosity will not let her ignore it.

"That is to prevent me from siring more children."

"Oh..." Althea presses her lips together. She is not too surprised given the oldest child he has produced. "Two is enough for you?"

"More than enough," Hadion replies then inhales sharply. "I have another mark on my back."

Hadion turns around and shows Althea his back. She stares at the faint white lines at his shoulder blades then the large black tattoo taking over the rest of his back.

"What is this one for?" She asks.

"For the magnification of my gifts and magic."

Althea should study the sigil on his back but instead eyes the curvature of his spine and the ripples of his muscles. Her fingers reach out and graze the natural line on his skin giving away he has natural wings. Hadion looks over his shoulder to Althea. She pulls her hand away. The corners of Hadion's lips twitch. He looks away from Althea and turns his view toward the water. Having gotten up. he walks into the sea.

"Althea, undress and get in with me," He calls to her. Althea looks toward him and sees his lower half covered.

"Hurry up, Althea." He waves at her. She begins removing her outer layer but before she can remove her chemise Hadion calls to Althea. "Stop taking so long and just come in."

Althea leaves on the chemise and goes into the water. She 'eeps' as she feels the cold water making Hadion laugh. He holds his hand out to her. She takes it and allows him to draw her further into the water. The water rises higher on her body than on his.

"Why do you want me in this freezing water?" Althea questions shivering.

"We can practice your water manipulation."

"Oh. What do you want me to try?"

"Let's practice making water orbs. See." Hadion holds his hand out and speaks his spell. The seawater rises and forms a ball that rises in the air without dropping any water. Althea holds out her hand and copies his words. Some of the water curls up but it falls back instead of becoming a ball. Althea continues to practice until she finally gets an orb though it does not rise off the water.

"I made an orb!" She smiles at Hadion.

"You need to be able to raise it."

"Why?"

"Well, water orbs can be used to transfer water quickly from one place to another and it can be used to help someone stuck in water be moved from the water. It can be used to imprison someone," Hadion explains the purpose. "So, you need to be able to raise it up and around."

"Oh, I see. I'll keep trying then," Althea nods and continues her work. Hadion watches her intently as she continues to try to make the orb rise. She begins to have her orb float up but it falls apart before she can move it too far.

"Ugh!" She groans as the orb falls once more.

"Breathe, Althea," Hadion comes behind her. He wraps one arm around her and places his hand on her chest while he uses his other hand to support her tired arm.

"Breathe with me," he begins to inhale. Althea closes her eyes and does as he does. The warmth of his wet body against hers makes her heart speed up a beat.

"Try again," he does not move. Althea breathes in deeply then tries again.

"I'm doing it!" Althea beams finally making her orb remain solid and float.

"Excellent!" He removes himself from her. "Do it three more times."

Althea nods and does as told. Three successes later leave Althea grinning in delight at her skill.

"Good. Now, I'm going to swim far. You need to put a water orb around me and move me to dry land," he tells her.

"I don't think I'm ready for that." Althea shakes her head.

"I believe in you." He pats her hand then takes off further into the water. He swims far. Althea can barely see his head.

"Try it now, Althea," He yells in the distance. Althea sighs before focusing on his distant head. Repeatedly, she tries to capture him with her watery orb but over and over she fails. She grows weaker with each try. The water pushing against her combined with the day and night's worth of practice have left her body shaking and exhausted.

Everything around Althea begins to spin. Which way is the water and which way are the blurring stars? Althea falls backward into the water swallowing her up.

"Althea. Althea," She feels something patting her face. Althea opens her eyes with Hadion over her and sand beneath her. His wet curls drip on her as his colorful eyes are wide but focused on her. Her skin begins to form goosebumps.

"What happened?" Althea questions.

"You fainted in the water. I got you out," He answers and keeps the hand that was patting her cheek against her. "Are you well?"

"Yes. I...I'm sorry to have fainted. I didn't mean to. I just was so tired." She blushes.

"You were pushed beyond your limit. It is my fault," he takes responsibility.

"Well, thank you for fishing me out of the water. I'm sure my ring would have kept me from drowning but I'm sure I would have woken up in a panic if I woke in the water," She chuckles.

"Your ring?" He looks down at her hand. "Right. Your ring."

Hadion sits back on the sand as Althea begins to sit up. Hadion runs his hand through his black curls and looks up to the sky. Althea's eyes cannot help being drawn to the teacher's figure.

"You're probably too weak to fly back. I'll carry you," He decides getting up. He offers his hand to her. She takes it only for him to pull her up to her feet. He cradles her in his arms and sprouts his wings before taking off.

"My dress," She looks down at the discarded piece of clothing.

"You have more," he responds, not returning for it or the shirt he left behind. Althea sticks close to him and secretly enjoys his holds. She stares at his bare chest she is pressed against. She stares at the six-pointed falling star on his chest and the other tattoos there. Her finger goes to the star. She feels the scar tissue with her fingertip. She remembers Zarin's unfinished scar on her chest and the story behind it.

Althea keeps her head against him and hears the beating of his heart. It is rather fast but she knows given the physical activity, it makes sense. She finds despite the fast beat, it is rather soothing. She finds her weary self growing more and more comfortable and relaxed. Before she realizes it, Althea falls asleep.

When Althea opens her eyes again, she finds herself in her room with the plants giving off their lights as they are enchanted to do. Hadion is laying her on her bed. She looks up at his handsome face.

"My chemise...it's dry," she realizes.

"I used a drying spell. You should rest now," he whispers. His eyes lower making her look down. Sometime between the beach and the bed, her chemise has slipped exposing her shoulder, collar, and the top of her chest. His fingers go to the slipping fabric. The brush of his skin against hers makes her skin tingle. She is not sure if he will pull it up or down. She breathes heavily unsure of what he will do. His eyes meet hers and her tongue darts out to wet her lips. His face comes closer to hers. Her skin warms and her heart pounds. Adrenaline begins to course in her veins but not from fear. She closes her eyes and waits for a specific touch on her lips.

What will he feel like? How will he taste? Her mind wonders in waiting. Mother said Father's kisses were like a warm, honey cinnamon bun to her lips and his taste was just as sweet. Elspeth Kenwyn said when she was kissed by Ortwin Bonham it was like having a wet sardine shoved in her mouth and he tasted like boiled cabbage. *Please, don't taste like boiled cabbage.*

"Stay warm and sleep." She hears him say and she opens her eyes. He has pulled up her chemise and covered her with a blanket. He moves to leave her but she grabs his hand. He looks back at her with raised eyebrows.

"You're cold." She feels his icy hands.

"So?" He shrugs. Althea holds his hand tightly and closes her eyes. She whispers a spell. She feels his hand turn from ice to a temperature more her own. She looks up at Hadion and smiles. His other hand goes toward her face but it does not reach it. He pulls his hand from hers.

"Good night, Althea." He leaves. Althea stares at the door. She almost calls out to him but covers her mouth.

"What are you doing, Althea?" She asks herself, having removed her hand. "Go to sleep."

She lies down but her mind goes to picturing Hadion above her and coming closer to her. She recalls how she thought he was to kiss her and how she was even fine with it. She covers her head with her blanket embarrassed.

"Why would you even be fine with that? He's a sorcerer and has two kids. One is your enemy and the other is your friend. Who cares if he is gorgeous and smart and sometimes kind and makes you feel great about yourself? He is-He is…" Althea scolds herself but pauses as she tries to find the right adjective but all negative ones leave her brain.

"Ugh," She groans and uncovers her head. She rolls over and looks at the plants around her. She closes her eyes tightly and does her best to push away any thoughts of her master so she can sleep.

Althea wakes and finds she has overslept. She can tell by how far the sun has risen outside the window. Though surprised Hadion let her sleep in so long, she rushes to dress in case he should appear. Once dressed and ready for another day of lessons, she sits on her bed and waits.

She waits and waits and waits.

Althea rises not sure if her waiting is all for naught. She walks to the door and grabs the handle. She gasps when she finds it unlocked. She opens the door and looks up and down the empty hall. She goes to Odile's door and knocks. There is no reply.

"This is weird," She murmurs to herself.

"Althea," Odile appears in the hallway with a piece of paper in her hands.

"There you are. Have you seen your father?"

"Well, no, but he did leave me this letter," Odile holds up the paper.

"Oh? He is not here?"

"No. According to this letter, he and Bardolph have been called to a meeting for sorcerers. I am left in charge of you and have been told to tell you to keep practicing your magic." Odile looks at the letter again. Althea crosses her arms not quite sure why she is growing upset with this news.

"Sorcerers have meetings?" Althea snorts as if it were the most ridiculous thing she has ever heard.

"Only a few of the more powerful ones. I'm sure they are planning to discuss what to do about the newly opened Estellen," Odile brings up the country Althea had only been in a few weeks prior.

"Why would they need to meet about Estellen?"

"No one has been able to access it for a century. It is a treasure trove and given their vulnerability, some sorcerers will probably want to try to take it over or at least wreak some havoc. So, they will probably talk about that stuff. I'm just speculating," Odile answers.

"Oh...I hope no one tries to harm them," Althea gives her thoughts.

"It's inevitable."

There is no comfort for Althea. *Poor Astrophel and Sir Artegal.*

"But I'm glad it's just going to be us for a little bit. I barely see you these past two weeks. It'll be nice to go about freely." Odile smiles.

"Yes."

"Want to eat?" Odile's question causes her stomach to rumble.

"Yes, please."

After a meal together, the women return to Odile's tower where they both take to reading books on magic. Though her mind should be focusing on the words on the page before her, Althea's mind keeps going back to her master. She thinks of his tattooed and masculine body against her. She imagines the rush of his fingertips against her chest and shoulder when he moves her sleeve. She recalls the shimmer in his eyes or the timbre of his voice. She does not forget her near kiss and her want for it. She slams her face down in her book on the table and groans.

"You bored out of your mind, too?" Odile walks over to Althea. Althea does not answer but just moans.

"Want to go for a walk?" Odile's question earns a nod from the girl with her face in the book.

"Let's go then." Odile snaps shut her book. Althea lifts her head and closes the book. Perhaps a walk will help clear her mind of that person.

"Oh, the sun's going down," Althea notices immediately as they step outside for their walk.

"Yeah. You overslept."

"Should we just wait to walk tomorrow then?"

"No way. The island can be lots of fun after dark. Come on." Odile hooks her arm to Althea's and makes her walk with her. They walk toward the setting sun.

"Where are we going to go?" Althea asks as they walk further and further from the palace.

"To visit people who do not care about stupid things like magic books."

Soon enough Althea sees where Odile has led her. She pauses at the top of the hill as she looks down at the lake by Sommerstern. Music plays and maidens in white dance.

"I don't think I'm allowed down there," Althea whispers to Odile as if any of the dancers would be able to hear her.

"Don't be silly." Odile pulls Althea with her and makes her go down the hill and toward the swan maidens.

The music is light and cheerful allowing for the dancers to hop about in their dance. They smile and hold each other's hands as they dance as they enjoy each other's company and freedom from her feathery forms. It is when a dancer catches sight of the approaching women the dancing is thrown off rhythm. The other dancers begin to stop and the musicians miss their notes and then stop. All stare at Althea and Odile. One runs inside the castle while the others stay still. The one Althea remembers to be called Darya comes upfront.

"She is not welcome here," Darya points to Althea while talking to Odile.

"Says who?" Odile is not intimidated by the tall woman.

"Says our princess. She told this girl to get out weeks ago," Darya smirks.

"Oh? And why would she ban a woman from this sanctuary of women?" Odile questions.

"Because she is von Rothbart's lover," Darya answers making Althea's cheek redden. Odile chortles.

"Are you kidding me?"

"We have seen him fly over us with her in his arms," Another maiden pipes up.

"He has flown with me in his arms too and I am not his lover." Odile rolls her eyes.

"And I have seen her naked with him in the daytime," yet another voices her observations. Althea only blushes more.

"That is how he punishes me!" Althea gives the excuse.

Some of the swan maidens cover their mouths truly upset by this fact. Odile is not fazed by the information.

"Odile," the princess of the swans steps out into the crowd. The dancers split to make way for their princess. The royal one looks at Althea and presses her lips together.

"Althea, what are you doing here?" The princess frowns.

"I brought her." Odile smiles.

"Why? von Rothbart will not be happy," The princess refers to the man who took Althea away from the castle the last time she was there.

"He is not on the island. Neither is Bardolph. They've gone off to a meeting of sorcerers," Odile informs the leader of the swans.

"Oh. Well...if he is gone then..." The princess smiles at Althea and takes Althea's hand. "I have someone who would like to meet you."

"My princess, surely you are not going to allow her here. She is so obviously a lover of von Rothbart." Darya stops the blondes and whispers.

"Darya, if I cast out anyone who has held affection for a sorcerer on this island then I would have had to ban all the girls from the castle including you," She reminds Darya making her blush then turns back to Althea and smiles while telling her to continue with her.

"Shall I make all the instruments play so we all can dance?" Odile asks the swan maidens that are left outdoors. Nods and smiles come and so Odile spells the instruments to play allowing all to dance.

"Thank you for standing up to Darya for me, your highness, but I am confused. Why are you welcoming me now when last time I was here, you cast me out," Althea inquires walking into the castle.

"Just call me 'Odette'. And I am sure in your time with Hadion, you have found it hard to argue with him and get your way," Odette replies.

"Yes. He always has to be in control," Althea huffs.

"Yes. But since he is not here, you can come just as Odile does," Odette refers to the sorceress in training and leads Althea into a parlor room. They take seats there.

"Why would Odile not be allowed her whenever she wishes? Didn't she create this place for you all?"

Odette laughs then stops.

"I do not mean to criticize Odile, but you have seen her skill with magic, correct?"

"Yes, but who else could have made this sanctuary? Certainly not Bardolph."

"No. No. Hadion did," Odette answers. Althea pauses.

Hadion made a sanctuary for all the abused lovers of his son on the island. Why?

"So, I must do what he says for he can take away this place as well," Odette shares.

"I see."

"I did not want to give you over to him. I am sorry. But I had to for the sake of the others."

"I understand."

"I hope he has been kind to you."

"Oh, very," Althea speaks without thinking then catches herself. "I mean better than I would have thought a sorcerer to treat me."

"You must be careful. Sorcerers can be extraordinarily beguiling." Odette warns.

"I find them to be extraordinarily vexing," Althea quips and earns a snicker from Odette.

"Yes. They can be."

"You said you had someone for me to meet," Althea recalls Odette's earlier words.

"Yes. I do. Do you remember why you came here last time?"

"Yes. I found that hurt man and was looking for help," Althea remembers. "How is he? Is he still here on the island? Is he alive? Is he also a swan?"

"He is alive and well. He has not been affected by the swan curse due to his gender. And he is still here. He has been asking to see you."

"Me? But I don't think he was even conscious when I was helping him. Why would he ask for me?"

"While he was recovering, he asked to know who saved him. I did not want any of my ladies to lie and so I told him of you. He has asked to meet with you so he can repay you for your service to him."

"Oh, I see."

"I will get him if you do not mind," Odette stands from her seat.

"I do not mind."

Odette leaves the room and returns shortly. With her comes a young man about Stella's age. He is tall and well-built. He wears a set of black pants and a simple white tunic. His complexion reminds Althea of tea with cream in it while his short hair is the color of licorice. In contrast to his dark hair and skin, his eyes are a brilliant and piercing ice blue. Althea is surprised at how handsome he looks now that he is not just some man lying on a beach nearly dead. Althea stands up.

"Are you the one who saved me?" He comes to her and takes her hands. Althea is surprised but not displeased by the sudden touch.

"Yes. I'm Althea," she introduces herself. He kneels before her, bows his head, and brings her hands to his forehead.

"I owe you my life. Ask me for anything I shall give to you." He looks up to her.

"Oh...uh, well...um, thank you?" Althea is unsure of how to respond. "But don't feel so indebted to me. I just did what anyone would have."

"Ah, but that is not true. I believe the sentiment that survival belongs to the fittest is a belief held by most these days. You could have left me to die but you suffered to save me. I owe you the greatest of debts. Tell me what I can give or do to repay you."

Althea takes her time to consider the offer.

"As kind as an offer this is, I am afraid what I want you cannot give me."

"And what would that be?"

"My brother. He is hidden here on the island, trapped in the form of a beast. All I want is to find him, free him of his beastly form and go home. But where he is cannot be easily accessed, the cure to his ailment is not easily made and leaving this place is not easily done at all as I am sure her highness can attest."

The man rises but not unhappily.

"You have presented me with a challenge, madame. I will accept it and repay my debt to you." He squeezes her hands.

"Oh, no. Please do not. It is incredibly dangerous." Althea tries to dissuade him.

"I am not afraid. I have squelched rebellions, dueled pirates, and slain the great ice owl that wreaked havoc on the mountains of Iscrown. When I was shipwrecked, it was only because a storm overcame us. I was setting out to kill the sea beast that has been destroying my nation's trade ships in the Icy Passage," He boasts.

"You must be a great warrior," Odette comments.

"Well, I-I had a little help." He looks back at the swan princess with rosy cheeks as he attempts to be humble.

"Still, I do not want to risk your life when it is not your burden," Althea tries again to dissuade him. "My sources have claimed him to be in a cave called the 'cave of terror'. One must be able to use magic to go there."

"Well, I happen to be of fairy blood. I am an earth and water elemental and unafraid of such ominously named places." The man holds his head high.

"But-"

"I shall find your brother and return him to you. I cannot promise to make him well or get you off this island since I have yet to find a way myself, but I will unite you two," The man swears.

"It will be dangerous for you to go alone," Althea voices her concern for the man she has already saved once.

"I will go with him," Odette volunteers, stepping up next to the man. "I know my way around this island and can lead him."

"Thank you, my princess." He smiles softly.

"But you should not endanger yourself either." Althea looks to Odette.

"My crown protects me as your ring does you, Althea. No harm will come to me." Odette pats Althea's hand where her ring is.

"Should we leave tonight to go on our search?" the young warrior questions.

"There you all are," Odile enters the room preventing an answer to be given. She stops as she sees the man. She looks him up and down then looks at Odette.

"Odile, this is Prince Sigfried of Norwin. Prince Sigfried, this is Odile," Odette makes the introduction. Althea's eyes enlarge learning of the man's title. The prince bows his head to Odile who nods to him. He looks her over and finds her not hard on his eyes.

"Are you another swan maiden?" He approaches Odile.

"No." Odile shakes her head.

"She is von Rothbart's daughter," Odette gives away the identity of the dark-haired girl. Prince Sigfried stops.

"But isn't he the one who has cursed you and this place?" Prince Sigfried steps back as if to shield Odette.

"He is but Odile means no harm." Odette gently touches the prince's arm then passes him. She comes to Odile and takes the younger woman's hands. "We are close, aren't we, Odile?"

"Yes."

"If you two are friends then so shall we be," Prince Sigfried comes closer to Odile with a smile. Odile's eyes go back and forth between the prince and Odette. Then she smirks.

"Come and dance with me, Siggy, so we may become fast friends." Odile lets go of Odette's hand and grabs the prince's.

"I am afraid I am already engaged to begin a journey this night that will prevent me from dancing, Odile." He takes his hand from hers and looks at Odette.

"We can go tomorrow morning. Go and enjoy yourself now," Odette encourages. Prince Sigfried does as Odette says. He walks away with Odile leaving Odette and Althea alone.

"I do not feel comfortable sending you two alone to find Basil. Even if you are not able to be injured, isn't he?" Althea takes hold of Odette's arm.

"He can."

"Let me go with you two. Hadion is gone so I am free to go about till he returns," Althea brings up her master.

"Are you sure you want to do that?" Odette questions.

"Yes."

"Then join us tomorrow morning." Odette pats Althea's hand that is on her arm still.

Althea nods accepting this.

"Let us go and join the others." Odette gestures to the door. Althea and Odette start to where the ladies dance. In the middle of them is Prince Sigfried and Odile dancing. Althea is amazed at the gracefulness of Odile's movements as well as the prince's. He lifts her several times allowing her to move as if she were flying without wings. The others dance beautifully as well.

"I am so surprised by how beautifully you dance," Althea comments to Odette.

"Oh, well, all but I and the musicians were part of an international dancing group."

"What? Even Darya?" Althea looks back at Odette with her mouth open.

"Yes. Darya and the other dancing girls were a part of the Royal Austvest Dancers years ago. Bardolph disguised himself as a dancer and joined the group. He succeeded in seducing each of them. He brought them all here to be a part of his harem. He also brought girls from other lands who are now musicians. I'm not fully aware of what all occurred in Bardolph's little harem but what I do know is those young women suffered some atrocities that no woman should," Odette shares the history of the young women.

Althea frowns having found pity for the young maidens.

"But Hadion returned to the island and learned of the goings on in the harem, he took the girls out and brought them to be in my care," She continues.

"He brought them to you? Then why are they so against him if he saved them?"

"He keeps them here as he does me. Is it common to like one's captor?" Odette sets out the question. Althea shakes her head to agree but keeps her lips pressed together. She could never admit the feelings she had started to feel for the sorcerer.

"Come. Let's dance." Odette takes Althea's hand to take her to dance.

CHAPTER 37

ALTHEA

"Wasn't that so much fun?" Odile grins as she and Althea walk arm in arm toward her castle.

"It was. You are a splendid dancer," Althea praises her friend.

"I know." Odile tosses back her hair. "You're not bad yourself."

"Yeah right. I dance like a goose with two left feet among you swans."

Odile laughs.

They reach Odile's home and quickly go to the dining room. They find a meal prepared for them. They are quick to sit and eat.

"What shall we do tomorrow?" Odile grins at Althea while stuffing another roll into her mouth.

"Actually, I was thinking tomorrow, I would go look for Basil. Would you come with me?" Althea brings up her plans.

Odile stops her chewing. She swallows the bread in her mouth.

"Are you sure you're ready to do that?" Odile questions.

"Yes. Do you feel ready?" Althea turns the question back to the young sorceress.

"I...I don't know. I think I may need more time..." Odile grows demure.

"I don't know if I can wait, especially since we don't know how long Hadion and Bardolph will be gone."

Odile sighs.

"I guess we could try to look for him," Odile concedes.

"Great!" Althea smiles, making Odile smile back.

"In the morning we can go and meet Odette and Prince Sigfried at Sommerstern Castle before we set off," Althea adds.

"Wait. What?" Odile tenses from head to toe.

"Remember, how I disappeared after your father's return? While I was wandering, I found and saved the prince. I brought him to Sommerstern Castle to be cared for by Odette. The prince claims he owes me a debt and he has offered to help find Basil here on the island. Odette volunteered to help. We are all going to go tomorrow to look for the cave of terror, as you called it, to get Basil," Althea gives more detail. Odile's face turns neither sour nor sweet. Her lips remain closed and neutral.

"The prince is a good dancer but I doubt he knows any magic and Odette will be a swan half of the time," Odile tries to point out the challenges.

"The prince told me he is a fairy blood and knows magic. And what if she is a swan part of the time? I don't think it will be too much of a hindrance," Althea tries to champion her cause for the additions of the prince and swan princess.

Odile purses her lips as she considers Althea's proposal. Althea waits for Odile's reply but knows no matter the answer, she will be going to look for Basil and she will be going with the prince and Odette.

"I guess it wouldn't hurt to have more help," Odile finally speaks, making Althea smile once more.

"Great. We should get to bed so we can rest up for tomorrow." Althea stands up. Odile joins her. They return to their rooms. Althea is quick to sleep despite her excitement for the next day.

Dressed simply and in multipurpose shoes, Althea and Odile arrive at Sommerstern Castle just as the sun comes up into the sky. Outside waiting for the two young women are Prince Sigfried and a white swan. Althea is surprised to see the swan wearing a crown.

"Good morning, ladies." The prince nods to the women. Althea nods back respectfully to him.

"Hello, Siggy. Odette," Odile casually greets them.

"Do either of you know which way we should go to get to this 'cave of terror'?" Prince Sigfried asks.

"I know the way. Follow me," Odile states and waves her arm for all to follow her. Odette takes to the sky to fly.

For hours they trek across the island. Althea inhales the perfume of the numerous island flowers. She enjoys the melody of the birds hiding in the blue, pink, purple, and green trees. She smiles whenever she spots one of the woodland beasts. It is when the group stops by a trickling waterfall for some fresh spring water that they take their first rest.

"Odette packed some provisions," Prince Sigfried opens his satchel and begins passing out some bread. Before he begins to eat, he tears up pieces to feed the swan.

"So, Siggy, where are you from again?" Odile asks watching him feed the swan.

"Norwin," He answers.

"Norwin? And why is a prince from Norwin doing here?"

"I was shipwrecked here. Althea found me and saved me."

"I see." Odile turns her eyes back to the prince. "So that is why you owe her a debt."

"Yes. A debt, I hope to pay soon."

"Would a proposal of marriage have not been a satisfactory enough payment for saving your life?" Odile questions. Althea blushes.

"Odile!" Althea hisses.

"What? Is not a prince's life worth more than a cursed peasant's? You're getting a raw deal for just settling for him finding your brother. You could get a whole kingdom," Odile gives her opinion.

"My brother is worth more than a whole kingdom to me," Althea replies. "You wouldn't understand that though since you hate your brother."

Odile looks down and takes a bite of her bread.

"You must be close to your brother," Odette speaks to Althea.

"Yes. I am close to him and my sister too." Althea thinks of her siblings.

"Where is your sister? Is she trapped on this island as well?" The prince inquires.

"No. She is far away and trying to come here. I suppose she is not having much luck given she is not here yet."

"Well, this place is not spelled to be found or spelled to let its inhabitants be released," Odile decides to speak again.

"But we will find a way," Prince Sigfried declares. Althea smiles and nods in agreement.

"The only way you can get off is if my father lets you go or you learn to make a portal," Odile chimes in.

"A portal?" Prince Sigfried repeats the word.

"That is what Bardolph brought me through when he kidnapped me from Zeemaa," Althea recalls.

"But portals require one to be strong with magic," Odette comments.

"I'm sure if I keep practicing with Hadion I'll be able to make one and you will too, Odile."

"You are learning magic from Hadion?" Odette turns her whole focus to Althea. Althea blushes a little as she thinks of her magic training with the now-absent sorcerer.

"Yes. He's teaching me magic. I have been learning so I can rescue my brother."

"I did not know you were a sorceress. I thought you were just a companion to Odile," Odette's voice is low and soft.

"We were companions but she is more of Hadion's little sorceress companion than mine now," Odile gives her input.

"I'm not a sorceress and we are still companions. I'm learning magic but I don't follow the Fallen or use blood or anything like that," Althea tries to clarify. Odette says nothing more but the silence does not put Althea at ease. It reminds her of her father. He just knew how going silent when she did something wrong made her feel more ashamed than her mother scolding her.

"We should get moving." Prince Sigfried suddenly stands up.

"I agree," Odette nods. The other maidens rise. Odile begins to lead the way again.

Althea looks up to the flying Odette a few times as they continue to sojourn. Her stomach forms knots as she wonders what Odette is thinking of her. In truth, she barely knows the swan woman but thinking she has displeased her makes her feel...ashamed.

Is there something wrong with me learning magic from Hadion? I am only doing it to save Basil...and because it is fun...and because it makes me feel special and powerful...and because I like spending time with Hadion. Is there truly anything wrong with that? And why does Odette even care? Hadion saved her swan maidens from Bardolph. And she is super welcoming to Odile who is a sorceress. She must not be greatly opposed to those who use magic that is not necessarily fairy magic. Perhaps it is because she does not know Hadion the same way I do. Odette may only see Hadion as a big, bad sorcerer who on occasion does the right thing. But I have spent so much time with him.

I know beyond his flirtatious and sometimes menacing facade is a patient, encouraging teacher who cares about me. He has pressed me to go beyond her comfort zone many times but I find I am better for it now. But he also can respect some limits even when I want him to cross them. Oh, if only he had kissed me...

Althea stops with a face redder than powdered paprika.

Why in the world am I thinking so much about Hadion? Who cares that he did not kiss me? I should not want that. It is wrong on so many levels. Also, he just got up and left me in the middle of training. I should be angry at him not pining. And why should I care if Odette doesn't like Hadion or if I'm learning magic? Who is Odette to me? Sure, she has offered to help find Baz despite not knowing each other well but Odette is...Odette is...There truly is not anything I can find wrong with Odette. Except for when she cast me out at Hadion's order, Odette has been nothing but kind to me. And there is nothing for Odette to gain by being kind to me.

"Are you well, Althea?" Odile looks back to Althea. Althea comes to her senses and sees she is much further back than she intended.

"Yes!" Althea calls back and runs to catch up to the group.

"We are almost there. We just have to climb up that mountain there and get to the cliffside." Odile points ahead to a mountain on the west coast of the island. The sun begins to slowly sink by it.

"I will be human soon. Maybe we should stop and wait for my change." Odette comes down from the sky.

"If you think it best then yes," Prince Sigfried is quick to acquiesce to the swan.

"I guess we could use a breather before we go up." Odile decides to go with Odette's suggestion. They rest at the bottom of the mountain they are about to climb. As the sun goes down and the moon rises, Odette's body begins to glitter and glow. With a bright light nearly blinding the others, she turns from swan to woman again. Unlike her usual white gown and lovely shoes, she wears pantaloons, a blouse, and boots. From the supply bag, Prince Sigfried pulls out a lantern that Althea uses magic to light. Odile then casts a spell to double the lantern. She takes the double in her hand.

"Ready?" She asks her companions. They nod and begin their ascension.

"So, if we get in there and we find your brother...how are we to break the spell on him?" Odette asks Althea.

"That's a good question," Althea remarks.

"Wait. You do not know how to cure your brother?" Prince Sigfried stops.

"Well, I know the All-Cure elixir would do it."

"Do you have some with you?" Odette questions.

"No..." Althea looks down.

"I do," Odile chimes in.

"What?" All look at her.

"I do," Odile calmly chimes in.

"You do?" All look to her.

"Yes. I snuck into my father's room and found this vial of All-Cure Elixir," Odile brings a small vial of glowing liquid out from her clothes. Althea's eyes light up seeing the concoction.

"Odile, you wonderful girl!" Althea beams making Odile smile.

"Well, if you say so," Odile giggles.

"How did you know he had it? How could a sorcerer have it? Only a virgin can stir it and a fairy must bless it. Your father is neither." Althea questions.

"My father bought it in his travels. Bardolph used to curse me when we were younger and whenever he did, my father gave me a little. I am sorry I did not tell you about it sooner," Odile laughs at the end of her explanation. Althea hugs Odile before they continue on the path. Odile is quick to lead as she tucks the vial back into her clothes. Prince Sigfried and Odette follow behind them.

"I have heard that elixir can cure any curse. If that is true then you should take it instead of her brother." Prince Sigfried looks to Odette.

"Oh, no. I couldn't." She shakes her head.

"Yes, you could. And who is more worthy of freedom than you?"

"You think too highly of me, sir."

"There is no other way for me to think of you, my lady. You should demand the vial and drink now. I'm sure von Rothbart's daughter can get her father to make another."

"It will not matter if I drank a thousand vials of that elixir. It would not work," she responds.

"What do you mean?"

"Because my curse is too specific. There is only one way to break my curse and nothing else including the All-Cure elixir or true love's kiss can break it," Odette answers.

"Tell me what way it is."

"A virginal man must make me a vow of everlasting love to me and prove it to the world," Odette answers. The prince takes her hand then stops. Odette stops and looks back at the man.

"Sigfried?"

"Odette, I-"

"Hurry up, you two! We are almost to the cave!" Odile yells back down at the couple.

"We need to be quicker," Odette pulls her hand from the prince. He nods and follows her up.

As the four reach nearer to the top Odile leads them carefully around the side toward the cliff. Part of it juts out just enough to allow them to stand together with the one side below them and a large cave on their other side.

"How did you know how to find this place again?" Althea asks Odile.

"Bardolph used to threaten to throw me in there if I annoyed him too much," Odile answers.

"This is the cave of terror? It looks like a plain old cave to me," Prince Sigfried remarks unimpressed.

"It is cursed though or at least that's what Bardolph told me." Odile keeps staring at the cave opening. They all stand there silent and unsure.

"Are we going in or not?" The prince looks at the women.

"Yes." Althea nods. She takes the first step.

"You can stay out here if you wish. It would keep you safer," Prince Sigfried speaks only to Odette.

"I cannot be harmed and neither can Althea. If anyone should stay behind it should be you and Odile." Odette points to the two lantern holders.

"I will not leave your side," Prince Sigfried swears.

"And I will not leave yours." Odile locks arms with Althea.

"Then let's go." Althea takes a step.

With lanterns raised to give light to the darkness, the troupe walks slowly into the dark cave. Althea finds the cave to have many stalactites hanging from the ceiling but the floor is smooth. Looking forward she sees only growing darkness.

"Oh!" Althea trips on a rock. As she does, an arrow flies over her bowed head. The arrow makes the other jump. Odette and Prince Sigfried jump to the side only for the floor to collapse beneath them as Odile lets go of Althea and falls against the wall. She does, and a hiss followed by a pungent gas begins to fill the cave.

"Althea," Odile chokes and drops the lantern that quickly loses its light. Althea gets off the ground but finds she cannot see around her, much less Odile.

"Odile? Odette? Prince Sigfried?" Althea calls.

"Al-Al-Althea!" Odile continues to choke and gasp.

"Odi-ahhh!" Althea screams as she falls through the floor.

Althea opens her eyes and finds herself atop numerous spikes. Bioluminescent mushrooms all around her give her enough light to see around her. She rolls off the spikes as her ring has protected her, but she cannot see back up from whence she came. She sees a great round tunnel filled with the glowing fungus though. She walks and softly calls out for the other members of her group. She walks further and further into the tunnel and finds the light growing greater and greater but not from the mushroom. Something else is giving light.

Althea enters a great dome with many other tunnels around it. Thousands of jewels shine in the light of the lit fires around the dome. She looks around with her mouth agape. Her fingers wiggle with the desire to start plucking the jewels to shove into her pockets. She begins to run her hands through the stone. She picks some up to admire them and poses them on different parts of her.

A whimper snaps her out of her focus on the pretty, shiny things. She quiets herself and listens. Another whimper comes. She drops the jewel in her hand. The whimpers continue. Althea talks toward another tunnel but finds the whimpering coming from a different one. She steps into the dark tunnel lit with glowing mushrooms. Instead, she makes a small fire in her hands like Hadion taught her.

Althea sees matted fur, a long tail, and a great black wing with holes in it all against a wall. From this creature comes the whimpering.

"Baz?" She called out softly. The beast stops whimpering.

"Baz? Is that you?" She asks and reaches out with her unlit hand. As soon as her hand touches his wing, her ring breaks and falls to the floor.

This must be Baz!

From behind the wing pops up a large head with red eyes as well as a fanged mouth. Immediately, it goes to bite her. Althea screams and backs up from the beast. It turns and begins to use its talons to crawl toward her whilst continuing to try to bite her. Althea runs out of the tunnel screaming in fear.

Making it out into the jewels area, she feels the creature's talons grab her by her shoulders. Up into the air she is taken before being thrown down into the pile of jewels. She looks back up and sees the red-eyed beast diving back down at her with a snarling mouth to consume her. She crosses her arms over her.

"Basil!" She cries out one last time.

CHAPTER 38

STELLA

Liboria, the capital of Koralia, is better known in the land as the Crimson City. It is apt given the view from the gray stone castle set on the cliff of one of the northern hills overlooking the city's center shows all the roofs have crimson red tile. Of course, the Crimson City could also refer to how Liboria was the sight of the bloodiest battle in the Great Fairy War resulting in the streets and the three rivers in the city flowing with crimson blood.

Liboria is far from a bleeding city on the day Stella and her companions enter it. As they ride upon the cobblestones through the eastern gate, they see banners of red, gold, and green strung from building to building. Flags depicting a golden eagle wearing a laurel crown flying in a crimson sky are raised high. Some have the country's motto, "Rising in Glory and Fortune" embroidered on the flags. Music plays through the city streets covered in scattered flower petals. There are no sullen faces, only jovial smiles.

Stella finds herself reminded of Maroro. The seaside capital of Soldoro and this landlocked one of Koralia are vastly different but the happy crowds, the vibrant colors, and the smell of wine and jasmine cause her mind to travel back. Before she left Soldoro with her siblings to find their ways in the world, there had been a grand celebration in Maroro to celebrate the wedding anniversary of King Heliodoro and Queen Paloma.

Upon the recommendation of Sir Artegal, the group finds lodging and boarding for their animals quickly. They have been traveling for a few days and have yet to stay in another village since Aura. Stella is sure she and Tyr would like to sleep in real beds over the hard ground.

As Stella, Zarin, and Tyr wait outside an inn with the animals, they watch the city's people who practically dance in the street with large cups of wine.

"Is this another Zola festival?" Tyr asks Zarin.

"No. That would have been weeks ago," Zarin shakes her head.

"Another holiday then?" Stella raises an eyebrow. She is unsure what sort of holiday it could be but then again, she is not familiar with Koralia or its holidays.

"Not that I know of but I am not too familiar with this place," Zarin shrugs.

A large group of dwarfs with wineskins in hand stumble along the road. A merry song leaves their lips though many of the lyrics are slurred. Behind them are three young men who do not sing but do drink. Tyr approaches them.

"Excuse me." Tyr stops three men who laugh and have their arms wrapped around each other.

"Huh?" They stop seeing Tyr on the road. They are all red-faced and have glazed eyes thanks to the beverage in their wineskins they barely hold.

"Why is there such a great celebration here?" Tyr asks.

"Don't you know?" One hiccups.

"I do not." Tyr shakes his head.

"Queen Ro-Ro-Roza-Ro..." The man tries to speak but struggles with the name then laughs along with his friends. Another tries to speak but only nonsense comes out.

Almost out of nowhere, a lady appears in a green and white dress with small red blossoms on it. Her brown curly hair bounces with each step she takes. She walks up to Tyr and shakes her head at the drunken men.

"Elon! Oren! Erez!" She calls them. They all turn and blush when they see the young woman. They hide their drinks behind their backs. They smile at her. She does not return it.

"You three better get the food Mother asked for or I'll tan each one of your hides!" She fusses grabbing their drinks then shooing them away. They go on their way grumbling and tripping.

"Excuse me, miss." Tyr catches the small woman's attention before she can walk away. The woman looks up at Tyr and looks him over. She smiles.

"Yes?" Her voice is far sweeter than it had been.

"What is the cause for all this celebration?"

"Oh! Queen Rosalia has finally given birth to a child," The woman informs Tyr.

"But why such a grand celebration?" Tyr questions it.

"The king and queen have been barren for years. It is a miracle our queen who is almost fifty has given birth. The king has declared this week to be one of festivities to celebrate," She informs him.

"Oh! That is something to celebrate. Thank you so much."

"Of course. Is there anything else you need help with?" She bats her green eyes at him. They sparkle.

"No." He shakes his head though his eyes stay on hers.

"If you do, please, let me know. I live just over there. Just ask for Yaara." She points to a doorway.

"Thank you."

"You're more than welcome." She winks then walks off. Tyr blushes and returns to Stella and Zarin who overheard all.

"Ah, Tyr, have you found a replacement for my sister as your great love?" Stella teases, only making Tyr's redness spread from his cheeks to his ears.

"First, your sister is not my great love though she is a fine woman. Second, I don't even know that woman."

"She seems to want to know you," Stella continues. Tyr rolls his eyes as his neck reddens now.

"Are you getting embarrassed, Tyr? How unlike you? You were all smoother than silk with Althea but now...I thought you knew women." Stella pokes him with her words and finger.

"Leave me be! It's just been a while since I've had the attention of a beautiful woman," Tyr turns from pink to scarlet.

"Awww. Are you saying we don't give you enough attention?" Stella pooches out her lower lip in a slightly mocking way.

"That is not what I am saying!" He becomes more flustered.

"Oh, come here, Tyr. We'll give you attention." Stella comes at him with arms wide open. Zarin joins it. Tyr rolls his eyes as the women embrace him laughing and patting his head like a child.

"I get it, Tyr. You think we are old hags." Stella shakes her head as if sad. Zarin covers her mouth to keep in a laugh. Sir Artegal and Prince Astrophel come out and notice the three. Prince Astrophel clears his throat. Stella and Zarin stop their teasing and look at the knight and prince.

"Is something the matter?" Prince Astrophel questions.

"No. Just teasing Tyr a little." Stella and Zarin let him go with smiles. Stella ruffles his hair a little. Prince Astrophel does not smile.

"Well, we have two rooms for the evening. Will you help me take the horses to be boarded, horse-boy?" Sir Artegal asks.

"Sure thing, Artie."

"I would like to start looking for the woman Mother Huldah told us to find," Stella speaks up before anyone walks away.

"I do not know if we will have much luck today given most people are out of their senses from celebrating," Tyr reasons.

"Still, I would like to try."

"Yes, I would too," Zarin takes Stella's arm.

"I will escort thee too." Prince Astrophel offers.

"What is the name of the woman you are looking for?" Tyr asks.

"Tzafrira," Zarin answers.

"Tza-how is it pronounced again?" Tyr does not know how to say it.

"Tzafrira," Zarin repeats. Tyr says the name to himself a few times so she can register it. "We can ask around here for such a person."

"Great idea, Zarin," Stella smiles.

"Shall we agree to meet her tonight before nightfall?" Sir Artegal asks. They all nod in agreement before parting ways.

Stella, Zarin, and Astrophel go further into the city. They do their best to find people not already too inebriated to ask about the woman they need. Most shops are closed, preventing them from asking the owners. It does not matter much though given no one knows of this person.

As the day goes on, more and more people are found unconscious on the streets making people take large steps over the others. Astrophel always offers a helping hand to his lady friends to prevent them from tripping. Reaching the city's center, there are many dancers out with a large band playing music. Food stalls and wine sellers are taking advantage of the celebrations. A few shops are open as well. Some declare sales in honor of the newborn prince.

"Let's separate so we can cover more shops," Stella recommends. Astrophel hesitates but seeing Zarin also agrees, he gives in to the idea. Zarin goes north, Astrophel west, and Stella south. Stella goes to many stores proving to be fruitless for answers. She reaches the last shop on her row. She steps inside.

"Hello?" Stella calls out but hears no answers. She ventures further still calling out in want of an answer. But no one answers. She knows the store's door was unlocked and open so it must mean it is not closed. But she sees no owner or other patrons.

"Hello?" She calls out again.

"Hello." A voice comes behind her. She turns around excitedly and then freezes seeing Bardolph in a mirror hanging on the wall near some hanging fabrics. She loses her excitement. She has not had any contact with the sorcerer since he came into her mirror in Aura.

"You look disappointed. Were you expecting someone else?" He asks.

"I did not expect you at all," Stella replies.

"Well, it's been a few days since we last spoke and I have missed you. When I saw you in my mirror, I knew I had to reach out."

"You didn't have to," She mutters.

"I did. I need to know, have you thought about my offer?" He leans forward eager for her answer. Stella feels a lump in her throat and a knot in her stomach. She swallows the lump.

"I have."

"And?" He bats his long eyelashes expectantly.

"Bardolph, I couldn't make you happy. If you make me leave the one I love, you'll never have what you want from me and we will both be miserable."

"You're still infatuated with that pretty boy prince, aren't you?" He purses his lips.

"It is not an infatuation."

Bardolph rolls his eyes.

"My dear, my dear, my dear...do not be swayed by the romance of a prince. He is a man like any other and will break your heart. Do you think he will really marry a peasant when a royal connection betters his land?"

"He is adamant about his intention to marry me."

"But won't you disappoint him? You know nothing about politics or running a country. You can't even make the hard choices."

He's not wrong...

"You should be mine. I want only to love you and be loved by you," Bardolph speaks tenderly.

"And to give you the new Starrling." She has not forgotten. He smirks.

"Well, yes, that too. What do you say? Will you be mine or will you keep everyone you love in harm's way for the sake of a prince you'll disappoint?"

Bardolph extends his hand out of the mirror. Stella stares at it.

"Just say yes and take my hand. I'll be able to pull you through here to me. Then I'll fix everything as I promised."

Stella lifts her hand as she contemplates accepting. He smiles as she comes closer to his hand.

Please, have courage, beloved...Do not give into fear. Stella has not forgotten Astrophel's words.

"No." Stella shakes her head.

"No?" Bardolph scowls.

"No."

"I will have you!" Bardolph grabs her wrist. He tries to pull her into the mirror. Her fingertips pass into the almost liquid surface. She looks at Bardolph before seeing a dark figure in the shadows behind the sorcerer. Sharp red eyes and a wide grin of needle-like teeth appear in the dark figure. Stella goes white at the sight.

Crash!

The mirror falls to the ground, shattering the glass and making Bardolph's arm disappear. Stella looks to see Prince Astrophel standing beside where the mirror hung. He helps her up.

"Let us go." He points to the door. She runs out of the shop with Astrophel close behind. Once out in the open square Stella clutches her chest and breathes heavily. Astrophel comes and puts his arm around her. Zarin comes up with a flower wreath in her hair as it had been given to her by a random person giving out such crowns.

"Hajnal-I mean Stella, what is wrong?" Zarin approaches doing her best to remember the name change she only recently learned about. Stella remains silent. She cannot believe what she saw.

"Bardolph tried to pull her through a mirror," Prince Astrophel answers. Stella stays quiet.

"Let us go back to the inn," Astrophel gives the location. Stella remains quiet and clings to Astrophel even as they go to her and Zarin's room. Stella sits on her bed but refuses to let go of Astrophel.

"What is wrong, Stella?" Zarin kneels before Stella. She takes her friend's hands.

"I saw. I saw something...someone...some creature behind Bardolph in the mirror. It was just the shape of him and his eyes and his teeth. But I felt...I felt like I was dying. I felt my skin rotting and burning, my lungs filling up to choke me, my bones breaking, and my blood draining. I could smell sulfur. Oh, it was...it was terrible," Stella begins to weep. Astrophel tightens his arms around her.

"Was it made of shadows?" Zarin asks.

"Yes," Stella nods. Zarin grimaces.

"What is it?"

"I think you saw one of the Fallen," Zarin states.

"Bardolph is a part of the Fallen and never made me feel like that," Stella questions Zarin's guess.

"No, not a follower of the Fallen. One of the Fallen. It was not just Eous who fell. There were many Starrlings that fell. They are mostly shadows now who stick closely to members of the Fallen. They can take shape and even show some features," Zarin explains.

"How does thou know this?" Prince Astrophel seeks knowledge.

"When I was to join the Fallen, I was to make a blood contract to Eous, the Fallen One, before one of his shadowy beings who would then become my guide. Hajnal-Stella already knows how I did not complete my ritual. But if Bardolph has, then his guide must be around and the figure you saw," Zarin explains further.

"But he did not have such a being with him in Foxglove Grove and I have never seen one with him before today."

"They are not constant. They appear when summoned or when they desire to do so," Zarin continues.

"Could it...could it appear here?" Stella wonders.

"They come to those who are open to them," Zarin squashes the fear.

"Then let our hearts be ever closed to them." Prince Astrophel rubs Stella's arm.

"All will be well, Stella," Zarin gives a small smile to encourage Stella.

"It may be but I cannot shake the feeling." Stella looks down. "I wish my mother were here. She always could make such ill feelings leave."

"She has the feeling gift as well?" Zarin asks. Stella nods.

"I miss her and my father. I miss them both. I miss all of my family." Stella grows teary-eyed again.

"Write to them. Tell them what troubles thy heart," Prince Astrophel suggests.

"I do not want to worry them. There is nothing they can do anyway. They are in Soldoro. Telling them of everything will only cause them anxiety and stress they can do nothing about," Stella reasons.

"They are probably plenty worried already if you have not written them since before you left your village. You should write them," Zarin urges.

"I would rather write them once I know we have found the way to Althea and Basil. I do not want to write them a letter holding no hope," Stella voices her concern.

"Start the letter and once we find the woman and the way, finish it," Prince Astrophel gives the solution.

Stella lets go of Astrophel. She gets off the bed and goes to her belongings. She finds a small clay bird, some parchment, and charcoal.

"What is that?" Astrophel looks at the bird.

"Galatea. She's a messenger bird. I write my letter, put it in the open mouth here, then when I heat Galatea, she will fly away and find whomever I ask. Upon finding that person, Galatea will relay the message. My mother's other made her. She made two birds actually, Galatea and Phila. We have been using them to communicate with our parents and Basil since we moved," Stella explains. She sits and begins writing to her parents while Astrophel holds the bird and looks it over.

"I will go see if Sir Artegal and Tyr have returned," Zarin excuses herself.

Astrophel sits silently watching Stella write. She pauses often as she tries to figure out the best way to phrase things. She asks the prince about his thoughts on certain details. As she nears the end she stops.

"Astro, I want to thank you for helping me. I was so afraid. I don't know what I would have done if you had not been there." Stella puts her hand on the prince's who has remained seated next to her on the bed.

"Keep me close so thou never have to know what it is like again." Astrophel stares into her eyes.

"I wish you would always reside at my side."

"Let me reside not just by thy side but in thy heart for there is where thou reside with me." He brings her hand to his chest. She feels the beat of his heart. She looks at their hands then at his face.

"You are already there. You have always been, beloved," She confesses.

"Stella!" Zarin comes back into the room.

"Yes?" Stella moves her hand from Astrophel who still stares at her.

"Tyr has found someone who can help us," Zarin smiles.

CHAPTER 39

STELLA

Stella, Zarin, and Astrophel come to the road before the inn. Sir Artegal immediately begins to walk in a guiding manner when they approach him. The knight stops rather quickly at the door where Tyr's admirer had pointed him earlier. Sir Artegal knocks on the door. The beautiful woman from before opens the door. She grins seeing Sir Artegal and even more so at seeing Prince Astrophel.

"Hello there," She greets them warmly.

"Hello, we are friends of Tyr. He said someone here could help us," Sir Artegal states their business.

"Oh, yes! Do come in." She opens the door widely to allow all inside the building. Yaara, as Stella and Zarin recall her name to be, closes the door behind them before taking on the role of their guide.

"Follow me. Your friend is in our kitchen."

As they walk through what appears to be a home, they find six sets of everything. The furniture is a mix of large and extra small furniture. They reach a back room where Tyr sits at a table staring at a platter with braided bread on it. A young girl stands on a step at the stove as she stirs a boiling pot. Like Yaara, she has curly brown hair and wears a green dress. Tyr smiles at his friends.

"Mother, here are the others Tyr spoke of," Yaara announces. The young cook turns revealing she is not a child but a lady dwarf.

"Welcome. Please sit and have some bread while we finish cooking." She smiles at the group. They take seats at the table but none sit in the sixth and smallest chair there. Yaara goes to help her mother with the food. The travelers take some of the braided bread. Stella and Zarin bite into the bread but Sir Artegal puts his hand on Prince Astrophel's wrist to prevent him from doing so. Astrophel does fight the action.

"How is it?" Yaara's mother asks.

"So delicious! I cannot stop eating it," Tyr continues to fill his mouth.

"Good. Good. So where are you all from?" the mother asks.

"Well, Stella is from Austvest and Zarin is originally from Gold Haven but has been living in Austvest. Those two are from Estellen. And I'm from Senyama but I always say I'm from Norwin," he blurts out their origins as he brings another piece to his mouth but he stops realizing what he has said.

"I did not mean to say any of that." Tyr looks at his companions, not sure if they are upset with him.

"Are thou a witch or a fairy?" Sir Artegal looks at the small woman.

"What?" She is surprised by the question.

"I felt the deception once thou told us to eat. Thou have put something in this food to make him tell the truth. Is it fairy magic or is it something darker that will harm him? Tell us now so we may help him." Sir Artegal will not have another incident like what happened with Captain Kolar. The small woman loses her surprise and smiles impressed.

"I see it now. You are fairies too. I should have known by the eyes, ears, and by how handsome you men are." She turns all the way around. "Do not worry. It is just some truth potion I mixed in with the bread. I like for my guests to not lie. I'm not a discerner unlike you, sir."

"I wish people would stop tricking me with food," Tyr huffs and pushes the food away. Stella and Zarin have no problem eating.

"You do not need to keep eating since you know the truth," Yaara tells the women.

"Oh, such a potion will not work on us. We are protected." Zarin shows their rings.

"So why has thou allowed us here and claimed to be able to help Tyr?" Prince Astrophel decides to question the women not in their party.

"He came to me to ask if I knew of some woman. I told him my mother would know something," Yaara answers.

"And how can thou help us?" Prince Astrophel looks at the little woman.

"I think we should eat first. Do not worry I did not spike anything else," The mother chuckles. She and her daughter begin to scoop food from the pot into bowls and pass it around the table. The mother takes her seat in the little chair as Yaara brings another chair to the table.

"It is supposed to be fish stew but my sons have still not returned with the fish and I doubt they will till after they sober up in the morning," the little woman is aware of her three sons' ways.

"It looks great," Tyr is honest and begins eating as do all.

"Now, tell us how thou can help us?" Astrophel repeats his question.

"Well, who are you looking for? I have been in Liboria for a long time. I will probably know for whom you are searching," She answers.

"We are looking for a woman called Tzafrira," Zarin speaks the name.

"Tzafrira? That is not a name I have heard in these parts. Are you sure that is who you are looking for?"

"Yes. It is the name my mistress gave me," Zarin answers.

"Your mistress?"

"I am a fairy apprentice," Zarin answers.

"Ah. And who is your mistress?"

"Mother-I mean Huldah Holle."

"Huldah Holle? Hm...and why is she sending you to this Tzafrira woman?"

"Because she knows how to find the way to the place east of the sun and west of the moon," Stella says. Yaara and her mother become still at the mention of the place.

"Why would you ever want to go to such a place?" Yaara gasps.

"I rejected a sorcerer's proposal and so he took my brother and sister. I have to find them but there is no known way to do it," Stella explains.

"That is unfortunate," Yaara remarks.

"How do you know they are not already dead?" The harsh question comes from the smaller woman.

Stella feels everything in herself go cold at the thought of her siblings being dead. She shakes it off.

"My sister has a ring of protection so she must be alive. My brother, however...I-I-I don't know." Stella looks down at her soup and tears come into her eyes. She truly is not sure if Basil is alive or dead now. Astrophel tenses but reaches under the table to take Stella's hand.

"Can thou help us or not?" Prince Astrophel cuts to the point.

"I'm sorry but I do not think I know a Tzafrira," the woman shakes her head.

"Thou art lying," Sir Artegal calls the woman out on her lies earning a glare.

"You know where she is, don't you?" Tyr puts down his spoon.

"I cannot help you," The woman stands up.

"Why not? Just tell us where she is and we will be on our way," Zarin lays out the next steps.

"I cannot and will not. Leave, if you cannot accept this." The woman points toward the door.

"Mother, maybe you should-"

"You can leave as well, Yaara." The woman points again. Yaara closes her mouth.

"Let us go. We can find someone else to help us." Sir Artegal stands. The others begin to stand up to leave. Stella's eyes lose control over the wetness in them.

"But what if we do not? What if we never find another connection to Tzafrira and we will never be able to find Basil and Althea?" Stella turns to the small woman and gets on her knees before her and grabs the woman's small hands. She stares into her eyes.

"Please, help me. I cannot live with myself knowing it is my fault they die at the hands of a foul sorcerer. Please, please, help me," Stella begs. The woman sighs overcome by Stella's exuded emotions of desperation.

"Fine. I will help you."

"Thank you! Thank you!" Stella embraces her.

"Where is this Tzafrira then?" Sir Artegal steps forward.

"She is here."

"Where?" Tyr looks around.

"I am Tzafrira and I...I know how to get east of the sun and west of the moon."

"H-How do you know the way?" Zarin is the one to ask the question on all of their minds.

"It's my kingdom."

The guests in Tzafrira's home look at each other rather surprised and confused. This woman is not only the person they have been seeking but is also from the land that is home to a sorcerer.

"If this place is your kingdom, why are you here and not there? Why has the sorcerer been able to kidnap my family and take it there?" Stella questions getting off her knees, suddenly wary of the woman.

"Have a seat," Tzafrira sighs and takes a seat herself. The others do as well.

"You called it 'East of the Sun and West of the Moon', but that is merely its nickname. We called my land the Isle of Fortune. My people came to it during the exile of Fairies from the Old Lands. However, dwarfs like myself were considered even worse than tall fairies," Tzafrira begins.

"Trolls," honest Tyr drops the slur used to describe fairy dwarfs. He immediately apologizes.

"It is true they called us trolls. Some still do. Anyway, the ship carrying the dwarfs was caught in a horrible storm and crashed on the shores of the most beautiful island. The dwarfs saw it was a goodly place and decided to build their new nation upon it using their magic. They also cast spells to prevent non-magical persons from entering it in fear of sailors from the Old Lands coming to it. The dwarfs lived in harmony for many years and found natural treasures in it. Twelve dwarfs decided they wanted to leave to see the world. When they did, they took some treasures. Of the twelve, ten returned and claimed the outside world was a horrid place and they should never leave the island in fear of death. The other two disagreed and thought we should be open to seeing the outside lands. But because of the fear of the ten, the dwarfs decided to not leave again. What the ten did not confess to though was they had bragged about their riches to the other lands. The people there wanted to come and take part in the island. Not wanting to lose their riches they ran away. Because people did learn of the treasure, people did begin to hunt for the island. But none could find it and joked it must rest somewhere East of the Sun and West of the Moon.

Now, of the two brave dwarfs, one left to go back out with his family and never returned. The other one did stay but began working on magic rings that could teleport him to other lands so that he could still see the world. He kept it a secret and passed on the rings to his descendants. One descendant, my mother Adina, was traveling by the ring and met a sorcerer who was interested in finding the hidden island and to learn more about the magic rings. She fell in love with him and showed him the way. He would come and go in secret as he pleased for years resulting in my birth. When I had come of age, the sorcerer returned and asked for the magic rings. My mother refused to give him the rings and so he killed her. He began to kill everyone as he searched for them. Using the rings, I escaped with a couple of people. But I lost the rings once I was away from the island. I came south to Koralia and never tried to return to my home again," Tzafrira shares her and her island's history. The group sits in silence absorbing the details.

"What was the name of the sorcerer?" Zarin speaks first.

"Kazimeer. Kazimeer Rumpelgeist," Tzafrira answers. Though Stella figures Bardolph to be too young to be this grown woman's father, she needed reassurance.

"How can you find the island without a ring to take you?" Tyr asks the more important question.

"When I came to Koralia, I met the descendants of the dwarfs who left our home. We agreed to never go back there alone and so we all took a fourth of the coordinates and kept it with us. We need to meet with the other three and then we will be able to find it," Tzafrira explains.

"Where are these other three people?" Sir Artegal does not want to waste any more time.

"Port Ermacora on the far west coast of Koralia," Tzafrira gives the location. Stella feels her anxiety building in her chest. Tzafrira sees Stella's downcast expression. "Is something wrong?"

"We have been traveling a long time. We keep having to go from one quest to another. What if we reach Port Ermacora and one if not all of the others we are to meet are gone? We will have to find them and then who knows what will happen while we search for them. It will also take us much time to get from here to the coast. So much could happen to Althea and Basil while we keep wandering around," Stella shares her concerns.

"I will write to my comrades in Port Ermacora and make sure they are there. And we shall not travel by traditional means to Port Ermacora. We travel in a manner much faster," Tzafrira takes Stella's hand to give her some reassurance.

"Mother, do you mean..." Yaara gains an excited grin. Tzafrira smiles and nods. Yaara squeals and claps in delight.

"And in what manner are we to travel?" Stella raises an eyebrow.

"We shall travel by airship," Tzafrira's eyes light up showing off her hazel eyes with specks of silver in them.

"Airship?" Sir Artegal and Prince Astrophel are baffled.

"Yes. It is faster than traveling by beast for we will not have to stop to rest. But we must prepare our belongings and food tonight so we will not need to stop." Tzafrira lets go of Stella's hand and steps toward her daughter. "Yaara, you need to round up your brothers and get them sober then I will need you to help me cook before we get our traveling gear and the ship ready. Oh, we will need to hurry to get ready by dawn."

"I can help cook. I used to work in a bakery," Stella volunteers.

"Excellent! Are you handy in the kitchen too?" Tzafrira looks to Zarin. She nods.

"Yaara, focus on getting your brothers sober then work on getting our gear together," Tzafrira changes Yaara's job.

"I can help her!" Tyr volunteers. Yaara smiles at him.

"We can as well," Prince Astrophel strives to be of help.

"What are we to do with our horses?" Sir Artegal references their original mode of transportation.

"We will not need them where we are going so do what you wish. We have boarding stables here or you can sell them or you can set them free. It matters not to me," Tzafrira answers. The prince and knight look at one another. Prince Astrophel holds his index and thumb a mere inch apart and the knight nods understanding the gesture.

"We should get going. My brothers could be anywhere," Yaara starts to walk away. Tyr is quick to jump to follow the woman. Astrophel and Artegal are a little slower to follow. Tzafrira opens a drawer and tosses two extra aprons to Stella and Zarin.

"Let's get to work, ladies," Tzafrira smiles at them.

With their labors finished, Tzafrira, Stella, and Zarin return to their room at the inn. Zarin is quick to remove her outer layers so she might be able to be in her sleeping attire. Stella goes to her unfinished letter. Stella gives her love and signs her name before rolling up the paper as small as she can. She gently pushes it into the bird's mouth.

"Zarin," Stella looks at her friend.

"Yes?"

"What are the words to make a fire?"

Zarin proceeds to tell her.

"Thank you." Stella moves toward the window of their room with the bird in hand. She repeats the words. Her hands heat up as does the clay bird. The clay seems to fade away revealing the bird to be a beautiful blue and orange kingfisher. The bird shakes and rubs itself against Stella's palm then looks up at her.

"Take my message to Amalthea and Lierre Sipos in Soldoro," Stella tells the bird. It jumps from Stella's hand and takes off out of the window.

"So that is how it works." Zarin watches, rather amazed.

"Yes. It is nice and saves on postage," Stella jokes.

"And it can find anyone just by giving a name and location?"

"Yes."

"Even if they have never been there before?"

"Yes. My mother said my grandmother made it with magic so it will always go to its desired location." Stella thinks about the details her mother gave her when she gifted Stella the little bird.

"That is amazing. And you mentioned earlier Althea has one."

"Yes, there is another, Phila. She is Althea's."

"Do you think Althea has hers with her now?"

"No...why do you ask?"

"If we have it, couldn't you send it to Althea, and she one back to you?" The query gives the sister some more hope.

"I could try!" Stella jumps off the bed and looks through the bags belonging to Althea. She finds the hidden and wrapped-up bird. She also takes more parchment to write. When she is finished, Stella rolls up the letter and puts it in the other bird's mouth. She did as she had before with her bird. When this kingfisher awakens it stares at Stella ready for the mission.

"Take this message to Althea Sipos in the place East of the Sun and West of the Moon."

Receiving the words, the bird hops and flies out of the window. Stella closes the window afterward.

"I wonder if it will make it," Stella stares out the glass.

"Even if it doesn't, we will." Zarin puts her hand on Stella's shoulder. Stella smiles back at her friend then both decide it is time for bed especially since Tzafrira told them they would need to meet her before dawn.

CHAPTER 40

STELLA

In the twilight before the dawn of the day, Stella and her traveling group were quickly led away from Tzafrira's house by Yaara and toward an open field atop one of the northern hills beyond Liboria's city walls. It is there the party sees Tzafrira there with four men. Three of which are Tzafrira's now sober sons. They are with a wicker basket that is extremely large and resembles a boat. It is attached to a giant, colorful, dome balloon. Between the balloon and basket is a fire. The ship stays on the ground as ropes keep it tethered to steel spikes embedded in the ground.

"What a sight," Prince Astrophel remarks, impressed by the airship.

"It truly is amazing." Sit Artegal admires the contraption.

"Much has been done while I was sleeping," Prince Astrophel astutely claims.

Tzafrira talks with a tall swarthy man with no hair but a full beard. He and Tzafrira turn their attention to the approaching people. Yaara runs to the bald man and receives a kiss on the cheek from him. Tzafrira frowns seeing their horses are with them.

"I told you we cannot take horses," Tzafrira gestures to the beasts.

"They will not be a problem," Sir Artegal pats his animal's neck.

"They are far too heavy." Tzafrira puts her hands on her hips.

"I will take care of it." Sir Artegal unloads his bags as do the others.

"Who is this?" Tyr points to the bald man.

"I'm Amerigo Arbore," the man introduces himself.

"My husband," Tzafrira gives his relation. Tyr smiles and offers his hand to the man.

"Tyr Dahl," the shifter introduces himself.

"No more time for such introductions. We need to get going."

Tzafrira points toward the airship as she had called it. The travelers bring their belongings to the ship and put them where Tzafrira directs. Sir Artegal returns to their oversized animals. He holds out his hands and in amazement, the others watch as he uses his words to only cause the animals to sleep but for them to also shrink the beasts to a size no greater than a walnut. The knight picks up the four small animals in his hand. He produces a jar that has grass inside and places them in there. He then turns to go toward the airship.

"How did you do that?"

"That was amazing!"

"Teach me!"

The three sons swarm to the knight. The knight is unable to answer as their father bids them to leave the man alone. Sir Artegal boards the airship along with his friends.

Yaara gives a quick hug to her father before joining the others on the ship. Tzafrira hugs each son before kissing her husband 'farewell' and joining the others on the airship. She closes the entry door.

"Find a spot along the railing and hold on," Tzafrira gives orders which are quickly followed. Tzafrira looks to Yaara and gives her a thumbs up. Yaara gives a thumbs up to her father who, like her brothers, stand at one of the four spikes holding the ropes keeping the basket on the ground. The men loosen the ropes from the spike but hold on tightly. Slowly they release the ropes as the fire in the middle rises pushing hot air into the balloon above them. This takes them higher and higher. Finally, the men below release the ropes. Yaara begins pulling up the released rope. Tzafrira starts one another. The other occupants are called on to help pull up the others. As they finish pulling in the ropes and rolling them up inside the basket, they can look and see the beginning of the sunrise. The dark sky has lightened to have a hue of yellow and orange at the horizon. As they begin to float away from the Arbores, the sun rises as a brilliant, golden orb shedding light on the land of Koralia.

Tzafrira takes to the wheel much like a water ship's that is connected to ropes and acts as a pulley to help direct the airship. She does have to stand on a stool. They steer westward.

"Feel free to walk about the ship. It may rock but it will not turn over," Yaara encourages movement seeing the still passengers. The friends begin to walk and move about. Yaara opens some of their ration packages to hand out some of the bread made in the night.

"Mmm...this must be the bread thou made." Astrophel looks to Stella.

"Yes. I can taste the excitement in it," Tyr comments praising Stella's food.

"Oh, thank you." Stella smiles and takes a bite. She feels the emotion in the food. She had been excited about their new chance to find her siblings when she made the bread and tastes it now which rekindles it in her.

"How long shall it take us to reach Port Ermacora by this airship?" Sir Artegal comes and stands by the small captain.

"We should arrive by tomorrow morning."

"So early? Is not the western coast about a week's ride from Liboria?" Sir Artegal questions.

"Yes, but that is with stops and varying terrain. Traveling by air we move faster and do not need to stop. It is a far more efficient way to travel."

"Fascinating. I have not seen anything like it before. Is this a common mode of travel nowadays?"

"No. But my people have always been innovators and people around here are afraid of new things like traveling by air."

"I can understand that."

"I remember that Tyr boy mentioning you and that other man are from Estellen. How can that be given the nation hasn't existed for about a century?" Tzafrira questions.

"It was merely blocked off from the rest of the Far Lands."

"Even so, how are you two here now?"

"Stella came and broke the curse that was upon my companion which in turn resulted in the lowering of the barrier around Estellen," Sir Artegal answers and points to Astrophel.

"He was cursed?"

"Yes."

"And it caused your land to be closed up? Why would a land be tied to one man?" Tzafrira continues to question him.

"He is no ordinary man. That man is His Royal Highness Prince Astrophel of Estellen." Sir Artegal gives the title.

"He is a prince? He does have that look about him." Tzafrira gazes upon Astrophel then looks to Stella, "And she broke his curse?"

"Yes. She also broke a curse that was upon Tyr."

"Hmmm…" Tzafrira smiles to herself. "I know she is Stella, she is Zarin, he is Tyr, and he is the prince. But what's your name?"

"Sir Artegal," He introduces himself.

"Sir? Well, well. Are there any other royals or gentry among us?" Tzafrira looks around the airship.

"No," the knight shakes his head.

"So why are a prince and knight traveling with a baker, ora-oculist, and some fellow from Senyama? What interest could the prince and knight of an only recently opened land want with going on a quest to find some girl's siblings?"

"I go where my prince does and he will go where his heart leads him. As Stella is in possession of his heart, he must follow her."

"She has stolen his heart? I thought you were fairies," Tzafrira's eyes widen. Sir Artegal lets out a hearty laugh.

"We are. And she did not take his physical heart," the knight clarifies. Tzafrira breathes easier.

"Good. If you were, I would wreck this ship and have us all die rather than take you to the Isle of Fortune," She states calmly. He knows she is not lying.

"So, do you fly often?" Tyr asks Yaara.

"Well, we fly a lot in summer and autumn when the gentry likes to get away to the coasts."

"Where's the furthest this vessel has traveled?" Zarin pipes into the conversation as she is next to the couple.

"Chrysonero."

"Chrysonero? Why?" Zarin wonders.

"King Prospero II's brother Prince Faustino is married to Princess Chryssa of Chrysonero. So, the king on occasion has hired us to take him to and from the islands to see his brother."

"If your services are in such a demand the king pays for them, why is it no one knew of Tzafrira when we asked of her?" Zarin remembers their earlier struggle.

"In Koralia, my mother is known as Mrs. Arbore or goes by Sarah instead of Tzafrira. No one but her family and the ones we are meeting in Port Ermacora know her true name. So, when you were asking for Tzafrira it made sense no one knew her," Yaara explains. Zarin and Tyr nod understandingly.

"So, how did you two get all the way here when you're from another continent and you're from across the Night Sea?" Yaara gestures to Zarin then Tyr.

"My mother sold me to a Sea Captain who took me away from Gold Haven. I escaped eventually and became a fairy apprentice. I met Stella and her sister then came with them to find your mother," Zarin briefly shares her process.

"Your mother sold you? I'm so sorry," Yaara apologizes.

"It is not your fault and it has led me to where I am now," Zarin smiles.

"And Sir Artegal just killed that captain so..." Tyr adds the tidbit making the young maiden look to the knight talking with her mother still.

"Oh...and what about you, Tyr? When you were telling the truth you said you were from Senyama," Yaara turns the attention back to Tyr. Zarin stares at the young man just as interested as Yaara given Tyr's lack of sharing.

"Well, I wasn't sold like Zarin here," Tyr tilts his head toward Zarin. The women stay silent waiting for him to continue.

"My...my sister helped smuggle me out of Senyama and onto a ship to Norwin," he releases a new fact about him.

"Why did she have to smuggle you out?" Yaara leans forward more interested. Tyr looks into her bright green eyes and sees the little flakes of silver in them. They have a little shine to them. It relaxes his muscles and tongue.

"I was going to be killed if I stayed so I left."

"Why would someone want to kill you?"

"My half-brother was trying to get revenge on my father and another half-brother of mine by killing all of us at a dinner party. My sister was able to intercept me and send me off. So, I claimed a new home and took a new name," Tyr finally gives some insight into his past.

"Tyr, that's awful," Stella steps up, having tuned in just in time to hear Tyr's story.

"It is what it is. Do not look at me with such pity. This is one reason I did not want to tell you all about my past." Tyr pulls from Stella's touch but not in such a matter too abrupt as to cause much offense.

"But isn't it better for your friends to know the truth as to better support you?" Yaara asks then looks to Astrophel. "Don't you agree, Astrophel?"

"I do. It is one reason why Sir Artegal and I have no secrets between us," Astrophel answers.

"You should try being more open with your friends, Tyr." Yaara tries to encourage the young man.

"I-I-I guess." He cannot help agreeing with the pretty woman.

As the ship sails through the air, Tzafrira directs much attention to great sights over the lush land of Koralia and scenic waterfalls. Yaara provides much information and commentary on what they see. It makes sense as she has often had to play tour guide for the guests her mother has had aboard.

As the day draws to an end, Tzafrira encourages the guests on her airship to take a rest. Sir Artegal and Tyr find their resting place near the front while Zarin and Stella take to the right. Yaara takes to the left. Only the yawning Tzafrira and Astrophel remain up.

"If thou would like to rest, I can steer the ship," Astrophel offers.

"No. No. You need to sleep and you've never flown an airship before," Tzafrira rejects his offers.

"I do not sleep, madam. And if it is like steering a water ship, I know how to do so." Astrophel tries again. Tzafrira pauses.

"Do you know how to navigate using the stars?"

"I am from the land that loves them." He grins. Tzafrira considers the offer.

"Well...given the fire is enchanted to not change and you seem confident enough...I suppose I can sleep for a few hours and let you try it," Tzafrira decides. Prince Astrophel smiles. She gives him the wheel. She removes herself from the stool and pulls it away. She is quick to critique and set Astrophel on the proper way to fly her airship. Once satisfied she starts to walk away.

"Keep her going west, young prince," Tzafrira bids then joins her daughter. It does not take long before Tzafrira's snore reaches Astrophel's ears. He keeps at his duty wanting only to keep safe his friends.

Stella, who finds the wicker flooring and thoughts of Bardolph uncomfortable, sits up with a sigh. She looks up at the balloon above her. She stands and looks over the edge so she can look up at the starry sky instead of the air-filled fabric.

"Stella," Astrophel calls to her in a whisper. She turns and looks at the prince steering the ship.

"Come here, beloved," he calls to her. Stella comes over quietly to not disturb Zarin.

"What is it, Astro?"

"Why art thou not asleep?" He questions her.

"Earlier Bardolph said things that I am afraid will be true." Stella is upfront with her problem.

"Did he threaten thy family again?"

"It's not that. He said something about my future...our future." Stella gestures to Astrophel and herself.

"Our future?" The prince is puzzled.

"He pointed out that even though you love me and want to marry me, I may prove to be...unable to do what is needed and expected of a prince's wife. I am a peasant after all."

Astrophel opens his mouth to speak but closes it only to open it again.

"I know I have told thee of my father over the years but I do not know if I told thee about his life before my mother."

Stella pauses to think.

"No, I do not think so."

"My father was a peasant. He worked on a farm with his brothers and sisters. He barely knew how to read. But when he married my mother, he was taught not only to read but all a king consort should. He has proven himself a worthy partner for a queen. My father says the most important job of a consort is not knowing how to rule but how to love. Being able to bring love to a marriage is far more important than bringing wealth, lands, or armies," Astrophel repeats the words of his father.

"I think I will like your father," Stella remarks.

"And he will like thee. My mother shall too."

"I don't know about that. They may be upset that I have delayed your return."

"They will love thee for breaking my curse then they will come to love thee for more."

"What is expected of your future wife?"

"Well...thou will be in charge of running our household, supervising servants, producing an heir, directing our children's education, managing our private treasury, being the hostess to all of our guests, and be a judge of our people's issues in the Queen's Court. So, thou will have to be knowledgeable of Estellen's laws and know when to be just or merciful," Astrophel lists the duties.

"I see...that is a great many things."

"But as my mother still lives and reigns, those duties are held by my father so we can have time before thou would step into all of those roles. I shall help thee as well as I am sure thou will help me with my duties," Astrophel offers his aid.

Stella nods thinking about the many responsibilities.

"If thou do not want this then...I can understand. It is not an easy life to be in a position where thou must not only help but lead people. If this is not a life thou wish to have then-" Astrophel considers the pressures.

"As long as you are by my side, I think I will try and do what will be expected." Stella cuts him off. He smiles at her reply.

"You said I will need to produce an heir."

"That is a duty we both must do. I do not want to sound too bold but I must confess it is something I look forward to doing with thee."

Stella blushes. She knows what it takes to produce a child. Her mother talked so pleasantly of it while some other women of Foxglove Grove complained of the "chore". She knows in her heart it will be no chore.

"I do as well," She makes him red.

"Of course, if we cannot have a child, I have already decided on my heir," Astrophel states.

"Oh? And who is that?"

"Sir Artegal."

"But is he not older than you?"

"Yes, but he has fairy blood and that could allow him to outlive me. So, if I should die childless then I leave Estellen to him."

"What is Sir Artegal to you?" The question jumps out of her mouth.

"By blood, he is a distant cousin, and by duty, he is my sworn protector. But to me, he is more than that. He is even more than a brother to me. He is the ribs around my heart. I should say behind my parents and thee, he is the one I hold closest in my heart. Why does thou ask?"

"I was curious. I was not sure how you two were related but I can tell he is someone dear to you."

"Yes. I trust him above all others and had Prince Caradoc not abdicated, Artegal would be the heir of Estellen and not I," Astrophel explains.

"I see."

"But I do hope we have children. We shall have as many as El-Yah grants us. I hope for fourteen," He voices his expectations.

"Fourteen!" Stella's head pops off Astrophel's shoulder.

He wants me to give birth to fourteen children!

"Seven daughters and seven sons. We will have the most beautiful children." Prince Astrophel's eyes light up with the thoughts of the possible progeny.

"That is far too many, Astrophel," Stella rejects his plan.

"Twelve then?"

"Two," Stella counters.

"Far too little."

"If you were the one to be expelling them from your body you would think differently," Stella pokes him.

"Well, as long as thou art in my bed so often that we should be having fourteen children, I shall be content with less," Astrophel sighs his thoughts aloud.

"Astro," Stella's face flushes. Astrophel's face reddens realizing what he has said.

Stella raises her hand to push back some loose hair that blew into her face. It is then her ring begins to glow. It heats up and suddenly it breaks in two and falls to the floor. She looks over to Zarin whose ring has done the same.

"Astro," Stella looks at her naked finger.

"Yes?"

"My ring of protection...it's gone."

ASUNDER

CHAPTER 41

STELLA

Zarin stares at her naked finger once Stella wakes her at dawn. Though the ring that was enchanted to protect her lies on the floor of the airship in pieces, she is not afraid. Instead, she smiles.

"Then Althea has found your brother," Zarin deduces.

"I guess she must have." Stella starts to smile as well but it falls. "But that also means she can be hurt now...as can we."

"We must take care to not put ourselves in harm's way then." Zarin takes Stella's hand. The older of the two nods in agreement.

"I will not let thee be harmed," Astrophel pledges, coming to the side of the women since Tzafrira has taken her spot to man the wheel. Stella smiles at the prince though she knows in her heart such a promise cannot always be kept.

"What is going on?" Tyr yawns as he approaches his party. Sir Artegal comes with the young shifter.

"Our rings are broken. Althea has found Basil." Stella shows her hand.

"Artegal, we must be even more vigilant now with them," Astrophel speaks to the knight who nods in agreement, his eyes going to his female friends.

"Mother, I can see the water." Yaara turns back to her mother as she is taken to the front of the boat. The traveling group walks to the front of the airship to look out. In the distance are scores of colorful structures leading up to the faint blue line of the sea.

"That is Port Ermacora. I told some of my associates to meet us in a field north of the port and the others at the port via a pigeon," Tzafrira informs them.

"How much longer till we reach the field?" Tyr looks back at the small lady.

"Not long. Why?"

"No reason." He turns away though his bladder knows the true cause for the question as to those of the other travelers.

As the airship flies to the northern quadrant of the port city, many of the citizens look up at the flying structure. Those who have seen it before do not look with the same awe as though they have only just now seen it. In the northern field just outside of the city, three persons look up at the airship. They do not look at it with awe but with expectation.

Tzafrira and Yaara begin to throw ropes over the sides of the airship before Tzafrira goes back to the fire, she manipulates the burning so it lessens. As the flames go down so does the ship. It slowly begins to float down toward the ground like a feather from a flying bird's wing.

The people below the airship take the ropes once they are in reach and pull at them. They secure them to metal spikes in the ground. Finally, the airship lands. The balloon stays inflated. Yaara opens the gate keeping the people separated from the field. The travelers carry out their belongings from the airship. Yaara goes to embrace the people who have come to meet them. Tzafrira is quick to greet them with hugs as well. A couple of the greeters are dwarfs like Tzafrira though at an age between Tzafrira and Yaara while the other two are young men of great stature nearer to Yaara's age. All of them however have golden skin and bright blond hair.

Sir Artegal releases the shrunken beasts from their jar and has them grow to their original size. He also awakens them. The newcomers look impressed by Sir Artegal's action.

"Well done, my good sir." One of the dwarf men comes to the knight.

"I thank thee," Sir Artegal responds.

"I'm Notos Zilberstein," He offers his hand to the much taller man.

"Sir Artegal Belamour," the knight takes the hand.

"A fairy knight?" He raises an eyebrow.

"Yes." Sir Artegal nods.

"Well, it is a pleasure to meet a real fairy knight." Notos smiles.

"Then you're going to bust when you find out who this is," Tzafrira gestures to Astrophel.

"And who is he?" Notos looks over to Astrophel.

"His Royal Highness, Prince Astrophel of Estellen," Tzafrira repeats what Sir Artegal told her.

"You're a prince?" The two young men of great height gawk.

"I can see it." Notos's female dwarf companion smiles, eying the prince.

"Anemone, stop leering," Yaara nudges the lady dwarf.

"I can't help it. He is extremely handsome and I am not wed…"

"Did you say Estellen? That place has been…" Notos begins.

"It has opened up and now this prince is on a quest to find the Isle of Fortune," Tzafrira interrupts Notos.

"I thought you said you said we were helping a maiden find her stolen family, not a prince find fortune," Notos crosses his arms.

"I seek no fortune but that which comes from finding my love's family," Prince Astrophel speaks up.

"His love?" Anemone frowns.

"He is pledged to that young woman there," Yaara whispers, pointing to Stella who stays close to Meteora.

"How disappointing," Anemone mutters.

"You have no intention of raiding the hidden treasures of our island?" Notos keeps his arms crossed.

"I do not need it," Prince Astrophel maintains his lack of interest.

"Hmm…" Notos keeps staring at the prince unsure if he believes him.

"I swear to El-Yah I have no interest in taking hidden treasures from thy island. I seek only to take away my love's family from there," Prince Astrophel swears, making the locals of Port Ermacora stare at him with widened eyes.

"If you swear it to El-Yah then I shall believe it." Notos drops his arms.

"Are your sons capable of dismantling and caring for the airship?" Tzafrira asks Notos.

"Yes. Take care of it, boys." Notos look to the young men who nod.

"We should get moving on then," Tzafrira starts to walk.

"May we have a reprieve for a few minutes?" Tyr's face is tense.

"Yes. I think we should," Zarin agrees with the shifter.

"Let us take five minutes then reconvene here," Tzafrira agrees to the motion. Tyr bolts for the near woods. The knight and prince do not move as quickly. The ladies take to the woods across the clearing from the wooded area where the men have gone.

Having found her relief, Stella begins to start back to the clearing. As she walks, she hears rustling in the trees. She looks up and smiles as a blue kingfisher flies down. She holds out her finger. The bird happily lands there.

"Galatea," She smiles. The bird begins to sing a message.

"My dearest Stella,

Your letter has left your father and me with mixed emotions. Before receiving this letter, Mrs. Kenwyn wrote to us to tell us of your brother's kidnapping and your curse. We would have come straight away to Austvest to help but shortly before this misfortune, your father became ill with purple fever. Even with the help of healers, he still needs time to recover. I have kept the news of the kidnapping from him to not worsen his condition.

I am in shock over the details you have written. I am horrified to know Althea has been taken as well. If you had not mentioned the ring of protection you both wear, I do not know what I would do.

In honesty, I am not happy you are on this journey. I wish you and Althea had come back to us on Soldoro. We could have spoken with King Heliodoro about finding Baz and punishing this sorcerer.

I approve of your plan to find the woman who knows the way to where Althea and Basil are. Still, if it were not for your father's illness, I would make him take King Heliodoro's army to meet you right now in Koralia to take with you to where Althea and Basil are. But such an amount of people will make it hard to travel and may threaten the sorcerer in a way that could further hurt your brother and sister. I do hope those with whom you are traveling are brave and skilled as you have written. I hope they help you and fight for you.

And do not think that in my shock, grief, and concern I did not notice your mentioning of a prince and his intentions toward you. My darling girl, if this prince loves you and you love him then your father and I give our blessing.

I pray El-Yah protects you and guides you. I will wait for word from you that you have found your sister and brother. Farewell, my precious Stella.

Love, Mother."

Galatea finishes the message and turns to clay. Stella carries her bird with her back out to the clearing. She puts Galatea away and mounts her horse. Her heart is heavy knowing of her father's ailment and her parents' distress. Still, there is some happiness in knowing she has her parents' support for more than just her quest.

The regroup party finally set off to the city of Port Ermacora. Only Stella, Zarin, and the men of Estellen ride while the dwarfs, Yaara, and Tyr all choose to walk. Stella is sure to keep her horse behind all the others. Astrophel slows down so he may be with her.

"Are thou well, beloved?" he asks. Her heart flutters at the pet name. It is by far the one she likes most.

"I am. I...I received my mother's response."

"That was swift!" He exclaims.

"Yes."

"And how did she take the news?"

"She is...afraid but hopeful," Stella answers.

"I see. I hope that soon we will be able to relieve her fears and fulfill her hopes."

"I do too."

"Hurry up, you two. You're dragging!" Tyr yells from a distance. The lovers realize they are far behind and speed up.

The city of Port Ermacora is colorful and lively with its painted buildings and hanging gardens from the buildings. The salespeople do their best to try to lure customers to their business. It is easy to spot visitors since the locals know how to navigate their way around the watery canals flowing through the city while the tourists are always falling in the water, clinging to walls, or asking for help. Tzafrira and Yaara have no problem walking as they have been to the port many times before but their guests stick closely to the wall. The riders even dismount to safely guide their mounts.

They reach the marina where most boats are skiffs or trows. Notos and Anemone lead them to a particularly large trow ship with orange sails and a blue flag depicting a golden, three-prong trident.

"I thought the sigil for Koralia was a golden Eagle with laurels flying on a red banner," Zarin points out the difference in flags.

"It is. That flag is the symbol for Chrysonero." Yaara looks back to Zarin.

"Why is a ship from Chrysonero here?"

"There is much trade between the islands and Koralia. Also, Notos and Anemone are from Chrysonero but only recently have begun to have an extended stay here," Yaara explains further.

The group ventures up the ramp to the ship and finds at the top another dwarf of golden hair and skin. Unlike Notos, he has a curly, thick beard. He grins, showing off several silver teeth. He quickly greets Tzafrira with a hug and kisses her cheeks then does the same with Yaara.

"Welcome to the *Aello*. I never thought I'd see the day you would ask me to take us to our family's island. Are we to finally make the island for all?" He speaks to Tzafrira.

"No. It is not for rediscovery that we are going, Boreas. These people are in desperate need." Tzafrira gestures to the travelers behind her. He looks over the group.

"They do not look to be in desperate need," Boreas whispers. "And they are not dwarfs. Why should they be going to our motherland?"

"The sorcerers there have that one's siblings. Be careful not to let her touch you or you will feel the overwhelming sadness and desperation she has. I was forced to agree to lead them back," Tzafrira whispers to Boreas who eyes Stella as that is the one Tzafrira motioned to as she spoke.

"Well, even if it is not necessarily to our benefit, I am excited for such an adventure. Notos, Anemone, and I have only ever heard tales of the island." Boreas keeps a jolly expression.

"I have only ever heard tales of it too, Boreas. I'm lucky Mother is taking me along," Yaara gives her input.

"No. Yaara, I want you to stay here with Euros, Aeolous and their mother." Tzafrira turns to her daughter to refute her words.

"What? I want to go."

"No. It will be too dangerous for you. You will stay with Boreas's family and watch over the airship till your father and brothers arrive to take it back to Liboria."

"No. It is my birthright to go to the island as is everyone whose blood comes from the dwarfs who found refuge there." Yaara puts her hand on her hips.

"Do not argue with me, Yaara," Tzafrira snaps at her daughter.

"So, you will take strangers you pity to the island you have told me of all of my life and swore never to return to but you will not take me?"

"Nereo, Neilos, take the horses below with the cargo," Boreas calls to two men on the ship to distract all from the fight beginning between mother and daughter. Sir Artegal is quick to volunteer to help with the animals. The two men are tall and tan with yellow hair. They smile and nod to Zarin and Stella, making Prince Astrophel put his hand on Stella's shoulder. The prince insists on taking the women to their cabin.

"I am trying to protect you, Yaara," Tzafrira lowers her voice.

"Let us escort you to where we will be staying," Anemone offers her and Notos's services to take them from the bickering Arbore women.

"It's so dangerous I should not go but you will take the Zilbersteins?" Yaara gestures to Boreas who quickly walks away.

"They are capable on the sea and know how to fight. You have heard of them facing the Golden Strait pirates. They can hold their own should something arise. They have also assured me for years they are willing to risk anything to find the island."

"I am of age and willing."

"You are still my daughter and I do not care how willing you are."

"What are you so afraid of? I can use magic and fight pirates."

"It is not pirates I fear. On that island are men far more evil and powerful than any you have ever known."

"If they are so evil and powerful that you think I could be harmed then why risk your own life over pity?"

Tzafrira pauses looking away from her daughter then returns her eyes to the green-eyed girl.

"I cannot tell you but what I can tell you is when I return, we will be living as our royal bloodline should."

"Huh?"

"Our family will have a better life, but you cannot come. You must get off this ship." Tzafrira points to the ramp.

"Mother, I-"

"Get off, Yaara," Tzafrira orders again.

"No, I-"

"Get off!" Tzafrira bellows and thrusts her hands forward. A huge gust of wind pushes Yaara back and makes her fall down the ramp. Tzafrira pulls up the ramp by herself, preventing the dizzy Yaara from getting back on the ship.

"Boreas, let's get sailing," Tzafrira yells over to the captain. The captain nods and starts barking orders to his men who quickly get the boat moving.

"Mother! Mother!" Yaara calls after the small woman but she does not answer. With Tzafrira's instructions, the ship heads out northwest.

Tzafrira allows herself to go below deck once the ship is further from the port and all are on deck. As she goes into the quarters she is to share with Stella and Zarin, she reaches into her pocket and pulls out a small, round mirror. It ripples like water when she pokes it.

"We are on our way. Do not forget to prepare what you owe me," She whispers.

CHAPTER 42

ALTHEA

Prince Sigfried opens his eyes having felt himself stop falling. He finds him atop Odette with her arms around him. His arms are cut up some from their fall down the rocky hole.

"Odette! Odette! Are you alright?" He pushes himself out of her embrace and caresses her face. She opens her eyes and smiles. She touches the hand on her cheek.

"I'm fine. Did my body break your fall enough to keep you well?" She checks on his well-being.

"Yes. You did not have to-"

"I cannot be harmed, Sigfried. I should take the blow." She lets go of his hand and sits up. The prince is quick to stand and help her up. They find them in a tunnel lit by glowing mushrooms. Prince Sigfried looks up and finds the ceiling above them and the hole from where they were spat to be far above them. Such a fall should leave one dead if not severally injured.

"We won't be able to get back up there. We must walk and look for the others," Odette points toward the tunnel before them.

"We should just try to find a way out of here. It'll be better for us to just forget them and go back to the Sommerstern Castle," he recommends instead taking her hand.

"You may go and forget but I will not." She pulls her hand out of his.

"They are sorceresses, Odette, and probably dead. I know Althea saved my life but...we should save ourselves. Who knows what else is down here." He tries to take her hand again but Odette keeps it from him.

"I thought you were brave and honorable. Was I mistaken? Are you truly just a coward and a vow breaker?" Odette questions. Prince Sigfried steps back as if her words were an arrow to his chest.

"I will continue alone. I want no vow breaker at my side." Odette takes her starting steps. He steps before her to block her.

"I am no vow breaker." He claims.

"Prove it then. Help unite Althea and her brother."

Prince Sigfried nods. The two walk side by side through the tunnel. The couple finds their tunnel ends as it brings them to a large dome room with a floor covered in pieces of jewels and some stalagmites. Screams draw their eyes up to a great animal throwing Althea down onto a mountain of jewels.

As Basil's sword-like talons are ready to pierce Althea when a stalagmite flies in the air and pierces his shoulder with such force it knocks him to the side. Althea rolls off the piles of jewels and lands at the feet of Odette. The woman in white helps Althea get to her own feet. Prince Sigfried stands with his hands out toward the beast. Althea sees Basil rising again despite the stone piercing his shoulder.

With great command in his voice, the prince causes more stalagmites to shake and break from the ground. They rise to face off the approaching beast. They fly toward the great animal who dodges many but a few still land in various spots causing him to cry out in pain. Prince Sigfried continues sending the stalagmites toward the monstrous Basil until he falls to the ground. He pants and wheezes as many of his piercings are on his chest. Blood leaks from him. One of his red eyes is closed but the other looks at Althea. She begins to see a purple flash in it. Althea starts to go for the beast but the prince grabs her arm.

"Don't approach him. I'll finish him off," the prince lets her go and starts walking toward the fallen creature. He causes more of the rocky formations to rise and follow him. Althea can hear the whimpering of her beastly brother.

"Stop. Don't kill him. He's my brother!" Althea goes to grab the prince's arm.

"He's your brother?" Prince Sigfried comments as he looks at his foe.

"He is! Do not harm him any further," Althea orders.

"Please, do as she says, Sigfried." Odette comes and softly puts her hand on the prince's shoulder. He has the stalagmites fall.

Dewy-eyed, Althea comes and kneels next to Basil. She stares at the damage done by Prince Sigfried as well as some of what she must assume was previously done by Bardolph. She puts her hand on his chest causing him to yowl. She removes it.

"Baz, it's me, Althea, your sister." She tries to remind him. A tear comes from his eye. His breathing continues to be noisy and erratic. She knows the wounds are too great. Her lip trembles.

"Where is Odile? We need her elixir now!" Althea looks back to the others.

"Odile!" Odette's eyes grow and she turns to run back toward a tunnel to go in search of the other maiden.

"I'm here!" Odile suddenly runs out of another tunnel. She appears to be unharmed in any way. Odette comes to Odile and puts her hands on either side of Odile's face as she begins looking over her body.

"You are not harmed?" Odette asks softly. Odile shakes her head and then walks beyond Odette toward Althea and the beastly Basil. She pulls out the vial of the elixir. It is now half empty. She comes to Althea and looks at the animal. She grimaces then kneels.

"I had to drink some or that gas would have killed me," Odile informs Althea who explains as to there is less elixir as she hands it over.

"Will it still work?" Althea inquires.

"We just have to try," Odile shrugs. Althea comes to Basil's large mouth. She opens the vial.

"You need to drink this. It will save you," Althea tells Basil. He just lays there panting. Althea pours what little liquid left into his mouth. He does not swallow but keeps panting.

"You can't waste it!" Althea takes hold of his jaw and snout. She forces his mouth closed. Basil thrashes about and claws at Althea. He tears at her back but Althea does not let go. Basil swallows then goes limp. Althea gets off him. All stare as he lies there unmoving. Suddenly, he begins shaking and convulsing. Prince Sigfried steps in front of Odette while Althea and Odile back up as well.

The stalagmites fly out of Basil's body making the others duck down. His body shrinks then grows then shrinks again. He turns onto his side. His fur sheds as he vomits up black liquid. His tail shrinks into his body as his head regains its original shape. His wings begin to be sucked back into his shoulder blades. His giant red eyes turn purple as they once were.

Basil lies fully human on his side. There is no mark on his naked body. He opens his purple eyes and starts to push himself from the ground. He rubs his eyes then looks at the onlookers.

"Althea?" He only recognizes his sister.

"Baz!" Althea runs to her brother and immediately takes him into her arms. She cries joyfully.

"Thea..." He holds her close then pulls back. He looks at his hands and sees the blood. "Thea, you're hurt," he notes.

"Who cares. You're you again," She smiles.

"I did it, didn't I? I'm sorry. I didn't recognize you. All I saw were shadows." Basil gains some tears in his violet eyes.

"It's okay, Baz. I'm fine," Althea tries to relieve him of his guilt.

"You need to be healed." He looks beyond Althea. "Do any of you have medical training?"

"I can heal her," Odile volunteers and quickly comes to Althea's side. Odile lays her hands on Althea's open wound making the blonde wince.

"Sorry," Odile apologizes but keeps her hands where they are. She closes her eyes to help her focus. Basil stares at Odile while Althea breathes easier as the pain begins to leave her. Odile opens her eyes and moves her hands.

"It's not perfect. You have a little scarring but at least you're not bleeding. I will get some healing ointment when we get back," Odile explains to Althea who cannot see her own back.

"Thank you," Both Althea and Basil say at the same time. Odile looks at Basil. With their eyes meeting, she starts to smile while her cheeks become flushed.

"You're welcome," She speaks to the Sipos brother.

"I'm-"

"Basil," Odile finishes for him.

"And you are?"

"Odile."

"Odile...beautiful." He cannot turn his eyes from hers nor she from his.

"Thank you."

Althea watches them then clears her throat. She leans to Basil's ear.

"Baz, you don't have any clothes on," Althea whispers, remembering his nakedness. Basil looks down and burns in embarrassment. He is quick to use his hands for coverage.

"Oh, I am not offended. It only makes sense you'd be naked after being freed from such a curse. Here, I have two layers on. You can wear one." She tries to not let him be ashamed and begins to remove one of the layers from her dress. Basil is quick to put it on not caring it is a woman's dress.

"Thank you. You are kind," he takes her hands. Odile bats her eyes at him. The other three in the cave stare at the young ones rather bewildered.

"Baz," Althea calls his name.

"Yes?" he looks back at his sister. Having looked away from Odile, Basil seems to come to his senses.

"I'm so sorry, I was so...mesmerized," Basil blushes and releases Odile's hands. He stands up as does she.

"We could see that. We need to try to get out of here," Althea states the current issue.

"Right. Where is Stella though?" he starts looking around.

"No!" Althea screams. Everyone jumps at her sudden outburst. Althea braces and waits for Basil to turn to stone.

"Althea?" Basil's voice draws her eyes back to him.

He's human...The curse is broken? It is broken!

"Stella's name was cursed. It must be broken now," She smiles then loses it. "She is not with us here. After you were taken, Bardolph kidnapped me and brought me to this island."

"Where is Stella then? Don't tell me that sorcerer has gotten her."

"No. Stella is safe as far as I know. She is searching for us. I last saw her in Zeemaa but she was headed for Koralia to find someone who knows the way here."

"I see. And are all of you victims of this wicked sorcerer too?" Basil looks to the others.

"I was shipwrecked and ended up here," the prince answers.

"I was cursed to be here by a sorcerer but not Bardolph," Odette clarifies.

"And you, Odile?" Basil looks to the youngest of the group.

"Um, well…" She looks away. "Bardolph is my half-brother…"

"Half-brother?"

"Yes, but I have no love for him," Odile insists.

"It is true," Althea confirms.

"I see. I'm sorry but I forgot to make introductions to you two. I'm Basil Sipos," He introduces himself to Odette and Sigfried.

"Prince Sigfried of Norwin," the prince introduces himself, earning wide eyes from Basil.

"I am Odette." Odette keeps it simple.

"It is good to meet you all, seeing as you are friends of my sister."

"You as well," Odette smiles.

"We need to get ourselves out of here." Prince Sigfried is not as congenial as Odette.

"But how? I don't know about you but the hole I fell in is far too high and centered for me to climb back to," Odile shares her concerns.

"Surely one of these tunnels leads to an exit," Odette rationalizes.

"One does but when I was in my beastly form. I was too small to leave through it." Basil remembers.

"Show us then," Prince Sigfried directs.

"Follow me."

Basil takes them down a tunnel lit by mushrooms like the others. They walk and walk and walk. Althea's unprotected body begins to feel the effects of trekking all day and her physical altercation with her brother. She wonders if it is just her who is growing weary. She glances over at Odette and Sigfried. Sigfried tries to hide a yawn but Odette acts fine. Odile is alert at the front with Basil.

"I am so sorry about my half-brother turning you into a beast and imprisoning you here."

"It is not you who needs to apologize. Besides, all things happen for a reason," Basil tries to stay positive.

"Yes, I agree."

"Are we close to the exit?" Althea calls up as she is behind the others.

"Oh, yes. I can see the crack now," Basil points ahead. They draw near a wall. At the bottom is a black mass. Coming even closer, all can see it is a small hole leading to a forest outside.

"This hole is tiny! Only a rabbit could fit through there!" Prince Sigfried exclaims.

"I've seen shadowy forms slip out of here many times. We can squeeze through." Basil is not fazed.

"Probably because the sorcerer is a shapeshifter and could slip through it," Prince Sigfried argues.

"That could be possible." Althea frowns.

"Then I'll go first," Basil volunteers himself and gets on his knees. He exhales all air he could have then tries to angle himself just right. Grunting and groaning he tries to fit through the hole. Alas, his body is just too big.

"I told you it was too small." Prince Sigfried crosses his arms as Basil struggles to get back out of the hole. Odile and Althea help pull him out.

"Sigfried, that isn't helpful," Odette softly scolds him.

"Sorry," the prince apologizes quietly.

"I think if I shift into a smaller animal I could get out," Odile speaks more to Althea than anyone else.

"I think I could too," Althea figures.

"You can't shift." Basil looks to Althea.

"I can now."

"What?" Basil raises an eyebrow.

"I'll tell you later, Baz."

"But us turning into small animals only lets out and keeps everyone else trapped," Odile points out the problem.

"Maybe we could shift into something small then something larger that would cause the hole to break and grow?"

"But that could cause a collapse on those going through the new hole if too much of the wall is broken."

"True."

"Sigfried, you can manipulate earthen things. Couldn't you make the wall collapse so we can go out?" Odette turns to the prince again with an idea.

"I guess I could give it a go. But you all need to step back."

Basil and the women move far back in the tunnel. The prince takes several deep breaths and holds out his hands. He speaks softly but quickly. The wall of stone begins to shake violently. Odette grabs onto Odile who clutches Althea who is held by her brother. A crack goes straight up the wall from the small hole then small ones come from the middle line. Sigfried steps back as it all shatters.

As the dust settles, they see a large opening that will allow them to leave the tunnel and go out into the woods. The prince smiles pleased with his work then looks back to Odette who smiles just as pleased.

"After you." He bows and extends his arm to allow Odette to go. She begins to walk out of the new exit with Odile. Althea, Basil, and the prince walk out only for the ground to shake. The rocks at the top of the exit fall. They all stare at the pile of stones.

"Let's make camp. It is late," Prince Sigfried recommends.

"Yes. Let's," Odette agrees.

Once the fire is going and all are settled, Odette is quick to fall asleep as is Odile who is between her and Althea. Prince Sigfried lies near Odette but not too close as it would be ungentlemanly. Basil and Althea sit up together despite Althea's fatigue.

"Thank you for saving me, Thea. I guess I still need my big sister's help."

"That's what big sisters do." Althea touches Basil's shoulder. He flinches.

"Are you hurt?"

"No. I...I have not been touched gently in a long time."

"What did he do to you?"

"He would just hurt me. I don't want to go into it, Thea. It is only upsetting."

"I am sorry, Baz."

"It is not your fault. I am sorry I attacked you. I could not see who you were. I only see shadows."

"It is fine. I am glad you are you now." She hugs him.

"You are not yourself. How do you think you can shift?" Basil asks her quietly to not wake anyone.

"I don't think it. I know it."

"But you don't have any magic talent. You never have."

"I do though. I just don't feel like you, Mother, and Stella. I can't do stuff with air like you, Stella, and Father either. But I can compel others."

"Compel?"

"I seem to be able to compel others to be more inclined to my wants. It is a gift just like feeling and controlling the air though more subtle."

"But how can compelling others allow you to shift?"

"As long as I have active fairy blood. I can do magic. I have been learning magic from Odile's father."

"Her father is a fairy?"

"No. Well, I mean he has fairy blood but he is not a fairy. He's a sorcerer."

"A sorcerer!" Basil exclaims loudly only for Althea to "shh" him.

"A sorcerer? Althea, you should not be learning magic from such a person. They deal with blood magic and follow the ways of the Fallen or the Thirteen. They curse and kill. No good comes from them or their magic. Please, tell me you have not turned from El-Yah," Basil speaks passionately but quietly and grabs Althea by her shoulders.

"I have not turned from El-Yah, but you're wrong about them. Well, at least Odile's father and Odile."

"Odile is a sorceress?" He looks at the sleeping maiden and frowns.

"She is in training like me. She has not made a blood oath to the Fallen and neither have I. I am just learning magic to help us. And my master has proved to be a great teacher and his magic has done more to help than hurt," She defends herself, Odile, and Hadion.

"Master?"

"My teacher is my master."

"You need not follow him any longer. You must stop before you are swayed over to the way of the Fallen, Althea."

"I know what I am doing, Baz, and I will not be swayed. I know what is true and right," Althea tries to reassure him but he gives no inclination to her words doing that.

"We must leave this place as soon as we can and go back to Soldoro," Basil decides.

"We can't just leave whenever we wish," Althea shakes her head.

"Why not?"

"We have to have permission from the master of the island. That is the way of its enchantment," Althea explains.

"Who is the master? Bardolph?"

"No. It's Odile and Bardolph's father. My master."

"Then ask him to let us leave," Basil gives the simple answer to the problem.

"It is not that simple. The master is away with Bardolph. If Bardolph comes home first and finds us waiting for his father, he could try to curse you again before we could leave. And I had a ring of protection that has protected me from Bardolph but once I found you the ring stopped working. Bardolph could hurt me now."

"Then should I hide till the master of the island comes back so you can ask him for permission?"

"That might be best," Althea agrees to the plan.

"And will this master of yours let us go? Most masters are not quick to be separated from their apprentices."

"I will find a way to persuade him. Then we will leave, go back to Soldoro, and find Stella," Althea makes the plan. Basil sighs.

"I suppose I will have to go along with your plan."

"It will work. I promise. Soon we will leave this island and go home to mother and father." She holds up a pinky to her brother. He takes it with his own pinky, therefore, sealing the promise.

CHAPTER 43

ALTHEA

Althea wakes with a poke to her face. She opens one eye to see her brother poking her face. She should be annoyed but instead, she is happy to see he is there and still human.

"She's awake. We can get going." Basil moves his finger from her face and looks back to the others in their traveling party. Althea yawns and stretches but is quick to get on her feet as she sees the fire is out and the others including the swan Odette are waiting for her. Basil has easily accepted the fact the blonde from last night is now a swan.

"Do we know where we are and where we are going?" Althea asks, turning her head so she can stretch her neck.

"I flew up earlier. We need to head east from this spot which is that way. I will fly above the trees to help lead the way." Odette uses her wing to point east then starts to fly above the trees again. Looking up, they can see her white wings. The group begins walking in the woods. They are not in the colorful woods for long as they are soon out on open grounds. Althea keeps to the back of the group as she does not have much energy thanks to her lack of sleep and rough night. Before her Odile and Basil walk side by side. She cannot hear what they say but she can see the way Odile sticks close to Basil.

"I've heard you're a piper. Is that true?" Odile asks Basil.

"Yes, as was my father and his father before him."

"Can you actually control animals with a little song?"

"Yes. I even had control over your half-brother at one point." Basil's chest swells.

"Truly?"

"Yes."

"Can you control people who are shifted in animal form?"

"Yes."

"Wow! Could you teach me how?" Odile grabs his arms eagerly. Basil's mouth opens to agree but it closes.

"Are you a sorceress?" he does not answer her question.

"Yes, well, in training."

"Althea says you have not made a blood oath yet. Is that true?"

"Yes."

"Do you intend to?"

Odile's hands slip from Basil's arm and go behind her back to hold each other.

"Well…it is expected." She looks more to the ground than at Basil.

"But is it what you want to do?" Basil presses.

"I don't know." She shrugs. "All of my family except my mother has made the oath. My father has encouraged it and is prepared to help me make it once I come of age."

"How old are you?"

"I'll be seventeen soon." She tries to appear a little older.

"You are sixteen."

"Yes, and how old are you?"

"Twenty."

"You're not much older than me."

Basil does not respond to her comment.

"You should think hard and search your heart before you make your decision," Basil advises her. Odile chuckles.

"You sound like my mother."

"You said she is not bound to the Fallen. Is she against you making your vow?"

"Yes, but she is biased. She dislikes anything that makes me more like my father."

"When it comes to this, she may have more reason than just a dislike for a likeness."

"I know. But I have to ask myself, is it better to disappoint my mother or disappoint my father?"

"Choose what will not disappoint yourself."

"I thought you would tell me to choose to follow your ways?" Odile leans close to him.

"Who am I to tell you what to do? I am practically a stranger to you. I do think it would be best to not follow the Fallen One but that is a choice you must make on your own. You are your own person and have your own free will," Basil replies, causing Odile to smile to herself.

"You know you never answered my question," Odile circles back to the earlier part of their conversation.

"What question?" he seems genuinely at a loss.

"If you could teach me how to play the pipe and control animals?"

"Ohhhh, right…" He recalls.

"So? Can you?"

"I can but I won't," He answers dismissively. The stunned Odile stops before running back to his side.

"What do you mean you won't?"

"It would be dangerous."

"Dangerous?"

"There aren't many pipers in the Far Lands. Teaching another is dangerous to my lucrative career," He reasons. Odile guffaws and rolls her eyes.

"Come on, Baz. I promise I won't go into the piping business." She grabs his arm.

"Then teaching you is rather pointless if you're not going to use it to pipe," he counters.

"Bazzzzzz," she playfully whines at him as if she has known for more than the few hours she has.

"Sorry," He shrugs though not truly sorry at all.

"Come on. Please." She purses her lower lip into a pout like a child and bats her eyes.

"Do you even have a pipe?" He questions.

"No, but I can make one. Watch." She is quick to grab a twig from the ground. She mutters some words and changes the wood into a smooth wooden pipe and hands it to Basil. He stares at it impressed. Althea, who has witnessed the act, is as amazed if not more than the others. Odile has never been one to do magic so easily and well. Althea keeps such a comment to herself.

"Let me try it out." He brings the pipe to his lips and begins blowing. From the newly formed instrument comes a cheery melody. Basil plays and walks on. His music is enjoyed by all who listen. Without any intent, now animals have come under his control. He plays until they break for a midday rest.

Odette flies down and rests next to Sigfried who feeds her then himself. Althea sits with her brother and friend. Odile excuses herself to relieve herself over a hill nearby.

"You play well," Prince Sigfried comments.

"Thank you."

"I overheard earlier you can control beasts including sorcerers who are in beast form. Is that correct?"

"Yes. Why?"

"We have an issue with a family of bear sorceresses in Norwin. My parents may desire to hire someone like you to help them. Would you be interested?" Prince Sigfried brings up the opportunity. Basil's eyes light up.

"I-I think I would be."

"Should we ever get off this island, come to Norwin and we can discuss it further."

"That sounds good to me." Basil smiles.

"But that will be after we return to Soldoro and find our sister Stella," Althea interjects.

"Yes. Right," Basil remembers his plans now. Sigfried nods in understanding.

"Odette, I did not discuss this with you earlier but I was hoping while I try to find a way off this island you would keep Basil with you and Sigfried at Sommerstern," Althea addresses the swan.

"We can keep him. But he must promise not to use his skills on me or my swan maidens." Odette looks at Basil.

"I swear by El-Yah." He raises his hand to make the oath.

"Whoa!" Sigfried and Althea exclaim as they see lightning flash across the clear sky.

"That's weird," Basil comments.

"Why is Odile running?" Althea sees Odile running over the hill and towards them. The group stands up. Odile reaches them and grabs onto Althea.

"What's wrong, Odile?"

"We need to get back to the palace now."

"Why?"

"Didn't you see the lightning?" She looks to the others as well.

"Yes, but what does that have to do with-"

"That means my father and Bardolph are home. We must hurry and get back so they don't come looking for us here," Odile interrupts.

"We will need to transform and fly back then. Basil, I will see you soon." Althea hugs Basil.

"You're going to leave me?" He holds onto her.

"I must. I will see you soon," Althea promises and lets him go. She nods to Odette and Sigfried and gives them a 'thank you'. Althea closes her eyes and focuses until she shifts into a white-gold phoenix. Her clothes fall to the ground. Basil is baffled by the transformation.

"I'll come to see you soon, Baz. I expect a pipe lesson," Odile states her expectations then shifts into a black swan. The two new birds take to the sky leaving behind the two men and the swan.

As quickly as they can, Odile and Althea fly back toward the castle. As they come nearer to the palace, Althea sees Hadion walking in the garden of the Thirteen. He looks up to the two young women in their avian forms. Althea begins to descend to join her master when she remembers her ring.

"Let's fly to your room." Althea turns to Odile as she begins to ascend again. Odile nods. They fly up to her open window. There they return to their human form. Odile still has her clothes on but Althea does not.

"We should bathe. We're dirty," Althea comments. Odile agrees and so they are quick to Odile's bathing room. As they wait for the water to rise, Althea tries to look over her shoulder to her back.

"Are the scars still there?" Althea asks Odile.

"It's not too noticeable."

"But my missing ring is," Althea looks at her hand.

"So?"

"So, your father will know I found Basil. He may become upset with me. And if Bardolph learns I have no ring he may hurt me," Althea explains.

"Right...well, let's make you another one," Odile suggests.

"How?"

"Get in the water and I'll be right back." Odile goes back to her room leaving Althea alone in the bathing room. She gets in the water as Odile directed. Odile is quick to return and holds up a ring. She puts it on Althea's finger once she joins her in the bath.

"This looks close enough to your old ring, right?"

Althea looks at the ring. It is bronze, not gold but it is close enough.

"It will work," Althea nods.

"Good."

Althea relaxes more now that she has something to cover up her actions. The women quickly finish their cleaning before returning to Odile's room to dress. Odile dons a teal pleated gown with fluttering sleeves. Althea puts on a navy kaftan with golden embroidery and sapphires on her shoulders, chest, and arms. They leave their hair loose and flowing. Odile adds a simple headband of rose-cut diamonds to her head before putting a gold jerkin with a large sapphire in the middle around Althea's head.

Knock. Knock.

Althea's heart jumps as she assumes who it could be at the door. Odile goes to open the door. Hadion enters the room. His colorful eyes flicker over to Althea before focusing on Odile.

"You're back," Odile states, then hugs Hadion. He allows Odile to hug him. As she does, he looks at Althea again.

"Welcome back," Althea greets him. Odile steps back from her father.

"I saw you two flying in shifted form. Good work," He praises them. Althea smiles accepting his words.

"How was your meeting?" Odile asks Hadion.

"Tedious." He runs a hand through his hair. "I'm starving. Have you two eaten?"

"Yes," Althea says as Odile claims the opposite.

"Then come eat with me, Odile. I have brought back some seals from the bear clan," Hadion beckons his daughter.

"Did they also send dried walrus?"

"Yes, and elk tongue." Hadion nods as he escorts her out.

"Ooh!" Odile squeals. After Odile and Hadion leave, Althea goes over to her room. She takes off the headpiece and lays on her bed. She is worn out and tries to get some rest but as she begins to drift her mind goes back to the last time she fell asleep in this bed. She thinks of her master over her, touching her and almost doing more. She sits up frustrated. She should not think of such things.

Althea puts the headpiece back on her head and walks out. She figures a walk through the castle may serve as a puzzle and distract her. She has yet to see all of the castle's rooms. Perhaps she can discover the aviary Odile and Hadion have mentioned to her in passing.

Althea begins walking through halls she is familiar with until she reaches those she is not. She finds many doors locked and the ones unlocked seem to be guest rooms. She is not quite sure how long she has wandered around or at this point where she is as she has gotten turned around a few times. She walks down another corridor and finds a door at the end. She gives the door a pull and smiles as she sees it is unlocked.

"Is this the aviary?" She asks herself, opening the door further.

"Althea!" The urgent call of her name causes her to spin around and let go of the door. Hadion swiftly approaches her.

"Hadion!" She yips. "I mean Master."

"What are you doing?" He slams his hand against the door behind her causing it to close all of the way and trap her between him and it.

"I was looking for the aviary," She answers innocently, looking up at him nervously.

"The aviary? Why would you think the aviary is down here?" He is baffled by her choice of location.

"I don't know where you keep birds."

"Then you should ask and not just wander around," He scolds.

"I'm sorry..." She is confused by his apparent aggravation with her.

"Don't do it again," he orders, then takes her by her hand.

"Where are we going?" She asks as he starts to pull her away.

"To the aviary," He answers, not looking back at her.

Hadion guides her through his home until he reaches a higher level. He opens a door and inside Althea finds a beautiful room filled with plants, open white cages, a few lounging chaises, and beautiful birds she cannot even name the species. She smiles admiring them.

"Now, you should know how to get here," he states. Althea nods to him.

"Thank you for showing me the way."

He nods back. Althea starts to walk further in but stops as her hand is still in Hadion's grip.

"Um, Master." She turns to him.

"Yes?"

"Do you need to keep my hand?" She asks. Hadion looks down and immediately releases her hand. He moves his hand behind his back. He clears his throat.

"Go and look around," he encourages.

"Okay." She walks as she tries to do before when his hold was still on her. Althea walks about admiring the birds. One with purple and pink feathers comes and lands on her shoulders. Another with blue and green comes to her other. She smiles when the pink one begins to rub its head against her cheek.

"Ah!" Althea yelps when a small black and gold bird swoops down and rips her headpiece from her head. The birds on her shoulders fly away. Hadion laughs at Althea's reaction.

"That bird robbed me! It just took Odile's headpiece! She will not be happy! What sort of place have you brought me to, Hadion?" Althea crosses her arms.

Hadion keeps a smile but then begins tittering. The thief comes flying down to Hadion with the headpiece in its mouth. It perches on his hand and listens to Hadion. Hadion points to Althea. The bird flies over to Althea and lets go of the sapphire in its mouth. Althea catches it in her hand. It tweets at Althea.

"Thank you?" Althea speaks to the waiting bird. It nods then flies off.

Hadion comes to Althea and takes the adornment from her hands. He puts it back on her head. Althea looks up at him as he returns the jewelry to its former place. She smiles.

"Thank you."

"You're welcome." He lets his hands fall from her head and return to his sides.

"I'm sorry I upset you earlier when I got lost. I didn't mean to," she apologizes.

"I know and I'm sorry I spoke harshly. It's just...that door leads to the time tower."

"Time tower? What is it?"

"It's a sort of...portal. From what I know the dwarfs who lived here before my father overtook this island, were dabbling in magic to allow them to transport not just to different locations but different points in time. Their experiments were done mostly there. My father tried to concoct his own experiment with the magic. We learned it does allow one to travel in time and to other places but one must be focused on the time and place they want to go or they will be lost to madness in the tower and die inside."

"How-how did he learn this?"

"My father took his first wife with him into it. My father randomly appeared on the other side of the island three days after he entered while only his wife's bones came out. He told me he and his wife both began to forget things. They became confused in the darkness and violent. He said he could feel himself dying as did his wife. But my father regained some composure and made it out." Hadion explains.

"Oh my. Did he ever go back in?"

"No. I think my father was truly afraid of it after that day."

"Have you ever gone in?"

"No. And no one should."

"Then why leave it unlocked?"

"It refuses to be locked. It wants to be found. It has this…magnetic way of drawing lost people into it. Many new servants have gone in and we have found some of their remains."

"Oh…" Althea frowns at this information.

"You must be careful, Althea." He puts his hand on her shoulder.

"I will be. I promise."

As she smiles, his hand travels up from her shoulder to her neck then her face. She leans into hand.

"Hadion," She stares at his eyes. They shine and shimmer like jewels in the sun. His scent she breathes in makes her heart pump a tad harder. The tip of his tongue pokes out for a second as he wet his lips. Her lips tingle in wanting to be smothered.

Hadion leans down and tenderly presses his lips upon hers. Soft, warm, and chaste, the kiss has Althea's heart pounding. Her stomach flutters and her skin prickles. Hadion's hand goes to cradle the base of her skull. Althea's arms slip around his neck and keep him against her.

A swipe on her lips from his tongue gives his request. Althea parts her lips. The kiss that had been so tender turns harder and hotter. Her lips feel as if they are burning but she likes it. She likes his unique taste, the softness of his lips, and the rush of his body against hers. His arms go wrap around her as hers go around his. With very little effort he is able to lay her on one of the chaises. She arches her back to feel more of him. The warmth in her body begins to spread from her body down to every extremity.

Hadion's mouth leaves her so it may attach itself to her neck. His passionate lips suck and search for exactly the right spot which he finds the moment Althea moans. Such foreign touches only make the warmth in her body strengthen.

"Hadion…" She grabs at his hair breathless. He lifts his head so he may once again look at her face. Lips swollen, cheeks flushed, eyes gleaming with want, Althea waits for his next move. Hadion removes himself from her and steps back covering his mouth and diverting his eyes from her.

"You should go," he says.

"What?" Althea sits up lost.

"Go. Go back to your room," He points to the door and turns his back to her.

"Did I do something wrong?" She gets off the table and comes behind him to touch his shoulder.

"Just go!" He points to the door again. Althea's eyes brim with hot tears but she runs out of the aviary. As she walks away, she starts smoothing her dress with her hands and wondering what she did to upset him.

Was I too noisy? Do I smell? Do I not kiss well? Oh no! Do I taste like cabbage?

Question after question fills her mind as she rushes back to her room. She sits on her bed and brings her knees to her chest.

"What did I do wrong? Is it because I'm so inexperienced he did not like it? Does he not like me?" She asks aloud to herself then stops.

"Why should I care if he likes me? I don't like him," she tells herself. She stops again and rolls to her side with her knees still up high. She covers her eyes.

"Oh, no. I do like him. This is terrible."

Odile comes to Althea's room when the hour comes to sup. She knocks then enters without waiting for a response.

"Althea, it's time to eat," Odile walks toward the bed.

"I'm not hungry."

"Yes, you are," Odile calls out her lie.

"I don't want to eat right now."

"Why?" Odile sits on the bed.

"I just want to be alone right now."

"Why?"

"Because I just want to be alone."

"You want me to eat up here with you."

"No."

"Are you sure?"

"Yes."

"Really?"

"Yes, Odile. Please leave," Althea finally sits up.

"Have you been crying?" Odile notices the red eyes.

"Yes. So please leave me alone," Althea turns her face from Odile.

"Why have you been crying?" Odile keeps pressing.

"Odile, I do not want to talk to you about it. Get, out" Althea points to the door. Odile stands up.

"Althea, I'm not leaving till you tell me why you are crying or you come with me to eat." Odile declares. Althea cannot tell Odile she is upset over her father.

"Fine. I'll come to eat," Althea gets out of the bed.

"Great," Odile smiles. "But let's put some salve on those eyes."

Odile runs and fetches a balm to put on Althea's eyes. Almost instantly the puffiness and redness disappear. The maidens go down to the dining room. A grand meal is laid out for them as usual. Hadion sits at the head of the table. Althea and Odile take their usual seats. Althea does not even look at Hadion. Bardolph does not join them. It is quiet as they eat as no one seems to have much to say.

"Master." A voice croaks and all eyes go to a greenish, toadlike servant who has come to the table.

"What is it, Bufote?" Hadion looks to the servant.

"We caught this bird trying to come into the castle. It keeps calling out a name," Bufote produces a kingfisher bird in his hands. He keeps the beak pinched to keep it quiet. The bird wriggles in his hand.

"Let me see it." Hadion takes the bird from Bufote. As the servant frees the bird, it flies away before Hadion can take hold of it. The bird is quick to land before Althea.

"Phila?" Althea stares excitedly at the bird she has known since childhood.

"Althea Sipos?" it says.

"Yes."

"Althea, I hope this letter finds you in good health and you are unharmed. I am doing my best to find you and Basil. I am currently in Koralia. I have met the woman Mother Huldah said to meet and she will be guiding us toward you soon. Please, keep holding on till I reach you. Please, write to me and give me proof you are alive and well. Your sister, Stella" the bird sings then turns into clay.

Odile and Hadion look at Althea and her bird. Althea stares at the bird and thinks of her sister.

Stella is coming for me. I need to find a way off this island and take Basil away. That is what I am supposed to do. Who cares about this strange affection for Hadion or learning more magic? I have saved Basil. I don't have to learn more magic now. I need to leave and be with my family. I need to be with the ones who love me and want me.

"That is a fine messenger. Did your sister make it?" Odile asks.

"No. My...my grandmother did."

"Ah."

"I should write to my sister." Althea stands up and takes the clay bird into her hands.

"That would be for naught," Hadion wipes his mouth with a napkin.

"Why would you say that?"

"Once it is in its living form, it will not be able to get beyond the barriers of the island," Hadion states. Althea frowns and thinks to herself she will keep it until she and Basil leave so she can tell Stella to stop and wait for them. Althea sits down. She focuses more on eating than on listening to Odile and Hadion's conversations.

"Well, I am full. Please excuse me. I think I'll go for a walk in the garden," Odile stands. Hadion nods to his daughter who leaves the room.

"I think I shall retire." Althea stands up, taking her bird in her hand.

"Wait." Hadion stands up.

"I am very tired and want to rest. Good night." Althea turns to leave. Hadion grabs her free hand. She looks back at him.

"Please don't touch me." She pulls her hand from him.

"Althea, about earlier-"

"It doesn't matter. We can pretend it didn't happen."

"I don't want to pretend it didn't."

"You don't?" She looks into his eyes.

"Althea, from the moment I saw you I've wanted you." He closes the space between them. His hands go to either side of her face but do not touch her. He lowers them.

"I have tried in vain to resist my...my feelings for you. But the more I am with you the more I...crave you, crave your company, your voice, your smile. Today I lost control. I took advantage of you but...but if you think you may want me to...say it. Let me know if I am alone in this," he almost pleads.

"I..." She hesitates but the more she looks into his eyes she knows she cannot hold back. "I crave you."

Hadion lets out a laugh of relief and finally takes her face in his hands. He presses his lips against hers. Their arms wrap around each other as their fingers go running through each other's hair. Althea drops her bird. Hearing the shatter, Althea pulls away.

"Oh no! Phila!" Althea kneels to pick up the pieces.

"I can fix her," Hadion takes a knee.

"You can?" Her eyes flutter hopefully.

"It will take some time though given it is not just a simple clay bird."

Althea nods. Hadion holds out his hands for the pieces. Althea carefully picks them up and puts them in his hands. They rise together.

"I'll take this to my room. You should...rest. I'll see you in the morning," he gives instructions. Althea nods.

"Good night," he kisses her cheek.

"Good night," She returns.

Althea practically flies to her room once Hadion is gone. She squeals in utter delight as she gets on her bed.

He likes me!

CHAPTER 44

ALTHEA

With their feelings known and mutual, Hadion has found a far more useful way to encourage the best from his pupil. Yes, positive reinforcement has increased Althea's success. Of course, the rewards for her are rewards for him as well.

Althea lies in the grass with her limbs around the man whose lips have overtaken her own. The green blades poke up and tickle her ears as Hadion's tongue tries to tickle her tonsils. The weight of him on her body feels as if it is how her body should always feel. Without him on her. Her body feels too light. Her body feels too cold without his body's warmth.

In the two weeks since their first kiss, Althea has grown more and more dependent on the times like this. She could care less about learning magic or anything else as long as she can have Hadion. She wants more and more of him. She wants more than his lips, more than his praise. She is not sure what it is she wants but she wants it.

"Althea, we must stop," he breaks the kiss.

"Huh? Why?" She does not remove her arms from his neck.

"We can't do this all day," He chuckles.

"I don't think that is a good enough reason," Althea rejects his answer. He laughs but pulls at her arms to free him.

"We have more important things to do today," he states finally free of her hold. He moves from her.

"Such as?" Althea sits up.

"We have a ball to attend." He begins to run his hands through his hair to fix where Althea's hand played too much.

"What?" She leans close to him excitedly.

"I have been asked to attend a ball at a fellow sorcerer's home. I thought you might want to go with me."

"Yes! Yes!" She nods fervently. "I haven't been to a ball since I lived in Soldoro and even then I only got to go once. Oh, please take me to the ball!"

"I will. We must get back so we can prepare," he stands up. He gives her his hand so she may rise. Althea holds onto his hand as they walk back toward the castle.

"What sort of ball do sorcerers have? Who is going? Do they dance as regular people do? Will there be food?" the stream of questions come without there being any space for him to answer it.

"It's just like any other ball with common dancing and food. There are just going to be people there who can use magic and do so freely. It should be just you and me going there since Odile is not old enough and Bardolph...well, I don't know his plans. He may go but separately from us," Hadion gives his answers.

"It'll be just us two going...how will we be able to get there?"

"I will show you later. But right now, we need to get you cleaned up and dressed," He looks over her wrinkled dress and wild hair.

Hadion escorts Althea up to Odile's bathing room before leaving. Having seen how Odile runs the water, Althea sets to preparing her bath. She adds rose, ylang ylang, and jasmine oils to her bath. She smiles at the perfumed aroma coming from her bath. She dips in and cleans herself and her hair. When she finishes, she covers herself and goes back to her room.

Althea smiles seeing a box on her bed. On top is a note from Hadion. She quickly opens the box after reading his message to dress herself.

She pulls out the gown and dresses in it quickly. She goes to look at the mirror in her room. The lilac satin gown has gold trim going vertically from the bodice to the hem on either side of the middle part of the dress where the fabric is a pale rose color. A secondary layer of sheer tulle with tiny sparkling diamonds starts at her waist as it comes from the diamond belt she had to fasten there. The bodice of the dress hugs tightly to her torso and the purple parts of it have small diamonds sewn into it making it appear as if it were glitter. Her skirt starts just under her belted waist and expands into an A-line skirt. Her balloon sleeves hang off her shoulders and are made of a lilac tulle and connect to her bodice. She goes back to the box and finds a pair of lilac slippers with rose tips covered in small diamonds and with gold trim. Sliding them on her feet she finds them soft as a rabbit's fur. She returns to her mirror.

As she looks herself over, she finds herself nearly perfect except for her hair. She is not sure what she should do with it. She knows who would know though. Althea leaves her room and knocks on Odile's door.

"Come in," Odile gives her permission. Althea enters and finds Odile sitting and reading. She looks up and stares at Althea.

"Wow. You look beautiful."

"Thank you," Althea accepts the compliment.

"Why are you all dressed up?" Odile stands and lets go of her book.

"Um, well, your father has asked me to go to a ball with him."

"A ball?"

"Yes. He made me this dress and everything but I am not sure what to do with my hair. I was hoping you could help me," Althea gestures to her golden hair.

"I can. Come and sit," Odile leads her to a chair. Odile fetches a box containing her many brushes and combs. She begins brushing Althea's hair.

"You smell nice. Rose, ylang ylang, and Jasmine, right?" Odile asks.

"Yes. That's exactly right. You've got a great sense of smell."

"Yes, I suppose so. It is a nice change for you."

"What do you mean?" Althea turns back to look at Odile.

"Well, lately you've been smelling like my father."

Althea quickly turns around to hide her face.

"I know you two are...more than teacher and student, Althea. I've seen you two kissing in corridors... and outdoors...and the dining room...and father's study," Odile lists the places. Althea covers her face.

"Oh, my goodness. Odile. I'm so sorry. I can't even explain it. I just...Hadion and I...I don't know what. I just like being with him and - and...don't hate me, Odile." Althea spins around and grabs Odile's hand.

"I don't hate you. If you truly like him, who am I to judge," Odile's words make Althea smile. "Just be more discreet. He is my father after all."

Althea nods.

"Now, turn back around so I can fix your hair." Odile twirls her finger around to indicate what she wants from Althea. Althea obeys.

With a little help of magic, Odile can put some curls into Althea's hair. She makes a braid to go around the back of Althea's head like a halo while the rest of her hair is left down in lovely curls. She had two loose ringlets come to either side of Althea's face. In the braid, Odile puts small diamond pins matching those on Althea's dress. She adds some color to Althea's lips, cheeks, and eyelids. With a flick of her finger, Althea's eyelashes grow and darken.

"I think my work here is done," Odile smiles proudly at her work. Althea rises to look in the mirror in Odile's room. She knows it to be herself though more beautiful.

"Odile, thank you!" Althea is quick to hug her stylist.

"It was nothing."

"Odile, have you seen-" Hadion walks into the door and stops. He stares at Althea. "Althea," he finishes the sentence and yet seems to begin another one.

"Is it time to go?" Althea asks.

"Y-yes," Hadion nods.

"Have fun," Odile wishes.

"Thank you." Althea smiles.

"Behave yourself, Odile."

"Behave yourself," Odile quips. Althea blushes.

"Let's go," Althea goes for the door so Hadion comes.

"You look beautiful." He comments as they walk.

"Thank you. You look handsome," she pays him a compliment as well. She is not lying. Hadion wears all black from his boots to his pants to his top. His high-collared hussar jacket is styled with golden filigree on his collar and goes down the middle of his torso as well as going out onto his shoulders and hips then around the back to cover his coat's tails. He has it as well on the cuffs of his coat. Althea notices a golden wolf's head with wings and ruby eyes pinned at the base of his collar as if to serve as a button.

"Thank you."

Alone, Althea lets her hand slip into his. He accepts the hold as they venture on.

"I must warn you where we go tonight will be filled with people who are delightful but devious. I am glad you have your ring of protection," He refers to her ring. Althea glances at it. Guilt starts to eat at her. She has not told him her ring is broken.

Would he be mad if he knew?

"Hadion...."

"Yes?"

"I..." Althea feels herself begin to sweat.

"What's wrong?" He stops to search her face.

"My ring is..." She starts to lift it toward him. He looks at it. "It's fake."

"I know," He replies.

"You know?" She cannot believe this.

"Yes. Ever since we returned, I've noticed how little bumps injure you and the magic coming from it has disappeared. Also, it is bronze, not gold," he states and removes the ring from her finger.

"Why didn't you say something?"

"Why didn't you?" He counters.

"I didn't want you to be mad at me."

"Why would I be mad? It is clear the time limit set on it expired," He assumes. Althea realizes she never did tell him how it was to break.

"Are you upset with me for not telling you?"

"I'm more disappointed than anything but then again I am happy now for it must mean you truly trust me to confess."

"I do trust you," She nods.

"But as I do not trust the people we are about to see, I am going to give you a temporary form of protection." He reaches into his pocket. Out of it, he pulls a gold chain. A tear-shaped opal with a diamond and gold setting hangs from it. Althea's eyes light up at the sight of it. He unhooks the chain before locking the clasp behind her neck and under her hair. His fingers run on the chain to the opal before laying the stone against her chest.

"This should protect you from physical harm and curses. Only when I take it off will you be unprotected," he gives her the details. Althea nods in understanding.

They go up to the room from where Althea remembers Bardolph brought her. It is dark except for a few candles. Althea's grip on Hadion's hand increases as her stomach tightens. She is not sure her stomach does this.

"Why are we in here?"

"This is where we make the portal to go places." Hadion removes his hand from hers.

"How?"

"Shall I teach you?"

"I am your student."

"First, we must start a fire."

Something moves in the shadows. The sound makes Althea jump.

"What was that?" Althea grabs Hadion's arm.

"It's just Amraphel." Hadion seems unbothered and lights a fire in the fireplace.

"Who?"

From the shadows emerges a figure. He is tall like Hadion with a pale face and long white hair. He wears a black cloak with a hood. His eyes are blood red and his mouth is wide.

"Hello, Althea," The new person greets Althea. She does not loosen her grip on Hadion.

"I'm Amraphel," He introduces himself and holds out his hand toward her. She does not take it.

"Shy are we?" He starts to grin revealing his sharp teeth. Hadion puts Althea behind him.

"Leave her be. She is new to this," Hadion speaks to Amraphel who lowers his hand.

"I hope you will not be so shy the next time we meet." Amraphel nods to Althea then slips back into the shadows and seemingly disappears. Hadion turns around to face the fire.

"Who was that?" Althea questions.

"I will tell you later. But now we must finish making the portal." Hadion pulls a dagger from his boot and cuts his hand. He lets a few drops go into the fire.

"What are you doing?" She gasps at his actions.

"We must give payment to cross. Then I must focus on where we are going." He puts his dagger away. He flexes his hand and it immediately heals. He takes Althea by the hand. She stares at Hadion who gazes at the fire. He inhales but by the time he exhales, the fire turns into a white oval. Hadion leads and they walk through the opening.

The two come out in the front lawn of a great manor. The house of the estate is made of gray stones and appears to be like a large rectangle of different portions connected. Large glass windows are appearing to glow from the outside. The sky holds a sun that is preparing to set.

The lawn around Althea and Hadion has large topiaries resembling different animals as well as beautiful flowers of every color to separate the gravel path from the grass where the topiaries are. Between the couple and the large home is a fountain. The base of the fountain is made of intertwining scale bodies of two marble basilisks whose two heads are high up in the air and twist once more together. Their open mouths project water.

"Where are we?" Althea inquires as they approach the house.

"The Grand Serpentine," he answers.

"Which is where?"

"Belterre."

"Belterre..." She repeats the name of the country.

It is not far from Soldoro. If this is on the coast of the country then only the windy channel separates me from Soldoro, from mother and father!

"So why are we here? I mean for what celebration is this ball?" Althea begins ascending the stairs leading to the main door while holding Hadion's arm.

"We are celebrating the blue moon coming out tonight."

"Why?"

"Don't worry about it," he says just as they reach the doors. The doors open on their own allowing Althea and Hadion to enter into a grand hall. Althea sees the hall with numerous men dressed much like Hadion but none are in black while the women there are in extravagant gowns. She immediately straightens her back and holds her head up high. Her hand is tight on Hadion's arm as they move down the stairs. Many eyes flicker to the new couple.

"Hadion," An older man approaches them. He wears an apricot version of Hadion's clothes with bronze filigree. Instead of a wolf pin, he has a bronze tiger with red eyes. His silver hair is long but his beard is short and cut close to his face. He walks with a cane made of alder wood but the hand is the bronze body of a tiger. His sharp, monolid eyes give away his country of origin. Next to him comes a young, beautiful woman. Her dress is white but painted with orange tiger lilies. The dress though loose and flowy clings to her chest where a white band embroidered with flowers is. Over the dress are tied on sleeves that are a sheer light orange that nearly reach the bottom of her dress's hem. Around her neck is a gold chain with a tiger's eye pendant. Her obsidian hair is mostly left down but a great portion has been pulled up into a bun with braided loops hanging down. In her large bun sticks out two gold hair pins with lilies on their ends. From them hang three gold chains. At the base of the front of the bun is a small tiara made of three golden lilies. Althea notices no tattoos on her body except in the middle of her forehead where there is an inked third eye. It reminds her of Madame Fennella's tattoo. It even has a golden iris like the woodland witch. The woman's eyes, like her male companion's, are brown with sparkles of silver and magenta in them.

"Torashi. Meihu," Hadion nods to the man then to the woman who nods in return. The older man begins to speak in a language Althea does not understand. Hadion responds in the same language. As the men converse, Meihu eyes Althea. Hadion mentions Althea's name and she earns a bow from the foreign couple. Althea bows in return but still has no idea what is being said. Soon Torashi and Meihu walk away.

"Who were those people you were speaking to?"

"That was Torashi and his granddaughter Meihu from the house of the Horang," Hadion answers.

"Horang?"

"One of the sons of Rastaban," Hadion speaks as if this should be common knowledge. Althea recalls the name of Rastaban. Anyone who knows the history of the Far Lands knows of Rastaban and his cause for the Great Fairy War. Althea does not recall anything about the sons of Rastaban.

"He had sons?"

"He had six sons: Horang, Nahash, Eltanin, Urs, Aldhanab, and Ulfhard. Their descendants have their own houses and have brought in other sorcerers and sorceresses into them. You will see tonight by the colors they wear to what house these people belong," Hadion takes his time to educate her.

"I guess the house of Horang is the one where they wear orange," Althea makes her educated guess. She sees many people in shades of orange. All look to be from Senyama like Torashi and Meihu.

"Yes, orange and bronze. The ones in blue and silver are for the house of Urs. The ones in green and brass are for the house of Nahash which is the hosting house tonight," Hadion points out.

"So that is only three. Shouldn't there be more?" Althea questions.

"Well, the house of Eltanin is gold and red. The house of Ulfhard is black and iron. The house of Aldhanab is white and copper. There are only two people in the world that are descendants of Aldhanab. The house of Eltanin was recently destroyed by the Ogres. Only a few remain to represent them. The house of Ulfhard is nearly extinct from the killing within their family. The last of them intermarried with some of the Eltanin and the Aldhanab house. They wear colors from each family to represent the lines," Hadion continues his lesson.

"I see none in the colors you have mentioned except for you," Althea keeps scanning the crowd.

"Well, only Bardolph, Odile, and I are from the combined houses of Ulfhard and Eltanin. My sister and her young son are the last of the Aldhanab line though they have the blood of Ulfhard and Eltanin as well." Hadion grabs a flute of sparkling wine from a passing servant dressed in gray.

"So why have you dressed me in these colors?"

"Because none belong to a house."

"Gold does."

"Well, it belongs to my house as I suppose you do too," He reasons. Althea blushes.

Did he just say I am his?

A bell rings and all begin to move.

"Where is everyone going?"

"It is time to go to the ballroom." Hadion puts down his flute and begins to escort Althea away. They join the others in a large ballroom. The polished floors have green and brass serpents intertwined in a complicated circular knot. The white walls reflect the amber hues of the candles around them. There are large windowed doors across from the doors allowing the guests inside the room. From the rectangle ceiling hangs two giant crystal chandeliers. An orchestra sits on a balcony above all.

"So now, our host, Thuban will come to greet us all and pick a partner for the first dance," Hadion shares a bit of information.

"What sort of dances will be done? And don't tell me 'common' ones," Althea whispers. Hadion snorts.

"Well, we waltz, quadrille, cotillion, canario, carole, saltarello," He lists off.

"Oh, well I do know some of those dances," Althea feels some relief and thankfulness to her mother for teaching her.

Into the middle of the dance floor comes a man dressed in emerald green with brass filigree. His brown hair barely reaches the top of his high collar. He looks around at the guests who have entered the room.

"That is Thuban. He is the current head of the house of Nahash," Hadion whispers to her the man's identity. "He is the one who wants to have this grand ball. He says it is for the blue moon but I think he is trying to calculate who he can convince to join his side in plotting to invade Estellen."

"What?" Althea grows concerned.

"Many have already disagreed with his plans but he will try to convince the non-blood House members to leave their covens and join his so he will have more power to take over Estellen," Hadion shares.

Althea can hardly believe it. She completely forgot how Odile said the sorcerers were meeting to talk about Estellen and its possible invasion. She would hate that for Astrophel's people.

"Would you join him?" Althea whispers looking up at Hadion.

"The dance is starting," Hadion switches the focus to the dance floor. Thuban has chosen Meihu to join him. The song is slow. Thuban holds Meihu by her hand and waist. They glide across the dance floor effortlessly. Althea admires the moves. She feels as she did when she was at the ball in Soldoro. She stood on the sidelines watching as the ladies of the court were taken to dance. She was asked by one lord but when she stepped on his toes, he howled so loudly that no one else asked her to dance for fear of losing a foot. She preferred the village dances.

"Shall we join them?" Hadion interrupts her memory. Althea sees many couples have taken to the floor.

"Yes." Althea nods and takes Hadion's hand. He leads her to the dance floor. He takes her by the waist and hand. She puts her other hand on his shoulder. He leads her in the steps. Althea keeps looking down to make sure she does mess up her steps.

"Althea," he calls her name softly.

"Hm?" She looks up.

"Is there something wrong with my face?" Hadion asks.

"What? No." Althea shakes her head.

"Then why don't you look me in the face?"

"Oh, I'm just trying to remember the steps. I don't want to step on your toes or anything," Althea confesses.

"Do not worry about the steps. My boots are steel tipped. You can stomp all over them if you wish." He smiles and Althea lets out a soft giggle of relief.

"Just look me in the eyes and I'll take care of the rest," he whispers. She looks into his eyes. The more she stares the more at ease she is and the more confident she feels. He spins her out and catches her from behind. His hand goes to her waist. She puts her hand atop his and leans back against him. She closes her eyes as they spin. Out she goes once more from him before he draws her back so they are face to face once more. They smile as they are rejoined together. It is then Althea realizes something.

"We're floating," She notes.

"We are." He does not look down but keeps looking at Althea.

"But how?" They float high in the ballroom.

"Magic, my dear," He laughs. They finish their dance and as the music ends, they descend back to the floor only to be applauded by the onlookers. Althea keeps her hand in Hadion's as many come up to praise their performance. She has no idea who these people are but their smiles and kind words make them only make Althea feel welcomed. More music begins and the people go to the dance floor.

"Shall we go again?" Hadion asks Althea who nods. The next few dances are for groups and are much faster pace but Althea does not mind. It makes her feel as if she is back in Foxglove Grove at a town dance. Except she isn't having to dance with lovestruck farm boys who just want a chance to touch her. No, now she is dancing with the only man she wants to touch her.

With their fifth dance finished Althea seems to pant. She begs for reprieve. They go to the side of the room away from the dance floor.

"I will get us drinks. Stay here," Hadion takes off. Althea watches the dancers happily.

"You are a marvelous dancer," She hears the praise.

"Oh, thank you." Althea turns to her side and sees a beautiful woman. Her hair is long, blonde, and loose about her. Her silk crimson dress clings to her body. Her dress is tied behind her neck by two small strings. Her dress is cut down the middle exposing her from neck to below her navel. She wears long golden necklaces and some gold chains in her hair. Her lips are painted the same shade of red as her dress. Her green eyes are flaked with various colors. Something about her eyes and face, even her body is so familiar to Althea but she knows she has never met this woman in her life.

"Livia." Althea hears Hadion say as he comes behind her with two glasses of wine.

"Hello, Hadion." She smiles. Althea remembers now. *This is Bardolph's mother.*

CHAPTER 45

ALTHEA

Althea's stomach churns as she comes to realize the divine blonde who approached her is the mother of her great enemy and therefore the former lover of Hadion. Livia's sparkling green eyes focus on Hadion who stands with two drinks in his hands. Althea cannot believe that this woman could be the mother of a man Althea's age with her unwrinkled skin and not matronly body. Then again, Althea was shocked to learn of Hadion's true age.

"I'm so glad you came tonight. I was hoping to see you." Livia passes Althea to come close to Hadion. She takes a glass from Hadion without asking. Althea can see Livia's uncovered back. Down her spine are small tattooed sigils much like Hadion's. In the middle of her back is the large scar star of the Fallen.

"I can't say the same," Hadion's voice does not carry a pleasant tone.

"You're so wicked, Hadion," Livia laughs good-naturedly and playfully pats his arm.

"But not half as vile as you, Livia," Hadion quips, earning another laugh from Livia.

"Oh, I've missed this. Now, tell me where our son is. Is he here tonight?" Livia brings up Bardolph.

"I don't know. We did not come together." Hadion shrugs.

"Hmm…Well, are you going to introduce me to this lovely creature you've brought with you tonight?" Livia turns her shimmering green eyes back to Althea. Her smile is dazzling and kind.

"I'm Althea," Althea introduces herself but does not extend a hand out to Livia.

"Althea? What a darling name," Livia compliments.

"And you are Livia, correct?" Althea name checks.

"Yes. Livia of the Eltanin house. What house are you from, Althea? I have yet to meet a seed of Rastaban that hails from a house of purple or pink." Livia points out the dress confused but interested.

"I am not from the line of Rastaban," Althea states rather confidently.

"She has joined my house," Hadion quickly adds.

"Is that so? How wonderful." Livia's eyes turn to Hadion. Her tone seems completely sincere and cheerful. Althea cannot help thinking she is genial and sweet. She is not like her son.

"Hadion! There you are!" The host of the evening, Thuban, comes up behind Hadion and lays his hand on Hadion's shoulder.

"Thuban." Hadion pulls his shoulder from the host's hand.

"Oh! Livia, it's good to see you," He nods to Livia then looks to Althea. He smiles handsomely. "Hello. You're the little flower who stole the thunder of my dance partner earlier."

"I'm sorry. I did not intend to do so," Althea apologizes.

"It is quite alright. Beautiful things are meant to be shown off. I am Thuban and you must be the famous Odile." He takes her hand and brings it to his lips.

"No, I am not." Althea pulls her hand from him once his lips leave it.

"You think I would dance in that manner with my daughter?" Hadion questions Thuban who shrugs.

"I know not what happens on your little island. But if girls like this flower grow there, I would like a visit to pluck one for myself," Thuban intends to compliment Althea. She verbally gags shocking all around her including herself.

"Are you well?" Thuban questions.

"I apologize. Your words did not sit well with my stomach," Althea responds, earning a chortle from Hadion who covers his mouth to suppress the sound. Livia smirks as well. Thuban loses his smile.

"Well, I guess you prefer vinegar to honey then." Thuban turns his attention away from Althea to Hadion. "Come with me, Hadion. The other heads of the houses have agreed to a quick meeting before the blue moon sets."

"I-" Hadion looks to Althea.

"Go and do your duty to your house, Hadion. I'll keep Althea company," Livia shoos Hadion away. Thuban pulls Hadion away but he keeps looking back to Althea. Althea watches as he is led away.

"So, Althea, how did you and Hadion meet?" Livia asks, drawing Althea's eyes away from Hadion's back and to herself.

"Oh, um, on his island."

"Really? How is that?" Livia turns her head to the side.

"Bardolph kidnapped me and brought me to the island. Odile took care of me and then I met Hadion and became his apprentice." Althea answers then realizes the villain in her story is the other woman's son again.

"That Bardolph." Livia shakes her head disapprovingly. "He is like a magpie, always snatching shiny things."

Althea says nothing as she is not wanting to upset the woman before her. She is rather surprised at Livia's reaction.

Is she not as bad as her son?

"I am sorry he did that. If I were able to be around, I would make sure he would stop. Boys need their mothers to teach them right from wrong especially when their fathers do not," Livia sighs.

"Why do you not live on the island when you are Bardolph's mother?" Althea wonders aloud.

"When men grow tired of their playthings, they are often cast aside," Livia answers without answering.

"He cast you out?"

"I wouldn't say that. I was...asked to leave...harshly."

"Why?" Althea keeps probing.

"You sure are a curious one." Livia takes a sip of her wine.

"I am a student so I'm always eager to learn," Althea makes the excuse.

"You are more than a student, aren't you?" Livia is quick to notice. Althea blushes.

"I knew it. Don't feel awkward about it. You're not the first of Hadion's lovers I have met since our parting," Livia laughs.

How many others have there been? Althea begins to wonder.

"What do you know of Hadion and my relationship?" Livia gets Althea's attention again.

"I know you were his stepmother but you two have a son. Now you live apart," Althea shares what he knows.

"I see. Well, I will have you know I was much closer to Hadion's age than to his father's. I was nineteen," Livia tries to explain the age difference to make it seem less disagreeable to Althea.

"I fell for Hadion. He was so kind and gentle, unlike his father. We had to pretend our baby was his father's. Kazimeer did learn the truth eventually and Hadion killed him. I thought with Kazimeer dead, Hadion and I would be together but his heart was turned from me. He was so enamored with Odile's mother that when she demanded my expulsion, he asked me to leave. It is truly sad. We could have been such good friends and shared Hadion. But she got selfish. I hope you being here means she has gotten past her jealousy and is sharing Hadion now."

"I do not share him."

"Really?" Livia looks surprised.

"Yes. I am his only lover."

"You're sure?"

"Yes. Odile's mother is gone."

"Gone? Gone from the island?" Livia seeks clarification.

"As far as I know."

"He let Odette leave?" Livia seems to struggle to process this.

"Odette?" Althea repeats the name.

"Yes, Odette. Odile's mother."

Fortunately, Althea does not hold a glass in her hand or she would have dropped it and let it shatter. It is as if the wind has been knocked from Althea. Her mouth opens slightly as she tries to process this new fact.

Odette, the one who seems to hate Hadion the most, is Odile's mother. The more she thinks about it the more it seems to make sense. She and Odile do have some similar features. Odette is always welcoming of Odile and when they were in the cave, Odette stuck close to Odile. Odile even turns into a swan-like Odette. How could I be so blind?

Her stomach's bile bubbles and grows. It threatens to jump out of her throat. Everything around her grows hot.

When did the ballroom get so crowded? It is so tight here. I can't breathe!

"Are you well? You look as though you are going to be sick," Livia comments.

"I need some air. Excuse me," Althea walks away from Livia. She walks out of the ballroom and toward the front doors. She sprints out the entryway, down the stairs, and into the garden. She runs from the main path as she sees others there. She goes where she hedges. Once in the quiet hedges alone, she vomits. She pants and wipes her tears once finished. She looks up to the night sky. The stars sparkle and the moon has a lovely hue. She cannot enjoy it. How could she?

Why didn't Hadion tell me Odette is his former lover? Why didn't Odile? Why didn't Odette? If they hate each other, why did they have Odile? Why would Hadion get rid of Livia but keep Odette? Why curse and keep Odette on the island? Does he hate her so much that he wants to see her suffer? Will he do this to me one day?

"I wish Mother or Stella were here..."

Althea takes a few deep breaths then decides to return to the great house. She goes back to the ballroom as that is the only place she knows to go. When she enters, she sees all are standing on the sidelines and the candles have all been dimmed. Thuban dances in the middle alone with a young woman. Unlike everyone else, this young woman is in a translucent dress. The blue light from the moon shines through the window onto the couple. Her dress shines in the moonlight. The maiden beams and practically glows herself as she dances.

"Althea. Althea." The said woman hears her name being whispered loudly. She sees Hadion walking through the crowd near her. When he reaches her, he takes hold of her arm.

"Where have you been?" He asks quietly.

"I needed some air." She looks back at the couple. "What is going on here?"

"It's not important but we should get going now," Hadion starts to try to pull her out.

"Why?" Althea does not move and likewise does not move her voice to a louder sound.

"We just need to get back," Hadion remains vague.

"Wait."

Thuban picks the woman up by the waist and thrusts her into the air where she floats. Althea's eyes go to her entrances as the maiden shimmers and sparkles like a star. Thuban stands at the bottom with his hands up toward her as he is using magic to keep her suspended in the air. Some men begin to bring a stone table into the floor underneath the floating woman.

"What are they doing?" Althea asks.

"We need to go now," he insists and begins to move Althea. He tries to block her view as well. Althea keeps moving so she can see. Hadion finally picks her up and throws her over his shoulder. Althea pushes up to look behind him. As Hadion reaches the exit, Althea notices those who brought the table now bring a knife and a large goblet.

"What are they doing?" Althea whispers.

Thuban moves his hands. The young woman falls. Althea hears the crack of her skull when she hits the table. The one wielding the knife raises. Before Althea can see what he does, Hadion gets her out the doors of the ballroom which closes behind them. Hadion puts her down.

"Did they just kill her?" Althea looks at the door trembling.

"Let's go." He takes her hand.

"We have to go back and help her." Althea pulls. Hadion tightens his hold. Althea hears cheers from behind it.

"It is finished now," Hadion states calmly.

"What is?" Althea looks back to the man who brought her.

"The sacrifice."

"They killed her?"

"Yes. A virgin bathed in a spring's blue moon will give the drinker of her blood a temporary surge in virility." Hadion does not take pleasure in this lesson. Althea grimaces at the information. Althea grips her swirling stomach.

"I'm going to be sick," She groans.

"I will take you home." He takes her hand. He walks her out of the house and outside starts a small fire with a wave of his hand. He cuts his hand and drips blood into it. The oval comes. He takes her by the hand and leads her through the oval. They arrive back at his castle.

"Shall I take you back to your room?" Hadion offers.

"I can make it on my own. I don't want you to see me vomit." She tries to gross him out a little.

"That doesn't bother me. I'll walk you to your room," He insists. Hadion does just that. They walk in silence. When they reach her door, they both stop. If it were any other night, he would kiss her but as she keeps her face turned from him, he does not.

"Althea, I'm sorry about tonight. I never meant for you to see that. I shouldn't have taken you there," Hadion finally speaks.

"Why did you take me when you knew that was the whole purpose of the party?"

"I had to go and I wanted you with me. I planned to leave before the sacrifice but I couldn't find you until it was too late," He explains.

"Had I not been there would you have participated in the sacrifice?"

"No. I have no interest in hurting innocent people for my pleasure," He does not even pause.

"Truly?"

"You don't believe me?" He begins to take some offense.

Althea does not answer. Hadion's jaw tightens.

"I think you need to rest." Hadion looks away from Althea.

"I agree." Althea opens her door. Hadion walks away. Althea goes into her room. It does not lock as Hadion has already gone. She undresses from the fine gown Hadion made. She puts on her nightgown and lies down on her bed. She holds her stomach as she thinks about the evening. It started as a dream but turned into a nightmare. Not only did Hadion take her to a party where people get murdered, but she also had to meet his former lover and learn about Hadion and Odette.

Had she not learned what she had from Livia, she may have believed Hadion was honest when he said he did not like hurting others for his pleasure.

Knowing now that he cursed and kept Odette for his pleasure, how can his words be truthful? What else is a lie with Hadion? And who else has covered them up?

Althea tosses and turns unable to find any comfort in her bed. She sits up and gets out of the bed. She puts on her slippers then cautiously steps out of her room. She looks around for a sign of Hadion or Odile. Sensing nothing, she goes to the stairwell. She goes down quickly and then runs out into the garden of the thirteen. She does not stop there. She walks as quickly as she can. She does not stop till she reaches Sommerstern Castle. The women are out dancing. Althea sees Basil playing his new flute as the women dance including Odile and Odette. Sigfried dances with the two women.

"Althea!" Basil stops playing to come to his sister. Althea instantly grabs him and pulls him into a tight hug.

"Althea, you are distressed. Is something wrong? Odile says you have been well but I see you are not. What has happened?" He asks pulling back.

"I'm sorry I have not been here. I-I am fine. I..."

"Althea, what are you doing here?" Odile has come up.

"I need to talk to Odette," Althea states.

"Oh...okay," Odile steps aside.

"I'll go with you." Basil takes Althea's arm.

"No. I need to speak with her alone." Althea pulls her arm from Basil and walks straight to Odette who has stayed by the prince.

"Althea," Odette smiles but Althea does not.

"I need to speak with you, alone," Althea speaks softly.

"Um...sure. Let us go inside," Odette agrees. She leads Odette into the sitting room where they sit together in silence. Odette waits for Althea to speak but Althea keeps looking at the carpet. It is a lovely carpet. The base is blue with white patterns making swans and flowers.

"Althea, are you alright?" Odette speaks first. Althea looks up to the other woman.

"I need you to be completely honest with me."

"Alright."

"Are you Odile's mother?"

"Yes," Odette answers after a long pause.

"You and Hadion were lovers?"

Odette turns her face at the question.

"At one point in our lives," Odette's voice is barely above a whisper.

"When did it end?" Althea's stomach turns again.

"When I was pregnant with Odile," Odette answers.

"When it ended, did he curse you?" Althea continues with her questions.

"Yes."

Althea closes her eyes.

Is Hadion this cruel? He cast out the mother of one of his children then cursed the other one? I have not given him a child or my body but if I do try to leave with Basil and he catches me, will he curse me too and enjoy it?

"Althea." Odette reaches across and touches Althea's arm. Althea looks up. "Why are you asking me these things?"

"I...I'm..." Althea is not sure how to say it to Odette. Odette pulls her hand away.

"You're in love with him," Odette states.

"What? No!" Althea is quick to deny this.

"No?"

"No. I like him though. I like him immensely. Tonight, he took me to a ball and I met someone who told me about you and Hadion. It made me begin to rethink things with Hadion. If he is willing to cast aside a woman for another then curse that woman, what will he do to me if things do not go as he likes?" Althea confides her fears with Odette.

"Was this woman Livia?" Odette gains a sour expression when she says the name.

"Yes."

Odette closes her eyes and pinches the skin at the top of her nose between her eyebrows.

"Althea, Livia is like an oleander: beautiful and sweet but poisonous. It is because of her virulent seed Bardolph grew into what he is," Odette speaks harshly about the other woman. Odette moves her fingers from her face. She takes Althea's hands again.

"She has painted an untrue portrait of how things were and are."

"Then tell me so I may see clearer."

Odette inhales and holds it before exhaling and letting Althea go again. She leans back in her chair and looks out the window near them. From here, Odette can see the swan maidens dancing still with Odile among them. Basil has begun to dance with Odile though he is not as skilled as Sigfried or the others.

"I was a princess of Aust, well now Austvest. My brother is King Eric II. Do you know of him?"

"Yes. I did not know he had a sister."

"Well, that is because the sorcerer Kazimeer came and stole me away many years ago. He disguised himself as a Count von Rothbart. I rejected his affection so he kidnapped me. I had a necklace of protection from my fairy godmother that protected my chastity from him. He could still hurt me and did so when I could not complete impossible tasks he set me to do.

His son, Hadion, would seek me out to help me. With his aid, I never failed and was never hurt. I fell in love with Hadion. Because I was in love with him, my necklace's blessing broke. With it gone, Hadion and I...acted on our love physically. I became with child. I was not fully sure of what was going on with my body and so I confided in Livia, who had been kind to me. She made me believe she was going to help me and Hadion. Instead, she exposed me before Kazimeer and Hadion. It was then that I learned the cruel truth," Odette pauses as her eyes begin to fill with tears.

"What?" Althea leans in.

"Hadion had been ordered by Kazimeer to seduce me and impregnate me to shame me. Livia was in on it too," Odette begins to shed her tears. Althea covers her mouth.

"I...I cannot tell you all that occurred after I learned the truth. Hadion put me in Sommerstern Castle to live. I had Odile. Hadion gave me this cursed crown so that in the day I was to be a swan incapable of being harmed and at night I would be human and unable to be harmed and unable to age. He told me the only way for it to break was for a virginal man to declare his love for me before the whole world. I know now that this curse is not truly a curse. It was a protection spell. He was trying to make sure that no one, including him, could hurt me again. Of course, then he had the falling out with his father where he killed him. Hadion wanted Odile to learn magic so he had his sister Odessa and then Livia teach her. But I caught Livia trying to kill Odile. That's when I told Hadion and he sent Livia away. Hadion may not have loved me but he loved Odile.

"Over the years, Hadion and I have come to arrangements such as me taking care of the women Bardolph hurt and having my curse extend to them. He takes care of Odile and lets her live in luxury but allows her to come to me whenever she wants. When you came to me, I was going to keep you but Hadion wanted you for Odile. I wanted Odile to be happy so I sent you away. I am sorry I was not more honest about that."

Pity grows in Althea. She pities Odette for her broken heart but she also pities Hadion. These two women he has been with are not ones he necessarily chose. Livia was his stepmother and chose him to groom and seduce. Odette was picked by his father and he was forced to beguile and betray her.

"I say all of this to explain Hadion is flawed and has made poor choices, he does try to protect those he cares for and if he cares for you then he will not try to hurt you. That is not his way. But I do warn you to know his true intentions now before you get your heart broken," Odette finishes.

If Odette is telling the truth, which I am more inclined to believe given I know Odette better than I know Livia, then Hadion's reason to get rid of Livia was for Odile's sake. His curse on Odette is not a curse of malice for his pleasure. So perhaps Hadion would not curse me. But Odette is right. I need to know if Hadion's affections are true. I hope they are.

"Thank you, Odette. I know it must not have been easy to share this," Althea expresses her gratitude.

"I am only doing what I wish someone had done with me," Odette answers.

"I need to go. Thank you." Althea stands and starts for the door.

"Althea." Odette stands and calls the other woman's name. Althea stops to look back at Odette.

"Yes?"

"Don't tell Sigfried we had this talk. He doesn't know about my past yet," Odette asks the favor.

"Shouldn't you tell him? The truth will hurt less now coming from you than later coming from someone else," Althea recommends. Odette looks down.

"I suppose you're right." Odette mumbles.

"I will keep my lips sealed, Odette," Althea does promise, earning a soft smile. Althea leaves the castle and then heads back toward the larger one while the dancing continues. She is sure not to be seen by Odile or Basil.

Coming closer to the castle, Althea hears a whoosh. Hadion descends before her with his large black wings out. He has a frowning lip but concerned eyes.

"Hadion."

"I thought you were ill. I came to talk to you more. What are you doing out here?" He questions her.

"I went to speak with Odette."

"Why?"

"Livia told me things that upset me and I had to know if they were true."

"What did Livia tell you?" His tone grows harsher.

"She told me about Odette. I went to Odette and she told me of your relationship and why you cursed her," Althea informs her of her deeds. Hadion gains a stony expression.

"So, you hate me more now?"

"No."

"You don't?"

"No...I don't. I don't like that you took me to a ball where people are to get murdered. I don't like that you had an affair with your stepmother or that you impregnated a poor girl at the behest of your father. I don't like that you don't tell me everything. I don't like that when I'm not with you I miss you terribly and want you. I don't like that I'm afraid that all you like about me is the fact I'm here and I like kissing. I don't like that I might get my heart broken by you. But despite all of that, I...I don't hate you. I...feel the opposite toward you. I...I love you," Althea reconciles it to herself in that instant she does.

Hadion stands silent as stone. Althea's palms sweat.

Why doesn't he say something? Anything. Anything would be better than silence between us.

"How could a heart like mine, be loved by one like yours?" He poses the question. As he reaches out and brushes some of her hair from her face. His fingers linger on her cheek.

"How could it not?" Althea replies with her own.

The faintest of smiles comes to his face. He lifts her chin with his finger and thumb so he can easily kiss her lips.

CHAPTER 46

Althea

Hadion pulls back from the young woman. He stares at the innocent maiden looking up at him with a hopeful smile. It has not passed him she has changed into a nightgown or that her eyes hold a gleam of willingness in them. It is a look he has been given more than once. He licks his lips and tastes her there.

"Althea, I-"

"Father? What are you doing out here?" Odile suddenly approaches. Hadion looks away from Althea to his daughter.

"I should ask you the same question," Hadion takes a step toward her.

"I was just visiting the swan maidens," she tells him her answer first.

"And I was just coming to look for Althea," Hadion replies to her.

"I see you have succeeded. Well, I'm exhausted. I think I will go back to the castle to sleep. Will you come too, Althea?" Odile reaches the other young woman in the field and yawns.

"Um..." Althea looks to Hadion for direction.

"You two should go rest. It is getting late," Hadion agrees with his daughter.

"You should get some rest too, Father. You look tired." Odile points to Hadion's face. He sticks his tongue in his cheek.

"I need to speak with Odette so I must go to Sommerstern," Hadion gives his second destination.

"Can't you talk to her tomorrow? I'm sure she and her maidens are preparing for bed," Odile tries to dissuade him.

"I won't disturb the maidens." Hadion spreads his wings and takes off to the sky. Odile frowns.

"I hope Baz and Siggy are hidden," Odile speaks mostly to herself but also to Althea. Althea pales now realizing she never did tell Hadion she rescued her brother.

"Should we go back to make sure they are safe?" Althea looks toward the way leading back to the castle.

"I think it will only make my father more suspicious," Odile frowns.

"I guess we must hope they are quick to hide," Althea feels some defeat.

"Let's go back to the castle so no more suspicions arise."

Althea nods in agreement. They begin their journey back to the castle. As they walk, Althea glances at Odile often. Though many things liken her appearance to her father such as her hair, forehead, and complexion. But so much of her is like Odette as well. Why did no one tell her?

"Odile," Althea speaks first.

"Yes?"

"Why didn't you tell me Odette was your mother?" the question makes Odile stop. Althea stops to turn around and faces Odile.

"What?"

"I know the truth. I know she is your mother. Why didn't you tell me? I thought we were friends." Althea's hurt comes out in her question.

"My father asked me not to mention it."

"Why would he do that?"

"Probably because he thought if you knew my mother was a woman stuck on this island, cursed to be a swan half of the day you would not develop an interest in him. I knew he liked you as soon as he wanted to make you his pupil and he asked me then as well for me not to say anything. I'm sorry I didn't tell you, but I didn't want to disobey him. Also, I like you. If you were to fall for my father then you would want to stay then we could be friends, always. So, I kept it a secret even more."

"You wanted me to fall in love with your father so you could keep me as a friend?"

"Yes..."

"That's rather selfish."

"I know and I am sorry. I hope this does not harm our friendship or make you hate me or my father."

"I don't hate either of you. Just...please, be honest with me from now on," Althea requests.

"I will. Now, let's get back. I need some sleep. Your brother had me dancing way too much," Odile locks her arm with Althea's so they walk together.

"Do you like my brother, Odile?"

Odile blushes. "He is handsome."

"I think he looks like an otter."

"I think otters are cute," Odile mumbles and Althea chuckles.

"But I tried to kiss him and he rejected me. He said he couldn't kiss me because he couldn't fall in love with me," Odile confides to Althea.

"He did? Why would he say that?"

"He said he can't fall in love with me because he can't marry me because I do not follow El-Yah. He said our differing faiths would always pose a challenge between us. He says we can be friends but nothing more. So, I told him about you and my father and..."

"You told him about us?" Althea interrupts.

"Yes. Was I not supposed to?"

"Um...I guess not..." Althea bites her lip.

"And he said he is not happy you would choose to be with someone who is not a follower of El-Yah but says that is up to you. Then we had a talk about whether or not I want to be a sorceress or not."

"Sounds like you two had a long talk."

"We did. I find him so easy to talk to and though he gives his opinions, he does not make me feel like mine are lesser for being different. I think I...I think I like him," Odile admits more to herself than to Althea. Althea smiles warmly.

"Well, who knows what all the future holds," Althea squeezes Odile closer to her.

***

Hadion lands at Sommerstern Castle and finds the grounds empty but the lights inside the castle are lit. He enters causing the maidens still up and wandering to cower or retreat.

"Odette. Odette," he calls out over and over until she comes out to him.

"What are you doing here?" Odette comes out.

"I want to talk."

"Let's go to the parlor," She gives a location before they go walking. As they sit Odette stares at the sorcerer who looks around the room.

"I see you haven't changed anything," He comments.

"There isn't anywhere to go to get new furnishings," She replies. Hadion presses his lips together.

"What is it you want to talk about? I'm sure it isn't about my decor," Odette seeks the purpose of this meeting.

"Althea says you told her about us."

"Only because she asked."

Hadion inhales and keeps silent.

"Are you upset with me for telling her?" Odette wonders about his silence.

"No." He shakes his head.

"Okay...So?" Odette is lost on why he is here.

"I know you hate me for what I did, but you did love me at one point, correct?"

Odette's face turns red though she is not sure if it is from anger or embarrassment.

"Why are you bringing that up?"

"Because I need to know at what point did I make you stop? At what point, what action, what truth made you stop?"

"Why does that matter?" Odette refuses to look at Hadion or answer his question. She stands up to go to the door.

"I need to know, Odette." Hadion grabs her by the wrist.

"Let me go!" She demands throwing her arm down to release his grip.

"Odette, tell me." He has not lost his grip.

"Let me go!" She yells again and pulls once more. Hadion pins her against the door. He looks deep into her beautiful blue eyes. They are so alike to Althea's but Althea's shimmer and are lighter. He knows he hasn't been this close to Odette in years. Odette breathes in his scent, the scent that once gave her hope and comfort but now sorrow and regret. Still, his eyes entrance her.

"Odette, please. Tell me when I lost you," He speaks softly.

"Why must you know?" She whispers with tears pricking her eyes.

"I don't want to repeat my mistakes," He claims and steps back bringing his face closer to hers. He can feel her fluttering heartbeat against his chest.

"You...you love her, don't you? You love Althea." Odette reads him. He steps back. Odette scoffs and has a tear roll down her cheek that she quickly wipes away.

"I just don't want to lose her. I need to know what I can do to keep her near. What must I hide and keep to myself?"

Odette rolls her eyes.

"Don't hide anything. She should know who and what you truly are."

Hadion looks away from her.

"And even though you want her here with you, you shouldn't keep her. She's not a bird to keep in a gilded cage and to sing at your request. She has her goals, her duties, and her promises. Let her be free and if she wants to stay at your side, she will," Odette gives her thoughts on the matter.

"And what if she doesn't come back to me?"

"Then she doesn't," Odette shrugs. Hadion sneers at this advice.

"This has not been helpful," He comments. Odette lets out a little laugh and another tear that she is quick to wipe away.

"It is helpful just not in the way you want it to be," Odette remarks.

"How can I know you are not advising this so I lose her? So you can hurt me again?"

"Me hurt you? Am I the one to curse and trap you here? Am I the one who beguiled you? I have not been the one to hurt, Hadion. We both know that!" Odette snaps at him. Hadion set a hard look.

"You don't know anything, Odette," He claims, then starts to grab the door to exit through it.

"I know you should set that girl free before she gets hurt more than she already has," Odette gives her last thought.

Hadion leaves without looking back at the swan princess. He is quick to be out of the castle and to fly back to the castle. He arrives in his room and brings in his wings. He thinks about what Odette has said and her advice.

"Hadion." He hears his voice. From a corner shadow in his room steps out Amraphel. He is not the white-haired figure he had been earlier for Althea. He appears to be nothing more than a cloak with floating red eyes and a wide smile of sharp teeth.

"Amraphel, what is it?"

"You seem vexed. What is wrong, friend?"

"Nothing, Amraphel," Hadion shakes his head.

"I know you lie. Tell me, Hadion. What vexes you? I can help."

"No. You cannot."

"Was not I the one who helped you remove your father? Is it not I who helps keep Odile protected from Bardolph? Is it not I who helps keep Odette and those others safe and sound here? I always help you, Hadion. Tell me what has caused you to be unhappy," Amraphel reaches out a shadowy hand to the sorcerer. Hadion avoids the touch. This being indeed helped him with his magic but it did come at a cost.

"My issue cannot be influenced or changed by magic."

"Oh, I don't know about that. A woman can be easily influenced with the right words and potions," Amraphel smiles.

"Woman? Why would you say that?" Hadion looks at the red eyes.

"It is this budding romance with Althea causing you distress."

Hadion looks away but does not verbally answer.

"You feel for her like you did for Odette, don't you?" Amraphel continues. "I can help you with her. I helped you attain Odette."

"I attained Odette on my own," Hadion refutes the dark one.

"You think a bastard of a bastard could win a princess without help? Remember, I told you what to say. I created the magic you did to wow her," Amraphel argues for his praise.

"It wasn't magic that made her love me. She said so," Hadion argues back.

"Tsk. Magic or not she doesn't love you anymore. If you had followed my instructions more closely back then she could have stayed yours. I hope you don't lose Althea as you did her," Amraphel brings up the new object of Hadion's desire.

"I didn't want to take away her free will with a love potion. I do not want to do that with Althea either," Hadion gives his reasoning for not following Amraphel. The shadow shrugs.

"Then why not ask her, of her own free will, for a blood bond," Amraphel suggests.

"She does not do blood magic."

"Because she could not draw her own blood. She can now. She can do many things now." Amraphel grins. Hadion knows exactly what the other being means.

"She would never agree to that sort of thing," Hadion rolls his eyes.

"How do you know if you don't ask?" Amraphel questions. Hadion cannot make eye contact as he does consider this.

If I ask Althea, would she accept? She has said she loves me. Would she want to if she loves me? But she may not agree to it if she knows all the details of my life and of what a blood bond would entail.

"Leave me, Amraphel. I am tired." Hadion waves off the other.

"As you wish." Amraphel bows out and then disappears into the shadows. When Hadion feels the creature's presence is gone, he exhales and lies on his bed. He stares at his ceiling. The moonlight makes it glow down on him.

Should I listen to Odette or Amraphel?

Hadion looks over to his desk where Althea's broken bird sits, having been untouched for the past fortnight. He rises and walks to it. He stares at the once-magical messenger. He recalls the last message it delivered.

Althea's sister is on her way here to collect Althea and find their brother. She claims to have a guide but the only person who can find it without his or Bardolph's guidance would be someone with the blood of his father. His sister Odessa would not need to bring such a person to the island. She is far too busy trying to take over her husband's country to care about bringing her half-nephew's choice of bride to him.

"The troll," Hadion whispers to himself. He recalls his father mentioning his dalliance with the troll queen of this island and having a child before he destroyed them all.

Did this secret half-sister survive? Is she coming back now to the island? Why would she come back? Why would she bring a stranger here to save a sister and brother that are not her own? Will she bring a force with her? Will Althea go away with her family and this troll when they come?

"Let her go." is what Odette has said to do. If he does, she will never find her way back to him. But if her sister comes, she will want to go especially if they find her brother. But he is still lost. The longer he is lost the longer they would have to stay to find him. But then Bardolph will also have more time with Althea's sister whom he claims to love. However, given all Althea has told him, this girl holds no love for Bardolph. For the sister to have to stay would be dangerous for her and make her want to leave even more quickly. It could also possibly create more animosity between Althea and himself.

"Perhaps..." he mumbles to himself.

If I were to find this brother of Althea's, free him, and heal him, I could condition his release to her sister in return for her to stay with me at least until she finishes her apprenticeship. I could just ask her to stay and be mine and still let her brother go so she cannot say I forced her to stay. Would she accept? Would she give up her family with the knowledge they are free and well without her and stay with me?

"I must find and heal that boy first," Hadion walks away from the desk. He leaves the room and down the stairs. He goes to his study.

"I will need the last of the All-Cure Elixir to heal him," He starts to go for where he keeps his best potions hidden. As he looks behind the bookshelf to his secret nook, he begins to frown. His fingers go over each vial of potion, elixir, serum, cordial, panacea, nostrum, salve, liniment, and tonic. He cannot find the one he needs. Someone has stolen from him. Why? He is not sure. But who? He has a clue.

Hadion leaves the study and anger boiling his blood, he marches straight for Bardolph's room. He waves his hand making the heavy door fly open. He easily finds his son in his bed beneath the sheets with a woman. Hadion rips off the sheet causing a shriek from the young woman and a snarl from Bardolph.

"What are you doing?" Bardolph barks at his father getting off the bed. The maiden grabs the pillows to cover herself. Hadion recognizes the young woman with long brown curls, a voluptuous figure, and silver eyes, Yrsa from House Urs. Now he knows Bardolph must have left to go to the Blue Moon Ball at Thuban's home.

"Where is it?" Hadion keeps his focus on his son, not the woman.

"Where is what?" Bardolph yells.

"The All-Cure elixir. I know you've taken it!" Hadion gets in his son's face.

"Why would I want some stupid elixir?"

"To break one of the many curses you have set on others," Hadion answers.

"Ha. If I curse someone, they're staying that way," Bardolph scoffs.

"Maybe it has been set on you and you have taken it to free yourself," Hadion suggests.

"As if anyone would dare to curse me," He rolls his eyes.

"Then who has taken it?"

"Probably Odile. Who else would think they could get away with it?" Bardolph accuses his sister. Hadion searches Bardolph's eyes and senses no deceit.

"I will go and ask her then," Hadion decides and looks at the young woman who has started to redress in a blue and silver gown. Hadion turns his attention back to Bardolph.

"I thought it was Althea's sister you wanted," The father whispers to his son.

"From behind they look the same," Bardolph replies with a smirk.

"Don't start a fallout with House Urs over your lack of control," Hadion warns his son who scoffs again.

"I know what I'm doing, Hadion. Go now. I want to finish what I started here," Bardolph nods toward the door. Hadion leaves, knowing he needs to question the younger of his two children.

Hadion is quick to reach his daughter's room. He opens the door softly and finds his daughter asleep in her bed. He sits on it and softly rubs his hand up and down her arm. He calls her name a few times before she stirs.

"Yeah?" She asks with eyes a quarter open.

"Did you take my All-Cure elixir?" He asks sweetly.

"Yeah," She answers truthfully though sleepily.

"Why?" He keeps his gentleness.

"To save Baz," She closes her eyes and smiles. The image of the young man comes to her mind. Hadion knows who this Baz person is.

"Did you save him?"

"Mhm," She nods.

"Where is he? Is he safe?"

"He's with..." She starts to drift off again.

"With?" He rubs.

"Swans," She gives one word.

"Swans?' Hadion repeats. He stands and backs out of the room quietly. Reaching the outside of the room, Hadion stares at Althea's door. He knows she must be a part of the theft as well as the hiding of the man.

Why didn't she tell him she found and saved her brother? Is that why Odile and her did not want me to go to Sommerstern Castle? Is he there? Odette must be hiding him. When did they free him? It must have been when I was gone. Is that why Althea has been so affectionate? Is that why she has claimed to love me? Is it all a lie to distract me from the truth? Is her love a lie?

CHAPTER 47

ALTHEA

Althea exits her room smiling and excited for the day. She happily greets Odile who leaves her room at the same time. They link arms as they start down the stairs to go for breakfast.

"Did you sleep well?" Odile asks Althea.

"Yes. Did you?"

"Not really. I had an awful dream."

"Really? What happened?"

"I was dancing with flying pink swans when a wolf was asking me about the elixir I took and why. Then the swans and I started flying to the blue moon but something stabbed me from behind and I fell to the ground which had turned to tar and no matter how much I struggled, I couldn't get out of it," Odile recalls the nightmare.

"That's terrible," Althea loses her smile.

"I know. Do you have dreams like that?"

"Not recently," Althea shakes her head. "Do you often have nightmares?"

"Not always but more recently I think it has increased."

"You have never mentioned this to me before," Althea furrows her eyebrows.

"I guess it just hasn't bothered me as much as last night's. Usually, I wake and go back to sleep to more pleasant dreams but not last night."

"Perhaps you should make a dreamless sleeping draught. I saw one in the potions book," Althea brings up the optional aid.

"Perhaps..."

They reach the dining room where breakfast is served. Hadion sits at the table with Bardolph. The older of the men only wears black boots, pants, and a white shirt. The younger is in black boots and pants, and a red shirt with an oblique neck and a belt around his waist. While Bardolph devours the salted pork and eggs before him, Hadion merely drinks a cup of black coffee.

"Good morning," Althea greets cheerfully and takes her seat. Odile does as well. Bardolph looks at Odile and smirks. Odile does not notice as she busies herself with filling her plate. Hadion looks over to Althea who smiles at him. She hopes he likes her appearance. She put on one of the dresses he made for her with an iridescent white fabric so it can match the opal pendant she still wears. Hadion does not return the greeting and looks away from Althea.

"Did you sleep well?" She asks him. He remains silent and drinks more coffee. Althea's smile falters at his lack of response. Bardolph snickers.

"What are you grinning about?" Odile notices her brother's happy reaction.

"Nothing." He shakes his head and keeps eating.

"Did I do something wrong?" Althea whispers to Hadion.

"Have you?" he speaks for the first time that day.

"I don't think so," she replies. He clenches his jaw and irritation comes to his eyes.

"Come then. It's time for one of your lessons." He stands up and sets his coffee down. Althea stands up as well though she has not eaten at all. Hadion keeps up a fast pace Althea struggles to match.

"What will I be learning about?" She asks to prepare herself mentally.

"You will find out," he replies vaguely. Up and up, they go till they reach the highest tower and the balcony there.

"Are we to fly again?" She asks.

"Yes. You won't be needing this." He reaches over and pulls out the necklace of protection he gave her. He shoves it into his pocket. Though surprised by the snatching, she has to assume he is right.

Hadion takes hold of her though his touch is not as gentle as it has been before.

Has it always been this rough and I did not notice because of the ring of protection?

Hadion takes her high into the sky with his wings spread out wide. He looks up and not at her. She holds onto him tighter when she feels herself slipping against him. Reaching a height making the castle look like a doll house rather than the giant building it is.

"Why are we up here so high?" She asks Hadion, her fingers curling so tightly into his fabric it might rip it.

"You need to let go of me. I am holding you," He reminds her. She relaxes her grip as she knows he will not let her fall. He never does.

"It's time," he says, though Althea is not sure of what he is talking about.

"Huh?" She raises an eyebrow. Hadion lets go.

"Haaaaaaaaaaaaaa!" Althea screams as she falls. Hadion stays high as he watches.

"Hadion! Hadion!" She cries out but he makes no move to come for her.

Why is he not coming for me? I'm not protected anymore. I could die! Why is he not coming?

"This is a lesson. This is a lesson," she tells herself as she closes her eyes. "What am I supposed to do? What am I supposed to do?"

It clicks and with a few deep breaths, she shifts from herself to a small white dove. She stops herself from falling and starts flying. Leveling out she exhales in relief. She looks up at Hadion only to see a falcon with its sharp claws coming at her. She flaps desperately to get out of the beast's grip. She flies swiftly and dodges the talons as it keeps swooping after her. She keeps trying to look for Hadion but cannot see him anywhere.

Why is he letting this happen?

Althea starts flying upward toward the sun in hopes of blinding the other bird. It grabs her by its own feet and throws her down back. As her little body starts falling backward, she shifts back into her human form. If she had not been so afraid of the falcon coming at her she would have noticed she was able to shift and keep her clothes on her body.

"I need to be a bigger bird," she tells herself seeing the bird coming at her still. She shifts again into a large, white gold phoenix. After taking this form, the falcon's claws catch her around her neck and chest. Its force pushes her down toward the earth. Despite her trying to peck at the claws and flap, she sees she will soon hit the trees below. She closes her eyes and holds her breath.

Bursting into flame, the falcon releases her. Her ashes fall through the trees to the ground where they pile up among a path of wild aconite flowers. The falcon comes and lands on the giant fig tree above and watches as out of the ashes emerges a tiny baby bird growing into a beautiful maiden with golden hair and a dress of white. She looks at herself amazed and smiling. She has not been harmed and is still dressed.

The falcon shifts back into Hadion who stays seated on the branch. She looks up at him. Her smile fades.

"You dropped me!" She points at him.

"You need to learn to fly on your own," he replies.

"Then you chased me. You tried to kill me!" She accuses him. He jumps down from the branch.

"I was merely testing your ability to defend yourself," He brushes off some soot from the cuffs of his shirt.

"You could have told me you were going to do that," She crosses her arms.

"In the real world, no one warns you of an attack. You need to know how to take care of yourself. You never know when you will be put in harm's way. That's why I attacked."

"I see. I should have known that was what you were trying to teach me," She starts to smile as if she had done something silly by not figuring out his lesson. "I should have known you would never try to hurt me."

"You think I would never hurt you?"

"No, just like I wouldn't hurt you." She shakes her head with an honest smile. Her smile is gone when his hand wraps around her neck and she is pushed against the fig tree within a second. He has a steady hold on her but does not squeeze.

"Liar," He calls her, voice breaking.

"What?" Althea gapes at him utterly lost.

"You're lying to me, Althea. You've been lying to me for weeks."

"What have I been lying about?" Althea wants to know what it is she must refute to prove her honesty.

"You don't love me. You're just trying to distract me as a way to cover up the fact you got Odile to steal from me so you could save your brother who you've been hiding at Odette's," He brings up Basil. Althea shuts her mouth and looks away from Hadion.

"I am right, aren't I? Come out and admit it, Althea," He demands.

"It is true I found Basil and have kept him at Odette's. But I did not ask Odile to steal the elixir. She did that on her own. I should have told you all this but I was afraid. I was afraid if you knew I freed Basil and lost my ring you would be mad at me for disobeying your orders. I was also afraid Bardolph would learn of this and hurt both me and my brother. So, I kept everything a secret."

"You don't trust me to keep you safe and unharmed?"

"I do now. But on that day, I wasn't sure. Then I held it in for so long that I just knew it was too long and I didn't want...well... this. I don't want you to think I don't trust you. I do. I'm sorry I stumbled with this. But do know that even though I kept this secret, I never lied to you about how I felt. I do love you, Hadion. Look in my eyes. You will see there is no lie there. I love you." She puts her hands on his forearm.

Hadion looks down at her and into her eyes. It is true he finds no deceit there. He can understand why she hid this all from him but it does not keep it from hurting. But even so, should this little pain keep him from her? Should he give her up and the love she is offering over this? Does he even want to be drawn back into the life-ruining phenomenon of love? All love has ever left him with are two unplanned children, his father's blood on his hands, and a broken heart. What will it leave him with this time? He knows it will not be another child but perhaps something worse. He should end it now. He should cast her aside and punish her for her deceit. He should spare himself from more pain.

"Please, forgive me, Hadion," she pleads sincerely. He takes her face in his hands and stares down at her. He knows what his decision is now. He knows what path he will be taking.

"Why must you do this to me?" He asks strained.

"Do what?" She does not understand.

"Draw me in when you are going to hurt me."

"I'm not going to hurt you." She means what she says.

"Yes, you will and I will let you. I will willingly and happily allow you to torture me. You will be the thorn in my side that I push in further for it means you are a part of me. You will be my dearest bane."

"Then you will be mine as well," She decides. Hadion kisses her hard and passionately. She wraps her arms around him as his arms move to wrap around her as well.

As their kiss deepens, Althea's knees buckle. He holds her tightly to his body so then with great ease lies her down among the purple aconites and ash. Their kiss breaks for a second as Hadion removes his shirt. As her hands go into his hair, his hands begin undoing her dress. Layers are shed from both parties as the flames of their passions consume them and give them the need to be unrestrained with materials.

When both are at their most vulnerable, they stop with heaving chests to look at one another. They are nearly at the point where two become one. A point with no reversal. His hungry eyes stare into her starving ones.

"Yes?" He phrases the single word as a hopeful and desperate question. Without hesitation, Althea repeats the word eagerly with a smile. One last kiss is given between the maid and man beneath the fig tree before they pass the point of no return.

CHAPTER 48

ALTHEA

Rivers of golden hair weave through the purple aconites while some curls against Althea's peaches and cream skin. She lies flat on her back as Hadion lies on his side looking at her. She has her face turned to look at his. His fingers lightly push her hair away from her cheek then he lets his hand rest on it.

Althea had never been sure of what to truly expect regarding lovemaking. Sure, she had been given a short, scientific summary by her mother about what the act would entail so Althea would not be ignorant. However, she did not know it would hurt some or it would make her entire body tingle as if she had been struck by lightning. She can understand now why her parents were always slipping away for private moments together.

"Althea," He whispers.

"Yes?"

"Will you...will you stay with me?"

"I don't plan to leave you yet, especially not undressed," She answers with a laugh.

"I mean...Will you stay with me and...share my life with me?" He clarifies. Althea pauses surprised by the question. Though feelings have been discussed and in her passionate haste she has given herself to him, she has been rather unthoughtful about the future, their future.

Ever since I left Foxglove Grove, I've wanted to reunite my family. But after we are what is there for me? Basil will probably go back to his travels and work as a piper. Stella will go with Prince Astrophel. What will I do? I'm no piper so I will not go with Basil. I would not go back to Foxglove Grove as I'm not the best baker and I'm sure the people will have agitated feelings toward me over Stella's curse. I could go with Stella to Estellen and live as the prince's sister-in-law. But what would I do besides play court? It would be the same if I went to Soldoro and joined Mother and Father in King Heliodoro's court. If I were to stay here, I could learn more magic and be with Hadion as well as Odile. I could have adventures of my own and still visit my family. Hadion and I could travel the world. I could go places I have only ever heard about in stories. I could also help Odette, Prince Sigfried, and the swan maidens be free. Life with Hadion would be so much better than a life without him. I just need to make sure he will allow for the release and freedom of the others. I must make sure even if I am happy the others are not suffering.

"Hadion, I will if you promise to help reunite my family and-" Althea starts.

"I can do that as long as afterward you are still with me," he is quick to agree with his own terms.

"I would stay with you after but let me finish my request. Besides reuniting my family, I will stay if you release Odette and all in Sommerstern Castle," Althea finishes her condition.

Hadion presses his lips together and turns from Althea and removes his hand from her face. He lies flat on his back. He stays silent and does not answer her. Althea cannot quite understand this lack of an answer.

What good does it do for him to keep them here?

"Hadion, what happened between you and Odette?" She asks him turning onto her side.

"You know what happened. Odette told you." He still does not look at her.

"I know Odette's view of events but I don't know your side or why you keep her and the others here. Please, tell me so I can understand." Althea puts her hand on his chest.

"I don't think you'll like it or me in it."

"Hadion, I want to know all about you and your stories even if I may not like them," She tries to encourage him to open up to her.

"You want to know all about me?"

"Yes. I do."

Hadion takes a deep breath with closed eyes then as he exhales he looks at her.

"My parents were not married or lovers. My father kidnapped and raped my mother. She managed to escape him but still had to give birth to me. She raised me with fairies like herself. She worked as a dressmaker and I would go out to keep sheep with my uncle and cousins. I don't remember too much about that time now but I was happy despite the horrible visions I would have about the future. My father came when I was about eight years of age. He killed all and took me here to this island. He wanted me to be a great and powerful sorcerer like him. He used to beat me to try to change my ways. My half-sister, Odessa, despised me as she had lost her father's favor when I started to show my power. I had no comfort in those times.

"When I was twelve, my father married Livia and brought her to the island. She was beautiful and young, barely nineteen. She was kind to me and I could see her struggling with my father who was cruel and mean even to her. When I turned thirteen, my father was away doing what he wanted and Livia came to me. She told me she loved me and introduced me to sex magic. It was with her influence I decided to start to follow the Fallen as she did. When my father returned, we kept on with our affair but she became pregnant. Unsure of the paternity, she claimed it to be my father's. Bardolph was born and I treated him as a brother.

"Years later, my father was tired of Livia and sought out new entertainment. He went to the newly united Austvest and kidnapped Odette from there. He made her a slave. I saw her and I...I fell in love. I wanted her and so I sought the council of Amraphel. In exchange for my oath to the Fallen, he would help me. He told me to not let her know I was the son of the man who kidnapped her so I pretended to be a slave on the island too. I helped her out with the impossible tasks my father gave her. She fell love in with me too.

"Livia learned of my love for Odette and encouraged me to act on my love. I thought Livia was truly happy for me so I followed her advice. Odette and I...we did what fools do in love. Odette became pregnant and before she could even tell me, she told Livia. Livia brought Odette before my father and me to announce it. My father was quick to claim that he had planned this to humiliate and humble Odette. No matter what I said, Odette could not believe that I was not a part of the plot.

"She gave birth to Odile prematurely. I healed her body but I could not fix her mind or heart. I feared harm from my father toward Odette and Odile so I built Sommerstern Castle and made Odette a crown of protection. I was still new to this advanced magic so I had to do a split spell. In the day she would be a swan unable to be harmed and at night she would be an unageing woman unable to be harmed. But with any protection spell, there has to be a deadline. I had seen in a vision a man more worthy of Odette than I and that he would love her. I made the spell to only be broken when this man loved her and proclaimed it before the world. Odile stayed with Odette at Sommerstern Castle until she began training with my sister Odessa.

"Odile and Bardolph proved to have the same gifts. Some of these gifts neither Livia nor my father had. He figured out Bardolph was mine. In his rage he tried to kill my children, Livia and me. I killed him to defend us. I became the master of the island and my sister left. Livia took over training Odile and tried to become my wife, but I loved Odette. Livia did not like the rejection and took it out of Odile. So, I sent Livia away. Bardolph then tried to harm Odile as retaliation. I spelled Sommerstern to keep Bardolph away. I also had Odile's chambers enchanted to keep Bardolph away from her.

"Over the years, Bardolph has grown more out of control. While I was traveling, he attempted to start a harem here with women from all over the Far Lands. When I came home and learned of what he was doing to them. I would tell you the horrors of his harem but I do not wish to make you sick. Anyway, I took the women from him, sent them to Sommerstern Castle to be in Odette's care, and spelled them to share in Odette's spell. I beat Bardolph for his heinous actions. He made a blood oath to me he would never bring a harem to this island and do such disgusting things to them again. So far, he has kept his promise and Odette has taken care of the women.

"I have tried to do what I think right both in raising Bardolph and Odile and in caring for Odette. I have provided for her and her new companions whom she has cared for like a mother. I suppose I keep her here because I...I am afraid if she were to go, she may soften her heart to another only for it to be broken again. Or she will meet the man more worthy of her love and she will...will never forgive me or love me again." Hadion finishes his recollection of the past and some introspection. Althea sits up having learned much of this man.

"Do you still love Odette?" She asks softly with genuine curiosity rather than judgment.

"Yes."

The single word makes a cold chill run-down Althea's spine.

He is in love with another woman. I should have known. He never did say he loved me. He has only said he wants me. Althea becomes all too aware of her nakedness now. She feels as she did the first time he made her undress, embarrassed and ashamed. She tries to subtly cover herself with her hair.

"You...you don't...you don't love me..." Althea looks down at her dress beneath her. What was once beautiful and white is not stained with blood and grass. There is soot on it too now.

"That's not it at all," he sits up. "I do...I do love you."

"How can you love me and love her?" She tries to not let her emotions get the better of her.

"My love for her is different from my love for you." He starts to reach to hold her face but she pulls back from him.

"How? How is it different?"

"Odette is my first love. I will always love her. But I don't love her like I love you."

"What does that mean?" Althea is shaking.

"She will always have a place in my heart but she is not at the forefront. You are. It is you I want to be with, the one I want to love and be loved by." He touches her hand.

"Do you mean that?" Althea looks into his eyes hopeful every word he has said is true.

"I do." He nods, smiling.

"Odette came to you and told you she loved you and wanted to be with you, would you take her back?" She questions.

"No. I would not cast you aside for her."

"How can I know that for sure?" Althea looks away from him.

"I will let her go."

"What?" Althea looks back at him.

"I will let her go and the others in Sommerstern Castle. I'll free them so they may go wherever they wish."

"Really?" Althea regains her smile.

"Yes."

"Oh, Hadion!" Althea kisses him.

"But I will have to warn them."

"Warn them about?"

"Once they leave the island, the protection part of the spell will not work. They will age and be able to be harmed except in their swan forms which they will still turn into until the man I predicted breaks Odette's spell," Hadion explains.

"I think that will be resolved soon."

"What do you mean?"

"Do not be upset but there is someone on the island who may break Odette's curse," Althea speaks cautiously.

"What?"

"When I ran away, I found a man on the beach who survived a shipwreck. Odette and the others have been caring for him ever since. I think he loves Odette."

Hadion clenches his jaw. Althea waits to see what he says or does. Of course, if now he expresses his want for this man gone and Odette to not be with him, Althea will have to doubt his claims of only wanting her.

"Is he worthy of her?" Hadion asks.

"Um...I suppose. He is handsome, brave, and a prince."

"A prince? From where?"

"Norwin."

"You seem to know much about him. Have you too been enchanted by him?" Hadion's tone gives away his jealousy.

"No. How could I when I have only eyes for you?"

"Get dressed. We will go meet this prince," Hadion decides. He and Althea both dress. Althea knows whatever will happen at Sommerstern Castle now will prove to her whether Hadion loves her or Odette.

Having dressed, Althea tries to pat off the soot since she cannot be rid of the blood or grass stains. She reddens at the idea that her rendezvous with Hadion will be obvious to all just by a look at her dress. The dressed Hadion spreads out his wings and holds out his hand to her.

"What is wrong?" Hadion asks when she does not immediately take his hand.

"My dress...it's...well, look." She shows him the flaws. He smirks to himself but clears his throat to cover it. He waves his hand at her dress and a spell flies from his mouth. The ash, blood, and grass disappear leaving her dress as pristine as before their elicit interaction. Althea smiles at the cleanliness.

"Come." He holds his hand out to her again. She takes it. With a gentler hold this time, he takes her to the sky with him. They fly directly to Sommerstern. The swans there fly away in terror. It is not even noon so the women are still swans. Hadion lets go of Althea before he stands at the door of the castle. He holds out his hands and speaks.

"What are you doing?" Althea is confused by his actions.

"If there is a man in this place, he will be drawn out before me," Hadion's eyes do not leave the castle. From the open door, Basil flies out not of his own will. He falls before Hadion. He looks to the sorcerer then Althea.

"The prince?" Hadion glances at Althea.

"My brother." Althea shakes her head.

"Brother?" Hadion arches his eyebrow. Basil glares at the sorcerer then looks at Althea. Althea hopes her feelings of regret can be felt by her silent brother.

Hadion keeps his hand outstretched. Finally, the prince flies out. He narrowly avoids hitting Basil. Hadion lowers his hands. He stares at the prince who glares back at him. The royal man is unable to move his body from his kneeling position on the ground as is Basil. Hadion squats down and takes Prince Sigfried's jaw in his hand.

"He doesn't look like much of a prince to me," Hadion comments.

"Are you Bardolph or von Rothbart?" the prince questions the identity of this man.

"The latter, and you are?"

"Prince Sigfried of Norwin," He answers.

"Norwin? I guess you take more after your Juardhin mother with that complexion. But I see Norwin in your eyes." Hadion keeps looking at his face.

"What do you want, von Rothbart?" the prince pulls his face from Hadion's grip.

"What do I want? Well, I certainly didn't want any men in this female sanctuary." He gestures to the castle.

"It is a prison, not a sanctuary," Prince Sigfried argues.

"I think Odette would disagree with you," Hadion refers to the mistress of the castle.

"Do not speak of her!"

Hadion smirks at the obvious anger of the prince.

"I may say and do whatever I wish when it comes to Odette," He eggs on the prince.

"Not if I have anything to do with it." Prince Sigfried tries to stand but cannot.

"As if you could do anything to stop me." Hadion leans in close to Prince Sigfried's ear. "If I wanted to, I could ravish Odette right in front of you, you wouldn't be able to do anything but watch."

"You cannot harm her! She is protected!" Prince Sigfried argues.

"By all but me. I am the one who put her curse on her. I am the only one immune to it," he whispers and pulls back from the prince grinning devilishly.

"You sick son of-" the prince begins to lash out. Hadion laughs.

"I do not know why you are getting so upset. She is just a woman," Hadion stands up.

"She is not just a woman. She is a beacon of hope, a lady of kindness and generosity. She is a comfort and joy to all. She is love itself!" He claims. Hadion is taken aback by the man's proclamations of the woman but he keeps a stony expression.

"You sound like a virgin newly in love," Hadion mocks him.

"So? I am. I am not ashamed of it." Prince Sigfried does not care what this man thinks of him.

"You are?"

"Yes, and I will break the spell on her. I will declare before the entire world I love her and she will be free of you!" Prince Sigfried proclaims his intentions. Hadion glances over and sees the crowned swan who has come near with her scared hoard of swans. He knows she has heard the words.

"Then you do not care despite you being a man of virtue that your lady love is not?"

"What?"

"Don't you know? Odette and I were once lovers. Odile is our child. Your love is sullied and more my lover than yours."

Prince Sigfried pauses hearing this news. He swallows the information then with a clear voice he gives his reply.

"I do not care if she has slept with every man south of Norwin and has had a hundred children. I love her. That will not change because of her past."

Hadion takes a deep breath. He looks over to Odette who is still out of the prince's sight. A tear is in her eye as well as in Althea's.

"Fine. Have her. Take her and the others from here. Break the curse and be done with me," Hadion speaks loudly so all can hear. All eyes widened at the announcement. Odette flies to Hadion and then lands before him.

"Do you mean it, Hadion?" She asks.

"Yes. I'll make sure you all can leave. I just don't want to listen to this lovesick nonsense anymore," Hadion plays it cool. Had she been in her human form, the princess may have hugged him in her gratitude. Hadion turns to Althea and holds out his hand.

"Let's go."

"Thea," Basil finally speaks to his sister.

"We'll talk later, Baz," Althea takes Hadion's hand.

They fly up, the men are released from their bind to the ground. Althea stares at Hadion as they fly. He keeps his eyes head.

He must love Odette... She thinks then smiles to herself as she finishes the thought. *But he does love me too.*

CHAPTER 49

ALTHEA

Althea patiently and happily assists Hadion in the preparation for the departure of Odette, her women, and Prince Sigfried. How can she not be when this means all are a step closer to a happily ever after?

Odile comes to her father and Althea as they stand by the sea where Hadion has constructed a boat. She flies down as a black swan then regains her human form.

"Odile, good, you're here. You can help us," Hadion states.

"Are you really going to let all of them go?" Odile comes to her father.

"Yes." Hadion nods knowing of what she speaks.

"Why?"

"What do you mean?" Hadion is surprised by this question.

"I am happy they all will be free but what changed your mind after all these years?"

Hadion's eyes flutter over toward Althea for a brief moment then back to Odile.

"It is time. I am sure you are already aware of the prince hidden there. He will break your mother's curse once they leave this island. So, I am letting them go and the others there because...well, why not?" Hadion shrugs.

"But you said it was dangerous to let those women go back because they could cause a revolt against sorcerers," Odile brings up the excuse her father once gave her.

"I will give them handsome compensation for their time and hope that will keep their mouths shut," He decides.

"Well, they are already looting Sommerstern Castle so..." Odile informs him.

"They are? Well, it will be for naught since it will all turn back to rocks and trees once I reverse the spell created the castle," Hadion chuckles.

"You truly are going to let them go?"

"Yes."

"When?"

"Soon."

"When is soon?" Althea brings up the question herself.

"There is much chaos that comes from a horde suddenly appearing and claiming to be held captive by sorcerers for years. I have to let the release of everyone be a slow and calm transition. I can't just put everyone on a ship and let them go wherever they want." Hadion gives a more complex answer than wanted.

"What is your plan?" Althea questions.

"I will release the prince first to go back to Norwin. Then Odette and the others later," Hadion gives his order of events.

"Siggy will not go without Odette," Odile shakes her head.

"Siggy?" Hadion raises an eyebrow at the name.

"Prince Sigfried," Althea gives the proper name.

"He and Odette are engaged. I doubt he will leave this island without her in hand. I doubt he would trust you to let her leave if he leaves first," Odile makes a point.

"Well, I am not sending them out together," Hadion refuses.

"Why?"

"Because of the curse attaching the maidens to Odette, they have to stick together and there is a limit on my power as to how many people I can send at a time. So, I cannot send Odette and the Prince at the same time and I cannot send the maidens at a different time than Odette." Hadion explains this to the satisfaction of his daughter and his lover.

"If they cannot go together then you should give the prince some sort of collateral to prove you will send Odette," Althea suggests a solution.

"And what would he accept as collateral?"

"What about...Odile? He knows you would come for her." Althea gestures to Odile. The girl's ear perk at the recommendation.

"No. She is not trained enough in magic to protect herself there. If he should change his mind and want to harm her. No. I will not send Odile," Hadion refuses. Odile frowns.

"So even after Odette is gone, you will not allow me to go visit her in Norwin?" Odile seizes the moment to ask about the future.

"Once you are of age and a sorceress you can go wherever you want and do whatever you want. But as of now, I am still not letting you go alone with that prince to Norwin as collateral," Hadion is clear.

"Then what?"

"Send me," Althea volunteers.

"What?" They both look to Althea.

"I'll go. I'll stay with him in Norwin until Odette comes," Althea prepares a plan and comes close.

"No. I do not want you to go either." Hadion shakes his head.

"Well, it's either Odile or me. Who else would you come for?"

Hadion scowls. Neither option is good but he understands why they would be the only suitable choices.

"Fine. I will send you with him but you will come back to me once the wedding ceremony is over," He sets the limit. Althea smiles and nods in agreement.

"Very well. I suppose I should inform them of this before they destroy my little castle," Hadion walks to his window. He pushes on the window on the balcony and it moves to let him leave. His wings take him away leaving the two women together.

"Althea."

"Yes?"

"Your brother and you will be able to leave soon. Do you think you will?"

"I have already talked to Hadion about reuniting my family but afterward I would like to come back and stay here with him and you. Would that be...would you be happy if I did?" Althea takes Odile's hands.

"I know my father would be and I would be too. But what about your family? I do not think your brother would be happy at all," Odile brings up Basil.

"I cannot control the emotions of others. If he is not happy for me then that is his choice. But I am happy. I think that's all that matters to me right now." Althea smiles.

"How different you two are," Odile comments.

"How do you mean?" Althea tilts her head to the side slightly.

"It's nothing. Siblings are just different. Look at me and Bardolph," Odile refers to herself and her brother.

"Yes. You two are vastly different."

"Yes. But you know what we should do?"

"What?"

"Get you ready to go with the prince. I will help get you dresses fit for a queen to wear in Norwin," Odile lets go of one of Althea's hands but keeps hold of the other so she can lead her back toward their rooms.

***

The next day, as the women sit and eat their breakfast with Hadion, he informs them of his meeting with Prince Sigfried and Odette. They listen intently.

"Althea, you and Prince Sigfried will go through the portal to Norwin. There, Prince Sigfried will begin wedding preparations for him and Odette. Then five evenings later, Odette and the maidens will come by ship through a portal. The maidens have all declared their desires to remain Odette's ladies-in-waiting after her marriage to Prince Sigfried. I will provide them all with small fortunes and fine dresses to take with them into their new lives," Hadion shares the details.

"That is generous of you." Althea smiles at Hadion.

"Your mother has asked for you to be in attendance at the wedding as her maid of honor," Hadion looks to Odile. Odile tries to hold back her smile.

"She did?"

"Yes."

"Well...will you let me?" She seeks her father's permission.

"Yes, but I will come for you and Althea right after the ceremony," Hadion gives his limit.

"Oh, thank you! Thank you!" She jumps up from her seat and hugs her father. He accepts it gladly.

"What is all this ridiculous cheer for so early this morning?" Bardolph walks into the dining room with circles under his eyes and a sneer on his face.

"I'm finally getting to leave!" Odile gushes before she can stop herself.

"You're going to leave? You're going to let her?" He looks at Hadion with a cocked brow.

"Yes. I am letting Odette go along with your former harem. They will be joining the Norwin court. Odile will go with them to witness the wedding between Odette and a prince there," Hadion informs his son. A look of true surprise comes over Bardolph then a little grin.

"Why do you look happy?" Odile is quick to question.

"Why should I not be happy? We will finally be rid of your dreary mother and those useless cows. I will even get a break from you for a time. This is great news. I want to make a toast." He comes to the table and grabs the glass of wine set out for him. He lifts his glass high into the air. He gestures for the others to copy him. They are slow to take their glasses in hand.

"To this upcoming union, may it end our ties to our mistakes of the past," Bardolph gives his toast and drinks. Hadion drinks as well though slowly. This union should indeed help right the wrongs of his past. Neither Odile nor Althea drinks. Bardolph drains his glass. He slams it down but does not break it.

"Are you really happy over this?" Althea questions it.

"Of course. I do not want your sister to run into any of them and have them tell her falsehoods about me. And I never did like Odette. I am happy indeed." Bardolph keeps his grin and takes his seat. He begins to eat. Odile and Althea start to lose their enthusiasm due to Bardolph's then remember they did not need to lose their happiness just because he is happy.

Odile finishes her breakfast and starts to go toward Sommerstern Castle to see what she can help with there. The next day Althea smiles at the little trunk she has packed with dresses borrowed from Odile. Now she knows Hadion will not come until after the wedding ceremony, she has made sure that one will be appropriate for a royal wedding. She has never been to a royal wedding. She has been to a few weddings in Foxglove Grove though.

"I wonder what Odette will wear," Althea thinks of the bride-to-be. She knows no matter what, Odette will look beautiful. Of course, when Althea gets married, she wants to wear a white with golden flowers patterned all over it and pearls on the trim at her bosom. She will have her hair down with some pieces pulled back into braids where white glass flowers with pearls in the centers will be placed. She will look absolutely beautiful walking the aisle to Hadion.

Althea stops fantasizing. She is not getting married and Hadion has made no indication he wants to wed. She should push matrimonial thoughts about herself from her mind.

"Althea." Hadion knocks at the open door.

"Hadion," She turns around and smiles at him.

"I see you packed," He sees her trunk as she approaches her.

"Yes. Odile wanted to last night."

"Ah."

"I'm thrilled to go to Norwin. I have never been there." Althea closes the trunk and moves it from her bed.

"I don't think you will like it there."

"Why do you say that?" Althea looks up to him seeking a reason she should have disliked the island nation.

"I mean I do not want you to like it there," He corrects his statement.

"Why?"

"Because I don't want you to enjoy any place where I am not with you," Hadion admits, making Althea smile.

"I am sure I will miserable without you there with me." Althea plays to his ego. "Will you be unhappy without me here?"

"Utterly," he says and pulls her against him. She giggles.

"Good. Now, is there anything I should take with me to Norwin?"

"Make sure you do not take this off," He touches her necklace. She nods obediently. "Also, I have one more gift for you." He lets her go.

"You do?"

"You cannot go to a royal wedding looking like a peasant. So, I have made you a dress," He smiles and goes out of the room for a moment. He steps back in with a box. He hands it to her for her to open. She lays it on the bed before removing the red ribbon and lid. She pulls out the dress.

The ball gown is a pale yellowish beige. The bottom hem and the neckline are scalloped. The long sleeves end at a point. Golden lines and purple dots and diamonds are painted on the fabric making her dress look like a snowflake. Up her bodice, the pattern that is around her skirt is made small to see what the snowflakes should look like when looked at directly.

"It is beautiful," She states, amazed by it.

"I'm glad you like it. Let me fold it and pack it for you," he takes it from her hands.

"You really do like to make dresses," Althea comments.

"Well, my mother was a dressmaker and I guess making dresses makes me feel...close to her," Hadion speaks softly as he carefully puts the dress away.

"Do you miss her much?"

"Here and there. I see her a lot when I look at Odile." He lets his hands linger on the dress. He closes her trunk and moves it off the bed. He faces Althea again.

"I'm glad you and Odile get along well and our relationship has not caused too much trouble." He brings up the friendship.

"Odile told me she wants me around."

"I am glad we will not have to have a problem then. When we all come back together, I want us to live happily and as peacefully as we can," He pushes back some of Althea's hair.

"But you will help reunite my family first, correct?" Althea reminds him.

"Yes. Of course. Whatever will make you happy, I will do," He promises then kisses her. She wraps her arms around his neck and deepens the kiss. It is easy for him to push her over to fall on top of her bed. Althea is eager to continue her physical education and Hadion is just as eager to teach her. With so much going on, they have only been act upon their affections a few times since their first encounter, but each time has left Althea feeling closer and closer to him. Now that she will be away from him for even this short time, she wants to make sure he knows her feelings are true and she will still be connected to him.

***

Evening comes to the island. Hadion and Althea wait out in front for the approaching Prince Sigfried, Odile, Basil, and the others from Sommerstern Castle. Prince Sigfried brings nothing but himself to the castle. Althea smiles when she sees all come. He hugs Odette and gives her a quick kiss before walking forward. Basil comes to Althea. She hugs her brother.

"Althea, what have you gotten yourself into?"

"Do not worry, Baz. Everything is going to be alright."

"Althea, I can feel your love for him and it's your life but...is this wise? He is a sorcerer and-"

"Baz, he's not like other sorcerers. When I come back, I'll show you," Althea pulls away.

"Follow me," Hadion directs. Into the castle, they go. Prince Sigfried tries not to give away his curiosity as he walks through the castle behind the sorcerer and his apprentice. They reach the dark room where Hadion took Althea the last time they traveled through the portal.

"Have you brought me here to kill me?" Prince Sigfried asks, looking around the dark room with obvious blood stains on the floor.

"Oh, no," Althea laughs and tries to ease the prince, "This is the way we can use the portal."

"Portal? How can you travel by portal when you do not have the Troll Queen's ring?" Prince Sigfried questions.

"How do you know I do not have that ring?" Hadion looks at the prince curiously after he lit the fire in the fireplace.

"It was my parents who were imprisoned by the troll queen before being set free by the troll princess and sent back to Norwin by the magic portal ring," Prince Sigfried brings up his family's history.

"Then the princess came back here and her mother destroyed the ring before my father overtook the island," Hadion finishes the tale.

"That is not the ending I was told," Prince Sigfried mumbles to himself.

"And what end did your parents give? They killed the trolls?" Hadion snickers.

"No. The troll princess gave the ring to my parents so they could hide it away. So that is why I am lost on how you can open a portal without it. It is safe in Norwin."

"I have to open it the old fashion way." Hadion pulls out a knife and cuts his hand. He does not show any indication of pain. He casts the blood into the fire. An oval begins to form.

"Help me take hold of Althea's trunk so she does not have to carry it," Hadion points to the trunk already in the room. The prince lifts it.

"Remember, you are to do nothing to harm her. She is your savior. And you must keep my name out of all of this," Hadion reminds the prince. Althea assumes it must be from a former conversation.

"I will." The prince nods.

"Take his arm, Althea, then walk through together," Hadion continues with his directions. Althea starts to take hold of Prince Sigfried's arm then stops to turn back to Hadion. She kisses him quickly on the lips then scampers back to the prince and takes his arm. They step into the opening of the fire.

Althea blinks several times and shivers as she and Prince Sigfried step onto some wet white sand. She looks behind her and sees the portal close. Althea lets go of the prince and begins to look around her. They are clearly on a beach. The water lapping at their feet is dark and cold. Ahead of them, the sandy beach meets much greenery. In the distance, they can see a great castle. It has many towers with rounded but still pointed tops. The tops remind her of the spiced chocolate droplets some of the bakeries would have in Soldoro. There are many lights lit on the castle.

"Is this your home?" Althea turns to Prince Sigfried.

"Yes." He smiles gazing upon his home. "Let's go."

Prince Sigfried takes her trunk upon his shoulder and starts walking. Althea sticks close to him as she does not know the way to this castle.

"Halt! Who goes there?" A voice barks when the prince and maiden reach the halfway point between the beach and the castle. The bark comes from a knight on a horse who is accompanied by another armed knight on horseback.

"It is I, Prince Sigfried," the prince answers.

"Prince Sigfried?" The talkative knight is surprised by the claim. He brings forth a lantern in his hand and holds it toward the young man. He stares at the dark-skinned man with piercing blue eyes.

"Your Highness!" the knight immediately dismounts and bows before the royal. The other knight joins.

"You may rise." Prince Sigfried motions for them to end their genuflection.

"Your Highness, all believe you are dead. We must bring you to the King and Queen at once!" The knight points back to the castle.

"That is my plan. Take this and tell them to prepare not only my room but one for my guest." Prince Sigfried hands off the trunk to the speaking knight and then nods back to Althea.

"I will do so, your highness!" the knight mounts his steed with the trunk and takes off.

"Take my horse, your highness," The other knight offers his beast.

"I shall pass this offer to my lady. She is far more delicate than I." Prince Sigfried gestures to Althea. The knight and prince help Althea sit on the horse. The knight leads the horse as he walks with the prince toward the castle.

Before they can even enter the gates, more knights come out with a tall blond man in a nightgown who runs toward the traveling group. The bearded man is fast to take Prince Sigfried into his arms. He squeezes him tightly and sheds many tears.

"My son! My son! My son! You are home! I thought you were dead but you are alive! Praise El-Yah! My son is home! He is home!" The man cries in praise.

"Father," Prince Sigfried hugs the king tightly.

"Come inside. Your mother will want to see you. She has been ill since we assumed your ship's wreckage," The king is quick to lead this son forward.

"I will. But a servant must make sure my friend is taken care of as well," Prince Sigfried has not forgotten Althea.

"Your friend?" The king looks to Althea who offers a smile. "Who are you, my dear?"

"Althea." She answers and bows her head to the king.

"She saved my life and helped me to return here." Prince Sigfried is quick to give this fact to his father.

"Oh, my dear. Thank you. Give her the finest room! Anything she asks, give it! Now come, son. We must get to your mother!" The king leads the prince inside. Servants flock to Althea to do as the king commands. They take her from the horse to a room where she is to be pampered.

The king takes his son up into the castle to his royal bedchamber. The king opens the door which is dimly lit by a few candles. Beneath a light blue canopy, is a bed holding a woman propped up on many pillows. Like Prince Sigfried, her skin is dark though at this moment it has become gray and soaked in sweat. Her hair is wrapped up in white silk. Her eyes stay closed while her plump lips stay parted so she may breathe heavily.

"Mother!" Sigfried comes to her side and takes her clammy hand.

"Sigfried?" She opens her eyes but has to blink several times before she can see him.

"Mother." He smiles at her.

"Is it truly you, Sigfried?" She asks tears coming to her eyes at the sight of him.

"It is. I am here, Mother," he kisses the back of her hand. She begins to cry then holds her arms open. He climbs onto the bed and hugs her.

"Oh, Sigfried, my darling boy. I have missed you so terribly," She weeps but color comes back to her as does her health. Her weak arms grow strong and tight.

"I missed you too, Mother," He is sure to tell her as he pulls back so he can breathe.

"What happened? Your ship never returned." She wipes her wet cheeks. The king comes to the bed now and sits.

"There was a terrible storm and the ship was destroyed. I was hurt and floated ashore on an island. I believe it is the exact island you two once were trapped on with the trolls." Prince Sigfried looks from one parent to the other.

"The island east of the sun and west of the moon?" the king leans in.

"Did the trolls help you?" the queen asks.

"No. There are no trolls there now. I was found and saved by the woman I brought back with me - Althea," the prince informs his parents.

"You have brought a woman home?" the queen's eyes widen.

"She is exceptionally beautiful," the king comments.

"Is she?" She looks at her husband.

"Though not as beautiful as you, my love," He is quick to flatter her ego.

"Will you marry her?" the queen turns her eyes back to her son.

"No."

"No? But she saved your life. You owe her a great debt as do we," the king reminds him of his princely duty.

"I have repaid my debt to her and I have found love with another."

"You have?" the queen smiles hearing the word 'love'.

"Yes. Her name is Odette."

"Odette? Bjorn, is not that the name of the princess who went missing from Austvest years ago?" the queen checks with her husband.

"Yes, I believe it is, Dusana," Bjorn nods.

"She is that princess. She was cursed and trapped on the island. She has not aged at all. And despite the circumstances, she is still kind and brave. I have asked her to marry me and she has accepted."

"That is wonderful news, son, but why is she not here? Why bring this other woman and not your betrothed?" King Bjorn questions.

"I have brought Althea as she was the only way I could get home. My darling Odette cannot come yet. The portal I had to come through will only allow a certain number of people at a time and when Odette comes, she will be bringing her ladies-in-waiting."

"When will she be coming?" Queen Dusana inquires.

"She will be coming in five days. And when she comes, I marry her that hour," Prince Sigfried answers.

"Five days! That's barely any time!" Queen Dusana exclaims.

"Well, that is when the portal will open to let her come and I will not delay wedding her," Prince Sigfried is staunch on the timeline.

"Then let me out of this bed. We have much work to do!" Queen Dusana pushes her son out of her way.

"It is late, my love, and you are not well," King Bjorn tries to stop his wife.

"I am well now that my son is home. And? What if it is night? We have a royal wedding to prepare for in less than a week! Do you know how much work that is?" Queen Dusana argues and starts putting on her dressing robe.

"We do not need too grand an affair, Mother. As long as we are wed, that is all that matters. Just having you two there and a priest is enough for me," Prince Sigfried gets off the bed.

"That is sweet, Frieddy, but we are having a royal wedding," Queen Dusana decides and walks away to start calling for servants.

"Mother..." Prince Sigfried starts to try to argue again but his father's hand goes onto his shoulder.

"Do not stop your mother. Here is your first piece of marriage advice, my son. If you marry a strong-willed woman, it is best not to try and stop her." King Bjorn pats his son's shoulder. "You should get some sleep. Tomorrow I am sure your mother will drag you into a thousand activities."

Prince Sigfried nods. His father walks with him to his own bedchamber. And though the prince is in his twenties, his father tucks him into his bed.

"Good night, my boy," King Bjorn smiles then leaves the room. Prince Sigfried exhales as his body eases being back in the room he has had since boyhood. He smiles to himself. Soon Odette will be with him and they will no longer have to be apart ever again.

CHAPTER 50

STELLA

Stella has been aboard the ship *Aello* for weeks, despite the jolly Zilberstein siblings and Tzafrira being able to manipulate the wind and waves to make them go faster. In all these weeks Stella still has yet to have Phila return to her with word from Althea. Focusing on learning magic has done well to distract Stella's mind from dreading the possible reasons for the lack of reply. Of course, she also finds much comfort from her friends and Astrophel.

Prince Astrophel finds he can spend time with his beloved in the night when the others sleep and only he, Stella, and whoever is in charge of sailing the ship are awake. It is at such times in the night when Stella and Astrophel can be alone they speak freely as they did in their dreams.

As Stella stands on the deck of the ship far from the man steering it, she looks out to the dark sky lit up by the numerous stars and moon. Lanterns light up the deck. A hand comes over her eyes startling her.

"Guess who." The voice she loves most asks. She smiles.

"Astro." She turns around to find the smiling prince with one hand behind his back. "What are you hiding?"

"I have something for thee," He brings his hand around to the front. Stella looks down at his hand and finds a spoon made of elder wood there.

"I made it for thee as a sign of my desire to marry thee." He holds it out to her. She takes it in her hand. The wood is carved so the bowl of the spoon is smooth and a heart shape. The stem twisted with large openings giving the illusion of it being knotted. Etched in the twisted stems are small morning glories. At the top is a second heart with a knot making a star in the middle of it.

"I wanted to do a more complicated design but I am not as skilled a craftsman as I wish." He hopes for her not to be disappointed. In truth, the spoon is not as smooth as it could be and there are imperfections in the line up the heart's sides and the evenness of the twisting wood. Stella holds it to her chest.

"It is perfect," She smiles, earning one in return.

"Thou like it?"

"Yes. Of course. You made me a love spoon." She looks down at it again. "Morning glories are my favorite flowers. And I know the hearts mean love and the twisted stem means we are two becoming one but what is about the eight-point star?"

"Well, stars are of great importance to me. It is the symbol of Estellen."

"And you included it in the spoon because..."

"Does thou know why the star is the symbol of Estellen?"

"Because of all the fallen stars in the land."

"Partly but no. When the people came to the Far Lands after being exiled, they thought they might die crossing the Night Sea. During one of the weeks of travel, it stormed every day and every night. The skies and sea were so dark no one knew if it were day or night. People feared they would never see any light again and they would be lost. One night the sky cleared and the people were able to look up and see a single star. Though it was faint and small, it filled the people with hope and joy. They remembered even amid their suffering and dark times there was still light, still hope. When more stars appeared, they remembered their way and sailed to their new home. We keep the star as our symbol to remind us to never lose hope even when it is darkest.

"I do think thy parents named thee aptly for I was stuck alone in darkness and then thou came into my life. Thou gave me hope and now I will follow wherever thou go. Thou art my guiding star of hope, Stella. That is why I included the star," Astrophel explains.

"I shall treasure this always." She keeps the spoon close to her chest.

"Will thou marry me then?"

"Yes." Stella smiles earning a brighter one back from Astrophel. He embraces her.

"I promise to love thee always and forever."

"And I you."

"But now this is made, I thought thou could finish making the All-Cure elixir since thou needed a lovespoon."

"Yes! Thank you. I almost forgot about it. I am trying to think of what is left we need. We have found the stardust, root of aconite, blue pearls, blessed spring water, and mustard seed. Now I have this spoon. We have a plethora of fairies who can bless it! I should go wake Zarin!"

Stella kisses Astrophel on the cheek and then runs off. Stella comes into the cabin where the women sleep in hammocks. She shakes Zarin till she wakes.

"What? What?" Zarin only has one eye open.

"We need to make the elixir! Astro just gave me this lovespoon and two blue pearls so I can mix the elixir. We have everything so let's make it now!" Stella gushes.

"Can it not wait till the morning?" Zarin yawns and rubs her eyes.

"Let us not waste any time. Isn't it better to do what we can today since we never know what tomorrow holds? Come on, Zarin." Stella's high energy is not matched by the sleepy, golden-eyed woman.

"Fine," Zarin slips out of her hammock. Zarin and Stella begin to gather the ingredients for the elixir from their bags.

"Let's go up to the deck," Zarin suggests to not bother the sleeping Tzafrira and Anemone.

Coming up to the deck, they are quickly noticed by the man steering the ship. He winks one of his blue eyes at them.

"Good evening, ladies," He smiles at them.

"Good evening, Nereo," they respond but pay him little attention.

"What are you doing back out here, Stella? I thought you were done for the night when you ran away from your pretty boy?" Nereo keeps talking to Stella who kneels to the ground with Zarin.

"I didn't run away from him. I just went to get Zarin," Stella answers Nereo.

"Oh, did you two come out to spend the night with me?" He wiggles his eyebrows. The women roll their eyes.

"We would hate to distract you from your duty, Nereo," Stella speaks to the man without looking at him since she is more interested in what she and Zarin are doing.

"I don't mind the distraction. I'd rather look at your bodies over the heavenly ones," he remarks.

"Is that so?" Prince Astrophel approaches Nereo with a serious expression.

"Ah, not this guy," Nereo groans to himself.

"These women are busy at work and do not need thy special attention," Prince Astrophel begins to admonish the sailor. Nereo is forced to listen to Astrophel while the women work on the elixir.

They take out a jar she has already filled with the water from the blessed spring. Stella adds in the blue pearls that she crushes in her hands while Zarin puts in the root of wolfsbane. Stella adds the dash of Stardust before lifting her love spoon.

"I mix this then you will bless it, right?" Stella checks with Zarin who has her spell book with her.

Stella takes the spoon and begins to stir the ingredients together in the jar. The liquid is a dark purple and sparkles faintly from the stardust. As Stella stirs, Zarin puts her hands toward the jar. She looks closely at her book then closes her eyes and opens her mouth to repeat the words she read.

"What are they doing over there?" Nereo looks around Astrophel at the young women. Prince Astrophel looks over his shoulder to see the women at the jar beginning to glow. Zarin's words become louder making the liquid in the jar glow more. She finally stops and opens her eyes. She smiles in delight at the luminous liquid. Stella stops stirring. Astrophel is quick to come to the women.

"We have done it!" Stella squeals and shares a hug with Zarin.

"Seal it and store it safely," Prince Astrophel is fast to advise. Zarin puts the lid on to secure it. Stella tears up happily and takes Astrophel's hand.

"We should get some rest," Zarin looks to Stella who nods.

"Yes," Stella finally agrees. She leaves her prince and goes back with Zarin. Zarin tucks away the jar of the elixir and climbs back into her hammock. Stella gets hers after tucking her cleaned-off spoon into her pocket. She cannot lose her smile. She is just another step closer to restoring her brother.

Even in the morning when the sky is dark with storm clouds and the wind rocks the boat back and forth, Stella does not lose her joy. She and Zarin proudly show the elixir to Sir Artegal and Tyr.

"This stuff will cure any curse?" Tyr looks at the jar of bright, sparkling liquid.

"Yes." Zarin nods.

"But how do you know you didn't mess up?"

"Well, we're not going to curse someone to find out if it works or not," Stella huffs at Tyr's doubt.

"Well, we could curse someone for a moment and try to drink and see if it works," Tyr suggests, earning a look of disgust from the women and a smack to the back of the head from Sir Artegal.

"What? It's a legitimate idea!" Tyr defends his suggestion.

"Woah!" The exclamation comes as they all feel a large bump against the ship. Stella grabs onto the prince who grabs his knight who catches himself against the wall of the room they are in. Tyr catches Zarin as they fall together. Fortunately, Zarin does not drop the jar.

"What was that?" Stella looks at the others around her.

"Maybe the water is getting rougher. I should put this away," Zarin gets up. She is quick to find her bag to put the jar away. She comes back to the group only for another bump to send her and the others to the floor.

"What is that?" Zarin asks this time. They regain their footing and start-up to the main deck. On top they see the black clouds pouring out rain, waves rising and curling before crashing, and the sailors trying to keep them from losing control of the water. They cling to the wall where their door is and look out at the soaked deck.

"Captain Boreas." Sir Artegal walks toward the small captain. His voice is barely heard over the howling wind.

"Sir Artegal," The captain tries to approach the knight but the strong wind and rain almost make him fall.

"Something is hitting the boat. Is it a whale?" Sir Artegal has to yell out his question to the senior of the ship.

"A what?" Captain Boreas yells back as he has not yet reached the knight.

"Is it a whale?"

"A what?" the captain can still not hear.

"A-" Before Sir Artegal can finish the ship is bumped once more sending almost all to the floor. They all slide as the ship begins to turn on its side. It rocks back to his even but bumpy self. Sir Artegal reaches Captain Boreas with much effort.

"Is a whale hitting us?" Sir Artegal is finally able to make out his question to the captain.

"I am not sure. I have never been this far north into the Endless Ocean. I do not know what lurks here," he admits.

"We need to get below deck," Tzafrira has reached the knight and captain with Notos and Anemone.

"None of our wind magic is working," Anemone informs them loudly.

"We need to get the boys to come with us," Boreas looks to his brother who nods in agreement. As Sir Artegal and the women start back to where Sir Artegal's group is, the Zilberstein brothers try to gather the sailors.

Before any can reach their destination a sharp, shrill scream and a bump draws all attention to the side of the ship. Upon and out of the water rises a large sea serpent.

Scales of emerald green, open jaws with teeth like a hundred swords, and eyes blood red, the beast stares down at the people on the boat. Its body tightens around the ship making the wood break.

"Leviathan," Tzafrira whispers to herself. Sir Artegal draws his sword in preparation.

"Get inside!" Sir Artegal shouts to Astrophel and the others. The prince is quick to open the door and push Stella and Zarin inside with him.

"Do not lose courage now, boys. Grab a weapon," Captain Boreas yells to his crew. Some of the sailors grab the cutlasses on them while others run to fetch harpoons. Captain Boreas and Notos draw swords while Anemone and Tzafrira start back for the door. Tyr stays glued to the wall with his eyes on the serpent.

Lightning flashes and down comes the open mouth of the creature. As it dives the men ready themselves to fight the beast. It tries to gobble up the men but they strike at it with swords and harpoons.

"Ahhhh!" Neilus screams as the beast catches him in his teeth. The serpent rises and throws Neilus into the air. The men try to cut at the beast's underbelly but their weapons fail. Its scales are too hard for mere metal.

Sir Artegal sprouts his great wings and takes to the sky. He catches Neilus and slashes at the serpent's open mouth though it causes it no pain. Sir Artegal goes down with the wounded sailor who can only lay there bleeding out from the punctures made by the fangs. Sir Artegal begins trying to heal him.

The serpent dives down again, its sights set on Sir Artegal. Sir Artegal leaves Neilus and takes to the sky to draw the attention back up from the ship. The serpent's body still crashes into the ship causing it to concave and start turning on its side. Some sailors fall into the water.

The Zilbersteins take to chanting and moving their arms. They try to move the wind to attack the beast and blow it back away from the ship and the flying knight. The sailors continue to try to hurt the beast with their weapons while Tzafrira attempts to drag the injured Neilus back away from the fighting.

Inside the cracking ship, Stella, Zarin, and Astrophel struggle to not fall with each bump and twist of the ship. They hold tightly to anything looking like a permanent structure.

"Zarin, get to the horses and unicorns. Free them in case the ship begins to fill with water," Stella charges Zarin with the task. She takes off toward the cargo storage.

"I will join the others on deck and fight," Astrophel states.

"I will go get my pipe to help," Stella starts to go to the cabin where the women sleep.

"Stella," Astrophel grabs her hand.

"Yes?"

He pulls her to him and kisses her quickly. She blinks several times after he pulls away.

"I needed a bit of courage," he smiles then takes off to the deck.

Stella maneuvers to the room where her pipe is hidden in the bags. She takes it out and is ready to start back when the roof caves in with the belly of the serpent. The ship splits with the beast's body which is quick to go into the water after its destruction. Stella feels the floor tilt and the room begins to take on water. She slides but takes hold of one of the hammocks fastened to the roof. She sees Zarin's bag of books and the jarred elixir sliding toward the water. She knows she needs to reach it. She extends her leg and tries to use her foot to get to the strap. Tzafrira and Neilus fall from the upper deck and to the edge of the flooring sinking. Neilus's lifeless body slides away into the water. Tzafrira is just far enough that if she grabs Stella's foot, she can be drawn up but she is also just far enough away Tzafrira's small arms will not be able to reach the bag and Stella at the same time.

"Help me! I can't swim!" Tzafrira looks up at Stella as she claws at the wooden floor that keeps dipping. Stella looks between the elixir and Tzafrira.

"Grab my foot!" Stella yells, moving her foot away from the strap and to the woman. Tzafrira grabs on and Stella strains to pull Tzafrira to her. Tzafrira grabs Stella's dress and gets to her feet. Stella watches as the bag holding the books and elixir slide into the dark water.

"Let's get out of here before we drown," Tzafrira fights against gravity and succeeds in making it to the door. Stella does too. The hallway has turned on its side but they walk quickly to a window.

They climb out and to the top of the back of the ship that is in the air. Stella looks out and sees many of the sailors in the water swimming away from the sinking ship and toward Zarin who clings to the horses and unicorns swimming in the water. She looks to the other side of the ship where the Zilbersteins and Astrophel stand. Astrophel's drawn sword is ablaze. In the sky, Sir Artegal still fights the beast.

"Tyr! Tyr!" Stella calls out not seeing the other members of their party.

"I am here," Tyr's reply is faint to Stella's ears. She looks over the edge where she and Tzafrira are to see Tyr clinging to the ship.

"Tyr, take my hand," Stella bends over to reach toward him. He does not reach back.

"Tyr, I need you to take my hand," She insists. He finally takes hold of her and she pulls him up with Tzafrira's help. Once Tyr is aboard, she brings her pipe to her lips. She takes several breaths before blowing into it. She plays the song she had played for the mermaids. She plays and plays but notices no change in the actions of the sea beast.

"Try another song," Tyr encourages her. She nods and changes the song. She tries three different melodies before finally finding a noise seeming to at least irritate the beast.

The sea serpent closes its eyes and screeches hearing the noise. Stella stands and plays louder. She plays and watches as the serpent begins to sway back and forth. It begins to sink back into the water as well. The sinking ship on which she stands shakes and causes her to lose her balance and fall over. Fortunately, Tyr catches her but unfortunately, her pipe flies out of her hands and thus the song stops. The sea serpent rises again and shoots straight for Stella, Tyr, and Tzafrira.

"No!" Astrophel cries seeing the attack. Stella clings to Tyr and braces herself. He pushes her away. She opens her eyes and finds herself in shock.

Tyr's body is no longer the manly one she has come to know. Instead, he is covered in black, white, and orange scales. His body is elongated to be like a serpent but his hands and feet have become huge with talons. His face has grown a giant snout with white whiskers. His eyes are large but still brown. He opens his mouth and shows his ivory teeth. He dips down into the water before shooting straight up. His teeth are buried in the neck of the serpent that nearly snatches Stella and Tzafrira.

The serpent hollers out but begins to twist its body around Tyr's new one. Tyr claws at the constricting body around him. He bites harder while he tries to push out of the serpent's hold.

Sir Artegal's armor and body change and distort as he goes from a flying knight to a flying lion. He flies down to Prince Astrophel who climbs upon his back. They fly toward the serpent fighting against Tyr.

Astrophel slashes at the beast with his fiery sword. The beast thrashes and the flaming steel cuts through his armor of scales. The serpent loosens just long enough for Tyr to escape its grasp. Tyr takes to the sky the dives back down to attack again. Working together the dragon, flying lion, and prince battle the serpent.

The Serpent evades a few hits but takes many blows. Sir Artegal and Prince Astrophel near the serpent as they intend to strike the head. But the tail of the beast comes from the sea and takes hold of Sir Artegal. It brings the men of Estellen toward its open jaws.

Tyr comes between the serpent and its meal but becomes caught about his neck by the creature. Astrophel jumps off Sir Artegal's back and onto Tyr's caught neck. He runs up the serpent's face before plunging his sword into its head. The serpent releases Sir Artegal and Tyr. It sways then begins falling backward. Astrophel pulls out his sword and holsters it. As the Sea Serpent falls, Sir Artegal swoops in and grabs Astrophel. The serpent falls and sinks back into his home.

"Stella!" Zarin calls Stella who stares at the fallen serpent. Stella sees a small row boat that had once been on the side of the ship is afloat in the water and now holds the living sailors and Zarin. The horses and unicorns swim independently in the water.

"Get in the boat!" Zarin waves.

"Take Tzafrira first," Stella points to the smaller woman. The boat comes closer. Stella holds Tzafrira's hand and helps lower her to Nereo who takes the little woman into the boat.

Stella looks back at the air at Tyr's dragon body. He begins to fall forward in his great form but in an instant, he is returned to his human form. He is limp and bleeding greatly.

"Catch him!" Stella cries out. Sir Artegal flies and Astrophel can take hold of the wounded Tyr. Sir Artegal flies the men down to the ship. The prince and unconscious Tyr are welcomed. Zarin immediately begins trying to heal Tyr while Astrophel removes his shirt to cover Tyr's shivering, naked body. Sir Artegal brings over the Zilbersteins while in his flying lion form before returning to his still armored-covered human form. He retracts his wings and sits on the boat breathing deeply from his fatigue. He closes his eyes to rest for a moment. There is a moment of rest for all.

CHAPTER 51

ALTHEA

On the island hidden from all, Odette stares at herself in the mirror. She has finished dressing in her bridal attire. Her ball gown is the grandest she has ever worn or seen. She is surprised at all the work. She has a large crinoline to keep the dress large and puffed out to give her a bell-shaped skirt. Her bodice and underskirt are made with delicate silk. Beautiful lace work goes from the hem up and through the bodice. The top of the bodice is scalloped and depicts crescent moons. Her sleeves are sheer but are spotted with small diamonds and pearls. At her shoulders, there are clusters of diamonds and pearls to give her a cap sleeve look before it goes down into the sheer ones. Her split overskirt is made of white swan feathers. They go from hip to hem and even throughout her bridal train which is several feet long. Despite its structure and grandeur, she does not feel much weight upon her.

Odette's hair has been left to run down her back as a golden waterfall. She still wears her crown of protection. Her feet are covered in the most comfortable, white, silk slippers.

"You are radiant," Odile comments, staring at her mother.

"Thank you," Odette looks back at Odile in the reflection of the mirror. Odile like the other swan maidens is dressed in cream-colored gowns with beautifully embroidered orange, yellow, and blue florals. The sleeves open like bells at her wrist then cling to her upper arms. A gold band separates the lower sleeve from the little puffs on her shoulders. Around her waist is a golden belt. Her dress opens to show her simple yellow kirtle. She is wearing some blue slippers. Her hair is kept up, bound by golden bands.

"You look dazzling as well, Odile," Odette compliments her daughter.

"Thank you. But today is not about me. It's all about you, Mother. I am so happy for you," Odile smiles. Odette turns around to face Odile directly.

"You are?" Odette comes and takes hold of Odile's hands.

"Why would I not be?"

"I was afraid you would be upset I am leaving this place...and I am leaving you," Odette brings up the sensitive topic.

"I am sad you are going but I am happy you are finally going to be free and happy. Besides, once I am of age, I will come and visit as long as I like," Odile brings up her plans.

"You better come or I shall be most unhappy," Odette claims. Odette brings one hand to cup Odile's cheek. Her eyes fill with tears.

"I don't know how I can go even that long without you, Odile."

"You'll forget me as soon as you lay eyes on your prince," Odile jokes.

"No. No. My darling girl, I can never forget my greatest treasure."

"Treasure?" Odile scoffs.

"Of all things El-Yah has given me, you are the greatest gift. If I have ever made it seem like you were less than that, I am sorry," Odette apologizes and a tear starts rolling from her eye.

"Do not cry! You cannot arrive red-eyed at your wedding. I know you love me and I love you. I always have and always will," Odile wipes at the tear.

"Oh, Odile," Odette pulls her daughter into a hug. "I love you. I love you."

"I love you too. But let me go. I do not want to ruin your dress," Odile pulls back. The daughter fixes the dress as Odette wipes at her face.

A knock comes to the door. Odette bids the knocker enter. Hadion walks inside dressed in a black doublet with silver peacock feathers embroidered on it. His undershirt is black as well. He wears black breeches with knee-long black boots. His black hair has been combed. He stares at Odette.

"Oh, Hadion, is there something wrong?" Odette asks.

"No. No. I was just coming to let you know everything is ready for your departure," He states.

"Oh, I forgot a necklace. I will meet you at the boat!" Odile excuses herself and runs out of the room. She must go quickly if she wants to get to her room at the main castle before it is time to leave given they are still at Sommerstern Castle. She leaves Hadion and Odette alone in the room together.

"You look...stunning," he compliments her.

"Thank you but the dress is all your work," She states looking down at her dress rather than at him.

"My handiwork is nothing compared to your natural beauty." He does not take the compliment.

"You flatter me," She keeps her eyes off him.

"As I should. Now, do remember once off this island your crown of protection will not protect you anymore."

"Oh, yes. You told me."

They stand in silence.

"Do you..." Odette starts then stops.

"Do I what?"

"Do you promise you will let Odile come to see me after all this?" Odette looks up.

"If she wants to after she comes of age, I will not stop her."

"Thank you."

They stand in silence again.

"Odette," Hadion breaks the silence this time.

"Yes?"

"I know these past few years you and I...we haven't...we haven't been on good terms but I...I..." He keeps pausing.

"You what?" She looks at him curious as to what he may say.

"I...I am glad you have found love and he will make you happy since I could not."

"I am glad too. And I am glad you have found someone to love you as well." Odette brings up Althea. "Please, don't break her heart like you broke mine."

Hadion shakes his head as he does not want to do that. They share a smile between them.

"It is time I believe. I will get your ladies to carry your train," He leaves the room. Soon many of Odette's pledged ladies-in-waiting come to help carry her massive dress. Down and out of Sommerstern Castle, they go and start for the nearest beach. It is a great walk but none care for they know soon they will be free of this island.

Reaching the moonlit beach, all the maidens and Odette begin to board the swan-shaped boat that awaits them. Hadion had told Odette he had charmed it to sail without a captain. She sees all her dearest friends around her before noticing Odile is not there.

"Where is Odile?" Odette asks her ladies. They look around and call out for the other girl.

"I'm here!" She yells as she runs toward the boat. She passes Hadion and boards the ship.

"You are all aboard and ready?" Hadion asks once Odile is on the boat. Each maiden looks to see if anyone else is missing.

"We are ready," Odette answers. Hadion spreads his wings and takes to the sky. He flies out to sea. With great skill he causes fire to appear on the water. The flames are green. He cuts his hand and gives blood to it. He chants over and over as the boat begins to sail from the beach out to the sea on its own. The women hold onto each other tightly as they sail toward the green fire on the water. An oval starts to form. Hadion chants until the swan ship passes through. He stops. The fire disappears and Hadion is left alone above the sea.

On the beaches of Norwin, fairy knights wait for the arrival of their prince's bride. The prince wanted to be there to greet her but tradition would not have it. And the concern the prince might be set up for an attack at sea by a sorcerer from the House of Urs was another reason for him to be forced to wait in the crystal garden with his parents as well. Althea was allowed to go with the knights to help identify the bride.

A bright flash of light and the appearance of a swan-like ship carrying many women cause all knights to be on guard. The ship lands on the beach and the knight surrounds it cautiously. Seeing all the maidens and the beautiful woman in white, the knights look to Althea for confirmation of whether or not this is the right ship. Althea smiles and nods seeing Odette and Odile among the women.

Odette and her ladies leave the ship. All keep Odette's dress lifted in their hands to not let it be soiled. Althea is quick to hug the bride.

"You are stunning!" Althea compliments the bride.

"Thank you. Where is Sigfried?" Odette asks after her intended.

"He is waiting, eagerly," Althea answers, "Follow me."

The group travels with many knights surrounding the new hoard of women. As they come to the castle grounds, all look on in amazement at the grandeur of the place. As they reach the hedges separating them from the crystal gardens, Althea has them stop. The knights disperse to cover other perimeters. The women finally let go of Odette's dress. They fix it so it has no flaw then they fix their own.

"I will go ahead and let Prince Sigfried know you are coming. You will know to start coming when you hear the music," Althea tells Odette, then goes on into the ceremony space.

The crystal garden is a stunning feature of the Norwin castle grounds. There are numerous sculptures made of crystal throughout the manicured lawn with flowers at their bases. The sculptures vary from beasts to people. All around, Queen Dusana made sure to have lanterns hung and lit. The crystals shine in the light. There is a long path from the outer hedge to the center of the garden. At the center is a pond with a great fountain spurting water in the middle. Before it is a grand gazebo made of silver and glass. It is so large it could be mistaken for a house. It is filled with people in wooden pews that were brought in. To one side are two thrones where King Bjorn and Queen Dusana sit. Prince Sigfried stands at the end of the aisle along with a priest of El-Yah.

Prince Sigfried is dressed in a white linen vyshyvanka with blue embroidery. His white linen pants have blue embroidery on their side as they go into his white, knee-high boots. Despite standing for over an hour before his guests, he is calm. He knows the one he loves is on her way to him. Seeing Althea coming down the aisle with a smile, he starts to smile. He knows Odette is here. Althea takes a seat as the prince signals to the band nearby it is time.

"The music is starting!" some of the maidens squeal in delight.

"Line up properly, girls. We must make sure we do not disappoint." Darya takes on her role as a leader. The many women straighten up and pair off so that they begin. The music is slow, sweet, and has a consistent enough beat the bridesmaids know when to step.

Darya sends them two by two around the hedge as she wants them to be perfect so she can be the last one with Odette and Odile. When it comes to her turn, Darya turns to kiss Odette on the cheek then goes around the hedge leaving the mother and daughter alone.

Odette smiles and takes a deep breath as she waits for her turn. She cannot believe in a few moments, she will be with Sigfried, free of her curse, and free to live.

"Mother," Odile turns to Odette.

"Yes, Odile?"

"May I have one more hug before we go down?" Odile asks.

"Of course," Odette opens her arms to Odile and wraps them around her.

"I just have one more thing to say to you," Odile whispers.

"What is it?"

"Goodbye."

"What?" Odette pulls back only to feel a sharp pain in her back. She cannot scream as the air is taken from her lungs. Odette looks at Odile confused, shocked, and betrayed. Odile grins devilishly at the bride. She brings forth the weapon. It is a black blade. Odile plunges it into Odette's chest. The bride falls to the ground. With a shimmy, Odile changes and becomes Odette. Quickly she turns the hedge and begins walking down the aisle.

All rise as they see the bride approaching. Many whisper about her beauty including the astonished king and queen. Althea is not surprised by the beauty of the bride but is surprised Odile has not come down yet. Perhaps she was not truly ready to see her mother marry another man.

When Odette reaches Prince Sigfried, he takes her hands. The priest beckons for all to sit. As Althea sits, she feels her back hit the hands of someone who must have been grabbing hold of her chair. She looks back to whisper an apology but is surprised when she sees a familiar face there.

Thuban?

"It's alright," the man behind her forgives Althea and moves his hand. Althea faces the front.

Surely, that man is not Thuban. I must just be seeing things.

"As per the request of the prince, we shall have no readings, songs, or a great to do. The couple wants only to make their vows," The priest informs all the guests. Since most have been waiting for at least an hour, they are more than happy to skip to the vows. The bridesmaids are eager and lean toward the couple in excited anticipation.

"I take you to be mine and I will be yours until death parts us," Odette keeps her vow short and simple.

Prince Sigfried smiles at the words then clears his throat before beginning his. He holds Odette's hand and turns toward the crowd.

"I, Prince Siegfried of Norwin, make a vow of everlasting love to my bride before the whole world. From this day forth I shall never love another and will be hers until death," He ends and looks to Odette who grins.

"By the power vested in me, I pronounce you man and wife. You may seal your union with a kiss," the priest smiles. Prince Sigfried is quick to lean forward and kiss his new wife. Cheers begin but then fade. Prince Sigfried pulls back confused as to why there are no sounds of joy. He looks before him and sees it is no longer Odette before him but instead, it is Odile. He pushes her back horrified.

"What are you doing? Where is Odette?" He looks panicked for his true bride.

"Why do you care? I am your wife now," Odile laughs.

"No. No. Odette is my wife."

"No. I am and I am the one to whom you have made this everlasting vow," She snickers.

"No. No. That vow is for Odette."

"What is going on?" King Bjorn stands up.

"Odile, what are you doing?" Althea stands as well.

"Where is Odette?" The swan maidens ask each other. Darya runs back down the aisle.

A shriek of horror comes from Darya by the hedge. All turn their eyes to see Darya on her knees by Odette who is bleeding out.

"What have you done?" Prince Sigfried screams at Odile before turning to go run for Odette but Odile grabs his arm and holds onto it tightly.

"You're not going anywhere, hubby," Odile's voice drops to a low octave.

"Let me go, you vile wretch!"

"Do you not want to be married to me?" Odile asks.

"Of course not! Let me go!" He roars.

"Then I guess it is time for us to part," Odile says and from nothing produces a black sword of shadow which she uses to run through the chest of the prince. Cries of horror escape Queen Dusana and other onlookers. King Bjorn draws his sword as do many in the crowd. One of the musicians blows his horn calling which causes the fairy knights to turn and come running. Odile pulls out the sword from Prince Sigfried's chest. It is then that Odile shifts once more. No longer is she a young maiden. Now she is Bardolph.

King Bjorn comes to Bardolph with a sword in hand. He starts to attack but Bardolph's shadow sword stops the king's. Those armed in the crowd start to head toward Bardolph to protect their king. Althea stands with them. It is then she sees more standing with shadow swords including the man behind her. She knows now it is Thuban. She also begins to see more people she recognizes from the Blue Moon Ball. She does not know how they slipped into this wedding. Without hesitation, a fight begins.

Fire, ice, earth, and blade are used to kill. Those without magic are soon slaughtered as are those without weapons like the bridesmaids. Althea tries to fight against the sorcerers who have slipped in along with the fairy knights who are the only ones who stand a chance against the magical foe.

Althea is blown back as she faces a woman twice her size. Though not hurt thanks to her necklace, she is stunned. She starts to get up and sees her opponent has been struck down by another. Althea looks around at the horrible scene before her. King Bjorn and Queen Dusana fight Bardolph over the body of their son. The king with his sword and the queen with magic. The bridesmaids lie dead on the floor with so many others. More and more of the wielders of shadow swords prevail. She looks back toward Darya who holds onto Odette. She sees now Odette holding Darya's hand.

Is she alive? If she is, she will not be for long. Bardolph's forces will soon win. Althea looks back to the brawling and trembles. *There is no way to win. There is no way.*

"No!" King Bjorn's cry draws Althea's eyes to him again. The queen has fallen. It is now Bardolph that swings his sword and removes the king's head from his shoulders. Althea loses her breath. She watches Bardolph pick up the crown from the severed head and place it on his head. He walks back up the aisle, passing those still trying to fight. He approaches Darya and Odette. Darya stands seeing Bardolph. She stands so her body is a shield of protection for Odette. Darya opens her mouth to speak but Bardolph beheads her. Bardolph kneels by Odette. He raises his sword to strike but stops. He smiles then stands and walks away. Althea hears laughter and cheers. She sees that all who had tried to protect and defend Norwin are dead while Thuban and others like him are not.

What am I to do? Will they try to kill me too since I am fighting for the prince's side?

Thuban looks over at Althea. The others notice her too. One takes a few steps as if he wants to come for her. Thuban puts out his hand to stop this man.

"Leave her. She's Hadion's girl. She knows the plot," Thuban says loudly. The others smile and nod their heads to her before walking off with Thuban toward the way Bardolph.

Althea falls to her knees.

This was all a plot; a plot among sorcerers; a plot of which Bardolph AND Hadion were part of this. They planned this all along. All along...

CHAPTER 52

ALTHEA

Odette gasps for air but her lungs are rapidly filling with her blood. She coughs only splattering blood out of her mouth as she does. Tears spill onto her pale face. Her ears register the din rising outside among the terrified people. Her eyes are slowly losing their focus and light. Darya comes to her and holds her in her arms. She holds Odette's hand.

"Odette, hold on. Please, hold on, Odette. Stay with me," Darya pleads with the fallen princess.

"Darya," Odette croaks.

"Please, stay with me. Don't leave me, Odette." Darya's tearful demands are hard for Odette to hear. Darya lies Odette on the ground. Odette turns her head and helplessly watches Darya lose her head.

Bardolph kneels. She does not understand what he is doing here. She can barely see him.

"Hadion sends his well wishes," Bardolph laughs then leaves her.

*Is this how it ends? Me lying on the ground bleeding out from the wounds inflicted by my daughter? Oh, Odile...why? Why have you done this? Why did you do this to me and Sigfried? Oh, Sigfried...*Her heart weeps. The prince lived up to his title. He was everything she had dreamed of as a child. He was exactly what Hadion had told her he would be: gentle, princely, brave, and earnest. He loved her. He loved her truly and she loves him. She loves with every beat of her now failing heart.

"Odette. Odette," Her name is called but it is not from Sigfried's lips. Her eyes turn as she feels arms begin to lift her body from the ground. It is not Sigfried or one of her loyal but now dead swan maidens.

"H-Hadion?" She recognizes the man with the kaleidoscope eyes. There is no relief in seeing him.

"Odette. What happened?" He dares to ask. He picks up her body and his hand goes to where her wound is. Odette's face contorts to display her anger and disgust. She feels some air left in her lungs.

"Y-you...you betrayed me...again...and you...you had Odile...betray me too," she sobs thinking of her daughter.

How could the child I loved so much destroy everything?

"What? Odile? What did Odile do?" Hadion genuinely appears confused.

"She-she killed...everyone...and now I...I am dying. She-she did this," Odile struggles to speak.

"But Odile would-would never do this."

"B-B-Bardolph said...you send your well wishes...You betrayed me again, Hadion," Odile feels another wave of tears coming.

"No. No. Odette, I didn't. I swore I never would again," Hadion caresses her face.

"But why would Odile-" Odette starts to ask but coughs more causing blood to splatter on Hadion.

"Let me heal you." He presses his hand harder into her chest.

"No. Take me to Sigfried," She orders weakly. Hadion lifts her and carries her carefully down the aisle to the prince who lies on the ground dead. He lowers himself and her so she may look upon him. More tears come.

"Sigfried," She starts to choke. She turns her eyes back to Hadion. "I want to be with Sigfried. Let me die and be with him."

"But-"

"Let me die...I suffered...for so long...please...let me be at peace..." Odette begs. Hadion moves his hand from the chest he has tried to keep healing to honor her request.

"Odette, I know Odile did not do this. She loves you too much," Hadion tries to speak of their daughter's innocence.

"Then who?"

Hadion pauses then his eyes grow dark in the knowledge of the truth.

"Bardolph," Hadion answers. Odette coughs again.

"Yes. He...he must have...cursed her..." Odette agrees.

"I am sorry, Odette. I am sorry," he repeats. Odette stares up at the man who in more ways than one is responsible for her years of suffering and now her death. His eyes, the ones she had thought so mesmerizing in her youth, are brimming with tears. His face is desperate and anguished. She has not seen this side of him since the night she first told him she hated him, the same night he prophesied about Sigfried. She may not have all her senses about her but there is something she senses from him. She knows now more truly than ever the truth of his heart.

"I forgive you," her voice is fading.

Hadion does not speak but sheds a tear.

"Odette, I love you. I always have and I always will," he confesses. Odette smiles then starts coughing more allowing more blood to come out. Hadion holds her as she wheezes and chokes. As she sees her struggling, Hadion brings his hand to her head. With a quick motion, he ends her suffering. Her body lays limp in his arms. He lays her down next to Prince Sigfried's body. He waves his hand over her face and the blood is removed leaving behind her beautiful face. He pushes back her hair so she can see her more clearly. He takes her hand and kisses it. Hadion stares at her for a moment longer. He lowers the hand and lays it on Prince Sigfried's. He wipes away his tears. Back on his feet, Hadion turns his back to the lovers.

Hadion looks around at the massacred wedding guests. He looks for Odile and Althea. He sees many blondes but none are the right maiden. He takes to the sky so he can search for the young women.

From his high position, Hadion can see as sorcerers are attacking and killing more knights around the area. He sees people running from the castle screaming. Some are slaughtered and some are corralled. He finally sees Althea who is running toward the beach. He flies straight toward Althea. He lands in front of her just as she comes onto the beach. Her eyes are red and her face is covered in tears with splatters of blood. Her dress is also ruined with splashes of blood. He sees she still wears her necklace so the blood must not be hers.

"Althea." He reaches for her.

"Don't touch me!" She slaps his hands away.

He hears the voices of people coming. He does not know if it is a friend or foe. He starts a fire and sheds blood.

"Come, Althea." He holds his hand out to her. She shakes her head. He grabs her and drags her through the portal.

"Get off me!" She barks at him and pulls her arm from him once they are back in the dark tower room of the castle.

"Althea, what is it?" He looks at her confused.

"What? I know the truth now, Hadion. I know."

"You know what?"

"I know you lied. I know you used us. You and Bardolph used me," She shouts at him.

"What are you talking about?"

"Don't play stupid, Hadion." She hisses at him.

"I don't know what you think I have done. Tell me!" He steps closer to her.

"You and Bardolph planned everything. You only pretended to release Odette and the others so Bardolph could disguise himself as Odile and kill everyone. Your friends were able to slip into the wedding as guests so they could help him. Is that why you were visiting with them at the ball? You let me come so I could keep on the illusion this was all amicable. You two did all of this to take over this land and hurt Odette. I thought you loved her. I thought you loved me. I see now it was all a lie. You are using me since you couldn't use Odette anymore and you're used me as a pawn in this game," Althea lets him know what she believes.

"I had no part in this, Althea."

"Don't play stupid with me, Hadion. You are not so foolish to not know of the coup your son and friends planned."

"I am. I had no part in it, Althea. I was just trying to make you happy."

"Liar!" She screams at him.

"I am not lying!" He grabs her arms forcibly.

"Let me go!" She kicks him in the crotch. He stumbles backward. She takes the opportunity to open the door and run out. Hadion recovers and chases her down the stairs. He keeps calling her name.

Althea makes it into a flat hallway when Hadion catches her. She tries to get away but he tackles her and pins her to the floor.

"Let me go! Let me go!" She thrashes. He slaps her, stunning her but not hurting her.

"Listen to me. I had no part in this. I never would do this. I loved Odette. I was ready for her to go with Sigfried. And I want no rule of Norwin. This is all reeks of Bardolph," He tries to reason with her.

"Then why did they spare me and say it is because I am yours? Why would they do that unless you are a part of their group?"

"They may think I am but I am not. Althea, I am just as surprised and horrified as you."

"No. You're lying to me now. You've always been lying to me," her voice breaks with the claim.

"I haven't."

"I don't believe you," she sobs.

Hadion stares into her red and wet eyes. She looks at him greatly pained and disgusted. He lets her go and sits up and off her. Althea sits up.

"You will never trust me again, will you?" He asks.

She swallows the lump in her throat.

"Then I suppose there is no reason for us to be together anymore," He stands up. Althea stands as well. There is an awkward coldness between them now. It is so different from the heat that threw them together.

"Get your brother and then I'll send you through a portal," Hadion speaks first.

"You're going to have us go?" Althea asks.

"Yes. But you will not trust me for it, so do what you want," he waves his hand flippantly. Althea is hesitant to start walking.

"Go!" He orders.

Althea holds herself as she walks away. She is chilled to the bone. She cannot unsee all that happened at the wedding. She cannot unhear the cries and screams. She cannot unlearn what she believes to be the truth. Her poor friends... How could she let herself be so blind? How could she be so stupid? She should have never let herself fall in love with him.

"What is that?" Althea looks ahead as she nears the entry hall of the castle. A lump of fabric lies on the floor. The closer she comes the clearer she sees it is not just a lump of fabric. It is Odile on the floor with blood coming from her. Althea comes to her knees.

"Odile! Odile!" She tries to shake the pale girl. Odile's breathing is shallow and faint. Althea sees Odile lying with her hands on her side from where the blood oozes.

"Help! Help!" Althea screams over and over not sure of what has happened or about what to do.

Hadion at first appears walking then seeing the girls, he runs. He falls and slides on his knees to their sides.

"What has happened?" He starts checking for Odile's pulse.

"I don't know. I just found her like this," Althea answers.

"Odile, what happened?" He leans so he can look at her face. She does not open her eyes but her mouth does.

"Bardolph," Odile lets out a single word. Hadion and Althea look at each other and then back to Odile. Hadion turns her so he can look at her wound. A stab wound is deep in her abdomen. Hadion puts his hands on it and starts to chant what he hopes will bring her healing.

"I...I have already been trying to heal myself," Odile tries to tell Hadion. Althea holds her hand.

"You've done an excellent job, Odile," Althea tries to speak positively to ease the girls. Hadion keeps up his chants. Odile breathes weakly.

"He...He didn't ruin it, did he? You were able to-to-to stop him, right?" Odile asks.

"Stop what?"

"Bardolph. He...He told me he was going to...going to kill all and start... start building his child's kingdom. He... stabbed me with his shadow sword and...and turned into me. Da," She looks over to Hadion, "You stopped him, right? You... went early and stopped him. Right, Da?"

Althea looks from Odile to Hadion. Did he really not know about any of it?

"You said he stabbed you with a shadow sword?" Hadion looks at her wound which heals then reopens continuously.

"Yes," Odile strains.

"What does it have to do with anything?" Althea whispers.

"Their wounds are not simple healing. I need stronger magic," he answers Althea.

"Tell me the words and I can help. We can combine our magic," She reaches over to put her hands on his. Hadion says the words and Althea says them with him. The wound starts to close but when Odile exhales it opens again. Repeatedly they try.

"Do you need help?" A voice comes from nowhere. Althea looks around and then catches sight of a figure coming out of the shadows. Althea feels sick as the cloaked figure comes and stands by Hadion.

"Yes. Help me," Hadion looks up. Amraphel kneels. Hadion and Althea move their hands. The one made of shadows comes to Odile. She winces feeling him then screams as his fingers go into her open flesh. Soon the flesh closes with a nasty scar and the screaming Odile faints.

"This will only last the night," Amraphel states.

"What? But you can heal her permanently," Hadion questions the spirit.

"It comes with a cost," Amraphel reminds the father.

"What is the cost?"

"A life for a life," Amraphel states.

"Whose life?" Hadion asks without hesitating.

"A child for this child," Amraphel gestures to Odile.

"A child?" Althea is horrified to think of a little boy or girl being killed.

"My child for my child," Hadion glances at Althea.

"Bardolph?" Althea brings up the absent son.

"Sacrifice him and the blood you take, give it to Odile. She will be healed," Amraphel gives the directions. "You have till noon tomorrow."

Amraphel disappears. Odile lies unconscious on the floor before Althea and Hadion. Althea looks to Hadion knowing now she was wrong about him. She reaches over to him.

"Hadion, I'm sorry. I was wrong about-" Her hand goes to his shoulder but he moves.

"Touch me not, woman," He speaks coldly to her. He scoops up Odile in his arms. As he stands, Althea does too.

"Where are you taking her?"

"To her room. She needs to rest," He answers.

"Let me come so I can care for her," Althea starts to follow.

"No. This is my duty. You can leave," Hadion does not even look at her.

"Hadion, I am not leaving her like this," Althea refuses.

"You will get out of this house and go to your brother," He orders.

"No," Althea stands her ground. Hadion begins to chant and Althea feels her body moving as if a great and terrible wind is blowing her. Soon she flies out of the doors of the castle that shut after her. Once again in control of her body, Althea runs to the doors and tries to open them. They do not budge.

"Hadion, let me in! Let me in! Please!" She bangs on them but he does not let her inside.

Instead, Hadion carries his daughter to her room. He changes her from her soiled gown to a chemise. He loosens her hair. With her covered up and asleep, Hadion is on his knees by her bed. He holds her hand in his. He stays by her side all night dreading the choice he is going to have to make.

Do I save my daughter or spare my son?

In the morning, Odile has still not awakened. Hadion goes down from the castle to the doors. He finds Althea there asleep on the steps. Basil is there too.

"Althea," He calls her name. She opens her eyes and looks up at him.

"Hadion!"

Basil wakes and stands up.

"What are you doing here?" He asks Basil.

"Althea told me what happened. Please, may I go see Odile?" Basil requests.

"Why?"

"Because she is my friend," Basil answers.

"Mine too," Althea gets to her feet.

"Go and keep her company," Hadion allows.

"Are you not going to as well?" Basil asks.

"I have something I must do," Hadion answers. "Althea, show your brother the way. He may not be able to get through since Odile has not permitted him but he can try."

Hadion starts to leave the Sipos siblings. Althea goes and grabs him by the elbow. He looks down at her.

"Hadion, I am sorry I didn't believe you," Althea apologizes.

"It is too late now," he replies.

Althea frowns deeply.

"Go to Odile. I don't want her to be alone," Hadion points in the direction the tower should be.

"You are leaving. Are you going to do as Amraphel said?"

"I must do what I can," Hadion turns away from Althea and continues walking. Althea watches Hadion's back till he disappears. She then takes Basil through the castle to where Odile's quarters should be.

"I can't move," Basil is prevented from going too far given an invisible barrier.

"Oh, right. Only those with permission from Odile can enter."

"I will have to wait here then," Basil resigns himself to his spot.

"I must go on into her," Althea states.

"Go. I will pray for her here," Basil takes to his knees.

With Basil's blessing, Althea goes on to Odile's room. Althea sits by her friend who lies still and breathes slowly. She takes her hand. She kisses the back of it then lowers it to have it rest in her lap.

"Please, don't die," Althea makes her request.

CHAPTER 53

STELLA

"Jump down," Nereo calls to Stella who is still atop the sinking piece of the ship. She prepares to jump when she hears a shrill roar from above. She looks up as do the others. Swooping down from the sky comes a flying wolf.

"No!" Stella screams but is caught in the clutches of the winged beast. He carries her high into the sky.

"Artegal!" Astrophel looks to his knight. The knight jumps up and changes back into his flying lion form. Astrophel climbs on his back and takes out his sword which begins to burn. They fly after the beast holding Stella.

"Bardolph!" Stella realizes who it is.

"Miss me?"

Lightning flashes about them as thunder rolls. Sir Artegal tries to cast a spell to slow down Bardolph with his lion paws but the wolf is swift and evasive. Stella tries to hit the Bardolph but a quick punch to the face knocks the maiden unconscious.

"Stella!" Astrophel calls out to his beloved as he chases the winged wolf. Bardolph holds Stella tightly to his chest with one of his hands before turning. He flies backward through the storm clouds and begins speaking his dark words. A ball of black flames flies from Bardolph's hand. It hits Prince Astrophel who flies back from Sir Artegal's back. As the prince falls from the sky covered in black flames, Sir Artegal dives down and catches him and the flaming sword before he can hit the water. Prince Astrophel screams in agony as the black flames burn him and soak into his skin.

Bardolph flies away.

***

Stella wakes and finds herself in a bed with sky-blue curtains hanging over her head. She sits up on the large but soft bed to look around. The room is large and lascivious with its whitewood furniture, golden fixtures, mirrors, and a crystal chandelier. Stella rubs her eyes as she tries to remember where she is.

"Ow," She groans when one of the hands rubbing her eyes goes down on her cheek. It is then she feels the pain in her face and remembers with whom she was last. She looks down and finds her curly hair loose and dry. She has not changed from her wet clothes but they are dry now. Further down she sees her ankle in a shackle attached to a chain going under the bed. She pulls her ankle to test how much give there is to the chain.

"Moving like that won't break you free," Bardolph's voice draws her eyes to the door next to the mirror wall. He closes the door and starts walking toward her. She grabs a pillow as it is the only thing she can easily grab to put between her and the man approaching her.

"That pillow won't do much to protect you from me," He smirks.

"Are you going to ravish me now or have you already had your way with me?" She questions not sure of what was done in her sleep.

"It crossed my mind to have you when you lay there all silent and defenseless but I'd rather have you alert and fully aware of what I do," He sits on the side of the bed. Stella gets the urge to vomit but does not.

"How did you find me? I was careful to have no more mirrors near me," Stella questions. Bardolph leans onto his bent arm to lounge on the bed.

"I was able to get in contact with someone else."

"Who? How?"

"Did you know my grandfather had many bastards? He killed most of them to gain power but two were left alive. One on purpose but the second escaped him. Even so, I was able to contact her once I knew her name. I must thank you for that. If I had not heard you using her name over and over while searching for her in Liboria, I would have never learned my aunt's true name."

"Are you talking about Tzafrira?" Stella puts the pieces of his puzzle together. He nods, increasing her sick feeling. Stella begins to shake her head from side to side.

"No. You must be lying. She...she would not have spoken to you."

"She tried to cast me off at first when I appeared in her mirror, but she could not ignore me for long when I brought up an offer she could not refuse."

"What offer?"

"Did she ever tell you about the teleportation rings?"

"She said she lost them," Stella recalls.

"She did because the king and queen of Norwin had them. They kept them locked away but my...friend Yrsa was able to find and steal them for me. I promised Tzafrira the rings in exchange for you. I told her to accept you when you came looking for a guide and keep in communication with me," Bardolph enlightens Stella.

"You must be lying. You have to be lying. She...she tried to refuse to take me until I begged and made her feel my anguish." Stella tries to defend the woman she has not known long.

"Do not be foolish, my dear. Why would she risk coming to a place she knows is overrun with her kin that would as soon as kill her as see her unless she had a deal that profited her in place?"

Stella squeezes the pillow at her chest tighter as tears prick her eyes.

Did we risk our lives only to be tricked? Did I lose the elixir to save a woman who was betraying me the whole time?

"Do not be too dismayed. That traitor will not get what she wants. I purposefully came while you were still out at sea so our bond can be undone. I will send another storm and make sure she is lost at sea. I will keep the rings," he offers words he believes to be of comfort. Stella sees the silver rings with garnets on his fingers.

"No. My friends are with her. I do not wish for any of them to die." Stella is quick to think of how Astrophel, Sir Artegal, Tyr, Zarin, and the innocent sailors are still with Tzafrira. Bardolph focuses his sparkling hazel eyes on Stella's.

"I suppose I could save them, for a price of course."

"You are never slow to make a deal," Stella remarks. He smiles and takes her hands in his. He does not move his eyes from her.

"I will save your friends, including your precious prince, from death at sea and release your siblings, but you must give yourself to me willingly."

I keep resisting and more people get hurt. If I choose myself again, I will lose my family, friends, and Astro. And losing Astro means his kingdom will lose its next king. Choosing Bardolph can lead to the New Starrling. Death is a definite here but this possible life is not. I must do what I can to save the ones I love. Astro will have to understand. El Yah, give me the courage to do what I fear. Stay with me as you promised.

"I will...I will marry you after you save my friends from the sea and release my siblings," She decides.

"I will save your friends then, after we are married, I will release your siblings," He sets his preferred terms.

"Fine," She agrees. Bardolph glows in delight.

"I am so glad you have finally come to your senses. I will go now and save your friends and send servants in to prepare you for our nuptials," he holds onto a wicked grin. He gets off the bed and with a snap of his fingers, her chain is broken.

"Wait." Stella holds up her hand. He stops and looks back at her.

"What is it, my bride?"

"I want proof you are keeping your word. I want to see you save them," Stella is clear about her wishes.

"I cannot risk you running off to be with them after I save them...I shall have you watch from the high tower with a telescope. Will that satisfy you?" He asks. She nods.

"Come then," He holds his hand out to her. She gets off the bed but does not take his hand. He grabs it anyway so he can lead her more easily. He takes her to the hall on the journey to the highest tower. Stella is amazed by the architecture around her.

Up they go until they reach the top room where there is a balcony and telescope. Bardolph brings her to the large, golden instrument. The frigid air makes Stella shiver but she can see that the castle overlooks the turbulent sea. He peers into the into the telescope to look for her friends.

"Are we east of the sun and west of the moon now?" Stella asks.

"No. We are in Norwin."

"Norwin? Why are we here?"

"As of yesterday, I am now the king."

Stella pales. *What happened to the real king?*

Bardolph pulls back from the telescope with a smile.

"After months of waiting, plotting and seducing those I needed, I finally have a kingdom for us, for our child. Our child will need a seat of power. I intended it to be Estellen but given their great abundance of fairies there, I opted to take over Norwin instead when the opportunity presented itself. My friends and I have rid this land of the nobility and royals and have enchanted the soldiers to be obedient. No one will dare to try to take Norwin back from us. Now, we have all we need to begin our future together as king and queen."

"This is terrible," Stella comments. He brings his hand to cup her cheek but she turns her face from his touch.

"You will come to accept it. Now, look into it and find your friends," Bardolph directs stepping away from the instrument. Stella goes to the telescope and peers into it. She scans the sea until she sees the row boat. It is full of people she knows. She only sees the back of Astrophel's head leaning against Sir Artegal's shoulder. There are two horses and two unicorns struggling to swim with the little boat.

"I have found them. You must save the animals as well. They are dear to me," Stella states.

"I will save them but I will need some compensation for the additional work," Bardolph replies. Stella looks back at him annoyed.

"You are already going to have me. What else could you want?" She frowns.

"In exchange for the beasts, you must give me the spoon in your pocket," he states. Her hand goes to her pocket where she feels the outline of Astrophel's gift. She clenches her teeth.

"Fine," She hands it over to the sorcerer. He smiles and breaks the spoon in half in his hands before tossing it off the balcony. Stella clutches her fists.

"Watch through the telescope and you will see me keep my part of the deal," he points back to the telescope. Bardolph begins to chant his dark words as he holds his hands out toward the sea. Stella's eye goes back to the glass so she can see what will happen to her friends. The water around them begins to rise. She sees the panic on their faces as the water begins to rise and form around them like a sphere. The watery sphere rises into the air and floats like a bubble. Stella moves her eye to follow it as it quickly sails through the air toward the island. The water bubble pops and drops out the rowboat of people and the four animals onto a beach. The people are soaked but alive.

"It is done now," Bardolph's voice comes to her ear but she does not respond. Instead, she watches as the people climb out of the boat. They are careful to help each other. Sir Artegal and Nereo help carry Astrophel out of the boat. His back is to her.

"Look this way," She whispers. She needs to see his face one last time.

"I have done what you wanted. Now, let us be wed and get to bed." Bardolph grabs Stella's wrist causing her to lose her hold on the telescope and lose sight of her friends. She does not see how soldiers approach the group.

"I want to go see them," Stella tries to pull away from his grip.

"No. You will fulfill your promise to me." He squeezes her wrist tightly. She winces in pain. She knows he is right. She must keep her end of the deal.

Bardolph takes her down from the tower. He walks her through grand hallways till they come into a grand room. Great white pillars are holding up a second floor. The crown moldings are gold. The floors have been set to hold a design of a dragon circling a snowflake. There are golden stairs leading to a massive golden chair with a blue cushion in the seat. A canopy of blue and white hangs above the throne. There are many people in the room but all grin and leer at Stella as she is brought in by Bardolph.

"Who are these people?"

"My new court," He answers. He stops once they go up the stairs. Stella grows sick in her stomach as she feels the disgusting desire in them.

"We shall wed now in the way of my people," Bardolph informs her and takes out a knife from a holster on his belt.

"The way of your people?"

"We shall make our vows and seal it with blood. Then we shall consummate," he explains. Stella pales at the plan.

"Don't we need an officiant or something?" Stella tries to postpone the wedding.

"No. But we will be witnessed." Bardolph turns to face his court. "My friends, come now and witness our union."

The people whisper but turn to look at the couple more directly. Stella wants to run and hide but how can she with all these people around and the lives of the ones she loves on the line?

"I come to you willingly and bind myself to you. I am yours and you are mine. So it shall be until death," he vows as he cuts his palm. He then holds out the knife to Stella.

"Cut your hand and repeat my words. We will mix out blood and be sealed together," Bardolph instructs. Stella shakily takes the blade. She starts to bring it to her hand. She looks at her unmarred hand and then the already bloodied blade. She glances at the onlookers before looking up at Bardolph. He stares at her eagerly.

"I come to you..." She speaks slowly and softly. She closes her eyes. She pauses. "I come to you," She repeats.

"Yes?" Bardolph grows impatient.

"I come to you willingly and bind myself to you. I am yours and you are mine. So it shall be until death," She recites the words with tears finally leaving her eyes.

I am sorry, Astro.

She cuts open the palm of her hand. Bardolph quickly takes her hand with his cut one.

"We are one and so we shall be until death," he states looking deeply into her eyes. Bardolph takes her face in his hands not caring he gets his blood on her face. He kisses her forcibly. His kisses are not like Astrophel's. Though Astrophel was passionate in his kisses, there was a tenderness that Bardolph does not have. Her heart mourns for the prince she loves. The crowd cheers in approval.

Overwhelming desire and happiness overflow from Bardolph. The emotions practically choke Stella as he kisses her. Bardolph, however, clearly feels the grief in his bride. She does not attempt to prevent her emotions from passing to him. How different it is from the first bite he took in her bakery.

It had been a consuming feeling yet subtle. It had made his stomach flutter, his extremities tingle, and his face feels fuzzy. He had been so cold then in one bite so warm. It was so warm, soft, and safe. Something he had never felt before in his life. It made him happy. It all came from her and then it passed with the digestion of his food. That is the feeling he should be having now with her but instead, she is cold and sinking like a rock in the sea.

She should be honored that of all the women in the world, he chose her. He has chosen her to be not only his wife and mother to his child but to be queen. Yrsa Urs was practically dying to take the position. She stole the rings for him and even helped encourage the other sorcerers to participate in his coup in taking over Norwin. When he and Stella have their all-gifted child, they will be able to take over the Far Lands and then the rest of the world. She should be happy to be the most esteemed woman in the world. She should be thankful he saved her from the peasant life and made her queen. She should love him.

She will regain those feelings. I can make her regain them. Bardolph thinks to himself.

"Bardolph!" The yell of the name draws all attention away from the couple and to the back of the room. There is a large, upright circle leading to a room that is not this throne room. From it emerges a man tall, dark, and devastatingly handsome. The circle closes behind the man.

"Hadion," Bardolph addresses the man. "You have arrived just in time. I am about to bed my new wife."

Hadion looks to Stella who is unaware of her trembling.

"A new kingdom and a new bride," Hadion walks toward the couple. The witnesses split so Hadion is not hindered. "Impressive."

"I think so." Bardolph smiles.

"It amazes me how at such a young age you have already surpassed so many including your grandfather. He would hate it but he would respect you. Never would he or I attempt such a grand coup to wipe out a nation's royal family and nobility to become a king. As a fellow sorcerer, I must say 'well done'." Hadion praises the groom. Stella can feel her new husband's pride growing in his chest.

"Thank you. I am sure there are no hard feelings over the loss of your royal whore and her friends," Bardolph brings up people of whom Stella knows nothing.

"I know it was what was necessary," Hadion says in a matter-of-fact tone.

"It was."

"And I am sure you will understand what I am about to do is necessary," Hadion put his hand on Bardolph's shoulder. The new king furrows his brow. Hadion holds out his unoccupied hand toward the crowd. Without saying a single word, black fire spews from his hand and consumes the witnesses who scream out in horror and agony as they burn. Hadion brings his hand to Bardolph's throat.

"We are going home," Hadion squeezes Bardolph's throat tightly and with his fire-wielding hand opens a circular portal back to what Stella must assume is their home. Bardolph kicks Hadion back and pushes Stella behind him.

"I am not going anywhere with you, old man," Bardolph holds out his hands toward Hadion.

"You may have surpassed Kazimeer but you are not yet as powerful as me. I am taking you back." Hadion is not fazed by Bardolph's raised hands.

"No." Bardolph bares his teeth.

From Bardolph's hand comes black fire just as Hadion had fired. Hadion merely waves his arms and is unharmed by the flames. In return, Hadion sends a lightning bolt, striking Bardolph in the shoulder. It does not stop Bardolph from making the wood on the floor open and swallowing Hadion's body up to his head. Bardolph spreads his wings and takes to the air. With his hand covered in black fire, he dives to strike Hadion. Hadion catches Bardolph with a clawed hand and slams him to the floor which extinguishes the fire in his hand. Bardolph shifts from man to great black wolf and bites at Hadion. Hadion shifts into a great black wolf as well. In their beastly forms, they fight. Stella steps backward to be out of their way. As the wolves perform their violent dance, Stella looks for some escape. Every time she tries to take a step toward a door, one or both of the wolves inadvertently block her.

"Ah!" Stella yelps as the tail of one of the wolves knocks her back and sends her flying through the circle portal and hits a stone table. When Stella gets up, she sees the portal has closed and she is now in a dark room lit only by candles.

"Hello, Stella," A voice greets her from the shadows. Instantly, her body feels as if she is burning, rotting, and aching. She turns around and sees a man who resembles Astrophel almost perfectly except his eyes are red and his teeth which are exposed as he smiles are sharp.

"You are not Astrophel."

"No, But I adopted this form to be more pleasing to your eyes," he admits then bows to her. "I am Amraphel."

"I do not care who you are."

"Oh, but you should," He walks toward her.

"Why?"

"Because I am the only one who can help you now," Amraphel states.

"Is that so?" Stella doubts him.

"Yes. I can help you and the ones you love."

"I can do that myself."

"No. No, you cannot." Amraphel locks his eyes with hers.

"What do you mean?"

"Right now, your prince and your friends are being prepared to be executed by the knights of Norwin."

"What!"

"Bardolph ordered the knights to come and kill them once he put them on the land."

"No. He promised to save them from death."

"Death at sea," Amraphel brings up the specifics. Stella's heart drops knowing this person is right.

How could I be so easily fooled?

"And then there is that whole ploy with your siblings," Amraphel brings up Althea and Basil.

"What about them?"

"Do you know where they are now?

"No."

"Well, I can take you to their bodies if you wish and you can 'free' them," He offers.

"You are saying they're dead?"

"What else could I be saying?" He answers her question with his own. Her eyes water and her body trembles. She looks down at her still-bleeding hand. She has married her worst enemy who not only is going to kill her friends and Astrophel but has already killed Althea and Basil. She drops to her knees.

All I have done...was for nothing. I waited too long. I should have agreed to marry Bardolph when he asked. No. I should have never left Soldoro. I should have stayed in Soldoro and clung to her mother and father all the days of my life. Why did I ever leave them? How can I tell them because of my stubbornness, pride, and selfishness Basil and Althea are dead?

"Do not weep, Stella, I can help you." Amraphel kneels before her.

"How?" Stella questions. He smiles.

"I can save your loved ones from death and resurrect your brother and sister," He claims. Stella stares at him confused.

"The dead cannot be resurrected by anyone but El-Yah." The mention of El-Yah makes Amraphel grimace momentarily.

"Your faith is endearing but flawed. I can bring anything back to life."

"But for a price, right?" Stella questions.

"Of course. Everything comes at a price." Amraphel upturns his palms and shrugs.

"What is the price?" Stella wipes the tears off her cheeks though it makes blood smear on her face.

"Life is so precious and so it requires something precious to regain it," Amraphel speaks slowly.

"What is the price?" Stella repeats.

"A life, or in this case, two lives," Amraphel answers.

"I must die so they can live?"

"Not necessarily. You can give your life in exchange for one of your siblings but still be one life short. Or you can find two lives to exchange for theirs and not lose your own."

"And whose lives should I offer? I have no power over any life but my own."

"You may not now but soon you could."

"Speak plainly," Stella snaps at him.

"In exchange for the lives of Basil and Althea, you can give me the lives of your first two children. You may not be pregnant yet but one day you will be. You do not even have to give birth to them for you to give their lives for your siblings. You will never have to meet them and therefore never have to miss them like you will miss Althea and Basil," Amraphel explains further.

"I just have to promise to trade the lives of my future children and you will resurrect my siblings?"

"Yes." He nods smiling then claps his hand before spreading them apart. A piece of paper appears with words all over it.

"This is?"

"A contract. You promise the lives of your first two children either born or unborn and in exchange, I help you with your siblings," Amraphel quickly explains the contract. "You just need to give it a drop of blood. You have your hand cut and ready to do so."

Stella looks at her hand and the contract. One drop and a promise of lives that might never come will bring back her siblings.

"One drop?" Stella asks.

"Yes. One drop," He leans closer. Stella looks into Amraphel's blood-red eyes.

"You're a liar and a terrible one at that. I can feel how you are only full of death. You cannot bring life. You are nothing but a disgusting, deceptive maggot," Stella states. Amraphel loses his smile and begins to scowl which distorts the face of his pretend form. He begins to grow and in doing so, the form like Astrophel's evaporates allowing Amraphel to be a big black shadow with a face. His dark figure begins to fill up the room and crowds Stella. Her throat begins to contract and deprive her of air. His eyes and mouth almost take up half the room. In one bite he could consume her.

"I come to you to offer you help and you insult me. Do you know who I am? I am Amraphel, prince of shadows, bringer of power. I was there when man was formed. I have given all which you pathetic dustlings have desired since man fell from favor. I have given kingdoms and gold mines to peasants. I have taken the greatest armies in the world and turned them back to dust. I have been worshiped and given the lives of countless firstborns for my favor. I know the secret to bringing back the dead. I can destroy you in a single instant. I am no maggot. I am a god!" His giant mouth gnashes his teeth at her. Stella should crumble in fear. She should beg for his mercy and spare herself from his wrath.

"You are no god," Stella whispers.

"How dare you!" He howls.

"You are no god! You are a shadow and I am not afraid of the dark." Stella stands firm and unwavering.

"I will destroy you for your insolence!" He threatens.

"You have no power over me. As El-Yah cast you out of his realm, I cast you, Amraphel, out from me in the name of El-Yah!" Stella proclaims and a bright light emerges from her raised hand. A light so bright and brilliant it is like a star.

Amraphel yells out, making the whole room shake violently. The darkness caused by Amraphel grows and encircles Stella. She does not shudder or cower. She repeats her words making her light brighter and brighter. Amraphel curses before disappearing.

Stella falls to the ground gasping for air. She regains control over her breathing and stands up to her feet. She looks at her hand no longer has the star but instead stardust. Her other hand is still bloody. She holds them to her heaving chest.

CHAPTER 54

STELLA & ALTHEA

In their winged wolf forms, Bardolph and Hadion violently try to tear each other apart and curse each other with great afflictions. Fangs and claws draw blood and rip flesh. Just when Hadion gets the upper hand, Bardolph resurges and takes it only for Hadion to take it again. Repeatedly they blast through this cycle and transference of power.

Bardolph jumps on Hadion's back and with his teeth takes hold of one of Hadion's wings. From the base, he rips it off causing Hadion to howl out in pain. Hadion turns and throws Bardolph off him. He pounces on his son and holds him down by the throat. Bardolph chokes from the pressure. As Hadion holds him down, he calls to the shadows. The shadows come and like ropes they encircle Bardolph. Bardolph tries to break free of them but the more he struggles the tighter they become. They squeeze him so tightly they dig into his body. He is forced to shrink back into his human form. Still, the shadowy ropes shrink with him. Hadion loses his wolfish form to take on his human one. Bardolph curses at his father but Hadion's ropes gag his son. Voiceless and forced to be still, Bardolph glares at his father.

"I am taking you and you are going to make things right," Hadion starts a fire while staring at his son. Bardolph snarls. Hadion uses the blood coming from where his wing used to be, to put in the fire. The portal opens. Hadion grabs Bardolph but his thick brown curls and drags him through the portal.

Passing through, Hadion stops when he sees Stella standing in the room. She stares back at him. They stand there in silence staring at each other.

"You are Stella?" Hadion speaks first.

"Yes."

"You will soon be free of your marriage to him. Your brother and sister are here in the castle. In my daughter, Odile's tower. Go to them," Hadion informs her.

"You will not harm me?"

"No. Go." He points to the door. Stella opens the door and takes off without another word.

Stella runs through stairwells and hallways not sure of where she is to go. She notices servants with animalistic features. They are sure to duck away when she comes near.

"You! Please, please, help me," She calls out to one squat, greenish servant. He tries to hop away but Stella reaches him and grabs his arm.

"Please, help me. Help me get to Odile's tower," She asks him.

"I-I don't know if I can help you. My masters may not like me helping you." He cowers, trying to pull away from him.

"Is your master Bardolph?" Stella asks and sends a chill through the toadish servant.

"One of them…" he nods.

"I am Bardolph's wife so I am now your Mistress," She shows him the gash in her hand, "Tell me how to get to the main exit."

"Uh, er, well, Mistress, you go straight to the left then right then left twice more then right then left once more before going right. You'll go up some stairs, down a hall, and find a door," the servant gives her the directions.

"Thank you," Stella gets up and starts moving. She repeats the directions out loud as she keeps moving. She can take her first left and updates her words.

"Right, left, left, right, left, right. Right, left, left, right, left, right, Right, left, left, left, right, left, right. Right, left, left, left, right, left," She blathers and turns several times. She runs upstairs, turns right, and comes to the end of the hall where there is a single door.

"I guess this is the way out," She quickly opens the door not caring that her blood stains the door.

Stella walks through the door thinking perhaps the darkness was simply due to a lack of lighting in a hallway passage to the beach. She finds nothing in here is normal. She walks but feels no floor. She looks back and sees no door or even a strip of light to indicate there was a door. There is nothing above her and nothing ahead of her. And though there is nothing, she walks ahead, or at least what she thinks is ahead.

Walking and walking, Stella does not grow tired but more confused. She is not sure of how long she has been in this place. Has it only been mere minutes or hours or days or longer?

Where am I? Why am I walking?

Stella sits down the lies down. She keeps looking upward. Her eyelids become heavy and she yawns. She wants to sleep. How odd for she was tired a min-no an hour- no… how long ago was it she had energy? What does it matter? She no longer has it now. All she wants is to sleep.

Yes, I need to sleep. I need to rest.

Stella begins to rub her sleepy eyes. She looks at her hands.

How funny... Even though there is no light she sees her hands perfectly as if they were out in the sun. She stares at her hands despite her tired eyes. She sees the wound on her hand is still there. She also notices her skin is...wrinkled and spotted. Her skin is thin. She can practically see her bones. Her wound is gone as is her flesh.

In fright, Stella looks at the rest of her and fingers her flesh aging and fading until there is nothing but bone. Her boney fingers try to touch her body but they begin to fade before she can touch anything. She is turning to dust!

"El-Yah! El-Yah save me!" She cries out with her last breath.

***

Cries of pain quickly draw Althea's attention to Odile's now contorting face. Odile moves the blanket and looks at Odile's abdomen. Blood has started coming out through her nightgown.

"Althea?" Odile looks at the blonde.

"I'm here, Odile." Althea squeezes her hand.

"Where is my father?" She asks weakly.

"He is trying to find a way to help you," Althea informs her. "Let me try the healing spell your father did yesterday."

Althea lifts the dress to put her hands on the wound. Odile grimaces at the touch. Althea starts the chant. She tries to focus solely on her task. The bleeding decreases but does not stop.

"It hurts," Odile whines.

"I'm sorry. I'm trying to help," Althea apologizes.

"I know but it...it hurts more the more you try," Odile states.

"But I can't give up on you, Odile. I need to keep you alive. Hadion will be back soon with a cure. Please, let me continue," Althea tries to encourage Odile.

"But it hurts so much." Odile has tears in her eyes.

"Maybe Basil could help ease you. He is just outside the barrier. If you let him in, he can calm you with his gift," Althea brings up her brother.

"Basil? He is here?" A faint smile comes to Odile's pale face.

"Yes. Give your permission and he can come."

"I give it," Odile breathes hard.

Althea jumps to her feet and runs to where the barrier keeps her brother away. He is on his knees with his eyes closed.

"Baz! Come!" Althea waves her bloody hand. Without hesitation, Basil stands and rushes through the invisible barrier. He follows Althea into Odile's bedroom. She smiles at Basil when he comes to her side. She gives him her hand which he takes. He looks at her hand and then at her face.

"What do you need from me, Odile?" He asks, taking a knee.

"Althea says you can make me feel better while she stays my wound. Will you help me?" Odile asks.

"I will do my best." He rubs the back of her hand. He breathes in and out slowly. Odile soon does as well. Althea puts her hands back on the wound. She starts her chant.

"What are you doing?" Basil turns his eyes from Odile to his sister.

"I'm saying the healing chant Hadion used," Althea answers.

"Do you even know what you're saying?"

"No, but it's the words of magic." Althea shakes her head.

"You are calling upon the Fallen One to stop her from death," Basil tells her. She is not sure how he knows what she has been saying. She is half surprised and half not that this magic calls on the aide of the Fallen One.

"That is all I know. I have to say it to help her until Hadion comes back with a cure," Althea enlightens him about the problem.

"Let me try to heal her." Basil stands.

"You don't know healing magic," Althea states.

"I have learned much on my journeys. Let me try," Basil walks to the side where the injury is. He then looks back to Odile's watchful eyes. "May I try, Odile?"

"Yes," She nods. Althea moves to the other side and takes Odile's hand. Basil sits on the bed and puts his hands on the wound. Odile grimaces. Basil closes his eyes and softly whispers words sounding like what Zarin used to say when they traveled together.

Basil speaks quietly and quickly. Odile winces at the pressure of his hands. Althea stares at the bloody connection and frowns. Doubt is practically written on her forehead.

He is a great piper and a feeler but he is not a healer. No one in our family is. He is not even well-trained in magic. Hadion has decades of experience and is a healer yet he could not heal Odile. Basil is going to fail.

Odile groans and moans. Althea's eyes stay on the red wound. They enlarge when she sees something black starting to come out around Basil's hands. Instead of blood, it is like black sludge seeping out. Odile's eyes are shut tight so she does not see it but Althea does and jumps back not sure what it is. She comes close again to look. The sludge begins to solidify once out of the body. It takes a shape like giant black maggots with teeth and slits holding red eyes.

"What are those?" Althea gawks at the nasty creatures.

Basil does not answer for he continues to pray however he does open his eyes and look at them. The inky creatures wiggle, writhe, and shriek as Basil speaks aloud. They start to shrivel and turn to dust. Odile begins to breathe more easily. The blood staining her body and dress begins to absorb back into her body, leaving her clean. Her skin begins to stitch back together. When her skin is as smooth as it had been before Bardolph's blade. Basil pulls his hands away. Odile lifts her dress to look at where her wound should be.

"It's gone, and I feel well," Odile states. Althea stares at the unmarred flesh and then at her brother.

"Oh! Basil!" Odile embraces the one who healed her. "Thank you."

Basil allows the hug and even returns it.

"How did you do it?" Althea asks confused.

How could Basil reverse this when Hadion could not? Even Amraphel could not.

"It is not by my power but El-Yah's," Basil states.

"El-Yah?" Odile pulls back.

"I called upon El-Yah and asked to heal you," Basil explains.

"And El-Yah let you heal me?"

"Yes."

"But I am not a follower," Odile looks down.

"That does not mean you are not loved by him," Basil's words lift Odile's eyes.

"But what has it cost you to heal me?" She asks.

"Nothing."

"Nothing? It can't be nothing, everything comes with a price."

"Not with El-Yah."

Odile absorbs his answer.

"What were those black things coming out of you?" Althea asks Odile.

"I don't know," Odile shakes her head.

"I've seen them once before when I was in Belterre. I do not know what they are called but I watched a fairy heal a wizard who had been 'healing' himself through the help of shadow spirits. But the shadow spirit's magic was stalling his death but filling him with these sorts of parasites," Basil recounts his former encounter.

"Do you think Amraphel put them in me?" Odile looks to Althea thinking of the shadowy spirit.

"I suppose," Althea has to assume.

"Well, now I am healed, Father does not have to find another cure. Where is he?"

"He has gone after Bardolph in Norwin."

"Bardolph is in Norwin?" Odile's face falls. Althea looks down sadly.

"Althea, what has happened?"

"I...I don't want to say," Althea turns her face completely from Odile. Odile grabs her arm tightly.

"What happened, Althea? You have to tell me," Odile begins to lose her well-being. Althea looks back with tears in her eyes. Gently and without much detail, Althea shares the news of Odette's demise as well as of the swan maidens, Prince Sigfried, and the Norwin nobility at the hands of Bardolph and his helpers.

Odile sits quietly with misty eyes. Althea tries to rub her to comfort her but Odile is not responsive. Althea opens her mouth to try to give words of comfort but the young maiden looks to Basil.

"They followed in El-Yah. Do you think my mother and the others are in paradise?" Odile asks Basil.

"Yes," Basil nods. Odile smiles but the tears finally come. She weeps and is quickly held by Basil and Althea.

***

Hadion throws Bardolph atop the stone table in the dark room his portal led to. Bardolph lies still waiting for his father to unbind him. With a snap of Hadion's fingers, the gag is gone but the ropes remain.

"Finally. Now, let me go," Bardolph demands. Hadion says nothing but walks over to a cupboard in the room to take out a cup.

"Hadion, release me and I promise I'll never kill another one of your old lovers again," Bardolph bargains. Hadion sets the cup on the table.

"Come on. She wasn't even into you anymore. She was marrying someone else. You have to get over Odette."

Hadion stays silent but keeps walking around the room lighting the fire in the fireplace.

"Are you upset about me taking over Norwin? I know you're against taking over countries but that is what we are supposed to do. As the seed of Rastaban, we should be trying to take over the Far Lands as he wanted to do. I know it will be the New Starrling to take over all of them but I thought I could help my child get started. You really can't be upset over me fulfilling what our ancestor wanted," Bardolph continues trying to pinpoint why his father is not letting him go.

Hadion comes toward Bardolph with a ceremonial knife. Bardolph stares at his weapon-wielding father.

"Wait. Why are you bringing that toward me? Is that the only thing to cut these ropes?" Bardolph tries to find a reason for the knife. Hadion begins to speak.

"In blood, there is life and power and so to have what I need; I must take it. Great Eous, the Fallen One, I give this blood to you so I may have the power in it for what I need. Take this life so another can have it."

"What are you doing? What are you saying?" Bardolph stares in fear at his father.

"It must be done, Bardolph, to save your sister," Hadion states.

"No! No! I-I can fix this. I have a child on the way. We can sacrifice it and give it to Eous. You don't need my blood," Bardolph frantically tries to argue.

"It must be you. Amraphel says it must be your blood," Hadion brings the knife to Bardolph's throat.

"Please! No! Spare me! Please! Father!" Bardolph cries.

"I'm sorry," Hadion apologizes but with great force and speed, his knife cuts Bardolph's throat. Hadion grabs the cup he set aside and brings it to the flowing blood to catch it. He looks at Bardolph's face as it rapidly loses its color. Tears fall but he is sure not to let them fall into the cup of blood. With the cup filled, Hadion leaves the room. He walks steadily toward Odile's tower. He cannot spill it.

As he walks, he hears two servants chittering nervously. He intends to ignore it as he is on his important mission. But the whispers reach his ears.

"I saw her go straight in the forbidden door," one says.

"Oh, well. I guess she's dead now," The other states.

"Who went into the forbidden door?" Hadion stops, his heart fearing the worst for Althea.

Has she gone looking for him and go into the time tower?

The servants bow before their master.

"It was a young maiden with brown hair and a bleeding hand. She went into the forbidden door to the forbidden tower," one servant informs him. He knows they speak of Stella. She must have gone through his original portal. He leaves the servants and rushes toward the time tower. He sees fleck of stardust and drops of blood. There is a bloody hand print on the door. He opens it and finds nothing.

She's dead. Althea will be upset but that issue is not as important as healing Odile. He thinks and quickens to Odile's room to find the door open. He sees Althea and Basil hugging Odile who is crying.

"Odile?" Hadion calls her. The Sipos siblings pull away. Basil moves completely to let the father be next to his daughter.

"Father," Odile looks at her father. He comes and sits on the bed with the cup.

"Here, drink this and you will be healed," Hadion tries to hand it to her.

"I am already healed," Odile states.

"No, Amraphel's healing was only temporary. This will heal you fully," Hadion insists.

"I am already fully healed. Basil healed me," Odile looks to Basil.

"What? Show me your wound," He starts to lift her dress. He looks at her abdomen and finds not even a trace of a former injury.

"How did you do this?" Hadion looks to Basil.

"I asked El-Yah to heal her," He answers.

"El-Yah? No. It costs a life to save a life," Hadion shakes his head and looks at the blood of his son in the cup.

"I asked and El-Yah gave," Basil states. Hadion's breathing becomes shaky. He puts the cup down on Odile's nightstand and then shoots up to grab Basil by the collar violently.

"Why did you not tell me you could heal her? Do you know what I have done to save her?" Hadion blares in the younger man's face.

"I did not know I could but once I saw her and heard my sister speaking to a false god, I knew I had to try," Basil is not afraid.

"You should have told me you could even try! You should have told me!" Hadion moves to start choking Basil.

"Hadion, let him go!" Althea comes and grabs Hadion's arm. He looks at Althea hatefully.

"This is all you and your sister's fault!" he drops Basil to the ground and turns to face Althea.

"What?"

"Your sister rejected Bardolph and drove him to these lengths and if you had just trusted I loved you and not needed a show of it, I would not have had to let Odette go. She would be alive and here. Bardolph would not have come up with his plot and Odile would not have been hurt. I should have never tried to prove anything to a faithless girl like you. You don't even trust in your own god how could you trust in me? I should have gotten rid of you the moment I laid eyes on you." Hadion walks toward Althea and backs her into a wall. His words are arrows in her chest.

"Hadion," Althea whispers heartbroken.

"Get your brother and get out. I never want to see you again," Hadion points toward the door.

"Hadion, please," Althea tries to touch him.

"Never touch me again." He pulls away.

"Father, please, don't do this," Odile gets out of the bed.

"Get back, Odile," Hadion orders. His daughter cowers and gets back on her bed. Hadion throws fire to Odile's fireplace. He cuts open his hand to give to the fire.

"Go through it now, and never come back," Hadion orders Basil and Althea. Basil takes his sobbing sister's hand.

"We should and then try to find Stella," Basil tells his sister.

"She is dead," Hadion states having overheard Basil's words.

"Dead?" Althea pales looking at the messenger.

"Yes. She went into the time tower and is dead."

"The what?" Basil has no idea what the older man has said.

"No. How could she have even gotten there?" Althea shakes her head.

"She came through the portal then ran off and went in there. You know as well as I those who enter die. I saw her blood. She is dead."

Althea covers her mouth and finds her knees weak when her brother catches her. Hadion's feet move to go to her but he stops himself. He looks away from Althea.

"It can't be true. Odile, tell me you sense he is lying," Althea looks at Odile. The younger girl shakes her head.

"He is not lying."

"Now get out," Hadion points to the portal again still not looking at Althea. Basil wraps his arm around his sister and takes Althea to the portal opening. Althea looks back at Hadion who has turned his eyes back to her. She parts her lips but when he looks away from her, she closes them. She steps through the portal with Bardolph. The portal closes.

"Father," Odile starts.

"Drink from the cup," Hadion orders, pointing to the cup of blood.

"No. I am healed," She shakes her head.

"Drink it!" He rushes over and grabs the cup.

"No," She cowers from him fearfully. Hadion grabs Odile and pulls her toward him. She tries pulling away to resist him.

"I killed your brother for this. Drink it!" He screams at her. He grabs her by her jaw and pins her to her headboard. He forces the cup to her lips. She keeps them shut tightly to resist it.

"Drink it! Drink it!" He keeps yelling but only makes her cry. He begins to cry as well. He moves his hand from her jaw and the cup from her mouth.

"I have to undo this. I must find a way." Hadion leaves his daughter. He hurries through the castle again to reach his tower. Bardolph is still on the table with his throat slit. He puts the cup down next to Bardolph's head. Hadion presses his wound to draw more blood.

"Amraphel! Amraphel!" He yells out to summon the being. There is no response. Hadion grabs the knife he used earlier and cuts himself more.

"Amraphel! Come! I summon you!" He demands.

"What do you want, child of Rastaban?" Only the voice comes to the room.

"You lied to me! You said only Bardolph's blood could heal Odile yet she was healed before she drank the blood." Hadion speaks to the disembodied voice.

"I did not. The only way you could heal her was with the blood of your child."

Hadion breathes heavily with hands tightening into fists.

"Now I have lost my son. You made me kill my son!"

"I did not make you do anything. You chose Odile over him. You wanted his blood."

Hadion looks at Bardolph's peaceful face and touches his face. It was only yesterday the young man was a baby.

"I thought it was the only way. I did not want to kill him. I didn't. He's my son, my boy...I did not want him dead."

"Even though he tried to kill Odile and did kill Odette whom you love."

"Yes," He keeps stroking Bardolph's head.

"I can give him back to you." The voice is right at his ear. Hadion can feel Amraphel's breath.

"Show me."

CHAPTER 55

ALTHEA

Althea and Basil walk out onto a beach. Althea knows where they are and it is not somewhere she wants to be. To be fair, she wants to be nowhere but in the past when she was with her family somewhere safe. Now it is just her and Basil on the island nation of Norwin. Stella is dead, her parents are far away, and the man she loves has ended things and cast her out from him and Odile. So much has happened in such a short time and grief is consuming her quickly as a fire does a leaf. Althea looks at her brother who has silent tears rolling down his face.

"What is the time tower?" Basil asks his sister.

"It is some dark magic spot. Those who go in it die. If Stella went in it, she is dead," Althea gives more information to her brother.

"But how could she have even ended up in it?"

"It has this strange pull that lures people in. It almost pulled me once but Hadion stopped me. Since no one was able to stop her then she is...she must be..."

"And Odile said he was not lying..."

"It must be true."

"And Stella is..."

"Yes," Althea nods. Basil covers his eyes to cover up his crying eyes from her. There is some blubbering from the young man. He keeps his eyes covered but it does not stop the tears and snot from rolling down. Althea cries too. They do come to hold each other as they weep.

"We must stop. We have to figure out where we are and what to do." Basil lets his sister go.

"I know where we are." Althea tries to wipe her face.

"Where are we?" Basil asks her.

"Norwin," Althea answers.

"Can we get home from here?"

"I...I don't know. Bardolph and other sorcerers took over the castle. I don't know who is in power. I don't know if we will be able to find help to get home," Althea looks down defeated.

"I will go look out then. I see a pier and boats down there," Basil volunteers wiping his nose with the back of his arm sleeve.

"No. I will go with you. If the sorcerers are still in power, they will think I am aligned with Hadion and will spare me," Althea explains. They walk together toward the distant pier and ships. As they come closer, they see the few ships are dozens and all are filling up quickly with people with the help of soldiers. These people have many bags and sacks with them. The people look fearful and desperate. Basil can feel the overwhelming anxiety from the masses as well as from the soldiers. They go up so they can walk on the boardwalk leading to the pier and ships. They stand among the families who slowly move toward a ticket booth. The soldiers make a corral to keep the people in a thick line.

"Do not pass each other."

"Stick with your family."

"Remain calm and move forward."

These words are repeated over and over by the soldiers. Mothers and Fathers hold tightly to their children's hands. Many of the elderly hold onto younger persons. Some soldiers have even stepped in to help the more disabled move in the line.

Basil and Althea's turn comes to the ticket booth. A soldier sits in it. He has a large book on his table with an inkwell and a ring of tickets. He holds his quill in his hand.

"How many are in your group?" he asks.

"Two."

"Names?"

"Basil and Althea Sipos," Basil answers. "But we have no money for a ticket."

"No one pays. This is an evacuation," The soldier states. He rips off two tickets and hands them to Basil. "You will take the Nadezhda. It will take you to Austvest."

"We want to go to Soldoro," Basil puts out the other name.

"All ships are going to Austvest."

"Oh." Basil nods accepting this.

"Next!" The ticket booth man yells. Basil and Althea step toward a soldier using his arms and hands to point them toward the ships. They pass many ships loaded with passengers. They near the one painted with the word 'Nadezhda'. They start up the ramp and hand their tickets to a man collecting them.

"Women, children, and sickly will be sharing quarters below and men will be kept up top here," a member of the crew informs them. They have no reason to argue. Still, they stay on deck as many others seem to be as well. They walk to the far side of the ship to stand next to the railing. Althea can see from the distance the castle is on fire. The smoke billows and makes great gray clouds in the sky.

"Althea?" a voice calls. Althea turns and sees a smiling Zarin.

"Zarin?" Althea cannot believe the woman is here. They are quick to embrace.

"How are you here?"

"The one who controls the place east of the sun and west of the moon sent my brother and me to come here through a portal," Althea answers and shows Basil.

"You are Basil?" Zarin smiles at Basil who nods.

"I am glad to see you succeeded in healing him," Zarin takes Althea's hand.

"As am I. But how are you here?"

"Well, we found the one who could lead us to the island. We were on our way to find you when a leviathan attacked us. Bardolph came afterwards and took Stella. We tried sailing on but a magic water orb picked us up and dropped us on a beach near here. Soldiers came after us and as they led us toward the castle, the spell over them seemed to break. Once it did, the soldiers told us the sorcerers had killed all the royals and had taken over the castle. Sir Artegal went with the soldiers to go fight the sorcerers while some started to alert the people of the city so they could evacuate.

"Sir Artegal said he went to the castle and found many dead sorcerers but one was still alive. From him, he learned it was Bardolph who took over Norwin but he and Stella went through a portal. He is sure Bardolph will return. The soldier then set fire to the castle as a deterrent. Sir Artegal came back to us so we could leave. He believes Stella and Bardolph must be on the island east of the sun and west of the moon now. We still have a guide who knows the way to the island. She and the sailors who were bringing us are another ship at the present though. But when we all reach Austvest we can get together, take another boat and go after Stella," Zarin gives the plan. Tears come to Althea's eyes again. Basil looks away from Zarin.

"Zarin, it would be of no use," Althea does not support the plan.

"Why not?"

"Before we left the island, we learned Stella did come to the island but she...she died," Althea hates the words coming from her mouth.

"What?" Zarin is not sure what her ears are hearing.

"She came through a portal to the island but she did not make it to us."

"Did Bardolph kill her?" Zarin brings up the sorcerer.

"No. No, she...went into the Time Tower. It is a place of such bad magic those who enter it die," Althea explains.

"But...she...she can't be dead. I-I have seen so many visions of her in the future. I've seen her with Prince Astrophel and me and-and- she can't be dead!" Zarin is quick to deny this.

"But she is," Althea tries to wipe away some of her tears.

"But..." Zarin's eyes fill with tears.

"Zarin, why are you crying?" Tyr walks toward the group. He pauses when he sees Althea. He grins. "Althea."

"Tyr." She addresses him back but cannot smile. His eyes are quick to go to Zarin.

"Zarin, why are you crying?" He asks again.

"They say Stella is dead," Zarin informs the shifter who frowns deeply.

"Dead?" Tyr repeats the word.

"But it just can't be possible. I've seen so much more with her. And my visions are never wrong. She just can't be," Zarin continues to deny this.

"Maybe this time they are wrong or were just things you hoped for," Tyr suggests. This does nothing to comfort Zarin.

"I am so sorry, Althea," Tyr takes Althea's hand. "Stella has been a true friend to me. A true friend..."

Althea just nods to accept the kind words but keeps her mouth shut as she is afraid only sobs will come out of it.

"How are we going to tell Astrophel?" Zarin thinks of the prince.

"Who?" Basil is the only one not to know the man.

"He is a prince who loves Stella," Althea answers.

"Who are you?" Tyr notices Basil.

"My brother," Althea answers.

"Ah. Well, I don't think he will be able to handle this especially now," Tyr comments.

"What has happened to him?" Althea grows concerned.

"Bardolph cursed him while they fought over Stella. He is below deck and ill. Since Sir Artegal's return from the castle, he has been with the prince," Zarin enlightens Althea.

"Sir Artegal believes the fairies in Estellen will be able to undo the curse. He said they would need to go to Estellen and then set back out to look for Stella. But if she is dead then...there will be no need to come back." Tyr must change the knight's plans.

"We should not tell Astrophel of Stella yet. I fear...I fear it will kill him," Zarin advises the others. The others nod in agreement.

Some whistles blow and some yelling from the crew letting down the sails lead to the Nadezhda leaving the port. Sir Artegal comes up from below deck as many start to go below. Sir Artegal approaches those he recognizes. He greets Althea kindly and is introduced to Basil.

"I am glad thou hast escaped. Pray, tell me Stella has escaped as well and is somewhere aboard," he looks around the deck. Once more Althea is forced to inform another of her sister's demise.

"Please, do not tell the prince about this. It would not do him well," Zarin touches the knight's arm.

"I understand. I will inform him once he is home and safe in Estellen. I will not worsen his condition with such grave tidings," Sir Artegal decides. He looks to Althea and Basil who he can easily tell is Stella's brother as they have such similar eyes.

"I am grieved to learn this news. I...I am quite fond of her. I hate I failed in protecting her when she needed it most. I...I am sorry. But I must hold on to the joy and the hope I will see her again when I leave this life as well. This joy and hope I do wish thou all to have as well," Sir Artegal's words bring a bittersweet smile to Basil.

"I do have it as well. Thank you for reminding me. Your words have given me some comfort," Basil speaks to the knight. Althea takes in the promise made to those who hold their faith in El-Yah. It is the promise she has been told all of her life. She believed it about her grandparents and Odette and Sigfried. She grasps this promise with her heart that it is true and in the life after this, she will see her sister again.

"A storm is coming. All women, children, and sickly get below deck," Some sailors start yelling out. Many pairs of eyes go to the sky and see the darkness there. Zarin and Althea are urged to go below.

"We should go be with Prince Astrophel," Zarin takes Althea's hand. They go below where it is crowded and loud. Tears come from many children and women. Zarin leads Althea to a hammock near the back. She sees A body in it. This person is wrapped up in so much white cloth he reminds Althea of a fly wrapped by a spider.

Is this truly the prince?

"This is the prince?" Althea asks Zarin in a whisper.

"Yes."

"Can he not be healed?" She asks. "Surely if he is this wrapped up, he must be badly hurt."

"I have tried but this curse is strong. The master fairies in Estellen will know what to do," Zarin assures Althea. Zarin comes to the hammock and lets the prince know she has come to keep him company.

"Zarin," His voice is faint.

"I have Althea with me here as well."

"Althea?" he reaches out. Althea touches his hand.

"I am here," Althea tells him.

"Where is Stella?"

"Safe," Althea tells Astrophel.

If she is dead, she is safe now.

"Is she here? Let me see Stella," he begins to move but as he does, he groans in pain.

"She is not here, Astrophel. But she is safe from Bardolph," Zarin tries to get the prince to ease. His body goes limp.

"As long as my beloved is safe, I am content," He states.

"She is. She is safe." Althea smiles at the prince though he cannot see through his bandages. Althea does not want to be there when the truth is told to the prince.

It is soon the ship begins to rock back and forth with the stormy waves. Many huddle together in fear. Some vomit with the great shaking. Althea stays close to Zarin and the prince.

Hours upon hours, the ship sails on in the storm though the wind and waves knock it about strongly. Althea is not fazed by the violent jostling. As she goes to scratch the back of her neck, her fingers find the necklace there, the necklace Hadion gave her.

Is this what has been keeping me from being ill? She keeps it on for if it is all that is keeping her from seasickness, she may as well not get sick and make matters worse for herself.

On and on the storm goes. Throughout the night, none can sleep because of the shaking, crying, and stench of sickness. When the boat does grow calm and almost still, Althea is quick to try and find her way up to the deck. She climbs out and finds the clouds receding and the sun beginning to rise. Men are drenched to the bone from the storm. Many lie down on the deck asleep. She sees Basil sitting on the ground with Sir Artegal and Tyr at the edge of the boat. She is quick to go to them.

"Are you all well?" She checks.

"Yes. Yes. Just exhausted," Basil nods.

"They had Basil and Artie manipulating the wind to get us through the storm faster," Tyr pats Sir Artegal on the shoulders.

"You need to rest then."

"There is not much time. The scout has seen land. We will arrive in Austvest soon." Sir Artegal informs Althea.

"You two must have greatly hastened our ship then if we are almost to Austvest," Althea is surprised.

"Yes. But the Icy Passage is narrow." Sir Artegal does not take much praise.

"I will be glad to be on solid ground after last night," Tyr wipes his wet forehead.

"Yes. Me as well," Basil nods.

Many of those kept below start to come up onto the deck as they had seen the door open to let them out. Among them comes Zarin. She comes to the ones she knows. She clutches her stomach but does not vomit unlike some who run to the edge of the boat.

"I see you have not fared as well as Althea," Tyr notices the difference in the demeanor of the women.

"I guess she has a stronger stomach," Zarin comments. "Has anyone said how far we are from Austvest?"

"We will be arriving soon enough. Our wind gifts were used to help move us along last night," Sir Artegal informs her.

"Oh good," Zarin smiles. "I shall be glad to be back in Austvest."

"As will I," Althea agrees.

"Since we have found your brother who is no longer cursed and Stella is... is our quest finished?" Tyr asks.

"I suppose it is." Althea looks away.

"What do you all plan to do now?" Tyr looks around the group.

"I will take Prince Astrophel home to Estellen to be cured. If any of thee wish to come, thou will be welcomed as a friend to the kingdom," Sir Artegal offers the others. Tyr smiles at this. Zarin's eyes become downcast.

"I wish I could go but I promised my mistress I would return to her and finish my fairy apprenticeship," Zarin rejects the invitation.

"I understand. It is best to keep our promises," Sir Artegal states.

"I have not known any of you for long but I thank you for the offer, Sir. But I want to see my parents. I need to see them and tell them what has happened," Basil speaks up next.

"Yes. We'll go home to them," Althea agrees with her brother.

Sir Artegal nods understandingly.

"Well, I'm probably not the one you want to go with you but I do want to go with you and the prince," Tyr is the only one to accept.

"I shall be glad to have thy company, Tyr." Sir Artegal pats the shapeshifter and then looks to the others. "If ever any of thee decide to come to Estellen, thou shall be welcomed."

When the ship docks in Austvest, those who had been on the quest wait till most are off the ship before carefully carrying the wrapped Prince Astrophel off. They are quick to find a tradesman selling a cart. Sir Artegal can conjure some money to give.

With the prince laid in the cart, Sir Artegal produces a vial holding tiny unicorns and horses in them, he lets them out and they grow big.

"Meteora," Basil is quick to go to his former horse. She happily accepts his rubs. Zarin pats her horse while Sir Artegal pets the unicorns. He soon hitches his magical beasts to the cart. Meteora and Safa have been left bridled, saddled, and ready to ride.

"I guess we will take turns riding Meteora," Basil comments as he realizes he and Althea will have to share a horse.

"I guess so."

"Don't do that. If you two are going to Soldoro, you will have a long journey. Take Safa," Zarin offers her horse to the siblings.

"We can't take your horse. You have a long journey back to Mother Huldah." Althea shakes her head.

"I will be fine. Take Safa. I insist," She puts the reins in Althea's hands.

"Zarin." Tyr walks from the cart to the golden-eyed woman.

"Yes?"

"I can't let you travel alone, especially now I see you have given up your horse. Let me come with you. I will be your steed," Tyr offers.

"But you wanted to travel with Sir Artegal and Prince Astrophel," Zarin looks at the knight and the cart.

"I can always join them later. Besides, I like you much more than that boring Artie," Tyr jokes. Zarin laughs and hugs him briefly.

"Is this alright with you, Sir Artegal?" Zarin asks the knight who is now losing his companion. The knight nods.

"Then it is settled." Tyr smiles.

Zarin and Althea hug once more before Althea mounts Safa. Zarin goes to Sir Artegal and touches his arm.

"I pray we meet again," Zarin tells him softly with their eyes locked.

"As do I."

With lovers, friends, and family lost, they part with heavy hearts and a sad conclusion: living "happily ever after" is a fantasy.

CHAPTER 56

STELLA

There is air. There is breath. There is warmth. Inhaling, Stella opens her eyes. No longer is she surrounded by darkness. She sees a small blue flame before her. It gives enough light that she can find her body is fully formed, healed, and upright. Her clothes are even clean. She walks toward the floating flame.

Where am I? Where are we going?

The flame bounces ahead. The more she walks, the warmer Stella becomes. When she breathes in, she smells salt from the sea. She can hear the crashing of waves and the calling of seagulls. The blue flame expands and brightens till it is an overwhelmingly bright wall. It rushes toward her. Stella closes her eyes.

Squinting, Stella finds herself no longer in the strange abyss or a wall of light. Instead, she stands on a golden beach before a blue sea. The sun shines above her as the birds fly there as well. It is far different from Norwin.

Stella soaks in the sun and its warmth. Strangely, it feels as if she has been cold for years and now can bask in the sun. A song of praise sings in her heart for she is alive and not of her own doing. Taking another look around, she sees she is alone.

Where is Astrophel? Where is everyone else? I must find them.

Our story has not come to an end, just a dramatic pause.

Our story will resume in Book 2 (coming soon).

Acknowledgements

I want to start by thanking you, dear Reader. Thank you for taking a chance on this story. Please keep an eye out for the second installment of this series.

Thank you to my friends for your encouragement over the years, but I especially want to thank Mary. Thank you for reading through every rough draft and lending a listening ear throughout the entire writing and publishing process. You are a true friend, and I am so grateful for you.

Thank you to my family for instilling a love of storytelling in me and being so supportive. There is no way I could do anything without your love and encouragement.

Thank you to my editor, Makenna Albert, for editing, to Inspirasi_artist for the map and interior art designs, and to Moomimar.art for your cover art design and beta-reading. You all have helped mold and polish this story for the better.

Last but not least, I want to thank God. As the greatest author of the best story ever told, You have blessed me to have experienced a fraction of what You do. You are the God of hope, love, grace, and redemption. You forgive what is unforgivable. Thank You for Your sacrifice on the cross and Your unshakeable love.

About the Author

M. L. Lyons has always been a storyteller with a heart for romance, adventure, and fantasy. When not toying with the lives of her characters, she enjoys traveling and spending time with her friends and family. She currently lives in North Carolina with her faithful dog, Fitz.